John Evelyn, William Bray

Diary and correspondence of John Evelyn, F. R. S

Vol. II

John Evelyn, William Bray

Diary and correspondence of John Evelyn, F. R. S
Vol. II

ISBN/EAN: 9783743401853

Manufactured in Europe, USA, Canada, Australia, Japa

Cover: Foto ©Raphael Reischuk / pixelio.de

Manufactured and distributed by brebook publishing software (www.brebook.com)

John Evelyn, William Bray

Diary and correspondence of John Evelyn, F. R. S

DIARY

AND

CORRESPONDENCE

OF

JOHN EVELYN, F.R.S.

TO WHICH IS SUBJOINED

𝕿𝖍𝖊 𝕻𝖗𝖎𝖛𝖆𝖙𝖊 𝕮𝖔𝖗𝖗𝖊𝖘𝖕𝖔𝖓𝖉𝖊𝖓𝖈𝖊

BETWEEN

KING CHARLES I. AND SIR EDWARD NICHOLAS,

AND BETWEEN

SIR EDWARD HYDE, AFTERWARDS EARL OF CLARENDON,

AND SIR RICHARD BROWNE.

EDITED FROM THE ORIGINAL MSS. AT WOTTON

BY WILLIAM BRAY, ESQ. F.A.S.

A NEW EDITION, IN FOUR VOLUMES.

CORRECTED, REVISED, AND ENLARGED.

VOL. II.

LONDON: GEORGE BELL & SONS, YORK STREET,
COVENT GARDEN.

1889.

LONDON :

PRINTED BY WILLIAM CLOWES AND SONS, LIMITED,

STAMFORD STREET AND CHARING CROSS.

CONTENTS.

LIST OF ILLUSTRATIONS

IN VOL. II.

DIARY

OF

JOHN EVELYN.

1665-6. 3rd January. I supped in Nonesuch House,[1] whither the office of the Exchequer was transferred during the plague, at my good friend's Mr. Packer's, and took an exact view of the plaster statues and bass-relievos inserted betwixt the timbers and puncheons of the outside walls of the Court; which must needs have been the work of some celebrated Italian. I much admired how they had lasted so well and entire since the time of Henry VIII., exposed as they are to the air; and pity it is they are not taken out and preserved in some dry place; a gallery would become them. There are some mezzo-relievos as big as the life; the story is of the Heathen Gods, emblems, compartments, &c. The palace consists of two courts, of which the first is of stone, castle like, by the Lord Lumleys (of whom it was purchased), the other of timber, a Gothic fabric, but these walls incomparably beautified. I observed that the appearing timber-puncheons, entrelices, &c., were all so covered with scales of slate, that it seemed carved in the wood and painted, the slate fastened on the timber in pretty figures,

[1] Of this famous summer residence of Queen Elizabeth not a vestige remains, but "the avenue planted with rows of fair elms." There is a small print of Nonesuch in Speed's Map of Surrey, but a larger one is given by Hoefnagle in his "Collection of Views, some in England, but chiefly abroad." Lysons has copied the latter in his *Environs of London*, edit. 1796, 153. Pepys mentions the Exchequer money being removed to Nonesuch, and describes the park and house as they then appeared. The building was subsequently pulled down, and its contents dispersed. A modern structure has been raised on its site.

that has, like a coat of armour, preserved it from rotting. There stand in the garden two handsome stone pyramids, and the avenue planted with rows of fair elms, but the rest of these goodly trees, both of this and of Worcester Park adjoining, were felled by those destructive and avaricious rebels in the late war, which defaced one of the stateliest seats his Majesty had.

12th January. After much, and indeed extraordinary mirth and cheer, all my brothers, our wives, and children, being together, and after much sorrow and trouble during this contagion, which separated our families as well as others, I returned to my house, but my wife went back to Wotton. I not as yet willing to adventure her, the contagion, though exceedingly abated, not as yet wholly extinguished amongst us.

29th. I went to wait on his Majesty, now returned from Oxford to Hampton-Court, where the Duke of Albemarle presented me to him; he ran towards me, and in a most gracious manner gave me his hand to kiss, with many thanks for my care and faithfulness in his service in a time of such great danger, when every body fled their employments; he told me he was much obliged to me, and said he was several times concerned for me, and the peril I underwent, and did receive my service most acceptably (though in truth I did but do my duty, and O that I had performed it as I ought!) After this, his Majesty was pleased to talk with me alone, near an hour, of several particulars of my employment, and ordered me to attend him again on the Thursday following at Whitehall. Then the Duke came towards me, and embraced me with much kindness, telling me if he had thought my danger would have been so great, he would not have suffered his Majesty to employ me in that station. Then came to salute me my Lord of St. Albans, Lord Arlington, Sir William Coventry, and several great persons; after which, I got home, not being very well in health.

The Court was now in deep mourning for the French Queen-Mother.

2nd February. To London; his Majesty now come to Whitehall, where I heard and saw my Lord Mayor (and brethren) make his speech of welcome, and the two Sheriffs were knighted.

6th February. My wife and family returned to me from the country, where they had been since August, by reason of the contagion, now almost universally ceasing. Blessed be God for His infinite mercy in preserving us! I, having gone through so much danger, and lost so many of my poor officers, escaping still myself that I might live to recount and magnify His goodness to me.

8th. I had another gracious reception by his Majesty, who called me into his bed-chamber, to lay before and describe to him my project of an Infirmary, which I read to him, who, with great approbation, recommended it to his Royal Highness.

20th. To the Commissioners of the Navy who, having seen the project of the Infirmary, encouraged the work, and were very earnest it should be set about immediately; but I saw no money, though a very moderate expense would have saved thousands to his Majesty, and been much more commodious for the cure and quartering of our sick and wounded, than the dispersing them into private houses, where many more chirurgeons and attendants were necessary, and the people tempted to debauchery.

21st. Went to my Lord Treasurer for an assignment of 40,000*l.* upon the two last quarters for support of the next year's charge. Next day, to Duke of Albemarle and Secretary of State, to desire them to propose it to the Council.

1st March. To London, and presented his Majesty my book intituled, " The pernicious Consequences of the new Heresy of the Jesuits against Kings and States."[1]

7th. Dr. Sancroft, since Archbishop of Canterbury, preached before the King about the identity and immutability of God, on Psalm cii. 27.

13th. To Chatham, to view a place designed for an Infirmary.

15th. My charge now amounted to near 7000*l.* [weekly].

22nd. The Royal Society re-assembled, after the dispersion from the contagion.

24th. Sent 2000*l.* to Chatham.

1st April. To London, to consult about ordering the natural rarities belonging to the repository of the Royal Society; referred to a Committee.

<hr>

[1] *Ante,* vol. i. p. 410.

10th April. Visited Sir William D'Oyly,[1] surprised with a fit of apoplexy, and in extreme danger.

11th. Dr. Bathurst preached before the King, from "I say unto you all, watch"—a seasonable and most excellent discourse. When his Majesty came from chapel, he called to me in the lobby, and told me he must now have me sworn for a Justice of Peace (having long since made me of the Commission); which I declined as inconsistent with the other service I was engaged in, and humbly desired to be excused. After dinner, waiting on him, I gave him the first notice of the Spaniards referring the umpirage of the peace betwixt them and Portugal to the French King, which came to me in a letter from France before the Secretaries of State had any news of it. After this, his Majesty again asked me if I had found out any able person about our parts that might supply my place of Justice of Peace (the office in the world I had most industriously avoided, in regard of the perpetual trouble thereof in these numerous parishes); on which I nominated one, whom the King commanded me to give immediate notice of to my Lord Chancellor, and I should be excused; for which I rendered his Majesty many thanks.—From thence, I went to the Royal Society, where I was chosen by twenty-seven voices to be one of their Council for the ensuing year; but, upon my earnest suit in respect of my other affairs, I got to be excused—and so home.

15th. Our parish was now more infected with the plague than ever, and so was all the country about, though almost quite ceased at London.

24th. To London about our Mint-Commission, and sat in the inner Court of Wards.

8th May. To Queenborough, where finding the Richmond frigate, I sailed to the buoy of the Nore to my Lord-General and Prince Rupert, where was the Rendezvous of the most glorious fleet in the world, now preparing to meet the Hollander.—Went to visit my cousin, Hales, at a sweetly-watered place at Chilston, near Bockton. The next morning,

---

[1] One of the Commissioners for the Sick and Wounded. Pepys records a wager which Sir William laid with him, of "a poll of ling, a brace of carps, and a pottle of wine, and Sir W. Pen, and Mr. Scowen to be at the eating of them."

to Leeds Castle, once a famous hold, now hired by me of my Lord Culpeper for a prison. Here I flowed the dry moat, made a new drawbridge, brought spring water into the court of the Castle to an old fountain, and took order for the repairs.

22nd May. Waited on my Lord Chancellor at his new palace; and Lord Berkeley's[1] built next to it.

24th. Dined with Lord Cornbury, now made Lord Chamberlain to the Queen; who kept a very honourable table.

1st June. Being in my garden at six o'clock in the evening, and hearing the great guns go thick off, I took horse and rode that night to Rochester; thence, next day towards the Downs and sea-coast, but meeting the Lieutenant of the Hampshire frigate, who told me what passed, or rather what had not passed, I returned to London, there being no noise, or appearance, at Deal, or on that coast of any engagement. Recounting this to his Majesty, whom I found at St. James's Park, impatiently expecting, and knowing that Prince Rupert was loose about three at St. Helen's Point at N. of the Isle of Wight, it greatly rejoiced him; but he was astonished when I assured him they heard nothing of the guns in the Downs, nor did the Lieutenant who landed there by five that morning.

3rd. Whit-Sunday. After sermon came news that the Duke of Albemarle was still in fight, and had been all Saturday, and that Captain Harman's ship (the Henry) was like to be burnt. Then a letter from Mr. Bertie that Prince Rupert was come up with his squadron (according to my former advice of his being loose and in the way), and put new courage into our fleet, now in a manner yielding ground; so that now we were chasing the chasers; that the Duke of Albemarle was slightly wounded, and the rest still in great danger. So, having been much wearied with my journey, I slipped home, the guns still roaring very fiercely.

[1] John, created Baron Berkeley, of Stratton, in 1658. He was Lord-Lieutenant of Ireland in 1670, and Ambassador to France in 1674. He died in 1678. His new house, next to the Lord Chancellor's, was well-known as Berkeley House—the neighbourhood of Piccadilly being the then favourite locality for what Evelyn styles "new palaces."

5th June. I went this morning to London, where came several particulars of the fight.

6th. Came Sir Daniel Harvey from the General, and related the dreadful encounter, on which his Majesty commanded me to despatch an extraordinary physician and more chirurgeons. It was on the solemn Fast-day when the news came; his Majesty being in the chapel made a sudden stop to hear the relation, which being with much advantage on our side, his Majesty commanded that public thanks should immediately be given as for a victory. The Dean of the chapel going down to give notice of it to the other Dean officiating; and notice was likewise sent to St. Paul's and Westminster-Abbey. But this was no sooner over, than news came that our loss was very great both in ships and men; that the Prince frigate was burnt, and as noble a vessel of 90 brass guns lost; and the taking of Sir George Ayscue, and exceeding shattering of both fleets; so as both being obstinate, both parted rather for want of ammunition and tackle than courage; our General retreating like a lion; which exceedingly abated of our former joy. There was, however, orders given for bonfires and bells; but, God knows, it was rather a deliverance than a triumph. So much it pleased God to humble our late over-confidence that nothing could withstand the Duke of Albemarle, who, in good truth, made too forward a reckoning of his success now, because he had once beaten the Dutch in another quarrel; and being ambitious to outdo the Earl of Sandwich, whom he had prejudicated as deficient in courage.

7th. I sent more chirurgeons, linen, medicaments, &c., to the several ports in my district.

8th. Dined with me Sir Alexander Fraser, prime physician to his Majesty; afterwards, went on board his Majesty's pleasure-boat, when I saw the London frigate launched, a most stately ship, built by the City to supply that which was burnt by accident some time since; the King, Lord Mayor and Sheriffs, being there with great banquet.

11th. Trinity Monday, after a sermon, applied to the re-meeting of the Corporation of the Trinity-House, after the late raging and wasting pestilence: I dined with them in their new room in Deptford, the first time since it was rebuilt.

15th June. I went to Chatham.—*16th.* In the Jemmy yacht (an incomparable sailer) to sea, arrived by noon at the fleet at the Buoy at the Nore, dined with Prince Rupert and the General.

17th. Came his Majesty, the Duke, and many Noblemen. After Council, we went to prayers. My business being despatched, I returned to Chatham, having lain but one night in the Royal Charles; we had a tempestuous sea. I went on shore at Sheerness, where they were building an arsenal for the fleet, and designing a royal fort with a receptacle for great ships to ride at anchor; but here I beheld the sad spectacle, more than half that gallant bulwark of the kingdom miserably shattered, hardly a vessel entire, but appearing rather so many wrecks and hulls, so cruelly had the Dutch mangled us. The loss of the Prince, that gallant vessel, had been a loss to be universally deplored, none knowing for what reason we first engaged in this ungrateful war; we lost besides nine or ten more, and near 600 men slain and 1100 wounded, 2000 prisoners; to balance which, perhaps we might destroy eighteen or twenty of the enemy's ships, and 700 or 800 poor men.

18th. Weary of this sad sight, I returned home.

2nd July. Came Sir John Duncomb[1] and Mr. Thomas Chicheley,[2] both Privy Councillors and Commissioners of His Majesty's Ordnance, to visit me, and let me know that his Majesty had in Council, nominated me to be one of the Commissioners for regulating the farming and making of saltpetre through the whole kingdom, and that we were to sit in the Tower the next day. When they were gone, came to see me Sir John Cotton, heir to the famous antiquary, Sir Robert Cotton: a pretended great Grecian, but had by no means the parts, or genius of his grandfather.

3rd. I went to sit with the Commissioners at the Tower, where our commission being read, we made some progress

[1] " Duncomb was a judicious man, but very haughty, and apt to raise enemies against himself. He was an able Parliament-man, but could not go into all the designs of the Court; for he had a sense of religion, and a zeal for the liberty of his country."—Bishop Burnet's *Hist. of his own Times.*

[2] Afterwards knighted. Pepys mentions him as one of the Masters of the Ordnance. He was also, as Evelyn tells us, a Member of the Privy Council.

in business, our Secretary being Sir George Wharton, that famous mathematician who wrote the yearly Almanack during his Majesty's troubles. Thence, to Painters' Hall, to our other commission, and dined at my Lord Mayor's.

4th July. The solemn Fast-day. Dr. Meggot preached an excellent discourse before the King on the terrors of God's judgments. After sermon, I waited on my Lord Archbishop of Canterbury and Bishop of Winchester, where the Dean of Westminster spoke to me about putting into my hands the disposal of fifty pounds, which the charitable people of Oxford had sent to be distributed among the sick and wounded seamen since the battle. Hence, I went to the Lord Chancellor's to joy him of his Royal Highness's second son, now born at St. James's; and to desire the use of the Star-chamber for our Commissioners to meet in, Painters' Hall not being so convenient.

12th. We sat the first time in the Star-chamber. There was now added to our commission Sir George Downing[1] (one that had been a great . . . against his Majesty, but now insinuated into his favour; and, from a pedagogue and fanatic preacher, not worth a groat, had become excessively rich), to inspect the hospitals and treat about prisons.

14th. Sat at the Tower with Sir J. Duncomb and Lord Berkeley, to sign deputations for undertakers to furnish their proportions of saltpetre.

17th. To London, to prepare for the next engagement of the fleets, now gotten to sea again.

22nd. Our parish still infected with the contagion.

25th. The fleets engaged. I dined at Lord Berkeley's, at St. James's, where dined my Lady Harrietta Hyde, Lord Arlington, and Sir John Duncomb.

29th. The pestilence now fresh increasing in our parish, I forbore going to church. In the afternoon came tidings

[1] Secretary to the Treasury, and Commissioner of the Customs. He had been recently made a baronet, and was now a zealous courtier; though, during the Commonwealth, as Cromwell's Resident in Holland, he had been no less zealous a republican. He subsequently went to Holland as Ambassador from the King. To him belongs the credit of having engaged Pepys about the year 1659, as one of the clerks in a department of the Exchequer then under his management. For his character, of which Evelyn speaks as we see, and Pepys leaves a somewhat doubtful impression, see Lord Clarendon's *Life*.

of our victory over the Dutch, sinking some, and driving others aground, and into their ports.

1st August. I went to Dr. Keffler, who married the daughter of the famous chymist, Drebbell,[1] inventor of the bodied scarlet. I went to see his iron ovens, made portable (formerly) for the Prince of Orange's army: supped at the Rhenish Wine-House with divers Scots gentlemen.

6th. Dined with Mr. Povey, and then went with him to see a country house he had bought near Brentford;[2] returning by Kensington; which house stands to a very graceful avenue of trees, but it is an ordinary building, especially one part.

8th. Dined at Sir Stephen Fox's[3] with several friends and, on the 10th, with Mr. Odart, Secretary of the Latin tongue.

17th. Dined with the Lord Chancellor, whom I intreated to visit the Hospital of the Savoy, and reduce it (after the great abuse that had been continued) to its original institution for the benefit of the poor, which he promised to do.

25th. Waited on Sir William D'Oyly, now recovered, as

[1] Cornelius Van Drebbell, born at Alkmaar, in Holland, in 1572; but in the reign of Charles I. settled in London, where he died in 1634. He was famous for other discoveries in science besides that mentioned by Evelyn—the most important of which was the thermometer. He also made improvements in microscopes and telescopes; and though, like many of his scientific contemporaries, something of an empiric, possessed a considerable knowledge of chemistry and of different branches of natural philosophy.

[2] This country house, situated near Hounslow, was called the Priory. There were three brothers of this name; sons of Justinian Povey, Auditor-General to Queen Anne of Denmark. The one mentioned by Evelyn was Thomas Povey, a Member of Parliament, Treasurer to the Commissioners for the affairs of Tangier, and Surveyor-General of the Victualling Department, in which offices he was succeeded by Pepys. He had previously held office under Cromwell, and was Treasurer and Receiver-General of the rents and revenues of the Duke of York. Pepys of course mentions him frequently.

[3] One of the most celebrated statesmen of the period comprised in the Diary. He was knighted in 1665, made Clerk of the Green Cloth, and Paymaster of the Forces by Charles II. He lost the favour of his successor by opposing the bill for a standing army, but was again employed in the reign of Queen Anne. Evelyn gives an interesting account of him at p. 156 of this volume. He was father of the first Earl of Ilchester, and of the first Baron Holland. He projected Chelsea College—the honour of which has generally been attributed to Nell Gwynne. He also founded a new church and a set of alms-houses at his seat, Farley, in Wilts. He was born in 1627, and died in 1716.

it were, miraculously. In the afternoon, visited the Savoy Hospital, where I stayed to see the miserably dismembered and wounded men dressed, and gave some necessary orders. Then to my Lord Chancellor, who had, with the Bishop of London and others in the commission, chosen me one of the three surveyors of the repairs of Paul's, and to consider of a model for the new building, or, if it might be, repairing of the steeple, which was most decayed.

26th August. The contagion still continuing, we had the Church-service at home.

27th. I went to St. Paul's church, where, with Dr. Wren, Mr. Pratt, Mr. May, Mr. Thomas Chicheley, Mr. Slingsby,[1] the Bishop of London, the Dean of St. Paul's,[2] and several expert workmen, we went about to survey the general decays of that ancient and venerable church, and to set down in writing the particulars of what was fit to be done, with the charge thereof, giving our opinion from article to article. Finding the main building to recede outwards, it was the opinion of Chicheley and Mr. Pratt that it had been so built *ab origine* for an effect in perspective, in regard of the height; but I was, with Dr. Wren, quite of another judgment, and so we entered it; we plumbed the uprights in several places. When we came to the steeple, it was deliberated whether it were not well enough to repair it only on its old foundation, with reservation to the four pillars; this Mr. Chicheley and Mr. Pratt were also for, but we totally rejected it, and persisted that it required a new foundation, not only in regard of the necessity, but for that the shape of what stood was very mean, and we had a mind to build it with a noble cupola, a form of church-building not as yet known in England, but of wonderful grace. For this purpose, we offered to bring in a plan and estimate, which, after much contest, was at last assented to, and that we should nominate a committee of able workmen to examine the present foundation. This concluded, we drew all up in writing, and so went with my Lord Bishop to the Dean's.

---

[1] He held the office of Master of the Mint. Other members of the family were employed about the Court. Arthur, son of Sir Guildford, was knighted, and subsequently made a baronet; and Sir Robert Slingsby was Comptroller of the Navy—a man much respected by Pepys.

[2] Dr. Sancroft, afterwards Archbishop of Canterbury.

28th August. Sat at the Star-chamber. Next day, to the Royal Society, where one Mercator, an excellent mathematician, produced his rare clock and new motion to perform the equations, and Mr. Rooke, his new pendulum.[1]

2nd September. This fatal night, about ten, began the deplorable fire, near Fish-street, in London.

3rd. I had public prayers at home. The fire continuing, after dinner, I took coach with my wife and son, and went to the Bankside in Southwark, where we beheld that dismal spectacle, the whole city in dreadful flames near the waterside; all the houses from the Bridge, all Thames street, and upwards towards Cheapside, down to the Three Cranes, were now consumed; and so returned, exceeding astonished what would become of the rest.

The fire having continued all this night (if I may call that night which was light as day for ten miles round about, after a dreadful manner), when conspiring with a fierce eastern wind in a very dry season, I went on foot to the same place ; and saw the whole south part of the City burning from Cheapside to the Thames, and all along Cornhill (for it likewise kindled back against the wind as well as forward), Tower-street, Fenchurch-street, Gracious-street,[1] and so along to Baynard's Castle, and was now taking hold of St. Paul's church, to which the scaffolds contributed exceedingly. The conflagration was so universal, and the people so astonished, that, from the beginning, I know not by what despondency, or fate, they hardly stirred to quench it; so that there was nothing heard, or seen, but crying out and lamentation, running about like distracted creatures, without at all attempting to save even their goods; such a strange consternation there was upon them, so as it burned

---

[1] Nicholas Mercator, the mathematician, must not be confounded with his namesake, so well known as the inventor of Mercator's Projection, who was both a geographer and a mathematician, and who died in 1594. Nicholas was born at Holstein in 1640; but, after the Restoration, settled in England, where his scientific attainments procured him the honour of being elected a Fellow of the Royal Society. He wrote several books on science. Laurence Rooke was Astronomy, and subsequently Geometry, Professor of Gresham College. He was born in 1623, and died 1662; having established, by several successful works his reputation as a man of science.

[2] Now Gracechurch-street.

both in breadth and length, the churches, public halls, Exchange, hospitals, monuments, and ornaments; leaping after
a prodigious manner, from house to house, and street to
street, at great distances one from the other. For the heat,
with a long set of fair and warm weather, had even ignited
the air, and prepared the materials to conceive the fire,
which devoured, after an incredible manner, houses, furniture, and every thing. Here, we saw the Thames covered
with goods floating, all the barges and boats laden with what
some had time and courage to save, as, on the other side,
the carts, &c., carrying out to the fields, which for many
miles were strewed with moveables of all sorts, and tents
erecting to shelter both people and what goods they could
get away. Oh, the miserable and calamitous spectacle! such
as haply the world had not seen since the foundation of it,
nor can be outdone till the universal conflagration thereof.
All the sky was of a fiery aspect, like the top of a burning
oven, and the light seen above forty miles round-about for
many nights. God grant mine eyes may never behold the
like, who now saw above 10,000 houses all in one flame!
The noise and cracking and thunder of the impetuous flames,
the shrieking of women and children, the hurry of people,
the fall of towers, houses, and churches, was like a hideous
storm; and the air all about so hot and inflamed, that at
the last one was not able to approach it, so that they were
forced to stand still, and let the flames burn on, which they
did, for near two miles in length and one in breadth. The
clouds also of smoke were dismal, and reached, upon computation, near fifty miles in length. Thus, I left it this afternoon burning, a resemblance of Sodom, or the last day. It
forcibly called to my mind that passage—*non enim hic habemus
stabilem civitatem:* the ruins resembling the picture of Troy.
London was, but is no more! Thus, I returned.

4*th September.* The burning still rages, and it is now
gotten as far as the Inner Temple. All Fleet-street, the Old
Bailey, Ludgate-hill, Warwick-lane, Newgate, Paul's-chain,
Watling-street, now flaming, and most of it reduced to
ashes; the stones of Paul's flew like grenados, the melting
lead running down the streets in a stream, and the very
pavements glowing with fiery redness, so as no horse, nor
man, was able to tread on them, and the demolition had

stopped all the passages, so that no help could be applied. The eastern wind still more impetuously driving the flames forward. Nothing but the Almighty power of God was able to stop them; for vain was the help of man.

5th September. It crossed towards Whitehall; but oh! the confusion there was then at that Court! It pleased his Majesty to command me, among the rest, to look after the quenching of Fetter-lane end, to preserve (if possible) that part of Holborn, whilst the rest of the gentlemen took their several posts, some at one part, and some at another (for now they began to bestir themselves, and not till now, who hitherto had stood as men intoxicated, with their hands across), and began to consider that nothing was likely to put a stop but the blowing up of so many houses as might make a wider gap than any had yet been made by the ordinary method of pulling them down with engines. This some stout seamen proposed early enough to have saved near the whole City, but this some tenacious and avaricious men, aldermen, &c., would not permit, because their houses must have been of the first. It was, therefore, now commended to be practised; and my concern being particularly for the Hospital of St. Bartholomew, near Smithfield, where I had many wounded and sick men, made me the more diligent to promote it; nor was my care for the Savoy less. It now pleased God, by abating the wind, and by the industry of the people, when almost all was lost infusing a new spirit into them, that the fury of it began sensibly to abate about noon, so as it came no farther than the Temple westward, nor than the entrance of Smithfield, north: but continued all this day and night so impetuous towards Cripplegate and the Tower, as made us all despair. It also brake out again in the Temple; but the courage of the multitude persisting, and many houses being blown up, such gaps and desolations were soon made, as, with the former three days' consumption, the back fire did not so vehemently urge upon the rest as formerly. There was yet no standing near the burning and glowing ruins by near a furlong's space.

The coal and wood-wharfs, and magazines of oil, rosin, &c., did infinite mischief, so as the invective which a little before I had dedicated to his Majesty and published,[1] giving warn-

[1] The *Fumifugium*. See *ante*, i. 374.

ing what probably might be the issue of suffering those shops to be in the City was looked upon as a prophecy.

The poor inhabitants were dispersed about St. George's Fields, and Moorfields, as far as Highgate, and several miles in circle, some under tents, some under miserable huts and hovels, many without a rag, or any necessary utensils, bed or board, who from delicateness, riches, and easy accommodations in stately and well-furnished houses, were now reduced to extremest misery and poverty.

In this calamitous condition, I returned with a sad heart to my house, blessing and adoring the distinguishing mercy of God to me and mine, who, in the midst of all this ruin, was like Lot, in my little Zoar, safe and sound.

6th September. Thursday. I represented to his Majesty the case of the French prisoners at war in my custody, and besought him that there might be still the same care of watching at all places contiguous to unseized houses. It is not indeed imaginable how extraordinary the vigilance and activity of the King and the Duke was, even labouring in person, and being present to command, order, reward, or encourage workmen ; by which he showed his affection to his people, and gained theirs. Having, then, disposed of some under cure at the Savoy, I returned to Whitehall, where I dined at Mr. Offley's,[1] the groom-porter, who was my relation.

7th. I went this morning on foot from Whitehall as far as London Bridge, through the late Fleet-street, Ludgate-hill by St. Paul's, Cheapside, Exchange, Bishopsgate, Aldersgate, and out to Moorfields, thence through Cornhill, &c., with extraordinary difficulty, clambering over heaps of yet smoking rubbish, and frequently mistaking where I was: the ground under my feet so hot, that it even burnt the soles of my shoes. In the meantime, his Majesty got to the Tower by water, to demolish the houses about the graff, which, being built entirely about it, had they taken fire and attacked the White Tower, where the magazine of powder lay, would undoubtedly not only have beaten down and destroyed all the bridge, but sunk and torn the vessels

---

[1] Dr. Offley was rector of Abinger, and has left traces of himself as donor of farms to Okewood Chapel, at Wotton, in the patronage of the Evelyn family.

in the river, and rendered the demolition beyond all expression for several miles about the country.

At my return, I was infinitely concerned to find that goodly Church, St. Paul's—now a sad ruin, and that beautiful portico (for structure comparable to any in Europe, as not long before repaired by the late King) now rent in pieces, flakes of large stones split asunder, and nothing remaining entire but the inscription in the architrave, showing by whom it was built, which had not one letter of it defaced! It was astonishing to see what immense stones the heat had in a manner calcined, so that all the ornaments, columns, friezes, capitals, and projectures of massy Portland stone, flew off, even to the very roof, where a sheet of lead covering a great space (no less than six acres by measure) was totally melted. The ruins of the vaulted roof falling, broke into St. Faith's, which being filled with the magazines of books belonging to the Stationers, and carried thither for safety, they were all consumed, burning for a week following. It is also observable that the lead over the altar at the east end was untouched, and among the divers monuments the body of one bishop remained entire. Thus lay in ashes that most venerable church, one of the most ancient pieces of early piety in the Christian world, besides near one hundred more. The lead, iron-work, bells, plate, &c., melted, the exquisitely wrought Mercers' Chapel, the sumptuous Exchange, the august fabric of Christ Church, all the rest of the Compamies' Halls, splendid buildings, arches, entries, all in dust; the fountains dried up and ruined, whilst the very waters remained boiling; the voragos of subterranean cellars, wells, and dungeons, formerly warehouses, still burning in stench and dark clouds of smoke; so that in five or six miles traversing about I did not see one load of timber unconsumed, nor many stones but what were calcined white as snow.

The people, who now walked about the ruins, appeared like men in some dismal desert, or rather, in some great city laid waste by a cruel enemy; to which was added the stench that came from some poor creatures' bodies, beds, and other combustible goods. Sir Thomas Gresham's statue, though fallen from its niche in the Royal Exchange, remained entire, when all those of the Kings since the Conquest were broken to pieces. Also the standard in Cornhill, and Queen Elizabeth's effigies, with some arms on Ludgate, continued with but little detriment, whilst the vast iron chains of the City-streets, hinges, bars, and gates of prisons, were many of them melted and reduced to cinders by the vehement heat. Nor was I yet able to pass through any of the narrow streets, but kept the widest; the ground and air, smoke and fiery vapour, continued so intense, that my hair was almost singed, and my feet unsufferably surbated. The bye-lanes and narrow streets were quite filled up with rubbish; nor could one have possibly known where he was, but by the ruins of some Church, or Hall, that had some remarkable tower, or pinnacle remaining.

I then went towards Islington and Highgate, where one might have seen 200,000 people of all ranks and degrees dispersed, and lying along by their heaps of what they could save from the fire, deploring their loss; and, though ready to perish for hunger and destitution, yet not asking one penny for relief, which to me appeared a stranger sight than any I had yet beheld. His Majesty and Council indeed took all imaginable care for their relief, by proclamation for the country to come in, and refresh them with provisions.

In the midst of all this calamity and confusion, there was, I know not how, an alarm begun that the French and Dutch, with whom we were now in hostility, were not only landed, but even entering the City. There was, in truth, some days before, great suspicion of those two nations joining; and now that they had been the occasion of firing the town. This report did so terrify, that on a sudden there was such an uproar and tumult that they run from their goods, and, taking what weapons they could come at, they could not be stopped from falling on some of those nations whom they casually met, without sense or reason. The clamour and peril grew so excessive, that it made the whole Court amazed, and they did with infinite pains and great difficulty, reduce and appease the people, sending troops of soldiers and guards, to cause them to retire into the fields again, where they were watched all this night. I left them pretty quiet, and came home sufficiently weary and broken. Their spirits thus a little calmed, and the affright abated, they now began to repair into the suburbs about the City, where such as had friends, or opportunity, got shelter for the present; to which his Majesty's proclamation also invited them.[1]

Still, the plague continuing in our parish, I could not, without danger, adventure to our church.

10th September. I went again to the ruins; for it was now no longer a city.

[1] Subjoined is the Ordinance to which Evelyn alludes, reprinted from the original half-sheet in black letter:

CHARLES R.

His Majesty, in his princely compassion and very tender care, taking into consideration the distressed condition of many of his good subjects, whom the late dreadful and dismal fire hath made destitute of habitations, and exposed to many exigencies and necessities; for present remedy and redress whereof, his Majesty intending to give further testimony and evidences of his grace and favour towards them, as occasion shall arise, hath thought fit to declare and publish his Royal pleasure: That, as great proportions of bread, and all other provisions as can possibly be furnished, shall be daily and constantly brought, not only to the markets formerly in use, but also to such markets as by his Majesty's late order and declaration to the Lord Mayor and Sheriffs of London and Middlesex have been appointed and ordained, *viz.*, Clerkenwell, Islington, Finsbury-fields, Mile-end Green, and Ratcliff; his Majesty being sensible that this will be for the benefit also of the towns and places adjoining, as being the best expedient to prevent the resort of such persons thereunto as may pilfer and disturb them. And whereas, also, divers of the said distressed persons have saved and preserved their goods, which nevertheless they know not how to dispose of, it is his Majesty's pleasure, that all Churches, Chapels, Schools, and other like public places, shall be free and open to receive the said goods, when they shall be brought to be there laid. And all Justices of the Peace within the several Counties of Middlesex, Essex and Surrey, are to see the same to be done accordingly. And likewise that all cities and towns whatsoever shall, without any contradiction, receive the said distressed persons, and permit them to the free exercise of their manual trades; his majesty resolving and promising that, when the present exigence shall be passed over, he will take such care and order, that the said persons shall be no burthen to their towns, or parishes And it is his Majesty's pleasure, that this his declaration be forthwith published, not only by the Sheriffs of London and Middlesex, but also by all other Sheriffs, Mayors, and other chief officers in their respective precincts and limits, and by the constables in every parish. And of this his Majesty's pleasure all persons concerned are to take notice, and thereunto to give due obedience to the utmost of their power, as they will answer the contrary at their peril. Given at our Court at Whitehall, the fifth day of September, in the eighteenth year of our reign, one thousand six hundred sixty-six. God save the King.

13th September. I presented his Majesty with a survey of the ruins, and a plot for a new City,[1] with a discourse on it; whereupon, after dinner, his Majesty sent for me into the Queen's bed-chamber, her Majesty and the Duke only being present. They examined each particular, and discoursed on them for near an hour, seeming to be extremely pleased with what I had so early thought on. The Queen was now in her cavalier riding-habit, hat and feather, and horseman's coat, going to take the air.

16th. I went to Greenwich Church, where Mr. Plume preached very well from this text: " Seeing, then, all these things shall be dissolved," &c. : taking occasion from the late unparalleled conflagration to mind us how we ought to walk more holy in all manner of conversation.

• *27th.* Dined at Sir William D'Oyly's, with that worthy gentleman, Sir John Holland, of Suffolk.

10th October. This day was ordered a general Fast through the Nation, to humble us on the late dreadful conflagration, added to the plague and war, the most dismal judgments that could be inflicted; but which indeed we highly deserved for our prodigious ingratitude, burning lusts, dissolute court, profane and abominable lives, under such dispensations of God's continued favour in restoring Church, Prince, and People from our late intestine calamities, of which we were altogether unmindful, even to astonishment. This made me resolve to go to our parish assembly, where our Doctor

---

[1] Evelyn has preserved his letter to Sir Samuel Tuke, on the subject of the fire, and his scheme for re-building the City. Part of his plan was to lessen the declivities, and to employ the rubbish in filling up the shore of the Thames to low-water mark, so as to keep the basin always full.—In another letter to Mr. Oldenburg, Secretary to the Royal Society, dated 22nd December 1666, he says, after mentioning his having presented his reflections on re-building the City to his Majesty, that " the want of a more exact plot, wherein I might have marked what the fire had spared, and accommodated my design to the remaining parts, made me take it as a *rasa tabula,* and to form mine idea thereof, accordingly : I have since lighted upon Mr. Hollar's late plan, which looking upon as the most accurate hitherto extant, has caused me something to alter what I had so crudely done, though for the most part I still persist in my former discourse, and which I here send you as complete as an imperfect copy will give me leave, and the supplement of an ill memory, for since that time I hardly ever looked on it, and it was finished within two or three days after the Incendium." •

preached on Luke, xix. 41: piously applying it to the occasion. After which, was a collection for the distressed losers
in the late fire.

18th October. To Court. It being the first time his Majesty
put himself solemnly into the Eastern fashion of vest, changing
doublet, stiff collar, bands and cloak, into a comely dress,
after the Persian mode, with girdles or straps, and shoe-
strings and garters into buckles, of which some were set with
precious stones,[1] resolving never to alter it, and to leave the
French mode, which had hitherto obtained to our great expense and reproach. Upon which, divers courtiers and gentlemen gave his Majesty gold by way of wager that he would
not persist in this resolution. I had sometime before presented an invective against that unconstancy, and our so
much affecting the French fashion, to his Majesty; in which
I took occasion to describe the comeliness and usefulness of
the Persian clothing, in the very same manner his Majesty
now clad himself. This pamphlet I entitled *Tyrannus, or
the Mode*, and gave it to the King to read. I do not impute to this discourse the change which soon happened, but
it was an identity that I could not but take notice of.

This night was acted my Lord Broghill's[2] tragedy, called
Mustapha, before their Majesties at Court, at which I was
present; very seldom going to the public theatres for many
reasons now, as they were abused to an atheistical liberty;
foul and undecent women now (and never till now) permitted
to appear and act, who inflaming several young noblemen
and gallants, became their misses, and to some, their wives.
Witness the Earl of Oxford, Sir R. Howard,[3] Prince Rupert,
the Earl of Dorset, and another greater person than any of
them, who fell into their snares, to the reproach of their noble
families, and ruin of both body and soul.[4] I was invited by

---

[1] This costume was shortly after abandoned, and laid aside; nor does
any existing portrait exhibit the King so accoutred.

[2] Richard Lord Broghill, created, shortly after this, Earl of Orrery;
he wrote several other plays besides that here noticed.

[3] Sir Robert Howard held the office of Auditor of the Exchequer; but
was more celebrated as an author, having written comedies, tragedies,
poems, histories, and translations. He was born in 1626, and died in 1698.

[4] Among the principal offenders here aimed at were Mrs. Margaret
Hughes, Mrs. Eleanor Gwynne, Mrs. Davenport, Mrs. Uphill, Mrs. Davis,
and Mrs. Knight. Mrs. Davenport (Roxolana) was "my Lord Oxford's

my Lord Chamberlain to see this tragedy, exceedingly well written, though in my mind I did not approve of any such pastime in a time of such judgments and calamities.

21st October. This season, after so long and extraordinary a drought in August and September, as if preparatory for the dreadful fire, was so very wet and rainy as many feared an ensuing famine.

28th. The pestilence, through God's mercy, began now to abate considerably in our town.

30th. To London to our office, and now had I on the vest and surcoat, or tunic, as it was called, after his Majesty had brought the whole court to it. It was a comely and manly habit, too good to hold, it being impossible for us in good earnest to leave the Monsieurs' vanities long.

31st. I heard the signal cause of my Lord Cleveland[1] pleaded before the House of Lords; and was this day forty-six years of age, wonderfully protected by the mercies of God, for which I render him immortal thanks.

14th November. I went my winter-circle through my district, Rochester and other places, where I had men quartered, and in custody.

15th. To Leeds Castle.

16th. I mustered the prisoners, being about 600 Dutch and French, ordered their proportion of bread to be augmented, and provided clothes and fuel. Monsieur Colbert, Ambassador at the Court of England, this day sent money from his master, the French King, to every prisoner of that nation under my guard.

17th November. I returned to Chatham, my chariot overturning on the steep of Bexley-Hill, wounded me in two places on the head; my son, Jack, being with me, was like to have been worse cut by the glass; but I thank God we both escaped without much hurt, though not without exceeding danger. — *18th*. At Rochester.—*19th*. Returned home.

23rd. At London, I heard an extraordinary case before

misss;" Mrs. Uphill was the actress alluded to in connection with Sir R. Howard; Mrs. Hughes ensnared Prince Rupert; and the last of the "misses" referred to by Evelyn was Nell Gwynne.

[1] Thomas Wentworth, created in Feb. 1626-7 Baron Wentworth of Nettlested, and Earl of Cleveland. He died in 1667

a Committee of the whole House of Commons, in the Commons' House of Parliament, between one Captain Taylor and my Lord Viscount Mordaunt,[1] where, after the lawyers had pleaded and the witnesses been examined, such foul and dishonourable things were produced against his Lordship, of tyranny during his government of Windsor Castle, of which he was Constable, incontinence, and sub-orning witnesses (of which last, one Sir Richard Breames was most concerned), that I was exceedingly interested for his Lordship, who was my special friend, and husband of the most virtuous lady in the world. We sat till near ten at night, and yet but half the Counsel had done on behalf of the Plaintiff. The question then was put for bringing-in of lights to sit longer. This lasted so long before it was determined, and raised such a confused noise among the Members, that a stranger would have been astonished at it. I admire that there is not a rationale to regulate such trifling accidents, which consume much time, and is a reproach to the gravity of so great an assembly of sober men.

27th November. Sir Hugh Pollard, Comptroller of the Household, died at Whitehall, and his Majesty conferred the white staff on my brother Commissioner for sick and wounded, Sir Thomas Clifford, a bold young gentleman, of a small fortune in Devon, but advanced by Lord Arlington, Secretary of State, to the great astonishment of all the Court. This gentleman was somewhat related to me by the marriage of his mother to my nearest kinsman, Gregory Coale,[2] and was ever my noble friend, a valiant and daring person, but by no means fit for a supple and flattering courtier.

28th. Went to see Clarendon House,[3] now almost

---

[1] John, second son of John, first Earl of Peterborough. He was raised to the Peerage in July, 1659, for his services in the cause of Charles II. He died June 5th, 1675. See the whole proceedings in this affair in the Journals of Lords and Commons, under date of 1666.

[2] Of this "nearest kinsman" and his family, seated at Petersham in Surrey, see Bray's History of that County, i. 439, 441, but his precise connection or kinsmanship with the Evelyns does not appear.

[3] Of which frequent mention, throughout his Diary and Letters, is made by Evelyn; since quite demolished. It was situated where Albemarle Street now is. After Lord Clarendon's exile the Duke of Albemarle occupied it, and two engraved views of it exist as it then stood; one a small one by John Dunstall, and another upon a very large scale, by J. Spilbergh.

finished, a goodly pile to see to, but had many defects
as to the architecture, yet placed most gracefully. After
this, I waited on the Lord Chancellor, who was now at
Berkshire House,[1] since the burning of London.

2nd December. Dined with me Monsieur Kiviet, a Dutch
gentleman-pensioner of Rotterdam, who came over for protection, being of the Prince of Orange's party, now not
welcome in Holland. The King knighted him for some
merit in the Prince's behalf. He should, if caught, have
been beheaded with Monsieur Buat, and was brother-in-
law to Van Tromp, the sea-general. With him came
Mr. Gabriel Sylvius, and Mr. Williamson, secretary to
Lord Arlington;[2] M. Kiviet came to examine whether the
soil about the river of Thames would be proper to make
clinker-bricks, and to treat with me about some accommodation in order to it.[3]

1666-7. 9th January. To the Royal Society, which
since the sad conflagration were invited by Mr. Howard to
sit at Arundel-House in the Strand, who, at my instigation,
likewise bestowed on the Society that noble library which
his grandfather especially, and his ancestors had collected.
This gentleman had so little inclination to books, that it was
the preservation of them from embezzlement.

24th. Visited my Lord Clarendon, and presented
my son, John, to him, now preparing to go to Oxford, of

[1] Berkshire or Cleveland House, belonging to the Howards Earls of
Berkshire. It was purchased and presented by Charles II. to Barbara
Duchess of Cleveland, and was then of great extent ; she, however, after-
wards sold part, which was divided into various houses.

[2] Williamson, already mentioned in a note (vol. i. p. 409), filled
several important offices. He was Keeper of the State Paper Office,
Under Secretary, and then Secretary of State. He was knighted ; subsequently elected President of the Royal Society; and as Sir Joseph
Williamson, continued a Member of Parliament during several sessions,
representing Thetford and Rochester. Pepys describes him in 1662-3
as "a pretty knowing man and a scholar, but it may be, thinks himself
to be too much so." He died in 1701. See Ante, vol. i. p. 409.

[3] Occasional references are made to it hereafter (24, 32, &c.) Monsieur
Kiviet, probably the same person described by Pepys as "Kevet, Burgo-
master of Amsterdam." He made a proposition, as Evelyn describes
it, "to wharf the whole river of Thames, or quay from the Temple to
the Tower, as far as the fire destroyed, with bricks, without piles, both
lasting and ornamental."

which his Lordship was Chancellor. This evening I heard rare Italian voices, two eunuchs and one woman, in his Majesty's green chamber, next his cabinet.

29th January. To London, in order to my son's Oxford journey, who, being very early entered both in Latin and Greek, and prompt to learn beyond most of his age, I was persuaded to trust him under the tutorage of Mr. Bohun, Fellow of New College, who had been his preceptor in my house some years before; but, at Oxford, under the inspection of Dr. Bathurst, President of Trinity College, where I placed him, not as yet thirteen years old. He was newly out of long coats.[1]

15th February. My little book, in answer to Sir George Mackenzie[2] on Solitude, was now published, entitled " Public Employment, and an active Life with its Appanages, preferred to Solitude."[3]

18th. I was present at a magnificent ball, or masque, in the theatre at the Court, where their Majesties and all the great lords and ladies danced, infinitely gallant, the men in their richly embroidered most becoming vests.

19th. I saw a Comedy acted at Court. In the afternoon, I witnessed a wrestling match for 1000*l.* in St. James's Park, before his Majesty, a vast assemblage of lords and other spectators, betwixt the western and northern men, Mr. Secretary Morice and Lord Gerard being the judges. The western men won. Many great sums were betted.

6th March. I proposed to my Lord Chancellor, Mon-

---

[1] In illustration of the garb which succeeded the " long coats " out of which lads of twelve or thirteen were thus suffered to emerge, it may be mentioned that there hung, some years ago, and perhaps may hang still, upon the walls of the Swan Inn at Leatherhead in Surrey, a picture of four children, dates of birth between 1640 and 1650, of whom a lad of about the age of young Evelyn is represented in a coat reaching to his ankles.

[2] A Scottish advocate, who wrote several works on the Scottish laws, and various essays and poetical pieces. He was born at Dundee in 1536, and died in London in 1691. He has frequent mention in the Diary and Correspondence. See the present vol. p. 306, and vol. iii. 193.

[3] Re-printed in " Miscellaneous Writings, pp. 501-509. In a letter to Cowley, 12th March, 1666, Evelyn apologises for having written against that life which he had joined with Mr. Cowley in so much admiring, assuring him he neither was nor could be serious in avowing such a preference.

sieur Kiviet's undertaking to wharf the whole river of Thames, or quay, from the Temple to the Tower, as far as. the fire destroyed, with brick, without piles, both lasting and ornamental.—Great frosts, snow, and winds, prodigious at the vernal equinox ; indeed it had been a year of prodigies in this nation, plague, war, fire, rain, tempest and comet.

14th March. Saw *The Virgin-Queen,*[1] a play written by Mr. Dryden.

22nd. Dined at Mr. Secretary Morice's,[2] who showed me his library, which was a well-chosen collection. This afternoon, I had audience of his Majesty, concerning the proposal I had made of building the Quay.

26th. Sir John Kiviet dined with me. We went to search for brick-earth, in order to a great undertaking.

4th April. The cold so intense, that there was hardly a leaf on a tree.

18th. I went to make court to the Duke and Duchess of Newcastle, at their house in Clerkenwell,[3] being newly come out of the north. They received me with great kindness, and I was much pleased with the extraordinary fanciful habit, garb, and discourse of the Duchess.

22nd. Saw the sumptuous supper in the banqueting-house at Whitehall, on the eve of St. George's day, where were all the companions of the Order of the Garter.

23rd. In the morning, his Majesty went to chapel with the Knights of the Garter, all in their habits and robes, ushered by the heralds ; after the first service, they went in procession, the youngest first, the Sovereign last, with the Prelate of the Order and Dean, who had about his neck the

---

[1] The *Virgin Queen* which Evelyn saw was Dryden's *Maiden Queen.* Pepys saw it on the night of its first production (twelve day's before Evelyn's visit) ; and was charmed by Nell Gwynne's Florimell. " So great a performance of a comical part was never, I believe, in the world before."

[2] Sir William Morice. General Monk, his kinsman, procured him, at the Restoration, the place of Secretary of State, which he resigned in 1668 He died in 1676.

[3] See Correspondence, vol. iii. p. 244-250, vol. iv. pp. 8, &c. Both Duke and Duchess are frequently mentioned by Evelyn. The Duke spent a princely fortune (with very ill reward) in the service of Charles I. and II., and is now chiefly remembered for his high-flown wife's fantastical account of him.

book of the Statutes of the Order; and then the Chancellor of the Order (old Sir Henry de Vic), who wore the purse about his neck; then the Heralds and Garter-King-at-Arms, Clarencieux, Black Rod. But before the Prelate and Dean of Windsor went the gentlemen of the chapel and choristers, singing as they marched; behind them two doctors of music in damask robes; this procession was about the courts at Whitehall. Then, returning to their stalls and seats in the chapel, placed under each knight's coat-armour and titles, the second service began. Then, the King offered at the altar, an anthem was sung; then, the rest of the Knights offered, and lastly proceeded to the banqueting-house to a great feast. The King sat on an elevated throne at the upper end at a table alone; the Knights at a table on the right hand, reaching all the length of the room; over-against them a cupboard of rich gilded plate; at the lower end, the music; on the balusters above, wind music, trumpets, and kettle-drums. The King was served by the lords and pensioners who brought up the dishes. About the middle of the dinner, the Knights drank the King's health, then the King, theirs, when the trumpets and music played and sounded, the guns going off at the Tower. At the Banquet, came in the Queen, and stood by the King's left hand, but did not sit. Then was the banqueting-stuff flung about the room profusely. In truth, the crowd was so great, that though I stayed all the supper the day before, I now stayed no longer than this sport began, for fear of disorder. The cheer was extraordinary, each Knight having forty dishes to his mess, piled up five or six high; the room hung with the richest tapestry.

25th April. Visited again the Duke of Newcastle, with whom I had been acquainted long before in France, where the Duchess had obligation to my wife's mother for her marriage there; she was sister to Lord Lucas, and maid of honour then to the Queen-Mother; married in our chapel at Paris. My wife being with me, the Duke and Duchess both would needs bring her to the very Court.

26th. My Lord Chancellor showed me all his newly finished and furnished palace and library; then, we went to take the air in Hyde-Park.

27th. I had a great deal of discourse with his Majesty

at dinner. In the afternoon, I went again with my wife to the Duchess of Newcastle, who received her in a kind of transport, suitable to her extravagant humour and dress, which was very singular.

8th May. Made up accounts with our Receiver, which amounted to 33,936*l.* 1*s.* 4*d.* Dined at Lord Cornbury's, with Don Francisco de Melos, Portugal Ambassador, and kindred to the Queen: Of the party were Mr. Henry Jermyn,[1] and Sir Henry Capel.[2] Afterwards I went to Arundel-House, to salute Mr. Howard's sons, newly returned out of France.

11th. To London; dined with the Duke of Newcastle, and sat discoursing with her Grace in her bed-chamber after dinner, till my Lord Marquis of Dorchester with other company came in, when I went away.

30th. To London, to wait on the Duchess of Newcastle (who was a mighty pretender to learning, poetry, and philosophy, and had in both published divers books) to the Royal Society,[3] whither she came in great pomp, and being received by our Lord President at the door of our meeting-room, the mace, &c., carried before him, had several experiments showed to her. I conducted her Grace to her coach, and returned home.

1st June. I went to Greenwich, where his Majesty was trying divers grenadoes shot out of cannon at the Castle-hill, from the house in the Park; they brake not till they hit the mark, the forged ones brake not at all, but the cast ones very well. The inventor was a German there present. At the same time, a ring was showed to the King, pretended to be a projection of mercury, and malleable, and said by the gentlemen to be fixed by the juice of a plant.

8th. To London, alarmed by the Dutch, who were fallen on our fleet at Chatham, by a most audacious enterprise entering the very river with part of their fleet, doing us

[1] In 1685 created Baron Jermyn of Dover.

[2] A leading member of the House of Commons, created April 11th, 1692, Baron Capel of Tewkesbury, afterwards Lord Lieutenant of Ireland.

[3] This may remind us of the visit of another great lady, Queen Christina, to one of the sittings of the French Academy, recorded by Monsieur Pellisson, in his History of that learned body.

not only disgrace, but incredible mischief in burning several of our best men-of-war lying at anchor and moored there, and all this through our unaccountable negligence in not setting out our fleet in due time. This alarm caused me, fearing the enemy might venture up the Thames even to London (which they might have done with ease, and fired all the vessels in the River, too), to send away my best goods, plate, &c., from my house to another place. The alarm was so great that it put both Country and City into fear, a panic, and consternation, such as I hope I shall never see more ; everybody was flying, none knew why or whither. Now, there were land-forces despatched with the Duke of Albemarle, Lord Middleton,[1] Prince Rupert, and the Duke, to hinder the Dutch coming to Chatham, fortifying Upnor Castle, and laying chains and bombs; but the resolute enemy brake through all, and set fire on our ships, and retreated in spite, stopping up the Thames, the rest of the fleet lying before the mouth of it.

14th June. I went to see the work at Woolwich, a battery to prevent them coming up to London, which Prince Rupert commanded, and sunk some ships in the river.

17th. This night, about two o'clock, some chips and combustible matter prepared for some fire-ships, taking flame in Deptford-yard, made such a blaze, and caused such an uproar in the Tower (it being given out that the Dutch fleet was come up, and had landed their men and fired the Tower), as had liked to have done more mischief before people would be persuaded to the contrary and believe the accident. Everybody went to their arms. These were sad and troublesome times.

24th. The Dutch fleet still continuing to stop up the river, so as nothing could stir out or come in, I was before the Council, and commanded by his Majesty to go with some others and search about the environs of the city, now exceedingly distressed for want of fuel, whether there could

---

[1] John Middleton was first a Parliamentary general, but subsequently fought for Charles II. at Worcester, and otherwise distinguished himself as a Royalist officer till the Restoration, when he was created Earl of Middleton. He was Commander-in-Chief of the Forces in Scotland, Governor of Edinburgh Castle, Commissioner of the Scottish Parliament, and finally Governor of Tangier, where he died in 1673.

be any peat, or turf, found fit for use. The next day, I went and discovered enough, and made my report that there might be found a great deal; but nothing further was done in it.

28th June. I went to Chatham, and thence to view not only what mischief the Dutch had done; but how triumphantly their whole fleet lay within the very mouth of the Thames, all from the North Fore-land, Margate, even to the buoy of the Nore—a dreadful spectacle as ever Englishmen saw, and a dishonour never to be wiped off! Those who advised his Majesty to prepare no fleet this spring deserved—I know what—but[1]—

Here in the river off Chatham, just before the town, lay the carcase of the London (now the third time burnt), the Royal Oak, the James, &c. yet smoking; and now, when the mischief was done, we were making trifling forts on the brink of the river. Here were yet forces, both of horse and foot, with general Middleton continually expecting the motions of the enemy's fleet. I had much discourse with him, who was an experienced commander. I told him I wondered the King did not fortify Sheerness[2] and the Ferry; both abandoned.

2nd July. Called upon by my Lord Arlington, as from his Majesty, about the new fuel. The occasion why I was mentioned, was from what I said in my *Sylva* three years before, about a sort of fuel for a need, which obstructed a patent of Lord Carlingford,[3] who had been seeking for it himself; he was endeavouring to bring me into the project, and proffered me a share. I met my Lord; and, on the 9th, by an order of Council, went to my Lord Mayor, to be assisting. In the mean time they had made an experiment of my receipt of *houllies*, which I mention in my book to be made at Maestricht, with a mixture of charcoal dust and loam, and which was tried with success at Gresham College

---

[1] "The Parliament giving but weak supplies for the war, the King, to save charges, is persuaded by the Chancellor, the Lord Treasurer, Southampton, the Duke of Albemarle, and the other ministers, to lay up the first and second-rate ships, and make only a defensive war in the next campaign. The Duke of York opposed this, but was over-ruled." Life of King James II., vol. i. p. 425.

[2] Since done. Evelyn's note.

[3] Theobald, second Viscount Taafe, created Earl of Carlingford, June 26, 1662.

(there being the exchange for the meeting of the merchants since the fire) for everybody to see. This done, I went to the Treasury for 12,000*l.* for the sick and wounded yet on my hands.

Next day, we met again about the fuel at Sir J. Armourer's in the Mews.

8th July. My Lord Brereton and others dined at my house, where I showed them proof of my new fuel, which was very glowing, and without smoke or ill smell.

10th. I went to see Sir Samuel Morland's[1] inventions and machines, arithmetical wheels, quench-fires, and new harp.

17th. The Master of the Mint and his lady, Mr. Williamson, Sir Nicholas Armourer,[2] Sir Edward Bowyer, Sir Anthony Auger, and other friends dined with me.

29th. I went to Gravesend; the Dutch fleet still at anchor before the river, where I saw five of his Majesty's men-at-war encounter above twenty of the Dutch, in the bottom of the Hope, chasing them with many broadsides given and returned towards the buoy of the Nore, where the body of their fleet lay, which lasted till about midnight. One of their ships was fired, supposed by themselves, she being run on ground. Having seen this bold action, and their braving us so far up the river, I went home the next day,

[1] Aubrey (in his account of Surrey, vol. i. p. 12) says: "Under the equestrian Statue of Charles II., in the great Court at Windsor, is an engine for raising water, contrived by Sir Samuel Morland, alias Morley. He was son of Sir Samuel Morland, of Sulhamsted Bannister, Berks, created Baronet by Charles II., in consideration of services performed during his exile. The son was a great mechanic, and was presented with a gold medal, and made *Magister Mechanicorum* by the King, in 1681. He invented the drum capstands, for weighing heavy anchors: the speaking trumpet, and other useful engines. He died and was buried at Hammersmith, 1696. There is a monument for the two wives of Sir Samuel Morland in Westminster Abbey. There is a print of the son, by Lombart, after Lely. This Sir Samuel, the son, built a large room in his garden at Vauxhall, which was much admired at that time. On the top was a punchinello, holding a dial." More to a similar effect will be found in Manning and Bray's History of Surrey. He receives frequent mention from Evelyn in his letters as well as this Diary. For further notice of inventions by him, see *post* 70, 120, 167, 185, and 350.

[2] Sir Nicholas (a different person from Sir James) Armourer was Equerry to Charles II. Pepys tells a curious anecdote of his inducing the King to drink the Duke of York's health on his knees. The Queen of Bohemia talks of him familiarly in her letters as Nick Armourer.

not without indignation at our negligence, and the nation's reproach. It is well known who of the Commissioners of the Treasuy gave advice that the charge of setting forth a fleet this year might be spared, Sir W. C. (William Coventry) by name.

1st August. I received the sad news of Abraham Cowley's death, that incomparable poet and virtuous man, my very dear friend, and was greatly deplored.

3rd. Went to Mr. Cowley's funeral, whose corpse lay at Wallingford House, and was thence conveyed to Westminster Abbey in a hearse with six horses and all funeral decency, near a hundred coaches of noblemen and persons of quality following; among these, all the wits of the town, divers bishops and clergymen. He was interred next Geoffry Chaucer, and near Spenser. A goodly monument is since erected to his memory.

Now did his Majesty again dine in the presence, in ancient state, with music and all the court-ceremonies, which had been interrupted since the late war.

8th. Visited Mr. Oldenburg, a close prisoner in the Tower, being suspected of writing intelligence. I had an order from Lord Arlington, Secretary of State, which caused me to be admitted. This gentleman was secretary to our Society, and I am confident will prove an innocent person.[1]

15th. Finished my account, amounting to 25,000*l.*

17th. To the funeral of Mr. Farringdon, a relation of my wife's.

There was now a very gallant horse to be baited to death with dogs; but he fought them all, so as the fiercest of them could not fasten on him, till the men run him through with their swords. This wicked and barbarous sport deserved to have been punished in the cruel contrivers to get money, under pretence that the horse had killed a man, which was false. I would not be persuaded to be a spectator.

21st. Saw the famous Italian puppet-play, for it was no other.

24th. I was appointed, with the rest of my brother Commissioners, to put in execution an order of Council for free-

---

[1] Henry Oldenburg, Secretary to the Royal Society. He was committed to the Tower, as Pepys informs us, "for writing news to a virtuoso in France," but was shortly afterwards liberated.

ing the prisoners-at-war in my custody at Leeds Castle, and taking off his Majesty's extraordinary charge, having called before us the French and Dutch agents. The Peace was now proclaimed, in the usual form, by the heralds-at-arms.

25th August. After evening service, I went to visit Mr. Vaughan,[1] who lay at Greenwich, a very wise and learned person, one of Mr. Selden's executors and intimate friends.

27th. Visited the Lord Chancellor, to whom his Majesty had sent for the seals a few days before; I found him in his bed-chamber, very sad. The Parliament had accused him, and he had enemies at Court, especially the buffoons and ladies of pleasure, because he thwarted some of them, and stood in their way; I could name some of the chief. The truth is, he made few friends during his grandeur among the royal sufferers, but advanced the old rebels. He was, however, though no considerable lawyer, one who kept up the form and substance of things in the Nation with more solemnity than some would have had. He was my particular kind friend, on all occasions. The Cabal, however, prevailed, and that party in Parliament. Great division at Court concerning him, and divers great persons interceding for him.

28th. I dined with my late Lord Chancellor, where also dined Mr. Ashburnham, and Mr. W. Legge, of the Bed-chamber;[2] his Lordship pretty well in heart, though now many of his friends and sycophants abandoned him.

In the afternoon, to the Lords Commissioners for money, and thence to the audience of a Russian Envoy in the Queen's presence-chamber, introduced with much state, the soldiers, pensioners, and guards in their order. His letters of credence brought by his secretary in a scarf of sarsenet, their vests sumptuous, much embroidered with pearls. He delivered his speech in the Russ language, but without the

---

[1] Afterwards, Lord Chief Justice.
[2] John Ashburnham, Groom of the Bedchamber to Charles I. and Charles II. Colonel William Legge, Treasurer and Superintendent of the Ordnance, Member for Southampton, and father of the first Lord Dartmouth, filled the same post. Pepys describes him as " a pleasant man, and that hath seen much of the world, and more of the Court." He was with Charles I. during the rebellion, and represented Sussex in Parliament. Another of the Ashturnhams filled the office of Cofferer. Pepys frequently alludes to both.

least action, or motion, of his body, which was immediately interpreted aloud by a German that spake good English: half of it consisted in repetition of the Czar's Titles, which were very haughty and oriental: the substance of the rest was, that he was only sent to see the King and Queen, and know how they did, with much compliment and frothy language. Then, they kissed their Majesties' hands, and went as they came; but their real errand was to get money.

29*th August.* We met at the Star-Chamber about exchange and release of prisoners.

7th September. Came Sir John Kiviet, to article with me about his brickwork.[1]

13*th.* Betwixt the hours of twelve and one, was born my second daughter, who was afterwards christened Elizabeth.

19*th.* To London, with Mr. Henry Howard, of Norfolk, of whom I obtained the gift of his Arundelian Marbles, those celebrated and famous inscriptions Greek and Latin, gathered with so much cost and industry from Greece, by his illustrious grandfather, the magnificent Earl of Arundel, my noble friend whilst he lived. When I saw these precious monuments miserably neglected, and scattered up and down about the garden, and other parts of Arundel House, and how exceedingly the corrosive air of London impaired them, I procured him to bestow them on the University of Oxford. This he was pleased to grant me; and now gave me the key of the gallery, with leave to mark all those stones, urns, altars, &c., and whatever I found had inscriptions on them, that were not statues. This I did; and getting them removed and piled together, with those which were incrusted in the garden walls, I sent immediately letters to the Vice-Chancellor of what I had procured, and that if they esteemed it a service to the University (of which I had been a member), they should take order for their transportation.

This done, 21*st*, I accompanied Mr. Howard to his villa at Albury, where I designed for him the plot of his canal and garden, with a crypt[2] through the hill.

24*th.* Returned to London, where I had orders to deliver the possession of Chelsea College (used as my prison during the war with Holland for such as were sent from the fleet

---

[1] *Ante,* pp. 22, 24.

[2] Still in part remaining (1820), but stopped up at the further end.

to London) to our Society, as a gift of his Majesty our founder.

8th October. Came to dine with me Dr. Bathurst, Dean of Wells, President of Trinity College, sent by the Vice-Chancellor of Oxford, in the name both of him and the whole University, to thank me for procuring the Inscriptions, and to receive my directions what was to be done to show their gratitude to Mr. Howard.

11th. I went to see Lord Clarendon, late Lord Chancellor and greatest officer in England, in continual apprehension what the Parliament would determine concerning him.

17th. Came Dr. Barlow, Provost of Queen's College and Protobibliothecus of the Bodleian library, to take order about the transportation of the Marbles.

25th. There were delivered to me two letters from the Vice-Chancellor of Oxford, with the Decree of the Convocation, attested by the Public Notary, ordering four Doctors of Divinity and Law to acknowledge the obligation the University had to me for procuring the *Marmora Arundeliana,* which was solemnly done by Dr. Barlow,[1] Dr. Jenkins,[2] Judge of the Admiralty, Dr. Lloyd, and Obadiah Walker,[3] of University College, who having made a large compliment from the University, delivered me the decree fairly written:

Gesta venerabili domo Convocationis Universitatis Oxon.; . . 17. 1667.   Quo die retulit ad Senatum Academicum Dominus Vicecancellarius, quantum Universitas deberet singulari benevolentiæ Johannis Evelini Armigeri, qui pro eâ pietate quâ Almam Matrem prosequitur non solum Suasu et Consilio apud inclytum Heroem Henricum Howard, Ducis Norfolciæ hæredem, intercessit, et Universitati pretiosissimum eruditæ antiquitatis thesaurum Marmora Arundeliana largiretur; sed egregium insuper in ijs colligendis asservandisq; navavit operam : Quapropter unanimi suffragio Venerabilis Domûs decretum est, ut eidem publicæ gratiæ per delegatos ad Honoratissimum Dominum Henricum Howard propediem mittendos solemnitèr reddantur.
Concordant superscripta cum originali collatione factâ per me Ben. Cooper, Notarium Publicum et Registarium Universitat Oxon.

    " SIR,
" We intend also a noble inscription, in which also honourable mention shall be made of yourself; but Mr. Vice-Chancellor commands

---

[1] Bishop of Lincoln.
[2] Afterwards Sir Leoline Jenkins, Secretary of State.
[3] Subsequently, head of that College. See *ante*, vol. i. pp. 257, 285; also, see *post*, under 1675, July; and 1686, May.

me to tell you that that was not sufficient for your merits; but, that if
your occasions would permit you to come down at the Act (when we
intend a dedication of our new Theatre), some other testimony should
be given both of your own worth and affection to this your old Mother;
for we are all very sensible that this great addition of learning and reputation to the University is due as well to your industrious care for the
University, and interest with my Lord Howard, as to his great nobleness and generosity of spirit.

"I am, Sir, your most humble servant,
"OBADIAH WALKER, Univ. Coll."

The Vice-Chancellor's letter to the same effect were too
vainglorious to insert, with divers copies of verses that were
also sent me. Their mentioning me in the inscription I
totally declined, when I directed the titles of Mr. Howard,
now made Lord, upon his Ambassage to Morocco.

These four doctors, having made me this compliment,
desired me to carry and introduce them to Mr. Howard,
at Arundel-House: which I did, Dr. Barlow (Provost of
Queen's) after a short speech, delivering a larger letter of
the University's thanks, which was written in Latin, expressing the great sense they had of the honour done them.
After this compliment handsomely performed and as nobly
received, Mr. Howard accompanied the Doctors to their
coach. That evening, I supped with them.

26th October. My late Lord Chancellor was accused by
Mr. Seymour in the House of Commons; and, in the evening, I returned home.

31st. My birth-day—blessed be God for all his mercies!
I made the Royal Society a present of the Table of Veins,
Arteries, and Nerves, which great curiosity I had caused to
be made in Italy, out of the natural human bodies, by a
learned physician, and the help of Veslingius (professor at
Padua), from whence I brought them in 1646.[1] For this
I received the public thanks of the Society; and they are
hanging up in their Repository with an inscription.

9th December. To visit the late Lord Chancellor.[2] I found

[1] See ante, vol. i. p. 224.
[2] This entry of the 9th December, 1667, is a mistake. Evelyn could
not have visited the "late Lord Chancellor" on that day. Lord Clarendon fled on Saturday, the 29th of November, 1667, and his letter
resigning the Chancellorship of the University of Oxford is dated from
Calais on the 7th of December. That Evelyn's book is not, in every
respect, strictly a diary, is shown by this and several similar passages

him in his garden at his new-built palace, sitting in his gout
wheel-chair, and seeing the gates setting up towards the
north and the fields. He looked and spake very disconso-
lately. After some while deploring his condition to me, I
took my leave. Next morning, I heard he was gone;
though I am persuaded that, had he gone sooner, though but
to Cornbury, and there lain quiet, it would have satisfied
the Parliament. That which exasperated them was his pre-
suming to stay and contest the accusation as long as it was
possible : and they were on the point of sending him to the
Tower.   '

10*th* *December*. I went to the funeral of Mrs. Heath, wife
of my worthy friend and schoolfellow.

21*st*. I saw one Carr pilloried at Charing-cross for a
libel, which was burnt before him by the hangman.

1667-8. 8*th* *January*. I saw deep and prodigious gaming
at the Groom-Porter's, vast heaps of gold squandered away
in a vain and profuse manner. This I looked on as a horrid
vice, and unsuitable in a Christian Court.

9*th*. Went to see the revels at the Middle Temple, which
is also an old riotous custom, and has relation neither to
virtue nor policy.

10*th*. To visit Mr. Povey, where were divers great Lords
to see his well-contrived cellar, and other elegancies.[1]

24*th*. We went to stake out ground for building a college
for the Royal Society at Arundel House, but did not finish
it, which we shall repent of.

4*th February*. I saw the tragedy of *Horace* (written by the
virtuous Mrs. Philips) acted before their Majesties. Betwixt
each act a masque and antique dance. The excessive gallantry of the ladies was infinite, those especially on that
. . . . Castlemaine, esteemed at 40,000*l*. and more, far
outshining the Queen.

15*th*. I saw the audience of the Swedish Ambassador
Count Donna, in great state in the banqueting-house.

3*rd March*. Was launched at Deptford, that goodly vessel,

already adverted to in the remarks prefixed to the present edition. If
the entry of the 18th of August, 1683, is correct, the date of Evelyn's
last visit to Lord Clarendon was the 28th of November, 1667. (See
p. 194 of the present volume.)

[1] See *ante*, p. 9, and vol. i. pp. 394, 403 ; and *post*, p. 111.

                                                              D 2

The Charles I was near his Majesty. She is longer than the Sovereign, and carries 110 brass cannon; she was built by old Shish, a plain honest carpenter, master-builder of this dock, but one who can give very little account of his art by discourse, and is hardly capable of reading,[1] yet of great ability in his calling. The family have been ship-carpenter. in this yard above 300 years.

12th March. Went to visit Sir John Cotton, who had m into his library, full of good MSS. Greek and Latin, but mos famous for those of the Saxon and English Antiquities, collected by his grandfather.

2nd April. To the Royal Society, where I subscribed 50,000 bricks, towards building a college. Amongst other libertine libels, there was one now printed and thrown about, a bold petition of the poor w——s to Lady Castlemaine.[2]

9th. To London, about finishing my grand account of the sick and wounded, and prisoners at war, amounting to above £34,000.

I heard Sir R. Howard impeach Sir William Penn,[3] in the House of Lords, for breaking bulk, and taking away rich goods out of the East India prizes, formerly taken by Lord Sandwich.

28th. To London, about the purchase of Ravensbourne Mills, and land around it, in Upper Deptford, of one Mr. Becher.

30th. We sealed the deeds in Sir Edward Thurland's chambers in the Inner Temple. I pray God bless it to me, it being a dear pennyworth; but the passion Sir R. Browne had for it, and that it was contiguous to our other grounds, engaged me!

13th May. Invited by that expert commander, Captain

---

[1] The like was to be said of Mr. Brindley, who executed such great works for the Duke of Bridgewater towards the close of the eighteenth century.

[2] Evelyn has been supposed himself to have written this piece.

[3] Father of the Founder of Pennsylvania, whom Evelyn in a subsequent page accuses of having published "a blasphemous book against the Deity of our blessed Lord." Sir William Penn held the rank of Admiral, and had distinguished himself in the battle with the Dutch in 1664, which gained him the honour of knighthood. He was Governor of Kinsale, and died in 1670.

Cox, master of the lately built Charles the Second, now the best vessel of the fleet, designed for the Duke of York, I went to Erith, where we had a great dinner.

16*th May*. Sir Richard Edgecombe, of Mount Edgecombe, by Plymouth, my relation, came to visit me ; a very virtuous and worthy gentleman.

19*th June*. To a new play with several of my relations, *The Evening Lover*,[1] a foolish plot, and very profane ; it afflicted me to see how the stage was degenerated and polluted by the licentious times.

2*nd July*. Sir Samuel Tuke, Bart.,[2] and the lady he had married this day, came and bedded at night at my house, many friends accompanying the bride.

23*rd*. At the Royal Society, were presented divers *glossa petras*, and other natural curiosities, found in digging to build the fort at Sheerness. They were just the same as they bring from Malta, pretending them to be viper's teeth, whereas, in truth, they are of a shark, as we found by comparing them with one in our Repository.

3*rd August*. Mr. Bramstone, (son to Judge B.), my old fellow-traveller, now Reader at the Middle Temple, invited me to his feast, which was so very extravagant and great as the like had not been seen at any time. There were the Duke of Ormond, Privy Seal, Bedford, Belasis, Halifax, and a world more of Earls and Lords.

14*th*. His Majesty was pleased to grant me a lease of a slip of ground out of Brick Close, to enlarge my fore-court, for which I now gave him thanks ; then, entering into other discourse, he talked to me of a new varnish for ships, instead of pitch, and of the gilding with which his new yacht was beautified. I showed his Majesty the perpetual motion sent to me by Dr. Stokes, from Cologne ; and then came in Monsieur Colbert, the French Ambassador.

19*th*. I saw the magnificent entry of the French Ambas-

---

[1] There is no play extant with this name ; and though the latter might be but a second title (for Evelyn frequently mentions only one name of a play that has two), it is next to certain that he here means Dryden's comedy of *An Evening's Love, or, The Mock Astrologer*, which is indeed sufficiently licentious. It was produced and printed in 1668, when Evelyn appears to have seen it.

[2] Evelyn's cousin, and a colonel in the army of Charles I. His seat was at Cressing Temple, Essex.

sador Co.bert, received in the Banqueting House. I had never seen a richer coach than that which he came in to Whitehall. Standing by his Majesty at dinner in the presence, there was of that rare fruit called the King-pine, growing in Barbadoes and the West Indies; the first of them I had ever seen.[1] His Majesty having cut it up, was pleased to give me a piece off his own plate to taste of; but, in my opinion, it falls short of those ravishing varieties of deliciousness described in Captain Ligon's History, and others; but possibly it might, or certainly was, much impaired in coming so far; it has yet a grateful acidity, but tastes more like the quince and melon than of any other fruit he mentions.

28th August. Published my book of *The Perfection of Painting*,[2] dedicated to Mr. Howard.

17th September. I entertained Signor Muccinigo, the Venetian Ambassador, of one of the noblest families of the State, this being the day of making his public entry, setting forth from my house with several gentlemen of Venice and others in a very glorious train. He staid with me till the Earl of Anglesea and Sir Charles Cotterell (Master of the Ceremonies) came with the King's barge to carry him to the Tower, where the guns were fired at his landing; he then entered his Majesty's coach, followed by many others of the nobility. I accompanied him to his house, where there was a most noble supper to all the company, of course. After the extraordinary compliments to me and my wife, for the civilities he received at my house, I took leave and returned. He is a very accomplished person. He is since Ambassador at Rome.

29th. I had much discourse with Signor Pietro Cisij, a Persian gentleman, about the affairs of Turkey, to my great satisfaction. I went to see Sir Elias Leighton's[3] project of a cart with iron axle-trees.

[1] See *ante,* as to the Queen-pine, vol. i. p. 374.
[2] Reprinted in Evelyn's "Miscellaneous Writings," pp. 553-562.
[3] The Sir Ellis Layton of Pepys. He was secretary to the Prize Office, and to the Duke of York. "A mad freaking fellow"—according to one authority—though a Doctor of Civil Law, and brother to the Bishop of Dumblane. According to another, "for a speech of forty words the wittiest man that ever he knew," and moreover "one of the best companions at a meal in the world."

8th November. Being at dinner, my sister Evelyn sent for me to come up to London to my continuing sick brother.

14th. To London, invited to the consecration of that excellent person, the Dean of Ripon, Dr. Wilkins, now made Bishop of Chester; it was at Ely-House, the Archbishop of Canterbury, Dr. Cosin Bishop of Durham, the Bishops of Ely, Salisbury, Rochester, and others officiating. Dr. Tillotson preached. Then, we went to a sumptuous dinner in the hall, where were the Duke of Buckingham, Judges, Secretaries of State, Lord-Keeper, Council, Noblemen, and innumerable other company, who were honourers of this incomparable man, universally beloved by all who knew him. This being the Queen's birth-day, great was the gallantry at Whitehall, and the night celebrated with very fine fireworks.

My poor brother continuing ill, I went not from him till the 17th, when, dining at the Groom Porters, I heard Sir Edward Sutton play excellently on the Irish harp; he performs genteelly, but not approaching my worthy friend, Mr. Clark, a gentleman of Northumberland, who makes it execute lute, viol, and all the harmony an instrument is capable of; pity it is that it is not more in use; but, indeed, to play well, takes up the whole man, as Mr. Clark has assured me, who, though a gentleman of quality and parts, was yet brought up to that instrument from five years old, as I remember he told me.

25th. I waited on Lord Sandwich, who presented me with a Sembrador he brought out of Spain, showing me his two books of observations made during his embassy and stay at Madrid; in which were several rare things he promised to impart to me.

27th. I dined at my Lord Ashley's (since Earl of Shaftesbury), when the match of my niece[1] was proposed for his only son, in which my assistance was desired for my Lord.

28th. Dr. Patrick preached at Covent Garden, on Acts xvii. 31, the certainty of Christ's coming to judgment, it being Advent; a most suitable discourse.

19th December. I went to see the old play of *Cataline* acted, having been now forgotten almost forty years.

20th. I dined with my Lord Cornbury, at Clarendon-

[1] Probably the daughter of his Brother, Richard, of Epsom, but who married Mr. Montagu.

House, now bravely furnished, especially with the pictures of most of our ancient and modern wits, poets, philosophers, famous and learned Englishmen; which collection of the Chancellor's I much commended, and gave his Lordship a catalogue of more to be added.[1]

[1] It will be well to subjoin here what is said by Evelyn, in a letter to the Lord Chancellor, dated 18th March, 1666-7:

"My Lord, your Lordship inquires of me what pictures might be added to the Assembly of the Learned and Heroic persons of England which your Lordship has already collected; the design of which I do infinitely more magnify than the most famous heads of foreigners, which do not concern the glory of our country; and it is my opinion the most honourable ornament, the most becoming and obliging, which your Lordship can think of to adorn your palace withal, such, therefore, as seem to be wanting, I shall range under these three heads:

THE LEARNED.

Sir Hen. Saville.   Geo. Ripley.
Abp. of Armagh.   Wm. of Occam.
Dr. Harvey.   Hadrian 4th.
Sir H. Wotton   Alex. Ales.
Sir T. Bodley.   Ven. Bede.
G. Buchanan.   Jo. Duns Scotus.
Jo. Barclay.   Alcuinus,
Ed. Spencer.   Ridley,
Wm. Lily.   Latimer, } martyrs.
Wm. Hooker.   Roger Ascham.
Dr. Sanderson.   Sir J. Checke.
Wm. Oughtred.   Ladies { Eliz. Joan Weston,*
M. Philips.   { Jane Grey.
Rog. Bacon.

POLITICIANS.

Sir Fra. Walsingham.   Card. Wolsey.
Earl of Leicester.   Sir T. Smith.
Sir W. Raleigh.   Card. Pole.

SOLDIERS.

Sir Fra. Drake.   Earl of Essex.
Sir J. Hawkins.   Talbot.
Sir Martin Frobisher.   Sir F. Greville.
Tho. Cavendish.   Hor. E. of Oxford.
Sir. Ph. Sidney.

Some of which, though difficult to procure originals of, yet haply copies

* For an account of Lady Joan Weston, less known than her companion, see Ballard's Learned Ladies. There is a very scarce volume of Latin Poems by her, printed at Prague, 1606, and Evelyn specially mentions her in his *Numismata*. She is often celebrated by the writers of her time.

31st December. I entertained my kind neighbours, according to custom, giving Almighty God thanks for His gracious mercies to me the past year.

1668-9. *1st January.* Imploring His blessing for the year entering, I went to church, where our Doctor preached on Psalm lxv. 12, apposite to the season, and beginning a new year.

· *3rd.* About this time one of Sir William Penn's sons had published a blasphemous book against the Deity of our Blessed Lord.

29th. I went to see a tall gigantic woman who measured 6 feet 10 inches high, at 21 years old, born in the Low Countries.

13th February. I presented his Majesty with my *History of the Four Impostors ;*[1] he told me of other like cheats. I gave my book to Lord Arlington, to whom I dedicated it. It was now that he began to tempt me about writing "the Dutch War."

15th. Saw Mrs. Phillips' *Horace*[2] acted again.

18th. To the Royal Society, when Signor Malpighi, an Italian physician and anatomist, sent this learned body the incomparable History of the Silkworm.

1st March. Dined at Lord Arlington's at Goring House, with the Bishop of Hereford.

might be found out upon diligent inquiries. The rest, I think, your Lordship has already in good proportion."

Writing on the same subject to Pepys, in a letter dated 12th August, 1689 (*Correspondence*, vol. iii. p. 294), Evelyn tells him that the Lord Chancellor, Clarendon, had collected Portraits of very many of our great men; and he proceeds to put them down, without order or arrangement, as he recollected them. He gives also there a list of Portraits which he recommended to be added, a little different from the list contained in the letter above-quoted ; and he adds, that "when Lord Clarendon's design of making this collection was known, everybody who had any of the portraits, or could purchase them at any price, strove to make their court by presenting them. By this means he got many excellent pieces of Vandyke, and other originals by Lely and other the best of our modern masters."

[1] Re-printed in Evelyn's " Miscellaneous Writings," pp. 563—620.

[2] *Ante,* p. 35. Mrs. Phillips was a poetess of celebrity in her time, known as " the matchless Orinda." The work mentioned by Evelyn, was her translation of P. Corneille's ' Horace,' which Pepys calls " a silly tragedy." Marcellus Malpighi was eminent for his discoveries respecting the economy of the liver and kidneys, and for his researches in vegetable physiology. He was born 1628, and died 1694.

4th March. To the Council of the Royal Society, about disposing my Lord Howard's library, now given to us.

16th. To London, to place Mr. Christopher Wase about my Lord Arlington.

18th. I went with Lord Howard of Norfolk, to visit Sir William Ducie at Charlton, where we dined; the servants made our coachmen so drunk, that they both fell off their boxes on the heath, where we were fain to leave them, and were driven to London by two servants of my Lord's. This barbarous custom of making the masters welcome by intoxicating the servants, had now the second time happened to my coachman.

My son came finally from Oxford.

2nd April. Dined at Mr. Treasurer's, where was (with many noblemen) Colonel Titus of the bed-chamber, author of the famous piece against Cromwell, *Killing no Murder.*

I now placed Mr. Wase with Mr. Williamson, Secretary to the Secretary of State, and Clerk of the Papers.

14th. I dined with the Archbishop of Canterbury, at Lambeth, and saw the library, which was not very considerable.

19th May. At a Council of the Royal Society our grant was finished, in which his Majesty gives us Chelsea College, and some land about it. It was ordered that five should be a quorum for a Council. The Vice-President was then sworn for the first time, and it was proposed how we should receive the Prince of Tuscany, who desired to visit the Society.

20th. This evening, at 10 o'clock, was born my third daughter, who was baptised on the 25th by the name of Susannah.

3rd June. Went to take leave of Lord Howard, going Ambassador to Morocco. Dined at Lord Arlington's, where were the Earl of Berkshire, Lord Saint John, Sir Robert Howard, and Sir R. Holmes.

10th. Came my Lord Cornbury, Sir William Pulteney,[1] and others to visit me. I went this evening to London, to carry Mr. Pepys to my brother Richard, now exceedingly

---

[1] A distinguished Parliament man, grandfather of the first Earl of Bath. He was a Commissioner of the Privy Seal under William III., and died in 1671.

afflicted with the stone, who had been sucessfully cut, and carried the stone as big as a tennis-ball to show him, and encourage his resolution to go through the operation.

30th June. My wife went a journey of pleasure down the river as far as the sea, with Mrs. Howard and her daughter, the Maid of Honour, and others, amongst whom that excellent creature, Mrs. Blagg.[1]

7th July. I went towards Oxford; lay at Little Wycomb.

8th. Oxford.

9th. In the morning, was celebrated the Encænia of the New Theatre, so magnificently built by the munificence of Dr. Gilbert Sheldon, Archbishop of Canterbury, in which was spent £25,000, as Sir Christopher Wren, the architect (as I remember), told me; and yet it was never seen by the benefactor, my Lord Archbishop having told me that he never did or ever would see it. It is, in truth, a fabric comparable to any of this kind of former ages, and doubtless exceeding any of the present, as this University does for colleges, libraries, schools, students, and order, all the Universities in the world. To the theatre is added the famous Sheldonian printing-house. This being at the Act and the first time of opening the Theatre (Acts being formerly kept in St. Mary's church, which might be thought indecent, that being a place set apart for the immediate worship of God, and was the inducement for building this noble pile), it was now resolved to keep the present Act in it, and celebrate its dedication with the greatest splendour and formality that might be; and, therefore, drew a world of strangers, and other company, to the University, from all parts of the nation.

The Vice-Chancellor, Heads of Houses, and Doctors, being seated in magisterial seats, the Vice-Chancellor's chair and desk, Proctors, &c. covered with brocatelle (a kind of brocade) and cloth of gold; the University Registrar read the founder's grant and gift of it to the University for their scholastic exercises upon these solemn occasions. Then

[1] Afterwards Mrs. Godolphin, whose life, written by Evelyn, has been published under the auspices of the Bishop of Oxford. The affecting circumstances of her death will be found recorded at p. 131 of the present volume.

followed Dr. South,[1] the University's orator, in an eloquent
speech. which was very long, and not without some malicious
and indecent reflections on the Royal Society, as under-
miners of the University; which was very foolish and untrue,
as well as unseasonable. But, to let that pass from an ill-
natured man, the rest was in praise of the Archbishop and
the ingenious architect. This ended, after loud music from
the corridor above, where an organ was placed, there followed divers panegyric speeches, both in prose and verse,
interchangeably pronounced by the young students placed
in the rostrums, in Pindarics, Eclogues, Heroics, &c., mingled
with excellent music, vocal and instrumental, to entertain
the ladies and the rest of the company. A speech was then
made in praise of academical learning. This lasted from
eleven in the morning till seven at night, which was concluded with ringing of bells, and universal joy and feasting.

10th July. The next day began the more solemn lectures
in all the faculties, which were performed in the several
schools, where all the Inceptor-Doctors did their exercises,
the Professors having first ended their reading. The assembly now returned to the Theatre, where the *Terræ filius*
(the *University Buffoon*) entertained the auditory with a
tedious, abusive, sarcastical rhapsody, most unbecoming the
gravity of the University, and that so grossly, that unless it
be suppressed, it will be of ill consequence, as I afterwards
plainly expressed my sense of it both to the Vice-Chancellor
and several Heads of Houses, who were perfectly ashamed
of it, and resolved to take care of it in future. The old
facetious way of rallying upon the questions was left off,
falling wholly upon persons, so that it was rather licentious
lying and railing than genuine and noble wit. In my life,
I was never witness of so shameful entertainment.

After this ribaldry, the Proctors made their speeches.
Then began the music art, vocal and instrumental, above in
the balustrade corridor opposite to the Vice-Chancellor's
seat. Then, Dr. Wallis, the mathematical Professor, made

---

[1] Robert South, D.D., prebendary of Westminster and Canon of
Christ-church, one of the most eloquent preachers of the seventeenth
century. Pepys alludes to his having been seized with a fainting fit in
the pulpit while preaching before the King. He nevertheless lived to
the age of eighty-three.

his oration, and created one Doctor of music according to the usual ceremonies of gown (which was of white damask), cap, ring, kiss, &c. Next followed the disputations of the Inceptor-Doctors in Medicine, the speech of their Professor, Dr. Hyde, and so in course their respective creations. Then disputed the Inceptors of Law, the speech of their Professor, and creation. Lastly, Inceptors of Theology: Dr. Compton (brother to the Earl of Northampton) being junior, began with great modesty and applause; so the rest. After which, Dr. Tillotson, Dr. Sprat, &c., and then Dr. Allestree's speech, the King's Professor, and their respective creations.[1] Last of all, the Vice-Chancellor, shutting up the whole in a panegyrical oration, celebrating their benefactor and the rest, apposite to the occasion.

Thus was the Theatre dedicated by the scholastic exercises in all the Faculties with great solemnity; and the night, as the former, entertaining the new Doctor's friends in feasting and music. I was invited by Dr. Barlow, the worthy and learned Professor of Queen's College.

11th July. The Act sermon was this forenoon preached by Dr. Hall, in St. Mary's, in an honest practical discourse against Atheism. In the afternoon, the church was so crowded, that not coming early I could not approach to hear.

[1] Thomas Hyde, D.D., Hebrew Reader, Keeper of the Bodleian Library, Prebend of Salisbury Cathedral, Regius Professor of Hebrew, and canon of Christchurch, Oxford; author of a Latin History of the Ancient Persians and Medes, and one of Walton's coadjutors in the great polyglot Bible. Born in 1638, and died in 1703.—Henry, son of Spencer Compton, Earl of Northampton, slain at the battle of Hopton Heath, commenced his career as a cornet of dragoons, but after a short time abandoned the army for the church, in which he raised himself by his talents to be Bishop of Oxford, and in 1675 was translated to the see of London. He was a zealous Protestant during the reign of James II., and not only was instrumental in bringing over William of Orange to this country, but placed the crown upon his head, on Archbishop Sancroft refusing to assist at the coronation. He wrote several works of a religious character, and a translation of the life of Donna Olympia Maldachina, from the Italian. He died in 1713.—Dr. Thomas Sprat, Bishop of Rochester, the biographer of Cowley, historian of the Royal Society, and author of sundry verses and sermons. Born in 1636, died 1713.—Richard Allestree was first designed for the church, but the Civil War forced him into the army. At the Restoration he returned to his original profession, in which he raised himself to considerable eminence. Born 1619, died 1680.

12th July. Monday. Was held the Divinity Act in the Theatre again, when proceeded seventeen Doctors, in all Faculties some.

13th. I dined at the Vice-Chancellor's, and spent the afternoon in seeing the rarities of the public libraries, and visiting the noble marbles and inscriptions, now inserted in the walls that compass the area of the Theatre, which were 150 of the most ancient and worthy treasures of that kind in the learned world. Now, observing that people approach them too near, some idle persons began to scratch and injure them, I advised that a hedge of holly should be planted at the foot of the wall, to be kept breast-high only to protect them; which the Vice-Chancellor promised to do the next season.

14th. Dr. Fell,[1] Dean of Christ-church and Vice-Chancellor, with Dr. Allestree, Professor, with beadles and maces before them, came to visit me at my lodging.—I went to visit Lord Howard's sons at Magdalen College.

15th. Having two days before had notice that the University intended me the honour of Doctorship, I was this morning attended by the beadles belonging to the Law, who conducted me to the Theatre, where I found the Duke of Ormond (now Chancellor of the University) with the Earl of Chesterfield and Mr. Spencer (brother to the late Earl of Sunderland). Thence, we marched to the Convocation-House, a convocation having been called on purpose; here, being all of us robed in the porch, in scarlet with caps and hoods, we were led in by the Professor of Laws, and presented respectively by name, with a short eulogy, to the Vice-Chancellor, who sate in the chair, with all the Doctors and Heads of Houses and masters about the room, which was exceeding full. Then, began the Public Orator his speech, directed chiefly to the Duke of Ormond, the Chancellor; but in which I had my compliment, in course. This ended, we were called up, and created Doctors according to the form, and seated by the Vice-Chancellor amongst the Doctors, on his right hand; then, the Vice-Chancellor made a short speech, and so, saluting our brother Doctors, the pageantry concluded, and the convocation was dissolved. So

[1] Afterwards Bishop of Oxford.

formal a creation of honorary Doctors had seldom been seen, that a convocation should be called on purpose, and speeches made by the Orator; but they could do no less, their Chancellor being to receive, or rather do them, this honour. I should have been made Doctor with the rest at the public Act, but their expectation of their Chancellor made them defer it. I was then led with my brother Doctors to an extraordinary entertainment at Doctor Mewes', head of St. John's College, and, after abundance of feasting and compliments, having visited the Vice-Chancellor and other Doctors, and given them thanks for the honour done me, I went towards home the 16th, and got as far as Windsor, and so to my house the next day.

4th August. I was invited by Sir Henry Peckham to his reading-feast in the Middle Temple, a pompous entertainment, where were the Archbishop of Canterbury, all the great Earls and Lords, &c. I had much discourse with my Lord Winchelsea, a prodigious talker; and the Venetian Ambassador.

17th. To London, spending almost the entire day in surveying what progress was made in re-building the ruinous City, which now began a little to revive after its sad calamity.

20th. I saw the splendid audience of the Danish Ambassador in the Banqueting-House at Whitehall.

23rd. I went to visit my most excellent and worthy neighbour, the Lord Bishop of Rochester, at Bromley, which he was now repairing, after the dilapidations of the late Rebellion.

2nd September. I was this day very ill of a pain in my limbs, which continued most of this week, and was increased by a visit I made to my old acquaintance, the Earl of Norwich, at his house in Epping Forest, where are many good pictures put into the wainscot of the rooms, which Mr. Baker, his Lordship's predecessor there, brought out of Spain; especially the History of Joseph, a picture of the pious and learned Picus Mirandula, and an incomparable one of old Breugel. The gardens were well understood, I mean the *potager*. I returned late in the evening, ferrying over the water at Greenwich.

26th. To church, to give God thanks for my recovery.

3rd Octeber. I received the Blessed Eucharist, to my unspeakable joy.

21st. To the Royal Society, meeting for the first time after a long recess, during vacation, according to custom ; where was read a description of the prodigious eruption of Mount Etna; and our English itinerant presented an account of his autumnal peregrination about England, for which we hired him, bringing dried fowls, fish, plants, animals, &c.

26th. My dear brother continued extremely full of pain, the Lord be gracious to him !

3rd November. This being the day of meeting for the poor, we dined neighbourly together.

25th. I heard an excellent discourse by Dr. Patrick, on the Resurrection; and afterwards, visited the Countess of Kent, my kinswoman.

8th December. To London, upon the second edition of my *Sylva*, which I presented to the Royal Society.

1669-70. *6th February.* Dr. John Breton, Master of Emmanuel College, in Cambridge (uncle to our vicar), preached on John i. 27; "whose shoe-lachet I am not worthy to unloose," &c., describing the various fashions of shoes, or sandals, worn by the Jews, and other nations : of the ornaments of the feet : how great persons had servants that took them off when they came to their houses, and bare them after them : by which pointing the dignity of our Saviour, when such a person as St. John Baptist acknowledged his unworthiness even of that mean office. The lawfulness, decentness, and necessity, of subordinate degrees and ranks of men and servants, as well in the Church as State : against the late levellers, and others of that dangerous rabble, who would have all alike.

3rd March. Finding my Brother [Richard] in such exceeding torture, and that he now began to fall into convulsion-fits, I solemnly set the next day apart to beg of God to mitigate his sufferings, and prosper the only means which yet remained for his recovery, he being not only much wasted, but exceedingly and all along averse from being cut (for the stone) ; but, when he at last consented, and it came to the operation, and all things prepared, his spirit and resolution failed.

6th March. Dr. Patrick[1] preached in Covent Garden church. I participated of the Blessed Sacrament, recommending to God the deplorable condition of my dear brother, who was almost in the last agonies of death. I watched late with him this night. It pleased God to deliver him out of this miserable life, towards five o'clock this Monday morning, to my unspeakable grief. He was a brother whom I most dearly loved, for his many virtues; but two years younger than myself, a sober, prudent, worthy gentleman. He had married a great fortune, and left one only daughter, and a noble seat at Woodcot, near Epsom. His body was opened, and a stone taken out of his bladder, not much bigger than a nutmeg. I returned home on the 8th, full of sadness, and to bemoan my loss.

20th. A stranger preached at the Savoy French church; the Liturgy of the Church of England being now used altogether, as translated into French by Dr. Durell.[2]

21st. We all accompanied the corpse of my dear brother to Epsom church, where he was decently interred in the chapel belonging to Woodcot House. A great number of friends and gentlemen of the country attended, about twenty coaches and six horses, and innumerable people.

22nd. I went to Westminster, where in the House of Lords I saw his Majesty sit on his throne, but without his robes, all the peers sitting with their hats on; the business of the day being the divorce of my Lord Ross. Such an occasion and sight had not been seen in England since the time of Henry VIII.[3]

[1] Simon Patrick, Prebendary of Westminster, Dean of Peterborough, Bishop of Chichester, thence removed to the see of Ely, and author of several religious works, in which he put himself forward as the champion of the Protestant party in the reign of James II. Born in 1626, died in 1707.

[2] John Durell, Dean of Windsor. He translated the Liturgy into the French and Latin languages, and was the author of a Vindication of the Church of England against schismatics. Born 1626, died 1683.

[3] Evelyn subjoins in a note: "When there was a project, 1669, for getting a divorce for the King, to facilitate it there was brought into the House of Lords a bill for dissolving the marriage of Lord Ross, on account of adultery, and to give him leave to marry again. This Bill, after great debates, passed by the plurality of only two votes, and that by the great industry of the Lord's friends, as well as the Duke's

5th May. To London, concerning the office of Latin Secretary to his Majesty, a place of more honour and dignity than profit, the reversion of which he had promised me.

21st. Came to visit me Mr. Henry Saville, and Sir Charles Scarborough.

26th. Receiving a letter from Mr. Philip Howard, Lord Almoner to the Queen,[1] that Monsieur Evelin, first physician to Madame (who was now come to Dover to visit the King her brother), was come to town, greatly desirous to see me ; but his stay so short, that he could not come to me, I went with my brother to meet him at the Tower, where he was seeing the magazines and other curiosities, having never before been in England : we renewed our alliance and friendship, with much regret on both sides that, he being to return towards Dover that evening, we could not enjoy one another any longer. How this French family, Ivelin, of Evelin, Normandy, a very ancient and noble house is grafted into our pedigree, see in the collection brought from Paris, 1650.

16th June. I went with some friends to the Bear Garden, where was cock-fighting, dog-fighting, bear and bull-baiting, it being a famous day for all these butcherly sports, or rather barbarous cruelties. The bulls did exceeding well, but the Irish wolf-dog exceeded, which was a tall greyhound, a stately creature indeed, who beat a cruel mastiff. One of the bulls tossed a dog full into a lady's lap as she sate in one of the boxes at a considerable height from the arena. Two poor dogs were killed, and so all ended with the ape on horseback, and I most heartily weary of the rude and dirty pastime, which I had not seen, I think, in twenty years before.

18th. Dined at Goring House, whither my Lord Arlington carried me from Whitehall with the Marquis of Wor-

cuemies, who carried it on chiefly in hopes it might be a precedent and inducement for the King to enter the more easily into their late proposals : nor were they a little encouraged therein, when they saw the King countenance and drive on the Bill in Lord Ross's favour. Of eighteen Bishops that were in the House, only two voted for the bill, of which one voted through age, and one was reputed Socinian."—The two Bishops favourable to the bill were Dr. Cosin, Bishop of Durham, and Dr. Wilkins, Bishop of Chester.

[1] Afterwards created Cardinal.

cester; there, we found Lord Sandwich, Viscount Stafford,[1] the Lieutenant of the Tower, and others. After dinner, my Lord communicated to me his Majesty's desire that I would engage to write the History of our late War with the Hollanders, which I had hitherto declined; this I found was ill taken, and that I should disoblige his Majesty, who had made choice of me to do him this service, and, if I would undertake it, I should have all the assistance the Secretary's office and others could give me, with other encouragements, which I could not decently refuse.

Lord Stafford rose from table, in some disorder, because there were roses stuck about the fruit when the dessert was set on the table; such an antipathy, it seems, he had to them as once Lady Selenger[2] also had, and to that degree that, as Sir Kenelm Digby tells us, laying but a rose upon her cheek when she was asleep, it raised a blister: but Sir Kenelm was a teller of strange things.

24*th June.* Came the Earl of Huntingdon and Countess, with the Lord Sherard, to visit us.

29*th.* To London, in order to my niece's marriage, Mary, daughter to my late brother Richard, of Woodcot, with the eldest son of Mr. Attorney Montague, which was celebrated at Southampton-House chapel, after which a magnificent entertainment, feast, and dancing, dinner and supper, in the great room there; but the bride was bedded at my sister's lodging, in Drury-Lane.

6*th July.* Came to visit me Mr. Stanhope, Gentleman-Usher to her Majesty, and uncle to the Earl of Chesterfield, a very fine man, with my Lady Hutcheson.

19*th.* I accompanied my worthy friend, that excellent man, Sir Robert Murray, with Mr. Slingsby, Master of the Mint, to see the latter's Seat and estate at Burrow-Green in Cambridgeshire, he desiring our advice for placing a new house, which he was resolved to build.[3] We set out in a

---

[1] Sir William Howard, created in November, 1640, Viscount Stafford In 1678, he was accused of complicity with the Popish Plot, and upon trial by his Peers in Westminster Hall, was found guilty, by a majority of twenty-four. He was beheaded, Dec. 29, 1680, on Tower Hill.

[2] St. Leger.

[3] It is probable that Slingsby did not build, and that after his misfortunes (see *post,* p. 281) it was sold. Lysons tells us, in his Magna

coach and six horses with him and his lady, dined about
midway at one Mr. Turner's, where we found a very noble
dinner, venison, music, and a circle of country ladies and
their gallants. After dinner, we proceeded, and came to
Burrow-Green that night. This had been the ancient seat
of the Cheekes (whose daughter Mr. Slingsby married),
formerly tutor to King Henry VI. The old house large and
ample, and built for ancient hospitality, ready to fall down
with age, placed in a dirty hole, a stiff clay, no water, next
an adjoining church-yard, and with other inconveniences.
We pitched on a spot of rising ground, adorned with venerable
woods, a dry and sweet prospect east and west, and fit for a
park, but no running water; at a mile distance from the old
house.

20th July. We went to dine at Lord Allington's,[1] who
had newly built a house of great cost, I believe little less
than £20,000.[2] His architect was Mr. Pratt. It is seated
in a park, with a sweet prospect and stately avenue; but
water still defective; the house has also its infirmities.
Went back to Mr. Slingsby's.

22nd. We rode out to see the great mere, or level, of
recovered fen land, not far off. In the way, we met Lord
Arlington going to his house in Suffolk, accompanied with
Count Ogniati, the Spanish minister, and Sir Bernard Gas-
coigne; he was very importunate with me to go with him to
Euston, being but fifteen miles distant; but, in regard of
my company, I could not. So, passing through Newmarket,
we alighted to see his Majesty's house there, now new-building; the arches of the cellars beneath are well turned by
Mr. Samuel, the architect, the rest mean enough, and hardly
fit for a hunting-house. Many of the rooms above had the

Britannia, that all which remains of an old brick mansion is now con-
verted into a farm-house.
  [1] Since Constable of the Tower. *Evelyn's Note.*
  [2] A.) Horseheath. The Allingtons were seated here before 1239:
Evelyn's friend, William, who built the house above referred to, had
been created an Irish Peer by the title of Lord Allington. Lysons says
the house cost 70,000*l.*, and with the estate was sold, in 1687, to Mr.
John Bromley for 42,000*l.*, who expended 30,000*l.* more on the building. His grandson was created Lord Montford, in 1741. In 1776,
the second Lord Montford sold the estate, the house being sold, in
1777, for the materials, to be pulled down. See *Lysons,* pp. 216, 217.

chimneys in the angles and corners, a mode now introduced by his Majesty, which I do at no hand approve of. I predict it will spoil many noble houses and rooms, if followed. It does only well in very small and trifling rooms, but takes from the state of greater. Besides, this house is placed in a dirty street, without any court or avenue, like a common one, whereas it might, and ought to have been built at either end of the town, upon the very carpet where the sports are celebrated; but, it being the purchase of an old wretched house of my Lord Thomond's, his Majesty was persuaded to set it on that foundation, the most improper imaginable for a house of sport and pleasure.[1]

We went to see the stables and fine horses, of which many were here kept at a vast expense, with all the art and tenderness imaginable.

Being arrived at some meres, we found Lord Wotton and Sir John Kiviet[2] about their draining-engines, having, it seems, undertaken to do wonders on a vast piece of marsh-ground they had hired of Sir Thomas Chicheley, (Master of the Ordnance). They much pleased themselves with the hopes of a rich harvest of hemp and cole-seed, which was the crop expected.

Here we visited the engines and mills both for wind and water, draining it through two rivers, or graffs, cut by hand, and capable of carrying considerable barges, which went thwart one the other, discharging the water into the sea. Such this spot had been the former winter; it was astonishing to see it now dry, and so rich that weeds grew on the banks, almost as high as a man and horse. Here, my Lord and his partner had built two or three rooms, with Flanders white bricks, very hard. One of the great engines was in the kitchen, where I saw the fish swim up, even to the very chimney-hearth, by a small cut through the room, and running within a foot of the very fire.

Having, after dinner, ridden about that vast level, pestered with heat and swarms of gnats, we returned over Newmarket Heath, the way being mostly a sweet turf and down, like Salisbury Plain, the jockeys breathing their fine barbs and racers, and giving them their heats.

---

[1] Sold by the Crown in 1816.   [2] *Ante*, pp. 22, 24, 32.

23rd July.   We returned from Burrow-green to London, staying some time at Audley End. to see that fine palace. It is indeed a cheerful piece of Gothic building, or rather *antico moderno*, but placed in an obscure bottom. The cellars and galleries are very stately. It has a river by it, a pretty avenue of limes, and in a park.

This is in Saffron Walden parish, famous for that useful plant, with which all the country is covered.

Dining at Bishop-Stortford, we came late to London.

5th August. There was sent me by a neighbour a servant-maid, who, in the last month, as she was sitting before her mistress at work, felt a stroke on her arm a little above the wrist for some height, the smart of which, as if struck by another hand, caused her to hold her arm awhile till somewhat mitigated; but it put her into a kind of convulsion, or rather hysteric fit. A gentleman coming casually in, looking on her arm, found that part powdered with red crosses, set in most exact and wonderful order, neither swelled nor depressed, about this shape,

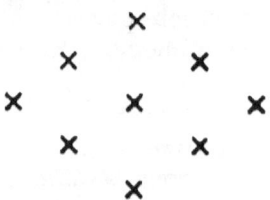

not seeming to be any way made by artifice, of a reddish colour, not so red as blood, the skin over them smooth, the rest of the arm livid and of a mortified hue, with certain prints as it were of the stroke of fingers. This had happened three several times in July, at about ten days' interval, the crosses beginning to wear out, but the successive ones set in other different, yet uniform order. The maid seemed very modest, and came from London to Deptford with her mistress, to avoid the discourse and importunity of curious people. She made no gain by it, pretended no religious fancies; but seemed to be a plain, ordinary, silent, working wench, somewhat fat, short, and high-coloured. She told me divers divines and physicians had seen her, but were unsatisfied; that she had taken some remedies against her fits, but they did her no good; she had never before had any its; once since, she seemed in her sleep to hear one say to her that she should tamper no more with them, nor trouble herself with any thing that happened, but put her trust in the merits of Christ only.

This is the substance of what she told me, and what I saw and curiously examined. I was formerly acquainted with the impostorious nuns of Loudun, in France, which made such noise amongst the Papists; I therefore thought this worth the notice. I remember Monsieur Monconys[1] (that curious traveller and a Roman Catholic) was by no means satisfied with the *stigmata* of those nuns, because they were so shy of letting him scrape the letters, which were Jesus, Maria, Joseph, (as I think,) observing they began to scale off with it, whereas this poor wench was willing to submit to any trial; so that I profess I know not what to think of it, nor dare I pronounce it anything supernatural.

26th August. At Windsor I supped with the Duke of Monmouth; and, the next day, invited by Lord Arlington, dined with the same Duke, and divers Lords. After dinner, my Lord and I had a conference of more than an hour alone in his bed-chamber, to engage me in the History. I showed him something that I had drawn up, to his great satisfaction, and he desired me to show it to the Treasurer.

28th. One of the Canons preached; then followed the offering of the Knights of the Order, according to custom; first the poor Knights, in procession, then, the Canons in their formalities, the Dean and Chancellor, then his Majesty (the Sovereign), the Duke of York, Prince Rupert; and, lastly, the Earl of Oxford, being all the Knights that were then at Court.

I dined with the Treasurer, and consulted with him what pieces I was to add; in the afternoon, the King took me aside into the balcony over the terrace, extremely pleased with what had been told him I had begun, in order to his commands, and enjoining me to proceed vigorously in it. He told me he had ordered the Secretaries of State to give me all necessary assistance of papers and particulars relating to it

[1] Balthasar de Monconys, a Frenchman, celebrated for his travels in the East, which he published in three volumes. His object was to dis-cover vestiges of the philosophy of Trismegistus and Zoroaster; in which, it is hardly necessary to add, he was not very successful.

and enjoïning me to make it a *little keen*, for that the Hollanders had very unhandsomely abused him in their pictures, books, and libels.

Windsor was now going to be repaired, being exceedingly ragged and ruinous. Prince Rupert, the Constable, had begun to trim up the keep or high round Tower, and handsomely adorned his hall with furniture of arms, which was very singular, by so disposing the pikes, muskets, pistols, bandoleers, holsters, drums, back, breast, and headpieces, as was very extraordinary. Thus, those huge steep stairs ascending to it had the walls invested with this martial furniture, all new and bright, so disposing the bandoleers, holsters, and drums, as to represent festoons, and that without any confusion, trophy-like. From the hall we went into his bed-chamber, and ample rooms hung with tapestry, curious and effeminate pictures, so extremely different from the other, which presented nothing but war and horror.

The King passed most of his time in hunting the stag, and walking in the park, which he was now planting with rows of trees.

13th September. To visit Sir Richard Lashford, my kinsman, and Mr. Charles Howard, at his extraordinary garden, at Deepden.

15th. I went to visit Mr. Arthur Onslow, at West Clandon, a pretty dry seat on the Downs, where we dined in his great room.

17th. To visit Mr. Hussey,[1] who, being near Wotton, lives in a sweet valley, deliciously watered.

23rd. To Albury, to see how that garden proceeded, which I found exactly done to the design and plot I had made, with the crypta through the mountain in the park, thirty perches in length. Such a Pausilippe[2] is nowhere in England. The canal was now digging, and the vineyard planted.

14th October. I spent the whole afternoon in private with the Treasurer, who put into my hands those secret pieces and transactions concerning the Dutch war, and particularly the expedition of Bergen, in which he had himself the chief part, and gave me instructions, till the King arriving from Newmarket, we both went up into his bed-chamber.

[1] At Sutton in Shere.
[2] A word adopted by Evelyn for a subterranean passage, from the famous grot of Pausilippo, at Naples.

21st October. Dined with the Treasurer; and, after dinner, we were shut up together. I received other [further] advices, and ten paper-books of despatches and treaties; to return which again I gave a note under my hand to Mr. Joseph Williamson, Master of the Paper-office.

31st. I was this morning fifty years of age; the Lord teach me to number my days so as to apply them to his glory! Amen.

4th November. Saw the Prince of Orange, newly come to see the King, his uncle; he has a manly, courageous, wise countenance, resembling his mother and the Duke of Glocester, both deceased.

I now also saw that famous beauty, but in my opinion of a childish, simple, and baby face, Mademoiselle Querouaille,[1] lately Maid of Honour to Madame, and now to be so to the Queen.

23rd. Dined with the Earl of Arlington, where was the Venetian Ambassador, of whom I now took solemn leave, now on his return. There were also Lords Howard, Wharton, Windsor, and divers other great persons.

24th. I dined with the Treasurer, where was the Earl of Rochester, a very profane wit.

15th December. It was the thickest and darkest fog on the Thames that was ever known in the memory of man, and I happened to be in the very midst of it. I supped with Monsieur Zulestein, late Governor to the late Prince of Orange.

1670-1. *10th January.* Mr. Bohun, my son's tutor, had been five years in my house, and now Bachelor of Laws, and Fellow of New College, went from me to Oxford to reside there, having well and faithfully performed his charge.

18th. This day, I first acquainted his Majesty with that incomparable young man, Gibbon,[2] whom I had lately met

[1] Henrietta, the King's sister, married to Philip, Duke of Orleans, was then on a visit here. Madame Querouaille came over in her train, on purpose to entice Charles into an union with Louis XIV.; a design which unhappily succeeded but too well. She became the King's mistress, was made Duchess of Portsmouth, and was his favourite till his death. See page 68.

[2] Better known by the name of Grinling Gibbons; celebrated for his exquisite carving. Some of his most astonishing work is at Chatsworth and at Petworth. Walpole in his *Catalogue of Painters*, thus speaks of him (and see Cunningham's *Lives of Sculptors*, iii. 1—16)

with in an obscure place by mere accident, as I was walking
near a poor solitary thatched house, in a field in our parish,

" *Grinling Gibbon.*—An original genius, a citizen of nature. There
is no instance before him of a man who gave to wood the loose and
airy lightness of flowers, and chained together the various productions
of the elements with the free disorder natural to each species. It is
uncertain whether he was born in Holland, or in England; it is said
that he lived in Bell-Savage Court, Ludgate Hill, and was employed
by Betterton, in decorating the Theatre, in Dorset Gardens. He lived
afterwards at Deptford, in the same house with a musician, where the
beneficent and curious Mr. Evelyn found and patronized both. This
gentleman, Sir P. Lely, and Bap. May, who was something of an architect himself, recommended Gibbon to Charles II., who was too indolent
to search for genius, and too indiscriminate in his bounty to confine it
to merit; but was always pleased when it was brought home to him.
He gave the artist a place in the Board of Works, and employed his
hand on ornaments of most taste in his palaces, particularly at Windsor.
Gibbon, in gratitude, made a present of his own bust in wood to Mr.
Evelyn, who kept it at his house in Dover-street. The piece that had
struck so good a judge was a large carving, in wood, of St. Stephen
stoned, long preserved in the sculptor's own house, and afterwards purchased and placed by the Duke of Chandos at Cannons."

Walpole is not quite correct, however, in such portions of this account
as relate to Evelyn. Gibbon, when young, was found by Evelyn in a
small house at Deptford, working on that famous piece from Tintoret
here said to represent the stoning of St. Stephen, and which seems,
from Evelyn's account, to have been his first performance of consequence. But it must have been afterwards that he lived in Belle-
Sauvage Yard, and that he worked on the Theatre in Dorset Gardens
Evelyn does not mention a musician, and says there was only an old
woman with him in the house at Deptford. It was Evelyn who recommended him to the King, to May the architect, and to Sir Christopher
Wren. Of the bust nothing is known at Wotton.

Subjoined is an original Letter, addressed by Grinling Gibbon to
Evelyn :

Honred
S[r] I wold beg the faver wen you see S[r] Joseff Williams [Williamson]
again you wold be pleased to speack to him that hee wold get mee to
Carve his Ladis sons hous my Lord Kildare for I onderstand it will
[be] verry considerabell ar If you haen Acquantans wich my Lord to
speack to him his sealf and I shall for Ev're be obliaged to You I
wold speack to S[lr] Josef my sealf but I knouw it would do better from
you

S[r] youre Most umbell
Sarvant

Lond 23 Mar. 1682.   G. GIBBON.

Upon receipt of this, Evelyn wrote to Lord Kildare, recommending
Gibbon ; and to Gibbon, enclosing the letter.

near Sayes Court. I found him shut in; but looking in at the window, I perceived him carving that large cartoon, or crucifix, of Tintoretto, a copy of which I had myself brought from Venice, where the original painting remains. I asked if I might enter; he opened the door civilly to me, and I saw him about such a work as for the curiosity of handling, drawing, and studious exactness, I˙ never had before seen in all my travels. I questioned him why he worked in such an obscure and lonesome place; he told me it was that he might apply himself to his profession without interruption, and wondered not a little how I found him out. I asked if he was unwilling to be made known to some great man, for that I believed it might turn to his profit; he answered, he was yet but a beginner, but would not be sorry to sell off that piece; on demanding the price, he said £100. In good earnest, the very frame was worth the money, there being nothing in nature so tender and delicate as the flowers and festoons about it, and yet the work was very strong; in the piece was more than one hundred figures of men, &c. I found he was likewise musical, and very civil, sober, and discreet in his discourse. There was only an old woman in the house. So, desiring leave to visit him sometimes, I went away.

Of this young artist, together with my manner of finding him out, I acquainted the King, and begged that he would give me leave to bring him and his work to Whitehall, for that I would adventure my reputation with his Majesty that he had never seen anything approach it, and that he would be exceedingly pleased, and employ him. The King said he would himself go see him. This was the first notice his Majesty ever had of Mr. Gibbon.

20th January. The King came to me in the Queen's withdrawing-room from the circle of ladies, to talk with me as to what advance I had made in the Dutch History. I dined with the Treasurer, and afterwards we went to the Secretary's Office, where we conferred about divers particulars.

21st. I was directed to go to Sir George Downing, who having been a public minister in Holland, at the beginning of the war, was to give me light in some material passages.

This year the weather was so wet, stormy, and unseasonable, as had not been known in many years.

9th February. I saw the great ball danced by the Queen and distinguished ladies at Whitehall Theatre. Next day, was acted there the famous play, called *The Siege of Granada,* two days acted successively; there were indeed very glorious scenes and perspectives, the work of Mr. Streeter, who well understands it.[1]

19th. This day dined with me Mr. Surveyor, Dr. Christopher Wren, and Mr. Pepys, Clerk of the Acts, two extraordinary, ingenious, and knowing persons, and other friends. I carried them to see the piece of carving which I had recommended to the King.

25th. Came to visit me one of the Lords Commissioners of Scotland for the Union.

28th. The Treasurer acquainted me that his Majesty was graciously pleased to nominate me one of the Council of Foreign Plantations, and give me a salary of £500 per annum, to encourage me.

29th. I went to thank the Treasurer, who was my great friend, and loved me; I dined with him and much company, and went thence to my Lord Arlington, Secretary of State, in whose favour I likewise was upon many occasions, though I cultivated neither of their friendships by any mean submissions. I kissed his Majesty's hand, on his making me one of that new-established Council.

1st March. I caused Mr. Gibbon to bring to Whitehall his excellent piece of carving, where being come, I advertised his Majesty, who asked me where it was; I told him in Sir Richard Browne's (my father-in-law) chamber, and that if it pleased his Majesty to appoint whither it should be brought, being large and though of wood heavy, I would take care for it. " No," says the King, "show me the way, I'll go to Sir Richard's chamber," which he immediately did, walking along the entries after me; as far as the ewry, ill he came up into the room, where I also lay. No sooner

---

[1] Evelyn here refers to Dryden's *Conquest of Granada.* Robert Streeter, an artist held in much esteem at this period, and enjoying the post of Serjeant Painter to the King, who was very fond of him, died in 1680. He is often mentioned by Evelyn. See *post*, pp. 85, 101, 142, and 178.

was he entered and cast his eye on the work, but he was astonished at the curiosity of it; and having considered it a long time, and discoursed with Mr. Gibbon, whom I brought to kiss his hand, he commanded it should be immediately carried to the Queen's side to show her. It was carried up into her bed-chamber, where she and the King looked on and admired it again; the King, being called away, left us with the Queen, believing she would have bought it, it being a crucifix; but, when his Majesty was gone, a French peddling woman, one Madame de Boord, who used to bring petticoats and fans, and baubles, out of France to the ladies, began to find fault with several things in the work, which she understood no more than an ass, or a monkey, so as in a kind of indignation, I caused the person who brought it to carry it back to the chamber, finding the Queen so much governed by an ignorant Frenchwoman, and this incomparable artist had his labour only for his pains, which not a little displeased me; and he was fain to send it down to his cottage again; he not long after sold it for 80*l*., though well worth 100*l*., without the frame, to Sir George Viner.

His Majesty's Surveyor, Mr. Wren, faithfully promised me to employ him.[1] I having also bespoke his Majesty for his work at Windsor, which my friend, Mr. May, the architect there, was going to alter, and repair universally; for, on the next day, I had a fair opportunity of talking to his Majesty about it, in the lobby next the Queen's side, where I presented him with some sheets of my history. I thence walked with him through St. James's Park to the garden, where I both saw and heard a very familiar discourse between . . . . . and Mrs. Nelly,[2] as they called an impudent comedian, she looking out of her garden on a terrace at the top of the wall, and . . . . . standing on the green walk under it. I was heartily sorry at this scene. Thence the King walked to the Duchess of Cleveland, another lady of pleasure, and curse of our nation.

---

[1] The carving in the Choir, &c. of St. Paul's Cathedral was executed by Gibbon.
[2] Nell Gwynne: there can be no doubt as to the name with which we are to fill up these blanks. This familiar interv'ew of Nelly and the King has afforded a subject for painters.

5th March. I dined at Greenwich, to take leave of Sir Thomas Linch, going Governor of Jamaica.

10th. To London, about passing my patent as one of the standing Council for Plantations, a considerable honour, the others in the Council being chiefly noblemen and officers of state.

2nd April. To Sir Thomas Clifford, the Treasurer, to condole with him on the loss of his eldest son, who died at Florence.

2nd May. The French King, being now with a great army of 28,000 men about Dunkirk, divers of the grandees of that Court, and a vast number of gentlemen and cadets, in fantastical habits, came flocking over to see our Court, and compliment his Majesty. I was present, when they first were conducted into the Queen's withdrawing-room, where saluted their Majesties the Dukes of Guise, Longueville, and many others of the first rank.

10th. Dined at Mr. Treasurer's,[1] in company with Monsieur De Grammont and several French noblemen, and one Blood, that impudent bold fellow who had not long before attempted to steal the imperial crown itself out of the Tower, pretending only curiosity of seeing the regalia there, when stabbing the keeper, though not mortally, he boldly went away with it through all the guards, taken only by the accident of his horse falling down. How he came to be pardoned, and even received into favour, not only after this, but several other exploits almost as daring both in Ireland and here, I could never come to understand. Some believed he became a spy of several parties, being well with the Sectaries and Enthusiasts, and did his Majesty services that way, which none alive could do so well as he; but it was

---

[1] This entry of 10th May, 1671, so far as it relates to Blood, and the stealing of the crown, &c., is a mistake. Blood stole the crown on the 9th of May, 1671—the very day before; and the "not long before" of Evelyn, and the circumstance of his being "pardoned," which Evelyn also mentions, can hardly be said to relate to only the day before. This is another of the passages to which frequent reference has been made, and which are explained in the advertisement to the present edition of the Diary. The Monsieur de Grammont, who was one of the party at the Treasurer's, was Philebert, Comte de Grammont, so well known by the Memoirs he dictated to his brother-in-law, Anthony, Count Hamilton. He died in 1707.

certainly the boldest attempt, so the only treason of this sort that was ever pardoned. This man had not only a daring but a villanous unmerciful look, a false countenance, but very well-spoken, and dangerously insinuating.

11*th May.* I went to Eltham, to sit as one of the Commissioners about the Subsidy now given by Parliament to his Majesty.

17*th.* Dined at Mr. Treasurer's [Sir Thomas Clifford] with the Earl of Arlington, Carlingford, Lord Arundel of Wardour, Lord Almoner to the Queen, a French Count and two abbots, with several more of French nobility; and now by something I had lately observed of Mr. Treasurer's con versation on occasion, I suspected him a little warping to Rome.

25*th.* I dined at a feast made for me and my wife by the Trinity Company, for our passing a fine of the land which Sir R. Browne, my wife's father, freely gave to found and build their college, or Alms-houses on, at Deptford, it being my wife's after her father's decease. It was a good and charitable work and gift, but would have been better bestowed on the poor of that parish, than on the seamen's widows, the Trinity Company being very rich, and the rest of the poor of the parish exceedingly indigent.

26*th.* The Earl of Bristol's house in Queen's Street [Lincoln's Inn Fields) was taken for the Commissioners of Trade and Plantations, and furnished with rich hangings of the King's. It consisted of seven rooms on a floor, with a long gallery, gardens, &c. This day we met the Duke of Buckingham, Earl of Lauderdale, Lord Culpeper, Sir George Carteret, Vice-Chamberlain, and myself, had the oaths given us by the Earl of Sandwich, our President. It was to advise and counsel his Majesty, to the best of our abilities, for the well-governing of his Foreign Plantations, &c., the form very little differing from that given to the Privy Council. We then took our places at the Board in the Council-Chamber, a very large room furnished with atlases, maps, charts, globes, &c. Then came the Lord Keeper, Sir Orlando Bridgeman, Earl of Arlington, Secretary of State, Lord Ashley, Mr. Treasurer, Sir John Trevor, the other Secretary, Sir John Duncomb, Lord Allington, Mr. Grey, son to the Lord Grey, Mr. Henry Broucher, Sir Humphrey

Winch, Sir John Finch, Mr. Waller, and Colonel Titus, of the Bedchamber,[1] with Mr. Slingsby, Secretary to the Council, and two Clerks of the Council, who had all been sworn some days before. Being all set, our Patent was read, and then the additional Patent, in which was recited this new establishment; then, was delivered to each a copy of the Patent, and of instructions: after which, we proceeded to business.

The first thing we did was, to settle the form of a circular letter to the Governors of all his Majesty's Plantations and Territories in the West Indies and Islands thereof, to give them notice to whom they should apply themselves on all occasions, and to render us an account of their present state and government; but, what we most insisted on was, to know the condition of New England, which appearing to be very independent as to their regard to Old England, or his Majesty, rich and strong as they now were, there were great debates in what style to write to them; for the condition of that Colony was such, that they were able to contest with all other Plantations about them, and there was fear of their breaking from all dependence on this nation; his Majesty, therefore, commended this affair more expressly. We, therefore, thought fit, in the first place, to acquaint ourselves as well as we could of the state of that place, by some whom we heard of that were newly come from thence, and to be informed of their present posture and condition; some of our Council were for sending them a menacing letter, which those who better understood the peevish and touchy humour of that Colony, were utterly against.

A letter was then read from Sir Thomas Modiford, Governor of Jamaica; and then the Council brake up.

Having brought an action against one Cocke, for money which he had received for me, it had been referred to an arbitration by the recommendation of that excellent good man, the Chief-Justice Hales;[2] but, this not succeeding, I

[1] Silas Titus, Author of *Killing no Murder.*
[2] Sir Matthew Hale, so famous as one of the justices of the bench in Cromwell's time. After the Restoration, he became Chief Baron of the Exchequer; then Chief Justice of the King's Bench; and died in 1676. The author of numerous works, not only on professional subjects, but on mathematics and philosophy.

went to advise with that famous lawyer, Mr. Jones, of Gray's Inn, and, 27th May, had a trial before Lord Chief Justice Hales; and, after the lawyers had wrangled sufficiently, it was referred to a new arbitration. This was the very first suit at law that ever I had with any creature, and oh, that it might be the last!

1st *June.* An installation at Windsor.

6th. I went to Council, where was produced a most exact and ample information of the state of Jamaica, and of the best expedients as to New England, on which there was a long debate; but at length it was concluded that, if any, it should be only a conciliating paper at first, or civil letter, till we had better information of the present face of things, since we understood they were a people almost upon the very brink of renouncing any dependence on the Crown.

19th. To a splendid dinner at the great room in Deptford Trinity House, Sir Thomas Allen chosen Master, and succeeding the Earl of Craven.

20th. To carry Colonel Middleton[1] to Whitehall, to my Lord Sandwich, our President, for some information which he was able to give of the state of the Colony in New England.

21st. To Council again, when one Colonel Cartwright, a Nottinghamshire man, (formerly in commission with Colonel Nicholls) gave us a considerable relation of that country; on which the Council concluded that in the first place a letter of amnesty should be despatched.

24th. Constantine Huygens, Seignor of Zuylichem, that excellent learned man, poet, and musician, now near eighty years of age, a vigorous brisk man,[2] came to take leave of me before his return into Holland with the Prince, whose Secretary he was.

[1] A coadjutor of Pepys at the Navy Board, and by him styled "a most honest and understanding man."

[2] He died in 1687, at the great age of 90 years and 6 months. Constantine and his son, Christian Huygens, were both eminent for scientific knowledge and classical attainments; Christian, particularly so; for he was the inventor of the pendulum, made an improvement in the air-pump, first discovered the ring and one of the satellites of Saturn, and ascertained the laws of collision of elastic bodies. He died in 1695. Constantine, the father, was a person of influence and distinction in Holland, and held the post of secretary to the Prince of Orange.

26th June. To Council, where Lord Arlington acquainted us, that it was his Majesty's proposal we should, every one of us, contribute £20 towards building a Council-chamber and conveniences somewhere in Whitehall, that his Majesty might come and sit amongst us, and hear our debates ; the money we laid out to be reimbursed out of the contingent monies already set apart for us, viz. £1000 yearly. To this we unanimously consented. There came an uncertain bruit from Barbadoes of some disorder there. On my return home I stepped in at the theatre to see the new machines for the intended scenes, which were indeed very costly and magnificent.

29th. To Council, where were letters from Sir Thomas Modiford, of the expedition and exploit of Colonel Morgan,[1] and others of Jamaica, on the Spanish Continent at Panama.

4th July. To Council, where we drew up and agreed to a letter to be sent to New England, and made some proposal to Mr. Gorges, for his interest in a plantation there.

24th. To Council. Mr. Surveyor brought us a plot for the building of our Council-chamber, to be erected at the end of the Privy-garden, in Whitehall.

3rd August. A full appearance at the Council. The matter in debate was, whether we should send a deputy to New England, requiring them of the Massachusets to re-store such to their limits and respective possessions, as had petitioned the Council; this to be the open commission only; but, in truth, with secret instructions to inform us of the condition of those Colonies, and whether they were of such power, as to be able to resist his Majesty and declare for themselves as independent of the Crown, which we were told, and which of late years made them refractory. Colonel Middleton, being called in, assured us they might be curbed by a few of his Majesty's first-rate frigates, to spoil their trade with the islands ; but, though my Lord President was not satisfied, the rest were, and we did resolve to advise his Majesty to send Commissioners with a formal commission for adjusting boundaries, &c., with some other instructions.

19th. To Council. The letters of Sir Thomas Modiford were read, giving relation of the exploit at Panama, which

---

[1] See *post,* p. 99.

was very brave; they took, burnt, and pillaged the town of vast treasures, but the best of the booty had been shipped off, and lay at anchor in the South Sea, so that, after our men had ranged the country sixty miles about, they went back to Nombre de Dios, and embarked for Jamaica. Such an action had not been done since the famous Drake.

I dined at the Hamburgh Resident's, and, after dinner, went to the christening of Sir Samuel Tuke's son, Charles, at Somerset-House, by a Popish priest, and many odd ceremonies. The godfathers were the King, and Lord Arundel of Wardour, and godmother, the Countess of Huntingdon.

29th August. To London, with some more papers of my progress in the Dutch War, delivered to the Treasurer.

September 1st. Dined with the Treasurer, in company with my Lord Arlington, Halifax, and Sir Thomas Strickland;[1] and, next day, went home, being the anniversary of the late dreadful fire of London.

13th. This night fell a dreadful tempest.

15th. In the afternoon at Council, where letters were read from Sir Charles Wheeler, concerning his resigning his government of St. Christopher's.

21st. I dined in the City, at the fraternity feast in Ironmongers' Hall,[2] where the four stewards chose their successors for the next year, with a solemn procession, garlands about their heads, and music playing before them; so, coming up to the upper tables where the gentlemen sat, they drank to the new stewards; and so we parted.

22nd. I dined at the Treasurer's, where I had discourse with Sir Henry Jones (now come over to raise a regiment of horse), concerning the French conquests in Lorraine; he told me the king sold all things to the soldiers, even to a handful of hay.

Lord Sunderland was now nominated Ambassador to Spain.

After dinner, the Treasurer carried me to Lincoln's Inn,

---

[1] Made a baronet by Charles I. on the field at Edgehill, where he commanded a regiment of infantry. After the Restoration he was member for the County of Westmoreland, and Privy Purse to Charles II. He was subsequently one of James II.'s Privy Council, and followed him into France, where he died in 1694.

[2] One of the grand court-days of that opulent Company, which is one of *twelve*.

to one of the Parliament Clerks, to obtain of him, that I
might carry home and peruse, some of the Journals, which
were accordingly delivered to me to examine about the late
Dutch war. Returning home, I went on shore to see the
Custom-House, now newly rebuilt since the dreadful conflagration.[1]

9th and 10th October. I went, after evening-service, to
London, in order to a journey of refreshment with Mr.
Treasurer, to Newmarket, where the King then was, in his
coach with six brave horses, which we changed thrice, first,
at Bishop-Stortford, and last, at Chesterford; so, by night,
we got to Newmarket, where Mr. Henry Jermain (nephew
to the Earl of St. Alban's) lodged me very civilly. We
proceeded immediately to Court, the King and all the
English gallants being there at their autumnal sports.
Supped at the Lord Chamberlain's; and, the next day, after
dinner, I was on the heath, where I saw the great match
run between Woodcock and Flatfoot, belonging to the
King, and to Mr. Eliot, of the Bedchamber, many thousands
being spectators; a more signal race had not been run for
many years.

This over, I went that night with Mr. Treasurer to Euston,
a palace of Lord Arlington's, where we found Monsieur
Colbert (the French Ambassador), and the famous new
French Maid of Honour, Mademoiselle Querouaille,[2] now
coming to be in great favour with the King. Here was
also the Countess of Sunderland, and several lords and
ladies, who lodged in the house.

During my stay here with Lord Arlington, near a fortnight, his Majesty came almost every second day with the
Duke, who commonly returned to Newmarket, but the
King often lay here, during which time I had twice the
honour to sit at dinner with him, with all freedom. It was
universally reported that the fair lady —— was bedded one
of these nights, and the stocking flung, after the manner of
a married bride; I acknowledge she was for the most part
in her undress all day, and that there was fondness and
toying with that young wanton; nay, it was said, I was at

[1] This new edifice was again destroyed by fire in 1718, and again
rebuilt, was a third time destroyed by fire in February 1814.
[2] *Ante*, p. 57.

the former ceremony; but it is utterly false; I neither saw nor heard of any such thing whilst I was there, though I had been in her chamber, and all over that apartment late enough, and was myself observing all passages with much curiosity. However, it was with confidence believed she was first made *a Miss*, as they call these unhappy creatures, with solemnity at this time.

On Sunday, a young Cambridge Divine preached an excellent sermon in the chapel, the King and the Duke of York being present.

16th October. Came all the great men from Newmarket, and other parts both of Suffolk and Norfolk, to make their court, the whole house filled from one end to the other with lords, ladies, and gallants; there was such a furnished table, as I had seldom seen, nor anything more splendid and free, so that for fifteen days there were entertained at least 200 people, and half as many horses, besides servants and guards, at infinite expense.

In the morning, we went hunting and hawking; in the afternoon, till almost morning, to cards and dice, yet I must say without noise, swearing, quarrel, or confusion of any sort. I, who was no gamester, had often discourse with the French Ambassador, Colbert, and went sometimes abroad on horseback with the ladies to take the air, and now and then to hunting; thus idly passing the time, but not without more often recess to my pretty apartment, where I was quite out of all this hurry, and had leisure when I would, to converse with books, for there is no man more hospitably easy to be withal than my Lord Arlington, of whose particular friendship and kindness I had ever a more than ordinary share. His house is a very noble pile, consisting of four pavilions after the French, beside a body of a large house, and, though not built altogether, but formed of additions to an old house (purchased by his Lordship of one Sir T. Rookwood) yet with a vast expense made not only capable and roomsome, but very magnificent and commodious, as well within as without, nor less splendidly furnished. The staircase is very elegant, the garden handsome, the canal beautiful, but the soil dry, barren, and miserably sandy, which flies in drifts as the wind sits. Here my Lord was pleased to advise with me about ordering his plantations of firs, elms, limés, &c., up his park, and in all other places and avenues. I persuaded him to bring his park so near as to comprehend his house within it; which he resolved upon, it being now near a mile to it. The water furnishing the fountains, is raised by a pretty engine, or very slight plain wheels, which likewise serve to grind his corn, from a small cascade of the canal, the inven-tion of Sir Samuel Morland. In my Lord's house, and especially above the staircase, in the great hall and some of the chambers and rooms of state, are paintings in fresco by Signor Verrio, being the first work which he did in England.

17th October. My Lord Henry Howard coming this night to visit my Lord Chamberlain, and staying a day, would needs have me go with him to Norwich, promising to convey me back, after a day or two; this, as I could not refuse, I was not hard to be persuaded to, having a desire to see that famous scholar and physician, Dr. T. Browne, author of the *Religio Medici* and *Vulgar Errors*, now lately knighted.[1] Thither, then, went my Lord and I alone, in his flying chariot with six horses; and, by the way, dis-coursing with me of several of his concerns, he acquainted me of his going to marry his eldest son to one of the King's natural daughters, by the Duchess of Cleveland; by which he reckoned he should come into mighty favour. He also told me that, though he kept that idle creature, Mrs. B——, and would leave £200 a year to the son he had by her, he would never marry her,[2] and that the King himself had cautioned him against it. All the world knows how he kept his promise, and I was sorry at heart to hear what now he confessed to me; and that a person and a family which I so much honoured for the sake of that noble and

[1] Beside the work mentioned by Evelyn, Sir Thomas Browne was the author of the famous treatise on "Urn Burial," and "The Garden of Cyrus." He was born in 1605, and died in 1682.

[2] For the manner in which my Lord Howard, when Duke of Norfolk, kept his word in the matter of Mrs. B[ickerton], see *post*, p. 125; also, p. 128. Evelyn's own reference to the text is another of the many evidences to which the reader's attention has been drawn, that his book partakes more of the character of Memoirs than a Diary, in the strict sense of that word. This title, indeed, is often given to it by himself. See *post*, p. 94.

illustrious friend of mine, his grandfather, should dishonour
and pollute them both with those base and vicious courses
he of late had taken since the death of Sir Samuel Tuke,
and that of his own virtuous lady (my Lady Anne Somerset, sister to the Marquis); who, whilst they lived, preserved this gentleman by their example and advice from
those many extravagances that impaired both his fortune
and reputation.

Being come to the Ducal Palace, my Lord made very
much of me; but I had little rest, so exceedingly desirous
he was to show me the contrivance he had made for the
entertainment of their Majesties, and the whole Court not
long before, and which, though much of it was but temporary,
apparently framed of boards only, was yet standing. As to
the palace, it is an old wretched building, and that part of
it newly built of brick, is very ill understood; so as I was
of opinion it had been much better to have demolished
all, and set it up in a better place, than to proceed any
farther; for it stands in the very market-place, and, though
near a river, yet a very narrow muddy one, without any
extent.

Next morning, I went to see Sir Thomas Browne (with
whom I had some time corresponded by letter, though I
had never seen him before); his whole house and garden
being a paradise and cabinet of rarities, and that of the
best collection, especially medals, books, plants, and natural
things. Amongst other curiosities, Sir Thomas had a collection of the eggs of all the fowl and birds he could procure,
that country (especially the promontory of Norfolk) being
frequented, as he said, by several kinds which seldom or
never go farther into the land, as cranes, storks, eagles, and
variety of water-fowl. He led me to see all the remarkable
places of this ancient city, being one of the largest, and
certainly, after London, one of the noblest of England, for
its venerable cathedral, number of stately churches, cleanness of the streets, and buildings of flint so exquisitely
headed and squared, as I was much astonished at; but he
told me they had lost the art of squaring the flints, in which
they so much excelled, and of which the churches, best
houses, and walls, are built. The Castle is an antique
extent of ground, which now they call Marsfield, and would

have been a fitting area to have placed the Ducal Palace in The suburbs are large, the prospects sweet, with other amenities, not omitting the flower-gardens, in which all the inhabitants excel. The fabric of stuffs brings a vast trade to this populous town.

Being returned to my Lord's, who had been with me all this morning, he advised with me concerning a plot to rebuild his house, having already, as he said, erected a front next the street, and a left wing, and now resolving to set up another wing and pavilion next the garden, and to convert the bowling-green into stables. My advice was, to desist from all, and to meditate wholly on rebuilding a handsome palace at Arundel House, in the Strand, before he proceeded farther here, and then to place this in the Castle, that ground belonging to his Lordship.

I observed that most of the church-yards (though some of them large enough) were filled up with earth, or rather the congestion of dead bodies one upon another, for want of earth, even to the very top of the walls, and some above the walls, so as the churches seemed to be built in pits.

18*th October.* I returned to Euston, in Lord Henry Howard's coach, leaving him at Norwich, in company with a very ingenious gentleman, Mr. White, whose father and mother (daughter to the late Lord Treasurer Weston, Earl of Portland) I knew at Rome, where this gentleman was born, and where his parents lived and died with much reputation, during their banishment in our civil broils.

21*st.* Quitting Euston, I lodged this night at Newmarket, where I found the jolly blades racing, dancing, feasting, and revelling, more resembling a luxurious and abandoned rout, than a Christian Court. The Duke of Buckingham was now in mighty favour, and had with him that impudent woman, the Countess of Shrewsbury,[1] with his band of fiddlers, &c.

Next morning, in company with Sir Bernard Gascoyne, and Lord Hawley, I came in the Treasurer's coach to Bishop-Stortford, where he gave us a noble supper. The following day, to London, and so home.

14*th November.* To Council, where Sir Charles Wheeler, late Governor of the Leeward Islands, having been com-

[1] See *post*, p. 141.

plained of for many indiscreet managements, it was resolved, on scanning many of the particulars, to advise his Majesty to remove him; and consult what was to be done, to prevent these inconveniences he had brought things to. This business staid me in London almost a week, being in Council, or Committee, every morning till the 25th.

27th November. We ordered that a proclamation should be presented to his Majesty to sign, against what Sir Charles Wheeler had done in St. Christopher's since the war, on the articles of peace at Breda. He was shortly afterwards recalled.

6th December. Came to visit me Sir William Haywood, a great pretender to English antiquities.

14th. Went to see the Duke of Buckingham's ridiculous farce and rhapsody, called *The Recital,*[1] buffooning all plays, yet profane enough.

23rd. The Councillors of the Board of Trade dined together at the Cock, in Suffolk Street.

1671-2. *12th January.* His Majesty renewed us our lease of Sayes Court pastures for ninety-nine years, but ought, according to his solemn promise[2] (as I hope he will still perform), have passed them to us in fee-farm.

23rd. To London, in order to Sir Richard Browne, my father-in-law, resigning his place as Clerk of the Council to Joseph Williamson, Esq., who was admitted, and was knighted. This place his Majesty had promised to give me many years before; but, upon consideration of the renewal of our lease and other reasons, I chose to part with it to Sir Joseph, who gave us and the rest of his brother-clerks a handsome supper at his house; and, after supper, a concert of music.

3rd February. An extraordinary snow; part of the week was taken up in consulting about the commission of prisoners of war, and instructions to our officers, in order to a second war with the Hollanders, his Majesty having made choice of the former commissioners, and myself amongst them.

11th. In the afternoon, that famous proselyte, Monsieur Brevall, preached at the Abbey, in English, extremely well

[1] The well-known play of *The Rehearsal* is meant.
[2] The King's engagement, under his hand, is now at Wotton.

and with much eloquence. He had been a Capuchin, but much better learned than most of that Order.

12th February. At the Council, we entered on enquiries about improving the Plantations by silks, galls, flax, senna, &c., and considered how nutmegs and cinnamon might be obtained, and brought to Jamaica, that soil and climate promising success. Dr. Worsley being called in, spake many considerable things to encourage it. We took order to send to the Plantations, that none of their ships should adventure homeward single, but stay for company and convoys. We also deliberated on some fit person to go as Commissioner to inspect their actions in New England, and, from time to time, report how that people stood affected.—In future, to meet at Whitehall.

20th. Dr. Parr, of Camberwell, preached a most pathetic funeral discourse and panegyric at the interment of our late pastor, Dr. Breton (who died on the 18th), on " Happy is the servant whom when his Lord cometh," &c. This good man, among other expressions, professed that he had never been so touched and concerned at any loss as at this, unless at that of King Charles our Martyr, and Archbishop Usher, whose chaplain he had been. Dr. Breton had preached on the 28th and 30th of January : on the Friday, having fasted all day, making his provisionary sermon for the Sunday following, he went well to bed; but was taken suddenly ill, and expired before help could come to him.

Never had a parish a greater loss, not only as he was an excellent preacher, and fitted for our great and vulgar auditory, but for his excellent life and charity, his meekness and obliging nature, industrious, helpful, and full of good works. He left near £400 to the poor in his will, and that what children of his should die in their minority, their portion should be so employed. I lost in particular a special friend, and one that had an extraordinary love to me and mine.

25th. To London, to speak with the Bishop, and Sir John Cutler,[1] our patron, to present Mr. Frampton (afterwards Bishop of Gloucester).

---

[1] An eminent citizen of London, and member of the Grocers' Company, who have a statue of him in their hall. There is another in the College of Physicians. He is severely handled by Pope, as all poetical readers know, yet Pepys appears to have thought well of him.

1st March. A full Council of Plantations, on the danger of the Leeward Islands, threatened by the French, who had taken some of our ships, and began to interrupt our trade. Also in debate, whether the new Governor of St. Christopher's should be subordinate to the Governor of Barbadoes. The debate was serious and long.

12th. Now was the first blow given by us to the Dutch convoy of the Smyrna fleet, by Sir Robert Holmes and Lord Ossory, in which we received little save blows, and a worthy reproach for attacking our neighbours 'ere any war was proclaimed, and then pretending the occasion to be, that some time before, the Merlin yacht chancing to sail through the whole Dutch fleet, their Admiral did not strike to that trifling vessel. Surely, this was a quarrel slenderly grounded, and not becoming Christian neighbours. We are like to thrive, accordingly. Lord Ossory several times deplored to me his being engaged in it ; he had more justice and honour than in the least to approve of it, though he had been over-persuaded to the expedition. There is no doubt but we should have surprised this exceeding rich fleet, had not the avarice and ambition of Holmes and Spragge separated themselves, and wilfully divided our fleet, on presumption that either of them was strong enough to deal with the Dutch convoy without joining and mutual help; but they so warmly plied our divided fleets, that whilst in conflict the merchants sailed away, and got safe into Holland.

A few days before this, the Treasurer of the Household, Sir Thomas Clifford,[1] hinted to me, as a confidant, that his

[1] "On the King's intention to have a Lord Treasurer (1672), instead of putting the Seals into Commission, the Duke of York desired Lord Arlington to join with him in proposing to the King the Lord Clifford for that considerable employment ; but he found Lord Arlington very cold in it, and endeavouring to persuade the Duke that the King did not intend the alteration ; and, the next day, he employed a friend to press the Duke to endeavour to get Sir Robert Car to be Commissioner in the room of Lord Shaftesbury (then appointed Lord Chancellor).

"Some few days after, the Duke proposed to his Majesty the Lord Clifford as Treasurer, which was well received, and he said he would do it, as thinking nobody fitter ; he also told the Duke that Lord Arlington had a mind to have that Staff: but he answered him that he had too

Majesty would *snut up the Exchequer* (and, accordingly, his
Majesty made use of infinite treasure there, to prepare for
an intended rupture) ; but, says he, it will soon be open
again, and everybody satisfied ; for this bold man, who had
been the sole adviser of the King to invade that sacred
stock (though some pretend it was Lord Ashley's counsel,
then Chancellor of the Exchequer), was so over-confident
of the success of this unworthy design against the Smyrna
merchants, as to put his Majesty on an action which not
only lost the hearts of his subjects, and ruined many widows
and orphans, whose stocks were lent him, but the reputation of his Exchequer for ever, it being before in such
credit, that he might have commanded half the wealth of
the nation.

The credit of this bank being thus broken, did exceedingly discontent the people, and never did his Majesty's
affairs prosper to any purpose after it, for as it did not
supply the expense of the meditated war, so it melted away,
I know not how.

To this succeeded the King's Declaration for an universal
toleration ; Papists, and swarms of Sectaries, now boldly
showing themselves in their public meetings. This was
imputed to the same council, Clifford warping to Rome as
was believed, nor was Lord Arlington clear of suspicion,
to gratify that party, but as since it has proved, and was

much kindness for him to let him have it, for he knew he was not fit for
the office; and should he give it him, it would be his ruin. A little
after, the King told the Duke that he found Lord Arlington was angry
with Lord Clifford, on knowing that he was to have the place; and
desired the Duke to persuade Lord Arlington not to let the world see
his discontent, and to endeavour to make them continue friends. They
promised the Duke to live friendly together ; but Lord Arlington kept
not his word, and was ever after cold, if not worse, towards him.

"Christmas coming on, the King spake to Lord Clifford and Lord
Arundel of Wardour, to persuade the Duke to receive the Sacrament
with him at that time (which the Duke had forborne for several months
before). They urged the King not to press it, and he then seemed satisfied : but the day before Christmas Eve, the King spoke again to Lord
Clifford to represent to the Duke what he had before said, which the
Lord Clifford did, but found the Duke was not to be moved in his
resolution of not going against his conscience."—*King James's Life, by
himself.*

then evidently foreseen, to the extreme weakening the
Church of England and its Episcopal Government, as it
was projected. I speak not this as my own sense, but
what was the discourse and thoughts of others, who were
lookers-on; for I think there might be some relaxations
without the least prejudice to the present Establishment,
discreetly limited, but to let go the reins in this manner,
and then to imagine they could take them up again as easily,
was a false policy, and greatly destructive. The truth is,
our Bishops slipped the occasion; for, had they held a steady
hand upon his Majesty's restoration, as they might easily
have done, the Church of England had emerged and
flourished, without interruption; but they were then remiss,
and covetous after advantages of another kind, whilst his
Majesty suffered them to come into a harvest, with which,
without any injustice, he might have remunerated innumerable gallant gentlemen for their services, who had ruined
themselves in the late rebellion.[1]

21st *March.* I visited the coasts in my district of Kent,
and divers wounded and languishing poor men, that had
been in the Smyrna conflict. I went over to see the new-
begun Fort of Tilbury; a royal work, indeed, and such as
will one day bridle a great city to the purpose, before they
are aware.

23rd. Captain Cox, one of the Commissioners of the
Navy, furnishing me with a yacht, I sailed to Sheerness to
see that fort also, now newly finished; several places on
both sides the Swale and Medway to Gillingham and Upnore, being also provided with redoubts and batteries, to
secure the station of our men-of-war at Chatham, and shut
the door when the steeds were stolen.

24th. I saw the chirurgeon cut off the leg of a
wounded sailor, the stout and gallant man enduring it with
incredible patience, without being bound to his chair, as
usual on such painful occasions. I had hardly courage
enough to be present. Not being cut off high enough, the
gangrene prevailed, and the second operation cost the poor
creature his life.

---

[1] Evelyn here alludes to the fines for renewals of leases not filled up
during the interregnum, and now to be immediately applied for. Bishop
Burnet says they were much misapplied. *Hist. of his own Times,* i. 304.

Lord! what miseries are mortal men subject to, and what confusion and mischief do the avarice, anger, and ambition of Princes, cause in the world!

25th March. I proceeded to Canterbury, Dover, Deal, the Isle of Thanet, by Sandwich, and so to Margate. Here we had abundance of miserably wounded men, his Majesty sending his chief chirurgeon, Sergeant Knight, to meet me, and Dr. Waldrond had attended me all the journey. Having taken order for the accommodation of the wounded, I came back through a country the best cultivated of any that in my life I had anywhere seen, every field lying as even as a bowling-green, and the fences, plantations, and husbandry, in such admirable order, as infinitely delighted me, after the sad and afflicting spectacles and objects I was come from. Observing almost every tall tree to have a weathercock on the top bough, and some trees half-a-dozen, I learned that, on a certain holyday, the farmers feast their servants; at which solemnity, they set up these cocks, in a kind of triumph.

Being come back towards Rochester, I went to take order respecting the building a strong and high wall about a house I had hired of a gentleman, at a place called Hartlip, for a prison, paying £50 yearly rent. Here I settled a Provost-Marshal and other officers, returning by Feversham. On the 30th, heard a sermon in Rochester cathedral, and so got to Sayes Court on the first of April.

4th April. I went to see the fopperies of the Papists at Somerset-House and York-House, where now the French Ambassador had caused to be represented our Blessed Saviour at the Pascal Supper with his Disciples, in figures and puppets made as big as the life, of wax-work, curiously clad and sitting round a large table, the room nobly hung, and shining with innumerable lamps and candles: this was exposed to all the world; all the City came to see it. Such liberty had the Roman Catholics at this time obtained.

16th. Sat in Council, preparing Lord Willoughby's commission and instructions as Governor of Barbadoes and the Caribbee Islands.

17th. Sat on business in the Star Chamber.

19th. At Council, preparing instructions for Colonel Stapleton, now to go Governor of St. Christopher's; and heard the complaints of the Jamaica merchants against the Spaniards, for hindering them from cutting logwood on the main land, where they have no pretence.

21st April. To my Lord of Canterbury, to entreat him to engage Sir John Cutler, the patron, to provide us a grave and learned man, in opposition to a novice.

30th. Congratulated Mr. Treasurer Clifford's new honour, being made a Baron.

2nd May. My son, John, was specially admitted of the Middle Temple by Sir Francis North, his Majesty's Solicitor-General, and since Chancellor. I pray God bless this beginning, my intention being that he should seriously apply himself to the study of the law.

10th. I was ordered, by letter from the Council, to repair forthwith to his Majesty, whom I found in the Pall-Mall, in St. James's Park, where his Majesty coming to me from the company, commanded me to go immediately to the sea-coast, and to observe the motion of the Dutch fleet and ours, the Duke and so many of the flower of our nation being now under sail, coming from Portsmouth, through the Downs, where it was believed there might be an encounter.

11th. Went to Chatham.—*12th.* Heard a sermon in Rochester Cathedral.

13th. To Canterbury; visited Dr. Bargrave,[1] my old fellow-traveller in Italy, and great virtuoso.

14th. To Dover; but the fleet did not appear till the 16th, when the Duke of York with his and the French squadron, in all 170 ships (of which above 100 were men-of-war), sailed by, after the Dutch, who were newly withdrawn. Such a gallant and formidable navy never, I think, spread sail upon the seas. It was a goodly yet terrible sight, to behold them as I did, passing eastward by the straits betwixt Dover and Calais in a glorious day. The wind was yet so high, that I could not well go aboard, and they were soon got out of sight. The next day, having visited our prisoners and the Castle, and saluted the Governor, I took horse for Margate. Here, from the North Foreland Light-

[1] Dean of Canterbury, and a great benefactor to the Cathedral Library there. Todd, in his *Life of Milton*, furnishes some curious particulars concerning him.

house top (which is a Pharos, built of brick, and having on
the top a cradle of iron, in which a man attends a great sea-
coal fire all the year long, when the nights are dark, for the
safeguard of sailors), we could see our fleet as they lay at
anchor.   The next morning, they weighed, and sailed out of
sight to the N.E.

19th May. Went to Margate; and, the following day,
was carried to see a gallant widow, brought up a farmeress,
and I think of gigantic race, rich, comely, and exceedingly
industrious.   She put me in mind of Deborah and Abigail,
her house was so plentifully stored with all manner of
country-provisions, all of her own growth, and all her conveniences so substantial, neat, and well understood; she
herself so jolly and hospitable; and her land so trim and
rarely husbanded, that it struck me with admiration at her
economy.

This town much consists of brewers of a certain heady
ale, and they deal much in malt, &c.   For the rest, it is
raggedly built, and has an ill haven, with a small fort of
little concernment, nor is the island well disciplined; but as
to the husbandry and rural part, far exceeding any part of
England for the accurate culture of their ground, in which
they exceed, even to curiosity and emulation.

We passed by Rickborough, and in sight of Reculvers,
and so through a sweet garden, as it were, to Canterbury.

24th.   To London, and gave his Majesty an account of
my journey, and that I had put all things in readiness upon
all events, and so returned home sufficiently wearied.

31st.   I received another command to repair to the sea-
side; so I went to Rochester, where I found many wounded,
sick, and prisoners, newly put on shore after the engagement on the 28th, in which the Earl of Sandwich, that incomparable person and my particular friend, and divers more
whom I loved, were lost.   My Lord (who was Admiral of
the Blue) was in the Prince, which was burnt, one of the
best men-of-war that ever spread canvass on the sea.   There
were lost with this brave man, a son of Sir Charles Cotterell
(Master of the Ceremonies), and a son of Sir Charles Harbord (his Majesty's Surveyor-General), two valiant and
most accomplished youths, full of virtue and courage, who
might have saved themselves; but chose to perish with my

Lord, whom they honoured and loved above their own lives.

Here, I cannot but make some reflections on things past. It was not above a day or two that going to Whitehall to take leave of his Lordship, who had his lodgings in the Privy-Garden, shaking me by the hand he bid me good-bye, and said he thought he should see me no more, and I saw, to my thinking, something boding in his countenance: " No," says he, " they will not have me live. Had I lost a fleet (meaning on his return from Bergen when he took the East India prize) I should have fared better; but, be as it pleases God—I must do something, I know not what, to save my reputation. Something to this effect, he had hinted to me; thus I took my leave. I well remember that the Duke of Albemarle, and my now Lord Clifford, had, I know not why, no great opinion of his courage, because, in former conflicts, being an able and experienced seaman (which neither of them were), he always brought off his Majesty's ships without loss, though not without as many marks of true courage as the stoutest of them; and I am a witness that, in the late war, his own ship was pierced like a colander. But the business was, he was utterly against this war from the beginning, and abhorred the attacking of the Smyrna fleet; he did not favour the heady expedition of Clifford at Bergen, nor was he so furious and confident as was the Duke of Albemarle, who believed he could vanquish the Hollanders with one squadron. My Lord Sandwich was prudent as well as valiant, and always governed his affairs with success and little loss; he was for deliberation and reason, they for action and slaughter without either; and for this, whispered as if my Lord Sandwich was not so gallant, because he was not so rash, and knew how fatal it was to lose a fleet, such as was that under his conduct, and for which these very persons would have censured him on the other side. This it was, I am confident, grieved him, and made him enter like a lion, and fight like one, too, in the midst of the hottest service, where the stoutest of the rest seeing him engaged, and so many ships upon him, durst not, or would not, come to his succour, as some of them, whom I know, might have done. Thus, this gallant person perished, to gratify the pride and envy of some I named.

Deplorable was the loss of one of the best accomplished persons, not only of this nation but of any other. He was learned in sea-affairs, in politics, in mathematics, and in music : he had been on divers embassies, was of a sweet and obliging temper, sober, chaste, very ingenious, a true nobleman, an ornament to the Court and his Prince; nor has he left any behind him who approach his many virtues.

He had, I confess, served the tyrant Cromwell, when a young man, but it was without malice, as a soldier of fortune; and he readily submitted, and that with joy, bringing an entire fleet with him from the Sound, at the first tidings of his Majesty's restoration. I verily believe him as faithful a subject as any that were not his friends. I am yet heartily grieved at this mighty loss, nor do I call it to my thoughts without emotion.

2nd June. Trinity-Sunday, I passed at Rochester; and, on the 5th, there was buried in the Cathedral Monsieur Rabiniére, Rear-Admiral of the French squadron, a gallant person, who died of the wounds he received in the fight. This ceremony lay on me, which I performed with all the decency I could, inviting the Mayor and Aldermen to come in their formalities. Sir Jonas Atkins was there with his guards; and the Dean and Prebendaries : one of his countrymen pronouncing a funeral oration at the brink of his grave, which I caused to be dug in the choir. This is more at large described in the Gazette of that day; Colonel Reymes, my colleague in commission, assisting, who was so kind as to accompany me from London, though it was not his district; for indeed the stress of both these wars lay more on me by far than on any of my brethren, who had littleto do in theirs.—I went to see Upnore Castle, which I found pretty well defended, but of no great moment.

Next day, I sailed to the fleet, now riding at the buoy of the Nore, where I met his Majesty, the Duke, Lord Arlington, and all the great men, in the Charles, lying miserably shattered; but the miss of Lord Sandwich redoubled the loss to me, and showed the folly of hazarding so brave a fleet, and losing so many good men, for no provocation but that the Hollanders exceeded us in industry, and in all things but envy.

At Sheerness, I gave his Majesty and his Royal Highness an account of my charge, and returned to Queenborough; next day, dined at Major Dorel's, Governor of Sheerness; thence, to Rochester; and the following day, home.

12th June. To London to his Majesty, to solicit for money for the sick and wounded, which he promised me.

19th. To London again, to solicit the same.

21st. At a Council of Plantations. Most of this week busied with the sick and wounded.

3rd July. To Lord Sandwich's funeral, which was by water to Westminster, in solemn pomp.

31st. I entertained the Maids of Honour (among whom there was one I infinitely esteemed for her many and extraordinary virtues[1]) at a comedy this afternoon, and so went home.

1st August. I was at the marriage of Lord Arlington's only daughter (a sweet child if ever there was any[2]) to the Duke of Grafton, the King's natural son by the Duchess of Cleveland; the Archbishop of Canterbury officiating, the King and all the grandees being present. I had a favour given me by my Lady; but took no great joy at the thing for many reasons.

18th. Sir James Hayes, Secretary to Prince Rupert, dined with me: after dinner, I was sent for to Gravesend to dispose of no fewer than 800 sick men. That night, I got to the fleet at the buoy of the Nore, where I spake with the King and the Duke; and, after dinner next day, returned to Gravesend.

1st September. I spent this week in soliciting for moneys, and in reading to my Lord Clifford my papers relating to the first Holland war.—Now, our Council of Plantations met at Lord Shaftesbury's (Chancellor of the Exchequer) to read and reform the draught of our new Patent, joining the Council of Trade to our political capacities. After this, I returned home, in order to another excursion

[1] Mrs. Blagg, whom Evelyn never tires of instancing and characterising as a rare example of piety and virtue, in so rare a wit, beauty, and perfection, in a licentious court and depraved age. She was afterwards married to Mr. Godolphin, and her life, written by Evelyn, has been edited and published by the Bishop of Oxford. *Ante,* p. 43. And see *post,* p. 130, &c.

[2] She was then only five years old.

to the sea-side, to get as many as possible of the men who were recovered on board the fleet.

8th September. I lay at Gravesend, thence to Rochester, returning on the 11th.

15th. Dr. Duport, Greek Professor of Cambridge, preached before the King on 1 Timothy, vi. 6. No great preacher, but a very worthy and learned man.

25th. I dined at Lord John Berkeley's,[1] newly arrived out of Ireland, where he had been Deputy; it was in his new house,[2] or rather palace; for I am assured it stood him in near £30,000. It is very well built, and has many noble rooms, but they are not very convenient, consisting but of one *Corps de Logis;* they are all rooms of state, without closets. The staircase is of cedar. the furniture is princely: the kitchen and stables are ill-placed, and the corridor worse, having no report to the wings they join to. For the rest, the fore-court is noble, so are the stables; and, above all, the gardens, which are incomparable by reason of the inequality of the ground, and a pretty piscina. The holly hedges on the terrace I advised the planting of. The porticos are in imitation of a house described by Palladio; but it happens to be the worst in his book, though my good friend, Mr. Hugh May, his Lordship's architect, effected it.

26th. I carried with me to dinner my Lord H. Howard (now to be made Earl of Norwich and Earl Marshal of England) to Sir Robert Clayton's, now Sheriff of London, at his new house,[3] where we had a great feast; it is built

---

[1] Lord Berkeley, of Stratton.

[2] Berkeley-House was burnt to the ground by accident. The site was on a farm called Hay-hill Farm, the names of which are preserved in Hay-street, Hill-street, and Farm-street. Devonshire House, Lansdowne House, Berkeley Square, &c., now occupy portions of the original estate. See p. 5.

[3] In the Old Jewry. Sir Robert built it to keep his shrievalty, which he did therein with great magnificence. Afterwards for some years it was the residence of Mr. Samuel Sharp, a famous surgeon in his time, and was then occupied (from 1806 to the close of the year 1811) by the London Institution, for their library and reading-rooms. This Institution, ultimately established by Charter, was finally settled in its present building on the north side of Moorfields, in 1818.—Streeter's paintings have been long placed in the family seat of the Claytons, at Marden, near Godstone, Surrey.

indeed for a great magistrate, at excessive cost. The cedar dining-room is painted with the history of the Giants' War, incomparably done by Mr. Streeter, but the figures are too near the eye.

6th October. Dr. Thistlethwait preached at Whitehall on Rev. v. 2,—a young, but good preacher. I received the blessed Communion, Dr. Blandford, Bishop of Worcester, and Dean of the Chapel, officiating. Dined at my Lord Clifford's, with Lord Mulgrave, Sir Gilbert Talbot, and Sir Robert Holmes.

8th. I took leave of my Lady Sunderland, who was going to Paris to my Lord, now ambassador there. She made me stay dinner at Leicester-House,[1] and afterwards sent for Richardson, the famous fire-eater. He devoured brimstone on glowing coals before us, chewing and swallowing them; he melted a beer-glass and eat it quite up; then, taking a live coal on his tongue, he put on it a raw oyster, the coal was blown on with bellows till it flamed and sparkled in his mouth, and so remained till the oyster gaped and was quite boiled. Then, he melted pitch and wax with sulphur, which he drank down, as it flamed; I saw it flaming in his mouth, a good while; he also took up a thick piece of iron, such as laundresses use to put in their smoothing boxes, when it was fiery hot, held it between his teeth, then in his hand, and threw it about like a stone; but this I observed, he cared not to hold very long; then, he stood on a small pot; and, bending his body, took a glowing iron with his mouth from between his feet, without touching the pot, or ground, with his hands; with divers other prodigious feats.

13th. After sermon (being summoned before), I went to my Lord Keeper's, Sir Orlando Bridgeman, at Essex House,[2] where our new patent was opened and read, constituting us that were of the Council of Plantations, to be now of the Council of Trade also, both united. After the patent was read, we all took our oaths, and departed.

[1] Then a handsome brick building, on the north side of Leicester-square, which many years later, in 1708, was occupied by the Imperial Ambassador, having been let to him by the Earl of Leicester.

[2] Which stood near St. Clement's Church in the Strand, and of which the site is still commemorated in Essex Street, Essex Place, Essex Court, and Devereux Court.

24th October. Met in Council, the Earl of Shaftesbury, now our President, swearing our Secretary and his clerks, which was Mr. Locke,[1] an excellent learned gentleman, and student of Christ Church, Mr. Lloyd, and Mr. Frowde. We dispatched a letter to Sir Thomas Linch, Governor of Jamaica, giving him notice of a design of the Dutch on that island.

27th. I went to hear that famous preacher, Dr. Frampton, at St. Giles's, on Psalm xxxix. 6. This divine had been twice at Jerusalem, and was not only a very pious and holy man, but excellent in the pulpit for the moving affections.

8th November. At Council, we debated the business of the consulate of Leghorn. I was of the Committee with Sir Humphry Winch, the chairman, to examine the laws of his Majesty's several plantations and colonies in the West Indies, &c.

15th. Many merchants were summoned about the consulate of Venice; which caused great disputes; the most considerable thought it useless. This being the Queen-Consort's birth-day, there was an extraordinary appearance of gallantry, and a ball danced at Court.

30th. I was chosen Secretary to the Royal Society.

21st December. Settled the consulate of Venice.

1672-3. *1st January.* After public prayers in the chapel at Whitehall, when I gave God solemn thanks for all his mercies to me the year past, and my humble supplications to him for his blessing the year now entering, I returned home, having my poor deceased servant (Adams) to bury, who died of a pleurisy.

3rd. My son now published his version of "Rapinus Hortorum."[2]

28th. Visited Don Francisco de Melos, the Portugal Ambassador, who showed me his curious collection of books

---

[1] The celebrated John Locke. When Lord Shaftesbury withdrew to Holland, Locke followed him, for which he was deprived of his student's place by an order from the King.

[2] "*Of Gardens.* Four Books. First written in Latin verse, by Renatus Repinus, and now made English. By I. E. London, 1673. Dedicated to Henry, Earle of Arlington, &c. &c. &c." The Dedication is re-printed in Evelyn's "Miscellaneous Writings," pp. 623, 624.

and pictures. He was a person of good parts, and a virtuous man.

6th February. To Council about reforming an abuse of the dyers with *saundus,* and other false drugs; examined divers of that trade.

23rd. The Bishop of Chichester[1] preached before the King on Coloss. ii. 14, 15, admirably well, as he can do nothing but what is well.

5th March. Our new vicar, Mr. Holden, preached in Whitehall chapel, on Psalm iv. 6, 7. This gentleman is a very excellent and universal scholar, a good and wise man; but he had not the popular way of preaching, nor is in any measure fit for our plain and vulgar auditory, as his predecessor was. There was, however, no comparison betwixt their parts for profound learning. But time and experience may form him to a more practical way than that he is in of University lectures and erudition; which is now universally left off for what is much more profitable.

15th. I heard the speech made to the Lords in their House by Sir Samuel Tuke, in behalf of the Papists, to take off the penal laws; and then dined with Colonel Norwood.

16th. Dr. Pearson, Bishop of Chester,[2] preached on Hebrews ix. 14; a most incomparable sermon from one of the most learned divines of our nation. I dined at my Lord Arlington's with the Duke and Duchess of Monmouth; she is one of the wisest and craftiest of her sex, and has much wit. Here was also the learned Isaac Vossius.[3]

During Lent, there is constantly the most excellent preaching by the most eminent bishops and divines of the nation.

[1] Dr. Peter Gunning, who held the Mastership of St. John's College, Cambridge, and afterwards the Bishopric of Ely. Burnet says of him that he was a man of great reading, a very honest, sincere man, but of no sound judgment. *Hist. of his own Times,* i. 297.
[2] Well known by his *Exposition of the Creed.*
[3] Born at Leyden, 1618. On coming to England, Charles II. gave him a canonry at Windsor, and the University of Oxford conferred on him the degree of Doctor of Laws. It was said of him by the King, "He is a strange man for a divine; there is nothing he refuses to believe, but the Bible." He died in 1688.

26th March. I was sworn a younger brother of the Trinity-House, with my most worthy and long acquainted noble friend, Lord Ossory (eldest son to the Duke of Ormond), Sir Richard Browne, my father-in-law, being now Master of that Society; after which there was a great collation.

29th. I carried my son to the Bishop of Chichester, that learned and pious man, Dr. Peter Gunning,[1] to be instructed by him before he received the Holy Sacrament, when he gave him most excellent advice, which I pray God may influence and remain with him as long as he lives; and O that I had been so blessed and instructed, when first I was admitted to that sacred ordinance!

30th. Easter-Day. Myself and son received the blessed Communion, it being his first time, and with that whole week's more extraordinary preparation. I beseech God to make him a sincere good Christian, whilst I endeavour to instil into him the fear and love of God, and discharge the duty of a father.

At the sermon *coram Rege*, preached by Dr. Sparrow, Bishop of Exeter, to a most crowded auditory; I staid to see whether, according to custom, the Duke of York received the Communion with the King; but he did not, to the amazement of every body. This being the second year he had forborne, and put it off, and within a day of the Parliament sitting, who had lately made so severe an Act against the increase of Popery, gave exceeding grief and scandal to the whole nation, that the heir of it, and the son of a martyr for the Protestant religion, should apostatize. What the consequence of this will be, God only knows, and wise men dread.

11th April. I dined with the plenipotentiaries designed for the treaty of Nimeguen.

17th. I carried Lady Tuke to thank the Countess of Arlington for speaking to his Majesty in her behalf, for being one of the Queen-Consort's women. She carried us up into her new dressing-room at Goring House, where was a bed, two glasses, silver jars, and vases, cabinets, and other so rich furniture as I had seldom seen; to this excess of superfluity were we now arrived, and that not only at

[1] *Ante,* p. 87.

Court, but almost universally, even to wantonness and profusion.

Dr. Compton, brother to the Earl of Northampton, preached on 1 Corinth. v. 11—16, showing the Church's power in ordaining things indifferent; this worthy person's talent is not preaching, but he is like to make a grave and serious good man.[1]

I saw her Majesty's rich toilet in her dressing-room, being all of massy gold, presented to her by the King, valued at £4000.

26th April. Dr. Lamplugh preached at St. Martin's, the Holy Sacrament following, which I partook of, upon obligation of the late Act of Parliament, enjoining everybody in office, civil or military, under penalty of £500, to receive it within one month before two authentic witnesses; being engrossed on parchment, to be afterwards produced in the Court of Chancery, or some other Court of Record; which I did at the Chancery-bar, as being one of the Council of Plantations and Trade; taking then also the oath of allegiance and supremacy, signing the clause in the said Act against Transubstantiation.

25th May. My son was made a younger brother of the Trinity-house. The new master was Sir J. Smith, one of the Commissioners of the Navy, a stout seaman, who had interposed and saved the Duke from perishing by a fire-ship in the late war.

28th. I carried one Withers, an ingenious shipwright, to the King, to show him some new method of building.

29th. I saw the Italian comedy at the Court, this afternoon.

10th June. Came to visit and dine with me my Lord Viscount Cornbury and his Lady; Lady Frances Hyde, sister to the Duchess of York; and Mrs. Dorothy Howard, Maid of Honour. We went, after dinner, to see the formal and formidable camp on Blackheath, raised to invade Holland; or, as others suspected, for another design. Thence, to the Italian glass-house at Greenwich, where glass was blown of finer metal than that of Murano, at Venice.

[1] Henry, sixth son of the second Earl of Northampton, educated at Oxford, began life as a cornet in Lord Oxford's regiment of guards, but afterwards took orders, and was successively Bishop of Oxford and London; in which last See he died, 1713, aged 81.

13th June. Came to visit us, with other ladies of rank, Mrs. Sedley,[1] daughter to Sir Charles, who was none of the most virtuous, but a wit.

19th. Congratulated the new Lord Treasurer, Sir Thomas Osborne, a gentleman with whom I had been intimately acquainted at Paris, and who was every day at my father-in-law's house and table there; on which account, I was too confident of succeeding in his favour, as I had done in his predecessor's; but such a friend shall I never find, and I neglected my time, far from believing that my Lord Clifford would have so rashly laid down his staff, as he did, to the amazement of all the world, when it came to the test of his receiving the Communion, which I am confident he forbore more from some promise he had entered into to gratify the Duke, than from any prejudice to the Protestant religion, though I found him wavering a pretty while.

23rd. To London, to accompany our Council, who went in a body to congratulate the new Lord Treasurer, no friend to it, because promoted by my Lord Arlington, whom he hated.

26th. Came visitors from Court to dine with me and see the army still remaining encamped on Blackheath.

6th July. This evening I went to the funeral of my dear and excellent friend, that good man and accomplished gentleman, Sir Robert Murray,[2] Secretary of Scotland. He was buried by order of his Majesty in Westminster Abbey.

25th. I went to Tunbridge Wells, to visit my Lord Clifford, late Lord Treasurer, who was there to divert his mind more than his body; it was believed that he had so engaged himself to the Duke, that rather than take the Test, without which he was not capable of holding any office, he would resign that great and honourable station. This, I am confident, grieved him to the heart, and at last broke it; for, though he carried with him music and people to divert him, and, when I came to see him, lodged me in his own apartment, and would not let me go from him, I found he was

---

[1] The Duke of York's mistress, afterwards created by him Countess of Dorchester. See *post,* pp. 128, 258.

[2] According to the testimony of his contemporaries, universally beloved and esteemed by men of all opinions, and the life and soul of the Royal Society. He delighted in every occasion of doing good, and Burnet refers enthusiastically to his superiority of genius and comprehension.

struggling in his mind; and, being of a rough and ambit.cus nature, he could not long brook the necessity he had brought on himself, of submission to this conjuncture. Besides, he saw the Dutch war, which was made much by his advice, as well as the shutting up of the Exchequer,[1] very unprosperous. These things his high spirit could not support. Having staid here two or three days, I obtained leave of my Lord to return.

In my way, I saw my Lord of Dorset's house at Knowle, near Sevenoaks, a great old-fashioned house.

30th July. To Council, where the business of transporting wool was brought before us.

31st. I went to see the pictures of all the judges and eminent men of the Long Robe, newly painted by Mr. Wright,[2] and set up in Guildhall, costing the City £1000. Most of them are very like the persons they represent, though I never took Wright to be any considerable artist.

13th August. I rode to Durdans, where I dined at my Lord Berkeley's of Berkeley-Castle, my old and noble friend, it being his wedding-anniversary, where I found the Duchess of Albemarle, and other company, and returned home on that evening, late.

15th. Came to visit me my Lord Chancellor, the Earl of Shaftesbury.

18th. My Lord Clifford, being about this time returned from Tunbridge, and preparing for Devonshire, I went to take my leave of him at Wallingford-House; he was packing up pictures, most of which were of hunting wild beasts, and vast pieces of bull-baiting, bear-baiting, &c. I found him in his study, and restored to him several papers of state, and others of importance, which he had furnished me with, on engaging me to write the History of the Holland War, with other private letters of his acknowledgments to my Lord Arlington, who from a private gentleman of a very noble family, but inconsiderable fortune, had advanced him from almost nothing. The first thing was his being in Parlia-

[1] Burnet, says the Earl of Shaftesbury, was the chief man in this advice. There is a story, among the gossip of that day, that Shaftesbury having formed the plan, Clifford got possession of it over a bottle of wine, and carried it to the King as his own.

[2] Michael Wright was a fashionable portrait-painter of the day, but not comparable to Lely.

ment, then knighted, then made one of the Commissioners
of sick and wounded, on which occasion, we sate long
together; then, on the death of Hugh Pollard, he was made
Comptroller of the Household and Privy Councillor, yet
still my brother Commissioner; after the death of Lord
Fitz-Harding, Treasurer of the Household, he, by letters to
Lord Arlington, which that Lord showed me, begged of his
Lordship to obtain it for him as the very height of his ambition.   These were written with such submissions and professions of his patronage, as I had never seen any more acknowledging.   The Earl of Southampton then dying, he was
made one of the Commissioners of the Treasury.   His
Majesty inclining to put it into one hand, my Lord Clifford,
under pretence of making all his interest for his patron, my
Lord Arlington, cut the grass under his feet, and procured
it for himself, assuring the King that Lord Arlington did
not desire it.   Indeed, my Lord Arlington protested to me
that his confidence in Lord Clifford made him so remiss, and
his affection to him was so particular, that he was absolutely
minded to devolve it on Lord Clifford, all the world knowing how he himself affected ease and quiet, now growing into
years, yet little thinking of this go-by.   This was the only
great ingratitude Lord Clifford showed, keeping my Lord
Arlington in ignorance, continually assuring him he was
pursuing his interest, which was the Duke's, into whose
great favour Lord Clifford was now gotten; but which certainly cost him the loss of all, namely, his going so irrevo-
cably far in his interest.

For the rest, my Lord Clifford was a valiant incorrupt
gentleman, ambitious, not covetous; generous, passionate,
a most constant sincere friend, to me in particular, so as
when he laid down his office, I was at the end of all my
hopes and endeavours.   These were not for high matters,
but to obtain what his Majesty was really indebted to my
father-in-law, which was the utmost of my ambition, and
which I had undoubtedly obtained, if this friend had
stood.   Sir Thomas Osborn, who succeeded him, though
much more obliged to my father-in-law and his family,
and my long and old acquaintance, being of a more haughty
and far less obliging nature, I could hope for little; a man
of excellent natural parts; but nothing of generous or
grateful.

Taking leave of my Lord Clifford, he wrung me by the hand, and, looking earnestly on me, bid me God-b'ye, adding, "Mr. Evelyn, I shall never see thee more." "No!" said I, "my Lord, what's the meaning of this? I hope I shall see you often, and as great a person again." "No, Mr. Evelyn, do not expect it, I will never see this place, this City, or Court again," or words of this sound. In this manner, not without almost mutual tears, I parted from him; nor was it long after, but the news was that he was dead, and I have heard from some who I believe knew, he made himself away, after an extraordinary melancholy. This is not confidently affirmed, but a servant who lived in the house, and afterwards with Sir Robert Clayton, Lord Mayor, did, as well as others, report it; and when I hinted some such thing to Mr. Prideaux, one of his trustees, he was not willing to enter into that discourse.

It was reported with these particulars, that, causing his servant to leave him unusually one morning, locking himself in, he strangled himself with his cravat upon the bed-tester; his servant, not liking the manner of dismissing him, and looking through the key-hole, (as I remember), and seeing his master hanging, brake in before he was quite dead, and taking him down, vomiting a great deal of blood, he was heard to utter these words, "Well; let men say what they will, there is a God, a just God above;" after which he spake no more. This, if true, is dismal. Really, he was the chief occasion of the Dutch war, and of all that blood which was lost at Bergen in attacking the Smyrna fleet, and that whole quarrel.

This leads me to call to mind what my Lord Chancellor Shaftesbury affirmed, not to me only, but to all my brethren the Council of Foreign Plantations, when not long after, this accident being mentioned as we were one day sitting in Council, his Lordship told us this remarkable passage: that, being one day discoursing with him when he was only Sir Thomas Clifford, speaking of men's advancement to great charges in the nation, "Well," says he, "my Lord, I shall be one of the greatest men in England. Don't impute what I say either to fancy, or vanity; I am certain that I shall be a mighty man; but it will not last long; I shall not hold it, but die a bloody death." "What," says my Lord, "your horoscope tells you so?" "No matter for that, it will be as I tell you." "Well," says my Lord Chancellor Shaftesbury, "if I were of that opinion, I either would not be a great man, but decline preferment, or prevent my danger."

This my Lord affirmed in my hearing, before several gentlemen and noblemen sitting in council at Whitehall. And I the rather am confident of it, remembering what Sir Edward Walker (Garter King-at-Arms)[1] had likewise affirmed to me a long time before, even when he was first made a Lord; that carrying his pedigree to Lord Clifford on his being created a peer, and, finding him busy, he bade him go into his study, and divert himself there till he was at leisure to discourse with him about some things relating to his family; there lay, said Sir Edward, on his table, his horoscope and nativity calculated, with some writing under it, where he read that he should be advanced to the highest degree in the state that could be conferred upon him, but that he should not long enjoy it, but should die, or expressions to that sense; and I think, (but cannot confidently say) a bloody death. This Sir Edward affirmed both to me and Sir Richard Browne; nor could I forbear to note this extraordinary passage in these memoirs.

14th September. Dr. Creighton, son to the late eloquent Bishop of Bath and Wells, preached to the Household on Isaiah, lvii. 8.

15th. I procured £4000 of the Lords of the Treasury, and rectified divers matters about the sick and wounded.

16th. To Council, about choosing a new Secretary.

17th. I went with some friends to visit Mr. Bernard Grenville, at Abs Court in Surrey; an old house in a pretty park.[2]

23rd. I went to see Paradise, a room in Hatton-Garden, furnished with a representation of all sorts of

---

[1] Celebrated for his knowledge of heraldry. He attended Charles II. into exile, and after the Restoration he became first Clerk of the Privy Council, and subsequently Garter King-at-Arms. Author, among other works, of *Iter Carolinum*, or an account of the Marches, &c., of King Charles I., *Military Discoveries, Historical Discoveries*, &c. He died in 1677. Pepys describes his bringing the Garter to the Earl of Sandwich, and his officiating at the coronation of Charles II.

[2] At Walton-on-Thames.

animals handsomely painted on boards, or cloth, and so cut cut and made to stand, move, fly, crawl, roar, and make their several cries. The man who showed it, made us laugh heartily at his formal poetry.

15th October. To Council, and swore in Mr. Locke, secretary, Dr. Worsley being dead.

27th. To Council, about sending succours to recover New York: and then we read the commission and instructions to Sir Jonathan Atkins, the new Governor of Barbadoes.

5th November. This night the youths of the City burnt the Pope in effigy, after they had made procession with it in great triumph, they being displeased at the Duke for altering his religion, and marrying an Italian lady.[1]

30th. On St. Andrew's day, I first saw the new Duchess of York, and the Duchess of Modena, her mother.

1st December. To Gresham College, whither the City had invited the Royal Society by many of their chief aldermen and magistrates, who gave us a collation, to welcome us to our first place of assembly, from whence we had been driven to give place to the City, on their making it their Exchange, on the dreadful conflagration, till their new Exchange was finished, which it now was. The Society having till now been entertained and having met at Arundel House.[2]

2nd. I dined with some friends, and visited the sick: thence, to an alms-house, where was prayers and relief, some very ill and miserable. It was one of the best days I ever spent in my life.

3rd. There was at dinner my Lord Lockhart, designed ambassador for France, a gallant and a sober person.

9th. I saw again the Italian Duchess and her brother, the Prince Reynaldo.

20th. I had some discourse with certain strangers, not unlearned, who had been born not far from Old Nineveh; they assured me of the ruins being still extant, and vast and

---

[1] The Princess Mary Beatrice D'Este, daughter of the Duke of Modena.

[2] One of the great houses by the Strand. It was pulled down at the end of the 17th century, but the family names and titles are retained in the streets which arose on its site, Howard, Norfolk, Arundel, and Surrey.

wonderful were the buildings, vaults, pillars, and magnificent fragments;[1] but they could say little of the Tower of Babel that satisfied me. But the description of the amenity and fragrancy of the country for health and cheerfulness, delighted me; so sensibly they spake of the excellent air and climate in respect of our cloudy and splenetic country.

24th December. Visited the prisoners at Ludgate, taking orders about the releasing of some.

30th. I gave Almighty God thanks for His infinite goodness to me the year past, and begged His mercy and protection the year following: afterwards, invited my neighbours to spend the day with me.

1673-4: 5th January. I saw an Italian opera in music, the first that had been in England of this kind.

9th. Sent for by his Majesty to write something against the Hollanders about the duty of the Flag and Fishery. Returned with some papers.

25th March. I dined at Knightsbridge, with the Bishops of Salisbury, Chester, and Lincoln, my old friends.

29th May. His Majesty's birth-day and Restoration. Mr. Demalhoy, Roger L'Estrange, and several of my friends, came to dine with me on the happy occasion.

27th June. Mr. Dryden, the famous poet and now laureate, came to give me a visit. It was the anniversary of my marriage, and the first day I went into my new little cell and cabinet, which I built below towards the south court, at the east end of the parlour.

9th July. Paid 360*l.* for purchase of Dr. Jacombe's son's share in the mill and land at Deptford, which I bought of the Beechers.

22nd. I went to Windsor with my wife and son to see my daughter Mary, who was there with my Lady Tuke, and to do my duty to his Majesty. Next day, to a great entertainment at Sir Robert Holmes's at Cranbourne Lodge, in the Forest; there were his Majesty, the Queen, Duke, Duchess, and all the Court. I returned in the evening with Sir Joseph Williamson, now declared Secretary of State. He was son of a poor clergyman somewhere in Cumberland, brought up at Queen's College, Oxford, of which he came to

[1] The remarkable discoveries of Mr. Layard give now a curious interest to this notice by Evelyn,

be a fellow ; then travelled with . . . . . and returning when
the King was restored, was received as a Clerk under Mr.
Secretary Nicholas. Sir Henry Bennett (now Lord Arlington) succeeding, Williamson is transferred to him, who
loving his ease more than business (though sufficiently able
had he applied himself to it) remitted all to his man Williamson ; and, in a short time, let him so into the secret of
affairs, that (as his Lordship himself told me) there was a
kind of necessity to advance him ; and so, by his subtlety,
dexterity, and insinuation, he got now to be principal Secretary ; absolutely Lord Arlington's creature, and ungrateful
enough. It has been the fate of this obliging favourite to
advance those who soon forgot their original. Sir Joseph
was a musician, could play at *Jeu de Goblets*, exceeding formal,
a severe master to his servants, but so inward with my Lord
O'Brien, that after a few months of that gentleman's death,
he married his widow,[1] who, being sister and heir of the Duke
of Richmond, brought him a noble fortune. It was thought
they lived not so kindly after marriage as they did before.
She was much censured for marrying so meanly, being herself allied to the Royal family.

6th August. I went to Groombridge, to see my old friend,
Mr. Packer ; the house built within a moat, in a woody
valley. The old house had been the place of confinement of
the Duke of Orleans, taken by one Waller (whose house it
then was) at the battle of Agincourt, now demolished, and a
new one built in its place, though a far better situation had
been on the south of the wood, on a graceful ascent. At
some small distance, is a large chapel, not long since built
by Mr. Packer's father, on a vow he made to do it on the
return of King Charles I. out of Spain, 1625, and dedicated
to St. Charles ; but what saint there was then of that name
I am to seek, for, being a Protestant, I conceive it was not
Borromeo.

[1] Lady Catherine Stuart, sister and heir to Charles Stuart, Duke of
Richmond and Lennox, the husband of Mrs. Frances Stuart, one of the
most admired beauties of the Court, with whom Charles the Second was
so deeply in love that he never forgave the Duke for marrying her, having already, it is thought, formed some similar intention himself. He
took the first opportunity of sending the Duke into an honourable
exile, as Ambassador to Denmark, where he shortly after died, leaving
no issue by the Duchess.

I went to see my farm at Ripe, near Lewes.

19th August. His Majesty told me how exceedingly the Dutch were displeased at my treatise of the *History of Commerce;*[1] that the Holland Ambassador had complained to him of what I had touched of the Flags and Fishery, &c., and desired the book might be called in; whilst, on the other side, he assured me he was exceedingly pleased with what I had done, and gave me many thanks. However, it being just upon conclusion of the treaty of Breda (indeed it was designed to have been published some months before and when we were at defiance), his Majesty told me he must recall it formally; but gave order that what copies should be publicly seized to pacify the Ambassador, should immediately be restored to the printer, and that neither he nor the vender should be molested. The truth is, that which touched the Hollander was much less than what the King himself furnished me with, and obliged me to publish, having caused it to be read to him before it went to the press; but the error was, it should have been published before the peace was proclaimed. The noise of this book's suppression made it presently be bought up, and turned much to the stationer's advantage. It was no other than the Preface prepared to be prefixed to my History of the whole War; which I now pursued no further.

21st. In one of the meadows at the foot of the long Terrace below the Castle [Windsor], works were thrown up to show the King a representation of the City of Maestricht, newly taken by the French. Bastions, bulwarks, ramparts, palisadoes, graffs, horn-works, counter-scarps, &c., were constructed. It was attacked by the Duke of Monmouth (newly come from the real siege) and the Duke of York, with a little army, to show their skill in tactics. On Saturday night, they made their approaches, opened trenches, raised batteries, took the counterscarp and ravelin, after a stout defence; great guns fired on both sides, grenadoes shot, mines sprung, parties sent out, attempts of raising the siege,

---

[1] Entitled " Navigation and Commerce, their Original and Progress, &c. By I. Evelyn, Esq., S.R.S." 8vo., 1674. Dedicated to the King. It was, in fact, only the introduction to the intended History of the Dutch War, and is reprinted in his " Miscellaneous Writings," pp. 625— 686.

prisoners taken, parleys ; and, in short, all the circumstances of a formal siege, to appearance, and, what is most strange, all without disorder, or ill accident, to the great satisfaction of a thousand spectators. Being night, it made a formidable show. The siege being over, I went with Mr. Pepys back to London, where we arrived about three in the morning.

15th *September*. To Council, about fetching away the English left at Surinam, &c., since our reconciliation with Holland.

21st. I went to see the great loss that Lord Arlington had sustained by fire at Goring House, this night consumed to the ground, with exceeding loss of hangings, plate, rare pictures, and cabinets ; hardly anything was saved of the best and most princely furniture that any subject had in England. My lord and lady were both absent at the Bath.

6th *October*. The Lord Chief Baron Turner, and Serjeant Wild, Recorder of London,[1] came to visit me.

20th. At Lord Berkeley's, I discoursed with Sir Thomas Modiford, late Governor of Jamaica, and with Colonel Morgan, who undertook that gallant exploit from Nombre de Dios to Panama, on the Continent of America; he told me 10,000 men would easily conquer all the Spanish Indies, they were so secure. They took great booty, and much greater had been taken, had they not been betrayed and so discovered before their approach, by which the Spaniards had time to carry their vast treasure on board ships that put off to sea in sight of our men, who had no boats to follow. They set fire to Panama, and ravaged the country sixty miles about. The Spaniards were so supine and unexercised, that they were afraid to fire a great gun.

31st. My birth-day, 54th year of my life. Blessed be God ! It was also preparation-day for the Holy Sacrament, in which I participated the next day, imploring God's protection for the year following, and confirming my resolutions of a more holy life, even upon the Holy Book. The Lord assist and be gracious unto me ! Amen.

[1] Sir Edward Turner, Speaker of the House of Commons, subsequently Solicitor-General, and Lord Chief Baron, died in 1675. Serjeant, afterwards Sir William Wild, was Member for the City of London, and Recorder.

15th November. The anniversary of my baptism: I first heard that famous and excellent preacher, Dr. Burnet (author of the *History of the Reformation*) on Colossians iii. 10, with such flow of eloquence and fulness of matter, as showed him to be a person of extraordinary parts.

Being her Majesty's birth-day, the Court was exceeding splendid in clothes and jewels, to the height of excess.

17th. To Council, on the business of Surinam, where the Dutch had detained some English in prison, ever since the first war, 1665.

19th. I heard that stupendous violin, Signor Nicholao (with other rare musicians), whom I never heard mortal man exceed on that instrument. He had a stroke so sweet, and made it speak like the voice of a man, and, when he pleased, like a concert of several instruments. He did wonders upon a note, and was an excellent composer. Here was also that rare lutanist, Dr. Wallgrave; but nothing approached the violin in Nicholao's hand. He played such ravishing things as astonished us all.

2nd December. At Mr. Slingsby's, Master of the Mint, my worthy friend, a great lover of music. Heard Signor Francisco on the harpsichord, esteemed one of the most excellent masters in Europe on that instrument; then, came Nicholao with his violin, and struck all mute, but Mrs. Knight, who sung incomparably, and doubtless has the greatest reach of any English woman; she had been lately roaming in Italy, and was much improved in that quality.

15th. Saw a comedy[1] at night, at Court, acted by the ladies only, amongst them Lady Mary and Ann, his Royal Highness's two daughters, and my dear friend, Mrs. Blagg,

---

[1] This was the Masque of *Calisto, or the Chaste Nymph*, by John Crowne. The performers in the piece were, the two daughters of the Duke of York, Lady Henrietta Wentworth (afterwards mistress to the Duke of Monmouth), Countess of Sussex, Lady Mary Mordaunt, Mrs. Blagg, who had been Maid of Honour to the Queen, and Mrs Jennings, then Maid of Honour to the Duchess of York, and afterwards the cele-brated Duchess of Marlborough. The Duke of Monmouth, Lord Dum-blaine, Lord Daincourt, were among the dancers; and Mrs. Davis, Mrs. Knight, Mrs. Butler, and other celebrated comedians of the day, also acted and sung in the performance. The Masque was printed (1675) in 4to.

who, having the principal part, performed it to admiration. They were all covered with jewels.

22nd December. Was at the repetition of the *Pastoral*, on which occasion Mrs. Blagg had about her near £20,000 worth of jewels, of which she lost one worth about £80, borrowed of the Countess of Suffolk. The press was so great, that it is a wonder she lost no more. The Duke made it good.

1674-5. *20th January.* Went to see Mr. Streeter, that excellent painter of perspective and landscape, to comfort and encourage him to be cut for the stone, with which that honest man was exceedingly afflicted.[1]

22nd March. Supped at Sir William Petty's, with the Bishop of Salisbury, and divers honourable persons. We had a noble entertainment in a house gloriously furnished; the master and mistress of it were extraordinary persons. Sir William was the son of a mean man somewhere in Sussex, and sent from school to Oxford, where he studied Philosophy, but was most eminent in Mathematics and Mechanics; proceeded Doctor of Physic, and was grown famous, as for his learning so for his recovering a poor wench that had been hanged for felony; and her body having been begged (as the custom is) for the anatomy lecture, he bled her, put her to bed to a warm woman, and, with spirits and other means, restored her to life.[2] The young scholars joined and made a little portion, and married her to a man who had several children by her, she living fifteen years after, as I have been assured. Sir William

---

[1] The King, who had a great regard for this artist, is said to have sent for a famous surgeon from Paris, on purpose to perform the operation.

[2] A full account of this event was given in a published pamphlet at the time, entitled " Newes from the Dead, or a true and exact Narration of the miraculous Deliverance of Anne Greene, who being executed at Oxford, Dec. 14, 1650, afterwards revived; and by the care of certain Physicians there, is now perfectly recovered. Oxford, the second Impression, with Additions, 4to. 1651." Added to the Narrative are several copies of Verses in Latin, English, and French, by Gentlemen of the University, commemorative of the event; amongst others, by Joseph Williamson, afterwards Secretary of State, by Christopher Wren, the famous architect, then of Wadham College, by Walter Pope, Dr. Ralph Bathurst (the last under other names), and many more. The pamphlet was reprinted, but very negligently, from the first and worst edition, in Morgan's *Phœnix Britannicus*, 4to.

came from Oxford to be tutor to a neighbour of mine;
thence, when the rebels were dividing their conquests in
Ireland, he was employed by them to measure and set out
the land, which he did on an easy contract, so much per
acre.   This he effected so exactly, that it not only furnished
him with a great sum of money; but enabled him to purchase an estate worth £4000 a year.   He afterwards married
the daughter of Sir Hardress Waller; she was an extraordinary wit as well as beauty, and a prudent woman.

Sir William, amongst other inventions, was author of
the double-bottomed ship,[1] which perished, and he was
censured for rashness, being lost in the Bay of Biscay in a
storm, when, I think, fifteen other vessels miscarried.   This
vessel was flat-bottomed, of exceeding use to put into
shallow ports, and ride over small depths of water.   It consisted of two distinct keels cramped together with huge
timbers, &c., so as that a violent stream ran between; it
bare a monstrous broad sail, and he still persists that it is
practicable, and of exceeding use; and he has often told me
he would adventure himself in such another, could he procure sailors, and his Majesty's permission to make a second
Experiment; which name the King gave the vessel at the
launching.

The Map of Ireland made by Sir William Petty is believed to be the most exact that ever yet was made of any
country.   He did promise to publish it; and I am told it
has cost him near £1000 to have it engraved at Amsterdam.
There is not a better Latin poet living, when he gives himself that diversion; nor is his excellence less in Council and
prudent matters of state; but he is so exceeding nice in
sifting and examining all possible contingencies, that he
adventures at nothing which is not demonstration.   There
was not in the whole world his equal for a superintendent
of manufacture and improvement of trade, or to govern a
plantation.   If I were a Prince, I should make him my
second Counsellor, at least.   There is nothing difficult to
him.   He is, besides, courageous; on which account, I cannot but note a true story of him, that when Sir Aleyn
Brodrick sent him a challenge upon a difference betwixt

---

[1] See *ante*, vol. i. pp. 400, 409.

them in Ireland, Sir William, though exceedingly purblind, accepted the challenge, and it being his part to propound the weapon, desired his antagonist to meet him with a hatchet, or axe, in a dark cellar; which the other, of course, refused.

Sir William was, with all this, facetious and of easy conversation, friendly and courteous, and had such a faculty of imitating others, that he would take a text and preach, now like a grave orthodox divine, then falling into the Presbyterian way, then to the fanatical, the Quaker, the monk and friar, the Popish priest, with such admirable action, and alteration of voice and tone, as it was not possible to abstain from wonder, and one would swear to hear several persons, or forbear to think he was not in good earnest an enthusiast and almost beside himself; then, he would fall out of it into a serious discourse; but it was very rarely he would be prevailed on to oblige the company with this faculty, and that only amongst most intimate friends. My Lord Duke of Ormond once obtained it of him, and was almost ravished with admiration; but by-and-bye, he fell upon a serious reprimand of the faults and miscarriages of some Princes and Governors, which, though he named none, did so sensibly touch the Duke, who was then Lieutenant of Ireland, that he began to be very uneasy, and wished the spirit laid which he had raised, for he was neither able to endure such truths, nor could he but be delighted. At last, he melted his discourse to a ridiculous subject, and came down from the joint stool on which he had stood; but my lord would not have him preach any more. He never could get favour at Court, because he outwitted all the projectors that came near him. Having never known such another genius, I cannot but mention these particulars, amongst a multitude of others which I could produce. When I, who knew him in mean circumstances, have been in his splendid palace, he would himself be in admiration how he arrived at it; nor was it his value or inclination for splendid furniture and the curiosities of the age, but his elegant lady could endure nothing mean, or that was not magnificent. He was very negligent himself, and rather so of his person, and of a philosophic temper. "What a to-do is here!" would he say, "I can lie in straw with as much satisfaction '

He is author of the ingenious deductions from the bills of mortality, which go under the name of Mr. Graunt; also of that useful discourse of the manufacture of wool, and several others in the register of the Royal Society. He was also author of that paraphrase on the 104th Psalm in Latin verse, which goes about in MS., and is inimitable. In a word, there is nothing impenetrable to him.

26th March. Dr. Brideoak was elected Bishop of Chichester, on the translation of Dr. Gunning to Ely.

30th. Dr. Allestree preached on Romans, vi. 3, the necessity of those who are baptized to die to sin; a very excellent discourse from an excellent preacher.

25th April. Dr. Barrow,[1] that excellent, pious, and most learned man, divine, mathematician, poet, traveller, and most humble person, preached at Whitehall to the household, on Luke, xx. 27, of love and charity to our neighbours.

29th. I read my first discourse *Of Earth and Vegetation* before the Royal Society as a lecture in course, after Sir Robert Southwell[2] had read his the week before *On Water.* I was commanded by our President, and the suffrage of the Society, to print it.

16th May. This day was my dear friend, Mrs. Blagg,[3] married at the Temple Church to my friend, Mr. Sidney Godolphin, Groom of the Bedchamber to his Majesty.

18th. I went to visit one Mr. Bathurst, a Spanish merchant, my neighbour.

31st. I went with Lord Ossory to Deptford, where we chose him Master of the Trinity Company.

2nd June. I was at a conference of the Lords and Commons in the Painted Chamber, on a difference about imprisoning some of their members; and, on the 3d, at another conference, when the Lords accused the Commons for their transcendant misbehaviour, breach of privilege, Magna

[1] Master of Trinity College, Cambridge; in which he succeeded Dr. John Pearson, made Bishop of Chester.

[2] Sent Envoy Extraordinary to Portugal, in 1665, and in the same capacity to Brussels, in 1671. He was subsequently Clerk of the Privy Council, and having shown much taste for learned and scientific researches, was five times elected President of the Royal Society. He died in 1702. His son Edward became Secretary of State.

[3] *Ante,* p. 43, &c., and see *post,* p. 130.

Charta, subversion of government, and other high, provoking, and diminishing expressions, showing what duties and
subjection they owed to the Lords in Parliament, by record
of Henry IV. This was likely to create a notable disturbance.

15th June. This afternoon came Monsieur Querouaille and
his lady, parents to the famous beauty and * * * * *
favourite at Court, to see Sir R. Browne, with whom they
were intimately acquainted in Bretagne, at the time Sir
Richard was sent to Brest to supervise his Majesty's sea-
affairs, during the later part of the King's banishment.
This gentleman's house was not a mile from Brest; Sir
Richard made an acquaintance there, and, being used very
civilly, was obliged to return it here, which we did. He
seemed a soldierly person and a good fellow, as the Bretons
generally are; his lady had been very handsome, and seemed
a shrewd understanding woman. Conversing with him in
our garden, I found several words of the Breton language
the same with our Welch. His daughter was now made
Duchess of Portsmouth, and in the height of favour; but he
never made any use of it.

27th. At Ely House, I went to the consecration of my
worthy friend, the learned Dr. Barlow, Warden of Queen's
College, Oxford, now made Bishop of Lincoln. After it,
succeeded a magnificent feast, where were the Duke of
Ormond, Earl of Lauderdale, the Lord Treasurer, Lord
Keeper, &c.

8th July. I went with Mrs. Howard and her two daughters towards Northampton Assizes, about a trial at law, in
which I was concerned for them as a trustee. We lay this
night at Henley-on-the-Thames, at our attorney, Mr. Stephens's, who entertained us very handsomely. Next day,
dining at Shotover, at Sir Timothy Tyrill's, a sweet place,
we lay at Oxford, where it was the time of the Act. Mr.
Robert Spencer, uncle to the Earl of Sunderland, and my
old acquaintance in France, entertained us at his apartment
in Christ Church, with exceeding generosity.

10th. The Vice-Chancellor, Dr. Bathurst (who had formerly taken particular care of my son), President of Trinity
College, invited me to dinner, and did me great honour all
the time of my stay. The next day, he invited me and all

my company, though strangers to him, to a very noble
feast. I was at all the academic exercises.—Sunday, at St.
Mary's, preached a Fellow of Brasen-nose, not a little magnifying the dignity of Churchmen.

11*th July*. We heard the speeches, and saw the ceremony
of creating Doctors in Divinity, Law, and Physic. I had,
early in the morning, heard Dr. Morison, Botanic Professor,
read on divers plants in the Physic Garden: and saw that
rare collection of natural curiosities of Dr. Plot's, of Magdalen Hall, author of *The Natural History of Oxfordshire*, all
of them collected in that shire, and indeed extraordinary,
that in one county there should be found such variety of
plants, shells, stones, minerals, marcasites, fowls, insects,
models of works, crystals, agates and marbles. He was
now intending to visit Staffordshire, and, as he had of
Oxfordshire, to give us the natural, topical, political, and
mechanical history. Pity it is that more of this industrious man's genius were not employed so to describe every
county of England; it would be one of the most useful
and illustrious works that was ever produced in any age or
nation.[1]

I visited also the Bodleian Library, and my old friend,
the learned Obadiah Walker, head of University College,
which he had now almost re-built, or repaired. We then
proceeded to Northampton, where we arrived the next day.

In this journey, went part of the way Mr. James Graham
(since Privy Purse to the Duke), a young gentleman exceedingly in love with Mrs. Dorothy Howard, one of the
Maids of Honour in our company.[2] I could not but pity
them both, the mother not much favouring it. This lady
was not only a great beauty, but a most virtuous and
excellent creature, and worthy to have been wife to the
best of men. My advice was required, and I spake to the
advantage of the young gentleman, more out of pity than

[1] Robert Morison, Physician to Charles II., Regius Professor of
Botany at Oxford, and author of "Præludium Botanicum," and of the
fragment of a "Historia Plantarum," which he left unfinished when he
died, in 1683. Robert Plot, Doctor of Laws, one of the Secretaries of
the Royal Society, Royal Historiographer, Keeper of the Archives of
the Heralds' College; celebrated for his "Natural Histories of Oxfordshire and Staffordshire." He died in 1696.

[2] He afterwards married her. See the next note.

that she deserved no better match; for, though he was a gentleman of good family, yet there was great inequality.

14th July. I went to see my Lord Sunderland's Seat at Althorpe, four miles from the ragged town of Northampton (since burnt, and well re-built). It is placed in a pretty open bottom, very finely watered and flanked with stately woods and groves in a park, with a canal, but the water is not running, which is a defect. The house, a kind of modern building, of freestone, within most nobly furnished; the apartments very commodious, a gallery and noble hall; but the kitchen being in the body of the house, and chapel too small, were defects. There is an old yet honourable gate-house standing awry, and out-housing mean, but designed to be taken away. It was moated round, after the old manner, but it is now dry, and turfed with a beautiful carpet. Above all, are admirable and magnificent the several ample gardens furnished with the choicest fruit, and exquisitely kept. Great plenty of oranges, and other curiosities. The park full of fowl, especially herns, and from it a prospect to Holmby House, which being demolished in the late civil wars, shows like a Roman ruin, shaded by the trees about it, a stately, solemn, and pleasing view.

15th. Our cause was pleaded in behalf of the mother, Mrs. Howard[1] and her daughters, before Baron Thurland, who had formerly been steward of Courts for me; we carried our cause, as there was reason, for here was an imprudent as well as disobedient son against his mother, by instigation, doubtless, of his wife, one Mrs. Ogle, (an ancient maid), whom he had clandestinely married, and who brought

[1] Mrs. Howard was widow of William, fourth son of the first Earl of Berkshire, being the daughter of Lord Dundas, a Scottish peer. They had one son, Craven Howard, and two daughters, Dorothy, who married Colonel James Graham, of Levens, in Westmoreland; and Anne, who married Sir Gabriel Sylvius, Knt. Craven married two wives, the first of whom was Anne Ogle, of the family of the Ogles of Pinchbeck, in the county of Lincoln. She was Maid of honour to Queen Catherine at the time. The two daughters are the ladies mentioned by Evelyn in the text; but he is not correct in calling Craven heir-apparent of the Earl of Berks, since, besides the uncle then in possession of the title, there was another uncle before him, who in fact inherited it, and did not die till many years after.

him no fortune, he being heir-apparent to the Earl of Berkshire. We lay at Brickhill, in Bedfordshire, and came late
the next day to our journey's end.

This was a journey of adventures and knight-errantry.
One of the lady's servants being as desperately in love with
Mrs. Howard's woman, as Mr. Graham was with her daughter,
and she riding on horseback behind his rival, the amorous
and jealous youth having a little drink in his pate, had here
killed himself had he not been prevented; for, alighting from
his horse, and drawing his sword, he endeavoured twice or
thrice to fall on it, but was interrupted by our coachman,
and a stranger passing by. After this, running to his rival,
and snatching his sword from his side (for we had beaten
his own out of his hand), and on the sudden pulling down
his mistress, would have run both of them through; we
parted them, not without some blood. This miserable creature poisoned himself for her not many days after they came
to London.

19th July. The Lord Treasurer's Chaplain preached at
Wallingford-House.

9th August. Dr. Sprat, prebend of Westminster, and Chaplain to the Duke of Buckingham, preached on the 3rd Epistle
of Jude, showing what the primitive faith was, how near it
and how excellent that of the Church of England, also the
danger of departing from it.

27th. I visited the Bishop of Rochester, at Bromley, and
dined at Sir Philip Warwick's, at Frogpoole [Frognall].

2nd September. I went to see Dulwich College, being the
pious foundation of one Alleyn, a famous comedian, in King
James's time. The chapel is pretty, the rest of the hospital
very ill contrived; it yet maintains divers poor of both sexes.
It is in a melancholy part of Camberwell parish. I came
back by certain medicinal Spa waters, at a place called
Sydenham Wells, in Lewisham parish, much frequented in
summer.

10th. I was casually showed the Duchess of Portsmouth's
splendid apartment at Whitehall, luxuriously furnished, and
with ten times the richness and glory beyond the Queen's;
such massy pieces of plate, whole tables, and stands of incredible value.

29th. I saw the Italian Scaramuccio act before the King

at Whitenall, people giving money to come in, which was very scandalous, and never so before at Court-diversions. Having seen him act before in Italy, many years past, I was not averse from seeing the most excellent of that kind of folly.

14th October. Dined at Kensington with my old acquaintance, Mr. Henshaw, newly returned from Denmark, where he had been left resident after the death of the Duke of Richmond, who died there Ambassador.

15th. I got an extreme cold, such as was afterwards so epidemical, as not only to afflict us in this island, but was rife over all Europe, like a plague. It was after an exceeding dry summer and autumn.

I settled affairs, my Son being to go into France with my Lord Berkeley, designed Ambassador-extraordinary for France and Plenipotentiary for the general treaty of peace at Nimeguen.

24th. Dined at Lord Chamberlain's with the Holland Ambassador L. Duras, a valiant gentleman whom his Majesty made an English Baron, of a cadet, and gave him his seat of Holmby, in Northamptonshire.[1]

27th. Lord Berkeley coming into Council, fell down in the gallery at Whitehall, in a fit of apoplexy, and being carried into my Lord Chamberlain's lodgings, several famous doctors were employed all that night, and with much ado he was at last recovered to some sense, by applying hot fire-pans and spirit of amber to his head; but nothing was found so effectual as cupping him on the shoulders. It was almost a miraculous restoration. The next day he was carried to Berkeley-House. This stopped his journey for the present, and caused my stay in town. He had put all his affairs and his whole estate in England into my hands during his intended absence, which though I was very unfit to undertake, in regard of many businesses which then took me up, yet, upon the great importunity of my lady and Mr. Godolphin (to whom I could refuse nothing) I did take it on me. It seems when he was Deputy in Ireland, not long before, he had been much wronged by one he left in trust with his affairs, and therefore wished for some unmercenary

[1] Since Earl of Faversham. See Baker's *Northamptonshire*, vol. i. p. 197.

friend who would take that trouble on him; this was to receive his rents, look after his houses and tenants, solicit supplies from the Lord Treasurer, and correspond weekly with him, more than enough to employ any drudge in England; but what will not friendship and love make one do?

31st October. Dined at my Lord Chamberlain's, with my Son. There were the learned Isaac Vossius, and Spanhemius,[1] son of the famous man of Heidelberg; nor was this gentleman less learned, being a general scholar. Amongst other pieces, he was author of an excellent treatise on Medals.

10th November. Being the day appointed for my Lord Ambassador to set out, I met them with my coach at New Cross. There were with him my Lady his wife, and my dear friend, Mrs. Godolphin, who, out of an extraordinary friendship, would needs accompany my lady to Paris, and stay with her some time, which was the chief inducement for permitting my Son to travel, but I knew him safe under her inspection, and in regard my Lord himself had promised to take him into his special favour, he having intrusted all he had to my care.

Thus, we set out, three coaches (besides mine), three waggons, and about forty horse. It being late, and my Lord as yet but valetudinary, we got but to Dartford, the first day, the next to Sittingbourne.

At Rochester, the major, Mr. Cony, then an officer of mine for the sick and wounded of that place, gave the ladies a handsome refreshment as we came by his house.

12th November. We came to Canterbury: and, next morning, to Dover.

There was in my Lady Ambassadress's company my Lady Hamilton, a sprightly young lady, much in the good graces of the family, wife of that valiant and worthy gentleman George Hamilton, not long after slain in the wars. She had been a maid of honour to the Duchess, and now turned Papist.

---

[1] Ezekiel Spanheim was born at Geneva in 1629. The Elector Palatine, Charles Louis, to whose son he had been tutor, sent him, after the peace of Ryswicke, ambassador to France, and thence to England, where he died in 1710. He was a learned author, as well as a celebrated diplomatist.

14th November. Being Sunday, my Lord having before delivered to me his letter of attorney, keys, seal, and his Will, we took solemn leave of one another upon the beach, the coaches carrying them into the sea to the boats, which delivered them to Captain Gunman's yacht, the Mary. Being under sail, the castle gave them seventeen guns, which Captain Gunman answered with eleven. Hence, I went to church, to beg a blessing on their voyage.

2nd December. Being returned home, I visited Lady Mordaunt at Parson's Green, my Lord her son being sick. This pious woman delivered to me £100 to bestow as I thought fit for the release of poor prisoners, and other charitable uses.

21st. Visited her Ladyship again, where I found the Bishop of Winchester, whom I had long known in France; he invited me to his house at Chelsea.

23rd. Lady Sunderland gave me ten guineas, to bestow in charities.

1675-6. *20th February.* Dr. Gunning, Bishop of Ely, preached before the King from St. John, xx. 21, 22, 23, chiefly against an anonymous book, called *Naked Truth*, a famous and popular treatise against the corruption in the Clergy, but not sound as to its quotations, supposed to have been the Bishop of Hereford's,[1] and was answered by Dr. Turner, it endeavouring to prove an equality of order of Bishop and Presbyter.

27th. Dr. Pritchard, Bishop of Gloucester, preached at Whitehall, on Isaiah, v. 5, very allegorically, according to his manner, yet very gravely and wittily.

29th. I dined with Mr. Povey, one of the Masters of Requests, a nice contriver of all elegancies, and exceedingly formal. Supped with Sir J. Williamson, where were of our Society Mr. Robert Boyle, Sir Christopher Wren, Sir William Petty, Dr. Holden, sub-dean of his Majesty's Chapel, Sir James Shaen, Dr. Whistler,[2] and our Secretary, Mr. Oldenburg.

4th March. Sir Thomas Linch was returned from his government of Jamaica.

[1] Dr. Herbert Croft.
[2] President of the College of Physicians. He accompanied Bulstrode Whitelock in his embassy to Sweden, and died in 1684. Pepys says that he found him " good company, and a very ingenious man."

16th March.. The Countess of Sunderland and I went by water to Parson's-green, to visit my Lady Mordaunt, and to consult with her about my Lord's monument. We returned by coach.

19th. Dr. Lloyd, late Curate of Deptford, but now Bishop of Llandaff, preached before the King, on 1 Cor., xv. 57, that though sin subjects us to death, yet through Christ we become his conquerors.

23rd. To Twickenham Park, Lord Berkeley's country-seat, to examine how the bailiffs and servants ordered matters.

24th. Dr. Brideoake,[1] Bishop of Chichester, preached a mean discourse for a Bishop. I also heard Dr. Fleetwood, Bishop of Worcester, on Matt., xxvi. 38, of the sorrows of Christ, a deadly sorrow caused by our sins; he was no great preacher.

30th. Dining with my Lady Sunderland, I saw a fellow swallow a knife, and divers great pebble stones, which would make a plain rattling one against another. The knife was in a sheath of horn.

Dr. North, son of my Lord North, preached before the King, on Isaiah, liii. 57, a very young but learned and excellent person. Note. This was the first time the Duke appeared no more in chapel, to the infinite grief and threatened ruin of this poor nation.

2nd April. I had now notice that my dear friend, Mrs. Godolphin, was returning from Paris. On the 6th, she arrived to my great joy, whom I most heartily welcomed.

28th. My wife entertained her Majesty at Deptford, for which the Queen gave me thanks in the withdrawing-room at Whitehall.

The University of Oxford presented me with the *Marmora Oxoniensia Arundeliana;* the Bishop of Oxford writing to desire that I would introduce Mr. Prideaux,[2] the editor (a young man most learned in antiquities) to the Duke of

[1] *Ante*, p. 104. Ralph Brideoake, Dean of Salisbury, succeeded Bishop Gunning in this see.

[2] The copy of Prideaux's book thus presented to Evelyn is still in the library at Wotton. Humphrey Prideaux was born in 1648, and became Dean of Norwich. He was the author of "The Connection of the History of the Old and New Testament," "The Life of Mahomet," and other works. He died in 1724.

Norfolk, to present another dedicated to his Grace, which I did, and we dined with the Duke at Arundel House, and supped at the Bishop of Rochester's with Isaac Vossius.

7th May. I spoke to the Duke of York about my Lord Berkeley's going to Nimeguen. Thence, to the Queen's Council at Somerset Honse, about Mrs. Godolphin's lease of Spalding, in Lincolnshire.

11th. I dined with Mr. Charleton, and went to see Mr. Montague's new palace near Bloomsbury, built by Mr. Hooke, of our Society, after the French manner.[1]

13th. Returned home, and found my son returned from France; praised be God!

22nd. Trinity Monday. A chaplain of my Lord Ossory's preached, after which we took barge to Trinity House in London. Mr. Pepys (Secretary of the Admiralty) succeeded my Lord as Master.

2nd June. I went with my Lord Chamberlain to see a garden,[2] at Enfield town ; thence, to Mr. Secretary Coventry's lodge in the Chase. It is a very pretty place, the house commodious, the gardens handsome, and our entertainment very free, there being none but my Lord and myself. That which I most wondered at was, that, in the compass of twenty-five miles, yet within fourteen of London, there is not a house, barn, church, or building, besides three lodges.[3] To this Lodge are three great ponds, and some few inclosures, the rest a solitary desert, yet stored with not less than 3000 deer. These are pretty retreats for gentlemen, especially for those who are studious and lovers of privacy.

We returned in the evening by Hampstead, to see Lord Wotton's house and garden (Bellsize House[4]), built with vast expense by Mr. O'Neale, an Irish gentleman who married Lord Wotton's mother, Lady Stanhope. The furniture is very particular for Indian cabinets, porcelain, and other solid and noble moveables. The gallery very fine, the gardens very large, but ill-kept, yet woody and

[1] Now the British Museum.
[2] Probably Dr. Robert Uvedale's. See an account of it in *Archæologia,* vol. xii. p. 188, and Robinson's *History of Enfield,* vol. i. p. 111.
[3] Enfield Chase was divided in 1777.
[4] In Park's *History of Hampstead* will be found notices of this house,

chargeable. The soil a cold weeping clay, not answering the expense.

12th June. I went to Sir Thomas Bond's new and fine house by Peckham ; it is on a flat, but has a fine garden and prospect through the meadows to London.

2nd July. Dr. Castillion, Prebend of Canterbury, preached before the King, on John, xv. 22, at Whitehall.

19th. Went to the funeral of Sir William Sanderson, husband to the Mother of the Maids,[1] and author of two large but mean histories of King James and King Charles the First. He was buried at Westminster.

1st August. In the afternoon, after prayers at St. James's Chapel, was christened a daughter of Dr. Leake's, the Duke's Chaplain : godmothers were Lady Mary, daughter of the Duke of York, and the Duchess of Monmouth : godfather, the Earl of Bath.

15th. Came to dine with me my Lord Halifax, Sir Thomas Meeres, one of the Commissioners of the Admiralty, Sir John Clayton, Mr. Slingsby, Mr. Henshaw, and Mr. Bridgeman.

25th. Dined with Sir John Banks at his house in Lincoln's Inn Fields, on recommending Mr. Upman to be tutor to his son going into France. This Sir John Banks was a merchant of small beginning, but had amassed £100,000.

26th. I dined at the Admiralty with Secretary Pepys, and supped at the Lord Chamberlain's. Here was Captain Baker, who had been lately on the attempt of the Northwest passage. He reported prodigious depth of ice, blue as a sapphire, and as transparent. The thick mists were their chief impediment, and cause of their return.

2nd September. I paid £1700 to the Marquis de Sissac, which he had lent to my Lord Berkeley, and which I heard the Marquis lost at play in a night or two.

The Dean of Chichester preached before the King, on Acts, xxiv. 16 ; and Dr. Crichton preached the second sermon before him on Psalm xc. 12, of wisely numbering our days, and well employing our time.

3rd. Dined at Captain Graham's, where I became ac-

---

[1] The author of a "History of Mary Queen of Scots," and of Histories of James and Charles I. He held the post of gentleman of the chamber, and his wife that of "mother of the maids." See *ante,* vol. i. p. 385.

quainted with Dr. Compton (brother to the Earl of Northampton), now Bishop of London, and Mr. North, son to the
Lord North, brother to the Lord Chief Justice and Clerk
of the Closet, a most hopeful young man.   The Bishop had
once been a soldier, had also travelled Italy, and became a
most sober, grave, and excellent prelate.

   6th September. Supped at the Lord Chamberlain's, where
also supped the famous beauty and errant lady, the Duchess
of Mazarine (all the world knows her story), the Duke
of Monmouth, Countess of Sussex (both natural children of
the King by the Duchess of Cleveland[1]), and the Countess
of Derby, a virtuous lady, daughter to my best friend, the
Earl of Ossory.

   10th.   Dined with me Mr. Flamsted, the learned astrologer and mathematician,[2] whom his Majesty had established
in the new Observatory in Greenwich Park, furnished with
the choicest instruments.   An honest, sincere man.

   12th.   To London, to take order about the building of a
house, or rather an apartment, which had all the conveniences of a house, for my dear friend, Mr. Godolphin and
lady, which I undertook to contrive and survey, and employ
workmen until it should be quite finished; it being just
over-against his Majesty's wood-yard by the Thames side,
leading to Scotland-yard.

   19th.   To Lambeth, to that rare magazine of marble, to
take order for chimney-pieces, &c., for Mr. Godolphin's
house.   The owner of the works had built for himself a
pretty dwelling-house ; this Dutchman had contracted with
the Genoese for all their marble.   We also saw the Duke
of Buckingham's glass-work, where they made huge vases

---

[1] Evelyn makes a slip here. The Duke of Monmouth's mother was,
it is well known, Lucy Walters, sometimes called Mrs. Barlow, and
heretofore mentioned in the Diary.   Nor is he more correct as to the
Countess of Sussex. Lady Anne Fitzroy, as she is called in the Peerage
books, was married to Lennard Dacre, Earl of Sussex, by whom she left
a daughter only, who succeeded on her father's death to the Barony of
Dacre.   On the other hand, the Duke of Southampton, the Duke of
Grafton, and the Duke of Northumberland, were all of them children of
Charles the Second by the Duchess of Cleveland.

[2] John Flamstead, author of " Historia Cœlestis Britannica," and
other works. A distinguished astronomer ; and in the comprehensive-
ness of his scientific knowledge, second only to Sir Isaac Newton. He
died in 1719.

of metal as clear, ponderous, and thick as crystal; also looking-glasses far larger and better than any that come from Venice.

9th October. I went with Mrs. Godolphin and my wife to Blackwall, to see some Indian curiosities; the streets being slippery, I fell against a piece of timber with such violence that I could not speak nor fetch my breath for some space: being carried into a house and let blood, I was removed to the water-side and so home, where, after a day's rest, I recovered. This being one of my greatest deliverances, the Lord Jesus make me ever mindful and thankful!

31st. Being my birth-day, and fifty-six years old, I spent the morning in devotion and imploring God's protection, with solemn thanksgiving for all his signal mercies to me, especially for that escape which concerned me this month at Blackwall. Dined with Mrs. Godolphin, and returned home through a prodigious and dangerous mist.

9th November. Finished the lease of Spalding, for Mr. Godolphin.

16th. My Son and I dining at my Lord Chamberlain's, he showed us amongst others that incomparable piece of Raphael's, being a Minister of State dictating to Guicciardini, the earnestness of whose face looking up in expectation of what he was next to write, is so to the life, and so natural, as I esteem it one of the choicest pieces of that admirable artist. There was a Woman's head of Leonardo da Vinci; a Madonna of old Palma, and two of Vandyke's, of which one was his own picture at length, when young, in a leaning posture; the other, an eunuch, singing. Rare pieces indeed!

4th December. I saw the great ball danced by all the gallants and ladies at the Duchess of York's.

10th. There fell so deep a snow as hindered us from church.

12th. To London, in so great a snow, as I remember not to have seen the like.

17th. More snow falling, I was not able to get to church.

1676-7, 8th February. I went to Roehampton, with my lady Duchess of Ormond. The garden and perspective is pretty, the prospect most agreeable.

15*th May*. Came the Earl of Peterborough, to desire me to be a trustee for Lord Viscount Mordaunt and the Countess, for the sale of certain lands set out by Act of Parliament, to pay debts.

12*th June*. I went to London, to give the Lord Ambassador Berkeley (now returned from the treaty at Nimeguen) an account of the great trust reposed in me during his absence, I having received and remitted to him no less than £20,000 to my no small trouble and loss of time, that during his absence, and when the Lord Treasurer was no great friend [of his] I yet procured him great sums, very often soliciting his Majesty in his behalf; looking after the rest of his estates and concerns entirely, without once accepting any kind of acknowledgment, purely upon the request of my dear friend, Mr. Godolphin. I returned with abundance of thanks and professions from my Lord Berkeley and my Lady.

29*th*. This business being now at an end, and myself delivered from that intolerable servitude and correspondence, I had leisure to be somewhat more at home and to myself.

3*rd July*. I sealed the deeds of sale of the manor of Blechingley to Sir Robert Clayton, for payment of Lord Peterborough's debts, according to the trust of the Act of Parliament.

16*th*. I went to Wotton.—22*nd*. Mr. Evans, curate of Abinger, preached an excellent sermon on Matt. v. 12. In the afternoon, Mr. Higham at Wotton catechised.

26*th*. I dined at Mr. Duncomb's, at Sheere, whose house stands environed with very sweet and quick streams.

29*th*. Mr. Bohun, my Son's late tutor, preached at Abinger, on Phil., iv. 8, very elegantly and practically.

5*th August*. I went to visit my Lord Brounker, now taking the waters at Dulwich.

9*th*. Dined at the Earl of Peterborough's the day after the marriage of my Lord of Arundel to Lady Mary Mordaunt, daughter to the Earl of Peterborough.

28*th*. To visit my Lord Chamberlain, in Suffolk; he sent his coach and six to meet and bring me from St. Edmund's Bury to Euston.

29*th*. We hunted in the Park and killed a very fat buck. —31*st*. I went a hawking.

4th September. I went to visit my Lord Crofts, now dying at St. Edmunds Bury, and took the opportunity to see this ancient town, and the remains of that famous monastery and abbey. There is little standing entire, save the gatehouse; it has been a vast and magnificent Gothic structure, and of great extent. The gates are wood, but quite plated over with iron. There are also two stately churches, one especially.

5th. I went to Thetford, to the borough-town, where stand the ruins of a religious house : there is a round mountain artificially raised, either for some castle, or monument, which makes a pretty landscape. As we went and returned, a tumbler showed his extraordinary address in the Warren. I also saw the Decoy; much pleased with the stratagem.

7th. There dined this day at my Lord's one Sir John Gaudy, a very handsome person, but quite dumb, yet very intelligent by signs, and a very fine painter; he was so civil and well bred, as it was not possible to discern any imperfection in him. His lady and children were also there, and he was at church in the morning with us.

9th. A stranger preached at Euston Church, and fell into a handsome panegyric on my Lord's new building the church, which indeed for its elegance and cheerfulness, is one of the prettiest country churches in England. My Lord told me his heart smote him that, after he had bestowed so much on his magnificent palace there, he should see God's House in the ruin it lay in. He has also re-built the parsonage-house, all of stone, very neat and ample.

10th. To divert me, my Lord would needs carry me to see Ipswich, when we dined with one Mr. Mann by the way, who was Recorder of the town. There were in our company my Lord Huntingtower, son to the Duchess of Lauderdale, Sir Edward Bacon, a learned gentleman of the family of the great Chancellor Verulam, and Sir John Felton, with some other Knights and Gentlemen. After dinner, came the Bailiff and Magistrates in their formalities with their maces to compliment my Lord, and invite him to the town-house, where they presented us a collation of dried sweetmeats and wine, the bells ringing, &c. Then, we went to see the town, and first, the Lord Viscount

Hereford's house, which stands in a park near the town, like that at Brussels, in Flanders; the house not great, yet pretty, especially the hall. The stews for fish succeed one another, and feed one the other, all paved at bottom. There is a good picture of the Blessed Virgin in one of the parlours, seeming to be of Holbein or some good master. Then we saw the Haven, seven miles from Harwich. The tide runs out every day, but the bedding being soft mud, it is safe for shipping and a station. The trade of Ipswich is for the most part Newcastle coals, with which they supply London; but it was formerly a clothing town. There is not any beggar asks alms in the whole place, a thing very extraordinary, so ordered by the prudence of the Magistrates. It has in it fourteen or fifteen beautiful churches: in a word, it is for building, cleanness, and good order, one of the best towns in England. Cardinal Wolsey was a butcher's son of Ipswich, but there is little of that magnificent Prelate's foundation here, besides a school and I think a library, which I did not see. His intentions were to build some great thing. We returned late to Euston, having travelled about fifty miles this day.

Since first I was at this place, I found things exceedingly improved. It is seated in a bottom between two graceful swellings, the main building being now in the figure of a Greek II with four pavilions, two at each corner, and a break in the front, railed and balustred at the top, where I caused huge jars to be placed full of earth to keep them steady upon their pedestals between the statues, which make as good a show as if they were of stone, and, though the building be of brick, and but two stories besides cellars, and garrets covered with blue slate, yet there is room enough for a full court, the offices and outhouses being so ample and well disposed. The King's apartment is painted *a fresco*, and magnificently furnished. There are many excellent pictures of the great masters. The gallery is a pleasant, noble room: in the break, or middle, is a billiard-table, but the wainscot, being of fir, and painted, does not please me so well as Spanish oak without paint. The chapel is pretty, the porch descending to the gardens. The orange-garden is very fine, and leads into the green-house, at the end of which is a hall to eat in, and the conservatory some

hundred feet long, adorned with maps, as the other side is
with the heads of the Cæsars, ill cut in alabaster; above,
are several apartments for my Lord, Lady, and Duchess,[1]
with kitchens and other offices below, in a lesser form;
lodgings for servants, all distinct, for them to retire to when
they please, and would be in private, and have no communi-
cation with the palace, which he tells me he will wholly
resign to his son-in-law and daughter, that charming young
creature.

The canal running under my lady's dressing-room chamber
window, is full of carps and fowl, which come and are fed
there. The cascade at the end of the canal turns a corn-
mill, that provides the family, and raises water for the
fountains and offices. To pass this canal into the opposite
meadows, Sir Samuel Morland has invented a screw-bridge,
which, being turned with a key, lands you fifty feet distant
at the entrance of an ascending walk of trees, a mile in
length, as it is also on the front into the park, of four rows
of ash-trees, and reaches to the park-pale, which is nine
miles in compass, and the best for riding and meeting the
game that I ever saw. There were now of red and fallow
deer almost a thousand, with good covert, but the soil barren
and flying sand, in which nothing will grow kindly. The
tufts of fir, and much of the other wood, were planted by my
direction, some years before. This seat is admirably placed
for field-sports, hawking, hunting, or racing. The mutton is
small, but sweet. The stables hold thirty horses and four
coaches. The out-offices make two large quadrangles, so as
servants never lived with more ease and convenience; never
master more civil. Strangers are attended and accommodated as at their home, in pretty apartments furnished with
all manner of conveniences and privacy.

There is a library full of excellent books; bathing-rooms,
elaboratory, dispensary, a decoy, and places to keep and fat
fowl in. He had now in his new church (near the garden)
built a dormitory, or vault, with several repositories, in which
to bury his family.

In the expense of this pious structure, the church is most
laudable, most of the Houses of God in this country resembling rather stables and thatched cottages than temples

---

[1] His daughter, wife of the Duke of Grafton.

in which to serve the Most High. He has built a lodge in the park for the keeper, which is a neat dwelling, and might become any gentleman. The same has he done for the par-son, little deserving it for murmuring that my Lord put him some time out of his wretched hovel, whilst it was building. He has also erected a fair inn at some distance from his palace, with a bridge of stone over a river near it, and re-paired all the tenants' houses, so as there is nothing but, neatness and accommodations about his estate, which I yet think is not above 1500*l*. a year. I believe he had now in his family one hundred domestic servants.

His lady (being one of the Brederode's daughters, grand-child to a natural son of Henry Frederick, Prince of Orange) is a good-natured and obliging woman. They love fine things, and to live easily, pompously, and hospitably; but, with so vast expense, as plunges my Lord into debts exceed-ingly. My Lord himself is given into no expensive vice but building, and to have all things rich, polite, and princely. He never plays, but reads much, having the Latin, French, and Spanish tongues in perfection. He has travelled much, and is the best-bred and courtly person his Majesty has about him, so as the public Ministers more frequent him than any of the rest of the Nobility. Whilst he was Secre-tary of State and Prime Minister, he had gotten vastly, but spent it as hastily, even before he had established a fund to maintain his greatness; and now beginning to decline in favour (the Duke being no great friend of his), he knows not how to retrench. He was son of a Doctor of Laws, whom I have seen, and, being sent from Westminster School to Oxford, with intention to be a divine, and parson of Arlington,[1] a village near Brentford, when Master of Arts, the Rebellion falling out, he followed the King's Army, and receiving an *honourable wound in the face*,[2] grew into favour, and was advanced from a mean fortune, at his Majesty's restoration, to be an Earl and Knight of the Garter, Lord Chamberlain of the Household, and first favourite for a long

[1] In Lord Clarendon's *Continuation of his Life* will be found the men-tion of a curious circumstance relating to Sir Henry Bennett's taking his title, when first created a Baron, from this place.

[2] A deep cut across his nose. He was obliged always to wear a black patch upon it, and so is represented in his portraits.

time, during which the King married his natural son, the
Duke of Grafton, to his only daughter and heiress, as before
mentioned, worthy for her beauty and virtue of the greatest
Prince in Christendom. My Lord is, besides this, a prudent
and understanding person in business, and speaks well; unfortunate yet in those he has advanced, most of them proving ungrateful. The many obligations and civilities I have
received from this noble gentleman, extracts from me this
character, and I am sorry he is in no better circumstances.

Having now passed near three weeks at Euston, to my
great satisfaction, with much difficulty he suffered me to
look homeward, being very earnest with me to stay longer ;
and, to engage me, would himself have carried me to Lynn-
Regis, a town of important traffic, about twenty miles beyond, which I had never seen ; as also the Travelling Sands,
about ten miles wide of Euston, that have so damaged the
country, rolling from place to place, and, like the Sands in
the Deserts of Lybia, quite overwhelmed some gentlemen's
whole estates, as the relation extant in print, and brought
to our Society, describes at large.

13th September. My Lord's coach conveyed me to Bury,
and thence baiting at Newmarket, stepping in at Audley-
End to see that house again, I slept at Bishop-Stortford;
and, the next day, home. I was accompanied in my journey
by Major Fairfax, of a younger house of the Lord Fairfax,
a soldier, a traveller, an excellent musician, a good-natured
well-bred gentleman.

18th. I preferred Mr. Phillips (nephew of Milton) to the
service of my Lord Chamberlain, who wanted a scholar to
read to and entertain him sometimes.

12th October. With Sir Robert Clayton to Marden, an
estate he had bought lately of my kinsman, Sir John Evelyn,
of Godstone, in Surrey; which from a despicable farm-house
Sir Robert had erected into a seat with extraordinary expense. It is in such a solitude among hills, as, being not
above sixteen miles from London, seems almost incredible,
the ways up to it are so winding and intricate. The gardens
are large, and well-walled, and the husbandry part made
very convenient and perfectly understood. The barns, the
stacks of corn, the stalls for cattle, pigeon-house, &c., of
most laudable example. Innumerable are the plantations

of trees, especially walnuts. The orangery and gardens are very curious. In the house are large and noble rooms. He and his lady (who is very curious in distillery) entertained me three or four days very freely. I earnestly suggested to him the repairing of an old desolate dilapidated church, standing on the hill above the house,[1] which I left him in good disposition to do, and endow it better; there not being above four or five houses in the parish, besides that of this prodigious rich Scrivener.[2] This place is exceeding sharp in the winter, by reason of the serpentining of the hills: and it wants running water; but the solitude much pleased me. All the ground is so full of wild thyme, marjoram, and other sweet plants, that it cannot be overstocked with bees; I think he had near forty hives of that industrious insect.

14th October. I went to church at Godstone, and to see old Sir John Evelyn's dormitory, joining to the church, paved with marble, where he and his lady lie on a very stately monument at length; he in armour of white marble.[3] The inscription is only an account of his particular branch of the family, on black marble.

[1] Woldingham. The Church consisted of one room about thirty feet long and twenty-one wide, without any tower, spire, or bell. It was considered as a Donative, not subject to the Bishop; and service was performed therein once a month. No churchwarden; two farm-houses, four cottages; and by the Population Return, even as late as 1811, the number of inhabitance was only fifty-eight. That disposition in Sir Robert Clayton which Evelyn fancied he saw, appears to have subsided; the church remained, some quarter of a century ago, as it was in Evelyn's time.

[2] The last member of the Company called Scriveners, named Ellis, died at the age of more than 90. Dr. Johnson speaks well of him. Their business comprehended that of a Banker, and what is now called a Conveyancer: they had money deposited with them for the purpose of making purchases, or lending on mortgage, and it was they who prepared the deeds. In the time of King Charles I., and during the civil wars and commonwealth, a gentleman of the name of Abbot in the City had a very great share of this business, and he had two clerks, named Clayton and Morris, who jointly succeeded to his interest in it, from which they acquired a great estate. Mr. Morris died first, and, having no children, left his property to his friend, who became Sir Robert Clayton. The first Editor of Evelyn's Diary had seen a deed attested by Mr. Abbot, as Scrivener, and by Mr. Morris and Mr. Clayton, as his servants. See post, p 144.

[3] It is a very fine monument, in perfect preservation.

15th October. Returned to London; in the evening, I saw the Prince of Orange, and supped with Lord Ossory.

23rd. Saw again the Prince of Orange; his marriage with the Lady Mary, eldest daughter to the Duke of York, by Mrs. Hyde, the late Duchess, was now declared.

11th November. I was all this week composing matters between old Mrs. Howard and Sir Gabriel Sylvius, upon his long and earnest addresses to Mrs. Anne, her second daughter,[1] Maid of Honour to the Queen. My friend, Mrs Godolphin (who exceedingly loved the young lady) was most industrious in it, out of pity to the languishing knight; so as though there were great differences in their years, it was at last effected, and they were married the 13th, in Henry VII.'s Chapel, by the Bishop of Rochester,[2] there being besides my wife and Mrs. Graham, her sister, Mrs. Godoiphin, and very few more. We dined at the old lady's, and supped at Mr. Graham's at St. James's.

15th. The Queen's birthday, a great Ball at Court, where the Prince of Orange and his new Princess danced.

19th. They went away, and I saw embarked my Lady Sylvius, who went into Holland with her husband, made Hoffmaester to the Prince, a considerable employment. We parted with great sorrow, for the great respect and honour I bore her, a most pious and virtuous lady.

27th. Dined at the Lord Treasurer's with Prince Rupert, Viscount Falkenburg, Earl of Bath, Lord O'Brien, Sir John Lowther, Sir Christopher Wren, Dr. Grew,[3] and other learned men.

30th. Sir Joseph Williamson, Principal Secretary of State, was chosen President of the Royal Society, after my Lord Viscount Brounker had possessed the chair now sixteen years successively, and therefore now thought fit to *change*, that prescription might not prejudice.

4th December. Being the first day of his taking the chair, he gave us a magnificent supper.

---

[1] *Ante,* p. 108, note.

[2] Dr. John Dolben, also Dean of Westminster, translated afterwards to York.

[3] Nehemiah Grew, a physician, who directed his researches towards botany, and one of the first who advocated the theory of different sexes in plants. Born 1628, died 1711.

20*th December.* Carried to my Lord Treasurer an account of the Earl of Bristol's Library, at Wimbledon, which my Lord thought of purchasing, till I acquainted him that it was a very broken collection, consisting much in books of judicial astrology, romances, and trifles.[1]

25*th.* I gave my Son an office, with instructions how to govern his youth; I pray God give him the grace to make a right use of it!

1677-8. *23rd January.* Dined with the Duke of Norfolk, being the first time I had seen him since the death of his elder brother, who died at Padua in Italy, where he had resided above thirty years. The Duke had now newly declared his marriage to his concubine, whom he promised me he never would marry.[2] I went with him to see the Duke of Buckingham, thence to my Lord Sunderland, now Secretary of State, to show him that rare piece of Vosterman's (son of old Vosterman), which was a view, or landscape of my Lord's palace, &c., at Althorpe, in Northamptonshire.

8*th February.* Supping at my Lord Chamberlain's I had a long discourse with the Count de Castel Mellor, lately Prime Minister in Portugal, who, taking part with his master, King Alphonso, was banished by his brother, Don Pedro, now Regent; but had behaved himself so uncorruptly in all his ministry that, though he was acquitted, and his estate restored, yet would they not suffer him to return. He is a very intelligent and worthy gentleman.

18*th.* My Lord Treasurer sent for me to accompany him to Wimbledon, which he had lately purchased of the Earl of Bristol; so breaking fast with him privately in his chamber, I accompanied him with two of his daughters, my Lord Conway, and Sir Bernard Gascoyne; and, having surveyed his gardens and alterations, returned late at night.

22*nd.* Dr. Pierce preached at Whitehall, on 2 Thessalonians, iii. 6, against our late schismatics, in a rational dis-

[1] Yet who can doubt that a library of this description, a " very broken collection " though it might then be considered, would now-a-days be deemed a curious collection, and an object of much competition? *Habent sua fata libelli!*

[2] The Duke had now taken his second wife, Mrs. Jane Bickerton, daughter of a Scotch gentleman, Mr. Robert Bickerton, who was Gentleman of the Wine-Cellar to King Charles II. *Ante,* p. 70, and *see post,* p. 128.

course, but a little over-sharp, and not at al proper for the auditory there.

22nd March. Dr. South preached *coram Rege*, an incomparable discourse on this text, " A wounded spirit who can bear." Note: Now was our Communion-table placed altarwise; the church steeple, clock, and other reparations finished.

16th April. I showed Don Emmanuel de Lyra (Portugal Ambassador) and the Count de Castel Mellor, the Repository of the Royal Society, and the College of Physicians.

18th. I went to see new Bedlam Hospital, magnificently built,[1] and most sweetly placed in Moorfields, since the dreadful fire in London.

28th June. I went to Windsor with my Lord Chamberlain (the castle now repairing with exceeding cost) to see the rare work of Verrio, an incomparable carving of Gibbons.

29th. Returned with my Lord by Hounslow Heath, where we saw the new-raised army encamped, designed against France, in pretence, at least; but which gave umbrage to the Parliament. His Majesty and a world of company were in the field, and the whole army in battalia; a very glorious sight. Now were brought into service a new sort of soldiers, called *Grenadiers*, who were dexterous in flinging hand grenados, every one having a pouch full; they had furred caps with coped crowns like Janizaries, which made them look very fierce, and some had long hoods hanging down behind, as we picture fools. Their clothing being likewise piebald, yellow and red.

8th July. Came to dine with me my Lord Longford, Treasurer of Ireland, nephew to that learned gentleman, my Lord Aungier, with whom I was long since acquainted: also the Lady Stidolph, and other company.

19th. The Earl of Ossory came to take his leave of me, going into Holland to command the English forces.

20th. I went to the Tower to try a metal at the Assay-

---

[1] Taken down in 1814, and a new one erected on the Surrey side of the Thames, in the road leading from St. George's Fields to Lambeth. On pulling it down, the foundations were found to be very bad, it having been built on part of the Town-ditch, and on a soil very unfit for the erection of so large a building. The patients were removed to the new building in August 1815.

master's, which only proved sulphur; then saw Monsieur Rotière, that excellent graver belonging to the Mint, who emulates even the ancients, in both metal and stone;[1] he was now moulding a horse for the King's statue, to be cast in silver, of a yard high. I dined with Mr. Slingsby, Master of the Mint.

23rd July. Went to see Mr. Elias Ashmole's library and curiosities, at Lambeth. He has divers MSS., but most of them astrological, to which study he is addicted, though I believe not learned, but very industrious, as his History of the order of the Garter proves. He showed me a toad included in amber. The prospect from a turret is very fine, it being so near London, and yet not discovering any house about the country. The famous John Tradescant bequeathed his Repository to this gentleman, who has given them to the University of Oxford, and erected a lecture on them, over the laboratory, in imitation of the Royal Society.[2]

Mr. Godolphin was made Master of the Robes to the King.

25th. There was sent me £70; from whom I knew not, to be by me distributed among poor people; I afterwards found it was from that dear friend (Mrs. Godolphin), who had frequently given me large sums to bestow on charities.

16th August. I went to Lady Mordaunt, who put £100 into my hand to dispose of for pious uses, relief of prisoners, poor, &c. Many a sum had she sent me on similar occasions; a blessed creature she was, and one that loved and feared God exemplarily.

[1] Doubtless Philip Rotière, who introduced the figure of Britannia into the coinage, taking for his model the King's favourite, Frances Stewart, Duchess of Richmond.

[2] The donation took effect in 1677, and a suitable building was erected by Sir Christopher Wren, bearing the name of the " Ashmolean Museum." This was the first public institution for the reception of Rarities in Art or Nature, established in England; and it possessed what, in the infancy of the study of Natural History in this country, might fairly be regarded as a valuable and superior collection. In the Museum are preserved good portraits of Ashmole, and of the Tradescant family, by Dobson, from which very poor and ill-executed engravings have been taken.

23rd August. Upon Sir Robert Reading's importunity, 1 went to visit the Duke of Norfolk, at his new Palace at Weybridge,[1] where he has laid out in building near £10,000, on a copyhold, and in a miserable, barren, sandy place by the street-side; never in my life had I seen such expense to so small purpose. The rooms are wainscotted, and some of them richly pargeted with cedar, yew, cypress, &c. There are some good pictures, especially that incomparable painting of Holbein's, where the Duke of Norfolk, Charles Brandon, and Henry VIII., are dancing with the three ladies, with most amorous countenances, and sprightly motion exquisitely expressed. It is a thousand pities, (as I told my Lord of Arundel his son) that that jewel should be given away.

24th. I went to see my Lord of St. Alban's house, at Byfleet, an old large building. Thence, to the paper-mills, where I found them making a coarse white paper. They cull the rags which are linen for white paper, woollen for brown; then they stamp them in troughs to a pap, with pestles, or hammers, like the powder-mills, then put it into a vessel of water, in which they dip a frame closely wired with wire as small as a hair and as close as a weaver's reed; on this they take up the pap, the superfluous water draining through the wire; this they dexterously turning, shake out like a pancake on a smooth board between two pieces of flannel, then press it between a great press, the flannel sucking out the moisture; then, taking it out, they ply and dry it on strings, as they dry linen in the laundry; then dip it in alum-water, lastly, polish and make it up in quires. They put some gum in the water in which they macerate the rags. The mark we find on the sheets is formed in the wire.

25th. After evening prayer, visited Mr. Sheldon, (nephew to the late Archbishop of Canterbury) and his pretty melancholy garden; I took notice of the largest

---

[1] This house was the property of Mrs. Bickerton, whom the Duke married. After his death, she married Mr. Maxwell, and they, together with Lord George Howard (her eldest son by the Duke), sold it to Mrs. Sedley, afterwards Countess of Dorchester, mistress to James II. The Countess. who bore a daughter to James II., afterwards married David Collyer, Earl of Portmore. See *post*, p. 258.

arbor thuyris I had ever seen. The place is finely watered, and there are many curiosities of India, shown in the house.

There was at Weybridge the Duchess of Norfolk, Lord Thomas Howard, (a worthy and virtuous gentleman, with whom my son was sometime bred in Arundel House) who was newly come from Rome, where he had been some time ; also one of the Duke's daughters, by his first lady. My Lord leading me about the house made no scruple of show-ing me all the hiding-places for the Popish priests, and where they said mass, for he was no bigoted Papist. He told me he never trusted them with any secret, and used Protestants only in all businesses of importance.

I went this evening with my Lord Duke to Windsor, where was a magnificent Court, it being the first time of his Majesty removing thither since it was repaired.

27th August. I took leave of the Duke, and dined at Mr. Henry Bruncker's, at the Abbey of Sheene, formerly a Monastery of Carthusians, there yet remaining one of their solitary cells with a cross. Within this ample enclosure are several pretty villas and fine gardens of the most excel-lent fruits, especially Sir William Temple's (lately Ambas-sador into Holland), and the Lord Lisle's, son to the Earl of Leicester, who has divers rare pictures, above all, that of Sir Brian Tuke's, by Holbein.

After dinner, I walked to Ham, to see the house and garden of the Duke of Lauderdale, which is indeed inferior to few of the best villas in Italy itself ; the house furnished like a great Prince's ; the parterres, flower-gardens, orange-ries, groves, avenues, courts, statues, perspectives, fountains, aviaries, and all this at the banks of the sweetest river in the world, must needs be admirable.

Hence, I went to my worthy friend, Sir Henry Capel, [at Kew] brother to the Earl of Essex ; it is an old timber-house ; but his garden has the choicest fruit of any plantation in England, as he is the most industrious and understanding in it.   .

29th. I was called to London to wait upon the Duke of Norfolk, who having at my sole request bestowed the Arundelian Library on the Royal Society, sent to me to take charge of the books, and remove them, only stipu-

lating that I would suffer the Herald's chief officer, Sir
William Dugdale, to have such of them as concerned
Heraldry and the Marshal's office, books of Armory and
Genealogies, the Duke being Earl Marshal of England. I
procured for our Society, besides printed books, near one
hundred MSS., some in Greek of great concernment. The
printed books being of the oldest impressions, are not the
less valuable ; I esteem them almost equal to MSS.
Amongst them, are most of the Fathers, printed at Basil,
before the Jesuits abused them with their expurgatory
Indexes; there is a noble MS. of Vitruvius. Many of
these books had been presented by Popes, Cardinals, and
great persons, to the Earls of Arundel and Dukes of
Norfolk ; and the late magnificent Earl of Arundel bought
a noble library in Germany, which is in this collection. I
should not, for the honour I bear the family, have persuaded the Duke to part with these, had I not seen how
negligent he was of them, suffering the priests and everybody to carry away and dispose of what they pleased ; so
that abundance of rare things are irrecoverably gone.

Having taken order here, I went to the Royal Society to
give them an account of what I had procured, that they
might call a Council and appoint a day to wait on the Duke
to thank him for this munificent gift.

3rd September. I went to London, to dine with Mrs
Godolphin, and found her in labour; she was brought to
bed of a son, who was baptised in the chamber, by the name
of Francis, the susceptors being Sir William Godolphin
(head of the family), Mr. John Hervey, Treasurer to the
Queen, and Mrs. Boscawen, sister to Sir William and the
father.

8th. Whilst I was at church came a letter from Mr.
Godolphin, that my dear friend his lady was exceedingly
ill, and desiring my prayers and assistance. My wife and
I took boat immediately, and went to Whitehall, where, to
my inexpressible sorrow, I found she had been attacked
with a new fever, then reigning this excessive hot autumn,
and which was so violent, that it was not thought she could
last many hours.

9th. She died in the 26th year of her age, to the inexpressible affliction of her dear husband, and all her relations,

but of none in the world more than of myself, who lost the
most excellent and inestimable friend that ever lived. Never
was a more virtuous and inviolable friendship; never a more
religious, discreet, and admirable creature, beloved of all,
admired of all, for all possible perfections of her sex. She
is gone to receive the reward of her signal charity, and all
other her Christian graces, too blessed a creature to converse
with mortals, fitted as she was, by a most holy life, to be received into the mansions above. She was for wit, beauty,
goodnature, fidelity, discretion, and all accomplishments, the
most incomparable person. How shall I ever repay the obligations to her for the infinite good offices she did my soul
by so often engaging me to make religion the terms and tie
of the friendship there was between us! She was the best
wife, the best mistress, the best friend, that ever husband
had. But it is not here that I pretend to give her character,
having designed to consecrate her worthy life to posterity.

Her husband, struck with unspeakable affliction, fell down
as dead. The King himself, and all the Court, expressed
their sorrow. To the poor and miserable, her loss was irre-
parable; for there was no degree but had some obligation
to her memory. So careful and provident was she to be prepared for all possible accidents, that (as if she foresaw her
end) she received the heavenly viaticum but the Sunday
before, after a most solemn recollection. She put all her
domestic concerns into the exactest order, and left a letter
directed to her husband, to be opened in case she died in
child-bed, in which with the most pathetic and endearing expressions of the most loyal and virtuous wife, she begs his
kindness to her memory might be continued by his care and
esteem of those she left behind, even to her domestic servants, to the meanest of which she left considerable legacies,
as well as to the poor. It was now seven years since she
was Maid of Honour to the Queen, that she regarded me as
a father, a brother, and what is more, a friend. We often
prayed, visited the sick and miserable, received, read, discoursed, and communicated in all holy offices together.
She was most dear to my wife, and affectionate to my
children. But she is gone! This only is my comfort,
that she is happy in Christ, and I shall shortly behold
K 2

her again ' She desired to be buried in the dormitory of his family, near three hundred miles from all her other friends. So afflicted was her husband at this severe loss, that the entire care of her funeral was committed to me. Having closed the eyes, and dropped a tear upon the cheek of my dear departed friend, lovely even in death, I caused her corpse to be embalmed and wrapped in lead, a plate of brass soldered thereon, with an inscription, and other circumstances due to her worth, with as much diligence and care as my grieved heart would permit me ; I then retired home for two days, which were spent in solitude and sad reflection.

17th September. She was, accordingly, carried to Godolphin, in Cornwall, in a hearse with six horses, attended by two coaches of as many, with about thirty of her relations and servants. There accompanied the hearse her husband's brother, Sir William, two more of his brothers, and three sisters: her husband was so overcome with grief, that he was wholly unfit to travel so long a journey, till he was more composed. I went as far as Hounslow with a sad heart; but was obliged to return upon some indispensable affairs. The corpse was ordered to be taken out of the hearse every night, and decently placed in the house, with tapers about it, and her servants attending, to Cornwall; and then was honourably interred in the parish church of Godolphin. This funeral cost not much less than £1000.

With Mr. Godolphin, I looked over and sorted his lady's papers, most of which consisted of Prayers, Meditations, Sermon-notes, Discourses, and Collections on several religious subjects, and many of her own happy composing, and so pertinently digested, as if she had been all her life a student in divinity. We found a diary of her solemn resolutions, tending to practical virtue, with letters from select friends, all put into exact method. It astonished us to see what she had read and written, her youth considered.

1st October. The Parliament and the whole Nation were

---

[1] Mr. Godolphin (afterwards Lord Godolphin) continued the steady friend of Mr. Evelyn, whose grandson married into his family. The infant now mentioned as born, carried on through a long life the friendly family intercourse thus earnestly begun ; and Evelyn, in redemption of the promise in the text, wrote Mrs. Godolphin's Life, which has lately been published under the auspices of the Bishop of Oxford.

alarmed about a conspiracy of some eminent Papists for the destruction of the King and introduction of Popery, discovered by one Oates and Dr. Tongue,[1] *which last I knew, being the translator of the "Jesuits' Morals;"* I went to see and converse with him at Whitehall, with Mr. Oates, one that was lately an apostate to the church of Rome, and now returned again with this discovery. He seemed to be a bold man, and, in my thoughts, furiously indiscreet; but everybody believed what he said; and it quite changed the genius and motions of the Parliament, growing now corrupt and interested with long sitting and court practices; but, with all this, Popery would not go down. This discovery turned them all as one man against it, and nothing was done but to find out the depth of this. Oates was encouraged, and everything he affirmed taken for gospel;—the truth is, the Roman Catholics were exceeding bold and busy everywhere, since the Duke forbore to go any longer to the chapel.

[1] Ezrael Tonge was bred in University College, Oxford, and being puritanically inclined, quitted the University; but in 1648 returned, and was made a Fellow. He had the living of Pluckley, in Kent, which he resigned in consequence of quarrels with his parishioners and Quakers. In 1657, he was made fellow of the newly-erected College at Durham, and that being dissolved in 1660, he taught school at Islington. He then went with Colonel Edward Harley to Dunkirk, and subsequently took a small living in Herefordshire (Lentwardine): but quitted it for St. Mary Stayning, in London, which, after the fire in 1666, was united to St. Michael, Wood Street. These he held till his death, in 1680. He was a great opponent of the Roman Catholics. Wood mentions several publications of his, among which are, *The Jesuits unmasked*, 1678; *Jesuitical Aphorisms*, 1678; and *The Jesuits' Morals*, 1680 (1670); the two latter translated from the French. (Wood's *Athen. Oxon.* vol. ii. p. 502.) Evelyn speaks of the last of these translations as having been executed by his desire: and it figures in a notable passage of Oates's testimony. Oates said, for example, "that Thomas Whitbread, a priest, on 13th June, 16 . . did tell the rector of St. Omer's that a Minister of the Church of England had scandalously put out the *Jesuits' Morals* in English, and had endeavoured to render them odious, and had asked the Rector whether he thought Oates might know him? and the Rector called the deponent, who heard these words as he stood at the chamber-door, and when he went into the chamber of the Provincial, he asked him 'If he knew the author of the Jesuits' Morals?' deponent answered, 'His person, but not his name.' Whitbread then demanded, whether he would undertake to poison, or assassinate the author; which deponent undertook, having £50 reward promised him, and appointed to return to England."

16th October. Mr Godolphin requested me to continue the trust his wife had reposed in me, in behalf of his little son, conjuring me to transfer the friendship I had for his dear wife, on him and his.

21st. The murder of Sir Edmondbury Godfrey, found strangled about this time, as was manifest, by the Papists, he being the Justice of the Peace, and one who knew much of their practices, as conversant with Coleman (a servant of the . . . . now accused), put the whole nation into a new ferment against them.

31st. Being my 58th of my age, required my humble addresses to Almighty God, and that he would take off His heavy hand, still on my family ; and restore comforts to us after the loss of my excellent friend.

5th November. Dr. Tillotson preached before the Commons at St. Margaret's. He said the Papists were now arrived at that impudence, as to deny that there ever was any such as the gunpowder-conspiracy ; but he affirmed that he himself had several letters written by Sir Everard Digby (one of the traitors), in which he gloried that he was to suffer for it ; and that it was so contrived, that of the Papists not above two or three should have been blown up, and they, such as were not worth saving.

15th. The Queen's birthday. I never saw the Court more brave, nor the nation in more apprehension and consternation. Coleman and one Staly had now been tried, condemned, and executed. On this, Oates grew so presumptuous, as to accuse the Queen of intending to poison the King ; which certainly that pious and virtuous lady abhorred the thoughts of, and Oates's circumstances made it utterly unlikely in my opinion. He probably thought to gratify some who would have been glad his Majesty should have married a fruitful lady ; but the King was too kind a husband to let any of these make impression on him. However, divers of the Popish peers were sent to the Tower, accused by Oates ; and all the Roman Catholic lords were by a new Act for ever excluded the Parliament ; which was a mighty blow. The King's, Queen's, and Duke's servants, were banished, and a test to be taken by everybody who pretended to enjoy any office of public trust, and who would not be suspected of Popery. I went with Sir William Godolp in, a member of the Commons' House, to the Bishop of Ely (Dr. Peter Gunning), to be resolved whether masses were idolatry, as the text expressed it, which was so worded, that several good Protestants scrupled, and Sir William, though a learned man and excellent divine himself, had some doubts about it. The Bishop's opinion was, that he might take it, though he wished it had been otherwise worded in the text.

1678-9. 15th January. I went with my Lady Sunderland to Chelsea, and dined with the Countess of Bristol [her mother] in the great house, formerly the Duke of Buckingham's, a spacious and excellent place for the extent of ground and situation in a good air.[1] The house is large, but ill-contrived, though my Lord of Bristol who purchased it after he sold Wimbledon to my Lord Treasurer, expended much money on it. There were divers pictures of Titian and Vandyke, and some of Bassano, very excellent, especially an Adonis and Venus, a Duke of Venice, a butcher in his shambles selling meat to a Swiss; and of Vandyke, my Lord of Bristol's picture, with the Earl of Bedford's at length, in the same table. There was in the garden a rare collection of orange-trees, of which she was pleased to bestow some upon me.

16th January. I supped this night with Mr. Secretary at one Mr. Houblon's, a French merchant, who had his house furnished en Prince, and gave us a splendid entertainment.[2]

25th. The Long Parliament, which had sat ever since the

---

[1] This mansion stood at the north end of Beaufort Row, extending westward about 100 yards from the water-side. It was originally called Buckingham-House: but in January 1682 was sold by Lady Anne Russell, daughter of Francis, Earl of Bedford, to Henry, Marquis of Worcester, created Duke of Beaufort in the same year; after whom it was known by the title of Beaufort-House. It continued to be the residence of this family till about the year 1720, when, having stood empty for several years, it was purchased by Sir Hans Sloane, in 1738, and was pulled down in 1740.—Faulkner's *History of Chelsea*.

[2] One of the most eminent of the merchants of London at this period. Two of James Houblon's sons obtained the honour of knighthood. Sir James became one of the members for the city, in 1648; Sir John was Lord Mayor, one of the Commissioners of the Admiralty, and Governor of the Bank of England. From the former descend the Houblons of Hallingbury-place, Essex, and of Culverthorpe, Lincoln. Pepys mentions "five brothers Houblon," and he adds, "mighty fine gentlemen they are all, and used me mighty respectfully."

Restoration, was dissolved by persuasion of the Lord Treasurer, though divers of them were believed to be his pensioner. At this, all the politicians were at a stand, they being very eager in pursuit of the late plot of the Papists.

30th January. Dr. Cudworth preached before the King at Whitehall, on 2 Timothy, iii. 5, reckoning up the perils of the last times, in which, amongst other wickedness, treasons should be one of the greatest, applying it to the occasion, as committed under a form of reformation and godliness; concluding that the prophecy did intend more particularly the present age, as one of the last times; the sins there enumerated, more abundantly reigning than ever.

2nd February. Dr. Durell, Dean of Windsor, preached to the household at Whitehall, on 1 Cor. xvi. 22; he read the whole sermon out of his notes, which I had never before seen a Frenchman do, he being of Jersey, and bred at Paris.

4th. Dr. Pierce, Dean of Salisbury, preached on 1 John, iv. 1, " Try the Spirits, there being so many delusory ones gone forth of late into the world;" he inveighed against the pernicious doctrines of Mr. Hobbes.

My Brother, Evelyn, was now chosen Knight for the County of Surrey, carrying it against my Lord Longford and Sir Adam Brown, of Bechworth Castle. The country coming in to give him their suffrages were so many, that I believe they eat and drank him out near £2000, by a most abominable custom.

1st April. My friend, Mr. Godolphin, was now made one of the Lords Commissioners of the Treasury, and of the Privy Council.

4th. The Bishop of Gloucester preached in a manner very like Bishop Andrews, full of divisions, and scholastical, and that with much quickness. The holy Communion followed.

20th. Easter-day. Our vicar preached exceeding well on 1 Cor. v. 7. The holy Communion followed, at which I and my daughter, Mary (now about fourteen years old), received for the first time. The Lord Jesus continue his grace unto her, and improve this blessed beginning!

24th. The Duke of York, voted against by the Commons for his recusancy, went over to Flanders; which made much discourse.

4th June. I dined with Mr. Pepys in the Tower, he hav-

Vandyk. pinx

WILLIAM HOWARD,

VISCOUNT STAFFORD.

OB. 1680.

ing been committed by the House of Commons for misde-
meanors in the Admiralty when he was Secretary ; I believe
he was unjustly charged.[1] Here I saluted my Lords Stafford and Petre, who were committed for the Popish plot.

7th June. I saw the magnificent cavalcade and entry of
the Portugal ambassador.

17th. I was godfather to a son of Sir Christopher Wren,
surveyor of his Majesty's buildings, that most excellent and
learned person, with Sir William Fermor, and my Lady Viscountess Newport, wife of the Treasurer of the Household.
Thence to Chelsea, to Sir Stephen Fox, and my lady, in
order to the purchase of the Countess of Bristol's house
there, which she desired me to procure a chapman for.

19th. I dined at Sir Robert Clayton's with Sir Robert
Viner,[2] the great banker.

22nd. There were now divers Jesuits executed about the
plot, and a rebellion in Scotland of the fanatics, so that there
was a sad prospect of public affairs.

25th. The new Commissioners of the Admiralty came
to visit me, viz., Sir Henry Capell, brother to the Earl of
Essex, Mr. Finch, eldest son to the Lord Chancellor, Sir
Humphry Winch, Sir Thomas Meeres, Mr. Hales, with some
of the Commissioners of the Navy. I went with them to
London.

1st July. I dined at Sir William Godolphin's, and with
that learned gentleman went to take the air in Hyde-Park,
where was a glorious cortège.

---

[1] Pepys was concerned in a contested election in 1684, and his opponent having accused him of being a Papist, the House of Commons
proceeded to make inquiry into the charge, but failed in the proof. By
Grey's Debates (vol. vii, 303—15), it would seem that another accusation brought against Pepys was the having sent information to the
French court of the state of the English Navy—a charge which has
been properly scouted as incredible. See Lord Braybrooke's last
edition of Pepys's Diary, published by Mr. Bohn, vol. i. pp. xxii—xxvi.

[2] A very wealthy banker, whom Pepys describes as living in great state
at Swakely House, Ickenham, Middlesex. When Lord Mayor, he entertained Charles II. at Guildhall ; and on his Majesty retiring, urged
him to "return and take t'other bottle." He was created a Baronet.
The crown was indebted to Sir Robert Viner, at the shutting of the
Exchequer, nearly half a million of money, for which he was awarded
25,000l. 9s. 4d. per annum, out of the excise.

3rd July. Sending a piece of venison to Mr. Pepys, still a prisoner, I went and dined with him.

6th. Now were there papers, speeches, and libels, publicly cried in the streets against the Dukes of York and Lauderdale, &c., obnoxious to the Parliament, with too much and indeed too shameful a liberty; but the people and Parliament had gotten head by reason of the vices of the great ones.

There was now brought up to London a child, son of one Mr. Wotton,[1] formerly amanuensis to Dr. Andrews, Bishop

---

[1] The Rev. Henry Wotton, minister of Wrentham, in Suffolk. This son was afterwards the celebrated William Wotton, the friend and defender of Dr. Bentley, and the antagonist of Sir William Temple, in the great Controversy about Ancient and Modern Learning. His early and extraordinary proficiency in letters, and general knowledge of every kind, was commemorated by his father in a pamphlet "On the Education of Children," addressed to King Charles II., and reprinted in 1753, with the attestations of several learned men who had examined him, to the truth of his uncommon abilities and wonderful acquisitions in the different languages, both ancient and modern. Nevertheless these eminent qualifications did not advance him in the line of his profession beyond a Fellowship at Cambridge, and the country parsonage of Milton, in Buckinghamshire, which was given him by the Earl of Nottingham, to whom he had been chaplain. Sir Philip Skippon, who lived at Wrentham, in Suffolk, in a letter to Mr. John Ray, Sept. 18, 1671, writes: "I shall somewhat surprise you with what I have seen in a little boy, William Wotton, five years old last month, son of Mr. Wotton, minister of this parish, who hath instructed his child within the last three quarters of a year in the reading the Latin, Greek, and Hebrew languages, which he can read almost as well as English, and that tongue he could read at four years and three months old, as well as most lads of twice his age." Sir Philip left also a draft of a longer letter to Mr. Ray, in which he adds, "He is not yet able to parse any language, but what he performs in turning the three learned tongues into English is done by strength of memory, so that he is ready to mistake when some words of different signification have near the same sound. His father hath taught him by no rules, but only uses his memory in remembering words."—He was admitted of Catherine Hall, Cambridge, April, 1676, some months before he was ten years old. He took the degree of B.A. when only twelve years and five months old. Dr. Burnet, Bishop of Sarum, recommended him to Dr. Lloyd, Bishop of St. Asaph, who took him as an assistant in making a catalogue of his books, and carried him to St. Asaph, and gave him the sinecure of Llandrillo, in Denbighshire. Swift laughed at him, but this he drew upon himself by having attacked the author of the *Tale of a Tub*. He published, as is well known, an answer to that great satire. He also

of Winton, who both read and perfectly understood Hebrew, Greek, Latin, Arabic, Syriac, and most of the modern languages; disputed in divinity, law, and all the sciences; was skilful in history, both ecclesiastical and profane; in politics; in a word, so universally and solidly learned at eleven years of age, that he was looked on as a miracle. Dr. Lloyd, one of the most deep learned divines of this nation in all sorts of literature, with Dr. Burnet, who had severely examined him, came away astonished, and they told me they did not believe there had the like appeared in the world. He had only been instructed by his father, who being himself a learned person, confessed that his son knew all that he himself knew. But, what was more admirable than his vast memory, was his judgment and invention, he being tried with divers hard questions, which required maturity of thought and experience. He was also dexterous in chronology, antiquities, mathematics. In sum, an *intellectus universalis*, beyond all that we read of Picus Mirandula, and other precocious wits, and yet withal a very humble child.

14*th July.* I went to see how things stood at Parson's Green, my Lady Viscountess Mordaunt (now sick in Paris, whither she went for health) having made me a trustee for her children, an office I could not refuse to this most excellent, pious, and virtuous lady, my long acquaintance.

15*th.* I dined with Mr. Sidney Godolphin, now one of the Lords Commissioners of the Treasury.

18*th.* I went early to the Old Bailey Sessions-house, to the famous trial of Sir George Wakeman, one of the Queen's physicians, and three Benedictine monks;[1] the first (whom I was well acquainted with, and take to be a worthy gentleman abhorring such a fact) for intending to poison the King; the others as accomplices to carry on the plot, to subvert the government, and introduce Popery. The Bench was crowded with the Judges, Lord Mayor Justices, and

compiled Memoirs of the Cathedral Churches of St. David and St. Asaph, which Browne Willis published. When very young, he remembered almost the whole of any discourse he had heard, and on a certain occasion he repeated to Bishop Lloyd one of his own sermons. He died in 1726, aged 61, and was buried at Buxted, in Sussex.

[1] William Marshal, William Rumley, and James Corker.—See State Trials, fol. vol. ii. p 918.

innumerable spectators. The chief accusers, Dr. Oates (as he called himself), and one Bedlow, a man of inferior note. Their testimonies were not so pregnant, and I fear much of it from hearsay, but swearing positively to some particulars, which drew suspicion upon their truth; nor did circumstances so agree, as to give either the Bench, or Jury, so entire satisfaction as was expected. After, therefore, a long and tedious trial of nine hours, the Jury brought them in not guilty, to the extraordinary triumph of the Papists, and without sufficient disadvantage and reflections on witnesses, especially Oates and Bedlow.

This was a happy day for the Lords in the Tower, who expecting their trial, had this gone against the prisoners at the bar, would all have been in the utmost hazard. For my part, I look on Oates as a vain, insolent man, puffed up with the favour of the Commons for having discovered something really true, more especially as detecting the dangerous intrigue of Coleman, proved out of his own letters, and of a general design which the Jesuited party of the Papists ever had and still have, to ruin the Church of England; but that he was trusted with those great secrets he pretended, or had any solid ground for what he accused divers noblemen of, I have many reasons to induce my contrary belief. That among so many commissions as he affirmed to have delivered to them from P. Oliva[1] and the Pope,—he who made no scruple of opening all other papers, letters, and secrets, should not only not open any of those pretended commissions, but not so much as take any copy or witness of any one of them, is almost miraculous. But the commons (some leading persons I mean of them) had so exalted him, that they took all he said for Gospel, and without more ado ruined all whom he named to be conspirators; nor did he spare whoever came in his way. But indeed the murder of Sir Edmundbury Godfrey, suspected to have been compassed by the Jesuits' party for his intimacy with Coleman (a busy person whom I also knew), and the fear they had that he was able to have discovered things to their prejudice, did so exasperate not only the Commons but all the nation, that much of these sharpnesses against the more

---

[1] Padrè Oliva, General of the Order of Jesuits.

honest Roman Catholics who lived peaceably, is to be imputed to that horrid fact.

The sessions ended, I dined or rather supped (so late it
was) with the Judges[1] in the large room annexed to the
place, and so returned home. Though it was not my
custom or delight to be often present at any capital trials,
we having them commonly so exactly published by those
who take them in short-hand, yet I was inclined to be at
this signal one, that by the ocular view of the carriages and
other circumstances of the managers and parties concerned,
I might inform myself, and regulate my opinion of a cause
that had so alarmed the whole nation.

22nd July. Dined at Clapham, at Sir D. Gauden's ; went
thence with him to Windsor, to assist him in a business with
his Majesty. I lay that night at Eton College, the Provost's lodgings (Dr. Craddock), where I was courteously
entertained.

23rd. To Court : after dinner, I visited that excellent
painter, Verrio, whose works in *fresco* in the King's palace,
at Windsor, will celebrate his name as long as those walls
last. He showed us his pretty garden, choice flowers, and
curiosities, he himself being a skilful gardener.

I went to Clifden, that stupendous natural rock, wood,
and prospect, of the Duke of Buckingham's,[2] and buildings
of extraordinary expense. The grots in the chalky rocks
are pretty : it is a romantic object, and the place altogether
answers the most poetical description that can be made of
solitude, precipice, prospect, or whatever can contribute to
a thing so very like their imaginations. The stand, somewhat like Frascati as to its front, and on the platform is a
circular view to the utmost verge of the horizon, which,
with the serpenting of the Thames, is admirable. The
staircase is for its materials singular ; the cloisters, de-
scents, gardens, and avenue through the wood, august and

---

[1] The Judges were, Lord Chief Justice North, Mr. Justice Atkins,
Mr. Justice Windham, Mr. Justice Pemberton, and Mr. Justice Dolben.

[2] —————————— Cliefden's proud alcove,
The bower of wanton Shrewsbury and Love.—POPE.
—The same Countess of Shrewsbury, who, when her husband challenged
the Duke, her paramour, is said to have held the horse of the latter, in
the habit of a page, while they fought.

stately; but the land all about wretchedly barren, and producing nothing but fern. Indeed, as I told his Majesty that evening (asking me how I liked Clifden) without flattery, that it did not please me so well as Windsor for the prospect and park, which is without compare; there being but one only opening, and that narrow, which led one to any variety, whereas that of Windsor is everywhere great and unconfined.

Returning, I called at my cousin Evelyn's, who has a very pretty seat in the forest, two miles by hither Clifden, on a flat, with gardens exquisitely kept, though large, and the house a staunch good old building, and what was singular, some of the rooms floored dove-tail-wise without a nail, exactly close. One of the closets is pargetted with plain deal, set in diamond, exceeding staunch and pretty.

7th August. Dined at the Sheriffs, when, the Company of Drapers and their wives being invited, there was a sumptuous entertainment, according to the forms of the city, with music, &c., comparable to any Prince's service in Europe.

8th. I went this morning to show my Lord Chamberlain, his Lady, and the Duchess of Grafton, the incomparable work of Mr. Gibbon, the carver, whom I first recommended to his Majesty, his house being furnished like a cabinet, not only with his own work, but divers excellent paintings of the best hands. Thence, to Sir Stephen Fox's, where we spent the day.

31st. After evening service, to see a neighbour, one Mr. Bohun, related to my son's late tutor of that name, a rich Spanish merchant, living in a neat place, which he has adorned with many curiosities, especially several carvings of Mr. Gibbon, and some pictures by Streeter.

13th September. To Windsor, to congratulate his Majesty on his recovery; I kissed the Duke's hand, now lately returned from Flanders[1] to visit his brother the King, on which there were various bold and foolish discourses, the Duke of Monmouth being sent away.

19th. My Lord Sunderland, one of the principal Secre-

---

[1] He returned the day before, the 12th of September. This is another of the indications that the entries of this Diary were not always made on the precise days they refer to.

taries of State, invited me to dinner, where was the King's natural son, the Earl of Plymouth, the Earl of Shrewsbury, Earl of Essex, Earl of Mulgrave, Mr. Hyde, and Mr. Godolphin. After dinner, I went to prayers at Eton, and visited Mr. Henry Godolphin, fellow there, and Dr. Craddock.

25th September. Mr. Slingsby and Signor Verrio came to dine with me, to whom I gave China oranges off my own trees, as good, I think, as were ever eaten.

6th October. A very wet and sickly season.

23rd. Dined at my Lord Chamberlain's, the King being now newly returned from his Newmarket recreations.

4th November. Dined at the Lord Mayor's; and, in the evening, went to the funeral of my pious, dear, and ancient learned friend, Dr. Jasper Needham, who was buried at St. Bride's church. He was a true and holy Christian, and one who loved me with great affection. Dr. Dove preached with an eulogy due to his memory. I lost in this person one of my dearest remaining sincere friends.

5th. I was invited to dine at my Lord Tiviotdale's, a Scotch Earl, a learned and knowing nobleman. We afterwards went to see Mr. Montague's new palace near Bloomsbury, built by our curator, Mr. Hooke, somewhat after the French; it was most nobly furnished, and a fine, but too much exposed garden.[1]

6th. Dined at the Countess of Sunderland's, and was this evening at the re-marriage of the Duchess of Grafton to the Duke (his Majesty's natural son), she being now twelve years old. The ceremony was performed in my Lord Chamberlain's (her father's) lodgings at Whitehall by the Bishop of Rochester, his Majesty being present. A sudden and unexpected thing, when everybody believed the first marriage would have come to nothing; but, the measure being determined, I was privately invited by my Lady, her mother, to be present. I confess I could give her little joy, and so I plainly told her, but she said the King would have it so, and there was no going back. This sweetest, hopefullest, most beautiful child, and most virtuous too, was sacrificed to a boy that had been rudely bred, without anything to encourage them but his Majesty's pleasure. I pray

[1] Now the British Museum. See *ante*, p. 113, and *post*, pp. 197 and 258.

God the sweet child find it to her advantage, who, if my augury deceive me not, will in few years be such a paragon as were fit to make the wife of the greatest Prince in Europe! I staid supper, where his Majesty sat between the Duchess of Cleveland (the mother of the Duke of Grafton) and the sweet Duchess the bride; there were several great persons and ladies, without pomp. My love to my Lord Arlington's family and the sweet child made me behold all this with regret, though as the Duke of Grafton affects the sea, to which I find his father intends to use him, he may emerge a plain, useful and robust officer; and, were he polished, a tolerable person; for he is exceeding handsome, by far surpassing any of the King's other natural issue.

8th November. At Sir Stephen Fox's, and was agreeing for the Countess of Bristol's house at Chelsea, within 500*l.*

18th. I dined at my Lord Mayor's, being desired by the Countess of Sunderland to carry her thither on a solemn day, that she might see the pomp and ceremony of this Prince of Citizens, there never having been any, who for the stateliness of his palace, prodigious feasting, and magnificence, exceeded him. This Lord Mayor's acquaintance had been from the time of his being apprentice to one Mr. Abbot, his uncle,[1] who being a scrivener, and an honest worthy man, one who was condemned to die at the beginning of the troubles forty years past, as concerned in the commission of array for King Charles I. had escaped with his life; I often used his assistance in money-matters. Robert Clayton, then a boy, his nephew, became, after his uncle Abbot's death, so prodigiously rich and opulent, that he was reckoned one of the wealthiest citizens. He married a free-hearted woman, who became his hospitable disposition; and, having no children, with the accession of his partner and fellow apprentice,[2] who also left him his estate, he grew excessively rich. He was a discreet magistrate, and though envied, I think without much cause. Some believed him guilty of hard dealing, especially with the Duke of Buckingham, much of whose estate he had swallowed, but I never saw any ill by him, considering the trade he was of. The reputation and known integrity of his uncle, Abbot, brought

[1] The Lord Mayor was now Sir Robert Clayton. See *an* , pp. 115, 116, and *note.*   [2] Mr. Morris.

all the royal party to him, by which ne got not only great
credit, but vast wealth, so as he passed this office with infinite magnificence and honour.

20th November. I dined with Mr. Slingsby, Master of the Mint,
with my wife, invited to hear music, which was exquisitely
performed by four of the most renowned masters : Du Prue,
a Frenchman, on the lute; Signor Bartholomeo, an Italian, on
the harpsichord; Nicholao on the violin ; but, above all, for
its sweetness and novelty, the *viol d'amore* of five wire strings
played on with a bow, being but an ordinary violin, played
on lyre-way, by a German. There was also a *flute douce*, now
in much request for accompanying the voice. Mr. Slingsby,
whose son and daughter played skilfully, had these meetings
frequently in his house.

21st. I dined at my Lord Mayor's, to accompany my
worthiest and generous friend, the Earl of Ossory ; it was
on a Friday, a private day, but the feast and entertainment might have become a King. Such an hospitable costume and splendid magistrature does no city in the world
show, as I believe.

23rd. Dr. Allestree preached before the household on
St. Luke, xi. 2; Dr. Lloyd on Matt. xxiii. 20, before the
King, showing with how little reason the Papists applied
those words of our blessed Saviour to maintain the pretended
infallibility they boast of. I never heard a more Christian
and excellent discourse ; yet were some offended that he
seemed to say the Church of Rome was a true church ; but
it was a captious mistake ; for he never affirmed anything
that could be more to their reproach, and that such was the
present Church of Rome, showing how much it had erred.
There was not in this sermon so much as a shadow for
censure, no person of all the clergy having testified greater
zeal against the errors of the Papists than this pious and
most learned person. I dined at the Bishop of Rochester's,
and then went to St. Paul's, to hear that great wit, Dr.
Sprat, now newly succeeding Dr. Outram, in the cure of St.
Margaret's. His talent was, a great memory, never making
use of notes, a readiness of expression in a most pure and
plain style of words, full of matter, easily delivered.

26th. I met the Earl of Clarendon with the rest of my
fellow executors of the will of my late Lady Viscountess

Mordaunt, namely, Mr. Laurence Hyde, one of the Commissioners of the Treasury, and lately Plenipotentiary-Ambassador at Nimeguen; Andrew Newport; and Sir Charles Wheeler; to examine and audit and dispose of this year's account of the estate of this excellent Lady, according to the direction of her Will.

27th November. I went to see Sir John Stonehouse, with whom I was treating a marriage between my son and his daughter-in-law.

28th. Came over the Duke of Monmouth from Holland unexpectedly to his Majesty; whilst the Duke of York was on his journey to Scotland, whither the King sent him to reside and govern. The bells and bonfires of the City at this arrival of the Duke of Monmouth publishing their joy, to the no small regret of some at Court. This Duke, whom for distinction they called the Protestant Duke (though the son of an abandoned woman), the people made their idol.

4th December. I dined, together with Lord Ossory and the Earl of Chesterfield, at the Portugal Ambassador's, now newly come, at Cleveland House, a noble palace, too good for that infamous . . . . . The staircase is sumptuous, and the gallery and garden; but, above all, the costly furniture belonging to the Ambassador, especially the rich Japan cabinets, of which I think there were a dozen. There was a billiard table, with as many more hazards as ours commonly have; the game being only to prosecute the ball till hazarded, without passing the port, or touching the pin; if one miss hitting the ball every time, the game is lost, or if hazarded. It is more difficult to hazard a ball, though so many, than in our table, by reason the bound is made so exactly even, and the edges not stuffed; the balls are also bigger, and they for the most part use the sharp and small end of the billiard-stick, which is shod with brass, or silver. The entertainment was exceeding civil; but, besides a good olio, the dishes were trifling, hashed and condited after their way, not at all fit for an English stomach, which is for solid meat. There was yet good fowls, but roasted to coal, nor were the sweetmeats good.

30th. I went to meet Sir John Stonehouse, and give him a particular of the settlement on my son, who now made his addresses to the young lady his daughter-in-law, daughter of Lady Stonehouse.

1679-80. 25*th January.* Dr. Cave, author of *Primitive Christianity*, &c., a pious and learned man,[1] preached at Whitehall to the household, on James, iii. 17, concerning the duty of grace and charity.

30*th.* I supped with Sir Stephen Fox, now made one of the Lords Commissioners of the Treasury.

19*th February.* The writings for the settling jointure and other contracts of marriage of my son were finished and sealed. The lady was to bring £5000, in consideration of a settlement of £500 a-year present maintenance, which was likewise to be her jointure, and £500 a-year after mine and my wife's decease. But, with God's blessing, it will be at the least £1000 a-year more in a few years. I pray God make him worthy of it, and a comfort to his excellent mother, who deserves much from him!

21*st. Shrove - Tuesday.* My son was married to Mrs. Martha Spencer, daughter to my Lady Stonehouse by a former gentleman, at St. Andrew's, Holborn, by our Vicar, borrowing the church of Dr. Stillingfleet, Dean of St. Paul's, the present incumbent. We afterwards dined at a house in Holborn; and, after the solemnity and dancing was done, they were bedded at Sir John Stonehouse's lodgings in Bow Street, Covent Garden.

26*th.* To the Royal Society, where I met an Irish Bishop with his Lady, who was daughter to my worthy and pious friend, Dr. Jeremy Taylor, late Bishop of Down and Connor; they came to see the Repository. She seemed to be a knowing woman, beyond the ordinary talent of her sex

3*rd March.* I dined at my Lord Mayor's, in order to the meeting of my Lady Beckford, whose daughter (a rich heiress) I had recommended to my brother of Wotton for his only son, she being the daughter of the lady by Mr. Eversfield, a Sussex gentleman.

16*th.* To London, to receive £3000 of my daughter-in-law's portion, which was paid in gold.

26*th.* The Dean of Sarum preached on Jerem., xlv. 5, an hour and a half from his common-place book, of kings and great men retiring to private situations. Scarce any thing of Scripture in it.

[1] Mr. William Cave; author also of "Lives of the Apostles and Martyrs," and "Historia Literaria." Born 1637, died 1713.

18th April. On the earnest invitation of the Earl of
Essex, I went with him to his house at Cashiobury, in
Hertfordshire. It was on Sunday, but going early from
his house in the square of St. James, we arrived by ten
o'clock; this he thought too late to go to church, and we
had prayers in his chapel. The house is new, a plain
fabric, built by my friend, Mr. Hugh May. There are
divers fair and good rooms, and excellent carving by Gibbon,
especially the chimney-piece of the library. There is in the
porch, or entrance, a painting by Verrio, of Apollo and the
Liberal Arts. One room pargetted with yew, which I liked
well. Some of the chimney mantels are of Irish marble,
brought by my Lord from Ireland, when he was Lord Lieutenant, and not much inferior to Italian. The tympanum,
or gable, at the front is a bass-relievo of Diana hunting, cut
in Portland stone, handsomely enough. I do not approve
of the middle doors being round: but, when the hall is
finished as designed, it being an oval with a cupola, together
with the other wing, it will be a very noble palace. The
library is large, and very nobly furnished, and all the books
are richly bound and gilded; but there are no MSS., except
the Parliament Rolls and Journals, the transcribing and
binding of which cost him, as he assured me, £500.

No man has been more industrious than this noble Lord
in planting about his seat, adorned with walks, ponds, and
other rural elegancies; but the soil is stony, churlish, and
uneven, nor is the water near enough to the house, though
a very swift and clear stream run within a flight-shot from
it in the valley, which may fitly be called Coldbrook, it
being indeed excessive cold, yet producing fair trouts. It is
pity the house was not situated to more advantage: but it
seems it was built just where the old one was, which I
believe he only meant to repair; this leads men into irre-
mediable errors, and saves but a little.

The land about is exceedingly addicted to wood, but the
coldness of the place hinders the growth. Black cherry-
trees prosper even to considerable timber, some being eighty
feet long; they make also very handsome avenues. There
is a pretty oval at the end of a fair walk, set about with
treble rows of Spanish chesnut-trees.

The gardens are very rare, and cannot be otherwise,

having so skilful an artist to govern them as Mr. Cooke, who is, as to the mechanic part, not ignorant in mathematics, and pretends to astrology. There is an excellent collection of the choicest fruit.

As for my Lord, he is a sober, wise, judicious, and ponder ing person, not illiterate beyond the rate of most noblemen in this age, very well versed in English History and affairs, industrious, frugal, methodical, and every way accomplished. His Lady (being sister of the late Earl of Northumberland) is a wise, yet somewhat melancholy woman, setting her heart too much on the little lady, her daughter, of whom she is over fond. They have a hopeful son at the Academy.

My Lord was not long since come from his Lord-Lieutenancy of Ireland, where he showed his abilities in administration and government, as well as prudence in considerably augmenting his estate without reproach. He had been Ambassador Extraordinary in Denmark, and, in a word, such a person as became the son of that worthy hero his father to be, the late Lord Capel, who lost his life for King Charles I.

We spent our time in the mornings in walking, or riding, and contriving [alterations], and the afternoons in the library, so as I passed my time for three or four days with much satisfaction. He was pleased in conversation to impart to me divers particulars of state, relating to the present times. He being no great friend to the D—— was now laid aside, his integrity and abilities being not so suitable in this conjuncture.—21st. I returned to London.

30th April. To a meeting of the executors of late Viscountess Mordaunt's estate, to consider of the sale of Parson's Green, being in treaty with Mr. Loftus, and to settle the half year's account.

1st May. Was a meeting of the feoffees of the poor of our parish. This year I would stand one of the collectors of their rents, to give example to others. My son was added to the feoffees.

This afternoon came to visit me Sir Edward Deering, of Surrendon, in Kent, one of the Lords of the Treasury, with his daughter, married to my worthy friend, Sir Robert Southwell, Clerk of the Council, now Extraordinary-Envoy to the Duke of Brandenburgh, and other Princes in Germany, as before he had been in Portugal, being a sober, wise, and virtuous gentleman.

13th May. I was at the funeral of old Mr. Shish, master-shipwright of his Majesty's Yard here, an honest and remarkable man, and his death a public loss, for his excellent success in building ships (though altogether illiterate), and for breeding up so many of his children to be able artists. I held up the pall with three knights, who did him that honour, and he was worthy of it. It was the custom of this good man to rise in the night, and to pray, kneeling in his own coffin, which he had lying by him for many years. He was born that famous year, the Gunpowder-plot, 1605.

14th June. Came to dine with us the Countess of Clarendon, Dr. Lloyd, Dean of Bangor (since Bishop of St. Asaph), Dr. Burnet, author of the History of the Reformation, and my old friend, Mr. Henshaw. After dinner, we all went to see the Observatory, and Mr. Flamsted, who showed us divers rare instruments, especially the great quadrant.

24th July. Went with my wife and daughter to Windsor, to see that stately court, now near finished. There was erected in the court the King on horseback, lately cast in copper, and set on a rich pedestal of white marble, the work of Mr. Gibbon, at the expense of Toby Rustate, a page[1] of the back stairs, who by his wonderful frugality had arrived to a great estate in money, and did many works of charity, as well as this of gratitude to his master, which cost him £1000. He is very simple, ignorant, but honest and loyal creature.

We all dined at the Countess of Sunderland's, afterwards to see Signor Verrio's garden, thence to Eton College, to salute the Provost, and heard a Latin speech of one of the Alumni (it being at the election) and were invited to supper; but took our leave, and got to London that night in good time.

26th. My most noble and illustrious friend, the Earl of Ossory, espying me this morning after sermon in the

---

[1] Mr. Tobias Rustate. He was a great benefactor to Jesus College, Cambridge; in particular by an endowment of scholarships there for the benefit of young students, orphan sons of Clergymen.

privy gallery, calling to me, told me he was now going his journey (meaning to Tangier, whither he was designed Governor, and General of the forces, to regain the losses we had lately sustained from the Moors, when Inchiquin was Governor). I asked if he would not call at my house (as he always did whenever he went out of England on any exploit). He said he must embark at Portsmouth, "wherefore let you and I dine together to-day; I am quite alone, and have something to impart to you; I am not well, shall be private, and desire your company."

Being retired to his lodgings, and set down on a couch, he sent to his secretary for the copy of a letter which he had written to Lord Sunderland (Secretary of State), wishing me to read it; it was to take notice how ill he resented it, that he should tell the King before Lord Ossory's face, that Tangier was not to be kept, but would certainly be lost, and yet added that it was fit Lord Ossory should be sent, that they might give some account of it to the world, meaning (as supposed) the next Parliament, when all such miscarriages would probably be examined; this Lord Ossory took very ill of Lord Sunderland, and not kindly of the King, who resolving to send him with an incompetent force, seemed, as his Lordship took it, to be willing to cast him away, not only on a hazardous adventure, but in most men's opinion, an impossibility, seeing there was not to be above 300 or 400 horse, and 4000 foot for the garrison and all, both to defend the town, form a camp, repulse the enemy, and fortify what ground they should get in. This touched my Lord deeply, that he should be so little considered as to put him on a business in which he should probably not only lose his reputation, but be charged with all the miscarriage and ill success; whereas, at first they promised 6000 foot and 600 horse effective.

My Lord, being an exceeding brave and valiant person, and who had so approved himself in divers signal battles, both at sea and land; so beloved and so esteemed by the people, as one they depended on, upon all occasions worthy of such a captain;—he looked on this as too great an indifference in his Majesty, after all his services, and the merits of his father, the Duke of Ormond, and a design of some who envied his virtue. It certainly took so deep root in his mind, that he who was the most void of fear in the world (and assured me he would go to Tangier with ten men if his Majesty commanded him) could not bear up against this unkindness. Having disburdened himself of this to me after dinner, he went with his Majesty to the Sheriffs at a great supper in Fishmongers' Hall; but, finding himself ill, took his leave immediately of his Majesty, and came back to his lodging. Not resting well this night, he was persuaded to remove to Arlington House, for better accommodation. His disorder turned to a malignant fever, which increasing, after all that six of the most able physicians could do, he became delirious, with intervals of sense, during which Dr. Lloyd (after Bishop of St. Asaph) administered the Holy Sacrament, of which I also participated. He died the Friday following, the 30th July, to the universal grief of all that knew or heard of his great worth, nor had any a greater loss than myself. Oft would he say I was the oldest acquaintance he had in England (when his father was in Ireland), it being now of about thirty years, contracted abroad, when he rode in the Academy in Paris, and when we were seldom asunder.

His Majesty never lost a worthier subject, nor father a better or more dutiful son; a loving, generous, good-natured, and perfectly obliging friend; one who had done innumerable kindnesses to several before they knew it; nor did he ever advance any that were not worthy; no one more brave, more modest; none more humble, sober, and every way virtuous. Unhappy England in this illustrious person's loss! Universal was the mourning for him, and the eulogies on him; I staid night and day by his bedside to his last gasp, to close his dear eyes! O sad father, mother, wife, and children! What shall I add? He deserved all that a sincere friend, a brave soldier, a virtuous courtier, a loyal subject, an honest man, a bountiful master, and good Christian, could deserve of his prince and country. One thing more let me note, that he often expressed to me the abhorrence he had of that base and unworthy action which he was put upon, of engaging the Smyrna fleet in time of peace, in which though he behaved himself like a great captain, yet he told me it was the only blot in his life, and troubled him exceedingly. Though he was commanded.

and never examined further when he was so, yet he always spake of it with regret and detestation. The Countess was at the seat of her daughter, the Countess of Derby, about 200 miles off.

30th August. I went to visit a French gentleman, one Monsieur Chardin,[1] who having been thrice in the East Indies, Persia, and other remote countries, came hither in our return-ships from those parts, and it being reported that he was a very curious and knowing man, I was desired by the Royal Society to salute him in their name, and to invite him to honour them with his company. Sir Joseph Hoskins and Sir Christopher Wren accompanied me. We found him at his lodgings in his Eastern habit, a very handsome person, extremely affable, a modest, well-bred man, not inclined to talk wonders. He spake Latin, and understood Greek, Arabic, and Persian, from eleven years' travels in those parts, whither he went in search of jewels, and was become very rich. He seemed about 36 years of age. After the usual civilities, we asked some account of the extraordinary things he must have seen in travelling over land to those places where few, if any, northern Europeans, used to go, as the Black and Caspian Sea, Mingrelia, Bagdat, Nineveh, Persepolis, &c. He told us that the things most worthy of our sight would be, the draughts he had caused to be made of some noble ruins, &c.; for that, besides his own little talent that way, he had carried two good painters with him, to draw landscapes, measure and design the remains of the palace which Alexander burnt in his frolic at Persepolis, with divers temples, columns, relievos, and statues, yet extant, which he affirmed to be sculpture far exceeding anything he had observed either at Rome, in Greece, or in any other part of the world where magnificence was in estimation. He said there was an inscription in letters not intelligible, though entire. He was sorry he could not gratify the curiosity of the Society at present, his things not being yet out of the ship; but would wait on them with them on his return from Paris,

---

[1] Better known as Sir John Chardin, he having, though a Frenchman, been knighted by Charles II. He was an enterprising traveller in the East, and his accounts of India and Persia were thought peculiarly interesting. He died in 1713.

whither he was going the next day, but with intention to return suddenly, and stay longer here, the persecution in France not suffering Protestants, and he was one, to be quiet.

He told us that Nineveh was a vast city, now all buried in her ruins, the inhabitants building on the subterranean vaults, which were, as appeared, the first stories of the old city;[1] that there were frequently found huge vases of fine earth, columns, and other antiquities; that the straw which the Egyptians required of the Israelites, was not to burn, or cover the rows of bricks as we use, but being chopped small to mingle with the clay, which being dried in the sun (for they bake not in the furnaces) would else cleave asunder; that in Persia are yet a race of Ignicolæ, who worship the sun and the fire as Gods; that the women of Georgia and Mingrelia were universally, and without any compare, the most beautiful creatures for shape, features, and figure, in the world, and therefore the Grand Seignor and Bashaws had had from thence most of their wives and concubines; that there had within these hundred years been Amazons amongst them, that is to say, a sort or race of valiant women, given to war; that Persia was extremely fertile; he spoke also of Japan and China, and of the many great errors of our late geographers, as we suggested matter for discourse. We then took our leaves, failing of seeing his papers; but it was told us by others that indeed he durst not open, or show them, till he had first showed them to the French King; but of this he himself said nothing.

2nd September. I had an opportunity, his Majesty being still at Windsor, of seeing his private library at Whitehall, at my full ease. I went with expectation of finding some curiosities, but, though there were about 1000 volumes, there were few of importance which I had not perused before. They consisted chiefly of such books as had from time to time been dedicated, or presented to him; a few histories, some Travels and French books, abundance of maps and sea charts, entertainments and pomps, buildings and pieces relating to the Navy, some mathematical instruments; but what was most rare, were three or four

[1] See *ante*, pp. 95, 96.

Romish breviaries, with a great deal of miniature and monkish painting and gilding, one of which is most exquisitely
done, both as to the figures, grotesques, and compartments,
to the utmost of that curious art. There is another in
which I find written by the hand of King Henry VII.,
his giving it to his dear daughter, Margaret, afterwards
Queen of Scots, in which he desires her to pray for his
soul, subscribing his name at length. There is also the
process of the philosophers' great elixir, represented in
divers pieces of excellent miniature, but the discourse is in
high Dutch, a MS. There is another MS. in quarto, of
above 300 years old, in French, being an institution of
physic, and in the botanical part the plants are curiously
painted in miniature; also a folio MS. of good thickness,
being the several exercises, as Themes, Orations, Translations, &c., of King Edward VI., all written and subscribed
by his own hand, and with his name very legible, and divers
of the Greek interleaved and corrected after the manner of
schoolboys' exercises, and that exceedingly well and proper;
with some epistles to his preceptor, which show that young
Prince to have been extraordinarily advanced in learning,
and as Cardan, who had been in England affirmed, stupen-
dously knowing for his age. There is likewise his Journal,[1]
no less testifying his early ripeness and care about the
affairs of state.

There are besides many pompous volumes, some embossed with gold, and intaglios on agates, medals, &c. I
spent three or four entire days, locked up, and alone, among
these books and curiosities. In the rest of the private lodgings contiguous to this, are divers of the best pictures of the
great masters, Raphael, Titian, &c., and, in my esteem, above
all, the *Noli me tangere* of our Blessed Saviour to Mary Magdalen after his Resurrection, of Hans Holbein; than which
I never saw so much reverence and kind of heavenly astonishment expressed in a picture.[2]

There are also divers curious clocks, watches, and pen-
dules of exquisite work, and other curiosities. An ancient

[1] Several extracts from this journal are made by Burnet in his *History
of the Reformation.*
[2] Now, with other pictures mentioned in the course of this Diary, is
the gallery at Hampton Court.

woman who made these lodgings clean, and had all the keys, let me in at pleasure for a small reward, by means of a friend.

6th September. I d.ned with Sir Stephen Fox, now one of the Lords Commissioners of the Treasury. This gentleman came first a poor boy from the choir of Salisbury, then he was taken notice of by Bishop Duppa, and afterwards waited on my Lord Percy (brother to Algernon Earl of Northumberland), who procured for him an inferior place amongst the Clerks of the Kitchen and Green-Cloth side, where he was found so humble, diligent, industrious, and prudent in his behaviour, that his Majesty being in exile, and Mr. Fox waiting, both the King and Lords about him frequently employed him about their affairs, and trusted him both with receiving and paying the little money they had. Returning with his Majesty to England, after great wants and great sufferings, his Majesty found him so honest and industrious, and withal so capable and ready, that, being advanced from Clerk of the Kitchen to that of the Green-Cloth, he procured to be Paymaster to the whole Army, and by his dexterity and punctual dealing he obtained such credit among the bankers, that he was in a short time able to borrow vast sums of them upon any exigence. The continual turning thus of money, and the soldiers' moderate allowance to him for keeping touch with them, did so enrich him, that he is believed to be worth at least £200,000, honestly got and unenvied; which is next to a miracle. With all this he continues as humble and ready to do a courtesy as ever he was.

He is generous, and lives very honourably, of a sweet nature, well-spoken, well-bred, and is so highly in his Majesty's esteem, and so useful, that being long since made a knight, he is also advanced to be one of the Lords Commissioners of the Treasury, and has the reversion of the Cofferer's place after Harry Brouncker. He has married his eldest daughter to my Lord Cornwallis, and gave her £12,000, and restored that entangled family besides. He matched his son to Mrs. Trollop, who brings with her (besides a great sum) near, if not altogether, £2000 per annum. Sir Stephen's lady (an excellent woman) is sister to Mr. Whittle, one of the King's chirurgeons. In a word, never was man

more fortunate than Sir Stephen; he is a handsome person,
virtuous, and very religious.[1]

23rd September. Came to my house some German strangers
and Signor Pietro, a famous musician, who had been long
in Sweden in Queen Christina's Court; he sung admirably
to a guitar, and had a perfect good tenor and base, and had
set to Italian composure many of Abraham Cowley's pieces
which showed extremely well. He told me that in Sweden
the heat in some part of summer was as excessive as the
cold in winter; so cold, he affirmed, that the streets of all
the towns are desolate, no creatures stirring in them for
many months, all the inhabitants retiring to their stoves.
He spake high things of that romantic Queen's learning and
skill in languages, the majesty of her behaviour, her exceeding wit, and that the histories she had read of other countries, especially of Italy and Rome, had made her despise
her own. That the real occasion of her resigning her crown
was the nobleman's importuning her to marry, and the
promise which the Pope had made her of procuring her to
be Queen of Naples, which also caused her to change her
religion; but she was cheated by his crafty Holiness,[2] working on her ambition; that the reason of her killing her
secretary at Fontainebleau, was, his revealing that intrigue
with the Pope. But, after all this, I rather believe it was
her mad prodigality and extreme vanity, which had consumed those vast treasures the great Adolphus, her father,
had brought out of Germany during his [campaigns] there
and wonderful successes; and that, if she had not voluntarily
resigned, as foreseeing the event, the Estates of her kingdom would have compelled her to do so.

30th October. I went to London to be private, my birth-
day being the next day, and I now arrived at my sixtieth
year; on which I began a more solemn survey of my whole
life, in order to the making and confirming my peace with
God, by an accurate scrutiny of all my actions past, as far
as I was able to call them to mind. How difficult and un-

[1] This notice of the founder of the peerages of Ilchester and Holland
contains much that, quite apart from the nice details of genealogy, might
sufficiently prove his kinship with the remarkable and genial represen-
tatives of those families in later times.
[2] Pope Alexander VII., of the family of Chighi, at Sienna.

certain, yet how necessary a work! The Lord be merciful to me, and accept me! Who can tell how oft he offendeth? Teach me, therefore, so to number my days, that I may apply my heart unto wisdom, and make my calling and election sure. Amen, Lord Jesus!

31st October. I spent this whole day in exercises. A stranger preached at Whitehall[1] on Luke xvi. 30, 31. I then went to St. Martin's, where the Bishop of St. Asaph preached on 1 Peter, iii. 15; the holy Communion followed, at which I participated, humbly imploring God's assistance in the great work I was entering into. In the afternoon, I heard Dr. Sprat, at St. Margaret's, on Acts, xvii. 11.

I began and spent the whole week in examining my life, begging pardon for my faults, assistance and blessing for the future, that I might, in some sort, be prepared for the time that now drew near, and not have the great work to begin when one can work no longer. The Lord Jesus help and assist me! I therefore stirred little abroad till the 5th November, when I heard Dr. Tenison, the now vicar of St. Martin's; Dr. Lloyd, the former incumbent, being made Bishop of St. Asaph.

7th November. I participated of the Blessed Communion, finishing and confirming my resolutions of giving myself up more entirely to God, to whom I had now most solemnly devoted the rest of the poor remainder of life in this world; the Lord enabling me, who am an unprofitable servant, a miserable sinner, yet depending on his infinite goodness and mercy accepting my endeavours.

15th. Came to dine with us Sir Richard Anderson, his lady, son, and wife, sister to my daughter-in-law.

30th. The anniversary election at the Royal Society, brought me to London, where was chosen President that excellent person and great philosopher, Mr. Robert Boyle, who indeed ought to have been the very first; but neither his infirmity nor his modesty could now any longer excuse him. I desired I might for this year be left out of the Council, by reason my dwelling was in the country. The Society according to custom dined together.

The signal day begun the trial (at which I was present)

---

[1] Probably to the King's household, very early in the morning, as the custom was.

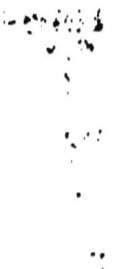

of my Lord Viscount Stafford, for conspiring the death of the King; second son to my Lord Thomas Howard Earl of Arundel and Surrey, Earl Marshal of England, and grandfather to the present Duke of Norfolk, whom I so well knew, and from which excellent person I received so many favours. It was likewise his birthday. The trial was in Westminster-Hall, before the King, Lords, and Commons.; just in the same manner as, forty years past, the great and wise Earl of Strafford (there being but one letter differing their names) received his trial for pretended ill government in Ireland, in the very same place, this Lord Stafford's father being then High-Steward. The place of sitting was now exalted some considerable height from the paved floor of the Hall, with a stage of boards. The throne, woolpacks for the Judges, long forms for the Peers, chair for the Lord Steward, exactly ranged, as in the House of Lords. The sides on both hands scaffolded to the very roof for the members of the House of Commons. At the upper end, and on the right side of the King's state, was a box for his Majesty, and on the left, others for the great ladies, and over head a gallery for ambassadors and public ministers. At the lower end, or entrance, was a bar, and place for the prisoner, the Lieutenant of the Tower of London, the axe-bearer and guards, my Lord Stafford's two daughters, the Marchioness of Winchester being one; there was likewise a box for my Lord to retire into. At the right hand, in another box, somewhat higher, stood the witnesses; at the left, the managers, in the name of the Commons of England, namely, Serjeant Maynard (the great lawyer, the same who prosecuted the cause against the Earl of Strafford forty years before, being now near eighty years of age), Sir William Jones, late Attorney-General, Sir Francis Winnington, a famous pleader, and Mr. Treby, now Recorder of London,[1] not appearing in their gowns as lawyers, but in their cloaks and swords, as representing the Commons of England : to these were joined Mr. Hampden, Dr. Sacheverell, Mr. Poule, Colonel Titus, Sir Thomas Lee, all gentlemen of quality, and noted parliamentary men. The two first days, in which

---

[1] Afterwards Chief Justice of the Common Pleas, and knighted. Sir George Treby was also member of Parliament for Plympton, in Devonshire, where he was born He died in 1702.

were read the commission and impeachment, were but a
tedious entrance into matter of fact, at which I was but
little present.   But, on Thursday, I was commodiously
seated amongst the Commons, when the witnesses were
sworn and examined.   The principal witnesses were Mr.
Oates (who called himself Dr.) Mr. Dugdale, and Turberville.
Oates swore that he delivered a commission to Viscount
Stafford from the Pope, to be Paymaster-General to an army
intended to be raised ;—Dugdale, that being at Lord Aston's,
the prisoner dealt with him plainly to murder his Majesty ;
and Turberville, that at Paris he also proposed the same to
him.

3rd December.   The depositions of my Lord's witnesses
were taken, to invalidate the King's witnesses ; they were
very slight persons, but, being fifteen or sixteen, they took
up all that day, and in truth they rather did my Lord injury
than service.

4th.   Came other witnesses of the Commons to cor-
roborate the King's, some being Peers, some Commons,
with others of good quality, who took off all the former day's objections, and set the King's witnesses *recti in
Curiâ.*

6th.   Sir William Jones summoned up the evidence ; to
him succeeded all the rest of the managers, and then Mr.
Henry Poule made a vehement oration.   After this my
Lord, as on all occasions, and often during the trial, spoke
in his own defence, denying the charge altogether, and that
he had never seen Oates, or Turberville, at the time and
manner affirmed : in truth, their testimony did little weigh
with me ; Dugdale's only seemed to press hardest, to which
my Lord spake a great while, but confusedly, without any
method.

One thing my Lord said as to Oates, which I confess
did exceedingly affect me : That a person who during his
depositions should so vauntingly brag that though he went
over to the Church of Rome, yet he was never a Papist,
nor of their religion, all the time that he seemed to apos-
tatise from the Protestant, but only as a spy ; though he
confessed he took their sacrament, worshipped images,
went through all their oaths, and discipline of their prose-
es, swearing secrecy and to be faithful, but with intent

to come over again and betray them ;—that such an hypo-
crite, that had so deeply prevaricated as even to turn
idolater (for so we of the Church of England termed it),
attesting God so solemnly that he was entirely theirs and
devoted to their interest, and consequently (as he pretended) trusted ;—I say, that the witness of such a profli-
gate wretch should be admitted against the life of a peer,—
this my Lord looked upon as a monstrous thing, and such
as must needs redound to the dishonour of our religion and
nation. And verily I am of his Lordship's opinion : such a
man's testimony should not be taken against the life of a
dog. But the merit of something material which he discovered against Coleman, put him in such esteem with the
Parliament, that now, I fancy, he stuck at nothing, and
thought everybody was to take what he said for gospel.
The consideration of this, and some other circumstances,
began to stagger me ; particularly how it was possible that
one who went among the Papists on such a design, and pretended to be intrusted with so many letters and commissions
from the Pope and the party, nay and delivered them to so
many great persons, should not reserve one of them to show,
nor so much as one copy of any commission, which he who
had such dexterity in opening letters might certainly have
done, to the undeniable conviction of those whom he accused ;
but, as I said, he gained credit on Coleman. But, as to
others whom he so madly flew upon, I am little inclined to
believe his testimony, he being so slight a person, so passionate, ill-bred, and of such impudent behaviour ; nor is it likely
that such piercing politicians as the Jesuits should trust
him with so high and so dangerous secrets.

7th December. On Tuesday, I was again at the trial, when
judgment was demanded ; and, after my Lord had spoken
what he could in denying the fact, the managers answering
the objections, the Peers adjourned to their House, and
within two hours returned again. There was, in the meantime, this question put to the judges, " whether there being
but one witness to any single crime, or act, it could amount
to convict a man of treason." They gave an unanimous
opinion that in case of treason they all were overt acts, for
though no man should be condemned by one witness for
any one act, yet for several acts to the same intent, it was

valid; which was my Lord's case. This being past, and the Peers in their seats again, the Lord Chancellor Finch (this day the Lord High-Steward) removing to the woolsack next his Majesty's state, after summoning the Lieutenant of the Tower to bring forth his prisoner, and proclamation made for silence, demanded of every peer (who were in all eighty-six) whether William, Lord Viscount Stafford, were guilty of the treason laid to his charge, or not guilty.

Then the Peer spoken to, standing up, and laying his right hand upon his breast, said Guilty, or Not guilty, upon my honour, and then sat down, the Lord Steward noting their suffrages as they answered upon a paper: when all had done, the number of Not guilty being but 31, the Guilty 55 : and then, after proclamation for silence again, the Lord Steward directing his speech to the prisoner, against whom the axe was turned edgeways and not before, in aggravation of his crime, he being ennobled by the King's father, and since received many favours from his present Majesty: after enlarging on his offence, deploring first his own unhappiness that he who had never condemned any man before should now be necessitated to begin with him, he then pronounced sentence of death by hanging, drawing, and quartering, according to form, with great solemnity and dreadful gravity ; and, after a short pause, told the prisoner that he believed the Lords would intercede for the omission of some circumstances of his sentence, beheading only excepted; and then breaking his white staff, the Court was dissolved. My Lord Stafford during all this latter part spake but little, and only gave their Lordships thanks after the sentence was pronounced ; and indeed behaved himself modestly, and as became him.

It was observed that all his own relations of his name and family condemned him, except his nephew, the Earl of Arundel, son to the Duke of Norfolk. And it must be acknowledged that the whole trial was carried on with exceeding gravity : so stately and august an appearance I had never seen before ; for, besides the innumerable spectators of gentlemen and foreign ministers, who saw and heard all the proceedings, the prisoner had the consciences of all the Commons of England for his accusers, and all the

Peers to be his Judges and Jury. He had likewise the assistance of what counsel he would, to direct him in his plea, who stood by him. And yet I can hardly think that a person of his age and experience should engage men whom he never saw before (and one of them that came to visit him as a stranger at Paris) *point blank* to murder the King: God only who searches hearts, can discover the truth. Lord Stafford was not a man beloved, especially of his own family.

12th December. This evening, looking out of my chamber-window towards the west, I saw a meteor of an obscure bright colour, very much in shape like the blade of a sword, the rest of the sky very serene and clear. What this may portend, God only knows; but such another phenomenon I remember to have seen in 1640, about the trial of the great Earl of Strafford, preceding our bloody Rebellion. I pray God avert his judgments! We have had of late several comets, which though I believe appear from natural causes, and of themselves operate not, yet I cannot despise them. They may be warnings from God, as they commonly are forerunners of his animadversions. After many days and nights of snow, cloudy and dark weather, the comet was very much wasted.

17th. My daughter-in-law was brought to bed of a son, christened Richard.

22nd. A solemn public Fast that God would prevent all Popish plots, avert his judgments, and give a blessing to the proceedings of parliament now assembled, and which struck at the succession of the Duke of York.

29th. The Viscount Stafford was beheaded on Tower-hill.

1680-1. 10th February. I was at the wedding of my nephew, John Evelyn of Wotton, married by the Bishop of Rochester at Westminster, in Henry VII.'s chapel, to the daughter and heir of Mr. Eversfield, of Sussex, her portion £8000. The solemnity was kept with a few friends only at Lady Beckford's, the lady's mother.

8th March. Visited and dined at the Earl of Essex's, with whom I spent most of the afternoon alone. Thence to my (yet living) godmother and kinswoman, Mrs. Keightley, sister to Sir Thomas Evelyn, and niece to my father, being now eighty-six years of age, sprightly, and in perfect health, her eyes serving her as well as ever, and of a comely countenance, that one would not suppose her above fifty.

27th March. The Parliament now convened at Oxford. Great expectation of his Royal Highness's case as to the succession, against which the House was set.

An extraordinary sharp cold spring, not yet a leaf on the trees, frost and snow lying: whilst the whole nation was in the greatest ferment.

11th April. I took my leave of Dr. Lloyd (Bishop of St. Asaph) at his house in Leicester Fields, now going to reside in his diocese.

12th. I dined at Mr. Brisbane's, Secretary to the Admiralty, a learned and industrious person, whither came Dr. Burnet, to thank me for some papers I had contributed towards his excellent History of the Reformation.

26th. I dined at Don Pietro Ronquillo's, the Spanish Ambassador, at Wild House,[1] who used me with extraordinary civility. The dinner was plentiful, half after the Spanish, half after the English way. After dinner, he led me into his bedchamber, where we fell into a long discourse concerning religion. Though he was a learned man in politics, and an advocate, he was very ignorant in religion, and unable to defend any point of controversy; he was, however, far from being fierce. At parting, he earnestly wished me to apply humbly to the Blessed Virgin to direct me, assuring me that he had known divers who had been averse from the Roman Catholic religion, wonderfully enlightened and convinced by her intercession. He importuned me to come and visit him often.

29th. But one shower of rain all this month.

5th May. Came to dine with me Sir William Fermor, of Northamptonshire, and Sir Christopher Wren, his Majesty's Architect and Surveyor, now building the Cathedral of St. Paul, and the Column in memory of the City's conflagration, and was in hand with the building of fifty parish churches. A wonderful genius had this incomparable person.

16th. Came my Lady Sunderland, to desire that I would

---

[1] Near Drury Lane.

propose a match to Sir Stephen Fox for her son, Lord Spencer, to marry Mrs. Jane, Sir Stephen's daughter. I excused myself all I was able; for the truth is, I was afraid he would prove an extravagant man: for, though a youth of extraordinary parts, and had an excellent education to render him a worthy man, yet his early inclinations to extravagance made me apprehensive, that I should not serve Sir Stephen by proposing it, like a friend; this being now his only daughter, well-bred, and likely to receive a large share of her father's opulence. Lord Sunderland was much sunk in his estate by gaming and other prodigalities, and was now no longer Secretary of State, having fallen into displeasure of the King for siding with the Commons about the succession; but which, I am assured, he did not do out of his own inclination, or for the preservation of the Protestant religion; but by mistaking the ability of the party to carry it. However, so earnest and importunate was the Countess, that I did mention it to Sir Stephen, who said that it was too great an honour, that his daughter was very young as well as my Lord, and he was resolved never to marry her without the parties' mutual liking; with other objections which I neither would nor could contradict. He desired me to express to the Countess the great sense he had of the honour done him, that his daughter and her son were too young; that he would do nothing without her liking, which he did not think her capable of expressing judiciously, till she was sixteen or seventeen years of age, of which she now wanted four years, and that I would put it off as civilly as I could.

20th May. Our new curate preached, a pretty hopeful young man, yet somewhat raw, newly come from college, full of Latin sentences, which in time will wear off. He read prayers very well.

25th. There came to visit me Sir William Walter and Sir John Elowes: and, the next day, the Earl of Kildare, a young gentleman related to my wife, and other company. There had scarce fallen any rain since Christmas.

2nd June. I went to Hampton Court, when the Surrey gentlemen presented their addresses to his Majesty, whose hand I kissed, introduced by the Duke of Albemarle. Being at the Privy Council, I took another occasion of discoursing with Sir Stephen Fox about his daughter and to revive that business, and at last brought it to this: That, in case the young people liked one the other, after four years, he first desiring to see a particular of my Lord's present estate if I could transmit it to him privately, he would make her portion €14,000, though to all appearance he might likely make it £50,000 as easily, his eldest son having no child, and growing very corpulent.

12th June. It still continued so great a drought as had never been known in England, and it was said to be universal.

14th August. No sermon this afternoon, which I think did not happen twice in this parish these thirty years; so gracious has God been to it, and indeed to the whole nation: God grant that we abuse not this great privilege. either by our wantonness, schism, or unfaithfulness, under such means as he has not favoured any other nation under Heaven besides !

23rd. I went to Wotton, and, on the following day, was invited to Mr. Denzil Onslow's at his seat at Purford, where was much company, and such an extraordinary feast, as I had hardly seen at any country gentleman's table. What made it more remarkable was, that there was not anything save what his estate about it did afford; as venison, rabbits, hares, pheasants, partridges, pigeons, quails, poultry, all sorts of fowl in season from his own decoy near his house, and all sorts of fresh fish. After dinner, we went to see sport at the decoy, where I never saw so many herons.

The seat stands on a flat, the ground pasture, rarely watered, and exceedingly improved since Mr. Onslow bought it of Sir Robert Parkhurst, who spent a fair estate. The house is timber, but commodious, and with one ample d ning-room, the hall adorned with paintings of fowl and huntings, &c., the work of Mr. Barlow, who is excellent in this kind from the life.[1]

30th. From Wotton I went to see Mr. Hussey,[2] (at Sutton in Shere), who has a very pretty seat well watered,

---

[1] This house has been pulled down many years. The estate is the property of the Onslow family.

[2] *Ante*, p. 56.

near my brother's. He is the neatest husband for curious ordering his domestic and field accommodations, and what pertains to husbandry, that I have ever seen, as to his granaries, tacklings, tools, and utensils, ploughs, carts, stables, wood-piles, wood-house, even to hen-roosts and hog-troughs. Methought, I saw old Cato, or Varro, in him; all substantial, all in exact order. The sole inconvenience he lies under, is the great quantity of sand which the stream brings along with it, and fills his canals and receptacles for fish too soon. The rest of my time of stay at Wotton was spent in walking about the grounds and goodly woods, where I have in my youth so often entertained my solitude; and so, on the 2nd of September, I once more returned to my home.

6th September. Died my pretty grandchild, and was interred on the 8th [at Deptford].

14th. Dined with Sir Stephen Fox, who proposed to me the purchasing of Chelsea College, which his Majesty had sometime since given to our Society, and would now purchase it again to build an hospital; or infirmary for soldiers there, in which he desired my assistance as one of the Council of the Royal Society.

15th. I had another opportunity of visiting his Majesty's private library, at Whitehall.

To Sir Samuel Morland's, to see his house and mechanics.[1]

17th. I went with Monsieur Faubert about taking the Countess of Bristol's house for an academy, he being lately come from Paris for his religion, and resolving to settle here.[2]

· In Lambeth, at what is now Vauxhall, where Sir Samuel Morland had fitted up a house. It contained a large room, furnished magnificently, and elaborate fountains constructed in the garden. He was much in favour with Charles the Second for services he had rendered to him while abroad, and this is probably the place to which it is said the King and his Ladies used to cross the water to go to. See Manning and Bray's *Hist. Surrey* iii. 489, 490, 491. Poor Sir Samuel became blind at last, and seems to have suffered from a sort of religious melancholy. See *post*, p. 350.

² He had a riding-house between Swallow Street (now replaced by Regent Street) and King Street; the passage by it between those streets is still called by his name.

23rd September. I went to see Sir Thomas Bond's fine ouse and garden, at Peckham.

2nd October. I went to Camberwell, where that good man Dr. Parr (late chaplain to Archbishop Usher) preached on Acts xvi. 30.

11th. To Fulham, to visit the Bishop of London, in whose garden I first saw the *Sedum arborescens* in flower, which was exceedingly beautiful.

5th November. Dr. Hooper preached on Mark xii. 16, 17, before the King, of the usurpation of the Church of Rome. This is one of the first rank of pulpit men in the nation.[1]

15th. I dined with the Earl of Essex who, after dinner in his study, where we were alone, related to me how much he had been scandalized and injured in the report of his being privy to the marriage of his Lady's niece, the rich young widow of the late Lord Ogle, sole daughter of the Earl of Northumberland; showing me a letter of Mr. Thynn's, excusing himself for not communicating his marriage to his Lordship. He acquainted me also with the whole story of that unfortunate lady being betrayed by her grandmother, the Countess of Northumberland, and Colonel Bret, for money; and that though, upon the importunity of the Duke of Monmouth, he had delivered to the grandmother a particular of the jointure which Mr. Thynn pretended he would settle on the lady, yet he totally discouraged the proceeding, as by no means a competent match for one that both by birth and fortune might have pretended to the greatest prince in Christendom; that he also proposed the Earl of Kingston, or the Lord Cranburn, but was by no means for Mr. Thynn.[2]

[1] George Hooper, afterwards Dean of Canterbury, Bishop of St. Asaph, and then translated to the see of Bath and Wells. He died in 1727.

[2] Thomas Thynne, Esq., of Longleat Hall, Wilts. He had married the young widow of Lord Ogle, but the marriage was never consummated; and he had previously seduced, under a promise of marriage, a young lady, who is said to have been in some way instrumental to his murder. Hence the burlesque epitaph:

" Here lies Tom Thynne of Longleat Hall,
Who never would have miscarried,
Had he married the woman he lay withal;
Or laid with the woman he married."

19*th November*. I dined with my worthy friend, Mr. Ers-
kine, Master of the Charter-house, uncle to the Duchess of
Monmouth; a wise and learned gentleman, fitter to have
been a privy councillor and minister of state than to have
been laid aside.

24*th*. I was at the audience of the Russian Ambassador
before both their Majesties in the Banqueting-house. The
presents were carried before him, held up by his followers
in two ranks before the King's State, and consisted of
tapestry (one suite of which was doubtlessly brought from
France as being of that fabric, the Ambassador having
passed through that kingdom as he came out of Spain), a
large Persian carpet, furs of sable and ermine, &c.; but
nothing was so splendid and exotic as the Ambassador
who came soon after the King's restoration.[1] This present
Ambassador was exceedingly offended that his coach was
not permitted to come into the Court, till, being told that
no King's Ambassador did, he was pacified, yet requiring
an attestation of it under the hand of Sir Charles Cotterell, the Master of the Ceremonies; being, it seems, afraid
he should offend his Master, if he omitted the least punctilio.
It was reported he condemned his son to lose his head for
shaving off his beard, and putting himself in the French
mode at Paris, and that he would have executed it, had not
the French King interceded—but qy. of this.

30*th*. Sir Christopher Wren chosen President [of the
Royal Society], Mr. Austine, Secretary, with Dr. Plot, the
ingenious author of the *History of Oxfordshire*. There was a
most illustrious appearance.

1681-2. 11*th January*. I saw the audience of the Morocco
Ambassador,[2] his retinue not numerous. He was received

‡ Assuming the truth of what Lord Essex conveyed to Evelyn in the
text, the inclinations of the wealthy heiress were not consulted in her
union; and this may have given rise to the suspicion that she encouraged Count Königsmarke's addresses, and was privy to his murderous
designs upon her husband.

[1] *Ante*, vol. i. p. 393.

[2] Named Hamet. He made his public entry through London the
fifth of this month. On the thirtieth of May following, he was entertained at Oxford; and, about the same time, dined with Elias Ashmole, who made him a present of a magnifying glass. July 14, the
Ambassador took his leave of the King, and on the 23rd of the same

in the Banqueting-house, both their Majesties being present
He came up to the throne without making any sort of
reverence, not bowing his head, or body. He spake by a
renegado Englishman, for whose safe return there was a
promise. They were all clad in the Moorish habit, cassocks
of coloured cloth, or silk, with buttons and loops, over this
an *alhaga*, or white woollen mantle, so large as to wrap
both head and body, a sash, or small turban, naked-legged
and armed, but with leather socks like the Turks, rich
scymitar, and large calico sleeved shirts. The Ambassador
had a string of pearls oddly woven in his turban. I fancy the
old Roman habit was little different as to the mantle and
naked limbs. He was a handsome person, well-featured, of
a wise look, subtle, and extremely civil. Their presents
were lions and ostriches;[1] their errand about a peace at
Tangier. But the concourse and tumult of the people was
intolerable, so as the officers could keep no order, which
these strangers were astonished at at first, there being
nothing so regular, exact, and performed with such silence,
as is on all these public occasions of their country, and
indeed over all the Turkish dominions.

14*th January*. Dined at the Bishop of Rochester's, at the
Abbey, it being his marriage-day, after twenty-four years.
He related to me how he had been treated by Sir William
Temple, foreseeing that he might be a delegate in the concern of my Lady Ogle now likely to come in controversy
upon her marriage with Mr. Thynn; also, how earnestly
the late Earl of Danby, Lord Treasurer, sought his friendship, and what plain and sincere advice he gave him from
time to time about his miscarriages and partialities; particularly his outing Sir John Duncomb from being Chancellor
of the Exchequer, and Sir Stephen Fox, above all, from
being Paymaster of the Army. The Treasurer's excuse

month embarked for his own country. His visit, as Evelyn tells us,
excited not only much interest in the Court circles, but great popular
curiosity. The proof of this remains indeed in the different prints
of him which exist, and among them a large and fine one by Robert
White.

[1] Sir John Reresby informs us in his *Memoirs*, "that the Ambassador's present consisted of two lions and thirty ostriches; at which his
Majesty laughed, and said he knew nothing more proper to send by
way of return than a flock of geese."

and reason was, that Fox's credit was so over-great
with the bankers and monied men, that he could procure
none but by his means; "for that reason," replied the
Bishop, " I would have made him my friend, Sir Stephen being a person both honest and of credit." He
told him likewise of his stateliness and difficulty of access,
and several other miscarriages, and which indeed made him
hated.

24th January. To the Royal Society, where at the Council
we passed a new law for the more accurate consideration of
candidates, as whether they would really be useful; also,
concerning the honorary members, that none should be
admitted but by diploma.

This evening, I was at the entertainment of the Morocco
Ambassador at the Duchess of Portsmouth's glorious apartments at Whitehall, where was a great banquet of sweetmeats and music; but at which both the Ambassador and his
retinue behaved themselves with extraordinary moderation
and modesty, though placed about a long table, a lady
between two Moors, and amongst these were the King's
natural children, namely, Lady Lichfield and Sussex, the
Duchess of Portsmouth, Nelly, &c., concubines, and cattle
of that sort, as splendid as jewels and excess of bravery
could make them; the Moors neither admiring nor seeming
to regard anything, furniture or the like, with any earnestness, and but decently tasting of the banquet. They drank
a little milk and water, but not a drop of wine; they also
drank of a sorbet and jacolatt;[1] did not look about, or stare
on the ladies, or express the least surprise, but with a
courtly negligence in pace, countenance, and whole behaviour, answering only to such questions as were asked with
a great deal of wit and gallantry, and so gravely took leave
with this compliment, that God would bless the Duchess of
Portsmouth and the Prince, her son, meaning the little
Duke of Richmond. The King came in at the latter end,
just as the Ambassador was going away. In this manner
was this slave (for he was no more at home) entertained by
most of the nobility in town, and went often to Hyde Park
on horseback, where he and his retinue showed their extra-

___
[1] Sherbet and chocolate.

ordinary activity in horsemanship, and flinging and catching
their lances at full speed; they rode very short, and could
stand upright at full speed, managing their spears with
incredible agility.   He went sometimes to the theatres,
where, upon any foolish or fantastical action, he could not
forbear laughing, but he endeavoured to hide it with extraordinary modesty and gravity.   In a word, the Russian
Ambassador, still at Court, behaved himself like a clown,
compared to this civil heathen.

   27th January. This evening, Sir Stephen Fox acquainted
me again with his Majesty's resolution of proceeding in the
erection of a Royal Hospital for emerited soldiers on that
spot of ground which the Royal Society had sold to his Majesty for 1300*l.*, and that he would settle 5000*l.* per annum
on it, and build to the value of 20,000*l.* for the relief and
reception of four companies, namely, 400 men, to be as in a
college, or monastery. I was therefore desired by Sir Stephen
(who had not only the whole managing of this, but was, as
I perceived, himself to be a grand benefactor, as well it became him who had gotten so vast an estate by the soldiers)
to assist him, and consult what method to cast it in, as to
the government.   So, in his study we arranged the governor,
chaplain, steward, house-keeper, chirurgeon, cook, butler,
gardener, porter, and other officers, with their several salaries
and entertainments.   I would needs have a library, and
mentioned several books, since some soldiers might possibly
be studious, when they were at leisure to recollect.   Thus we
made the first calculations, and set down our thoughts to
be considered and digested better, to show his Majesty and
the Archbishop.   He also engaged me to consider of what
laws and orders were fit for the government, which was to be
in every respect as strict as in any religious convent.

   After supper, came in the famous treble, Mr. Abel, newly
returned from Italy ; I never heard a more excellent voice ;
one would have sworn it had been a woman's, it was so high,
and so well and skilfully managed, being accompanied by
Signor Francesco on the harpsichord.

   28th.   Mr. Pepys, late Secretary to the Admiralty,
showed me a large folio containing the whole mechanic part
and art of building royal ships and men of war, made by
Sir Anthony Dean, being so accurate a piece from the very

keel to the lead block, rigging, guns, victualling, manning, and even to every individual pin and nail, in a method so astonishing and curious, with a draught, both geometrical and in perspective, and several sections, that I do not think the world can show the like. I esteem this book as an extraordinary jewel.

7th February. My daughter, Mary, began to learn music of Signor Bartholomeo, and dancing of Monsieur Isaac, reputed the best masters.

Having had several violent fits of an ague, recourse was had to bathing my legs in milk up to the knees, made as hot as I could endure it; and sitting so in it in a deep churn, or vessel, covered with blankets, and drinking *carduus* posset, then going to bed and sweating, I not only missed that expected fit, but had no more, only continued weak, that I could not go to church till Ash-Wednesday, which I had not missed, I think, so long in twenty years, so gracious had God been to me.

After this warning and admonition, I now began to look over and methodise all my writings, accompts, letters, papers; inventoried the goods, and other articles of the house, and put things into the best order I could, and made my will; that now, growing in years, I might have none of these secular things and concerns to distract me, when it should please Almighty God to call me from this transitory life. With this, I prepared some special meditations and devotions for the time of sickness. The Lord Jesus grant them to be salutary for my poor soul in that day, that I may obtain mercy and acceptance!

1st March. My second grandchild was born, and christened the next day by our vicar at Sayes Court, by the name of John.[1] I beseech God to bless him!

2nd. Ash-Wednesday. I went to church: our vicar preached on Proverbs, showing what care and vigilance was required for the keeping of the heart upright. The Holy Communion followed, on which I gave God thanks for his gracious dealing with me in my late sickness, and affording me this blessed opportunity of praising Him in the congregation, and receiving the cup of salvation with new and serious resolutions.

[1] Who became his successor, and was created a baronet in 1713. See *Lysons,* iv. **377.**

Came to see and congratulate my recovery, Sir John Lowther, Mr. Herbert, Mr. Pepys, Sir Anthony Deane, and Mr. Hill.

10th March. This day was executed Colonel Vrats, and some of his accomplices, for the execrable murder of Mr. Thynn,[1] set on by the principal Koningsmark. He went to execution like an undaunted hero, as one that had done a friendly office for that base coward, Count Koningsmark, who had hopes to marry his widow, the rich Lady Ogle, and was acquitted by a corrupt jury, and so got away. Vrats told a friend of mine who accompanied him to the gallows, and gave him some advice, that he did not value dying of a rush, and hoped and believed God would deal with him like a gentleman. Never man went, so unconcerned for his sad fate.

24th. I went to see the corpse of that obstinate creature, Colonel Vrats, the King permitting that his body should be transported to his own country, he being of a good family, and one of the first embalmed by a particular art, invented by one William Russell, a coffin-maker, which preserved the body without disbowelling, or to appearance using any bituminous matter. The flesh was florid, soft, and full, as if the person were only sleeping. He had now been dead near fifteen days, and lay exposed in a very rich coffin lined with lead, too magnificent for so daring and horrid a murderer.

At the meeting of the Royal Society were exhibited some pieces of amber sent by the Duke of Brandenburg, in one of which was a spider, in another a gnat, both very entire. There was a discourse of the tingeing of glass, especially with red, and the difficulty of finding any red colour effectual to penetrate glass, among the glass-painters; that the most diaporous, as blue, yellow, &c., did not enter into the substance of what was ordinarily painted, more than very shallow, unless incorporated in the metal itself, other reds and whites not at all beyond the superfices.

5th April. To the Royal Society, where at a Council was regulated what collections should be published monthly, as formerly the transactions, which had of late been discontinued, but were now much called for by the curious abroad and at home.

[1] Who lies buried in Westminster Abbey; the manner of his death being represented on his monument.

12th April. I went this afternoon with several of the Roya.
Society to a supper which was all dressed, both fish and
flesh, in Monsieur Papin's digestors, by which the hardest
bones of beef itself, and mutton, were made as soft as cheese,
without water or other liquor, and with less than eight ounces
of coals, producing an incredible quantity of gravy ; and for
close of all, a jelly made of the bones of beef, the best for
clearness and good relish, and the most delicious that I had
ever seen, or tasted. We eat pike and other fish bones, and
all without impediment ; but nothing exceeded the pigeons,
which tasted just as if baked in a pie, all these being stewed
in their own juice, without any addition of water save what
swam about the digestor, as *in balneo ;* the natural juice of
all these provisions acting on the grosser substances, reduced
the hardest bones to tenderness ; but it is best descanted
with more particulars for extracting tinctures, preserving
and stewing fruit, and saving fuel, in Dr. Papin's book, published and dedicated to our Society, of which he is a member.
He is since gone to Venice with the late Resident here (and
also a member of our Society), who carried this excellent
mechanic, philosopher, and physician, to set up a philosophical meeting in that city. This philosophical supper
caused much mirth amongst us, and exceedingly pleased all
the company. I sent a glass of the jelly to my wife, to
the reproach of all that the ladies ever made of their best
hartshorn.[1]

The season was unusually wet, with rain and thunder.

25th May. I was desired by Sir Stephen Fox and Sir
Christopher Wren to accompany them to Lambeth, with the
plot and design of the College to be built at Chelsea, to have
the Archbishop's approbation. It was a quadrangle of 200
feet square, after the dimensions of the larger quadrangle at
Christ-Church, Oxford, for the accommodation of 440 persons, with governor and officers. This was agreed on.

The Duke and Duchess of York were just now come to
London, after his escape and shipwreck, as he went by sea
for Scotland.

[1] Denys Papin, a French physician and mathematician, who possessed
so remarkable a knowledge of mathematics, that he very nearly brought
the invention of the steam-engine into working order. He assisted Mr.
Boyle in his pneumatic experiments, and was afterwards mathematical
professor at Marpurg. He died in 1710.

28th May. At the Rolls' chapel preached the famous Dr.
Burnet on 2 Peter, i. 10, describing excellently well what
was meant by election ; viz. not the effect of any irreversible
decree, but so called because they embraced the Gospel
readily, by which they became elect, or precious to God. It
would be very needless to make our calling and election
sure, were they irreversible and what the rigid Presbyterians
pretend. In the afternoon, to St. Lawrence's church, a new
and cheerful pile.

29th. I gave notice to the Bishop of Rochester of what
Maimburg had published about the motives of the late
Duchess of York's perversion, in his History of Calvinism ;
and did myself write to the Bishop of Winchester[1] about it,
who being concerned in it, I urged him to set forth his vindication.

31st. The Morocco Ambassador being admitted an honorary member of the Royal Society, and subscribing his name
and titles in Arabic, I was deputed by the Council to go and
compliment him.

19th June. The Bantam,[2] or East India Ambassadors, (at
this time we had in London the Russian, Moroccan, and Indian Ambassadors,) being invited to dine at Lord George
Berkeley's (now Earl), I went to the entertainment to con-
template the exotic guests. They were both very hard-
favoured, and much resembling in countenance some sort of
monkeys. We eat at two tables, the Ambassadors and in-
terpreter by themselves. Their garments were rich Indian
silks, flowered with gold, *viz.* a close waistcoat to their knees,
drawers, naked legs, and on their heads caps made like fruit-
baskets. They wore poisioned daggers at their bosoms, the
hafts carved with some ugly serpents' or devils' heads, exceeding keen, and of Damascus metal. They wore no
sword. The second Ambassador (sent it seems to succeed
in case the first should die by the way in so tedious a journey), having been at Mecca, wore a Turkish or Arab sash, a
little part of the linen hanging down behind his neck, with

[1] Dr. Morley.
[2] The name of one was Pungearon Nia Para, of the other Kaia Nebbe,
or Keay Nabee. There are prints existing of both, representing them
exactly as here described. There were others in the embassy, but probably of inferior degree.

some other difference of habit, and was half a negro, bare
legged and naked feet, and deemed a very holy man. They
sate crossed-legged like Turks, and sometimes in the posture
of apes and monkeys; their nails and teeth as black as jet,
and shining, which being the effect, as to their teeth, of per-
petually chewing betel to preserve them from the tooth-ache.
much raging in their country, is esteemed beautiful.

The first ambassador was of an olive hue, a flat face,
narrow eyes, squat nose, and Moorish lips, no hair appeared;
they wore several rings of silver, gold, and copper on their
fingers, which was a token of knighthood, or nobility. They
were of Java Major, whose princes have been turned Ma-
homedans not above fifty years since; the inhabitants are
still pagans and idolaters. They seemed of a dull and heavy
constitution, not wondering at any thing they saw; but
exceedingly astonished how our law gave us propriety in
our estates, and so thinking we were all kings, for they could
not be made to comprehend how subjects could possess any
thing but at the pleasure of their Prince, they being all
slaves; they were pleased with the notion, and admired our
happiness. They were very sober, and I believe subtle in
their way. Their meat was cooked, carried up, and they
attended by several fat slaves, who had no covering save
drawers, which appeared very uncouth and loathsome. They
eat their pilaw, and other spoon-meat, without spoons, taking
up their pottage in the hollow of their fingers, and very
dexterously flung it into their mouths without spilling a
drop.

17th July. Came to dine with me, the Duke of Grafton
and the young Earl of Ossory, son to my most dear deceased
friend.

30th. Went to visit our good neighbour, Mr. Bohun,[1]
whose whole house is a cabinet of all elegancies, especially
Indian; in the hall are contrivances of Japan screens, instead of wainscot; and there is an excellent pendule clock
enclosed in the curious flower-work of Mr. Gibbon, in the
middle of the vestibule. The landscapes of the screens represent the manner of living, and country of the Chinese
But, above all, his lady's cabinet is adorned on the fret

[1] This was at Lee.   See Hasted's *History of Kent*, vol. i. p. 67.

ceiling, and chimney-piece, with Mr. Gibbon's best carving.
There are also some of Streeter's best paintings, and many
rich curiosities of gold and silver as growing in the mines.
The gardens are exactly kept, and the whole place very
agreeable and well watered. The owners are good neigh-
·bours, and Mr. Bohun has also built and endowed an hospital for eight poor people, with a pretty chapel, and every
necessary accommodation.

1st August. To the Bishop of London at Fulham, to review
the additions which Mr. Marshall had made to his curious
book of flowers in miniature, and collection of insects.

4th. With Sir Stephen Fox, to survey the foundations of
the Royal Hospital begun at Chelsea.

9th. The Council of the Royal Society had it recommended to them to be trustees and visitors, or supervisors,
of the Academy which Monsieur Faubert did hope to procure to be built by subscription of worthy gentlemen and
noblemen, for the education of youth, and to lessen the vast
expense the nation is at yearly by sending children into
France to be taught military exercises. We thought good
to give him all the encouragement our recommendation
could procure.

15th. Came to visit me Dr. Rogers, an acquaintance of
mine long since at Padua. He was then Consul of the
English nation, and student in that University, where he
proceeded Doctor in Physic; presenting me now with the
Latin oration he lately made upon the famous Dr. Harvey's
anniversary in the College of Physicians, at London.

20th. This night I saw another comet, near Cancer, very
bright, but the stream not so long as the former.

29th. Supped at Lord Clarendon's, with Lord Hyde, his
brother, now the great favourite, who invited himself to dine
at my house the Tuesday following.

30th October. Being my birthday, and I now entering my
great climacterical of 63, after serious recollections of the
years past, giving Almighty God thanks for all his merciful
preservations and forbearance, begging pardon for my sins
and unworthiness, and his blessing on me the year entering; I went with my Lady Fox to survey her building, and
give some directions for the garden at Chiswick;[1] the archi-

---

[1] See Lysons' *Environs,* ii. p. 209.

tect is Mr. May; somewhat heavy and thick, and not so well
understood; the garden much too narrow, the place without
water, near a highway, and near another great house of my
Lord Burlington, little land about it, so that I wonder at the
expense; but women will have their will.

25th November. I was invited to dine with Monsieur
Lionberg, the Swedish Resident, who made a magnificent
entertainment, it being the birthday of his King. There
dined the Duke of Albemarle, Duke of Hamilton, Earl of
Bath, Earl of Aylesbury, Lord Arran, Lord Castlehaven, the
son of him who was executed fifty years before, and several
great persons. I was exceedingly afraid of drinking (it
being a Dutch feast), but the Duke of Albemarle being
that night to wait on his Majesty, excess was prohibited;
and, to prevent all, I stole away and left the company as
soon as we rose from table.

.28th. I went to the Council of the Royal Society, for
the auditing the last year's accompt, where I was surprised
with a fainting fit that for a time took away my sight;
but God being merciful to me, I recovered it after a short
repose.

30th. I was exceedingly endangered and importuned to
stand the election,[1] having so many voices, but by favour of
my friends, and regard of my remote dwelling, and now
frequent infirmities, I desired their suffrages might be transferred to Sir John Hoskins, one of the Masters of Chancery; a most learned virtuoso as well as lawyer, who accordingly was elected.

7th December. Went to congratulate Lord Hyde (the
great favourite), newly made Earl of Rochester,[2] and lately
marrying his eldest daughter to the Earl of Ossory.

18th. I sold my East India adventure of £250 principal
for £750 to the Royal Society, after I had been in that
company twenty-five years, being extraordinary advanta-
geous, by the blessing of God.

23rd January, 1682-3. Sir Francis North, son to the Lord
North, and Lord Chief Justice, being made Lord Keeper
on the death of the Earl of Nottingham, the Lord Chancellor, I went to congratulate him. He is a most knowing,

[1] For President of the Royal Society.
[2] Laurence, second son of the Chancellor.

:earned, and ingenious man, and, besides being an excellent person, of an ingenious and sweet disposition, very skilful in music, painting, the new philosophy, and politer studies.

29th January. Supped at Sir Joseph Williamson's, where was a select company of our Society, Sir William Petty, Dr. Gale (that learned schoolmaster of St. Paul's),[1] Dr. Whistler, Mr. Hill, &c. The conversation was philosophical and cheerful, on divers considerable questions proposed; as of the hereditary succession of the Roman Emperors; the Pica mentioned in the preface to our Common Prayer, which signifies only the Greek Kalendarium. These were mixed with lighter subjects.

2nd February. I made my court at St. James's, when I saw the sea-charts of Captain Collins,[2] which that indus-trious man now brought to show the Duke, having taken all the coasting from the mouth of the Thames, as far as Wales, and exactly measuring every creek, island, rock, soundings, harbours, sands, and tides, intending next spring to proceed till he had finished the whole island, and that measured by chains and other instruments: a most exact and useful undertaking. He affirmed, that of all the maps put out since, there are none extant so true as those of Joseph Norden, who gave us the first in Queen Elizabeth's time; all since him are erroneous.

12th. This morning, I received the news of the death of my father-in-law, Sir Richard Browne, Knt. and Bart., who died at my house at Sayes Court this day at ten in the morning, after he had laboured under the gout and dropsy for near six months, in the 78th year of his age. The funeral was solemnized on the 19th at Deptford, with as much decency as the dignity of the person, and our rela-tion to him, required; there being invited the Bishop of Rochester, several noblemen, knights, and all the fraternity

---

[1] Dr. Thomas Gale; he was Greek Professor at Cambridge, Master of St. Paul's School, London, and subsequently Dean of York. He was the author of several scholastic works; and was counted among the most learned men of his time. Born in 1636: died in 1702.

[2] Probably a John Collins, who had been in the naval service of Venice, and who was employed at this time as an accountant in some of the government offices, was a contributor to the Transactions of the Royal Society, and wrote several mathematical works.

of the Trinity Company, of which he had been Master, and
others of the country. The vicar preached a short but
proper discourse on Psalm xxxix. 10, on the frailty of our
mortal condition, concluding with an ample and well-de-
served eulogy on the defunct, relating to his honourable
birth and ancestors, education, learning in Greek and Latin,
modern languages, travels, public employments, signal
loyalty, character abroad, and particularly the honour of
supporting the Church of England in its public worship
during its persecution by the late rebels' usurpation and
regicide, by the suffrages of divers Bishops, Doctors of the
church, and others, who found such an asylum in his house
and family at Paris, that in their disputes with the Papists
(then triumphing over it as utterly lost) they used to argue
for its visibility and existence from Sir R. Browne's chapel
and assembly there. Then he spake of his great and loyal
sufferings during thirteen years' exile with his present
Majesty, his return with him in the signal year 1660 ; his
honourable employment at home, his timely recess to recollect himself, his great age, infirmities, and death.

He gave to the Trinity-Corporation that land in Deptford
on which are built those alms-houses for twenty-four widows
of emerited seamen. He was born the famous year of the
Gunpowder Treason, in 1605, and being the last [male] of his
family, left my wife, his only daughter, heir. His grandfather, Sir Richard Browne, was the great instrument under
the great Earl of Leicester (favourite to Queen Elizabeth)
in his government of the Netherland. He was Master of
the Household to King James, and Cofferer ; I think was
the first who regulated the compositions through England
for the King's Household, provisions, progresses,[1] &c. which
was so high a service, and so grateful to the whole nation,
that he had acknowledgments and public thanks sent him
from all the counties ; he died by the rupture of a vein in
a vehement speech he made about the compositions in a
Parliament of King James. By his mother's side he was a

[1] Notice was taken of this in a previous passage of the Diary. The
different counties were bound to supply provisions of various kinds,
and these were collected by officers called purveyors, whose extortions
often excited the attention of Parliament. For a particular account of
their practices, see *Archæologia*, vol. iii. p. 349.

Gunson, Treasurer of the Navy in the reigns of Henry the
Eighth, Queen Mary, and Queen Elizabeth, and, as by his
large pedigree appears, related to divers of the English
nobility. Thus ended this honourable person, after so many
changes and tossings to and fro, in the same house where
he was born. "Lord teach us so to number our days, that
we may apply our hearts unto wisdom!"

By a special clause in his will, he ordered that his body
should be buried in the church-yard under the south-east
window of the chancel, adjoining to the burying places of
his ancestors, since they came out of Essex into Sayes
Court, he being much offended at the novel custom of
burying every one within the body of the church and
chancel; that being a favour heretofore granted to martyrs
and great persons; this excess of making churches charnel-
houses being of ill and irreverend example, and prejudicial
to the health of the living, besides the continual disturbance
of the pavement and seats, and several other indecencies.
Dr. Hall, the pious Bishop of Norwich, would also be so
interred,[1] as may be read in his testament.

16*th March.* I went to see Sir Josiah Child's prodigious
cost in planting walnut-trees about his seat,[2] and making
fishponds, many miles in circuit, in Epping Forest, in a
barren spot, as oftentimes these suddenly monied men for
the most part seat themselves. He from a merchant's
apprentice, and management of the East India Company's
stock, being arrived to an estate ('tis said) of £200,000;
and lately married his daughter to the eldest son of the
Duke of Beaufort, late Marquis of Worcester, with £50,000
portional present, and various expectations.

I dined at Mr. Houblon's,[3] a rich and gentle French
merchant, who was building a house in the Forest, near Sir
J. Child's, in a place where the late Earl of Norwich dwelt
some time, and which came from his lady, the widow of
Mr. Baker. It will be a pretty villa, about five miles from
Whitechapel.

[1] As was afterwards, at Fulham, Dr. Compton, Bishop of London,
who used to say, "The church-yard for the dead, the church for the
living."

[2] Where Wanstead House stood.

[3] The family were eminent merchants in the time of Queen Elizabeth.
—Morant's *Essex*, vol. ii. p. 513.

18th March. I went to hear Dr. Horneck preach at the Savoy Church, on Phil. ii. 5. He was a German born, a most pathetic preacher, a person of a saint-like life, and hath written an excellent treatise on Consideration.[1]

20th. Dined at Dr. Whistler's, at the Physicians' College, with Sir Thomas Millington, both learned men; Dr. W. the most facetious man in nature, and now Censor of the College. I was here consulted where they should build their library; it is pity this College is built so near Newgate Prison, and in so obscure a hole,[2] a fault in placing most of our public buildings and churches in the City, through the avarice of some few men, and his Majesty not overruling it, when it was in his power after the dreadful conflagration.

21st. Dr. Tenison preached at Whitehall on 1 Cor., vi. 12; I esteem him to be one of the most profitable preachers in the Church of England, being also of a most holy conversation, very learned and ingenious. The pains he takes and care of his parish will, I fear, wear him out, which would be an inexpressible loss.[3]

24th. I went to hear Dr. Charleton's lecture on the heart in the Anatomy Theatre at the Physicians' College.[4]

30th. To London, in order to my passing the following week, for the celebration of the Easter now approaching, there being in the Holy Week so many eminent preachers officiating at the Court and other places.

6th April. Good Friday. There was in the afternoon, according to custom, a sermon before the King, at Whitehall; Dr. Sprat preached for the Bishop of Rochester.

[1] The full title is "*The great Law of Consideration,* or a Discourse wherein the nature, usefulness, and absolute necessity of Consideration, in order to a truly serious and religious life, are laid open." It went through several editions.

[2] This fault was not amended till our own day. The new College in Pall Mall East was opened by Sir Henry Halford in 1825.

[3] Dr. Thomas Tenison succeeded Tillotson in the archiepiscopal See of Canterbury, having before been Vicar of St. Martin's in the Fields, and Bishop of Lincoln. He lived to a great age.

[4] Walter Charleton was with Charles II. during his exile, in the capacity of physician, and returned with him at the Restoration. He wrote on natural history, antiquities, theology, medicine, and natural philosophy. Died 1707.

17th April. I was at the launching of the last of the thirty
ships ordered to be new built by Act of Parliament, named
the Neptune, a second rate, one of the goodliest vessels of
the whole navy, built by my kind neighbour, young Mr.
Shish, his Majesty's master shipwright of this dock.

1st May. I went to Blackheath, to see the new fair, being
the first procured by the Lord Dartmouth. This was the
first day, pretended for the sale of cattle, but I think in
truth to enrich the new tavern at the bowling-green, erected
by Snape,[1] his Majesty's farrier, a man full of projects.
There appeared nothing but an innumerable assembly of
drinking people from London, pedlars, &c., and I suppose it
too near London to be of any great use to the country.

March was unusually hot and dry, and all April excessively wet.

I planted all the out-limits of the garden and long walks
with holly.[2]

9th. Dined at Sir Gabriel Sylvius's, and thence to
visit the Duke of Norfolk, to ask whether he would part
with any of his cartoons and other drawings of Raphael, and
the great masters; he told me if he might sell them all
together he would, but that the late Sir Peter Lely (our
famous painter) had gotten some of his best. The person
who desired me to treat for them was Vander Douse,
grandson to that great scholar, contemporary and friend of
Joseph Scaliger.

16th. Came to dinner and visit me Sir Richard Anderson,
of Pendley, and his lady, with whom I went to London.

8th June. On my return home from the Royal Society,
I found Mr. Wilbraham, a young gentleman of Cheshire.

11th. The Lord Dartmouth was elected Master of the
Trinity House; son to George Legge, late Master of the
Ordnance, and one of the Grooms of the Bedchamber; a
great favourite of the Duke's, an active and understanding
gentleman in sea-affairs.

---

[1] Mr. Granger mentions a print of this person by White, and says he
was father of Dr. Snape, of Eton; members of the same family had
been serjeant-farriers to the Sovereign for three hundred years.

[2] Evelyn adds a note: " 400 feet in length, 9 feet high, 5 in diameter,
in my now ruined garden, thanks to the Czar of Muscovy."—*Sylva,*
book ii. chap. vi.

13*th June*. To our Society, where we received the Count de Zinzendorp, Ambassador from the Duke of Saxony, a fine young man: we showed him divers experiments on the Magnet, on which subject the Society were upon.

16*th*. I went to Windsor, dining by the way at Chiswick, at Sir Stephen Fox's, where I found Sir Robert Howard (that universal pretender), and Signor Verrio, who brought his draught and designs for the painting of the staircase of Sir Stephen's new house.

That which was new at Windsor since I was last there, and was surprising to me, was the incomparable fresco painting in St. George's Hall, representing the legend of St. George, and triumph of the Black Prince, and his reception by Edward III.; the volto, or roof, not totally finished; then the Resurrection in the Chapel, where the figure of the Ascension is, in my opinion, comparable to any paintings of the most famous Roman masters; the Last Supper, also over the altar. I liked the contrivance of the unseen organ behind the altar, nor less the stupendous and beyond all description the incomparable carving of our Gibbon, who is, without controversy, the greatest master both for invention and rareness of work, that the world ever had in any age; nor doubt I at all that he will prove as great a master in the statuary art.

Verrio's invention is admirable, his ordnance full and flowing, antique and heroical; his figures move; and, if the walls hold (which is the only doubt by reason of the salts which in time and in this moist climate prejudice, the work will preserve his name to ages.

There was now the terrace brought almost round the old Castle; the grass made clean, even, and curiously turfed; the avenues to the new park, and other walks, planted with elms and limes, and a pretty canal, and receptacle for fowl; nor less observable and famous is the throwing so huge a quantity of excellent water to the enormous height of the Castle, for the use of the whole house, by an extraordinary invention of Sir Samuel Morland.[1]

17*th June*. I dined at the Earl of Sunderland's with the Earls of Bath, Castlehaven, Lords Viscounts Falconberg Falkland, Bishop of London, the Grand Master of Malta,

[1] See *ante*, p. 167.

brother to the Duke de Vendôme (a young wild spark), and Mr. Dryden, the poet. After evening prayer, I walked in the park with my Lord Clarendon, where we fell into discourse of the Bishop of Salisbury (Dr. Seth Ward), his subtlety, &c. Dr. Durell, late Dean of Windsor, being dead, Dr. Turner, one of the Duke's chaplains was made dean.

- I visited my Lady Arlington, Groom of the Stole to her Majesty, who being hardly set down to supper, word was brought her that the Queen was going into the park to walk, it being now near eleven at night; the alarm caused the Countess to rise in all haste, and leave her supper to us.

By this one may take an estimate of the extreme slavery and subjection that courtiers live in, who have not time to eat and drink at their pleasure. It put me in mind of Horace's *Mouse*, and to bless God for my own private condition.

Here was Monsieur de l'Angle, the famous minister of Charenton, lately fled from the persecution in France, concerning the deplorable condition of the Protestants there.

18*th June*. I was present, and saw and heard the humble submission and petition of the Lord Mayor, Sheriffs, and Aldermen, on behalf of the City of London, on the *quo warranto* against their charter, which they delivered to his Majesty in the presence-chamber. It was delivered kneeling, and then the King and Council went into the council-chamber, the Mayor and his brethren attending still in the presence-chamber. After a short space, they were called in, and my Lord Keeper made a speech to them, exaggerating the disorderly and riotous behaviour in the late election, and polling for Papillon and Du Bois after the Common-hall had been formally dissolved: with other misdemeanours, libels on the government, &c., by which they had incurred his Majesty's high displeasure: and that but for this submission, and under such articles as the King should require their obedience to, he would certainly enter judgment against them, which hitherto he had suspended. The things required were as follows: that they should neither elect Mayor, Sheriffs, Aldermen, Recorder, Common Serjeant, Town-Clerk, Coroner, nor Steward of Southwark, without his Majesty's approbation; and that if they presented any his Majesty did not like, they should proceed in wonted manner to a second choice; if that was disapproved, his Majesty to nominate them; and if within five days they thought good to assent to this, all former miscarriages should be forgotten. And so they tamely parted with their so ancient privileges after they had dined and been treated by the King. This was a signal and most remarkable period. What the consequences will prove, time will show. Divers of the old and most learned lawyers and judges were of opinion that they could not forfeit their charter, but might be personally punished for their misdemeanours; but the plurality of the younger judges and rising men judged it otherwise.

The Popish Plot also, which had hitherto made such a noise, began now sensibly to dwindle, through the folly, knavery, impudence, and giddiness of Oates, so as the Papists began to hold up their heads higher than ever, and those who had fled, flocked to London from abroad. Such sudden changes and eager doings there had been, without anything steady or prudent, for these last seven years.

19th June. I returned to town in a coach with the Earl of Clarendon,[1] when passing by the glorious palace of his father, built but a few years before, which they were now demolishing, being sold to certain undertakers, I turned my head the contrary way till the coach had gone past it, lest I might minister occasion of speaking of it; which must needs have grieved him, that in so short a time their pomp was fallen.

28th. After the Popish Plot, there was now a new and (as they called it) a Protestant Plot discovered, that certain Lords and others should design the assassination of the King and the Duke as they were to come from Newmarket, with a general rising of the nation, and especially of the City of London, disaffected to the present Government. Upon which were committed to the Tower, the Lord Russell, eldest son of the Earl of Bedford, the Earl of Essex, Mr. Algernon Sidney, son to the old Earl of Leicester, Mr. Trenchard, Hampden, Lord Howard of Escrick, and others.

---

[1] Henry Hyde, the second Earl, appointed Lord-Lieutenant of Ireland in 1686, and died October 31, 1709, a Governor of the Charter-House, High Steward of the University of Oxford, and F.R.S.

A proclamation was issued against my Lord Grey, the Duke
of Monmouth, Sir Thomas Armstrong, and one Ferguson,
who had escaped beyond sea; of these some were said to be
for killing the King, others for only seizing on him, and persuading him to new counsels, on the pretence of the danger
of Popery, should the Duke live to succeed, who was now
again admitted to the councils and cabinet secrets. The
Lords Essex and Russell were much deplored, for believing
they had any evil intention against the King, or the Church;
some thought they were cunningly drawn in by their enemies for not approving some late counsels and management
relating to France, to Popery, to the persecution of the Dissenters, &c. They were discovered by the Lord Howard of
Escrick and some false brethren of the club, and the design
happily broken; had it taken effect, it would, to all appearance, have exposed the Government to unknown and dangerous events; which God avert!

Was born my grand-daughter at Sayes Court, and christened by the name of Martha Maria, our Vicar officiating.
I pray God bless her, and may she choose the better part!

13th July. As I was visiting Sir Thomas Yarborough and
his Lady[1] in Covent Garden, the astonishing news was
brought to us of the Earl of Essex having cut his throat,
having been but three days a prisoner in the Tower, and
this happening on the very day and instant that Lord
Russell was on his trial, and had sentence of death. This
accident exceedingly amazed me, my Lord Essex being so
well known by me to be a person of such sober and religious
deportment, so well at his ease, and so much obliged to the
King. It is certain the King and Duke were at the Tower,
and passed by his window about the same time this morning, when my Lord asking for a razor, shut himself into a
closet, and perpetrated the horrid act. Yet it was wondered by some how it was possible he should do it in the
manner he was found, for the wound was so deep and wide,
that being cut through the gullet, wind-pipe, and both the
iugulars, it reached to the very vertebræ of the neck, so
that the head held to it by a very little skin as it were; the
gapping too of the razor, and cutting his own fingers, was a

[1] The lady was Mary Blagg, of whom Count Hamilton says so much;
and sister of Mr. Blagg, of whom Evelyn speaks so much

little strange; but more, that having passed the jugulars he should have strength to proceed so far, that an executioner could hardly have done more with an axe. There were odd reflections upon it.[1]

The fatal news coming to Hicks's Hall upon the article of my Lord Russell's trial, was said to have had no little influence on the Jury and all the Bench to his prejudice. Others said that he had himself on some occasions hinted that in case he should be in danger of having his life taken from him by any public misfortune, those who thirsted for his estate should miss of their aim; and that he should speak favourably of that Earl of Northumberland,[2] and some others, who made away with themselves; but these are discourses so unlike his sober and prudent conversation, that I have no inclination to credit them. What might instigate him to this devilish act, I am not able to conjecture. My Lord Clarendon, his brother-in-law, who was with him but the day before, assured me he was then very cheerful, and declared it to be the effect of his innocence and loyalty; and most believe that his Majesty had no severe intentions against him, though he was altogether inexorable as to Lord Russell and some of the rest. For my part, I believe the crafty and ambitious Earl of Shaftesbury had brought them into some dislike of the present carriage of matters at Court, not with any design of destroying the monarchy (which Shaftesbury had in confidence and for unanswerable reasons told me he would support to his last breath, as having seen and felt the misery of being under mechanic tyranny), but perhaps of setting up some other whom he might govern, and frame to his own platonic fancy, without much regard to the religion established under the hierarchy, for which he had no esteem; but when he perceived those whom he had engaged to rise, fail of his expectations, and the day past, reproaching his accomplices that a second day for an exploit of this nature was never

---

[1] Bishop Burnet, after making inquiry, by desire of the Countess, declares that he does not believe that Essex was murdered. *Own Times,* vol. i. p. 569.

[2] Henry Percy, eighth Earl of Northumberland, shot himself in the Tower, to which he had been committed on a charge of high treason, in June 1585.

successful, he gave them the slip, and got into Holland, where the fox died, three months before these unhappy Lords and others were discovered or suspected. Every one deplored Essex and Russell, especially the last, as being thought to have been drawn in on pretence only of endeavouring to rescue the King from his present councillors, and secure religion from Popery, and the nation from arbitrary government, now so much apprehended; whilst the rest of those who were fled, especially Ferguson and his gang, had doubtless some bloody design to get up a Commonwealth, and turn all things topsy-turvy. Of the same tragical principles is Sydney.

I had this day much discourse with Monsieur Pontaq, son to the famous and wise prime President of Bordeaux. This gentleman was owner of that excellent vignoble of Pontaq and O'Brien, from whence come the choicest of our Bourdeaux wines; and I think I may truly say of him, what was not so truly said of St. Paul, that much learning had made him mad. He had studied well in philosophy, but chiefly the Rabbins, and was exceedingly addicted to cabalistical fancies, an eternal hablador [romancer], and half distracted by reading abundance of the extravagant Eastern Jews. He spake all languages, was very rich, had a handsome person, and was well-bred, about forty-five years of age.[1]

14th July. I visited Mr. Fraser, a learned Scots gentleman, whom I had formerly recommended to Lord Berkeley for the instruction and government of his son, since dead at sea. He had now been in Holland at the sale of the learned Heinsius's library, and showed me some very rare and curious books, and some MSS., which he had purchased to good value. There were three or four Herbals in miniature,

---

[1] In a later page of the Diary (post, p. 339) Evelyn describes himself and certain members of the Royal Society all dining "at Pontac's as usual." Pontac's was a famous French eating-house, now existing only in the verse of Dryden, the prose of Swift and Defoe, and other such imperishable records. Defoe describes its name as derived from the owner of the most celebrated claret vintage of France; the president of the parliament of Bourdeaux; the "M. Pontaq" above referred to, established it; and Swift, who dined at it seventeen years after the dinner mentioned by Evelyn, tells Stella that the wine was charged seven shillings a flask. "Are not these pretty rates?"

accurately done, divers Roman antiquities of Verona, and very many books of Aldus's impression.

15th July. A stranger, and old man, preached on Jerem. vi. 8, the not hearkening to instruction, portentous of desolation to a people; much after Bishop Andrews's method, full of logical divisions, in short and broken periods, and Latin sentences, now quite out of fashion in the pulpit, which is grown into a far more profitable way, of plain and practical discourses, of which sort this nation, or any other, never had greater plenty or more profitable (I am confident); so much has it to answer for thriving no better on it.

The public was now in great consternation on the late plot and conspiracy; his Majesty very melancholy, and not stirring without double guards; all the avenues and private doors about Whitehall and the Park shut up, few admitted to walk in it. The Papists, in the mean time, very jocund; and indeed with reason, seeing their own plot brought to nothing, and turned to ridicule, and now a conspiracy of Protestants, as they called them.

The Turks were likewise in hostility against the German Emperor, almost masters of the Upper Hungary, and drawing towards Vienna. On the other side, the French King (who it is believed brought in the infidels) disturbing his Spanish and Dutch neighbours, having swallowed up almost all Flanders, pursuing his ambition of a fifth universal monarchy; and all this blood and disorder in Christendom had evidently its rise from our defections at home, in a wanton peace, minding nothing but luxury, ambition, and to procure money for our vices. To this add our irreligion and atheism, great ingratitude, and self-interest; the apostacy of some, and the suffering the French to grow so great, and the Hollanders so weak. In a word, we were wanton, mad, and surfeiting with prosperity; every moment unsettling the old foundations, and never constant to any thing. The Lord in mercy avert the sad omen, and that we do not provoke him till he bear it no longer!

This summer did we suffer twenty French men-of-war to pass our Channel towards the Sound, to help the Danes against the Swedes, who had abandoned the French interest, we not having ready sufficient to guard our coasts, or take cognizance of what they did; though the nation never had more, or a better navy, yet the sea had never so slender a fleet.

19th July. George, Prince of Denmark, who had landed this day, came to marry the Lady Anne, daughter to the Duke; so I returned home, having seen the young gallant at dinner at Whitehall.

20th. Several of the conspirators of the lower form were executed at Tyburn; and the next day,

21st. Lord Russell was beheaded in Lincoln's-Inn-Fields, the executioner giving him three butcherly strokes. The speech he made, and the paper which he gave the Sheriff declaring his innocence, the nobleness of the family, the piety and worthiness of the unhappy gentleman, wrought much pity, and occasioned various discourses on the plot.

25th. I again saw Prince George of Denmark : he had the Danish countenance, blonde, of few words, spake French but ill, seemed somewhat heavy, but reported to be valiant, and indeed he had bravely rescued and brought off his brother, the King of Denmark, in a battle against the Swedes, when both these Kings were engaged very smartly.

28th. He was married to the Lady Anne at Whitehall. Her court and household to be modelled as the Duke's, her father, had been; and they to continue in England.

1st August. Came to see me Mr. Flamsted, the famous astronomer, from his Observatory at Greenwich, to draw the meridian from my pendule, &c.

2nd. The Countesses of Bristol and Sunderland, aunt and cousin-german of the late Lord Russell, came to visit me, and condole his sad fate. The next day, came Colonel Russell, uncle to the late Lord Russell, and brother to the Earl of Bedford, and with him Mrs. Middleton, that famous and indeed incomparable beauty, daughter to my relation, Sir Robert Needham.

19th. I went to Bromley to visit our Bishop,[1] and excellent neighbour, and to congratulate his now being made Archbishop of York. On the 28th, he came to take his leave of us, now preparing for his journey and residence in his province.

28th. My sweet little grandchild, Martha Maria, died, and on the 29th was buried in the parish church.

[1] Dr. John Dolbein.

2nd September. This morning, was read in the church, after the office was done, the Declaration setting forth the late conspiracy against the King's person.

3rd. I went to see what had been done by the Duke of Beaufort on his late purchased house at Chelsea, which I once had the selling of for the Countess of Bristol; he had made great alterations, but might have built a better house with the materials and the cost he had been at.

Saw the Countess of Monte Feltre, whose husband I had formerly known; he was a subject of the Pope's, but becoming a Protestant he resided in England, and married into the family of the Savilles, of Yorkshire. The Count, her late husband, was a very learned gentleman, a great politician, and a goodly man. She was accompanied by her sister, exceedingly skilled in painting, nor did they spare for colour / on their own faces. They had a great deal of wit.

9th. It being the day of public thanksgiving for his Majesty's late preservation, the former declaration was again read, and there was an office used, composed for the occasion. A loyal sermon was preached on the divine right of Kings, from Psalm cxliv. 10. "Thou hast preserved David from the peril of the sword."

15th. Came to visit me the learned anatomist, Dr. Tyson,· with some other Fellows of our Society.

16th. At the elegant villa and garden of Mr. Bohun, at Lee. He showed me the zinnar tree, or platanus, and told me that since they had planted this kind of tree about the city of Ispahan, in Persia, the plague, which formerly much infested the place, had exceedingly· abated of its mortal effects, and rendered it very healthy.

18th. I went to London, to visit the Duchess of Grafton, now great with child, a most virtuous and beautiful lady. Dining with her at my Lord Chamberlain's, met my Lord of St. Alban's, now grown so blind, that he could not see to

[1] Doctor Edward Tyson, a learned physician, born at Clevedon, Somersetshire, in 1649, who became reader of the anatomical lecture in Surgeons' Hall, and physician to the hospitals of Bethlehem and Bridewell, which offices he held at his death, Aug. 1, 1708. He was an ingenious writer, and has left various Essays in the Philosophical Transactions and Hook's Collections. He published also "The Anatomy of a Porpoise dissected at Gresham College," and the "Anatomy of a Pigmy compared with a Monkey, an Ape, and a Man," 4to., 1698-9.

take his meat. He has lived a most easy life, in plenty even
abroad, whilst his Majesty was a sufferer; he has lost immense sums at play, which yet, at about eighty years old, he
continues, having one that sits by him to name the spots on
the cards. He eat and drank with extraordinary appetite.
He is a prudent old courtier, and much enriched since his
Majesty's return.

After dinner, I walked to survey the sad demolition of
Clarendon-House, that costly and only sumptuous palace of
the late Lord Chancellor Hyde, where I have often been so
cheerful[1] with him, and sometimes so sad:[1] happening to make
him a visit but the day before he fled from the angry Parliament, accusing him of mal-administration, and being envious
at his grandeur, who from a private lawyer came to be father-
in-law to the Duke of York, and as some would suggest,
designing his Majesty's marriage with the Infanta of Portugal, not apt to breed. To this they imputed much of our
unhappiness; and that he, being sole minister and favourite
at his Majesty's restoration, neglected to gratify the King's
suffering party, preferring those who were the cause of our
troubles. But perhaps as many of these things were inju-
riously laid to his charge, so he kept the government far
steadier than it has proved since. I could name some who I
think contributed greatly to his ruin,—the buffoons and the
misses, to whom he was an eye-sore. It is true he was
of a jolly temper, after the old English fashion; but France
had now the ascendant, and we were become quite another
nation. The Chancellor gone, and dying in exile, the Earl
his successor sold that which cost £50,000 building, to the
young Duke of Albemarle for £25,000, to pay debts which
how contracted remains yet a mystery, his son being no way
a prodigal. Some imagine the Duchess his daughter had
been chargeable to him. However it were, this stately
palace is decreed to ruin, to support the prodigious waste the
Duke of Albemarle had made of his estate, since the old man
died.   He sold it to the highest bidder, and it fell to
certain rich bankers and mechanics, who gave for it and the
ground about it, £35,000; they design a new town, as it

---

[1] An engraving of the south or principal front of this noble mansion,
copied from an extremely rare print, is given in Smith's Sixty-two Additional Plates to his Antiquities of Westminster, 4to., 1807.

were, and a most magnificent piazza [square]. It is said they
have already materials towards it with what they sold of the
house alone, more worth than what they paid for it. See the
vicissitudes of earthly things! I was astonished at this
demolition, nor less at the little army of labourers and arti-
ficers levelling the ground, laying foundations, and contriving
great buildings at an expense of £200,000, if they perfect
their design.[1]

19th *September.* In my walks I stepped into a goldbeater's
workhouse, where he showed me the wonderful ductility of
that spreading and oily metal. He said it must be finer
than the standard, such as was old angel-gold, and that of
such he had once to the value of £100 stamped with the
agnus dei, and coined at the time of the holy war; which had
been found in a ruined wall somewhere in the north, near to
Scotland, some of which he beat into leaves, and the rest
sold to the curiosi in antiquities and medals.

23rd. We had now the welcome tidings of the King of
Poland raising the siege of Vienna, which had given terror
to all Europe, and utmost reproach to the French, who it is
believed brought in the Turks for diversion, that the French
King might the more easily swallow Flanders, and pursue
his unjust conquest on, the empire, whilst we sat unconcerned
and under a deadly charm from somebody.

There was this day a collection for rebuilding Newmarket,

[1] In a letter to Lord Cornbury, dated Sayes Court, 20th January,
1665-6, Evelyn having then just returned from a visit to Clarendon
House, says: "I went with prejudice and a critical spirit, incident to those
who fancy they know anything in art; I acknowledge that I have never
seen a nobler pile. My old friend and fellow-traveller (inhabitants and
contemporaries at Rome) has perfectly acquitted himself. It is, without
hyperbole, the best contrived, the most useful, graceful, and magnificent
house in England; I except not Audley-End, which though larger and
full of gaudy barbarous ornaments, does not gratify judicious spectators.
Here is state and use, solidity and beauty, most symmetrically com-
bined together. Nothing abroad pleases me better, nothing at home
approaches it. I have no design to gratify the architect beyond what I
am obliged as a professed honourer of virtue wheresoever it is conspicuous; but when I had seriously contemplated every room (for I went
into them all, from the cellar to the platform on the roof), seen how well
and judiciously the walls were erected, the arches cut and turned, the
timber braced, their scantlings and contignations disposed, I was most
highly satisfied, and do acknowledge myself to have much improved by
what I observed."

consumed by an accidental fire, which removing his Majesty
thence sooner than was intended, put by the assassins, who
were disappointed of their rendezvous and expectation by a
wonderful providence. This made the King more earnest to
render Winchester the seat of his autumnal field-diversions
for the future, designing a palace there, where the ancient
castle stood; infinitely indeed preferable to Newmarket
for prospects, air, pleasure, and provisions. The surveyor
has already begun the foundation for a palace, estimated to
cost £35,000, and his Majesty is purchasing ground about
it to make a park, &c.

4th October. I went to London, on receiving a note from
the Countess of Arlington, of some considerable charge or
advantage I might obtain by applying myself to his Majesty
on this signal conjuncture of his Majesty entering-up judgment against the City-charter; the proposal made me I
wholly declined, not being well satisfied with these violent
transactions, and not a little sorry that his Majesty was so
often put upon things of this nature against so great a City,
the consequence whereof may be so much to his prejudice;
so I returned home. At this time, the Lord Chief-Justice
Pemberton was displaced. He was held to be the most
learned of the judges, and an honest man. Sir George
Jeffreys was advanced, reputed to be most ignorant, but most
daring. Sir George Treby, Recorder of London, was also
put by, and one Genner, an obscure lawyer, set in his place.
Eight of the richest and chief aldermen were removed, and
all the rest made only justices of the peace, and no more
wearing of gowns, or chains of gold; the Lord Mayor and
two Sheriffs holding their places by new grants as *custodes*,
at the King's pleasure. The pomp and grandeur of the
most august City in the world thus changed face in a moment; which gave great occasion of discourse and thoughts
of hearts, what all this would end in. Prudent men were
for the old foundations.

Following his Majesty this morning through the gallery,
I went with the few who attended him, into the Duchess
of Portsmouth's *dressing-room* within her bed-chamber,
where she was in her morning loose garment, her maids
combing her, newly out of her bed, his Majesty and the
gallants standing about her; but that which engaged my

curiosity, was the rich and splendid furniture of this woman's apartment, now twice or thrice pulled down and rebuilt to satisfy her prodigal and expensive pleasures, whilst her Majesty's does not exceed some gentlemen's ladies in furniture and accommodation.   Here I saw the new fabric of French tapestry, for design, tenderness of work, and incomparable imitation of the best paintings, beyond any thing I had ever beheld.   Some pieces had Versailles, St. Germains, and other palaces of the French King, with huntings, figures, and landscapes, exotic fowls, and all to the life rarely done.   Then for Japan cabinets, skreens, pendule clocks, great vases of wrought plate, tables, stands, chimney-furniture, sconces, branches, braseras, &c., all of massy silver and out of number, besides some of her Majesty's best paintings.

Surfeiting of this, I dined at Sir Stephen Fox's and went contented home to my poor, but quiet villa.   What contentment can there be in the riches and splendour of this world, purchased with vice and dishonour?

10th October.   Visited the Duchess of Grafton, not yet brought to bed, and dining with my Lord Chamberlain (her father), went with them to see Montague-House,[1] a palace lately built by Lord Montague, who had married the most beautiful Countess of Northumberland.[2]   It is a stately and ample palace.   Signor Verrio's fresco paintings, especially the funeral pile of Dido, on the staircase, the labours of Hercules, fight with the Centaurs, his effeminacy with Dejanira, and Apotheosis or reception among the gods, on the walls and roof of the great room above,— I think exceeds any thing he has yet done, both for design, colouring, and exuberance of invention, comparable to the greatest of the old masters, or what they so celebrate at Rome.   In the rest of the chamber are some excellent paintings of Holbein, and other masters.   The garden is large, and in good air, but the fronts of the house not answerable to the inside.   The court at entry, and wings

---

[1] *Ante*, pp. 113 and 143; *post*, p. 259.
[2] He was made Earl of Montagu by King William, and Duke by Queen Anne.   His wife was Lady Elizabeth, daughter of Thomas Wriothesley, Earl of Southampton, widow of Joceline Percy, the 11th and last Earl of Northumberland (of that family).

for offices seem too near the street, and that so very narrow and meanly built, that the corridor is not in proportion to the rest, to hide the court from being overlooked by neighbours; all which might have been prevented, had they placed the house further into the ground, of which there was enough to spare. But on the whole it is a fine palace, built after the French pavilion-way, by Mr. Hooke, the Curator of the Royal Society. There were with us my Lady Scroope, the great wit, and Monsieur Chardine, the celebrated traveller.

13th October. Came to visit me my old and worthy friend, Mr. Packer, bringing with him his nephew Berkeley, grandson to the honest judge. A most ingenious, virtuous, and religious gentleman, seated near Worcester, and very curious in gardening.

17th. I was at the court-leet of this manor, my Lord Arlington his Majesty's High-Steward. [1]

26th. Came to visit and dine with me, Mr. Brisbane, Secretary to the Admiralty, a learned and agreeable man.

30th. I went to Kew to visit Sir Henry Capell, brother to the late Earl of Essex; but he being gone to Cashiobury, after I had seen his garden [2] and the alterations therein, I returned home. He had repaired his house, roofed his hall with a kind of cupola, and in a niche was an artificial fountain; but the room seems to me over-melancholy, yet might be much improved by having the walls well painted à fresco. The two green-houses for oranges and myrtles communicating with the rooms below, are very well contrived. [3] There is a cupola made with pole-work between two elms at the end of a walk, which being covered by plashing the trees to them, is very pretty; for the rest there are too many fir-trees in the garden.

17th November. I took a house in Villiers Street, York Buildings, for the winter, having many important concerns to dispatch, and for the education of my daughters.

23rd. The Duke of Monmouth, till now proclaimed traitor on the pretended plot for which Lord Russell was lately beheaded, came this evening to Whitehall and rendered himself, on which were various discourses.

---

[1] The manor of Deptford-le-Strond, alias West Greenwich.
[2] *Archæologia*, vol. xii. p. 185.
[3] Of late years this plan has been frequently adopted.

ALGERNON SIDNEY.

ⁿB 1000

26*th November.* I went to compliment the Duchess of Grafton, now lying-in of her first child, a son,[1] which she called for, that I might see it. She was become more beautiful, if it were possible, than before, and full of virtue and sweetness. She discoursed with me of many particulars, with great prudence and gravity beyond her years.

29*th.* Mr. Forbes showed me the plot of the garden making at Burleigh, at my Lord Exeter's, which I looked on as one of the most noble that I had seen.

The whole court and town in solemn mourning for the death of the King of Portugal, her Majesty's brother.

30*th.* At the anniversary dinner of the Royal Society the King sent us two does. Sir Cyril Wych was elected President.

5*th December.* I was this day invited to a wedding of one Mrs. Castle, to whom I had some obligation, and it was to her fifth husband, a Lieutenant-Colonel of the City. She was the daughter of one Burton, a broom-man, by his wife, who sold kitchen-stuff in Kent Street, whom God so blessed that the father became a very rich, and was a very honest man; he was sheriff of Surrey,[2] where I have sat on the bench with him. Another of his daughters was married to Sir John Bowles; and this daughter was a jolly friendly woman. There was at the wedding the Lord Mayor, the Sheriff, several Aldermen and persons of quality; above all, Sir George Jeffreys, newly made Lord Chief Justice of England, with Mr. Justice Withings, danced with the bride, and were exceeding merry. These great men spent the rest of the afternoon, till eleven at night, in drinking healths, taking tobacco, and talking much beneath the gravity of Judges, who had but a day or two before condemned Mr. Algernon Sydney, who was executed the 7th on Tower-Hill, on the single witness of that monster of a man, Lord Howard of Escrick, and some sheets of paper taken in Mr. Sydney's study, pretended to be written by him, but not fully proved, nor the time

[1] Charles, who succeeded his father, killed in Ireland in 1690. This son was Lord Lieutenant of Ireland, Lord Chamberlain, Privy Counsellor, K.G., &c. in the reigns of Anne, George I. and George II. There is a fine whole-length mezzotinto of him by Faber.
[2] In 1673.

when, but appearing to have been written before his
Majesty's restoration, and then pardoned by the Act of
Oblivion; so that though Mr. Sydney was known to be a
person obstinately averse to government by a monarch
(the subject of the paper was in answer to one by Sir E.
Filmer), yet it was thought he had very hard measure
There is this yet observable, that he had been an inveterate
enemy to the last king, and in actual rebellion against
him; a man of great courage, great sense, great parts,
which he showed both at his trial and death; for, when
he came on the scaffold, instead of a speech, he told them
only that he had made his peace with God, that he came not
thither to talk, but to die; put a paper into the sheriff's
hand, and another into a friend's; said one prayer as short
as a grace, laid down his neck, and bid the executioner do
his office.

The Duke of Monmouth, now having his pardon, refuses
to acknowledge there was any treasonable plot; for which
he is banished Whitehall. This was a great disappointment
to some who had prosecuted Trenchard, Hampden, &c.,
that for want of a second witness were come out of the Tower
upon their *habeas corpus*.

The King had now augmented his guards with a new sort
of dragoons, who carried also grenadoes, and were habited
after the Polish manner, with long peaked caps, very fierce
and fantastical.

7th December. I went to the Tower, and visited the Earl
of Danby, the late Lord High Treasurer, who had been imprisoned four years: he received me with great kindness.
I dined with him, and stayed till night. We had discourse
of many things, his Lady railing sufficiently at the keeping
her husband so long in prison. Here I saluted the Lord
Dumblaine's wife,[1] who before had been married to Emerton,
and about whom there was that scandalous business before
the delegates.

23rd. The small-pox very prevalent and mortal; the
Thames frozen.

26th. I dined at Lord Clarendon's, where I was to

---

[1] Peregrine, Viscount Dumblaine, youngest son of the Earl of Danby,
so created in his father's life-time, and afterwards inheritor of his title
and estate.

meet that ingenious and learned gentleman, Sir George Wheeler, who has published the excellent description of Africa and Greece, and who, being a knight of a very fair estate and young, had now newly entered into Holy Orders.

27th December. I went to visit Sir John Chardin, a French gentleman, who had travelled three times by land into Persia, and had made many curious researches in his travels, of which he was now setting forth a relation. It being in England this year one of the severest frosts that has happened of many years, he told me the cold in Persia was much greater, the ice of an incredible thickness; that they had little use of iron in all that country, it being so moist (though the air admirably clear and healthy) that oil would not preserve it from rusting, so that they had neither clocks nor watches; some padlocks they had for doors and boxes.

30th. Dr. Sprat, now made Dean of Westminster, preached to the King at Whitehall, on Matt. vi. 24. Recollecting the passages of the past year, I gave God thanks for his mercies, praying his blessing for the future.

1683-4. *1st January.* The weather continuing intolerably severe, streets of booths were set upon the Thames; the air was so very cold and thick, as of many years there had not been the like. The small-pox was very mortal.

2nd. I dined at Sir Stephen Fox's: after dinner came a fellow who eat live charcoal, glowingly ignited, quenching them in his mouth, and then champing and swallowing them down. There was a dog also which seemed to do many rational actions.

6th. The river quite frozen.

9th. I went across the Thames on the ice, now become so thick as to bear not only streets of booths, in which they roasted meat, and had divers shops of wares, quite across as in a town, but coaches, carts, and horses passed over. So I went from Westminster-stairs to Lambeth, and dined with the Archbishop: where I met my Lord Bruce, Sir George Wheeler, Colonel Cooke, and several divines. After dinner and discourse with his Grace till evening prayers, Sir George Wheeler and I walked over the ice from Lambeth-stairs to the Horse-ferry.

10th. I visited Sir Robert Reading, where after supper

we had music, but not comparable to that which Mrs. Bridgeman made us on the guitar with such extraordinary skill and dexterity.

16th January. The Thames was filled with people and tents, selling all sorts of wares as in the City.

24th. The frost continuing more and more severe, the Thames before London was still planted with booths in formal streets, all sorts of trades and shops furnished, and full of commodities, even to a printing-press, where the people and ladies took a fancy to have their names printed, and the day and year set down when printed on the Thames :[1] this humour took so universally, that it was estimated the printer gained £5 a day, for printing a line only, at sixpence a name, besides what he got by ballads, &c. Coaches plied from Westminster to the Temple, and from several other stairs to and fro, as in the streets, sleds, sliding with skates, a bull-baiting, horse and coach-races, puppet-plays and interludes, cooks, tippling, and other lewd places, so that it seemed to be a bacchanalian triumph, or carnival on the water, whilst it was a severe judgment on the land, the trees not only splitting as if lightning-struck, but men and cattle perishing in divers places, and the very seas so locked up with ice, that no vessels could stir out or come in. The fowls, fish, and birds, and all our exotic plants and greens, universally perishing. Many parks of deer were destroyed, and all sorts of fuel so dear, that there were great contributions to preserve the poor alive. Nor was this severe weather much less intense in most parts of Europe, even as far as Spain and the most southern tracts. London, by reason of the excessive cold-ness of the air hindering the ascent of the smoke, was so filled with the fuliginous steam of the sea-coal, that hardly could one see across the streets, and this filling the lungs with its gross particles, exceedingly obstructed the breast, so as one could scarcely breathe. Here was no water to be had from the pipes and engines, nor could the brewers

---

[1] Curiosity collectors still show these cards of Frost Fair. One may be described. Within a treble border is printed, " Mons' et Mad" Justel. Printed on the river of Thames being frozen. In the 36th year of King Charles the II., February the 5th, 1683." v. s. is added with a pen, probably by the holder of the card.

and divers other tradesmen work, and every moment was full of disastrous accidents.

4th February. I went to Sayes Court to see how the frost had dealt with my garden, where I found many of the greens and rare plants utterly destroyed. The oranges and myrtles very sick, the rosemary and laurels dead to all appearance, but the cypress likely to endure it.

5th. It began to thaw, but froze again. My coach crossed from Lambeth to the Horse-ferry at Milbank, Westminster. The booths were almost all taken down; but there was first a map or landscape cut in copper representing all the manner of the camp, and the several actions, sports, and pastimes thereon, in memory of so signal a frost.[1]

7th. I dined with my Lord Keeper [North], and walking alone with him some time in his gallery, we had discourse of music. He told me he had been brought up to it from a child, so as to sing his part at first sight. Then speaking of painting, of which he was also a great lover, and other ingenious matters, he desired me to come oftener to him.

8th. I went this evening to visit that great and knowing virtuoso, Monsieur Justell.[2] The weather was set in to an absolute thaw and rain; but the Thames still frozen.

10th. After eight weeks missing the foreign posts, there came abundance of intelligence from abroad.

12th. The Earl of Danby, late Lord-Treasurer, together with the Roman Catholic Lords impeached of high treason in the Popish Plot, had now their *habeas corpus*, and came out upon bail, after five years' imprisonment in the Tower. Then were also tried and deeply fined Mr. Hampden and

---

[1] Various representations of this curious scene of Frost Fair, both in wood and copper-plate engravings, preserve some idea of what it must have been.

[2] Henry Justell, created LL.D. by the University of Oxford, on presenting to the University the MSS. of his father, Christopher Justell, a learned writer on ecclesiastical antiquities and canon law. Both were born in France; but on the revocation of the edict of Nantes, the son fled to England, and was appointed Keeper of the King's Library. He published several works. Born, 1620; died, 1693.

others, for being supposed of the late plot, for which Lord Russell and Colonel Sidney suffered; as also the person who went about to prove that the Earl of Essex had his throat cut in the Tower by others; likewise Mr. Johnson, the author of that famous piece called Julian.[1]

15*th February.* News of the Prince of Orange having accused the Deputies of Amsterdam of *crimen læsæ Majestatis*, and being pensioners to France.

Dr. Tenison communicated to me his intention of erecting a library in St. Martin's parish, for the public use, and desired my assistance, with Sir Christopher Wren, about the placing and structure thereof, a worthy and laudable design. He told me there were thirty or forty young men in Orders in his parish, either governors to young gentlemen or chaplains to noblemen, who being reproved by him on occasion for frequenting taverns or coffee-houses, told him they would study or employ their time better, if they had books. This put the pious Doctor on this design; and indeed a great reproach it is that so great a city as London should not have a public library becoming it. There ought to be one at St. Paul's; the west end of that church (if ever finished) would be a convenient place.

23*rd.* I went to Sir John Chardin, who desired my assistance for the engraving the plates, the translation, and printing his History of that wonderful Persian Monument near Persepolis, and other rare antiquities, which he had caused to be drawn from the originals in his second journey into Persia, which we now concluded upon. Afterwards, I went with Sir Christopher Wren to Dr. Tenison, where we made the drawing and estimate of the expense of the library, to be begun this next spring near the Mews.[2]

---

[1] Samuel Johnson, a clergyman, who was distinguished by the rigour of his writings against the Court; particularly by his "Julian the Apostate," directed at the Duke of York, a recent convert to Popery. For these he was fined and imprisoned, put in the pillory, whipped at the cart's tail, and degraded from the priesthood: nevertheless, he was not silenced; and he lived to see the Revolution, which placed William of Orange on the throne; whereupon he received a present of £1000, and a pension of £300 per annum, for the joint lives of himself and his son. He died in 1703.

[2] It occupied a spacious room, which was well furnished with books, and has remained under the care of the Vicar of St. Martin's. To the Clergy in the City, Sion College is more peculiarly appropriated.

Great expectation of the Prince of Orange's attempts in Holland to bring those of Amsterdam to consent to the new levies, to which we were no friends, by a pseudo-politic adherence to the French interest.

26th February. Came to visit me Dr. Turner, our new Bishop of Rochester.

28th. I dined at Lady Tuke's, where I heard Dr. Walgrave (physician to the Duke and Duchess) play excellently on the lute.

7th March. Dr. Meggot, Dean of Winchester, preached an incomparable sermon (the King being now gone to Newmarket), on Heb. xii. 15, showing and pathetically pressing the care we ought to have lest we come short of the grace of God. Afterwards, I went to visit Dr. Tenison at Kensington, whither he was retired to refresh, after he had been sick of the small pox.

15th. At Whitehall preached Mr. Henry Godolphin, a prebend of St. Paul's, and brother to my dear friend Sydney, on Isaiah lv. 7. I dined at the Lord Keeper's, and brought him to Sir John Chardin, who showed him his accurate drafts of his travels in Persia.

28th. There was so great a concourse of people with their children to be touched for the Evil, that six or seven were crushed to death by pressing at the chirurgeon's door for tickets. The weather began to be more mild and tolerable; but there was not the least appearance of any spring.

30th. Easter day. The Bishop of Rochester preached before the King; after which his Majesty, accompanied with three of his natural sons, the Dukes of Northumberland, Richmond, and St. Alban's (sons of Portsmouth, Cleveland, and Nelly), went up to the altar; the three boys entering before the King within the rails, at the right hand, and three Bishops on the left: London (who officiated), Durham, and Rochester, with the Sub-dean, Dr. Holder. The King, kneeling before the altar, making his offering, the Bishops first received, and then his Majesty; after which he retired to a canopied seat on the right hand. Note, there was perfume burnt before the office began. I had received the sacrament at Whitehall early with the Lords and Household, the Bishop of London officiating. Then went to St. Martin's, where

Dr. Tenison preached (recovered from the small-pox) ; then went again to Whitehall as above. In the afternoon, went to St. Martin's again.

4th April. I returned home with my family to my house at Sayes Court, after five months' residence in London; hardly the least appearance of any spring.

30th. A letter of mine to the Royal Society concerning the terrible effects of the past winter being read, they desired it might be printed in the next part of their Transactions.[1]

10th May. I went to visit my brother in Surrey. Called by the way at Ashted, where Sir Robert Howard (Auditor of the Exchequer) entertained me very civilly at his new-built house, which stands in a park on the Down, the avenue south ; though down hill to the house, which is not great, but with the out-houses very convenient. The staircase is painted by Verrio with the story of Astrea ; amongst other figures is the picture of the Painter himself, and not unlike him ; the rest is well done, only the columns did not at all please me ; there is also Sir Robert's own picture in an oval ; the whole in *fresco*. The place has this great defect, that there is no water but what is drawn up by horses from a very deep well.

11th. Visited Mr. Higham, who was ill, and died three days after. His grandfather and father (who christened me), with himself, had now been rectors of this parish 101 years, viz. from May, 1583.

12th. I returned to London, where I found the Commissioners of the Admiralty abolished, and the office of Admiral restored to the Duke, as to the disposing and ordering all sea business; but his Majesty signed all petitions, papers, warrants, and commissions, that the Duke, not acting as admiral by commission or office, might not incur the penalty of the late Act against Papists and Dissenters holding offices, and refusing the oath and test. Every one was glad of this change, those in the late Commission being utterly ignorant in their duty, to the great damage of the Navy.

[1] This was done in the *Transactions*, No. 158. See it at length in the *Biog. Brit.* (Kippis's ed.), vol. v., p. 623. An Abstract of it is also reprinted in Evelyn's " Miscellaneous Writings," pp. 692—696.

The utter ruin of the Low Country was threatened by the siege of Luxemburg, if not timely relieved, and by the obstinacy of the Hollanders, who refused to assist the Prince of Orange, being corrupted by the French.

16th May. I received £600 of Sir Charles Bickerstaff for the fee-farm of Pilton, in Devon.

26th. Lord Dartmouth was chosen Master of the Trinity Company, newly returned with the fleet from blowing up and demolishing Tangier. In the sermon preached on this occasion, Dr. Can observed that, in the 27th chapter of the Acts of the Apostles, the casting anchor out of the fore-ship had been cavilled at as betraying total ignorance: that it is very true our seamen do not do so; but in the Mediterranean their ships were built differently from ours, and to this day it was the practice to do so there.

Luxemburg was surrendered to the French, which makes them master of all the Netherlands, gives them entrance into Germany, and a fair game for universal monarchy; which that we should suffer, who only and easily might have hindered, astonished all the world. Thus is the poor Prince of Orange ruined, and this nation and all the Protestant interest in Europe following, unless God in His infinite mercy, as by a miracle, interpose, and our great ones alter their counsels. The French fleet were now besieging Genoa, but after burning much of that beautiful city with their bombs, went off with disgrace.

11th June. My cousin, Verney, to whom a very great fortune was fallen, came to take leave of us, going into the country; a very worthy and virtuous young gentlemen.

12th. I went to advise and give directions about the building two streets in Berkeley Gardens, reserving the house and as much of the garden as the breadth of the house. In the meantime, I could not but deplore that sweet place (by far the most noble gardens, courts, and accommodations, stately porticos, &c., any where about the town) should be so much straitened and turned into tenements. But that magnificent pile and gardens contiguous to it, built by the late Lord Chancellor Clarendon, being all demolished, and designed for piazzas and buildings, was some excuse for my Lady Berkeley's resolution of letting out her ground also for so excessive a price as was offered, advancing near £1000 per annum in mere ground-rents; to such a mad intemperance was the age come of building about a city, by far too disproportionate already to the nation:[1] I having in my time seen it almost as large again as it was within my memory.

22nd June. Last Friday, Sir Thomas Armstrong was executed at Tyburn for treason, without trial, having been outlawed and apprehended in Holland, on the conspiracy of the Duke of Monmouth, Lord Russell, &c., which gave occasion of discourse to people and lawyers, in regard it was on an outlawry that judgment was given and execution.[2]

2nd July. I went to the Observatory at Greenwich, where Mr. Flamsted took his observations of the eclipse of the sun, now almost three parts obscured.

There had been an excessive hot and dry spring, and such a drought still continued as never was in my memory.

13th. Some small sprinkling of rain; the leaves dropping from the trees as in autumn.

25th. I dined at Lord Falkland's, Treasurer of the Navy, where after dinner we had rare music, there being amongst others, Signor Pietro Reggio, and Signor John Baptist, both famous, one for his voice, the other for playing on the harpsichord, few if any in Europe exceeding him. There was also a Frenchman who sung an admirable bass.

26th. I returned home, where I found my Lord Chief Justice [Jefferies], the Countess of Clarendon, and Lady Catherine Fitzgerald, who dined with me.

10th August. We had now rain after such a drought as no man in England had known.

24th. Excessive hot. We had not had above one or two considerable showers, and those storms, these eight or

---

[1] What would Evelyn think if he could see what is now called London?

[2] When brought up for judgment, Armstrong insisted on his right to a trial, the act giving that right to those who came in within a year, and the year not having expired. Jeffries refused it; and when Armstrong insisted that he asked nothing but law, Jeffries told him he should have it to the full, and ordered his execution in six days. When Jeffries went to the King at Windsor soon after, the King took a ring from his finger and gave it to Jeffries. *Burnet*, ii. 989.

nine months. Many trees died for the want of refreshment.

31*st August.* Mr. Sidney Godolphin was made Baron Godolphin.

26*th September.* The King being returned from Winchester, there was a numerous Court at Whitehall.

At this time the Earl of Rochester was removed from the Treasury to the Presidentship of the Council; Lord Godolphin was made first Commissioner of the Treasury in his place; Lord Middleton (a Scot) made Secretary of State, in the room of Lord Godolphin. These alterations being very unexpected and mysterious, gave great occasion of discourse.

There was now an Ambassador from the King of Siam, in the East Indies, to his Majesty.

22*nd October.* I went with Sir William Godolphin to see the rhinoceros, or unicorn, being the first that I suppose was ever brought into England. She belonged to some East India merchants, and was sold (as I remember) for above £2000. At the same time, I went to see a crocodile, brought from some of the West India Islands, resembling the Egyptian crocodile.

24*th.* I dined at Sir Stephen Fox's with the Duke of Northumberland. He seemed to be a young gentleman of good capacity, well-bred, civil, and modest: newly come from travel, and had made his campaign at the siege of Luxemburg. Of all his Majesty's children (of which he had now six Dukes) this seemed the most accomplished and worth the owning. He is extraordinary handsome and well-shaped. What the Dukes of Richmond and St. Alban's will prove, their youth does not yet discover; they are very pretty boys.

26*th.* Dr. Goodman preached before the King on James ii. 12, concerning the law of liberty: an excellent discourse and in good method. He is author of *The Prodigal Son*, a treatise worth reading, and another of the old religion.

27*th.* I visited the Lord Chamberlain, where dined the *black Baron* and Monsieur Flamerin, who had so long been banished France for a duel.

28*th.* I carried Lord Clarendon through the City, amidst

all the squibs and bacchanalia of the Lord Mayor's show, to the Royal Society, where he was proposed a member; and then treated him at dinner.

I went to St. Clement's, that pretty built and contrived church, where a young divine gave us an eloquent sermon on 1 Cor. vi. 20, inciting to gratitude and glorifying God for the fabric of our bodies and the dignity of our nature.

2nd November. A sudden change from temperate warm weather to an excessive cold rain, frost, snow, and storm, such as had seldom been known. This winter weather began as early and fierce as the past did late; till about Christmas there then had been hardly any winter.

4th. Dr. Turner, now translated from Rochester to Ely upon the death of Dr. Peter Gunning, preached before the King at Whitehall on Romans iii. 8, a very excellent sermon, vindicating the Church of England against the pernicious doctrines of the Church of Rome. He challenged the producing but of five clergymen who forsook our Church and went over to that of Rome, during all the troubles and rebellion in England, which lasted near twenty years; and this was to my certain observation a great truth.

15th. Being the Queen's birth-day, there were fireworks on the Thames before Whitehall, with pageants of castles, forts, and other devices of girandolas, serpents, the King and Queen's arms and mottoes, all represented in fire, such as had not been seen here. But the most remarkable was the several fires and skirmishes in the very water, which actually moved a long way, burning under the water, now and then appearing above it, giving reports like muskets and cannon, with grenados and innumerable other devices. It is said it cost £1,500. It was concluded with a ball, where all the young ladies and gallants danced in the great hall. The court had not been seen so brave and rich in apparel since his Majesty's Restoration.

30th. In the morning, Dr. Fiennes, son of the Lord Say and Seale, preached before the King on Joshua xxi. 11.

3rd December. I carried Mr. Justell and Mr. Slingsby (Master of the Mint), to see Mr. Sheldon's collection of medals. The series of Popes was rare, and so were several amongst the moderns, especially that of John Huss's martyrdom at Constance; of the Roman Emperors, Consulars;

some Greek, &c., in copper, gold, and silver ; not many
truly antique; a medallion of Otho Paulus Æmilius, &c.,
ancient. They were held at a price of £1,000 ; but not
worth, I judge, above £200.

7th December. I went to see the new church at St. James's,
elegantly built ; the altar was especially adorned, the white
marble enclosure curiously and richly carved, the flowers
and garlands about the walls by Mr. Gibbons, in wood : a
pelican with her young at her breast; just over the altar in
the carved compartment and border environing the purple
velvet fringed with I. H. S. richly embroidered, and most
noble plate, were given by Sir R. Geere, to the value (as
was said) of 200*l.* There was no altar anywhere in England, nor has there been any abroad, more handsomely
adorned.

17th. Early in the morning I went into St. James's Park
to see three Turkish, or Asian horses, newly brought over,
and now first showed to his Majesty. There were four, but
one of them died at sea, being three weeks coming from Hamburgh. They were taken from a Bashaw at the siege of
Vienna, at the late famous raising that leaguer. I never
beheld so delicate a creature as one of them was, of somewhat a bright bay, two white feet, a blaze ; such a head,
eyes, ears, neck, breast, belly, haunches, legs, pasterns, and
feet, in all regards, beautiful, and proportioned to admiration ; spirited, proud, nimble, making halt, turning with that
swiftness, and in so small a compass, as was admirable. With
all this so gentle and tractable as called to mind what I remember Busbequius speaks of them, to the reproach of our
grooms in Europe, who bring up their horses so churlishly,
as makes most of them retain their ill habits. They trotted
like does, as if they did not feel the ground. Five hundred
guineas was demanded for the first ; 300 for the second ; and
200 for the third, which was brown. All of them were choicely
shaped, but the two last not altogether so perfect as the
first.

It was judged by the spectators, among whom was the
King, Prince of Denmark, Duke of York, and several of the
Court, noble persons skilled in horses, especially Monsieur
Faubert and his son (provost masters of the Academy, and
esteemed of the best in Europe), that there were never seen

any horses in these parts to be compared with them. Add t͞o all this, the furniture, consisting of embroidery on the saddle, housings, quiver, bow, arrows, scymitar, sword, mace, or battle-axe, *à la Turcisq;* the Bashaw's velvet mantle furred with the most perfect ermine I ever beheld; all which, iron-work in common furniture being here of silver, curiously wrought and double gilt, to an incredible value. Such and so extraordinary was the embroidery, that I never saw any thing approaching it. The reins and headstall were of crimson silk, covered with chains of silver gilt. There was also a Turkish royal standard of a horse's tail, together with all sorts of other caparisons belonging to a general's horse, by which one may estimate how gallantly and magnificently those infidels appear in the field; for nothing could be seen more glorious. The gentleman (a German) who rid the horse, was in all this garb. They were shod with iron made round and closed at the heel, with a hole in the middle about as wide as a shilling. The hoofs most entire.

18*th December.* I went with Lord Cornwallis to see the young gallants do their exercise, Mr. Faubert having newly railed in a manage, and fitted it for the academy. There were the Dukes of Norfolk and Northumberland, Lord New-ourgh, and a nephew of (Duras) Earl of Feversham. The exercises were, 1, running at the ring; 2, flinging a javelin at a Moor's head; 3, discharging a pistol at a mark; lastly, taking up a gauntlet with the point of a sword; all these performed in full speed. The Duke of Northumberland hardly missed of succeeding in every one, a dozen times, as I think. The Duke of Norfolk did exceeding bravely. Lords Newburgh and Duras seemed nothing so dexterous. Here I saw the difference of what the French call "*bel homme à cheval,*" and "*bon homme à cheval;*" the Duke of Norfolk being the first, that is rather a fine person on a horse, the Duke of Northumberland being both in perfection, namely, a graceful person and an excellent rider. But the Duke of Norfolk told me he had not been at this exercise these twelve years before. There were in the field the Prince of Den-mark, and the Lord Lansdowne, son of the Earl of Bath, who had been made a Count of the Empire last summer for his service before Vienna.

20*th.* A villainous murder was perpetrated by Mr.

St. John, eldest son to Sir Walter St. John, a worthy gentleman, on a knight of quality,[1] in a tavern. The offender was
sentenced and reprieved. So many horrid murders and
duels were committed about this time as were never before
heard of in England; which gave much cause of complaint
and murmurings.

1684-5. 1*st* *January*. It proved so sharp weather, and
so long and cruel a frost, that the Thames was frozen
across, but the frost was often dissolved, and then froze
again.

11*th*. A young man preached upon St. Luke xiii. 5, after
the Presbyterian tedious method and repetition.

24*th*. I dined at Lord Newport's, who has some excellent
pictures, especially that of Sir Thomas Hanmer, by Vandyke,
one of the best he ever painted; another of our English
Dobson's painting;[2] but, above all, Christ in the Virgin's
lap, by Poussin, an admirable piece; with something of most
other famous hands.

25*th*. Dr. Dove preached before the King. I saw this
evening such a scene of profuse gaming, and the King in
the midst of his three concubines, as I have never before
seen—luxurious dallying and profaneness.

27*th*. I dined at Lord Sunderland's, being invited to hear
that celebrated voice of Mr. Pordage, newly come from
Rome; his singing was after the Venetian recitative, as
masterly as could be, and with an excellent voice both treble
and bass; Dr. Walgrave accompanied it with his *theorbo lute*,
on which he performed beyond imagination, and is doubtless
one of the greatest masters in Europe on that charming
instrument. Pordage is a priest, as Mr. Bernard Howard
told me in private.

There was in the room where we dined, and in his bed-
chamber, those incomparable pieces of Columbus, a Flagel-

---

[1] Sir William Estcourt. The catastrophe arose from a sudden quarrel,
and great doubts arose whether the offence was more than manslaughter;
but St. John was advised to plead guilty, and then had a pardon, for
which he paid 1600*l*. Exactly 100 years before, one of his family had
been tried for a similar offence and acquitted, but he was obliged to go
abroad, though he was afterwards employed. *Hist. of Surrey*, iii. 330,
App. cxx.
[2] William Dobson, a clever portrait painter, who succeeded Vandyke
in the employments he held under Charles I. He died in 1646.

lation, the Grammar-school, the Venus and Adonis of Titian;
and of Vandyke's that picture of the late Earl of Digby
(father of the Countess of Sunderland), and Earl of Bedford,
Sir Kenelm Digby, and two ladies of incomparable performance; besides that of Moses and the burning bush of Bassano, and several other pieces of the best masters. A marble
head of M. Brutus, &c.

28th January. I was invited to my Lord Arundel of Wardour (now newly released of his six years' confinement in
the Tower on suspicion of the plot called Oates's Plot),
where after dinner the same Mr. Pordage entertained us
with his voice, that excellent and stupendous artist, Signor
John Baptist, playing to it on the harpsichord. My daughter
Mary being with us, she also sung to the great satisfaction
of both the masters, and a world of people of quality
present.

She did so also at my Lord Rochester's the evening following, where we had the French boy so famed for his singing,
and indeed he had a delicate voice, and had been well taught.
I also heard Mrs. Packer (daughter to my old friend) sing
before his Majesty and the Duke, privately, that stupendous
bass, Gosling, accompanying her, but hers was so loud as
took away much of the sweetness. Certainly never woman
had a stronger or better ear, could she possibly have governed
it. She would do rarely in a large church among the nuns.

4th February. I went to London, hearing his Majesty had
been the Monday before (2nd February) surprised in his
bed-chamber with an apoplectic fit, so that if, by God's providence, Dr. King (that excellent chirurgeon as well as physician) had not been accidentally present to let him blood
(having his lancet in his pocket), his Majesty had certainly
died that moment; which might have been of direful consequence, there being nobody else present with the King save
this Doctor and one more, as I am assured. It was a mark
of the extraordinary dexterity, resolution, and presence of
mind in the Doctor, to let him blood in the very paroxysm,
without staying the coming of other physicians, which regu-
larly should have been done, and for want of which he must
have a regular pardon, as they tell me.[1] This rescued his

---

[1] Burnet tells us that the Privy Council approved of what he had
done, and ordered him 1000*l.*, but it was never paid him. There are

Majesty for the instant, but it was only a short reprieve.
He still complained, and was relapsing, often fainting, with
sometimes epileptic symptoms, till Wednesday, for which
he was cupped, let blood in both jugulars, and both vomit
and purges, which so relieved him, that on Thursday hopes
of recovery were signified in the public Gazette, but that
day about noon, the physicians thought him feverish. This
they seemed glad of, as being more easily allayed and methodically dealt with than his former fits; so as they prescribed the famous Jesuit's powder; but it made him worse,
and some very able doctors who were present did not think
it a fever, but the effect of his frequent bleeding and other
sharp operations used by them about his head, so that probably the powder might stop the circulation, and renew his
former fits, which now made him very weak. Thus he passed
Thursday night with great difficulty, when complaining of a
pain in his side, they drew twelve ounces more of blood from
him; this was by six in the morning on Friday, and it gave
him relief, but it did not continue, for being now in much
pain, and struggling for breath, he lay dozing, and, after some
conflicts, the physicians despairing of him, he gave up the
ghost at half an hour after eleven in the morning, being the
sixth of February, 1685, in the 36th year of his reign, and
54th of his age.

Prayers were solemnly made in all the churches, especially in both the Court Chapels, where the chaplains relieved
one another every half quarter of an hour from the time he
began to be in danger till he expired, according to the form
prescribed in the Church-offices. Those who assisted his
Majesty's devotions were, the Archbishop of Canterbury,
the Bishops of London, Durham, and Ely, but more especially Dr. Ken, the Bishop of Bath and Wells.[1] It is said

two good portraits of Dr. King engraved, in which the above-named
instance of his skill and promptitude is noticed.
[1] The account given of this by Charles's brother and successor, is, that
when the King's life was wholly despaired of, and it was time to prepare for another world, two Bishops came to do their function, who
reading the prayers appointed in the Common Prayer-Book on that occasion, when they came to the place where usually they exhort a sick
person to make a confession of his sins, the Bishop of Bath and Wells,
who was one of them, advertised him, *It was not of obligation*; and
after a short exhortation, asked him if he was sorry for his sins? which

'they exceedingly urged the receiving Holy Sacrament, but his Majesty told them he would consider of it, which he did so long till it was too late. Others whispered that the Bishops and Lords, except the Earls of Bath and Feversham, being ordered to withdraw the night before, Huddleston, the priest, had presumed to administer the Popish offices. He gave his breeches and keys to the Duke, who was almost continually kneeling by his bed side, and in tears. He also recommended to him the care of his natural children, all except the Duke of Monmouth, now in Holland, and in his displeasure. He entreated the Queen to pardon him (not without cause) ; who a little before had sent a bishop to excuse her not more frequently visiting him, in regard of her excessive grief, and withal that his Majesty would forgive it if at any time she had offended him. He spake to the Duke to be kind to the Duchess of Cleveland, and especially Portsmouth, and that Nelly might not starve.

Thus died King Charles II., of a vigorous and robust constitution, and in all appearance promising a long life. He was a prince of many virtues, and many great imperfections ; debonaire, easy of access, not bloody nor cruel ; his countenance fierce, his voice great, proper of person, every motion became him ;. a lover of the sea, and skilful in shipping ; not affecting other studies, yet he had a laboratory, and knew of many empirical medicines, and the easier

the King saying he was, the Bishop pronounced the absolution, and then, asked him if he pleased to receive the Sacrament ? to which the King made no reply ; and being pressed by the Bishop several times, gave no other answer but that it was time enough, or that he would think of it.

King James adds, that he stood all the while by the bed-side, and seeing the King would not receive the sacrament from them, and knowing his sentiments, he desired the company to stand a little from the bed, and then asked the King whether he should sent for a priest, to which the King replied, "For God's sake, brother, do, and lose no time." The Duke said he would bring one to him ; but none could be found except father Huddleston, who had been so assistant in the King's escape from Worcester ; he was brought up a back staircase, and the company were desired to withdraw, but he (the Duke of York) not thinking fit that he should be left alone with the King, desired the Earl of Bath, a Lord of the Bedchamber, and the Earl of Feversham, Captain of the Guard, should stay ; the rest being gone, father Huddleston was introduced, and administered the sacrament.—*Life of James II.*

mechanical mathematics; he loved lanting and building, and brought in a politer way of living, which passed to luxury and intolerable expense. He had a particular talent in telling a story, and facetious passages, of which he had innumerable; this made some buffoons and vicious wretches too presumptuous and familiar, not worthy the favour they abused. He took delight in having a number of little spaniels follow him and lie in his bed-chamber, where he often suffered the bitches to puppy and give suck, which rendered it very offensive, and indeed made the whole court nasty and stinking. He would doubtless have been an excellent prince, had he been less addicted to women, who made him uneasy, and always in want to supply their unmeasurable profusion, to the detriment of many indigent persons who had signally served both him and his father. He frequently and easily changed favourites to his great prejudice.

As to other public transactions, and unhappy miscarriages, 'tis not here I intend to number them; but certainly never had King more glorious opportunities to have made himself, his people, and all Europe happy, and prevented innumerable mischiefs, had not his too easy nature resigned him to be managed by crafty men, and some abandoned and profane wretches who corrupted his otherwise sufficient parts, disciplined as he had been by many afflictions during his banishment, which gave him much experience and knowledge of men and things; but those wicked creatures took him from off all application becoming so great a King. The history of his reign will certainly be the most wonderful for the variety of matter and accidents, above any extant in former ages: the sad tragical death of his father, his banishment and hardships, his miraculous restoration, conspiracies against him, parliaments, wars, plagues, fires, comets, revolutions abroad happening in his time, with a thousand other particulars. He was ever kind to me, and very gracious upon all occasions, and therefore I cannot without ingratitude but deplore his loss, which for many respects, as well as duty, I do with all my soul.

His Majesty being dead, the Duke, now King James II., went immediately to Council, and before entering into any business, passionately declaring his sorrow, told their Lordships, that since the succession had fallen to him, he wou.d endeavour to follow the example of his predecessor in his clemency and tenderness to his people; that, however he had been misrepresented as affecting arbitrary power, they should find the contrary; for that the laws of England had made the King as great a monarch as he could desire; that he would endeavour to maintain the Government both in Church and State, as by law established, its principles being so firm for monarchy, and the members of it showing themselves so good and loyal subjects;[1] and that, as he would never depart

[1] This is the substance (and very nearly the words employed) of what is stated by King James II. in the MS. printed in his life; but in that MS. are some words which Evelyn has omitted. For example, after speaking of the members of the Church of England as good and loyal subjects, the King adds, *and therefore I shall always take care to defend and support it.* James then goes on to say, that being desired by some present to allow copies to be taken, he said he had not committed it to writing; on which Mr. Finch (then Solicitor-General and afterwards Earl of Aylesford) replied, that what his Majesty had said had made so deep an impression on him, that he believed he could repeat the very words, and if his Majesty would permit him, he would write them down; which the King agreeing to, he went to a table and wrote them down, and this being shown to the King, he approved of it, and it was immediately published. The King afterwards proceeds to say : No one can wonder that Mr. Finch should word the speech as strong as he could in favour of the Established Religion, nor that the King in such a hurry should pass it over without reflection; for though his Majesty intended to promise both security to their religion and protection to their persons, he was afterwards convinced it had been better expressed by assuring them he never would endeavour to alter the Established Religion, than that he would endeavour to preserve it, and that he would rather support and defend the professors of it, than the religion itself; they could not expect he should make a conscience of supporting what in his conscience he thought erroneous : his engaging not to molest the professors of it, nor to deprive them or their successors of any spiritual dignity, revenue, or employment, but to suffer the ecclesiastical affairs to go on in the track they were in, was all they could wish or desire from a Prince of a different persuasion; but having once approved that way of expressing it which Mr. Finch had made choice of, he thought it necessary not to vary from it in the declarations or speeches he made afterwards, not doubting but the world would understand it in the meaning he intended.——'Tis true, afterwards *it was* pretended he kept not up to this engagement; but had they deviated no further from the duty and allegiance which both nature and repeated oath obliged them to, *than he did from his word*, they had still remained as happy a people as they really were during his short reign in England.'—*Life of James the Second*, ii. 435. The words printed in italics in this extract are from the interlineations of the son of King James the Second.

from the just rights and prerogatives of the Crown, so he would never invade any man's property; but as he had often adventured his life in defence of the nation, so he would still proceed, and preserve it in all its lawful rights and liberties.

This being the substance of what he said, the Lords desired it might be published, as containing matter of great satisfaction to a jealous people upon this change, which his Majesty consented to. Then were the Council sworn, and a Proclamation ordered to be published that all officers should continue in their stations, that there might be no failure of public justice, till his further pleasure should be known. Then the King rose, the Lords accompanying him to his bedchamber, where, whilst he reposed himself, tired indeed as he was with grief and watching, they returned again into the Council-chamber to take order for the *proclaiming* his Majesty, which (after some debate) they consented should be in the very form his grandfather, King James I., was, after the death of Queen Elizabeth; as likewise that the Lords, &c., should proceed in their coaches through the city for the more solemnity of it. Upon this was I, and several other Gentlemen waiting in the Privy gallery, admitted into the Council-chamber to be witness of what was resolved on. Thence with the Lords, the Lord Marshal and Heralds, and other Crown-officers being ready, we first went to Whitehall-gate, where the Lords stood on foot bare-headed, whilst the Herald proclaimed his Majesty's title to the Imperial Crown and succession according to the form, the trumpets and kettle-drums having first sounded three times, which ended with the people's acclamations. Then a herald called the Lords' coaches according to rank, myself accompanying the solemnity in my Lord Cornwallis's coach, first to Temple Bar, where the Lord Mayor and his brethren met us on horseback, in all their formalities, and proclaimed the King; hence to the Exchange in Cornhill, and so we returned in the order we set forth. Being come to Whitehall, we all went and kissed the King and Queen's hands. He had been on the bed, but was now risen and in his undress. The Queen was in bed in her apartment, but put forth her hand, seeming to be much afflicted, as I believe she was, having deported herself so decently upon all occasions since she came into England, which made her universally beloved

Thus concluded this sad and not joyful day.

I can never forget the inexpressible luxury and profane-ness, gaming, and all dissoluteness, and as it were total for-getfulness of God (it being Sunday evening), which this day se'nnight I was witness of, the King sitting and toy-ing with his concubines, Portsmouth, Cleveland, and Maza-rine, &c., a French boy singing love-songs,[1] in that glorious gallery, whilst about twenty of the great courtiers and other dissolute persons were at Basset round a large table, a bank of at least 2000 in gold before them; upon which two gen-tlemen who were with me made reflections with astonish-ment. Six days after, was all in the dust

It was enjoined that those who put on mourning should wear it as for a father, in the most solemn manner.

10th February. Being sent to by the Sheriff of the County to appear and assist in proclaiming the King, I went the next day to Bromley, where I met the Sheriff and the Com-mander of the Kentish Troop, with an appearance, I sup-pose, of above 500 horse, and innumerable people, two of his Majesty's trumpets, and a Serjeant with other officers, who having drawn up the horse in a large field near the town, marched thence, with swords drawn, to the market-place, where, making a ring, after sound of trumpets and silence made, the High Sheriff read the proclaiming titles to his bailiff, who repeated them aloud, and then, after many shouts of the people, his Majesty's health being drunk in a flint glass of a yard long, by the Sheriff, Commander, Officers, and chief Gentlemen, they all dispersed, and I returned.

13th. I passed a fine on selling of Honson Grange in Staffordshire, being about £20 per annum, which lying so great a distance, I thought fit to part with it to one Burton, a farmer there. It came to me as part of my daughter-in-law's portion, this being but a fourth part of what was di-vided between the mother and three sisters.

14th. The King was this night very obscurely buried[2]

---

[1] *Ante,* p. 214.

[2] The reasons are stated in the *Life of King James the Second.* "The funeral could not be performed with so great solemnity as some persons expected, because his late Majesty dying in, and his present Majesty pro-fessing, a different religion from that of his people, it had been a diffi-cult matter to reconcile the greater ceremonies which must have been performed according to the rites of the Church of England, with the

in a vault under Henry the Seventh's Chapel at Westminster, without any manner of pomp, and soon forgotten after all this vanity, and the face of the whole Court was exceedingly changed into a more solemn and moral behaviour; the new King affecting neither profaneness nor buffoonery. All the great officers broke their staves over the grave, according to form.

15th February. Dr. Tenison preached to the Household. The second sermon should have been before the King; but he, to the great grief of his subjects, did now, for the first time, go to mass publicly in the little Oratory at the Duke's lodgings, the doors being set wide open.

16th. I dined at Sir Robert Howard's, Auditor of the Exchequer, a gentleman pretending to all manner of arts and sciences, for which he had been the subject of comedy, under the name of Sir Positive ;¹ not ill-natured, but insufferably boasting. He was son to the late Earl of Berkshire.

17th. This morning his Majesty restored the staff and key to Lord Arlington, Chamberlain; to Mr. Savell, Vicechamberlain; to Lords Newport and Maynard, Treasurer and Comptroller of the Household; Lord Godolphin made Chamberlain to the Queen; Lord Peterborough Groom of the Stole, in place of the Earl of Bath; the Treasurer's staff to the Earl of Rochester; and his brother, the Earl of Clarendon, Lord Privy Seal, in the place of the Marquis of Halifax, who was made President of the Council; the Secretaries of State remaining as before.

19th. The Lord Treasurer and the other new Officers were sworn at the Chancery Bar and the Exchequer.

The late King having the revenue of excise, customs, and other late duties granted for his life only, they were now farmed and let to several persons, upon an opinion that the late King might let them for three years after his decease;

obligation of not communicating with it in spiritual things; to avoid, therefore, either disputes on the one hand, or scandal on the other, it was thought more prudent to do it in a more private manner; though at the same time there was no circumstance of state and pomp omitted which possibly could be allowed of. All the Privy Council, all the household, and all the Lords about town attended at the funeral."

¹ Evelyn here means Sir Positive At-All, in Shadwell's comedy of the *Sullen Lovers*, which Pepys also tells us was meant for Sir Robert Howard, Dryden's brother-in-law.

some of the old Commissioners refused to act. The lease was made but the day before the King died;[1] the major part of the Judges (but, as some think, not the best lawyers,) pronounced it legal, but four dissented.

The Clerk of the Closet had shut up the late King's private oratory next the Privy-chamber above, but the King caused it to be opened again, and that prayers should be said as formerly.

22nd February. Several most useful Tracts against Dissenters, Papists, and Fanatics, and Resolutions of Cases were now published by the London Divines.

4th March. Ash-Wednesday. After evening prayers, I went to London.

5th. To my grief, I saw the new pulpit set up in the Popish Oratory at Whitehall for the Lent preaching, mass being publicly said, and the Romanists swarming at Court with greater confidence than had ever been seen in England since the Reformation, so that everybody grew jealous as to what this would tend.

A Parliament was now summoned, and great industry used to obtain elections which might promote the Court-interest, most of the Corporations being now, by their new charters, empowered to make what returns of members they pleased.

There came over divers envoys and great persons to condole the death of the late King, who were received by the Queen-Dowager on a bed of mourning, the whole chamber, ceiling and floor, hung with black, and tapers were lighted, so as nothing could be more lugubrious and solemn. The Queen-Consort sate under a state on a black foot-cloth, to entertain the circle (as the Queen used to do), and that very decently.

6th. Lent Preachers continued as formerly in the Royal Chapel.

7th. My daughter, Mary, was taken with the small-pox,

---

[1] James, in his Life, makes no mention of this lease, but only says he continued to collect them, which conduct was not blamed: but, on the contrary, he was thanked for it, in an address from the Middle Temple, penned by Sir Bartholomew Shore, and presented by Sir Humphrey Mackworth, carrying great authority with it; nor did the Parliament find fault.

and there soon was found no hope of her recovery. A great
affliction to me: but God's holy will be done!

10th March. She received the blessed Sacrament; after
which, disposing herself to suffer what God should determine
to inflict, she bore the remainder of her sickness with extraordinary patience and piety, and more than ordinary resignation and blessed frame of mind. She died the 14th, to
our unspeakable sorrow and affliction, and not to our's only,
but that of all who knew her, who were many of the best
quality, greatest and most virtuous persons. The justness
of her stature, person, comeliness of countenance, gracefulness of motion, unaffected, though more than ordinary beautiful, were the least of her ornaments compared with those
of her mind. Of early piety, singularly religious, spending
a part of every day in private devotion, reading, and other
virtuous exercises ; she had collected and written out many
of the most useful and judicious periods of the books she
read in a kind of common-place, as out of Dr. Hammond
on the New Testament, and most of the best practical treatises. She had read and digested a considerable deal of
history, and of places. The French tongue was as familiar
to her as English ; she understood Italian, and was able to
render a laudable account of what she read and observed,
to which assisted a most faithful memory and discernment ;
and she did make very prudent and discreet reflections upon
what she had observed of the conversations among which
she had at any time been, which being continually of persons of the best quality, she thereby improved. She had
an excellent voice, to which she played a thorough-bass on
the harpsichord, in both which she arrived to that perfection,
that of the scholars of those two famous masters, Signors
Pietro and Bartholomeo, she was esteemed the best ; for the
sweetness of her voice and management of it added such an
agreeableness to her countenance, without any constraint or
concern, that when she sung, it was as charming to the eye
as to the ear ; this I rather note, because it was a universal
remark, and for which so many noble and judicious persons
in music desired to hear her, the last being at Lord Arundel's,
of Wardour.

What shall I say, or rather not say, of the cheerfulness
and agreeableness of her humour ? condescending to the

meanest servant in the family, or others, she still kept up
respect, without the least pride. She would often read to
them, examine, instruct, and pray with them if they were
sick, so as she was exceedingly beloved of everybody.
Piety was so prevalent an ingredient in her constitution (as
I may say), that even amongst equals and superiors she no
sooner became intimately acquainted, but she would endeavour to improve them, by insinuating something religious,
and that tended to bring them to a love of devotion ; she
had one or two confidants with whom she used to pass
whole days in fasting, reading, and prayers, especially
before the monthly communion, and other solemn occasions.
She abhorred flattery, and, though she had abundance of
wit, the raillery was so innocent and ingenious that it was
most agreeable ; she sometimes would see a play, but since
the stage grew licentious, expressed herself weary of them,
and the time spent at the theatre was an unaccountable
vanity. She never played at cards without extreme importunity and for the company ; but this was so very seldom, that I cannot number it among anything she could
name a fault.

No one could read prose or verse better or with more
judgment; and as she read, so she wrote, not only most
correct orthography, with that maturity of judgment and
exactness of the periods, choice of expressions, and familiarity of style, that some letters of hers have astonished me
and others, to whom she has occasionally written. She had
a talent of rehearsing any comical part or poem, as to them
she might be decently free with ; was more pleasing than
heard on the theatre ; she danced with the greatest grace I
had ever seen, and so would her master say, who was Monsieur Isaac ; but she seldom showed that perfection, save in
the gracefulness of her carriage, which was with an air of
sprightly modesty not easily to be described. Nothing
affected, but natural and easy as well in her deportment as
in her discourse, which was always material, not trifling,
and to which the extraordinary sweetness of her tone,
even in familiar speaking, was very charming. Nothing
was so pretty as her descending to play with little children,
whom she would caress and humour with great delight.
But she most affected to be with grave and sober men, of

whom she might learn something, and improve herself.
I have been assisted by her in reading and praying by
me ; comprehensive of uncommon notions, curious cf
knowing everything to some excess, had I not sometimes
repressed it.

Nothing was so delightful to her as to go into my
Study, where she would willingly have spent whole days,
for as I said she had read abundance of history, and all
the best poets, even Terence, Plautus, Homer, Virgil,
Horace, Ovid; all the best romances and modern poems ;
she could compose happily, and put in pretty symbols,
as in the *Mundus Muliebris*, wherein is an enumeration
of the immense variety of the modes and ornaments
belonging to the sex. But all these are vain trifles to
the virtues which adorned her soul; she was sincerely
religious, most dutiful to her parents, whom she loved
with an affection tempered with great esteem, so as we
were easy and free, and never were so well pleased as when
she was with us, nor needed we other conversation; she
was kind to her sisters, and was still improving them by
her constant course of piety. Oh, dear, sweet, and desirable
child, how shall I part with all this goodness and virtue
without the bitterness of sorrow and reluctancy of a
tender parent ! Thy affection, duty, and love to me was
that of a friend as well as a child. Nor less dear to thy
mother, whose example and tender care of thee was
unparalleled, nor was thy return to her less conspicuous;
Oh ! how she mourns thy loss ! how desolate hast thou
left us ! To the grave shall we · both carry thy memory !
God alone (in whose bosom thou art at rest and happy !)
give us to resign thee and all our contentments (for thou
indeed wert all in this world) to His blessed pleasure !
Let Him be glorified by our submission, and give us grace
to bless Him for the graces he implanted in thee, thy
virtuous life, pious and holy death, which is indeed the
only comfort of our souls, hastening through the infinite
love and mercy of the Lord Jesus to be shortly with thee,
dear child, and with thee and those blessed saints like
thee, glorify the Redeemer of the world to all eternity !
Amen.

It was in the 19th year of her age that this sickness

happened to her. An accident contributed to this disease; she had an apprehension of it in particular, which struck ner but two days before she came home, by an imprudent gentlewoman whom she went with Lady Falkland to visit, who, after they had been a good while in the house, told them she had a servant sick of the small pox (who indeed died the next day); this my poor child acknowledged made an impression on her spirits. There were four gentlemen of quality offering to treat with me about marriage, and I freely gave her her own choice, knowing her discretion. She showed great indifference to marrying at all, for truly, says she to her mother (the other day), were I assured of your life and my dear father's, never would I part from you; I love you and this home, where we serve God, above all things, nor ever shall I be so happy; I know and consider the vicissitudes of the world, I have some experience of its vanities, and but for decency more than inclination, and that you judge it expedient for me, I would not change my condition, but rather add the fortune you design me to my sisters, and keep up the reputation of our family. This was so discreetly and sincerely uttered that it could not but proceed from an extraordinary child, and one who loved her parents beyond example.

At London, she took this fatal disease, and the occasion of her being there was this: my Lord Viscount Falkland's Lady having been our neighbour (as he was Treasurer of the Navy), she took so great an affection to my daughter, that when they went back in the autumn to the City, nothing would satisfy their incessant importunity but letting her accompany my Lady, and staying sometime with her; it was with the greatest reluctance I complied. Whilst she was there, my Lord being musical, when I saw my Lady would not part with her till Christmas, I was not unwilling she should improve the opportunity of learning of Signor Pietro, who had an admirable way both of composure and teaching. It was the end of February before I could prevail with my Lady to part with her; but my Lord going into Oxfordshire to stand for Knight of the Shire there, she expressed her wish to come home, being tired of the vain and empty conversation of the town, the theatres, the court, and trifling visits which consumed so much precious time, and made her sometimes miss of that regular course of piety that gave her the greatest satisfaction. She was weary of this life, and I think went not thrice to Court all this time, except when her mother or I carried her. She did not affect showing herself, she knew the Court well, and passed one summer in it at Windsor with Lady Tuke, one of the Queen's women of the bed-chamber (a most virtuous relation of hers); she was not fond of that glittering scene, now become abominably licentious, though there was a design of Lady Rochester and Lady Clarendon to have made her a maid of honour to the Queen as soon as there was a vacancy. But this she did not set her heart upon, nor indeed on any thing so much as the service of God, a quiet and regular life, and how she might improve herself in the most necessary accomplishments, and to which she was arrived at so great a measure.

This is the little history and imperfect character of my dear child, whose piety, virtue, and incomparable endowments deserve a monument more durable than brass and marble. Precious is the memorial of the just. Much I could enlarge on every period of this hasty account, but that I ease and discharge my overcoming passion for the present, so many things worthy an excellent Christian and dutiful child crowding upon me. Never can I say enough, oh dear, my dear child, whose memory is so precious to me!

This dear child was born at Wotton, in the same house and chamber in which I first drew my breath, my wife having retired to my brother there in the great sickness that year upon the first of that month, and the very hour that I was born, upon the last: viz. October.

16th March. She was interred in the south-east end of the church at Deptford, near her grandmother and several of my younger children and relations. My desire was she should have been carried and laid among my own parents and relations at Wotton, where I desire to be interred myself, when God shall call me out of this uncertain transitory life, but some circumstances did not permit it. Our vicar, Dr. Holden, preached her funeral sermon on Phil. i. 21. "For to me to live is Christ, and to die is gain," upon which he made an apposite discourse, as those who heard it

assured me (for grief suffered me not to be present), concluding with a modest recital of her many virtues and signal
piety, so as to draw both tears and admiration from the
hearers. I was not altogether unwilling that something of
this sort should be spoken, for the edification and encouragement of other young people.

Divers noble persons honoured her funeral, some in person, others sending their coaches, of which there were six
or seven with six horses, viz., the Countess of Sunderland,
Earl of Clarendon, Lord Godolphin, Sir Stephen Fox, Sir
William Godolphin, Viscount Falkland, and others. There
were distributed amongst her friends about sixty rings.

Thus lived, died, and was buried the joy of my life, and
ornament of her sex and of my poor family! God Almighty
of His infinite mercy grant me the grace thankfully to
resign myself and all I have, or had, to His divine pleasure,
and in His good time, restoring health and comfort to my
family: "teach me so to number my days, that I may apply
my heart to wisdom," be prepared for my dissolution, and
that into the hands of my blessed Saviour I may recommend
my spirit! Amen!

On looking into her closet, it is incredible what a number
of collections she had made from historians, poets, travellers,
&c., but, above all, devotions, contemplations, and resolutions
on these contemplations, found under her hand in a book
most methodically disposed; prayers, meditations, and devotions on particular occasions, with many pretty letters to
her confidants; one to a divine (not named) to whom she
writes that he would be her ghostly father, and would not
despise her for her many errors and the imperfections of her
youth, but beg of God to give her courage to acquaint him
with all her faults, imploring his assistance and spiritual
directions. I well remember she had often desired me to
recommend her to such a person; but I did not think fit to
do it as yet, seeing her apt to be scrupulous, and knowing
the great innocency and integrity of her life.

It is astonishing how one who had acquired such substantial and practical knowledge in other ornamental parts
of education, especially music, both vocal and instrumental,
in dancing, paying and receiving visits, and necessary conversation, could accomplish half of what she has left; but,

as she never affected play or cards, which consume a world
of precious time, so she was in continual exercise, which yet
abated nothing of her most agreeable conversation. But
she was a little miracle while she lived, and so she died!

26th March. I was invited to the funeral of Captain Gunman, that excellent pilot and seaman, who had behaved
himself so gallantly in the Dutch war. He died of a
gangrene, occasioned by his fall from the pier of Calais.
This was the Captain of the yacht carrying the Duke (now
King) to Scotland, and was accused for not giving timely
warning when she split on the sands, where so many
perished; but I am most confident he was no ways guilty,
either of negligence, or design, as he made appear not
only at the examination of the matter of fact, but in the
Vindication he showed me, and which must needs give
any man of reason satisfaction. He was a sober, frugal,
cheerful, and temperate man; we have few such seamen left.

8th April. Being now somewhat composed after my great
affliction, I went to London to hear Dr. Tenison (it being on
a Wednesday in Lent) at Whitehall. I observed that
though the King was not in his seat above in the chapel,
the Doctor made his three congees, which they were not
used to do when the late King was absent, making then one
bowing only. I asked the reason; it was said he had a
special order so to do. The Princess of Denmark was in
the King's closet, but sate on the left hand of the chair, the
Clerk of the Closet standing by his Majesty's chair, as if he
had been present.

I met the Queen-Dowager going now first from White.
hall to dwell at Somerset-house.

This day my brother of Wotton and Mr. Onslow were
candidates for Surrey against Sir Adam Brown and my
cousin Sir Edward Evelyn, and were circumvented in their
election by a trick of the Sheriff's,[1] taking advantage of my
brother's party going out of the small village of Leatherhead
to seek shelter and lodging, the afternoon being tempestuous,
proceeding to the election when they were gone; they ex-

[1] Mr. Samuel Lewen. His name does not appear in the History of
Surrey among the land-owners of the county, but it is stated that in
1709 Sir William Lewen purchased the Rectory of Ewell, and that he
was Lord Mayor of London in 1717.

pecting the next morning; whereas before and then they exceeded the other party by many hundreds, as I am assured. The Duke of Norfolk led Sir Edward Evelyn's and Sir Adam Brown's party. For this parliament, very mean and slight persons (some of them gentlemen's servants, clerks, and persons neither of reputation nor interest) were set up; but the country would choose my brother whether he would or no, and he missed it by the trick above-mentioned. Sir Adam Brown was so deaf, that he could not hear one word. Sir Edward Evelyn[1] was an honest gentleman, much in favour with his Majesty.

10th April. I went early to Whitehall to hear Dr. Tillotson, Dean of Canterbury, preaching on Eccles. ix. 18. I returned in the evening, and visited Lady Tuke, and found with her Sir George Wakeman, the physician, whom I had seen tried and acquitted,[2] amongst the plotters for poisoning the late King, on the accusation of the famous Oates; and surely I believed him guiltless.

14th. According to my custom, I went to London to pass the holy week.

17th. Good-Friday. Dr. Tenison preached at the new church at St. James's, on 1 Cor. xvi. 22, upon the infinite love of God to us, which he illustrated in many instances. The Holy Sacrament followed, at which I participated. The Lord make me thankful! In the afternoon, Dr. Sprat, Bishop of Rochester, preached in Whitehall chapel, the auditory very full of Lords, the two Archbishops, and many others, now drawn to town upon occasion of the coronation and ensuing parliament. I supped with the Countess of Sunderland and Lord Godolphin, and returned home.

23rd. Was the coronation of the King and Queen. The solemnity was magnificent as is set forth in print.[3] The Bishop of Ely preached; but, to the sorrow of the people, no Sacrament, as ought to have been. However, the King

---

[1] His seat was at Long Ditton, near Kingston, which town had surrendered its charter to King Charles II. about a month before his death. King James appointed Sir Edward Evelyn one of the new corporation.

[2] Ante, p. 139.

[3] By Francis Sandford, illustrated with engravings, folio.

begins his reign with great expectations, and hopes of much reformation as to the late vices and profaneness of both Court and country. Having been present at the late King's coronation, I was not ambitious of seeing this ceremony.

3rd May. A young man preached, going chaplain with Sir J. Wiburn, Governor of Bombay, in the East Indies.

7th. I was in Westminster Hall when Oates, who had made such a stir in the kingdom, on his revealing a plot of the Papists, and alarmed several parliaments, and had occasioned the execution of divers priests, noblemen,[1] &c., was tried for perjury at the King's Bench; but, being very tedious, I did not endeavour to see the issue, considering that it would be published. Abundance of Roman Catholics were in the Hall in expectation of the most grateful conviction and ruin of a person who had been so obnoxious to them, and, as I verily believe, had done much mischief and great injury to several by his violent and ill-grounded proceedings; whilst he was at first so unreasonably blown up and encouraged, that his insolence was no longer sufferable.

Mr. Roger L'Estrange (a gentleman whom I had long known, and a person of excellent parts, abating some affectations) appearing first against the Dissenters in several Tracts, had now for some years turned his style against those whom (by way of hateful distinction) they called Whigs and Trimmers, under the title of Observator, which came out three or four days every week, in which sheets, under pretence to serve the Church of England, he gave suspicion of gratifying another party, by several passages which rather kept up animosities than appeased them, especially now that nobody gave the least occasion.[2]

10th. The Scots valuing themselves exceedingly to have been the first parliament called by his Majesty, gave the

[1] *Ante,* p. 140.
[2] In the first Dutch war, while Evelyn was one of the Commissioners for sick and wounded, L'Estrange in his Gazette mentioned the barbarous usage of the Dutch prisoners of war: whereupon Evelyn wrote him a very spirited letter, desiring that the Dutch Ambassador (who was then in England) and his friends would visit the prisoners, and examine their provisions; and he required L'Estrange to publish that vindication in his next number.

excise and customs to him and his successors for ever; the Duke of Queensberry making eloquent speeches, and especially minding them of a speedy suppression of those late desperate Field-Conventiclers who had done such unheard-of assassinations. In the meantime, elections for the ensuing parliament in England were thought to be very indirectly carried on in most places. God grant a better issue of it than some expect !

16*th May*. Oates was sentenced to be whipped and pilloried with the utmost severity.

21*st*. I dined at my Lord Privy Seal's with Sir William Dugdale, Garter King-at-Arms, author of the *Monasticon* and other learned works ; he told me he was 82 years of age, and had his sight and memory perfect.[1] There was shown a draft of the exact shape and dimensions of the crown the Queen had been crowned withal, together with the jewels and pearls, their weight and value, which amounted to £100,658 sterling, attested at the foot of the paper by the jeweller and goldsmith who set them.

22*nd*. In the morning, I went with a French gentleman, and my Lord Privy Seal, to the House of Lords, where we were placed by his Lordship next the Bar, just below the Bishops, very commodiously both for hearing and seeing. After a short space, came in the Queen and Princess of Denmark, and stood next above the Archbishops, at the side of the House on the right hand of the throne. In the interim, divers of the Lords, who had not finished before, took the test and usual oaths, so that her Majesty, the Spanish and other Ambassadors, who stood behind the throne, heard the Pope and the worship of the Virgin Mary, &c., renounced very decently, as likewise the prayers which followed, standing all the while. Then came in the King, the crown on his head, and being seated, the Commons were introduced, and the House being full, he drew forth a paper containing his speech, which he read distinctly enough, to this effect: "That he resolved to call a Parliament from the moment of his brother's decease, as the best means to settle all the concerns of the nation, so as to be most easy and happy to himself and his subjects ;

[1] Sir Isaac Heard, Garter King-at-Arms, who died in 1822, had similarly retained possession of his faculties to the great age of 92.

that he would confirm whatever he had said in his declaration at the first Council concerning his opinion of the principles of the Church of England, for their loyalty, and would defend and support it, and preserve its government as by law now established; that, as he would invade no man's property, so he would never depart from his own prerogative; and, as he had ventured his life in defence of the nation, so he would proceed to do still; that, having given this assurance of his care of our religion (his word was *your* religion) and property (which he had not said by chance, but solemnly), so he doubted not of suitable returns of his subjects' duty and kindness, especially as to settling his revenue for life, for the many weighty necessities of government, which he would not suffer to be precarious; that some might possibly suggest that it were better to feed and supply him from time to time only, out of their inclination to frequent parliaments; but that that would be a very improper method to take with him, since the best way to engage him to meet oftener would be always to use him well, and therefore he expected their compliance speedily, that this session being but short, they might meet again to satisfaction."

At every period of this, the House gave loud shouts. Then he acquainted them with that morning's news of Argyle's being landed in the West Highlands of Scotland from Holland, and the treasonous Declaration he had published, which he would communicate to them, and that he should take the best care he could it should meet with the reward it deserved, not questioning the parliament's zeal and readiness to assist him as he desired; at which there followed another *Vive le Roi*, and so his Majesty retired.

So soon as the Commons were returned and had put themselves into a grand committee, they immediately put the question, and unanimously voted the revenue to his Majesty for life. Mr. Seymour made a bold speech against many elections, and would have had those members who (he pretended) were obnoxious, to withdraw, till they had cleared the matter of their being legally returned; but no one seconded him. The truth is, there were many of the new members whose elections and returns were universally

censured, many of them being persons of no condition, or
interest, in the nation, or places for which they served,
especially in Devon, Cornwall, Norfolk, &c., said to have
been recommended by the Court, and from the effect of
the new charters changing the electors. It was reported
that Lord Bath carried down with him [into Cornwall]
no fewer than fifteen charters, so that some called him the
Prince Elector : whence Seymour told the House in his
speech that if this was digested, they might introduce what
religion and laws they pleased, and that though he never
gave heed to the fears and jealousies of the people before,
he was now really apprehensive of Popery. By the printed
list of members of 505, there did not appear to be above 135
who had been in former Parliaments, especially that lately
held at Oxford.

In the Lords' House, Lord Newport made an exception
against two or three young Peers, who wanted some months,
and some only four or five days, of being of age.

The Popish Lords, who had been sometime before released from their confinement about the plot, were now
discharged of their impeachment, of which I gave Lord
Arundel of Wardour joy.

Oates, who had but two days before been pilloried at
several places and whipped at the cart's tail from Newgate
to Aldgate, was this day placed on a sledge, being not able
to go by reason of so late scourging, and dragged from
prison to Tyburn, and whipped again all the way, which
some thought to be severe and extraordinary ; but, if he
was guilty of the perjuries, and so of the death of many
innocents, (as I fear he was,) his punishment was but what
he deserved. I chanced to pass just as execution was doing
on him. A strange revolution !

Note : there was no speech made by the Lord Keeper
[Bridgman] after his Majesty, as usual.

It was whispered he would not be long in that situation,
and many believe the bold Chief Justice Jefferies, who was
made Baron of Wem, in Shropshire, and who went thorough
stitch in that tribunal, stands fair for that office. I gave
him joy the morning before of his new honour, he having
always been very civil to me.

24th May. We had hitherto not any rain for many months,

so as the caterpillars had already devoured all the winter-fruit through the whole land, and even killed several greater old trees. Such two winters and summers I had never known.

4th June. Came to visit and take leave of me Sir Gabriel Sylvius, now going Envoy-extraordinary into Denmark, with his Secretary and Chaplain, a Frenchman, who related the miserable persecution of the Protestants in France; not above ten churches left them, and those also threatened to be demolished; they were commanded to christen their children within twenty-four hours after birth, or else a Popish priest was to be called, and then the infant brought up in Popery. In some places, they were thirty leagues from any minister, or opportunity of worship. This persecution had displeased the most industrious part of the nation, and dispersed those into Switzerland, Burgundy, Holland, Germany, Denmark, England, and the Plantations. There were with Sir Gabriel, his lady, Sir William Godolphin and sisters, and my Lord Godolphin's little son, my charge. I brought them to the water-side where Sir Gabriel embarked, and the rest returned to London.

14th. There was now certain intelligence of the Duke of Monmouth landing at Lyme, in Dorsetshire, and of his having set up his standard as King of England. I pray God deliver us from the confusion which these beginnings threaten!

Such a dearth for want of rain was never in my memory.

17th. The Duke landed with but 150 men; but the whole kingdom was alarmed, fearing that the disaffected would join them, many of the trained bands flocking to him. At his landing, he published a Declaration, charging his Majesty with usurpation and several horrid crimes, on pretence of his own title, and offering to call a free Parliament. This declaration was ordered to be burnt by the hangman, the Duke proclaimed a traitor, and a reward of £5000 to any who should kill him.

At this time, the words engraved on the monument in London, intimating that the Papists fired the City, were erased and cut out.

The exceeding drought still continues.

18th June. I received a warrant to send out a horse with twelve days' provisions, &c.

28th. We had now plentiful rain after two years' excessive drought and severe winters.

Argyle taken in Scotland, and executed, and his party dispersed.

2nd July. No considerable account of the troops sent against the Duke, though great forces sent. There was a smart skirmish; but he would not be provoked to come to an encounter, but still kept in the fastnesses.

Dangerfield whipped, like Oates, for perjury.

8th. Came news of Monmouth's utter defeat, and the next day of his being taken by Sir William Portman and Lord Lumley with the militia of their counties. It seems the Horse, commanded by Lord Grey, being newly raised and undisciplined, were not to be brought in so short a time to endure the fire, which exposed the Foot to the King's, so as when Monmouth had led the Foot in great silence and order, thinking to surprise Lieutenant-General Lord Feversham newly encamped, and given him a smart charge, interchanging both great and small shot, the Horse, breaking their own ranks, Monmouth gave it over, and fled with Grey, leaving their party to be cut in pieces to the number of 2000. The whole number reported to be above 8000; the King's but 2700. The slain were most of them *Mendip-miners*, who did great execution with their tools, and sold their lives very dearly, whilst their leaders flying were pursued and taken the next morning, not far from one another. Monmouth had gone sixteen miles on foot, changing his habit for a poor coat, and was found by Lord Lumley in a dry ditch covered with fern-brakes, but without sword, pistol, or any weapon, and so might have passed for some countryman, his beard being grown so long and so gray as hardly to be known, had not his George discovered him, which was found in his pocket. It is said he trembled exceedingly all over, not able to speak. Grey was taken not far from him. Most of his party were Anabaptists and poor cloth-workers of the country, no gentlemen of account being come in to him. The arch-*boutefeu*, Ferguson, Matthews, &c., were not yet found. The £5000 to be given to who-

RIley Pinx

WILLIAM CAVENDISH.

FIRST DUKE OF DEVONSHIRE

OB. 1707.

ever should bring Monmouth in, was to be distributed among
the militia by agreement between Sir William Portman and
Lord Lumley. The battle ended, some words, first in jest,
then in passion, passed between Sherrington Talbot (a
worthy gentleman, son to Sir John Talbot, and who had
behaved himself very handsomely) and one Captain Love,
both commanders of the militia, as to whose soldiers fought
best, both drawing their swords and passing at one another.
Sherrington was wounded to death on the spot, to the great
regret of those who knew him. He was Sir John's only son.

9th July. Just as I was coming into the lodgings at
Whitehall, a little before dinner, my Lord of Devonshire
standing very near His Majesty's bedchamber-door in the
lobby, came Colonel Culpeper, and in a rude manner looking at my Lord in the face, asked whether this was a time
and place for excluders to appear; my Lord at first took
little notice of what he said, knowing him to be a hot-
headed fellow, but he reiterating it, my Lord asked Culpeper whether he meant him; he said yes, he meant his
Lordship. My Lord told him he was no excluder (as indeed he was not); the other affirming it again, my Lord
told him he lied; on which Culpeper struck him a box on
the ear, which my Lord returned, and felled him. They
were soon parted, Culpeper was seized, and his Majesty,
who was all the while in his bedchamber, ordered him to be
carried to the Green-Cloth Officer, who sent him to the
Marshalsea, as he deserved. My Lord Devon had nothing
said to him.

I supped this night at Lambeth at my old friend's Mr.
Elias Ashmole's, with my Lady Clarendon, the Bishop of
St. Asaph, and Dr. Tenison, when we were treated at a
great feast.

10th. The Count of Castel Mellor, that great favourite
and prime minister of Alphonso, late King of Portugal, after
several years' banishment, being now received to grace and
called home by Don Pedro, the present King, as having been
found a person of the greatest integrity after all his sufferings, desired me to spend part of this day with him, and assist
him in a collection of books and other curiosities, which he
would carry with him into Portugal.

Mr. Hussey,[1] a young gentleman who made love to my late dear child, but whom she could not bring herself to answer in affection, died now of the same cruel disease, for which I was extremely sorry, because he never enjoyed himself after my daughter's decease, nor was I averse to the match, could she have overcome her disinclination.

15th July. I went to see Dr. Tenison's library [in St. Martin's].

Monmouth was this day brought to London and examined before the King, to whom he made great submission, acknowledged his seduction by Ferguson, the Scot, whom he named the bloody villain. He was sent to the Tower, had an interview with his late Duchess, whom he received coldly, having lived dishonestly with the Lady Henrietta Wentworth for two years. He obstinately asserted his conversation with that debauched woman to be no sin; whereupon, seeing he could not be persuaded to his last breath, the divines who were sent to assist him thought not fit to administer the Holy Communion to him. For the rest of his faults he professed great sorrow, and so died without any apparent fear. He would not make use of a cap or other circumstance, but lying down, bid the fellow to do his office better than to the late Lord Russell, and gave him gold; but the wretch made five chops before he had his head off; which so incensed the people, that had he not been guarded and got away, they would have torn him to pieces.

The Duke made no speech on the scaffold (which was on Tower-Hill), but gave a paper containing not above five or six lines, for the King, in which he disclaims all title to the Crown, acknowledges that the late King, his father, had indeed told him he was but his base son, and so desired his Majesty to be kind to his wife and children. This relation I had from Dr. Tenison (Rector of St. Martin's), who, with the Bishops of Ely and Bath anc Wells, were sent to him by his Majesty, and were at the execution.

Thus ended this quondam Duke, darling of his father and the ladies, being extremely handsome and adroit; an

[1] Son of Mr. Peter Hussey, of Sutton in Shere, Surrey. See *ante,* p. 56 and p. 166.

excellent soldier and dancer, a favourite of the people, of an easy nature, debauched by lust; seduced by crafty knaves, who would have set him up only to make a property, and taken the opportunity of the King being of another religion, to gather a party of discontented men. He failed, and perished.

He was a lovely person, had a virtuous and excellent lady that brought him great riches, and a second dukedom in Scotland. He was Master of the Horse, General of the King his father's army, Gentleman of the Bed-chamber, Knight of the Garter, Chancellor of Cambridge; in a word, had accumulations without end. See what ambition and want of principles brought him to! He was beheaded on Tuesday, 14th July. His mother, whose name was Barlow, daughter of some very mean creatures, was a beautiful strumpet, whom I had often seen at Paris; she died miserably without anything to bury her; yet this Perkin had been made to believe that the King had married her, a monstrous and ridiculous forgery! And to satisfy the world of the iniquity of the report, the King his father (if his father he really was, for he most resembled one Sidney [1] who was familiar with his mother) publicly and most solemnly renounced it, to be so entered in the Council Book some years since, with all the Privy Councillors' attestation.[2]

[1] Mr. Robert Sydney, commonly called handsome Sydney, related to the Earl of Leicester of that name.

[2] The *Life of James the Second* contains an account of the circumstances of the Duke of Monmouth's birth, which may be given in illustration of the statements of the text. Ross, tutor to the Duke of Monmouth, is there said to have proposed to Bishop Cosins to sign a certificate of the king's marriage to Mrs. Barlow, though her own name was Walters: but this the Bishop refused. She was born of a gentleman's family in Wales, but having little means and less grace, came to London to make her fortune. Algernon Sydney, then a Colonel in Cromwell's army, had agreed to give her fifty broad pieces (as he told the Duke of York); but being ordered hastily away with his regiment, he missed his bargain. She went into Holland, where she fell into the hands of his brother, Colonel Robert Sydney, who kept her for some time, till the king hearing of her, got her from him. On which the Colonel was heard to say, Let who will have her, she is already sped; and, after being with the king, she was so soon with child, that the world had no cause to doubt whose child it was, and the rather that when he grew to be a man, he very much resembled the colonel both in stature and countenance, even to a wart on his face. However, the king owned the child. In

Had it not pleased God to dissipate this attempt in the beginning, there would in all appearance have gathered an irresistible force which would have desperately proceeded to the ruin of the Church and Government; so general was the discontent and expectation of the opportunity. For my own part, I looked upon this deliverance as most signal. Such an inundation of fanatics and men of impious principles must needs have caused universal disorder, cruelty, injustice, rapine, sacrilege, and confusion, an unavoidable civil war, and misery without end. Blessed be God, the knot was happily broken, and a fair prospect of tranquillity for the future, if we reform, be thankful, and make a right use of this mercy!

18th July. I went to see the muster of the six Scotch and English regiments whom the Prince of Orange had lately sent to his majesty out of Holland upon this rebellion, but which were now returning, there having been no occasion for their use. They were all excellently clad and well disciplined, and were encamped on Blackheath with their tents: the King and Queen came to see them exercise, and the manner of their encampment, which was very neat and magnificent.

By a gross mistake of the Secretary of his Majesty's Forces, it had been ordered that they should be quartered in private houses, contrary to an Act of Parliament, but, on my informing his Majesty timely of it, it was prevented.

The two horsemen which my son and myself sent into the county-troops, were now come home, after a month's being out to our great charge.

20th. The Trinity-Company met this day, which should have been on the Monday after Trinity, but was put off by reason of the Royal Charter being so large, that it could not be ready before. Some immunities were superadded. Mr. Pepys, Secretary to the Admiralty, was a second time chosen Master. There were present the Duke of Grafton, Lord Dartmouth, Master of the Ordnance, the Commissioners of the Navy, and Brethren of the Corporation. We went to church, according to custom, and then took barge

the king's absence, she behaved so loosely, that on his return from his escape at Worcester he would have no further commerce with her, and she became a common prostitute at Paris.

to the Trinity-House, in London, where we had a great dinner, above eighty at one table.

7th August. I went to see Mr. Watts, keeper of the Apothecaries' garden of simples at Chelsea, where there is a collection of innumerable rarities of that sort particularly, besides many rare annuals, the tree bearing Jesuit's bark, which had done such wonders in quartan agues. What was very ingenious was the subterranean heat, conveyed by a stove under the conservatory, all vaulted with brick, so as he has the doors and windows open in the hardest frosts, secluding only the snow.

15th. Came to visit us Mr. Boscawen, with my Lord Godolphin's little son, with whose education hitherto his father had entrusted me.

27th. My daughter Elizabeth died of the small-pox, soon after having married a young man, nephew of Sir John Tippett, Surveyor of the Navy, and one of the Commissioners. The 30th, she was buried in the church at Deptford. Thus, in less than six months were we deprived of two children for our unworthiness and causes best known to God, whom I beseech from the bottom of my heart that he will give us grace to make that right use of all these chastisements, that we may become better, and entirely submit in all things to his infinite wise disposal. Amen!

3rd September. Lord Clarendon (Lord Privy Seal) wrote to let me know that the King being pleased to send him Lord-Lieutenant into Ireland, was also pleased to nominate me one of the Commissioners to execute the office of Privy Seal during his Lieutenancy there, it behoving me to wait upon his Majesty to give him thanks for this great honour.

5th. I accompanied his Lordship to Windsor (dining by the way of Sir Henry Capel's at Kew), where his Majesty receiving me with extraordinary kindness, I kissed his hand. I told him how sensible I was of his Majesty's gracious favour to me, that I would endeavour to serve him with all sincerity, diligence, and loyalty, not more out of my duty than inclination. He said he doubted not of it, and was glad he had the opportunity to show me the kindness he had for me. After this, came abundance of great men to give me joy.

6th. Sunday. I went to prayer in the chapel, and heard

Dr. Standish. The second sermon was preached by Dr. Creighton, on 1 Thess. iv. 11, persuading to unity and peace, and to be mindful of our own business, according to the advice of the apostle. Then I went to hear a Frenchman who preached before the King and Queen in that splendid chapel next St. George's Hall. Their Majesties going to mass, I withdrew to consider the stupendous painting of the Hall, which, both for the art and invention, deserve the inscription in honour of the painter, Signor Verrio. The history is Edward the Third receiving the Black Prince, coming towards him in a Roman triumph. The whole roof is the history of St. George. The throne, the carvings, &c. are incomparable, and I think equal to any, and in many circumstances exceeding any, I have seen abroad.

I dined at Lord Sunderland's, with (amongst others) Sir William Soames, designed Ambassador to Constantinople.

About 6 o'clock, came Sir Dudley and his brother Roger North, and brought the Great Seal from my Lord Keeper, who died the day before at his house in Oxfordshire. The King went immediately to council; everybody gues , g who was most likely to succeed this great officer; most believing it could be no other than my Lord Chief Justice Jefferies, who had so vigorously prosecuted the late rebels, and was now gone the Western Circuit, to punish the rest that were secured in the several counties, and was now near upon his return. I took my leave of his Majesty, who spake very graciously to me, and supping that night at Sir Stephen Fox's, I promised to dine there the next day.

15*th September*. I accompanied Mr. Pepys to Portsmouth, whither his Majesty was going the first time since his coming to the Crown, to see in what state the fortifications were. We took coach and six horses, late after dinner, yet got to Bagshot[1] that night. Whilst supper was making ready I went and made a visit to Mrs. Graham,[2] some time Maid of Honour to the Queen Dowager, now wife to James Graham, Esq., of the privy purse to the King; her house[3] being a walk in the forest, within a little quarter of a mile from Bagshot town. Very importunate she was that I would sup, and abide there that night; but, being obliged by my com-

---

[1] A distance of 26 miles.   [2] Miss Howard, see *ante*, p. 108.
          [3] Bagshot Park.

panion, I returned to our inn, after she had showed me her house, which was very commodious, and well-furnished, as she was an excellent house-wife, a prudent and virtuous lady. There is a park full of red deer about it. Her eldest son was now sick there of the small-pox, but in a likely way of recovery, and other of her children run about, and among the infected, which she said she let them do on purpose that they might whilst young pass that fatal disease she fancied they were to undergo one time or other, and that this would be the best : the severity of this cruel distemper so lately in my poor family confirming much of what she affirmed.

16th September. The next morning, setting out early, we arrived soon enough at Winchester to wait on the King, who was lodged at the Dean's (Dr. Meggot). I found very few with him besides my Lords Feversham, Arran, Newport, and the Bishop of Bath and Wells. His Majesty was discoursing with the Bishops concerning miracles, and what strange things the Saludadors[1] would do in Spain, as by creeping into heated ovens without hurt, and that they had a black cross in the roof of their mouths, but yet were commonly notorious and profane wretches ; upon which his Majesty further said, that he was so extremely difficult of miracles, for fear of being imposed upon, that if he should chance to see one himself, without some other witness, he should apprehend it a delusion of his senses. Then they spake of the boy who was pretended to have a wanting leg restored him, so confidently asserted by Fr. de Santa Clara

[1] Evelyn subjoins this note :—" As to that of the Saludador (of which likewise I remember Sir Arthur Hopton, formerly Ambassador at Madrid, had told me many like wonders), Mr. Pepys passing through Spain, and being extremely inquisitive of the truth of these pretended miracles of the Saludadors, found a very famous one at last, to whom he offered a considerable reward if he would make a trial of the oven, or any other thing of that kind, before him ; the fellow ingenuously told him, that finding he was a more than ordinary curious person, he would not deceive him, and so acknowledged that he could do none of the feats really, but that what they pretended was all a cheat, which he would easily discover, though the poor superstitious people were easily imposed upon ; yet have these impostors an allowance of the Bishops to practice their jugglings. This Mr. Pepys affirmed to me ; but, said he, I did not conceive it fit to interrupt his Majesty, who so solemnly told what they pretended to do. J. E."

R 2

and others. To all which the Bishop added a great miracle happening in Winchester to his certain knowledge, of a poor miserably sick and decrepit child (as I remember long kept unbaptized), who, immediately on his baptism, recovered; as also of the salutary effect of King Charles his Majesty's father's blood, in healing one that was blind.

There was something said of the second sight[1] happening to some persons, especially Scotch; upon which his Majesty, and I think Lord Arran, told us that Monsieur . . . . . . a French nobleman, lately here in England, seeing the late Duke of Monmouth come into the playhouse at London, suddenly cried out to somebody sitting in the same box, *Voilà Monsieur comme il entre sans tête!* Afterwards his Majesty spoke of some relics that had effected strange cures, particularly a piece of our blessed Saviour's cross, that healed a gentleman's rotten nose by only touching. And speaking of the golden cross and chain taken out of the coffin of St. Edward the Confessor at Westminster,[2] by one of the singing-men, who, as the scaffolds were taken down after his Majesty's coronation, espying a hole in the tomb, and something glisten, put his hand in, and brought it to the dean, and he to the King; his Majesty began to put the Bishop in mind how earnestly the late King (his brother) called upon him during his agony, to take out what he had in his pocket. I had thought, said the King, it had been for some keys, which might lead to some cabinet that his Majesty would have me secure; but, says he, you well remember that I found nothing in any of his pockets but a cross of gold, and a few insignificant papers; and thereupon he showed us the cross, and was pleased to put it into my hand. It was of gold, about three inches long, having on one side a crucifix enamelled and embossed, the rest was graved and garnished with goldsmiths' work, and two pretty broad table amethysts (as I conceived), and at the bottom a pendant pearl; within was enchased a little fragment, as was thought, of the true cross, and a Latin inscription in

[1] Several very curious letters on this subject are printed in *Pepys' Diary*, edited by Lord Braybrooke, published by Mr. Bohn.

[2] See a Narrative on the same subject among the Illustrations at the end of this volume.

gold and Roman Letters.[1] More company coming in, this discourse ended. I may not forget a resolution which his Majesty made, and had a little before entered upon it at the Council Board at Windsor or Whitehall, that the negroes in the Plantations should all be baptized, exceedingly declaiming against that impiety of their masters prohibiting it, out of a mistaken opinion that they would be *ipso facto* free ; but his Majesty persists in his resolution to have them christened, which piety the Bishop blessed him for.

I went out to see the new palace the late King had begun, and brought almost to the covering. It is placed on the side of the hill, where formerly stood the old Castle. It is a stately fabric, of three sides and a corridor, all built of brick, and cornished, windows and columns at the break and entrance of free-stone.[2] It was intended for a hunting-house when his Majesty should come to these parts, and has an incomparable prospect. I believe there had already been £20,000 and more expended ; but his now Majesty did not seem to encourage the finishing it at least for a while.

Hence to see the Cathedral, a reverend pile, and in good repair. There are still the coffins of the six Saxon Kings, whose bones had been scattered by the sacrilegious rebels of 1641, in expectation, I suppose, of finding some valuable relics, and afterwards gathered up again and put into new chests, which stand above the stalls of the choir.

[1] There is a pamphlet giving an account of this finding and presenting to the King, under the name of George Taylour; but the writer's name was Henry Keepe. See *Gough's Topography*.

[2] The first stone of this palace was laid by March 23, 1683, by King Charles in person, who, during the remainder of his reign, spent most of his time at Winchester, for the purpose of inspecting and forwarding the work. Upon Charles's death, an immediate stop was put to the building by James II. It was equally neglected by King William ; but Queen Anne, after surveying it herself, intended to complete it in favour of her husband, George, Prince of Denmark, upon whom it was settled, had he lived until she could afford the sums necessary for this purpose. The first public use to which it appears to have been applied, was that of a place of confinement for French prisoners in the war of 1756, during which 5,000 of them, at a time, were occasionally detained in it. In the year 1792, it was occupied by a certain number of French clergy banished from their native soil ; and, in 1796, it was fitted up as barracks for the residence of troops, to which purpose it is still applied.

17th September. Early next morning, we went to Portsmouth, something before his. Majesty arrived. We found all the road full of people, the women in their best dress, in expectation of seeing the King pass by, which he did, riding on horseback a good part of the way. The Mayor and Aldermen with their mace, and in their formalities, were standing at the entrance of the fort, a mile on this side of the town, where the Mayor made a speech to the King, and then the guns of the fort were fired, as were those of the garrison, as soon as the King was come into Portsmouth. All the soldiers (near 3,000) were drawn up, and lining the streets and platform to God's-house (the name of the Governor's residence), where, after he had viewed the new fortifications and ship-yard, his Majesty was entertained at a magnificent dinner by Sir . . . . Slingsby, the Lieutenant-Governor, all the gentlemen in his train sitting down at table with him, which I also had done had I not been before engaged to Sir Robert Holmes, Governor of the Isle of Wight, to dine with him at a private house, where likewise we had a very sumptuous and plentiful repast of excellent venison, fowl, fish, and fruit.

After dinner, I went to wait on his Majesty again, who was pulling on his boots in the Town-hall adjoing the house where he dined, and then having saluted some ladies, who came to kiss his hand, he took horse for Winchester, whither he returned that night. This hall is artificially hung round with arms of all sorts, like the hall and keep at Windsor. Hence, to see the ship-yard and dock, the fortifications, and other things.

Portsmouth, when finished, will be very strong, and a noble quay. There were now thirty-two men-of-war in the harbour. I was invited by Sir R. Beach, the Commissioner, where, after a great supper, Mr. Secretary and myself lay that night, and the next morning set out for Guildford, where we arrived in good hour, and so the day after to London.

I had twice before been at Portsmouth, the Isle of Wight, &c., many years since. I found this part of Hampshire bravely wooded, especially about the house and estate of Colonel Norton, who though now in being, having formerly made his peace by means of Colonel Legg, was formerly a very fierce commander in the first Rebellion. His house is large, and standing low, on the road from Winchester to Portsmouth.

By what I observed in this journey, is that infinite industry, sedulity, gravity, and great understanding and experience of affairs, in his Majesty, that I cannot but predict much happiness to the nation, as to its political government; and, if he so persist, there could be nothing more desired to accomplish our prosperity, but that he was of the national religion.

30th September. Lord Clarendon's commission for Lieutenant of Ireland was sealed this day.

2nd October. Having a letter sent me by Mr. Pepys with this expression at the foot of it, " I have something to show you that I may not have another time," and that I would not fail to dine with him, I accordingly went. After dinner, he had me and Mr. Houblon (a rich and considerable merchant, whose father had fled out of Flanders on the persecution of the Duke of Alva) into a private room, and told us that being lately alone with his Majesty, and upon some occasion of speaking concerning my late Lord Arlington dying a Roman Catholic, who had all along seemed to profess himself a Protestant, taken all the tests, &c., till the day (I think) of his death, his Majesty said that as to his inclinations he had known them long wavering, but from fear of losing his places, he did not think it convenient to declare himself. There are, says the King, those who believe the Church of Rome gives dispensations for going to church, and many like things, but that is not so; for if that might have been had, he himself had most reason to make use of it. *Indeed,* he said, as to *some matrimonial cases, there are now and then dispensations,* but hardly in any cases else.

This familiar discourse encouraged Mr. Pepys to beg of his Majesty, if he might ask it without offence, and for that his Majesty could not but observe how it was whispered among many whether his late Majesty had been reconciled to the Church of Rome; he again humbly besought his Majesty to pardon his presumption, if he had touched upon a thing which did not befit him to look into. The King ingenuously told him that he both was and died a Roman

Catholic, and that he had not long since declared it was
upon some politic and state reasons, best known to himsel.
(meaning the King his brother), but that he was of that persuasion: he bid him follow him into his closet, where opening a cabinet, he showed him two papers, containing about
a quarter of a sheet, on both sides written, in the late King's
own hand, several arguments opposite to the doctrine of
the Church of England, charging her with heresy, novelty,
and the fanaticism of other Protestants, the chief whereof
was, as I remember, our refusing to acknowledge the primacy and infallibility of the Church of Rome; how impossible it was that so many ages should never dispute it, till
of late; how unlikely our Saviour would leave his Church
without a visible Head and guide to resort to, during his
absence; with the like usual topic; so well penned as to
the discourse as did by no means seem to me to have been
put together by the late King, yet written all with his own
hand, blotted and interlined, so as, if indeed it was not given
him by some priest, they might be such arguments and reasons as had been inculcated from time to time, and here recollected; and, in the conclusion, showing his looking on
the Protestant religion (and by name the Church of England) to be without foundation, and consequently false and
unsafe.   When his Majesty had shown him these originals,
he was pleased to lend him the copies of these two papers,
attested at the bottom in four or five lines under his own
hand.

These were the papers I saw and read. This nice and
curious passage I thought fit to set down. Though all
the arguments and objections were altogether weak, and
have a thousand times been answered by our divines; they
are such as their priests insinuate among their proselytes,
as if nothing were Catholic but the Church of Rome, no
salvation out of that, no reformation sufferable, bottoming
all their errors on St Peter's successors' unerrable dictator-
ship, but proving nothing with any reason, or taking notice
of any objection which could be made against it. Here all
was taken for granted, and upon it a resolution and preference implied.

I was heartily sorry to see all this, though it was no other
than was to be suspected, by his late Majesty's too great indif-

ference, neglect, and course of life, that he had been perverted, and for secular respects only professed to be of another belief, and thereby giving great advantage to our
adversaries, both the Court and generally the youth and
great persons of the nation becoming dissolute and highly
profane.   God was incensed to make his reign very troublesome and unprosperous, by wars, plagues, fires, loss of reputation by an universal neglect of the public for the love of
a voluptuous and sensual life, which a vicious Court had
brought into credit.   I think of it with sorrow and pity,
when I consider how good and debonair a nature that unhappy Prince was; what opportunities he had to have
made himself the most renowned King that ever swayed
the British sceptre, had he been firm to that Church for
which his martyred and blessed father suffered; and had he
been grateful to Almighty God, who so miraculously restored him, with so excellent a religion; had he endeavoured
to own and propagate it as he should have done, not only
for the good of his Kingdom, but of all the Reformed
Churches in Christendom, now weakened and near ruined
through our remissness and suffering them to be supplanted,
persecuted, and destroyed, as in France, which we took no
notice of.   The consequence of this, time will show, and I
wish it may proceed no further.   The emissaries and instruments of the Church of Rome will never rest till they have
crushed the Church of England, as knowing that alone to
be able to cope with them, and that they can never answer
her fairly, but lie abundantly open to the irresistible force
of her arguments, antiquity and purity of her doctrine, so
that albeit it may move God, for the punishment of a nation
so unworthy, to eclipse again the profession of her here, and
darkness and superstition prevail, I am most confident the
doctrine of the Church of England will never be extinguished, but remain visible, if not eminent, to the consummation of the world. I have innumerable reasons that confirm
me in this opinion, which I forbear to mention here.

In the mean time, as to the discourse of his Majesty
with Mr. Pepys, and those papers, as I do exceedingly
prefer his Majesty's free and ingenuous profession of what
is own religion is, beyond concealment upon any politic
accounts, so I think him of a most sincere and honest

nature, one on whose word one may rely, and that he
makes a conscience of what he promises, to perform it.
In this confidence, I hope that the Church of England may
yet subsist, and when it shall please God to open his eyes
and turn his heart (for that is peculiarly in the Lord's hands)
to flourish also.   In all events, whatever do become of the
Church of England, it is certainly, of all the Christian professions on the earth, the most primitive, apostolical, and
excellent.

   8th October.   I had my picture drawn this week by the
famous Kneller.[1]

   14th.   I went to London about finishing my lodgings at
Whitehall.

   15th.   Being the King's birth-day, there was a solemn
ball at Court, and before it music of instruments and voices.
I happened by accident to stand the very next to the Queen
and the King, who talked with me about the music.

   18th.   The King was now building all that range
from east to west by the court and garden to the street, and
making a new chapel for the Queen, whose lodgings were to
be in this new building, as also a new Council-chamber and
offices next the south end of the Banqueting-house.   I returned home, next morning, to London.

   22nd.   I accompanied my Lady Clarendon to her house
at Swallowfield,[2] in Berks, dining by the way at Mr. Graham's lodge at Bagshot;[3] the house, new repaired and capacious enough for a good family, stands in a park.

   Hence, we went to Swallowfield; this house is after the
ancient building of honourable gentlemen's houses, when
they kept up ancient hospitality, but the gardens and waters
as elegant as it is possible to make a flat by art and industry,
and no mean expense, my lady being so extraordinarily skilled
in the flowery part, and my lord, in diligence of planting;

   [1] An engraving from this portrait, now at Wotton, forms the Frontispiece to the first volume of these Memoirs.

   [2] Sir William Backhouse died seised of the manor of Swallowfield, in
1669. His widow, daughter and heiress of Mr. William Backhouse, married Henry, Earl of Clarendon, who became possessed of this estate.
The celebrated Lord Chancellor resided at his son's house at Swallowfield after his retirement from public life, and there wrote portions of
his *History of the Rebellion.*

   [3] *Ante,* p. 242.

so that I have hardly seen a seat which shows more tokens of it than what is to be found here, not only in the delicious and rarest fruits of a garden, but in those innumerable timber trees in the ground about the seat, to the greatest ornament and benefit of the place. There is one orchard of 1000 golden, and other cider pippins; walks and groves of elms, limes, oaks, and other trees. The garden is so beset with all manner of sweet shrubs, that it perfumes the air. The distribution also of the quarters, walks, and parterres, is excellent. The nurseries, kitchen-garden full of the most desirable plants; two very noble orangeries well furnished; but, above all, the canal and fish ponds, the one fed with a white, the other with a black running water, fed by a quick and swift river, so well and plentifully stored with fish, that for pike, carp, bream, and tench, I never saw anything approaching it. We had at every meal carp and pike of a size fit for the table of a Prince, and what added to the delight was, to see the hundreds taken by the drag, out of which, the cook standing by, we pointed out what we had most mind to, and had carp that would have been worth at London twenty shillings a piece. The waters are flagged about with *Calamus aromaticus*, with which my lady has hung a closet, that retains the smell very perfectly. There is also a certain sweet willow and other exotics : also a very fine bowling-green, meadow, pasture, and wood; in a word, all that can render a country-seat delightful. There is besides a well-furnished library in the house.

26th October. We returned to London, having been treated with all sorts of cheer and noble freedom by that most religious and virtuous lady. She was now preparing to go for Ireland with her husband, made Lord-Deputy, and went to this country-house and ancient seat of her father and family, to set things in order during her absence; but never were good people and neighbours more concerned than all the country (the poor especially) for the departure of this charitable woman; every one was in tears, and she as unwilling to part from them. There was amongst them a maiden of primitive life, the daughter of a poor labouring man, who had sustained her parents (some time since dead) by her labour, and has for many years refused marriage, or to receive any assistance from the parish, besides the little hermitage my lady gives her rent-free; she lives on four-pence a-day, which she gets by spinning; says she abounds and can give alms to others, living in great humility and content, without any apparent affectation, or singularity; she is continually working, praying, or reading, gives a good account of her knowledge in religion, visits the sick; is not in the least given to talk; very modest, of a simple not unseemly behaviour; of a comely countenance, clad very plain. but clean and tight. In sum, she appears a saint of an ex-traordinary sort, in so religious a life, as is seldom met with in villages now-a-days.

29th October. I was invited to dine at Sir Stephen Fox's with my Lord Lieutenant, where was such a dinner for variety of all things as I had seldom seen, and it was so for the trial of a master-cook whom Sir Stephen had recommended to go with his Lordship into Ireland; there were all the dainties not only of the season, but of what art could add, venison, plain solid meat, fowl, baked and boiled meats, banquet [dessert], in exceeding plenty, and exquisitely dressed. There also dined my Lord Ossory and Lady (the Duke of Beaufort's daughter), my Lady Treasurer, Lord Cornbury, and other visitors.

28th. At the Royal Society, an urn full of bones was presented, dug up in a highway, whilst repairing it, in a field in Camberwell, in Surrey; it was found entire with its cover, amongst many others, believed to be truly Roman and ancient.

Sir Richard Bulkeley described to us a model of a chariot he had invented, which it was not possible to overthrow in whatever uneven way it was drawn, giving us a wonderful relation of what it had performed in that kind, for ease, ex-pedition, and safety; there were some inconveniences yet to be remedied—it would not contain more than one person; was ready to take fire every ten miles; and being placed and playing on no fewer than ten rollers, it made a most prodigious noise, almost intolerable. A remedy was to be sought for these inconveniences.

31st. I dined at our great Lord Chancellor Jefferies, who used me with much respect. This was the late Chief Jus-tice who had newly been the Western Circuit to try the Monmouth conspirators, and had formerly done such severe justice amongst the obnoxious in Westerminster Hall, for which his Majesty dignified him by creating him first a Baron, and now Lord Chancellor. He had some years past been conversant in Deptford; is of an assured and undaunted spirit, and has served the Court-interest on all the hardiest occasions; is of nature cruel, and a slave of the Court.

3rd November. The French persecution of the Protestants raging with the utmost barbarity, exceeded even what the very heathens used : innumerable persons of the greatest birth and riches leaving all their earthly substance, and hardly escaping with their lives, dispersed through all the countries of Enrope. The French tyrant abrogated the Edict of Nantes which had been made in favour of them, and without any cause; on a sudden demolishing all their churches, banishing, imprisoning, and sending to the galleys all the ministers; plundering the common people, and exposing them to all sorts of barbarous usage by soldiers sent to ruin and prey on them; taking away their children; forcing people to the Mass, and then executing them as relapsers; they burnt their libraries, pillaged their goods, eat up their fields and substance, banished or sent the people to the galleys, and seized on their estates. There had now been numbered to pass through Geneva only (and that by stealth, for all the usual passages were strictly guarded by sea and land) 40,000 towards Switzerland. In Holland, Denmark, and all about Germany, were dispersed some hundred thousands; besides those in England, where, though multitudes of all degree sought for shelter and welcome as distressed ' Christians and confessors, they found least encouragement, by a fatality of the times we were fallen into, and the uncharitable indifference of such as should have embraced them; and I pray it be not laid to our charge. The famous Claude[1] fled to Holland; Allix[2] and several more came to

---

[1] John Claude, a celebrated French Protestant minister, and a distinguished controversial writer; who, at the revocation of the Edict of Nantes, was ordered to quit France in four-and-twenty hours. One of his books was burned, by the direction of James II., by the hangman, in the Old Exchange, on May 5th, 1686. He died the following year.

[2] Mr. Peter Allix, a minister of the Reformed Church at Charenton, came over with his whole family, and met with great encouragement here. He was the author of several learned discourses in defence of Protestantism. His eldest son, John Peter Allix, became a Doctor of Divinity,

London, a. 1 persons of great estates came over, who had forsaken all. France was almost dispeopled, the bankers so broken, that the tyrant's revenue was exceedingly diminished, manufactures ceased, and everybody there, save the Jesuits, abhorred what was done, nor did the Papists themselves approve it. What the further intention is, time will show; but doubtless portending some revolution.

I was showed the harangue which the Bishop of Valentia on Rhone made in the name of the Clergy, celebrating the French King, as if he was a God, for persecuting the poor Protestants, with this expression in it, "That as his victory over heresy was greater than all the conquests of Alexander and Cæsar, it was but what was wished in England; and that God seemed to raise the French King to this power and magnanimous action, that he might be in capacity to assist in doing the same here." This paragraph is very bold and remarkable; several reflecting on Archbishop Usher's prophecy as now begun in France, and approaching the orthodox in all other reformed churches. One thing was much taken notice of, that the Gazettes which were still constantly printed twice a week, informing us what was done all over Europe, never spake of this wonderful proceeding in France; nor was any relation of it published by any, save what private letters and the persecuted fugitives brought. Whence this silence, I list not to conjecture; but it appeared very extraordinary in a Protestant country that we should know nothing of what Protestants suffered, whilst great collections were made for them in foreign places, more hospitable and Christian to appearance.

5th November. It being an extraordinary wet morning, and myself indisposed by a very great rheum, I did not go to church, to my very great sorrow, it being the first Gunpowder Conspiracy anniversary that had been kept now these eighty years under a prince of the Roman religion. Bonfires were forbidden on this day; what does this portend!

9th. Began the Parliament. The King in his speech required continuance of a standing force instead of a militia,

and, after passing through different preferments, was in 1730 made Dean of Ely, died in 1758, and was buried in his church of Castle Camps in Cambridgeshire.

and indemnity and dispensation to Popish officers from the Test; demands very unexpected and unpleasing to the Commons. He also required a supply of revenue, which they granted; but returned no thanks to the King for his speech, till farther consideration.

12th November. The Commons postponed finishing the bill for the Supply, to consider the Test, and Popish officers; this was carried but by one voice.

14th. I dined at Lambeth, my Lord Archbishop carrying me with him in his barge; there were my Lord Deputy of Ireland, the Bishops of Ely and St. Asaph, Dr. Sherlock, and other divines; Sir William Hayward, Sir Paul Rycaut, &c.

20th. The Parliament was adjourned to February, several both of Lords and Commons excepting against some passage of his Majesty's speech relating to the Test, and continuance of Popish officers in command. This was a great surprise in a parliament which people believed would have complied in all things.

Popish pamphlets and pictures sold publicly; no books nor answers to them appearing till long after.

21st. I resigned my trust for composing a difference between Mr. Thynn and his wife.

22nd. Hitherto was a very wet warm season.

4th December. Lord Sunderland was declared President of the Council, and yet to hold his Secretary's place. The forces disposed into several quarters through the kingdom are very insolent, on which are great complaints.

Lord Brandon, tried for the late conspiracy, was condemned and pardoned; so was Lord Grey, his accuser and witness.

Persecution in France raging, the French insolently visit our vessels, and take away the fugitive Protestants; some escape in barrels.

10th. To Greenwich, being put into the new Commission of Sewers.

13th. Dr. Patrick, Dean of Peterborough, preached at Whitehall, before the Princess of Denmark; who, since his Majesty came to the Crown, always sat in the King's closet, and had the same bowings and ceremonies applied to the place where she was, as his Majesty had when there in person.

Dining at Mr. Pepys's, Dr. Slayer showed us an experi
ment of a wonderful nature, pouring first a very cold liquor
into a glass, and super-fusing on it another, to appearance
cold and clear liquor also ; it first produced a white cloud,
then boiling, divers coruscations and actual flames of fire
mingled with the liquor, which being a little shaken together, fixed divers suns and stars of real fire, perfectly
globular, on the sides of the glass, and which there stuck
like so many constellations, burning most vehemently, and
resembling stars and heavenly bodies, and that for a long
space. It seemed to exhibit a theory of the eduction of
light out of the chaos, and the fixing or gathering of the
universal light into luminous bodies. This matter, or
phosphorus, was made out of human blood and urine,
elucidating the vital flame, or heat, in animal bodies. A
very noble experiment!

16*th December.* I accompanied my Lord Lieutenant as
far as St. Alban's, there going out of town with him near
200 coaches of all the great officers and nobility. The next
morning taking leave, I returned to London.

18*th.* I dined at the great entertainment his Majesty
gave the Venetian Ambassadors, Signors Zenno and Jus-
tiniani, accompanied with ten more noble Venetians of
their most illustrious families, Cornaro, Maccenigo, &c.,
who came to congratulate their Majesties coming to the
Crown. The dinner was most magnificent and plentiful, at
four tables, with music, kettle-drums, and trumpets, which
sounded upon a whistle at every health. The banquet
[dessert] was twelve vast chargers piled up so high that
those who sat one against another could hardly see each
other. Of these sweetmeats, which doubtless were some
days piling up in that exquisite manner, the Ambassadors
touched not, but leaving them to the spectators who came
out of curiosity to see the dinner, were exceedingly pleased
to see in what a moment of time all that curious work was
demolished, the comfitures voided, and the tables cleared.
Thus his Majesty entertained them three days, which (for
the table only) cost him £600, as the Clerk of the Green
Cloth (Sir William Boreman) assured me. Dinner ended,
I saw their procession, or cavalcade, to Whitehall, innumerable coaches attending. The two Ambassadors had four

coaches of their own, and fifty footmen (as I remember), besides other equipage as splendid as the occasion would permit, the Court being still in mourning. Thence, I went to the audience which they had in the Queen's presence-chamber, the Banqueting-house being full of goods and furniture till the galleries on the garden-side, council-chamber, and new chapel, now in building, were finished. They went to their audience in those plain black gowns and caps which they constantly wear in the city of Venice. I was invited to have accompanied the two Ambassadors in their coach to supper that night, returning now to their own lodgings, as no longer at the King's expense; but, being weary, I excused myself.

19th December. My Lord Treasurer made me dine with him, where I became acquainted with Monsieur Barillon, the French Ambassador, a learned and crafty advocate.

20th. Dr. Turner, brother to the Bishop of Ely, and sometime tutor to my son, preached at Whitehall on Mark viii. 38, concerning the submission of Christians to their persecutors, in which were some passages indiscreet enough, considering the time, and the rage of the inhuman French tyrant against the poor Protestants.

22nd. Our patent for executing the office of Privy Seal during the absence of the Lord Lieutenant of Ireland, being this day sealed by the Lord Chancellor, we went afterwards to St. James's, where the Court then was on occasion of building at Whitehall; his Majesty delivered the seal to my Lord Tiviot and myself, the other Commissioners not being come, and then gave us his hand to kiss. There were the two Venetian Ambassadors and a world of company; amongst the rest the first Popish Nuncio[1] that had been in England since the Reformation; so wonderfully were things changed, to the universal jealousy.

24th. We were all three Commissioners sworn on our knees by the Clerk of the Crown, before my Lord Chancellor, three several oaths; allegiance, supremacy, and the oath belonging to the Lord Privy Seal, which last we took standing. After this, the Lord Chancellor invited us all to

---

[1] Ferdinand, Count D'Ada, made afterwards a Cardinal for his services in this embassy. There is a good mezzotinto print of him.

dinner, but it being Christmas-eve we desired to be excused, intending at three in the afternoon to seal divers things which lay ready at the office; so attended by three of the Clerks of the Signet, we met and sealed. Amongst other things was a pardon to West, who being privy to the late conspiracy, had revealed the accomplices to save his own neck. There were also another pardon and two indenizations; and so agreeing to a fortnight's vacation, I returned home.

31st December. Recollecting the passages of the year past, and having made up accompts, humbly besought Almighty God to pardon those my sins which had provoked Him to discompose my sorrowful family; that he would accept of our humiliation, and in his good time restore comfort to it. I also blessed God for all his undeserved mercies and preservations, begging the continuance of his grace and preservation.—The winter had hitherto been extraordinary wet and mild.

1685-6. *1st January.* Imploring the continuance of God's providential care for the year now entered, I went to the public devotions. The Dean of the Chapel and Clerk of the Closet put out, viz., Bishop of London[1] and . . ., and Rochester[2] and Durham[3] put in their places; the former had opposed the toleration intended, and shown a worthy zeal for the reformed religion as established.

6th. I dined with the Archbishop of York, where was Peter Walsh, that Romish priest so well known for his moderation, professing the Church of England to be a true member of the Catholic Church. He is used to go to our public prayers without scruple, and did not acknowledge the Pope's infallibility, only primacy of order.

19th. Passed the Privy Seal, amongst others, the creation of Mrs. Sedley[4] (concubine to ——) Countess of Dor-

[1] Compton.   [2] Sprat.   [3] Crewe.
[4] Catharine, daughter of Sir Charles Sedley, Bart., one of the famous knot of wits and courtiers of King Charles's time—he was also a poet, and wrote some dramatic pieces. The Countess had a daughter by King James II., and was afterwards married to David, Earl of Portmore, by whom she had two sons, and died in 1717. Lord Dorset's well-known verses, "Tell me, Dorinda, why so gay," &c. are addressed to this lady. Her father's sarcasm, when he voted for filling up the vacant throne with the Prince and Princess of Orange, is well known; "King James made my daughter a Countess, and I have been helping to make his daughter a Queen." See *ante*, p. 128.

chester, which the Queen took very grievously, so as for two dinners, standing near her, I observed she hardly eat one morsel, nor spake one word to the King, or to any about her, though at other times she used to be extremely pleasant, full of discourse and good humour. The Roman Catholics were also very angry: because they had so long valued the sanctity of their religion and proselytes.

Dryden, the famous play-writer, and his two sons, and Mrs. Nelly (miss to the late ——), were said to go to mass; such proselytes were no great loss to the Church.

This night was burnt to the ground my Lord Montague's palace in Bloomsbury, than which for painting and furniture there was nothing more glorious in England. This happened by the negligence of a servant airing, as they call it, some of the goods by the fire in a moist season; indeed, so wet and mild a season had scarce been seen in man's memory.

At this Seal there also passed the creation of Sir Henry Waldegrave[1] to be a Peer. He had married one of the King's natural daughters by Mrs. Churchill. These two Seals my brother Commissioners passed in the morning before I came to town, at which I was not displeased. We likewise passed Privy Seals for £276,000 upon several accounts, pensions, guards, wardrobes, privy purse, &c., besides divers pardons, and one more which I must not forget (and which by Providence I was not present at) one Mr. Lytcott to be Secretary to the Ambassador to Rome. We being three Commissioners, any two were a quorum.

21st January. I dined at my Lady Arlington's, Groom of the Stole to the Queen Dowager, at Somerset House, where dined the Countesses of Devonshire, Dover, &c.; in all eleven ladies of quality, no man but myself being there.

24th. Unheard-of cruelties to the persecuted Protestants of France, such as hardly any age has seen the like, even among the Pagans.

6th February. Being the day on which his Majesty began

---

[1] He was the fourth Baronet. He was created 30th January, 1686, Baron Waldegrave, being at that time Comptroller of the King's Household; and died at Paris, in 1689.

his reign, by order of Council it was to be solemnized with
a particular office and sermon, which the Bishop of Ely [1]
preached at Whitehall on Numb. xi. 12; a Court oration
upon the Regal Office. It was much wondered at, that
this day, which was that of his late Majesty's death,
should be kept as a festival, and not the day of the
present King's coronation. It is said to have been formerly
the custom, though not till now since the reign of King
James I.

The Duchess of Monmouth, being in the same seat with
me at church, appeared with a very sad and afflicted countenance.

8th February. I took the Test in Westminster-Hall, before
the Lord Chief Justice. I now came to lodge at Whitehall, in the Lord Privy Seal's lodgings.

12th. My great Cause was heard by my Lord Chancellor,
who granted me a re-hearing. I had six eminent lawyers,
my antagonist three, whereof one was the smooth-tongued
Solicitor,[2] whom my Lord Chancellor reproved in great
passion for a very small occasion. Blessed be God for His
great goodness to me this day!

19th. Many bloody and notorious duels were fought
about this time. The Duke of Grafton killed Mr.
Stanley, brother to the Earl of [Derby], indeed upon an
almost insufferable provocation. It is to be hoped that
his Majesty will at last severely remedy this unchristian
custom.

Lord Sunderland was now Secretary of State, President of
the Council, and Premier-Minister.

1st March. Came Sir Gilbert Gerrard to treat with me
about his son's marrying my daughter, Susannna. The father
being obnoxious, and in some suspicion and displeasure of
the King, I would receive no proposal till his Majesty had
given me leave, which he was pleased to do; but, after several
meetings we brake off, on his not being willing to secure
any thing competent for my daughter's children; besides
that I found most of his estate was in the coal-pits as
far off as Newcastle, and on leases from the Bishop of Dur-

---

[1] Dr. Francis Turner.
[2] Finch, called *Silver Tongue*, from his manner of speaking.

ham, who had power to make concurrent leases, with other difficulties. ·

7th March. Dr. Frampton, Bishop of Gloucester, preached on Psalm xliv. 17, 18, 19, showing the several afflictions of the Church of Christ from the primitives to this day, applying exceedingly to the present conjuncture, when many were wavering in their minds, and great temptations appearing through the favour now found by the Papists, so as the people were full of jealousies and discouragement. The Bishop magnified the Church of England, exhorting to constancy and perseverance.

10th. A Council of the Royal Society about disposing of Dr. Ray's[1] book of Fishes, which was printed at the expense of the Society.

12th. A docket was to be sealed, importing a lease of twenty-one years to one Hall, who styled himself his Majesty's printer (he lately turned Papist) for the printing Missals, Offices, Lives of Saints, Portals, Primers, &c., books expressly forbidden to be printed or sold, by divers Acts of Parliament ; I refused to put my seal to it, making my exceptions, so it was laid by.

14th. The Bishop of Bath and Wells[2] preached on John vi. 17, a most excellent and pathetic discourse : after he had recommended the duty of fasting and other penitential duties, he exhorted to constancy in the Protestant religion, detestation of the unheard-of cruelties of the French, and stirring up to a liberal contribution. This sermon was the more acceptable, as it was unexpected from a Bishop who had undergone the censure of being inclined to Popery, the contrary whereof no man could show more. This indeed did all our Bishops, to the disabusing and reproach of all their delators : for none were more zealous against Popery than they were.

16th. I was at a review of the army about London, in

---

[1] John Ray, the celebrated naturalist, and author, among other works, of " The Wisdom of God manifested in the Works of the Creation." He was a liberal contributor to the Transactions of the Royal Society, ot which he was elected a fellow in 1667. Born in 1628, died in 1705.

[2] Thomas Ken, the deprived Bishop ; born at Berkhampstead, Herts, in July, 1637, and died at Longleat in Wiltshire, then the seat of Lord Viscount Weymouth, March 19, 1710-11.

Hyde Park, about 6000 horse and foot, in excellent order; his Majesty and infinity of people being present.

17th March. I went to my house in the country, refusing to be present at what was to pass at the Privy Seal the next day. In the morning, Dr. Tenison preached an incomparable discourse at Whitehall, on Timothy ii. 3, 4.

24th. Dr. Cradock (Provost of Eaton) preached at the same place on Psalm xlix. 13, showing the vanity of earthly enjoyments.

28th. Dr. White, Bishop of Peterborough, preached in a very eloquent style, on Matthew xxvi. 29, submission to the will of God on all accidents, and at all times.

29th. The Duke of Northumberland (a natural son of the late King by the Duchess of Cleveland) marrying very meanly, with the help of his brother Grafton, attempted in vain to spirit away his wife.

A Brief was read in all churches for relieving the French Protestants, who came here for protection from the unheard-of cruelties of the King.

2nd April. Sir Edward Hales, a Papist, made Governor of Dover Castle.[1]

15th. The Archbishop of York [2] now died of the small-pox, aged 62, a corpulent man. He was my special loving friend, and whilst Bishop of Rochester (from whence he was translated) my excellent neighbour. He was an inexpressible loss to the whole church, and that Province especially, being a learned, wise, stout, and most worthy prelate; I look on this as a great stroke to the poor Church of England, now in this defecting period.

18th. In the afternoon, I went to Camberwell, to visit Dr. Parr. After sermon, I accompanied him to his house, where he showed me the Life and Letters of the late learned Primate of Armagh (Usher), and among them that letter of Bishop Bramhall's to the Primate, giving notice of the Popish practices to pervert this nation, by sending a hundred priests into England, who were to conform themselves to all sectaries and conditions for the more easily dispersing

---

[1] Not taking the Test, Burnet tells us, his coachman was set up to inform against him and claim the 500*l.* penalty. When this was to be brought to trial, the judges were secretly asked their opinions, and such as were not clear with the Court were turned out. Half of them were dismissed.   [2] Dr. John Dolben

their doctrine amongst us.   This letter was the cause of the whole impression being seized, upon pretence that it was a political or historical account of things not relating to theology, though it had been licensed by the Bishop; which plainly showed what an interest the Papists now had,—that a Protestant book, containing the life and letters of so emi-. nent a man, was not to be published.   There were also many letters to and from most of the learned persons his correspondents in Europe.   The book will, I doubt not, struggle through this unjust impediment.

Several Judges were put out, and new complying ones put in.

25th April. This day was read in our church the Brief for a collection for relief of the Protestant French so cruelly, barbarously, and inhumanly oppressed without any thing being laid to their charge.   It had been long expected, and at last with difficulty procured to be published, the interest of the French Ambassador obstructing it.

5th May. There being a Seal, it was feared we should be required to pass a docket dispensing with Dr. Obadiah Walker and four more, whereof one was an apostate curate of Putney,[1] the others officers of University College, Oxford, who hold their masterships, fellowships, and cures, and keep public schools, and enjoy all former emoluments, notwithstanding they no more frequented or used the public forms of prayers, or communion, with the Church of England, or took the Test or oaths of allegiance and supremacy, contrary to twenty Acts of Parliament; which dispensation being also contrary to his Majesty's own gracious declaration at the beginning of his reign, gave umbrage (as well it might) to every good Protestant; nor could we safely have passed it under the Privy Seal, wherefore it was done by immediate warrant, signed by Mr. Solicitor.

This Walker was a learned person, of a monkish life, to whose tuition I had more than thirty years since recommended the sons of my worthy friend, Mr. Hyldyard, of Horsley in Surrey,[2] believing him to be far from what he proved—a hypocritical concealed Papist—by which he per-

[1] Edward Sclater; who first apostatized from Protestantism, and then, in 1689, read his recantation from Popery, and again became a Protestant.   [2] See *ante*, vol. i. p. 285.

verted the eldest son of Mr. Hyldyard, Sir Edward Hale's eldest son, and several more, to the great disturbance of the whole nation, as well as of the University, as by his now public defection appeared. All engines being now at work to bring in Popery, which God in mercy prevent!

This day was burnt in the old Exchange, by the common hangman, a translation of a book written by the famous Monsieur Claude, relating only matters of fact concerning the horrid massacres and barbarous proceedings of the French King against his Protestant subjects, without any refutation of any facts therein; so mighty a power and ascendant here had the French Ambassador, who was doubt-less in great indignation at the pious and truly generous charity of all the nation, for the relief of those miserable sufferers who came over for shelter.

About this time also, the Duke of Savoy, instigated by the French King to extirpate the Protestants of Piedmont, slew many thousands of those innocent people, so that there seemed to be an universal design to destroy all that would not go to mass, throughout Europe. *Quod Avertat D. O. M.!* No faith in Princes!

12th May. I refused to put the Privy Seal to Doctor Walker's license for printing and publishing divers Popish books, of which I complained both to my Lord of Canterbury (with whom I went to advise in the Council-Chamber), and to my Lord Treasurer that evening at his lodgings. My Lord of Canterbury's[1] advice was, that I should follow my own conscience therein; Mr. Treasurer's, that if in conscience I could dispense with it, for any other hazard he believed there was none. Notwithstanding this, I persisted in my refusal.

29th. There was no sermon on this anniversary, as there usually had been ever since the reign of the present King.

2nd June. Such storms, rain, and foul weather, seldom known at this time of the year. The camp at Hounslow Heath, from sickness and other inconveniences of weather, forced to retire to quarters; the storms being succeeded by excessive hot weather, many grew sick. Great feasting there, especially in Lord Dunbarton's quarters. There

[1] Dr. Sancroft. Burnet describes him as a timid man.

were many jealousies and discourses of what was the meaning of this encampment.

A seal this day; mostly pardons and discharges of Knight-Baronets' fees, which having been passed over for so many years, did greatly disoblige several families who had served his Majesty. Lord Tyrconnel gone to Ireland, with great powers and commissions, giving as much cause of talk as the camp, especially nineteen new Privy-Councillors and Judges being now made, amongst which but three Protestants, and Tyrconnell made General.

New Judges also here, among which was Milton, a Papist (brother to that Milton who wrote for the Regicides), who presumed to take his place without passing the Test.[1] Scotland refused to grant liberty of mass to the Papists there.

The French persecution more inhuman than ever. The Protestants in Savoy successfully resist the French dragoons sent to murder them.

The King's chief physician in Scotland apostatizing from the Protestant religion, does of his own accord publish his recantation at Edinburgh.[2]

11th *June.* I went to see Middleton's receptacle of water at the New River, and the new Spa Wells near.

20th. An extraordinary season of violent and sudden rain. The camp still in tents.

24th. My Lord-Treasurer settled my great business with Mr. Pretyman, to which I hope God will at last give a prosperous issue.

25th. Now his Majesty, beginning with Dr. Sharp and Tully,[3] proceeded to silence and suspend divers excellent divines for preaching against Popery.

[1] Christopher Milton, made a Baron of the Exchequer. He did not hold his office long. From weakness of constitution, Dr. Johnson remarks, he retired before he had done any disreputable act.

[2] Burnet informs us in his *Own Times,* that this Sir Robert Sibbald, the most learned antiquary in Scotland, who had lived in a course of philosophical virtue, but in great doubt as to revealed religion, was prevailed upon by the Earl of Perth to turn Papist; but he soon became ashamed of having done so, on so little inquiry. Upon this he proceeded to London for some months, retiring from all company, and underwent a deep course of study, by which he came to a conviction of the errors of Popery. He then returned to Scotland, and published, as Evelyn tells us, his recantation openly in a church.

[3] John Sharp, Dean of Norwich, famous for having been one of the first

27th June. I had this day been married thirty-nine years—blessed be God for all His mercies!

The new very young Lord Chief-Justice Herbert declared on the bench, that the government of England was entirely in the King; that the Crown was absolute; that penal laws were powers lodged in the Crown to enable the King to force the execution of the law, but were not bars to bind the King's power; that he could pardon all offences against the law, and forgive the penalties, and why could he not dispense with them; by which the Test was abolished? Every one was astonished. Great jealousies as to what would be the end of these proceedings.

6th July. I supped with the Countess of Rochester, where was also the Duchess of Buckingham and Madame de Governè, whose daughter was married to the Marquis of Halifax's son. She made me a character of the French King and Dauphin, and of the persecution; that they kept much of the cruelties from the King's knowledge; that the Dauphin was so afraid of his father, that he durst not let anything appear of his sentiments; that he hated letters and priests, spent all his time in hunting, and seemed to take no notice of what was passing.

This lady was of a great family and fortune, and had fled hither for refuge.

8th. I waited on the Archbishop at Lambeth, where I dined and met the famous preacher and writer, Dr. Allix,[1] doubtless a most excellent and learned person. The Archbishop and he spoke Latin together, and that very readily.

11th. Dr. Meggot, Dean of Winchester, preached before the Household in St. George's Chapel at Windsor, the late King's glorious chapel now seized on by the mass-priests. Dr. Cartwright, Dean of Ripon, preached before the great men of the Court in the same place.

We had now the sad news of the Bishop of Oxford's[2] death, an extraordinary loss to the poor Church at this

victims to the intolerance of James II., who caused him to be suspended for preaching against Popery. After the revolution he was made Dean of Canterbury, and subsequently Archbishop of York. Born 1644. Died 1713.—George Tully, another champion of Protestantism, whom James endeavoured to silence by persecution. He died in 1697.

[1] Allix, of whom see *ante*, p. 253.
[2] Dr. John Fell, also Dean of Christchurch.

time. Many candidates for his Bishopric and Deanery, Dr.
Parker, South, Aldrich, &c.   Dr. Walker (now apostatizing)
came to Court, and was doubtless very busy.

13th July. Note, that standing by the Queen at basset
(cards), I observed that she was exceedingly concerned for
the loss of £80; her outward affability much, changed to
stateliness, since she has been exalted.

The season very rainy and inconvenient for the camps.
His Majesty very cheerful.

14th. Was sealed at our office the Constitution of certain
Commissioners to take upon them full power of all Ecclesiastical affairs, in as unlimited a manner, or rather greater,
than the late High Commission-Court, abrogated by Parliament; for it had not only faculty to inspect and visit all
Bishops' dioceses, but to change what laws and statutes
they should think fit to alter among the Colleges, though
founded by private men; to punish, suspend, fine, &c., give
oaths and call witnesses. The main drift was to suppress
zealous preachers. In sum, it was the whole power of a
Vicar-General—note the consequence! Of the Clergy the
Commissioners were the Archbishop of Canterbury [San-
croft], Bishop of Durham [Crewe], and Rochester [Sprat];
of the Temporals, the Lord Treasurer, the Lord Chancellor
[Jefferies] (who alone was ever to be of the quorum), the
Chief Justice [Herbert], and Lord President [Earl of Sun-
derland].

18th July. I went to see Sir John Chardin, at Greenwich.

4th August. I dined at Signor Verrio's, the famous Italian
painter, now settled in his Majesty's garden at St. James's,
which he had made a very delicious Paradise.

8th. Our vicar gone to dispose of his country living in
Rutlandshire, having St. Dunstan in the East given him by
the Archbishop of Canterbury.

I went to visit the Marquis Ravigné, now my neighbour at
Greenwich, retired from the persecution in France. He was
the Deputy of all the Protestants of that kingdom in the
Parliament of Paris, and several times Ambassador in this and
other Courts; a person of great learning and experience.[1]

---

[1] His son was with King William in Ireland, and was made Earl of
Galway, but was dismissed through the violence of party, being a Frenchman. though his conduct had been in every respect unexceptionable, as
will appear hereafter.

8th September. Dr. Compton, Bishop of London, was on Monday suspended, on pretence of not silencing Dr. Sharp of St. Giles's, for something of a sermon in which he zealously reproved the doctrine of the Roman Catholics. The Bishop having consulted the civilians, they told him he could not by any law proceed against Dr. Sharp without producing witnesses, and impleaded according to form ; but it was overruled by my Lord Chancellor, and the Bishop sentenced without so much as being heard to any purpose. This was thought a very extraordinary way of proceeding, and was universally resented, and so much the rather for that two Bishops, Durham[2] and Rochester,[3] sitting in the Commission and giving their suffrages, the Archbishop of Canterbury refused to sit amongst them. He was only suspended *ab officio*, and that was soon after taken off. He was brother to the Earl of Northampton, had once been a soldier, had travelled in Italy, but became a sober, grave, and excellent Prelate.

12th. Buda now taken from the Turks ; a form of Thanksgiving was ordered to be used in the (as yet remaining) Protestant chapels and church of Whitehall and Windsor.

The King of Denmark was besieging Hamburgh, no doubt by the French contrivance, to embroil the Protestant Princes in a new war, that Holland, &c., being engaged, matter for new quarrel might arise : the unheard-of persecution of the poor Protestants still raging more than ever.

22nd September. The Danes retire from Hamburgh, the Protestant Princes appearing for their succour, and the Emperor sending his Minatories to the King of Denmark, and also requiring the restoration of the Duke of Saxe Gotha. Thus it pleased God to defeat the French designs, which were evidently to kindle a new war.

14th October. His Majesty's birth-day ; I was at his rising in his bedchamber, afterwards in the park, where four companies of guards were drawn up. The officers, &c. wonderfully rich and gallant ; they did not head their troops, but their next officers, the colonels being on horseback by the King whilst they marched. The ladies not less splendid at

---

¹ Crewe.   ² Sprat : he afterwards would not sit.

Court, where there was a ball at night; but small appearance of quality. All the shops both in the City and
suburbs were shut up, and kept as solemnly as any holiday.
Bonfires at night in Westminster,)ut forbidden in the
City.

17th October. Dr. Patrick, Dean of Peterborough, preached
at Covent Garden Church on Ephes. v. 18, 19, showing the
custom of the primitive saints in serving God with hymns,
and their frequent use of them upon all occasions: per-
stringing the profane way of mirth and intemperance of
this ungodly age. Afterwards, I visited my Lord Chief
Justice of Ireland, with whom I had long and private discourse concerning the miserable condition that kingdom
was like to be in, if Tyrconnel's counsel should prevail at
Court.

23rd. Went with the Countess of Sunderland to Cran-
bourn, a lodge and walk of my Lord Godolphin's in Windsor
Park. There was one room in the house spared in the
pulling down the old one, because the late Duchess of York
was born in it; the rest was built and added to it by Sir
George Carteret, Treasurer of the Navy; and since, the
whole was purchased by my Lord Godolphin, who spake to
me to go see it, and advise what trees were fit to be cut
down to improve the dwelling, being environed with old
rotten pollards, which corrupt the air. It stands on a
knoll, which though insensibly rising, gives it a prospect
over the Keep of Windsor, about three miles N. E. of it.
The ground is clayey and moist; the water stark naught; the
park is pretty; the house tolerable, and gardens convenient.
After dinner, we came back to London, having two coaches
both going and coming, of six horses apiece, which we
changed at Hounslow.

24th. Dr. Warren preached before the Princess at
Whitehall, on 5th Matthew, of the blessedness of the pure
in heart, most elegantly describing the bliss of the beatifical
vision. In the afternoon, Sir George Wheeler, Knight and
Baronet, preached on the 4th Matt. upon the necessity of
repentance, at St. Margaret's, an honest and devout discourse, and pretty tolerably performed. This gentleman
coming from his travels out of Greece, fell in love with the
daughter of Sir Thomas Higgins, his Majesty's resident a*

Venice, niece to the Earl of Bath, and married her. When they returned into England, being honoured with knighthood, he would needs turn preacher, and took orders. He published a learned and ingenious book of his travels, and is a very worthy person, a little formal and particular, but exceedingly devout.[1]

27th October. There was a triumphant show of the Lord Mayor both by land and water, with much solemnity, when yet his power has been so much diminished, by the loss of the City's former charter.

5th November. I went to St. Martin's in the morning, where Dr. Birch preached very boldly against the Papists, from John xvi. 2. In the afternoon, I heard Dr. Tillotson in Lincoln's Inn chapel, on the same text, but more cautiously.

16th. I went with part of my family to pass the melancholy winter in London at my son's house in Arundel Buildings.

5th December. I dined at my Lady Arlington's, Groom of the Stole to the Queen Dowager, at Somerset House, where dined divers French noblemen, driven out of their country by the persecution.

16th. I carried the Countess of Sunderland to see the rarities of one Mr. Charlton in the Middle Temple, who showed us such a collection as I had never seen in all my travels abroad, either of private gentlemen, or princes. It consisted of miniatures, drawings, shells, insects, medals, natural things, animals (of which divers, I think 100, were kept in glasses of spirits of wine), minerals, precious stones,

---

[1] Sir George Wheeler was born whilst his parents were in exile at Breda for their attachment to Charles I. He was of Lincoln College, Oxford. On his return from his travels in Asia and Greece, he was knighted. Having presented several antiquities which he had collected to the University of Oxford, in 1683, they gave him his degree of A.M. He took orders against the advice of powerful friends, but from an earnest desire to be useful as a parish priest; and he well fulfilled his intentions. He became Rector of Houghton-le-Spring, in Durham, the living which had been so exemplarily filled by the "Northern Apostle," Bernard Gilpin, whose example he worthily followed. Bishop Crewe also gave him a stall in Durham Cathedral. He died 18th January, 1723. His descendants are seated at Otterden, in Kent. See Surtees' History of Durham (1816), where a full account and a portrait of him are given.

vessels, curiosities in amber, crystal, agate, &c.; all being very perfect and rare of their kind, especially his books of birds, fish, flowers, and shells, drawn and miniatured to the life. He told us that one book stood him in £300; it was painted by that excellent workman, whom the late Gaston, Duke of Orleans, employed. This gentleman's whole collection, gathered by himself, travelling over most parts of Europe, is estimated at £8,000. He appeared to be a modest and obliging person.[1]

29th. I went to hear the music of the Italians in the new chapel, now first opened publicly at Whitehall for the Popish Service. Nothing can be finer than the magnificent marble work and architecture at the end, where are four statues, representing St. John, St. Peter, St. Paul, and the Church, in white marble, the work of Mr. Gibbon, with all the carving and pillars of exquisite art and great cost. The altar-piece is the Salutation; the volto in *fresco*, the Assumption of the Blessed Virgin, according to their tradition, with our Blessed Saviour, and a world of figures painted by Verrio. The throne where the King and Queen sit is very glorious, in a closet above, just opposite to the altar. Here we saw the Bishop in his mitre and rich copes, with six or seven Jesuits and others in rich copes, sumptuously habited, often taking off and putting on the Bishop's mitre, who sat in a chair with arms pontifically, was adored and censed by three Jesuits in their copes; then he went to the altar and made divers cringes, then censing the images and glorious tabernacle placed on the altar, and now and then changing place: the crosier, which was of silver, was put into his hand with a world of mysterious ceremony, the music playing, with singing. I could not have believed I should ever have seen such things in the King of England's palace, after it had pleased God to enlighten this nation; but our great sin has, for the present, eclipsed the blessing, which I hope He will in mercy and His good time restore to its purity.

Little appearance of any winter as yet.

---

[1] This collection was afterwards purchased by Sir Hans Sloane, and now forms part of the British Museum. *Gent. Mag.,* Nov. 1816, p. 325, from Mr. Bagford's papers in the British Museum.

1686-7. 1*st January.* Mr. Wake[1] preached at St. Martin's on 1 Tim. iii. 16, concerning the mystery of godliness. He wrote excellently, in answer to the Bishop of Meaux.

3*rd.* A Seal to confirm a gift of £4,000 per annum for 99 years to the Lord Treasurer out of the Post-office, and £1,700 per annum for ever out of Lord Gray's estate.

There was now another change of the great officers. The Treasury was put into commission, two professed Papists amongst them, viz., Lords Bellasis and Dover, joined with the old ones, Lord Godolphin, Sir Stephen Fox, and Sir John Ernley.

17*th.* Much expectation of several great men declaring themselves Papists. Lord Tyrconnel gone to succeed the Lord-Lieutenant [Clarendon] in Ireland, to the astonishment of all sober men, and to the evident ruin of the Protestants in that kingdom, as well as of its great improvement going on. Much discourse that all the White Staff officers and others should be dismissed for adhering to their religion. Popish Justices of the Peace established in all counties, of the meanest of the people ; Judges ignorant of the law, and perverting it—so furiously do the Jesuits drive, and even compel Princes to violent courses, and destruction of an excellent government both in Church and State. God of his infinite mercy open our eyes, and turn our hearts, and establish His truth with peace! The Lord Jesus defend His little flock, and preserve this threatened church and nation !

24*th.* I saw the Queen's new apartment at Whitehall, with her new bed, the embroidery of which cost £3,000. The carving about the chimney-piece, by Gibbon, is incomparable.

30*th.* I heard the famous eunuch, Cifaccio, sing in the new Popish chapel this afternoon ; it was indeed very rare, and with great skill. He came over from Rome, esteemed one of the best voices in Italy. Much crowding—little devotion.

---

[1] William III. recognised the services of the Rev. William Wake in the cause of the Protestant Church of England, by presenting him with valuable preferments. He was King's Chaplain, Rector of St. James's Westminster, Dean of Exeter, Bishop of Lincoln, and finally, Archbishop of Canterbury. Born 1657, died 1737.

27th February. Mr. Chetwin preached at Whitehall on Rom. i. 18, a very quaint neat discourse of Moral righteousness.

2nd March. Came out a proclamation for universal liberty of conscience in Scotland, and dispensation from all tests and laws to the contrary, as also capacitating Papists to be chosen into all offices of trust. The mystery operates.

3rd. Dr. Meggot, Dean of Winchester, preached before the Princess of Denmark, on Matt. xiv. 23. In the afternoon, I went out of town to meet my Lord Clarendon, returning from Ireland.

10th. His Majesty sent for the Commissioners of the Privy Seal this morning into his bedchamber, and told us that though he had thought fit to dispose of the Seal into a single hand, yet he would so provide for us, as it should appear how well he accepted our faithful and loyal service, with many gracious expressions to this effect; upon which we delivered the Seal into his hands. It was by all the world both hoped and expected, that he would have restored it to my Lord Clarendon; but they were astonished to see it given to Lord Arundel, of Wardour, a zealous Roman Catholic. Indeed it was very hard, and looked very unkindly, his Majesty (as my Lord Clarendon protested to me, on my going to visit him and long discoursing with him about the affairs of Ireland) finding not the least failure of duty in him during his government of that kingdom, so that his recall plainly appeared to be from the stronger influence of the Papists, who now got all the preferments.

Most of the great officers, both in the court and country, Lords and others, were dismissed, as they would not promise his Majesty their consent to the repeal of the test and penal statutes against Popish Recusants. To this end, most of the Parliament-men were spoken to in his Majesty's closet, and such as refused, if in any place of office or trust, civil or military, were put out of their employments. This was a time of great trial; but hardly one of them assented, which put the Popish interest much backward. The English clergy everywhere preached boldly against their superstition and errors, and were wonderfully followed by the people. Not one considerable proselyte was made in all this time. The party were exceedingly put to the worst by

the preaching and writing of the Protestants in many excellent treatises, evincing the doctrine and discipline of the
reformed religion, to the manifest disadvantage of their
adversaries. To this did not a little contribute the sermon
preached at Whitehall before the Princess of Denmark and
a great crowd of people, and at least thirty of the greatest
nobility, by Dr. Ken, Bishop of Bath and Wells,[1] on John
viii. 46 (the gospel of the day), describing through his whole
discourse the blasphemies, perfidy, wresting of Scripture,
preference of tradition before it, spirit of persecution, superstition, legends and fables of the Scribes and Pharisees, so
that all the auditory understood his meaning of a parallel
between them and the Romish priests, and their new Trent
religion. He exhorted his audience to adhere to the written
Word, and to persevere in the Faith taught in the Church
of England, whose doctrine for Catholic and soundness he
preferred to all the communities and churches of Christians
in the world; concluding with a kind of prophecy, that
whatever it suffered, it should after a short trial emerge to
the confusion of her adversaries and the glory of God.

I went this evening to see the order of the boys and
children at Christ's Hospital. There were near 800 boys
and girls so decently clad, cleanly lodged, so wholesomely
fed, so admirably taught, some the mathematics, especially
the forty of the late King's foundation, that I was delighted
to see the progress some little youths of thirteen or fourteen years of age had made. I saw them at supper, visited
their dormitories, and much admired the order, economy,
and excellent government of this most charitable seminary.
Some are taught for the Universities, others designed for
seamen, all for trades and callings. The girls are instructed
in all such work as becomes their sex and may fit them for
good wives, mistresses, and to be a blessing to their gene-

[1] A prelate remarkable for his benevolence and piety, and the only
person in England known to have interceded for the sufferers from the
cruelty of Colonel Kirke, on the suppression of Monmouth's rebellion;
urging the King with tears to put a stop to the dreadful butchery. He
was one of the seven bishops sent by James II. to the Tower; yet he
refused to acknowledge James's successor, on the ground that it would
be a breach of his Consecration Oath, and suffered for his conscientious
scruples the penalty of deprivation. He was born in 1637, and died
in 1711.

ration. They sung a psalm before they sat down to supper in the great Hall, to an organ which played all the time, with such cheerful harmony, that it seemed to me a vision of angels. I came from the place with infinite satisfaction, having never seen a more noble, pious, and admirable charity. All these consisted of orphans only.[1] The foundation was of that pious Prince King Edward VI., whose picture (held to be an original of Holbein) is in the court where the Governors meet to consult on the affairs of the Hospital, and his statue in white marble stands in a niche of the wall below, as you go to the church, which is a modern, noble and ample fabric. This foundation has had, and still has, many bene-factors.

16*th March.* I saw a trial of those devilish, murdering, mischief-doing engines called bombs, shot out of the mortar-piece on Blackheath. The distance that they are cast, the destruction they make where they fall, is prodigious.

20*th.* The Bishop of Bath and Wells (Dr. Ken) preached at St. Martin's to a crowd of people not to be expressed, nor the wonderful eloquence of this admirable preacher; the text was Matt. xxvi. 36 to verse 40, describing the bitter-ness of our Blessed Saviour's agony, the ardour of his love, the infinite obligations we have to imitate his patience and resignation; the means by watching against temptations, and over ourselves with fervent prayer to attain it, and the ex-ceeding reward in the end. Upon all which he made most pathetical discourses. The Communion followed, at which I was participant. I afterwards dined at Dr. Tenison's with the Bishop and that young, most learned, pious, and ex-cellent preacher, Mr. Wake.[2] In the afternoon, I went to hear Mr. Wake at the new-built church of St. Anne, on Mark viii. 34, upon the subject of taking up the cross, and strenuously behaving ourselves in time of persecution, as this now threatened to be.

His Majesty again prorogued the Parliament, foreseeing it would not remit the laws against Papists, by the extra-ordinary zeal and bravery of its members, and the free re-nunciation of the great officers both in court and state, who would not be prevailed with for any temporal concern.

---

[1] This is by no means the case now.
[2] Afterwards Arch:ishop of Canterbury.

25th. Good Friday. Dr. Tenison preached at St. Martin's on 1 Peter ii. 24. During the service, a man came into near the middle of the church, with his sword drawn, with several others in that posture ; in this jealous time it put the congregation into great confusion ; but it appeared to be one who fled for sanctuary, being pursued by bailiffs.

8th April. I had a re-hearing of my great cause at the Chancery in Westminster Hall, having seven of the most learned Counsel, my adversary five, among which were the Attorney-General and late Solicitor Finch, son to the Lord Chancellor Nottingham. The accompt was at last brought to one article of the surcharge, and referred to a Master. The cause lasted two hours and more.

10th. In the last week, there was issued a Dispensation from all obligations and tests, by which Dissenters and Papists especially had public liberty of exercising their several ways of worship, without incurring the penalty of the many Laws and Acts of Parliament to the contrary. This was purely obtained by the Papists, thinking thereby to ruin the Church of England, being now the only Church which so admirably and strenuously opposed their superstition. There was a wonderful concourse of people at the Dissenters' meeting-house in this parish, and the parish-church [Deptford] left exceeding thin. What this will end in, God Almighty only knows ; but it looks like confusion, which I pray God avert.

11th. To London about my suit, some terms of accommodation being proposed.

19th. I heard the famous singer, Cifaccio, esteemed the best in Europe. Indeed, his holding out and delicateness in extending and loosing a note with incomparable softness and sweetness, was admirable ; for the rest I found him a mere wanton, effeminate child, very coy, and proudly conceited, to my apprehension. He touched the harpsichord to his voice rarely well. This was before a select number of particular persons whom Mr. Pepys invited to his house ; and this was obtained by particular favour and much difficulty, the Signor much disdaining to show his talent to any but princes.

24th. At Greenwich, at the conclusion of the Church-service, there was a French sermon preached after the use of the English Liturgy translated into French, to a congregation of about 100 French Refugees, of whom Monsieur Ruvigny was the chief, and had obtained the use of the church, after the parish - service was ended. The preacher pathetically exhorted to patience, constancy, and reliance on God amidst all their sufferings, and the infinite rewards to come.

2nd May. I dined with Mynheer Diskvelts, the Holland Ambassador, a prudent and worthy person. There dined Lord Middleton, principal Secretary of State, Lord Pembroke, Lord Lumley, Lord Preston, Colonel Fitzpatrick, and Sir John Chardin. After dinner, the Ambassador discoursed of and deplored the stupid folly of our politics, in suffering the French to take Luxemburg, it being a place of the most concern to have been defended, for the interest not only of the Netherlands, but of England.

12th. To London. Lord Sunderland being Lord President and Secretary of State, was made Knight of the Garter and prime favourite.—This day there was such a storm of wind as had seldom happened, being a sort of hurricane. It kept the flood out of the Thames, so that people went on foot over several places above bridge. Also an earthquake in several places in England about the time of the storm.

26th. To London, about my agreement with Mr. Pretyman, after my tedious suit.

2nd June. I went to London, it having pleased his Majesty to grant me a Privy Seal for 6,000*l.*, for discharge of the debt I had been so many years persecuted for, it being indeed for money drawn over by my father- in- law, Sir R. Browne, during his residence in the Court of France, and so with a much greater sum due to Sir Richard from his Majesty ; and now this part of the arrear being paid, there remains yet due to me, as executor of Sir Richard, above 6,500*l.* more ; but this determining an expensive Chancery suit has been so great a mercy and providence to me, (through the kindness and friendship to me of Lord Godolphin, one of the Lords Commissioners of the Treasury,) that I do acknowledge it with all imaginable thanks to my gracious God.

6th. I visited my Lady Pierpoint, daughter to Sir John

Evelyn [1] of Deane [in Wilts], now widow of Mr. Pierpoint,
and mother of the Earl of Kingston. She was now engaged in the marriage of my cousin, Evelyn Pierpoint, her
second son.

There was about this time brought into the Downs a vast
treasure, which was sunk in a Spanish galleon about forty-
five years ago, somewhere near Hispaniola, or the Bahama
islands, and was now weighed up by some gentlemen, who
were at the charge of divers, &c., to the enriching them beyond all expectation. The Duke of Albemarle's share
[Governor of Jamaica] came to, I believe, 50,000*l.*[2] Some
private gentlemen who adventured 100*l.* gained from 8,000*l.*
to 10,000*l.* His Majesty's tenth was 10,000*l.*

The Camp was now again pitched at Hounslow, the Commanders profusely vying in the expense and magnificence of
tents.

12th June. Our Vicar preached on 2 Peter ii. 21, upon the
danger of relapsing into sin. After this, I went and heard
M. Lamot, an eloquent French preacher at Greenwich,
on Prov. xxx. 8, 9, a consolatory discourse to the poor and
religious refugees who escaped out of France in the cruel
persecution.

16th. I went to Hampton-Court to give his Majesty
thanks for his late gracious favour, though it was but
granting what was due. Whilst I was in the Council-
Chamber, came in some persons, at the head of whom was a
formal man with a large roll of parchment in his hand, being
an *Address* (as he said, for he introduced it with a speech)
of the people of Coventry, giving his Majesty their great
acknowledgments for his granting a liberty of conscience;
he added that this was not the application of one party only,
but the unanimous address of Church of England men,
Presbyterians, Independents, and Anabaptists, to show how
extensive his Majesty's grace was, as taking in all parties to
his indulgence and protection, which had removed all dis-

---

[1] This Evelyn Pierpoint was married in the same month to Lady
Mary Fielding. The issue of the marriage was the celebrated Lady
Mary Wortley Montagu.

[2] The Duke's share amounted to considerably more; not less, it was
said, than 90,000. A medal was struck on this occasion, which is engraved in Evelyn's book on that subject, No. LXXXVII. p. 151.

sensions and animosities, which would not only unite them in bonds of Christian charity, but exceedingly encourage their future industry, to the improvement of trade, and spreading his Majesty's glory throughout the world; and that now he had given to God his empire, God would establish his; with expressions of great loyalty and submission; and so he gave the roll to the King, which being returned to him again, his Majesty caused him to read. The address was short, but much to the substance of the speech of their foreman, to whom the King, pulling off his hat, said that what he had done in giving liberty of conscience, was, what was ever his judgment ought to be done; and that, as he would preserve them in their enjoyment of it during his reign, so he would endeavour to settle it by law, that it should never be altered by his successors. After this, he gave them his hand to kiss. It was reported the subscribers were above 1000.

But this is not so remarkable as an Address of the week before (as I was assured by one present), of some of the *Family of Love.* His Majesty asked them what this worship consisted in, and how many their party might consist of; they told him their custom was to read the Scripture, and then to preach; but did not give any further account, only said that for the rest they were a sort of refined Quakers, but their number very small, not consisting, as they said, of above threescore in all, and those chiefly belonging to the Isle of Ely.

18*th June.* I dined at Mr. Blathwaite's (two miles from Hampton). This gentleman is Secretary of War, Clerk of the Council, &c., having raised himself by his industry from very moderate circumstances. He is a very proper, handsome person, very dexterous in business, and, besides all this, has married a great fortune. His income by the Army, Council, and Secretary to the Committee of Foreign Plantations, brings him in above 2,000*l.* per annum.

23*rd.* The Privy Seal for 6,000*l.* was passed to me, so that this tedious affair was dispatched.—Hitherto, a very windy and tempestuous summer.—The French sermons to the refugees were continued at Greenwich Church.

19*th July.* I went to Wotton. In the way, I dined at Ashted, with my Lady Mordaunt.

5th August. I went to see Albury, now purchased by
Mr. Finch (the King's Solicitor, and son to the late Lord
Chancellor); I found the garden which I first designed for
the Duke of Norfolk, nothing improved.

15th. I went to visit Lord Clarendon at Swallowfield,
where was my Lord Cornbury just arrived from Denmark,
whither he had accompanied the Prince of Denmark two
months before, and now come back. The miserable tyranny
under which that nation lives, he related to us; the King
keeps them under an army of 40,000 men, all Germans, he
not daring to trust his own subjects. Notwithstanding this,
the Danes are exceeding proud, the country very poor and
miserable.

22nd August. Returned home to Sayes Court from Wotton, having been five weeks absent with my brother and
friends, who entertained us very nobly. God be praised for
His goodness, and this refreshment after my many troubles,
and let His mercy and providence ever preserve me. Amen.

3rd September. The Lord Mayor sent me an Officer
with a staff, to be one of the Governors of St. Thomas's
Hospital.

Persecution raging in France; divers churches there fired
by lightning, priests struck, consecrated hosts, &c., burnt
and destroyed, both at St. Maloes and Paris, at the grand
procession on Corpus Christi-day.

13th. I went to Lambeth, and dined with the Archbishop. After dinner, I retired into the library, which I
found exceedingly improved; there are also divers rare manuscripts in a room apart.

6th October. I was godfather to Sir John Chardin's son,
christened at Greenwich Church, named John. The Earl
of Bath and Countess of Carlisle, the other sponsors.

29th. An Anabaptist, a very odd ignorant person, a mechanic, I think, was Lord Mayor.[1] The King and Queen,
and Dadi,[2] the Pope's Nuncio, invited to a feast at Guildhall. A strange turn of affairs, that those who scandalized
the Church of England as favourers of Popery, should
publicly invite an emissary from Rome, one who represented
the very person of their Antichrist!

10th December. My son was returned out of Devon,

[1] Sir John Peake.   [2] Count D'Ada. *Ante,* page 257.

where he had been on a commission from the Lords of the Treasury about a concealment of land.

20*th December*. I went with my Lord Chief Justice Herbert, to see his house at Walton-on-Thames :[1] it is a barren place. To a very ordinary house he had built a very handsome library, designing more building to it than the place deserves, in my opinion. He desired my advice about laying out his gardens, &c. The next day, we went to Weybridge, to see some pictures of the Duchess of Norfolk's, particularly the statue, or child in gremio, said to be of Michel Angelo ; but there are reasons to think it rather a copy, from some proportion in the figures ill taken. It was now exposed to sale.

1687-8. 12*th January*. Mr. Slingsby, Master of the Mint, being under very deplorable circumstances on account of his creditors, and especially the King, I did my endeavour with the Lords of the Treasury to be favourable to him.

My Lord Arran, eldest son to the Duke of Hamilton, being now married to Lady Ann Spencer, eldest daughter of the Earl of Sunderland, Lord President of the Council, I and my family had most glorious favours sent us, the wedding being celebrated with extraordinary splendour.

15*th*. There was a solemn and particular office used at our, and all the churches of London and ten miles round, for a thanksgiving to God, for her Majesty being with child.

22*nd*. This afternoon I went not to church, being employed on a religious treatise I had undertaken.[2]

Post annum 1588 — 1660 — 1688, Annus Mirabilis Tertius.[3]

30*th*. Being the Martyrdom-day of King Charles the First, our curate made a florid oration against the murder

[1] This is a mistake ; the house was Oatlands in Weybridge. He followed the fortunes of King James, who gave him his great Seal. He was attainted, and Oatlands given to his brother, Admiral Herbert. He published an apology for the judgment he had given in favour of the King's dispensing powers, which was answered by Mr. Attwood and Sir Robert Atkins. Manning and Bray's *Hist. of Surrey*, ii. 786.

[2] What this was does not appear ; but there are several of Evelyn's composition remaining in MS.

[3] This seems to have been added after the page was written.

of that excellent Prince, with an exhortation to obedience from the example of David, 1 Samuel xxvi. 6.

12th February. My daughter. Evelyn going in the coach to visit in the City, a jolt (the door being not fast shut) flung her quite out in such manner, as the hind wheels passed over her a little above her knees. Yet it pleased God, besides the bruises of the wheels, she had no other harm. In two days, she was able, to walk, and soon after perfectly well ; through God Almighty's great mercy to an excellent wife and a most dutiful and discreet daughter-in-law.

17th. I received the sad news. of my niece Montague's death at Woodcot on the 15th.

15th March. I gave in my account about the Sick and Wounded, in order to have my quietus.

23rd. Dr. Parker, Bishop of Oxford, who so lately published his extravagant treatise about transubstantiation, and for abrogating the Test and Penal Laws, died. He was esteemed a violent, passionate, haughty man, but yet being pressed to declare for the Church of Rome, he utterly refused it. A remarkable end!

The French *Tyrant* now finding he could make no proselytes amongst those Protestants of quality, and others, whom he had caused to be shut up in dungeons, and confined to nunneries and monasteries, gave them, after so long trial, a general releasement, and leave to go out of the kingdom, but utterly taking their estates and their children ; so that great numbers came daily into England and other places, where they were received and relieved with very considerate Christian charity. This Providence and goodness of God to those who thus constantly held out, did so work upon those miserable poor souls who to avoid the persecution signed their renunciation, and to save their estates went to mass, that reflecting on what they had done, they grew so affected in their conscience, that not being able to support it, they in great numbers through all the French provinces, acquainted the magistrates and lieutenants that being sorry for their apostacy, they were resolved to return to their old religion ; that they would go no more to mass, but peaceably assemble when they could, to beg pardon and worship God, but so without weapons as not to give the least umbrage of rebel-

lion or sedition, imploring their pity and commiseration; and, accordingly, meeting so from time to time, the dragoon-missioners, Popish officers and priests, fell upon them, murdered and put them to death, whoever they could lay hold on; they without the least resistance embraced death, torture, or hanging, with singing psalms and praying for their persecutors to the last breath, yet still continuing the former assembling of themselves in desolate places, suffering with incredible constancy, that through God's mercy they might obtain pardon for this lapse. Such examples of Christian behaviour have not been seen since the primitive persecutions; and doubtless God will do some signal work in the end, if we can with patience and resignation hold out, and depend on His Providence.

24th March. I went with Sir Charles Littleton to Sheen, a house and estate given him by Lord Brounker; one who was ever noted for a hard, covetous, vicious man; but for his worldly craft and skill in gaming few exceeded him. Coming to die, he bequeathed all his land, house, furniture, &c. to Sir Charles, to whom he had no manner of relation, but an ancient friendship contracted at the famous siege of Colchester, forty years before. It is a pretty place, with fine gardens, and well-planted, and given to one worthy of them, Sir Charles being an honest gentleman and soldier. He is brother to Sir Henry Littleton of Worcestershire, whose great estate he is likely to inherit, his brother being without children. They are descendants of the great lawyer of that name, and give the same Arms and motto. He is married to one Mrs. Temple, formerly Maid of Honour to the late Queen, a beautiful lady, and he has many fine children, so that none envy his good fortune.

After dinner, we went to see Sir William Temple's near to it; the most remarkable things are his orangery and gardens, where the wall-fruit-trees are most exquisitely nailed and trained, far better than I ever noted.

There are many good pictures, especially of Vandyke's, in both these houses, and some few statues and small busts in the latter.

From thence to Kew, to visit Sir Henry Capell's, whose orangery and myrtetum are most beautiful and perfectly well kept. He was contriving very high palisadoes of reeds to shade his oranges during the summer, and painting those reeds in oil.

1st April. In the morning, the first sermon was by Dr. Stillingfleet, Dean of St. Paul's (at Whitehall), on Luke x. 41, 42. The holy Communion followed, but was so interrupted by the rude breaking in of multitudes zealous to hear the second sermon, to be preached by the Bishop of Bath and Wells, that the latter part of that holy office could hardly be heard, or the sacred elements be distributed without great trouble. The Princess being come, he preached on Mich. vii, 8, 9, 10, describing the calamity of the reformed church of Judah under the Babylonian persecution, for her sins, and God's delivery of her on her repentance; that as Judah emerged, so should the now Reformed Church, whenever insulted and persecuted. He preached with his accustomed action, zeal, and energy, so that people flocked from all quarters to hear him.

15th. A dry, cold, backward spring; easterly winds.

The persecution still raging in France, multitudes of Protestants, and many very considerable and great persons flying hither, produced a second general contribution, the Papists, by God's Providence, as yet making small progress amongst us.

29th. The weather was, till now, so cold and sharp, by an almost perpetual east wind, which had continued many months, that there was little appearance of any spring, and yet the winter was very favourable as to frost and snow.

2nd May. To London, about my petition for allowances upon the account of Commissioner for Sick and Wounded in the former war with Holland.

8th. His Majesty, alarmed by the great fleet of the Dutch (whilst we had a very inconsiderable one), went down to Chatham; their fleet was well prepared, and out, before we were in any readiness, or had any considerable number to have encountered them, had there been occasion, to the great reproach of the nation; whilst, being in profound peace, there was a mighty land-army, which there was no need of, and no force at sea, where only was the apprehension; but the army was doubtless kept and increased, in order to bring in and countenance Popery, the King beginning to discover his intention, by many instances

pursued by the Jesuits, against his first resolution to alter
nothing in the Church-Establishment, so that it appeared
there can be no reliance on Popish promises.

18th May. The King enjoining the n inisters to read his Declaration for giving liberty of conscien e (as it was styled) in
all the churches of England, this evening, six Bishops, Bath
and Wells,[1] Peterborough,[2] Ely,[3] Chichester,[4] St. Asaph,[5]
and Bristol,[6] in the name of all the rest of the Bishops,
came to his Majesty to petition him, that he would not
impose the reading of it to the several congregations within
their dioceses ; not that they were averse to the publishing
it for want of due tenderness towards Dissenters, in relation
to whom they should be willing to come to such a temper as
should be thought fit, when that matter might be considered and settled in Parliament and Convocation ; but that,
the declaration being founded on such a dispensing power
as might at pleasure set aside all laws ecclesiastical and
civil, it appeared to them illegal, as it had done to the Parliament in 1661 and 1672, and that it was a point of such
consequence, that they could not so far make themselves
parties to it, as the reading of it in church in time of Divine
Service amounted to.

The King was so far incensed at this address, that he
with threatening expressions commanded them to obey him
in reading it at their perils, and so dismissed them.

20th. I went to Whitehall Chapel, where, after the
morning Lessons, the Declaration was read by one of the
Choir who used to read the Chapters. I hear it was in the
Abbey Church, Westminster, but almost universally forborne throughout all London : the consequences of which
a little time will show.

25th. All the discourse now was about the Bishops refusing to read the injunction for the abolition of the Test,
&c. It seems the injunction came so crudely from the
Secretary's office, that it was neither sealed nor signed in
form, nor had any lawyer been consulted, so as the Bishops,
who took all imaginable advice, put the Court to great
difficulties how to proceed against them. Great were the

[1] Thomas Ken. [2] Thomas White. [3] Francis Turner. [4] John Lake.
[5] William Lloyd. [6] Sir John Trelawny, Bart.

consults, and a proclamation was expected all this day; but nothing was done. The action of the Bishops was universally applauded, and reconciled many adverse parties, Papists only excepted, who were now exceedingly perplexed, and violent courses were every moment expected. Report was, that the Protestant secular Lords and Nobility would abet the Clergy.

The Queen Dowager, hitherto bent on her return into Portugal, now on the sudden, on allegation of a great debt owing her by his Majesty disabling her, declares her resolution to stay.

News arrived of the most prodigious earthquake that was almost ever heard of, subverting the city of Lima and country in Peru, with a dreadful inundation following it.

8th June. This day, the Archbishop of Canterbury, with the Bishops of Ely, Chichester, St. Asaph, Bristol, Peterborough, and Bath and Wells, were sent from the Privy Council prisoners to the Tower, for refusing to give bail for their appearance, on their not reading the Declaration for liberty of conscience; they refused to give bail, as it would have prejudiced their peerage. The concern of the people for them was wonderful, infinite crowds on their knees begging their blessing, and praying for them, as they passed out of the barge along the Tower-wharf.

10th. A *young Prince* born, which will cause disputes.

About two o'clock, we heard the Tower-ordnance discharged, and the bells ring for the birth of a Prince of Wales. This was very surprising, it having been universally given out that her Majesty did not look till the next month.

13th. I went to the Tower to see the Bishops, visited the Archbishop and Bishops of Ely, St. Asaph, and Bath and Wells.

14th. Dined with the Lord Chancellor.

15th. Being the first day of Term, the Bishops were brought to Westminster on Habeas Corpus, when the indictment was read, and they were called on to plead; their Counsel objected that the warrant was illegal; but, after long debate, it was over-ruled, and they pleaded. The Court then offered to take bail for their appearance; but this they refused, and at last were dismissed on their own recogni-

tances to appear that day fortnight; the Archbishop in
£200, the Bishops £100 each.

17th June. Was a day of thanksgiving in London and ten
miles about for the young Prince's birth; a form of prayer
made for the purpose by the Bishop of Rochester.

29th. They appeared; the trial lasted from nine in the
morning to past six in the evening, when the Jury retired
to consider of their verdict, and the Court adjourned to
nine the next morning. The Jury were locked up till
that time, eleven of them being for an acquittal; but one
(Arnold, a brewer) would not consent. At length he agreed
with the others. The Chief Justice, Wright, behaved with
great moderation and civility to the Bishops. Alibone, a
Papist, was strongly against them; but Holloway and
Powell being of opinion in their favour, they were acquitted.
When this was heard, there was great rejoicing; and there
was a lane of people from the King's Bench to the water-
side, on their knees, as the Bishops passed and repassed, to
beg their blessing. Bonfires were made that night, and
bells rung, which was taken very ill at Court, and an appearance of nearly sixty Earls and Lords, &c., on the bench, did
not a little comfort them; but indeed they were all along
full of comfort and cheerful.

Note, they denied to pay the Lieutenant of the Tower
(Hales, who used them very surlily) any fees, alleging that
none were due.

The night was solemnized with bonfires, and other fireworks, &c.

2nd July. The two judges, Holloway and Powell, were
displaced.

3rd. I went with Dr. Godolphin and his brother Sir
William to St. Alban's, to see a library he would have
bought of the widow of Dr. Cartwright, late Archdeacon of
St. Alban's, a very good collection of books, especially in
divinity; he was to give £300 for them. Having seen the
great Church, now newly repaired by a public contribution,
we returned home.

8th. One of the King's chaplains preached before the
Princess on Exodus xiv. 13, "Stand still, and behold the
salvation of the Lord," which he applied so boldly to the
present conjuncture of the Church of England, that more

.could scarce be said to encourage desponders. The Popish priests were not able to carry their cause against their learned adversaries, who confounded them both by their disputes and writings.

12th July. The camp now began at Hounslow; but the ·nation was in high discontent.

Colonel Titus, Sir Henry Vane (son of him who was executed for his treason), and some other of the Presbyterians and Independent party, were sworn of the Privy Council, from hopes of thereby diverting that party from going over to the Bishops and Church. of England, which now they began to do, foreseeing the design of the Papists to descend and take in their most hateful of heretics (as they at other times expressed them to be) to effect their own ends, now evident; the utter extirpation of the Church of England first, and then the rest would follow.

17th. This night the fire-works were played off, that had been prepared for the Queen's up-sitting. We saw them to great advantage; they were very fine, and cost some thousands of pounds, in the pyramids, statues, &c.; but were spent too soon for so long a preparation.

26th. I went to Lambeth to visit the Archbishop, whom I found very cheerful.

10th August. Dr. Tenison now told me there would suddenly be some great thing discovered. This was the Prince of Orange intending to come over.

15th. I went to Althorpe, in Northamptonshire, seventy miles. A coach and four horses took up me and my son at Whitehall, and carried us to Dunstable, where we arrived and dined at noon, and from thence another coach and six horses carried us to Althorpe, four miles beyond Northampton, where we arrived by seven o'clock that evening. Both these coaches were hired for me by that noble Countess of Sunderland, who invited me to her house at Althorpe,[1] where she entertained me and my son with very extraordinary kindness; I staid till the Thursday.

18th. Dr. Jeffryes, the minister of Althorpe, who was my Lord's Chaplain when ambassador in France, preached the shortest discourse I ever heard; but what was defec-

---

[1] See a former visit to this place, p. 107.

tive in the amplitude of his sermon, he had supplied in the
largeness and convenience of the parsonage-house, which
the Doctor (who had at least £600 a year in spiritual advancement) had new built, and made fit for a person of
quality to live in, with gardens and all accommodation according therewith.

My lady carried us to see Lord Northampton's Seat, a
very strong large house, built with stone, not altogether
modern. They were enlarging the garden, in which was
nothing extraordinary, except the iron gate opening into the
park, which indeed was very good work, wrought in flowers,
painted with blue and gilded. There is a noble walk of
elms towards the front of the house by the bowling-green.
I was not in any room of the house besides a lobby looking
into the garden, where my Lord and his new Countess (Sir
Stephen Fox's daughter, whom I had known from a child)
entertained the Countess and her daughter the Countess of
Arran (newly married to the son of the Duke of Hamilton),
with so little good grace, and so dully, that our visit was
very short, and so we returned to Althorpe, twelve miles
distant.

The house, or rather palace, at Althorpe, is a noble uniform pile in form of a half H, built of brick and freestone,
balustred and à la moderne ; the hall is well, the staircase excellent ; the rooms of state, galleries, offices and furniture,
such as may become a great prince. It is situate in the
midst of a garden, exquisitely planted and kept, and all this
in a park walled in with hewn stone, planted with rows and
walks of trees, canals and fish-ponds, and stored with game.
And, what is above all this, governed by a lady, who without any show of solicitude, keeps everything in such admirable order, both within and without, from the garret to the
cellar, that I do not believe there is any in this nation, or
in any other, that exceeds her in such exact order, without
ostentation, but substantially great and noble. The meanest
servant is lodged so neat and cleanly ; the service at the
several tables, the good order and decency—in a word, the
entire economy is perfectly becoming a wise and noble person. She is one who for her distinguished esteem of me
from a long and worthy friendship, I must ever honour and
celebrate. I wish from my soul the Lord her husband

(whose parts and abilities are otherwise conspicuous) was as
worthy of her, as by a fatal apostasy and court-ambition he
has made himself unworthy! This is what she deplores, and
it renders her as much affliction as a lady of great soul and
much prudence is capable of. The Countess of Bristol, her
mother, a grave and honourable lady, has the comfort of
seeing her daughter and grandchildren under the same economy, especially Mr. Charles Spencer,[1] a youth of extraordinary hopes, very learned for his age, and ingenious, and
under a governor of great worth. Happy were it, could as
much be said of the elder brother, the Lord Spencer, who,
rambling about the world, dishonours both his name and his
family, adding sorrow to sorrow to a mother, who has taken
all imaginable care of his education. There is a daughter
very young married to the Earl of Clancarty, who has a
great and fair estate in Ireland, but who yet gives no great
presage of worth,—so universally contaminated is the youth
of this corrupt and abandoned age! But this is again re-
compensed by my Lord Arran, a sober and worthy gentleman, who has espoused the Lady Ann Spencer, a young lady
of admirable accomplishments and virtue.

23rd August. I left this noble place and conversation,
my lady having provided carriages to convey us back in the
same manner as we went, and a dinner being prepared at
Dunstable against our arrival. Northampton, having been
lately burnt and re-edified, is now become a town that for
the beauty of the buildings, especially the church and town-
house, may compare with the neatest in Italy itself.

Dr. Sprat, Bishop of Rochester, wrote a very honest and
handsome letter to the Commissioners Ecclesiastical, excusing himself from sitting any longer among them, he by no
means approving of their prosecuting the Clergy who refused
to read the Declaration for liberty of conscience, in prejudice
of the Church of England.

The Dutch make extraordinary preparations both at sea
and land, which with the no small progress Popery makes
among us, puts us to many difficulties. The Popish Irish

---

[1] The eldest son dying without issue, this Charles succeeded to the
title and estate, and marrying to his second wife one of the daughters
and at length coheiress to John Duke of Marlborough, his son by her
succeeded to that title.

soldiers commit many murders and insults; the whole nation disaffected, and in apprehensions.

After long trials of the doctors to bring up the little Prince of Wales by hand (so many of her Majesty's children having died infants) not succeeding, a country-nurse, the wife of a tile-maker, is taken to give it suck.

18*th September.* I went to London, where I found the Court in the utmost consternation on report of the Prince of Orange's landing; which put Whitehall into so panic a fear, that I could hardly believe it possible to find such a change.

Writs were issued in order to a Parliament, and a declaration to back the good order of elections, with great professions of maintaining the Church of England, but without giving any sort of satisfaction to the people, who showed their high discontent at several things in the Government.

Earthquakes had utterly demolished the ancient Smyrna, and several other places in Greece, Italy, and even in the Spanish Indies, forerunners of greater calamities. God Almighty preserve His Church and all who put themselves under the shadow of His wings, till these things be overpast!

30*th.* The Court in so extraordincry a consternation, on assurance of the Prince of Orange's intention to land, that the writs sent forth for a Parliament were recalled.

7*th October.* Dr. Tenison preached at St Martin's on 2 Tim. iii. 16, showing the Scriptures to be our only rule of faith, and its perfection above all traditions. After which, near 1,000 devout persons partook of the Communion. The sermon was chiefly occasioned by a Jesuit, who in the Masshouse on the Sunday before had disparaged the Scripture and railed at our translation, which some present contradicting, they pulled him out of the pulpit, and treated him very coarsely, insomuch that it was like to create a great disturbance in the City.

Hourly expectation of the Prince of Orange's invasion heightened to that degree, that his Majesty thought fit to abrogate the Commission for the dispensing Power (but retaining his own right still to dispense with all laws) and restore the ejec'ed Fellows of Magdalen College, Oxford.

In the mean time, he called over 5,000 Irish, and 4,000 Scots, and continued to remove Protestants and put in Papists at Portsmouth and other places of trust, and retained the Jesuits about him, increasing the universal discontent. It brought people to so desperate a pass, that they seemed passionately to long for and desire the landing of that Prince, whom they looked on to be their deliverer from Popish tyranny, praying incessantly for an east wind, which was said to be the only hindrance of his expedition with a numerous army ready to make a descent. To such a strange temper, and unheard-of in former times, was this poor nation reduced, and of which I was an eye-witness. The apprehension was (and with reason) that his Majesty's forces would neither at land nor sea oppose them with that vigour requisite to repel invaders.

The late imprisoned Bishops were now called to reconcile matters, and the Jesuits hard at work to foment confusion among the Protestants by their usual tricks. A letter was sent to the Archbishop of Canterbury,[1] informing him, from

---

[1] By Evelyn himself. The letter was as follows:

"My Lord, The honour and reputation which your Grace's piety, prudence, and signal courage, have justly merited and obtained, not only from the sons of the Church of England, but even universally from those Protestants amongst us who are Dissenters from her discipline; God Almighty's providence and blessing upon your Grace's vigilancy and extraordinary endeavours will not suffer to be diminished in this conjuncture. The conversation I now and then have with some in place, who have the opportunity of knowing what is doing in the most secret recesses and cabals of our Church's adversaries, obliges me to acquaint you, that the calling of your Grace and the rest of the Lords Bishops to Court, and what has there of late been required of you, is only to create a jealousy and suspicion amongst well-meaning people of such compliances, as it is certain they have no cause to apprehend. The plan of this and of all that which is to follow of seeming favour thence, is wholly drawn by the Jesuits, who are at this time more than ever busy to make divisions amongst us, all other arts and mechanisms having hitherto failed them. They have, with other things, contrived that your Lordships the Bishops should give his Majesty advice separately, without calling any of the rest of the Peers, which, though maliciously suggested, spreads generally about the town. I do not at all question but your Grace will speedily prevent the operation of this venom, and that you will think it highly necessary so to do; that your Grace is also injoined to compose a form of prayer, wherein the Prince of Orange is expressly to be named the Invader; of this I

good hands, of what was contriving by them. A paper of what the Bishops advised his Majesty was published. The Bishops were enjoined to prepare a form of prayer against the feared invasion. A pardon published. Soldiers and mariners daily pressed.

14th October. The King's Birthday. No guns from the Tower as usual. The sun eclipsed at its rising. This day signal for the victory of William the Conqueror against Harold, near Battel, in Sussex. The wind, which had been hitherto west, was east all this day. Wonderful expectation of the Dutch fleet. Public prayers ordered to be read in the churches against invasion.

28th. A tumult in London on the rabble demolishing a Popish chapel that had been set up in the City.

29th. Lady Sunderland acquainted me with his Majesty's taking away the Seals from Lord Sunderland, and of her being with the Queen to intercede for him. It is conceived that he had of late grown remiss in pursuing the interest of the Jesuitical counsels; some reported one thing, some another; but there was doubtless some secret betrayed, which time may discover.

There was a Council called, to which were summoned the Archbishop of Canterbury, the Judges, the Lord Mayor, &c.

presume not to say anything; but for as much as in all the Declarations, &c. which have hitherto been published in pretended favour of the Church of England, there is not once the least mention of the *Reformed* or *Protestant Religion*, but only of the *Church of England as by Law established*, which Church the Papists tell us is the *Church of Rome*, which is (say they) the Catholic Church of England—that only is established by Law; the Church of England in the *Reformed* sense so established, is but by an usurped authority. The antiquity of *that* would by these words be explained, and utterly defeat this false and subdolous construction, and take off all exceptions whatsoever; if, in all extraordinary offices, upon these occasions, the words *Reformed* and *Protestant* were added to that of the *Church of England by Law established*. And whosoever threatens to invade or come against us, to the prejudice of that Church, in God's name, be they Dutch or Irish, let us heartily pray and fight against them. My Lord, this is, I confess, a bold, but honest period: and, though I am well assured that your Grace is perfectly acquainted with all this before, and therefore may blame my impertinence, as that does ἀλλοτριοεπισκοπεῖν; yet I am confident you will not reprove the zeal of one who most humbly begs your Grace's pardon, with your blessing. Lond., 10 Oct. 1688." (From a copy in Evelyn's handwriting.) See *post*, p. 298.

The Queen Dowager, and all the ladies and lords who were present at the Queen Consort's labour, were to give their testimony upon oath of the Prince of Wales's birth, recorded both at the Council-Board and at the Chancery a day or two after. This procedure was censured by some as below his Majesty to condescend to, on the talk of the people. It was remarkable that on this occasion the Archbishop, Marquis of Halifax, the Earls of Clarendon and Nottingham, refused to sit at the Council-table amongst Papists, and their bold telling his Majesty that whatever was done whilst such sat amongst them was unlawful and incurred *præmunire* ;—at least, if what I heard be true.

30th October. I dined with Lord Preston, made Secretary of State, in the place of the Earl of Sunderland.

Visited Mr. Boyle, when came in the Duke of Hamilton and Earl of Burlington. The Duke told us many particulars of Mary Queen of Scots, and her amours with the Italian favourite, &c.

31st. My birthday, being the 68th year of my age. O blessed Lord, grant that as I grow in years, so may I improve in grace! Be Thou my Protector this following year, and preserve me and mine from those dangers and great confusions that threaten a sad revolution to this sinful nation! Defend Thy Church, our holy religion, and just laws, disposing his Majesty to listen to sober and healing counsels, that if it be Thy blessed will, we may still enjoy that happy tranquillity which hitherto Thou hast continued to us! Amen, Amen!

1st November. Dined with Lord Preston, with other company, at Sir Stephen Fox's. Continual alarms of the Prince of Orange, but no certainty. Reports of his great losses of horse in the storm, but without any assurance. A man was taken with divers papers and printed manifestoes, and carried to Newgate, after examination at the Cabinet-Council. There was likewise a Declaration of the States for satisfaction of all Public Ministers at the Hague, except to the English and the French. There was in that of the Prince's an expression, as if the Lords both Spiritual and Temporal had invited him over, with a deduction of the causes of his enterprise. This made his Majesty convene my Lord of Canterbury and the other Bishops now in town, to give an account of what was in the manifesto, and to enjoin them to clear themselves by some public writing of this disloyal charge.

2nd November. It was now certainly reported by some who saw the fleet, and the Prince embark, that they sailed from the Brill on Wednesday morning, and that the Princess of Orange was there to take leave of her husband.

4th. Fresh reports of the Prince being landed somewhere about Portsmouth, or the Isle of Wight, whereas it was thought it would have been northward. The Court in great hurry.

5th. I went to London; heard the news of the Prince having landed at Torbay, coming with a fleet of near 700 sail, passing through the Channel with so favourable a wind, that our navy could not intercept, or molest them. This put the King and Court into great consternation, they were now employed in forming an army to stop their further progress, for they were got into Exeter, and the season and ways very improper for his Majesty's forces to march so great a distance.

The Archbishop of Canterbury and some few of the other Bishops and Lords in London, were sent for to Whitehall, and required to set forth their abhorrence of this invasion. They assured his Majesty they had never invited any of the Prince's party, or were in the least privy to it, and would be ready to show all testimony of their loyalty; but, as to a public declaration, being so few, they desired that his Majesty would call the rest of their brethren and Peers, that they might consult what was fit to be done on this occasion, not thinking it right to publish any thing without them, and till they had themselves seen the Prince's Manifesto, in which it was pretended he was invited in by the Lords Spiritual and Temporal. This did not please the King; so they departed.

A Declaration was published, prohibiting all persons to see or read the Prince's Manifesto, in which was set forth at large the cause of his expedition, as there had been one before from the States.

These are the beginnings of sorrow, unless God in His mercy prevent it by some happy reconciliation of all dissensions among us. This, in all likelihood, nothing can

effect except a free Parliament; but this we cannot hope to
see, whilst there are any forces on either side. I pray God
to protect and direct the King for the best and truest interest of his people!—I saw his Majesty touch for the evil,
Piten the Jesuit, and Warner officiating.

14th November. The Prince increases every day in force.
Several Lords go in to him. Lord Cornbury carries some regiments, and marches to Honiton, the Prince's head-quarters.
The City of London in disorder; the rabble pulled down
the nunnery newly bought by the Papists of Lord Berkeley,
at St. John's. The Queen prepares to go to Portsmouth
for safety, to attend the issue of this commotion, which has
a dreadful aspect.

18th. It was now a very hard frost. The King goes to
Salisbury to rendezvous the army, and return to London.
Lord Delamere appears for the Prince in Cheshire. The
nobility meet in Yorkshire. The Archbishop of Canterbury and some Bishops, and such Peers as were in London,
address his Majesty to call a Parliament. The King invites
all foreign nations to come over. The French take all the
Palatinate, and alarm the Germans more than ever.

29th. I went to the Royal Society. We adjourned the
election of a President to 23rd April, by reason of the
public commotions, yet dined together as of custom this
day.

2nd December. Dr. Tenison preached at St. Martin's on
Psalm xxxvi. 5, 6, 7, concerning Providence. I received the
blessed Sacrament. Afterwards, visited my Lord Godolphin, then going with the Marquis of Halifax and Earl of
Nottingham as Commissioners to the Prince of Orange; he
told me they had little power. Plymouth declared for the
Prince. Bath, York, Hull, Bristol, and all the eminent
nobility and persons of quality through England, declare for
the Protestant religion and laws, and go to meet the Prince,
who every day sets forth new Declarations against the
Papists. The great favourites at Court, Priests and Jesuits,
fly or abscond. Every thing, till now concealed, flies
abroad in public print, and is cried about the streets. Expectation of the Prince coming to Oxford. The Prince
of Wales and great treasure sent privily to Portsmouth, the
Earl of Dover being Governor. Address from the Fleet

not grateful to his Majesty. The Papists in offices lay down their commissions, and fly. Universal consternation amongst them; it looks like a revolution.

7th December. My son went towards Oxford. I returned home.

9th. Lord Sunderland meditates flight. The rabble demolished all Popish chapels, and several Papist lords and gentlemen's houses, especially that of the Spanish Ambassador, which they pillaged, and burnt his library.[1]

13th. The King flies to sea, puts in at Feversham for ballast; is rudely treated by the people; comes back to Whitehall.

The Prince of Orange is advanced to Windsor, is invited by the King to St. James's, the messenger sent was the Earl of Faversham, the General of the Forces, who going without trumpet, or passport, is detained prisoner by the Prince, who accepts the invitation, but requires his Majesty to retire to some distant place, that his own guards may be quartered about the Palace and City. This is taken heinously, and the King goes privately to Rochester; is persuaded to come back; comes on the Sunday; goes to mass, and dines in public, a Jesuit saying grace (I was present).

17th. That night was a Council; his Majesty refuses to assent to all the proposals; goes away again to Rochester.

18th. I saw the King take barge to Gravesend at twelve o'clock—a sad sight! The Prince comes to St. James's, and fills Whitehall with Dutch guards. A Council of Peers meet about an expedient to call a Parliament; adjourn to the House of Lords. The Chancellor, Earl of Peterborough, and divers others taken. The Earl of Sunderland flies; Sir Edward Hales, Walker, and others, taken and secured.

All the world go to see the Prince at St. James's, where there is a great Court. There I saw him, and several of my acquaintance who came over with him. He is very stately, serious, and reserved. The English soldiers sent out of town to disband them; not well pleased.

24th. The King passes into France, whither the Queen and child were gone a few days before.

[1] The Spanish Ambassador's house, at this time, was Wild House, Drury Lane.

26th December. The Peers and such Commoners as were members of the Parliament at Oxford, being the last of Charles II. meeting, desire the Prince of Orange to take on him the disposal of the public revenue till a convention of Lords and Commons should meet in full body, appointed by his circular letters to the shires and boroughs, 22nd January. I had now quartered upon me a Lieutenant-Colonel and eight horses.

30th. This day prayers for the Prince of Wales were first left off in our church.

1688-9. 7th January. A long frost and deep snow; the Thames almost frozen over.

15th. I visited the Archbishop of Canterbury, where I found the Bishops of St. Asaph,[1] Ely,[2] Bath and Wells,[3] Peterborough,[4] and Chichester,[5] the Earls of Aylesbury and Clarendon, Sir George Mackenzie Lord-Advocate of Scotland, and then came in a Scotch Archbishop, &c. After prayers and dinner, divers serious matters were discoursed, concerning the present state of the Public, and sorry I was to find there was as yet no accord in the judgments of those of the Lords and Commons who were to convene; some would have the Princess made Queen without any more dispute, others were for a Regency; there was a Tory party (then so called), who were for inviting his Majesty again upon conditions; and there were Republicans who would make the Prince of Orange like a Stadtholder. The Romanists were busy among these several parties to bring them into confusion: most for ambition or other interest, few for conscience and moderate resolutions. I found nothing of all this in this assembly of Bishops, who were pleased to admit me into their discourses; they were all for a Regency, thereby to salve their oaths, and so all public matters to proceed in his Majesty's name, by that to facilitate the calling of a Parliament, according to the laws in being. Such was the result of this meeting.

My Lord of Canterbury gave me great thanks for the advertisement I sent him in October,[6] and assured me they took my counsel in that particular, and that it came very seasonably.

[1] Lloyd.   [2] Turner.   [3] Ken.   [4] White.   [5] Lake.   [6] *Ante*, p. 292.

I found by the Lord-Advocate that the Bishops of Scotland (who were indeed little worthy of that character, and
had done much mischief in that Church) were now coming
about to the true interest, in this conjuncture which threatened to abolish the whole hierarchy in that kingdom ; and
therefore the Scottish Archbishop and Lord-Advocate
requested the Archbishop of Canterbury to use his best
endeavours with the Prince to maintain the Church there in
the same state, as by law at present settled.

It now growing late, after some private discourse with
his Grace, I took my leave, most of the Lords being gone.

The trial of the bishops was now printed.

The great convention being assembled the day before,
falling upon the question about the Government, resolved that
King James having by the advice of the Jesuits and other
wicked persons endeavoured to subvert the laws of Church
and State, and deserted the kingdom, carrying away the
seals, &c., without any care for the management of the
government, had by demise abdicated himself and wholly
vacated his right ; they did therefore desire the Lords' concurrence to their vote, to place the crown on the next heir,
the Prince of Orange, for his life, then to the Princess, his
wife, and if she died without issue, to the Princess of Denmark, and she failing, to the heirs of the Prince, excluding
for ever all possibility of admitting a Roman Catholic.

27th January. I dined at the Admiralty, where was brought
in a child not twelve years old, the son of one Dr. Clench,
of the most prodigious maturity of knowledge, for I cannot
call it altogether memory, but something more extraordinary.[1] Mr. Pepys and myself examined him, not in any
method, but with promiscuous questions, which required
judgment and discernment to answer so readily and pertinently. There was not any thing in chronology, history,
geography, the several systems of astronomy, courses of the
stars, longitude, latitude, doctrine of the spheres, courses
and sources of rivers, creeks, harbours, eminent cities,
boundaries and bearings of countries, not only in Europe,
but in any other part of the earth, which he did not readily

[1] See a similar account of the afterwards celebrated William Wotton,
ante, p. 138. This Dr. Clench was murdered in a hackney coach, and
a man named Harrison was executed for the murder.

resolve and demonstrate his knowledge of, readily drawing
out with a pen anything he would describe. He was able
not only to repeat the most famous things which are left us
in any of the Greek or Roman histories, monarchies, repub-
lics, wars, colonies, exploits by sea and land, but all the
sacred stories of the Old and New Testament; the succession of all the monarchies, Babylonian, Persian, Greek,
Roman, with all the lower Emperors, Popes, Heresiarchs,
and Councils, what they were called about, what they determined, or in the controversy about Easter, the tenets of the
Gnostics, Sabellians, Arians, Nestorians; the difference
between St. Cyprian and Stephen about re-baptization;
the schisms. We leaped from that to other things totally
different, to Olympic years, and synchronisms; we asked
him questions which could not be resolved without considerable meditation and judgment, nay of some particulars
of the Civil Laws, of the Digest and Code. He gave a
stupendous account of both natural and moral philosophy,
and even in metaphysics.

. Having thus exhausted ourselves rather than this wonderful child, or angel rather, for he was as beautiful and lovely
in countenance as in knowledge, we concluded with asking
him if, in all he had read or heard of, he had ever met with
anything which was like this expedition of the Prince of
Orange, with so small a force to obtain three great kingdoms without any contest. After a little thought, he told
us that he knew of nothing which did more resemble it than
the coming of Constantine the Great out of Britain, through
France and Italy, so tedious a march, to meet Maxentius,
whom he overthrew at Pons Milvius with very little conflict,
and at the very gates of Rome, which he entered and was
received with triumph, and obtained the empire, not of three
kingdoms only, but of all the then known world. He was
perfect in the Latin authors, spake French naturally, and
gave us a description of France, Italy, Savoy, Spain, ancient
and modernly divided; as also of ancient Greece, Scythia,
and northern countries and tracts: we left questioning
further. He did this without any set or formal repetitions,
as one who had learned things without book, but as if he
minded other things, going about the room, and toying with
a parrot there, and as he was at dinner (*tanquam aliud agens,*

as it were) seeming to be full of play, of a lively, sprightly temper, always smiling, and exceeding pleasant, without the least levity, rudeness, or childishness.

His father assured us he never imposed anything to charge his memory by causing him to get things by heart, not ever the rules of grammar; but his tutor (who was a Frenchman) read to him, first in French, then in Latin; that he usually played amongst other boys four or five hours every day, and that he was as earnest at his play as at his study. He was perfect in arithmetic, and now newly entered into Greek. In sum (*horresco referens*), I had read of divers forward and precocious youths, and some I have known, but I never did either hear or read of anything like to this sweet child, if it be right to call him child who has more knowledge than most men in the world. I counselled his father not to set his heart too much on this jewel,

Immodicis brevis est ætas, et rara senectus,

as I myself learned by sad experience in my most dear child Richard,[1] many years since, who dying before he was six years old, was both in shape and countenance and pregnancy of learning, next to a prodigy.

29th January. The votes of the House of Commons being carried up by Mr. Hampden, their chairman, to the Lords, I got a station by the Prince's lodgings at the door of the lobby to the House, and heard much of the debate, which lasted very long. Lord Derby was in the chair (for the House was resolved into a grand committee of the whole House); after all had spoken, it came to the question, which was carried by three voices against a Regency, which 51 were for, 54 against; the minority alleging the danger of dethroning Kings, and scrupling many passages and expressions in the vote of the Commons, too long to set down particularly. Some were for sending to his Majesty with conditions: others that the King could do no wrong, and that the mal-administration was chargeable on his ministers. There were not more than eight or nine bishops, and but two against the Regency; the archbishop was absent, and the clergy now began to change their note, both in pulpit

[1] *Ante,* vol. i. p. 342.

and discourse, on their old passive obedience, so as people began to talk of the bishops being cast out of the House. In short, things tended to dissatisfaction on both sides; add to this, the morose temper of the Prince of Orange, who showed l..tle countenance to the noblemen and others, who expected a more gracious and cheerful reception when they made the.r court. The English army also was not so in order, and firm to his interest, nor so weakened but that it might give interruption. Ireland was in an ill posture as well as Scotland. Nothing was yet done towards a settlement. God of His infinite mercy compose these things, that we may be at last a Nation and a Church under some fixed and sober establishment!

30th January. The anniversary of King Charles the First's *martyrdom;* but in all the public offices and pulpit prayers, the collects, and litany for the King and Queen were curtailed and mutilated. Dr. Sharp preached before the Commons, but was disliked, and not thanked for his sermon.

31st. At our church (the next day being appointed a Thanksgiving for deliverance by the Prince of Orange, with prayers purposely composed), our lecturer preached in the afternoon a very honest sermon, showing our duty to God for the many signal deliverances of our Church, without touching on politics.

6th February. The King's coronation-day was ordered not to be observed, as hitherto it had been.

The Convention of the Lords and Commons now declare the Prince and Princess of Orange King and Queen of England, France, and Ireland (Scotland being an independent kingdom), the Prince and Princess being to enjoy it jointly during their lives; but the executive authority to be vested in the Prince during life, though all proceedings to run in both names, and that it should descend to their issue, and for want of such, to the Princess Anne of Denmark and her issue, and in want of such, to the heirs of the body of the Prince, if he survive, and that failing, to devolve to the Parliament, as they should think fit. These produced a conference with the Lords, when also there was presented heads of such new laws as were to be enacted. It is thought on these conditions they will be proclaimed.

There was much contest about the King's abdication, and

whether he had vacated the government. The Earl of Nottingham and about twenty Lords, and many Bishops,
entered their protests, but the concurrence was great against
them.

The Princess hourly expected. Forces sending to Ireland, that kingdom being in great danger by the Earl of
Tyrconnel's army, and expectations from France coming to
assist them, but that King was busy in invading Flanders,
and encountering the German Princes. It is likely that
this will be the most remarkable summer for action, which
has happened in many years.

21st *February*. Dr. Burnet preached at St. James's on the
obligation to walk worthy of God's particular and signal
deliverance of the Nation and Church.

I saw the *new Queen* and *King* proclaimed the very next
day after her coming to Whitehall, Wednesday, 13th February, with great acclamation and general good reception.
Bonfires, bells, guns, &c. It was believed that both, especially the Princess, would have showed some (seeming) reluctance at least, of assuming her father's Crown, and made
some apology, testifying by her regret that he should by his
mismanagement necessitate the Nation to so extraordinary
a proceeding, which would have showed very handsomely to
the world, and according to the character given of her piety ;
consonant also to her husband's first declaration, that there
was no intention of deposing the King, but of succouring
the Nation ; but nothing of all this appeared ; she came
into Whitehall laughing and jolly, as to a wedding, so as to
seem quite transported. She rose early the next morning,
and in her undress, as it was reported, before her women
were up, went about from room to room to see the convenience of Whitehall ; lay in the same bed and apartment where
the late Queen lay, and within a night or two sat down to
play at basset, as the Queen her predecessor used to do. She
smiled upon and talked to everybody, so that no change
seemed to have taken place at Court since her last going
away, save that infinite crowds of people thronged to see
her, and that she went to our prayers. This carriage was
censured by many. She seems to be of a good nature, and
that she takes nothing to heart : whilst the Prince her husband has a thoughtful countenance, is wonderful serious and

silent, and seems to treat all persons alike gravely, and to be very intent on affairs: Holland, Ireland, and France calling for his care.

Divers Bishops and Noblemen are not at all satisfied with this so sudden assumption of the Crown, without any previous sending, and offering some conditions to the absent King; or, on his not returning, or not assenting to those conditions, to have proclaimed him Regent; but the major part of both Houses prevailed to make them King and Queen immediately, and a crown was tempting. This was opposed and spoken against with such vehemence by Lord Clarendon (her own uncle), that it put him by all preferment, which must doubtless have been as great as could have been given him. My Lord of Rochester his brother, overshot himself, by the same carriage and stiffness, which their friends thought they might have well spared when they saw how it was like to be overruled, and that it had been sufficient to have declared their dissent with less passion, acquiescing in due time.

The Archbishop of Canterbury and some of the rest, on scruple of conscience and to salve the oaths they had taken, entered their protests and hung off, especially the Archbishop, who had not all this while so much as appeared out of Lambeth. This occasioned the wonder of many who observed with what zeal they contributed to the Prince's expedition, and all the while also rejecting any proposals of sending again to the absent King; that they should now raise scruples, and such as created much division among the people, greatly rejoicing the old courtiers, and especially the Papists.

Another objection was, the invalidity of what was done by a Convention only, and the as yet unabrogated laws; this drew them to make themselves on the 22nd [February] a Parliament, the new King passing the Act with the crown on his head. The lawyers disputed, but necessity prevailed, the Government requiring a speedy settlement.

Innumerable were the crowds, who solicited for, and expected offices; most of the old ones were turned out. Two or three white staves were disposed of some days before, as Lord Steward, to the Earl of Devonshire; Trea.

surer of the Household, to Lord Newport; Lord Chamberlain to the King, to my Lord of Dorset; but there were as yet none in offices of the Civil Government save the Marquis of Halifax as Privy Seal. A council of thirty was chosen, Lord Derby president, but neither Chancellor nor Judges were yet declared, the new Great Seal not yet finished.

8th March. Dr. Tillotson, Dean of Canterbury, made an excellent discourse on Matt. v. 44, exhorting to charity and forgiveness of enemies; I suppose purposely, the new Parliament being furious about impeaching those who were obnoxious, and as their custom has ever been, going on violently, without reserve, or moderation, whilst wise men were of opinion the most notorious offenders being named and excepted, an Act of Amnesty would be more seasonable, to pacify the minds of men in so general a discontent of the nation, especially of those who did not expect to see the government assumed without any regard to the absent King, or proving a spontaneous abdication, or that the birth of the Prince of Wales was an imposture; five of the Bishops also still refusing to take the new oath.

In the mean time, to gratify the people, the Hearth-Tax was remitted for ever; but what was intended to supply it, besides present great taxes on land, is not named.

The King abroad was now furnished by the French King with money and officers for an expedition to Ireland. The great neglect in not more timely preventing that from hence, and the disturbances in Scotland, give apprehensions of great difficulties, before any settlement can be perfected here, whilst the Parliament dispose of the great offices amongst themselves. The Great Seal, Treasury and Admiralty put into commission of many unexpected persons, to gratify the more; so that by the present appearance of things (unless God Almighty graciously interpose and give success in Ireland and settle Scotland) more trouble seems to threaten the nation than could be expected. In the interim, the new King refers all to the Parliament in the most popular manner, but is very slow in providing against all these menaces, besides finding difficulties in raising men to send abroad; the former army, which had never seen any service hitherto, receiving their pay and passing their summer in an idle scene of a camp at Hounslow, unwilling to engage, and many disaffected, and scarce to be trusted.

29th March. The new King much blamed for neglecting Ireland, now like to be ruined by the Lord Tyrconnel and his Popish party, too strong for the Protestants. Wonderful uncertainty where King James was, whether in France or Ireland. The Scots seem as yet to favour King William, rejecting King James's letter to them, yet declaring nothing positively. Soldiers in England discontented. Parliament preparing the coronation-oath. Presbyterians and Dissenters displeased at the vote for preserving the Protestant religion as established by law, without mentioning what they were to have as to indulgence.

The Archbishop of Canterbury and four[1] other Bishops refusing to come to Parliament, it was deliberated whether they should incur *Præmunire;* but it was thought fit to let this fall, and be connived at, for fear of the people, to whom these Prelates were very dear, for the opposition they had given to Popery.

Court-offices distributed amongst Parliament-men. No considerable fleet as yet sent forth. Things far from settled as was expected, by reason of the slothful, sickly temper of the new King, and the Parliament's unmindfulness of Ireland, which is likely to prove a sad omission.

The Confederates beat the French out of the Palatinate, which they had most barbarously ruined.

11th April. I saw the procession to and from the Abbey-Church of Westminster, with the great feast in Westminster-Hall, at the coronation of King William and Queen Mary. What was different from former coronations, was some alteration in the coronation-oath. Dr. Burnet, now made Bishop of Sarum, preached with great applause. The Parliament-men had scaffolds and places which took up the one whole side of the Hall. When the King and Queen

---

[1] Burnet names only three besides the Archbishop, namely, Thomas of Worcester, Lake of Chichester, Ken of Bath and Wells. He says (in his *Own Times*) that at the first landing of the Prince, Ken declared heartily for him, and advised all to go to him; but went with great heat into the notion of a Regent. After this, he changed his mind, came to town with intent to take the oaths, but again changed, and never did take them.

had dined, the ceremony of the Champion, and other services
by tenure were performed. The Parliament-men were
feasted in the Exchequer-chamber, and had each of them a
gold medal given them, worth five-and-forty shillings. On
one side were the effigies of the King and Queen inclining
one to the other; on the reverse was Jupiter throwing a
bolt at Phäeton, the words, " *Ne totus absumatur :*" which
was but dull, seeing they might have had out of the poet
something as apposite. The sculpture was very mean.

Much of the splendour of the proceeding was abated by
the absence of divers who should have contributed to it,
there being but five Bishops, four Judges (no more being
yet sworn), and several noblemen and great ladies wanting;
the feast, however, was magnificent. The next day the
House of Commons went and kissed their new Majesties'
hands in the Banqueting-house.

12*th April.* I went with the Bishop of St. Asaph to visit
my Lord of Canterbury at Lambeth, who had excused himself from officiating at the coronation, which was performed
by the Bishop of London, assisted by the Archbishop of
York. We had much private and free discourse with his
Grace concerning several things relating to the Church,
there being now a bill of comprehension to be brought
from the Lords to the Commons. I urged that when they
went about to reform some particulars in the Liturgy,
Church discipline, Canons, &c., the baptizing in private
houses without necessity might be reformed, as likewise so
frequent burials in churches; the one proceeding much
from the pride of women, bringing that into custom which
was only indulged in case of imminent danger, and out of
necessity during the rebellion, and persecution of the clergy
in our late civil wars; the other from the avarice of ministers, who, in some opulent parishes, made almost as much
of permission to bury in the chancel and the church, as of
their livings, and were paid with considerable advantage
and gifts for baptising in chambers. To this they heartily
assented, and promised their endeavour to get it reformed,
utterly disliking both practices as novel and indecent.

We discoursed likewise of the great disturbance and
prejudice it might cause, should the new oath, now on the
anvil, be imposed on any, save such as were in new office,

x 2

without any retrospect to such as either had no office, or had been long in office, who it was likely would have some scruples about taking a new oath, having already sworn fidelity to the government as established by law. This we all knew to be the case of my Lord Archbishop of Canterbury, and some other persons who were not so fully satisfied with the Convention making it an abdication of King James, to whom they had sworn allegiance.

King James was now certainly in Ireland with the Marshal d'Estrades, whom he made a Privy Councillor; and who caused the King to remove the Protestant Councillors, some whereof, it seems, had continued to sit, telling him that the King of France his master would never assist him if he did not immediately do it; by which it is apparent how the poor Prince is managed by the French.

Scotland declares for King William and Queen Mary, with the reasons of their setting aside King James, not as abdicating, but forfeiting his right by mal-administration; they proceeded with much more caution and prudence than we did, who precipitated all things to the great reproach of the nation, all which had been managed by some crafty illprincipled men. The new Privy Council have a Republican spirit, manifestly undermining all future succession of the crown and prosperity of the Church of England, which yet I hope they will not be able to accomplish so soon as they expect, though they get into all places of trust and profit.

21st April. This was one of the most seasonable springs, free from the usual sharp east winds that I have observed since the year 1660 (the year of the Restoration), which was much such an one.

26th. I heard the lawyers plead before the Lords the writ of error in the judgment of Oates, as to the charge against him of perjury, which after debate they referred to the answer of Holloway, &c., who were his Judges. I then went with the Bishop of St. Asaph to the Archbishop at Lambeth, where they entered into discourse concerning the final destruction of Antichrist, both concluding that the third trumpet and vial were now pouring out. My Lord St. Asaph considered the killing of the two witnesses, to be the utter destruction of the Cevennes Protestants by the French and Duke of Savoy, and the other the Waldenses and Pyrenean Christians, who by all appearance from good history had kept the primitive faith from the very Apostles' time till now. The doubt his Grace suggested was, wh:ther it could be made evident that the present persecution had made so great a havoc of those faithful people as of the other, and whether there were not yet some among them in being who met together, it being stated from the text, Apoc. xi., that they should both be slain together. They both. much approved of Mr. Mede's way of interpretation, and that he only failed in resolving too hastily on the King of Sweden's (Gustavus Adolphus) success in Germany. They agreed that it would be good to employ some intelligent French minister[1] to travel as far as the Pyrenees to understand the present state of the Church there, it being a country where hardly any one travels.

There now came certain news that King James had not only landed in Ireland, but that he had surprised Londonderry, and was become master of that kingdom, to the great shame of our Government, who had been so often solicited to provide against it by timely succour, and which they might so easily have done. This is a terrible beginning of more troubles, especially should an army come thence into Scotland, people being generally disaffected here and every where else, so that the sea and land-men would scarce serve without compulsion.

A new oath was now fabricating for all the clergy to take, of obedience to the present Government, in abrogation of the former oaths of allegiance, which it is foreseen many of the Bishops and others of the clergy will not take. The penalty is to be the loss of their dignity and spiritual preferment. This is thought to have been driven on by the Presbyterians, our new governors. God in mercy send us help, and direct the counsels to His glory and good of His Church !

Public matters went very ill in Ireland : confusion and dissension amongst ourselves, stupidity, inconstancy, emulation, the governors employing unskilful men in greatest offices, no person of public spirit and ability appearing,— threaten us with a very sad prospect of what may be the conclusion, without God's infinite mercy.

[1] They sent two. See afterwards.

A fight by Admiral Herbert with the French, he imprudently setting on them in a creek as they were landing men in Ireland, by which we came off with great slaughter and little honour—so strangely negligent and remiss were we in preparing a timely and sufficient fleet. The Scots Commissioners offer the crown to the *new King and Queen* on conditions.—Act of Poll-money came forth, sparing none.—Now appeared the Act of Indulgence for the Dissenters, but not exempting them paying dues to the Church of England Clergy, or serving in office according to law, with several other clauses.—A most splendid embassy from Holland to congratulate the King and Queen on their accession to the crown.

4th June. A solemn fast for success of the fleet, &c.

6th. I dined with the Bishop of Asaph; Monsieur Capellus, the learned son of the most learned Ludovicus, presented to him his father's works, not published till now.

7th. I visited the Archbishop of Canterbury, and staid with him till about seven o'clock. He read to me the Pope's excommunication of the French King.

9th. Visited Dr. Burnet, now Bishop of Sarum; got him to let Mr. Kneller draw his picture.

16th. King James's declaration was now dispersed, offering pardon to all, if on his landing, or within twenty days after, they should return to their obedience.

Our fleet not yet at sea, through some prodigious sloth, and men minding only their present interest; the French riding masters at sea, taking many great prizes to our wonderful reproach. No certain news from Ireland; various reports of Scotland; discontents at home. The King of Denmark at last joins with the Confederates, and the two Northern Powers are reconciled. The East India Company likely to be dissolved by Parliament for many arbitrary actions. Oates acquitted of perjury, to all honest men's admiration.

20th. News of *a Plot* discovered, on which divers were sent to the Tower and secured.

23rd. An extraordinary drought, to the threatening of great wants as to the fruits of the earth.

8th July. I sat for my picture to Mr. Kneller, for Mr. Pepys, late Secretary to the Admiralty, holding my *Sylva* in my right hand.[1] It was on his long and earnest request, and is placed in his library. Kneller never painted in a more masterly manner.

11*th June.* I dined at Lord Clarendon's, it being his lady's wedding-day, when about three in the afternoon there was an unusual and violent storm of thunder, rain, and wind; many boats on the Thames were overwhelmed, and such was the impetuosity of the wind as to carry up the waves in pillars and spouts most dreadful to behold, rooting up trees and ruining some houses. The Countess of Sunderland afterwards told me that it extended as far as Althorpe at the very time, which is seventy miles from London. It did no harm at Deptford, but at Greenwich it did much mischief.

16*th July.* I went to Hampton Court about business, the Council being there. A great apartment and spacious garden with fountains was beginning in the park at the head of the canal.

19*th.* The Marshal de Schomberg went now as General towards Ireland, to the relief of Londonderry. Our fleet lay before Brest. The Confederates passing the Rhine, besiege Bonn and Mayence, to obtain a passage into France. A great victory got by the Muscovites, taking and burning Perecop. A new rebel against the Turks threatens the destruction of that tyranny. All Europe in arms against France, and hardly to be found in history so universal a face of war.

The Convention (or Parliament as some called it) sitting, exempt the Duke of Hanover from the succession to the crown, which they seem to confine to the present new King, his wife, and Princess Anne of Denmark, who is so monstrously swollen, that it's doubted whether her being thought with child may prove a *tympany* only, so that the unhappy family of the Stuarts seems to be extinguishing; and then what government is likely to be next set up is unknown, whether regal and by election, or otherwise, the Republicans and Dissenters from the Church of England evidently looking that way.

The Scots have now again voted down Episcopacy there.

[1] Now at Wotton. A copy of it was given by the late Sir Frederick Evelyn to the Earl of Harcourt, a few years ago.

—Great discontents through this nation at the slow proceedings of the King, and the incompetent instruments
and officers he advances to the greatest and most necessary
charges.

23rd *August*. Came to visit me Mr. Firmin.[1]

25th. Hitherto it has been a most seasonable summer.—
Londonderry relieved after a brave and wonderful holding
out.

21st *September*. I went to visit the Archbishop of Canterbury since his suspension, and was received with great kindness.—A dreadful fire happened in Southwark.

2nd *October*. Came to visit us the Marquis de Ruvigné,
and one Monsieur le Coque, a French refugee, who left
great riches for his religion; a very learned, civil person;
he married the sister of the Duchess de la Force.—Otto-
bone, a Venetian Cardinal, eighty years old, made Pope.[2]

31st. My birthday, being now sixty-nine years old.
Blessed Father, who hast prolonged my years to this great
age, and given me to see so great and wonderful revolutions,
and preserved me amidst them to this moment, accept, I
beseech thee, the continuance of my prayers and thankful
acknowledgments, and grant me grace to be working out my
salvation and redeeming the time, that Thou mayst be
glorified by me here, and my immortal soul saved whenever
Thou shall call for it, to perpetuate Thy praises to all
eternity, in that heavenly kingdom where there are no more
changes or vicissitudes, but rest, and peace, and joy, and
consummate felicity, for ever. Grant this, O heavenly
Father, for the sake of Jesus thine only Son and our
Saviour. Amen!

5th *November*. The Bishop of St. Asaph, Lord-Almoner,
preached before the King and Queen, the whole discourse

---

[1] He was a man of the most amiable character, and unbounded
charity : a great friend of Sir Robert Clayton, who, after his death,
erected a monument for him in a walk which he had formed at Sir
Robert's seat at Marden, in Surrey. He was very fond of gardens, and
so far of a congenial spirit with Mr. Evelyn; and though Unitarian in
creed, he lived in intimacy with many of the most eminent clergy. His
life was printed in a small volume. See more of him in Manning and
Bray's *History of Surrey*, vol. ii. pp. 804, 805.

[2] Peter Otthobonus succeeded Innocent XI. as Pope in 1689, by the
title of Alexander VIII.

being an historical narrative of the Church of England's several deliverances, especially that of this anniversary, signalised by being also the birthday of the Prince of Orange, his marriage (which was on the 4th), and his landing at Torbay this day. There was a splendid ball and other rejoicings.

10th November. After a very wet season, the winter came on severely.

17th. Much wet, without frost, yet the wind north and easterly.—A Convocation of the Clergy meet about a reformation of our Liturgy, Canons, &c., obstructed by others of the clergy.

27th. I went to London with my family, to winter at Soho, in the great square.

1689-90. 11th January. This night there was a most extraordinary storm of wind, accompanied with snow and sharp weather; it did great harm in many places, blowing down houses, trees, &c., killing many people. It began about two in the morning, and lasted till five, being a kind of hurricane, which mariners observe have begun of late years to come northward. This winter has been hitherto extremely wet, warm, and windy.

12th. There was read at St. Ann's Church an exhortatory letter to the clergy of London from the Bishop, together with a Brief for relieving the distressed Protestants, the Vaudois, who fled from the persecution of the French and Duke of Savoy, to the Protestant Cantons of Switzerland.

The Parliament was unexpectedly prorogued to 2nd April to the discontent and surprise of many members who, being exceeding averse to the settling of any thing, proceeding with animosities, multiplying exceptions against those whom they pronounced obnoxious, and producing as universal a discontent against King William and themselves, as there was before against King James.—The new King resolved on an expedition into Ireland in person. About 150 of the members who were of the more royal party, meeting at a feast at the Apollo Tavern near St. Dunstan's, sent some of their company to the King, to assure him of their service; he returned his thanks, advising them to repair to their several counties and preserve the peace during his absence,

and assuring them that he would be steady to his resolution
of defending the Laws and Religion established. — The
great Lord suspected to have counselled this prorogation,
universally denied it. However, it was believed the chief
a dviser was the Marquis of Carmarthen,[1] who now seemed
to be most in favour.

: *2nd February.* The Parliament was dissolved by proclamation, and another called to meet the 20th of March.
This was a second surprise to the former members; and
now the Court-party, or, as they call themselves, Church of
England, are making their interests in the country. The
Marquis of Halifax lays down his office of Privy Seal, and
pretends to retire.

16*th.* The Duchess of Monmouth's chaplain preached
at St. Martin's an excellent discourse, exhorting to peace
and sanctity, it being now the time of very great division
and dissension in the nation; first, amongst the Churchmen, of whom the moderate and sober part were for a
speedy reformation of divers things, which it was thought
might be made in our Liturgy, for the inviting of Dissenters; others more stiff and rigid, were for no condescen-
sion at all. Books and pamphlets were published every day
pro and *con.;* the Convocation were forced for the present
to suspend any further progress.—There was fierce and
great carousing about being elected in the new Parliament.
—The King persists in his intention of going in person for
Ireland, whither the French are sending supplies to King
James, and we, the Danish horse to Schomberg.

19*th.* I dined with the Marquis of Carmarthen (late
Lord Danby), where was Lieutenant-general Douglas, a very
considerate and sober commander, going for Ireland. He
related to us the exceeding neglect of the English soldiers,
suffering severely for want of clothes and necessaries this
winter, exceedingly magnifying their courage and bravery
during all their hardships. There dined also Lord Lucas,
Lieutenant of the Tower, and the Bishop of St. Asaph.—
The Privy Seal was again put in commission, Mr. Cheny
(who married my kinswoman, Mrs. Pierrepoint), Sir Thomas
Knatchbull, and Sir P. W. Pultney.—The imprudence of

---

[1] Osborn, Lord Danby, afterwards Duke of Leeds.

both sexes was now become so great and universal, persons of all ranks keeping their courtesans publicly, that the King had lately directed a letter to the Bishops to order their clergy to preach against that sin, swearing, &c., and to put the ecclesiastical laws in execution without any indulgence.

25th February. I went to Kensington, which King William had bought of Lord Nottingham, and altered, but was yet a patched building, but with the garden, however, it is a very sweet villa, having to it the park and a straight new way through this park.

7th March. I dined with Mr. Pepys, late Secretary to the Admiralty, where was that excellent shipwright and seaman (for so he had been, and also a Commission of the Navy), Sir Anthony Deane. Amongst other discourse, and deploring the sad condition of our navy, as now governed by inexperienced men since this Revolution, he mentioned what exceeding advantage we of this nation had by being the first who built frigates, the first of which ever built was that vessel which was afterwards called " The Constant Warwick," and was the work of Pett¹ of Chatham, for a trial of making a vessel that would sail swiftly ; it was built with low decks, the guns lying near the water, and was so light and swift of sailing, that in a short time he told us she had, ere the Dutch war was ended, taken as much money from privateers as would have laden her ; and that more such being built, did in a year or two scour the Channel from those of Dunkirk and others which had exceedingly infested it. He added that it would be the best and only infallible expedient to be masters of the sea, and able to destroy the greatest navy of any enemy if, instead of building huge great ships and second and third rates, they would leave off building such high decks, which were for nothing but to gratify gentlemen-commanders, who must have all their effeminate accommodations, and for pomp ; that it would be the ruin of our fleets, if such persons were continued in command, they neither having experience nor being capable of learning, because they would not submit to the fatigue and inconvenience which those who were bred seamen would undergo, in those so otherwise useful swift frigates. These being to encounter the greatest ships would be able to protect, set on, and bring off, those who should manage the fire-ships , and the Prince who should first store himself with numbers of such fire-ships would, through the help and countenance of such frigates, be able to ruin the greatest force of such vast ships as could be sent to sea, by the dexterity of working those light, swift ships to guard the fire-ships. He concluded there would shortly be no other method of sea-fight ; and that great ships and men-of-war, however stored with guns and men, must submit to those who should encounter them with far less number. He represented to us the dreadful effect of these fire-ships ; that he continually observed in our late maritime war with the Dutch that, when an enemy's fire-ship approached, the most valiant commander and common sailors were in such consternation, that though then, of all times, there was most need of the guns, bombs, &c., to keep the mischief off, they grew pale and astonished, as if of a quite other mean soul, that they slunk about, forsook their guns and work as if in despair, every one looking about to see which way they might get out of their ship, though sure to be drowned if they did so. This he said was likely to prove hereafter the method of sea-fight, likely to be the misfortune of England if they continued to put gentlemen-commanders over experienced seamen, on account of their ignorance, effeminacy, and insolence.

9th March. Preached at Whitehall Dr. Burnet, late Bishop of Sarum, on Heb. iv. 13, anatomically describing the texture of the eye ; and that, as it received such innumerable sorts of spies through so very small a passage to the brain, and that without the least confusion or trouble, and accordingly judged and reflected on them ; so God who made this sensory, did with the greatest ease and at once see all that was done through the vast universe, even to the very thought as well as action. This similitude he continued with much perspicuity and aptness ; and applied it accordingly, for the admonishing us how uprightly we ought to live and behave ourselves before such an allseeing Deity ; and how we were to conceive of other His attributes, which we could have no idea of than by comparing them by what we were able to conceive of the nature and power of things, which were the objects of our senses ; and therefore it was

Martin Luz.

that in Scripture we attribute those actions and affections of God by the same of man, not as adequately or in any proportion like them, but as the only expedient to make some resemblance of His divine perfections; as when the Scripture says, "God will remember the sins of the penitent no more:" not as if God could forget anything, but as intimating he would pass by such penitents and receive them to mercy.

I dined at the Bishop of St. Asaph's, Almoner to the new Queen, with the famous lawyer Sir George Mackenzie (late Lord Advocate of Scotland), against whom both the Bishop and myself had written and published books, but now most friendly reconciled.[1] He related to us many particulars of Scotland, the present sad condition of it, the inveterate hatred which the Presbyterians show to the family of the Stuarts, and the exceeding tyranny of those bigots who acknowledge no superior on earth, in civil or divine matters, maintaining that the people only have the right of government; their implacable hatred to the Episcopal Order and Church of England. He observed that the first Presbyter-dissents from our discipline were introduced by the Jesuits' order, about the 20 of Queen Eliz., a famous Jesuit amongst them feigning himself a Protestant, and who was the first who began to pray extempore, and brought in that which they since called, and are still so fond of, praying by the Spirit. This Jesuit remained many years before he was discovered, afterwards died in Scotland, where he was buried at ...... having yet on his monument, "*Rosa inter spinas.*"

11*th March.* I went again to see Mr. Charlton's curiosities,[2] both of art and nature, and his full and rare collection of medals, which taken altogether, in all kinds, is doubtless one of the most perfect assemblages of rarities that can be any where seen. I much admired the contortions of the Thea root, which was so perplexed, large, and intricate, and withal hard as box, that it was wonderful to consider.—The French have landed in Ireland.

16*th.* A public fast.

[1] Sir George, as we have seen (*ante*, p. 23), had written in praise of a Private Life, which Mr. Evelyn answered by a book in praise of Public Life and Active Employment. See the present vol., p. 23, note.

[2] *Ante*, p. 270.

24th May.   City charter restored. Divers exempted from pardon.

4th June.   King William set forth on his Irish expedition, leaving the Queen regent.

10th.   Mr. Pepys read to me his Remonstrance, showing with what malice and injustice he was suspected with Sir Anthony Deane about the timber, of which the thirty ships were built by a late Act of Parliament, with the exceeding danger which the fleet would shortly be in, by reason of the tyranny and incompetency of those who now managed the Admiralty and affairs of the Navy, of which he gave an accurate state, and showed his great ability.

18th.   Fast-day. Visited the Bishop of St. Asaph; his conversation was on the Vaudois in Savoy, who had been thought so near destruction and final extirpation by the French, being totally given up to slaughter, so that there were no hopes for them; but now it pleased God that the Duke of Savoy, who had hitherto joined with the French in their persecution, being now pressed by them to deliver up Saluzzo and Turin as cautionary towns, on suspicion that he might at last come into the Confederacy of the German Princes, did secretly concert measures with, and afterwards declared for, them. He then invited these poor people from their dispersion amongst the mountains whither they had fled, and restored them to their country, their dwellings, and the exercise of their religion, and begged pardon for the ill-usage they had received, charging it on the cruelty of the French who forced him to it. These being the remainder of those persecuted Christians which the Bishop of St. Asaph had so long affirmed to be the two witnesses spoken of in the Revelation, who should be killed and brought to life again, it was looked on as an extraordinary thing that this prophesying Bishop should persuade two fugitive ministers of the Vaudois [1] to return to their country, and furnish them with 20*l.* towards their journey, at that very time when nothing but universal destruction was to be expected, assuring them and showing them from the Apocalypse, that their countrymen should be returned safely to their country before they arrived. This happening contrary to all expectation and appearance, did exceedingly credit the Bishop'

[1] *Ante,* p. 308.

confidence how that prophecy of the witnesses should come
to pass, just at the time, and the very month, he had spoken
of some years before.

I afterwards went with him to Mr. Boyle and Lady Ranelagh his sister, to whom he explained the necessity of it so
fully, and so learnedly made out, with what events were
immediately to follow, viz. the French King's ruin, the calling of the Jews to be near at hand, but that the Kingdom
of Antichrist would not yet be utterly destroyed till 30
years, when Christ should begin the Millenium, not as personally and visibly reigning on earth, but that the true religion and universal peace should obtain through all the
world. He showed how Mr. Brightman, Mr. Mede, and
other interpreters of these events failed, by mistaking and
reckoning the year as the Latins and others did, to consist
of the present calculation, so many days to the year, whereas the Apocalypse reckons after the Persian account, as
Daniel did, whose visions St. John all along explains as
meaning only the Christian Church.

24th June. Dined with Mr. Pepys, who the next day was
sent to the Gate-house,[1] and several great persons to the
Tower, on suspicion of being affected to King James; amongst
them was the Earl of Clarendon, the Queen's uncle. King
William having vanquished King James in Ireland, there
was much public rejoicing. It seems the Irish in King
James's army would not stand, but the English - Irish and
French made great resistance. Schomberg was slain, and
Dr. Walker,[2] who so bravely defended Londonderry. King
William received a slight wound by the grazing of a cannon
bullet on his shoulder, which he endured with very little
interruption of his pursuit. Hamilton, who broke his word
about Tyrconnel, was taken. It is reported that King James
is gone back to France. Drogheda and Dublin surrendered,

[1] Poor Pepys, as the reader knows, had already undergone an imprisonment, with perhaps just as much reason as the present, on the
absurd accusation of having sent information to the French Court of
the state of the English Navy. See *ante*, p. 136.

[2] George Walker, an Irish clergyman, who distinguished himself more
in the camp than in the pulpit, and after successfully defending Protestant Londonderry against the Popish army under James II, accompanied William III. during his decisive campaign against his father-in-
law, till he was slain at the battle of the Boyne.

and if King William be returning, we may say of him as Cæsar said, " *Veni, vidi, vici.*" But to alloy much of this, the French fleet rides in our channel, ours not daring to interpose, and the enemy threatening to land.

27th June. I went to visit some friends in tne Tower, when asking for Lord Clarendon, they by mistake directed me to the Earl of Torrington,[1] who about three days before had been sent for from the fleet, and put into the Tower for cowardice and not fighting the French fleet, which having beaten a squadron of the Hollanders, whilst Torrington did nothing, did now ride masters of the sea, threatening a descent.

20th July. This afternoon a camp of about 4000 men was begun to be formed on Blackheath.

· *30th.* I dined with Mr. Pepys, now suffered to return to his house, on account of indisposition.

1st August. The Duke of Grafton[2] came to visit me, going to his ship at the mouth of the river, in his way to Ireland (where he was slain).

3rd. The French landed some soldiers at Teignmouth, in Devon, and burnt some poor houses.—The French fleet still hovering about the western coast, and we having 300 sail of rich merchant-ships in the bay of Plymouth, our fleet begin to move towards them, under three admirals. The country in the west all on their guard.—A very extraordinary fine season; but on the 12th was a very great storm of thunder and lightning, and on the 15th the season much changed to wet and cold.—The militia and trained bands, horse and foot, which were up through England, were dismissed.— The French King having news that King William was slain, and his army defeated in Ireland, caused such a triumph at Paris, and all over France, as was never heard of; when, in the midst of it, the unhappy King James being vanquished,·

---

[1] Arthur Herbert, grandson of the celebrated Lord Herbert of Cherbury. In 1689, William raised him to the Peerage for his eminent naval services, with the titles of Baron Torbay and Earl of Torrington; but not succeeding against the French fleet near Beachy Head, he was sent to the Tower, tried by a Court-martial, and, though acquitted, never again employed. He died April 14, 1716.

[2] Henry Fitzroy, second natural son of Charles II. by the Duchess of Cleveland. His Grace was ancestor of the present Duke.

oy a speedy flight and escape, himself brought the news of his own defeat.

15th August. I was desired to be one of the bail of the Earl of Clarendon, for his release from the Tower, with divers noblemen. The Bishop of St. Asaph expounds his prophecies to me and Mr. Pepys, &c. The troops from Blackheath march to Portsmouth.—That sweet and hopeful youth, Sir Charles Tuke, died of the wounds he received in the fight of the Boyne, to the great sorrow of all his friends, being (I think) the last male of that family, to which my wife is related. A more virtuous young gentleman I never knew; he was learned for his age, having had the advantage of the choicest breeding abroad, both as to arts and arms; he had travelled much, but was so unhappy as to fall in the side of the unfortunate King.

The unseasonable and most tempestuous weather happening, the naval expedition is hindered, and the extremity of wet causes the siege of Limerick to be raised, King William returned to England.—Lord Sidney[1] left Governor of what is conquered in Ireland, which is near three parts [in four].

17th. A public fast.—An extraordinary sharp, cold, east wind.

12th October. The French General, with Tyrconnel and their forces, gone back to France, beaten out by King William.—Cork delivered on discretion. The Duke of Grafton was there mortally wounded and dies.—Very great storms of wind. The 8th of this month Lord Spencer wrote me word from Althorpe, that there happened an earthquake the day before in the morning, which, though short, sensibly, shook the house. The Gazette acquainted us that the like happened at the same time, half-past seven, at Barnstaple, Holyhead, and Dublin. We were not sensible of it here.

26th. Kinsale at last surrendered, meantime King James's party burn all the houses they have in their power, and amongst them that stately palace of Lord Ossory's, which lately cost, as reported, £40,000. By a disastrous accident, a third-rate ship, the Breda, blew up and destroyed all on

---

[1] Henry, youngest brother of Robert, second Earl of Leicester; created in 1689, Baron Sidney and Viscount Sidney, and in 1694 Earl of Romney. He died in 1704.

board; in it were twenty-five prisoners of war. She was to have sailed for England the next day.

3rd November. Went to the Countess of Clancarty,[1] to condole with her concerning her debauched and dissolute son, who had done so much mischief in Ireland, now taken and brought prisoner to the Tower.

16th. Exceeding great storms, yet a warm season.

23rd. Carried Mr. Pepys's memorials to Lord Godolphi now resuming the commission of the Treasury to the wonder of all his friends.

1st December. Having been chosen President of the Royal Society, I desired to decline it, and with great difficulty devolved the election on Sir Robert Southwell, Secretary of State to King William in Ireland.

20th. Dr. Hough, President of Magdalen College, Oxford, who was displaced with several of the Fellows for not taking the oath imposed by King James, now made a Bishop.[2] —Most of this month cold and frost.— One Johnson, a Knight, was executed at Tyburn for being an accomplice with Campbell, brother to Lord Argyle, in stealing a young heiress.

1690-1. 4th January. This week a *plot* was discovered for a general rising against the new Government, for which (Henry) Lord Clarendon and others were sent to the Tower. The next day, I went to see Lord Clarendon. The Bishop of Ely[3] searched for.—Trial of Lord Preston, as not being an English Peer, hastened at the Old Bailey.

18th. Lord Preston condemned about a design to bring in King James by the French. Ashton executed. The Bishop of Ely, Mr. Graham, &c., absconded.

[1] Elizabeth Fitzgerald, daughter of the Earl of Kildare. Her son, the third Earl, for the services he had rendered James II., forfeited in the reign of his successor the whole of his vast estates.

[2] In 1699, Dr. Hough was translated to Lichfield and Coventry: in 1717, he became Bishop of Worcester, which he held till 1743 when he died, 8th May, at the great age of 93. His conversation and familiar letters, at the close of his life, had the cheerfulness and spirit of youth. He was a genuine patriot; the delight of the Church; a thorn in the side of oppression; a pillar of religion; a father of the indigent; a friend to all. His Memoirs were published in a quarto volume, in 1812, by Mr. Wilmot.

[3] Dr. Turner, who, though one of the six Bishops sent to the Tower for the petition to the King, declined taking the oaths to William and Mary.

13th *March.* I went to visit Monsieur Justell and the Library at St. James's, in which that learned man had put the MSS. (which were in good number) into excellent order, they having lain neglected for many years. Divers medals had been stolen and embezzled.

21st. Dined at Sir William Fermor's, who showed me many good pictures. After dinner, a French servant played rarely on the lute. Sir William had now bought all the remaining statues collected with so much expense by the famous Thomas, Earl of Arundel, and sent them to his seat at Easton, near Towcester.[1]

25th. Lord Sidney, principal Secretary of State, gave me a letter to Lord Lucas, Lieutenant of the Tower, to permit me to visit Lord Clarendon; which this day I did, and dined with him.

10th *April.* This night, a sudden and terrible fire burnt down all the buildings over the stone-gallery at Whitehall to the water-side, beginning at the apartment of the late Duchess of Portsmouth (which had been pulled down and rebuilt no less than three times to please her), and consuming other lodgings of such lewd creatures, who debauched both King Charles II. and others, and were his destruction. The King returned out of Holland just as this accident happened—Proclamation against Papists, &c.

16th. I went to see Dr. Sloane's curiosities, being an universal collection of the natural productions of Jamaica, consisting of plants, fruits, corals, minerals, stones, earth, shells, animals, and insects, collected with great judgment; several folios of dried plants, and one which had about 80 several sorts of ferns, and another of grasses; the Jamaica pepper, in branch, leaves, flower, fruit, &c. This collection,[2]

[1] They are now at Oxford, having been presented to the University in 1755 by Henrietta, Countess-dowager of Pomfret, widow of Thomas, the first Earl.

[2] It now forms part of the collections in the British Museum. In 1707, he published the first volume of his *Natural History of Jamaica,* in folio, with numerous plates ; but the second volume did not appear till 1725. Dr. Sloane, better known as Sir Hans Sloane, having been created a Baronet by George I., was an eminent physician and naturalist, Physician-general to the Army, Physician in Ordinary to the King, and in 1727 was elected President of the Royal Society. His monument may be seen in the churchyard of old St. Luke's, Chelsea, near the river. His extensive museum and library were purchased for 20,000l., and transferred to the British Museum. Born 1660, died in 1752.

with his Journal and other philosophical and natural discourses and observations, indeed very copious and extraordinary, sufficient to furnish a history of that island, to which I encouraged him.

19th April. The Archbishop of Canterbury, and Bishops of Ely, Bath and Wells, Peterborough, Gloucester, and the rest who would not take the oaths to King William, were now displaced; and, in their rooms, Dr. Tillotson, Dean of St. Paul's, was made Archbishop: Patrick removed from Chichester to Ely; Cumberland[1] to Gloucester.

22nd. I dined with Lord Clarendon in the Tower.

24th. I visited the Earl and Countess of Sunderland, now come to kiss the King's hand, after his return from Holland. This is a mistery. The King preparing to return to the army.

7th May. I went to visit the Archbishop of Canterbury [Sancroft] yet at Lambeth. I found him alone, and discoursing of the times, especially of the new designed Bishops; he told me that by no canon or divine law they could justify the removing the present incumbents; that Dr. Beveridge, designed Bishop of Bath and Wells, came to ask his advice; that the Archbishop told him, though he should give it, he believed he would not take it; the Doctor said he would; why then, says the Archbishop, when they come to ask, say *Nolo*, and say it from the heart; there is nothing easier than to resolve yourself what is to be done in the case: the Doctor seemed to deliberate. What he will do I know not, but Bishop Ken, who is to be put out, is exceedingly beloved in his diocese; and, if he and the rest should insist on it, and plead their interest as freeholders, it is believed there would be difficulty in their case, and it may endanger a schism and much disturbance, so as wise men think it had been better to have let them alone, than to have proceeded with this rigour to turn them out for refusing to swear against their consciences. I asked at parting, when his Grace removed; he said that he had not yet received any summons, but I found the house altogether disfurnished, and his books packing up.

---

[1] A mistake. Dr. Edward Fowler was made Bishop of Gloucester in the place of Dr. Robert Frampton, deprived for not taking the oaths.

1st June. I went with my son, and brother-in-law, Glanville, and his son, to Wotton, to solemnize the funeral of
my nephew, which was performed the next day very decently
and orderly by the herald, in the afternoon, a very great
appearance of the country being there. I was the chief
mourner; the pall was held by Sir Francis Vincent, Sir
Richard Onslow, Mr. Thomas Howard (son to Sir Robert,
and Captain of the King's Guard), Mr. Hyldiard, Mr.
James, Mr. Herbert, nephew to Lord Herbert of Cherbury,
and cousin-german to my deceased nephew. He was laid in
the vault at Wotton church, in the burying-place of the
family. A great concourse of coaches and people accompanied the solemnity.

10th. I went to visit Lord Clarendon, still prisoner in
the Tower, though Lord Preston being pardoned was released.

17th. A fast.

11th July. I dined with Mr. Pepys, where was Dr. Cumberland, the new Bishop of Norwich,[1] Dr. Lloyd having
been put out for not acknowledging the Government. Cumberland is a very learned, excellent man.—Possession was
now given to Dr. Tillotson, at Lambeth, by the Sheriff;
Archbishop Sancroft was gone, but had left his nephew to
keep possession; and he refusing to deliver it up on the
Queen's message, was dispossessed by the Sheriff, and imprisoned. This stout demeanour of the few Bishops who
refused to take the oaths to King William, animated a great
party to forsake the churches, so as to threaten a schism;
though those who looked further into the ancient practice,
found that when (as formerly) there were Bishops displaced
on secular accounts, the people never refused to acknowledge the new Bishops, provided they were not heretics.
The truth is, the whole clergy had till now stretched the
duty of passive obedience, so that the proceedings against
these Bishops gave no little occasion of exceptions; but
this not amounting to heresy, there was a necessity of receiving the new Bishops, to prevent a failure of that order
in the Church.—I went to visit Lord Clarendon in the

[1] A mistake. Dr. Cumberland was made Bishop of Peterborough,
and Dr. John Moore succeeded Dr. Lloyd in the see of Norwich.

Tower, but he was gone into the country for air by the Queen's permission, under the care of his warden.

18*th July.* To London to hear Mr. Stringfellow preach his first sermon in the new-erected church of Trinity, in Conduit Street; to which I did recommend him to Dr. Tenison for the constant preacher and lecturer. This church, formerly built of timber on Hounslow-Heath by King James for the mass-priests, being begged by Dr. Teni son, rector of St. Martin's, was set up by that public-minded, charitable, and pious man near my son's dwelling in Dover Street, chiefly at the charge of the Doctor. I know him to be an excellent preacher and a fit person. This church, though erected in St. Martin's, which is the Doctor's parish, he was not only content, but was the sole industrious mover, that it should be made a separate parish, in regard of the neighbourhood having become so populous. Wherefore to countenance and introduce the new minister, and take possession of a gallery designed for my son's family, I went to London, where,

19*th*, in the morning Dr. Tenison preached the first sermon, taking his text from Psalm xxvi. 8. "Lord, I have loved the habitation of thy house, and the place where thine honour dwelleth." In concluding, he gave that this should be made a parish-church so soon as the Parliament sate, and was to be dedicated to the Holy Trinity,[1] in honour of the three undivided Persons in the Deity; and he minded them to attend to that faith of the Church, now especially that Arianism, Socinianism, and Atheism began to spread amongst us.—In the afternoon, Mr. Stringfellow preached on Luke vii. 5, "The centurion who had built a synagogue." He proceeded to the due praise of persons of such public spirit, and thence to such a character of pious benefactors in the person of the generous centurion, as was comprehensive of all the virtues of an accomplished Christian, in a style so full, eloquent, and moving, that I never

[1] This was never made a parish-church, but still remains a chapel, and is private property. But, under the Act for building fifty new churches, one was built in the street between Conduit Street and Hanover Square, the first stone being laid 20th June, 1712; it was dedicated to St. George, and part of St. Martin's was made a separate parish, now called St. George's, Hanover Square.

heard a sermon more apposite to the occasion. He modestly insinuated the obligation they had to that person who should be the author and promoter of such public works for the benefit of mankind, especially to the advantage of religion, such as building and endowing churches, hospitals, libraries, schools, procuring the best editions of useful books, by which he handsomely intimated who it was that had been so exemplary for his benefaction to that place. Indeed, that excellent person, Dr. Tenison, had also erected and furnished a public library,[1] [in St. Martin's]; and set up two or three free-schools at his own charges. Besides this, he was of an exemplary holy life, took great pains in constantly preaching, and incessantly employing himself to promote the service of God both in public and private. I never knew a man of a more universal and generous spirit, with so much modesty, prudence, and piety.

The great victory of King William's army in Ireland was looked on as decisive of that war. The French General, St. Ruth, who had been so cruel to the poor Protestants in France, was slain, with divers of the best commanders; nor was it cheap to us, having 1,000 killed, but of the enemy 4 or 5,000.

26th July. An extraordinary hot season, yet refreshed by some thunder-showers.

28th. I went to Wotton.

2nd August. No sermon in the church in the afternoon, and the curacy ill-served.

16th. A sermon by the curate; an honest discourse, but read without any spirit, or seeming concern; a great fault in the education of young preachers.—Great thunder and lightning on Thursday, but the rain and wind very violent.—Our fleet come in to lay up the great ships; nothing done at sea, pretending that we cannot meet the French.

13th September. A great storm at sea; we lost the Coronation and Harwich, above 600 men perishing.

14th October. A most pleasing autumn.—Our navy come in without having performed any thing, yet there has been great loss of ships by negligence, and unskilful men governing the fleet and Navy-board.

[1] *Ante*, p. 204.

7th November. I visited the Earl of Dover, who having made his peace with the King, was now come home. The relation he gave of the strength of the French King, and the difficulty of our forcing him to fight, and any way making impression into France. was very wide from what we fancied.

8th—30th. An extraordinary dry and warm season, without frost, and like a new spring; such as had not been known for many years. Part of the King's house at Kensington was burnt.

6th December. Discourse of another *plot*, in which several great persons were named, but believed to be a sham.— A proposal in the House of Commons that every officer in the whole nation who received a salary above £500 or otherwise by virtue of his office, should contribute it wholly to the support of the war with France, and this upon their oaths.

25th. My daughter-in-law was brought to bed of a daughter.

26th. An exceeding dry and calm winter, no rain for many past months.

28th. Dined at Lambeth with the new Archbishop. Saw the effect of my green-house furnace, set up by the Archbishop's son-in-law.

30th. I again saw Mr. Charlton's collection[1] of spiders, birds, scorpions, and other serpents, &c.

1691-2. 1st January. This last week died that pious admirable Christian, excellent philosopher, and my worthy friend, Mr. Boyle, aged about 65—a great loss to all that knew him, and to the public.

6th. At the funeral of Mr. Boyle, at St. Martin's. Dr. Burnet, Bishop of Salisbury, preached on Eccles. ii. 26. He concluded with an eulogy due to the deceased, who made God and religion the scope of all his excellent talents in the knowledge of nature, and who had arrived to so high a degree in it, accompanied with such zeal and extraordinary piety, which he showed in the whole course of his life, particularly in his exemplary charity on all occasions— that he gave £1,000 yearly to the distressed refugees of

---

[1] *Ante,* pp. 270, 317.

France and Ireland; was at the charge of translating the
Scriptures into the Irish and Indian tongues, and was now
promoting a Turkish translation, as he had formerly done of
Grotius "on the Truth of the Christian Religion" into
Arabic, which he caused to be dispersed in the Eastern
countries; that he had settled a fund for preachers who
should preach expressly against Atheists, Libertines, So-
cinians, and Jews; that he had in his will given £8,000 to
charitable uses; but that his private charities were extraordinary. He dilated on his learning in Hebrew and Greek,
his reading of the Fathers, and solid knowledge in theology,
once deliberating about taking Holy Orders, and that at
the time of restoration of King Charles II., when he
might have made a great figure in the nation as to secular
honour and titles, his fear of not being able to discharge so
weighty a duty as the first, made him decline that, and his
humility the other. He spake of his civility to strangers,
the great good which he did by his experience in medicine
and chemistry, and to what noble ends he applied himself
to his darling studies; the works both pious and useful
which he published; the exact life he led, and the happy
end he made. Something was touched of his sister, the
Lady Ranelagh, who died but a few days before him. And
truly all this was but his due, without any grain of flattery.

This week, a most execrable murder was committed on
Dr. Clench, father of that extraordinary learned child whom
I have before noticed.[1] Under pretence of carrying him
in a coach to see a patient, they strangled him in it; and,
sending away the coachman under some pretence, they left
his dead body in the coach, and escaped in the dusk of the
evening.

12th January. My grand-daughter was christened by
Dr. Tenison, now Bishop of Lincoln, in Trinity Church,
being the first that was christened there. She was named
Jane.

24th. A frosty and dry season continued; many persons
die of apoplexies, more than usual.—Lord Marlborough,
Lieutenant-General of the King's army in England, Gen-

[1] *Ante,* p. 299. A man named Henry Harrison was tried for the
murder of Dr. Clench, convicted, and hanged; but he left a paper,
which was printed, denying his guilt.

tleman of the Bed-chamber, &c., dismissed from all his charges, military and other, for his excessive taking of bribes, covetousness, and extortion on all occasions from his inferior officers.—Note, this was the Lord who was entirely advanced by King James, and was the first who betrayed and forsook his master. He was son of Sir Winston Churchill of the Green-cloth.

7th February. An extraordinary snow fell in most parts.

13th. Mr. Boyle having made me one of the trustees for his charitable bequests, I went to a meeting of the Bishop of Lincoln, Sir Rob. . . . . . wood, and Serjeant Rotheram, to settle that clause in the will which related to charitable uses, and especially the appointing and electing a minister to preach one sermon the first Sunday in the month, during the four summer months, expressly against Atheists, Deists, Libertines, Jews, &c., without descending to any other controversy whatever, for which £50 per annum is to be paid quarterly to the preacher; and, at the end of three years, to proceed to a new election of some other able divine, or to continue the same, as the trustees should judge convenient. We made choice of one Mr. Bentley,[1] chaplain to the Bishop of Worcester (Dr. Stillingfleet). The first sermon was appointed for the first Sunday in March, at St. Martin's; the second Sunday in April, at Bow-church, and so alternately.

28th. Lord Marlborough[2] having used words against the King, and been discharged from all his great places, his wife was forbid the Court, and the Princess of Denmark was desired by the Queen to dismiss her from her service; but she refusing to do so, goes away from Court to Sion-house.—Divers new Lords made; Sir Henry Capel,[3] Sir William Fermor,[4] &c.—Change of Commissioners in the Treasury.—The Parliament adjourned, not well satisfied

[1] Afterwards the celebrated scholar and critic, Librarian to the King, and Master of Trinity College, Cambridge.

[2] So celebrated in the reign of Queen Anne as John, first Duke of Marlborough. The real cause of his dismissal from his employments by William III. was not the one mentioned by Evelyn, but a quarrel between Queen Mary and her sister, the Princess Anne, in which her friend Lady Marlborough was involved.

[3] Lord Capel, of Tewkesbury.

[4] Baron Leominster; afterwards Earl of Pomfret.

with affairs.   The business of the East India Company,
which they would have reformed, let fall.—The Duke of
Norfolk does not succeed in his endeavour to be divorced.[1]

20th March. My son was made one of the Commissioners
of the Revenue and Treasury of Ireland, to which employment he had a mind, far from my wishes.—I visited the
Earl of Peterborough, who showed me the picture of the
Prince of Wales, newly brought out of France, seeming in
my opinion very much to resemble the Queen his mother,
and of a most vivacious countenance.

April. No spring yet appearing.   The Queen-dowager
went out of England towards Portugal, as pretended, against
the advice of all her friends.

4th. Mr. Bentley preached Mr. Boyle's lecture at St.
Mary-le-Bow.   So excellent a discourse against the Epi-
curean system is not to be recapitulated in a few words.
He came to me to ask whether I thought it should be
printed, or that there was anything in it which I desired to
be altered.   I took this as a civility, and earnestly desired
it should be printed, as one of the most learned and con-
vincing discourses I had ever heard.

6th. A fast.—King James sends a letter written and
directed by his own hand to several of the Privy Council,
and one to his daughter the Queen Regent, informing them
of the Queen being ready to be brought to bed, and summoning them to be at the birth by the middle of May,
promising as from the French King, permission to come and
return in safety.

21th. Much apprehension of a French invasion, and of an
universal rising.   Our fleet begins to join with the Dutch.
Unkindness between the Queen and her sister.   Very cold
and unseasonable weather, scarce a leaf on the trees.

5th May. Reports of an invasion were very hot, and
alarmed the City, Court, and people; nothing but securing
suspected persons, sending forces to the sea-side, and hastening out the fleet.   Continued discourse of the French
invasion, and of ours in France.   The eastern wind so constantly blowing, gave our fleet time to unite, which had
been so tardy n preparation, that, had not God thus

wonderfully favoured the enemy would in all probability have fallen upon us. Many daily secured, and proclamations out for more conspirators.

8th May. My kinsman, Sir Edward Evelyn, of Long Ditton,[1] died suddenly.

12th. A fast.

13th. I dined at my cousin Cheny's, son to my Lord Cheny, who married my cousin Pierpoint.

15th. My niece, M. Evelyn, was now married to Sir Cyril Wyche, Secretary of State for Ireland.[1] — After all our apprehensions of being invaded, and doubts of our success by sea, it pleased God to give us a great naval victory, to the utter ruin of the French fleet, their admiral and all their best men of war, transport-ships, &c.

29th. Though this day was set apart expressly for celebrating the memorable birth, return, and restoration of the late King Charles II., there was no notice taken of it, nor any part of the office annexed to the Common Prayer-Book made use of, which I think was ill done, in regard his restoration not only redeemed us from anarchy and confusion, but restored the Church of England as it were miraculously.

9th June. I went to Windsor to carry my grandson to Eton School, where I met my Lady Stonehouse and other of my daughter-in-law's relations, who came on purpose to see her before her journey into Ireland. We went to see the Castle, which we found furnished and very neatly kept, as formerly, only that the arms in the guard-chamber and keep were removed and carried away.—An exceeding great storm of wind and rain, in some places stripping the trees of their fruit and leaves as if it had been winter; and an extraordinary wet season, with great floods.

23rd July. I went with my wife, son, and daughter, to Eton, to see my grandson, and thence to my Lord Godolphin's, at Cranburn, where we lay, and were most honourably entertained. The next day to St. George's Chapel, and returned to London late in the evening.

25th. To Mr. Hewer's at Clapham, where he has an excellent, useful, and capacious house on the Common,

---

[1] See *post*, pp. 367-8.

built by Sir Den. Gauden, and by him sold to Mr. Hewer, who got a very considerable estate in the Navy, in which, from being Mr. Pepys's clerk, he came to be one of the principal officers, but was put out of all employment on the Revolution, as were all the best officers, on suspicion of being no friends to the change; such were put in their places, as were most shamefully ignorant and unfit. Mr. Hewer lives very handsomely and friendly to every body.[1] —Our fleet was now sailing on their long pretence of a descent on the French coast; but, after having sailed one hundred leagues, returned, the admiral and officers disagreeing as to the place where they were to land, and the time of year being so far spent,—to the great dishonour of those at the helm, who concerted their matters so indiscreetly, or, as some thought, designedly.

This whole summer was exceeding wet and rainy; the like had not been known since the year 1648; whilst in Ireland they had not known so great a drought.

16th July. I went to visit the Bishop of Lincoln, when, amongst other things, he told me that one Dr. Chaplin, of University College in Oxford, was the person who wrote the Whole Duty of Man; that he used to read it to his pupil, and communicated it to Dr. Sterne,[2] afterwards Archbishop of York, but would never suffer any of his pupils to have a copy of it.

19th August. A fast.—Came the sad news of the hurricane and earthquake, which has destroyed almost the whole Island of Jamaica, many thousands having perished.

11th. My son, his wife, and little daughter, went for Ireland, there to reside as one of the Commissioners of the Revenue.

14th. Still an exceeding wet season.

15th September. There happened an earthquake, which, though not so great as to do any harm in England, was universal in all these parts of Europe. It shook the house

[1] Much will be found concerning him in the *Diary and Correspondence of Samuel Pepys*, edited by Lord Braybrooke, published by Mr. Bohn.

[2] Richard Sterne, grandfather of the author of "Tristram Shandy." He attended Archbishop Laud to the scaffold as his chaplain. On the Restoration he was created Bishop of Carlisle, and subsequently Archbishop of York. He assisted in the Polyglott and in the revisal of the Book of Common Prayer. Born 1596, died 1683.

at Wotton, but was not perceived by any save a servant or two, who were making my bed, and another in a garret. I and the rest being at dinner below in the parlour, were not sensible of it. The dreadful one in Jamaica this summer was profanely and ludicrously represented in a puppet-play, or some such lewd pastime, in the fair of Southwark, which caused the Queen to put down that idle and vicious mock show.

1st October. This season was so exceedingly cold, by reason of a long and tempestuous north-east wind, that this usually pleasant month was very uncomfortable. No fruit ripened kindly.—Harbord dies at Belgrade; Lord Paget sent Ambassador in his room.

6th November. There was a vestry called about repairing or new building of the church [at Deptford], which I thought unseasonable in regard of heavy taxes, and other improper circumstances, which I there declared.

10th. A solemn Thanksgiving for our victory at sea, safe return of the King, &c.

20th. Dr. Lancaster, the new Vicar of St. Martin's, preached.

A signal robbery in Hertfordshire of the tax-money bringing out of the north towards London. They were set upon by several desperate persons, who dismounted and stopped all travellers on the road, and guarding them in a field, when the exploit was done, and the treasure taken, they killed all the horses of those whom they stayed, to hinder pursuit, being sixteen horses. They then dismissed those that they had dismounted.

14th December. With much reluctance we gratified Sir J. Rotherham, one of Mr. Boyle's trustees, by admitting the Bishop of Bath and Wells[1] to be lecturer for the next year, instead of Mr. Bentley, who had so worthily acquitted himself. We intended to take him in again the next year.

1692-3. January. Contest in Parliament about a self-denying Act, that no Parliament-man should have any office: it wanted only two or three voices to have been carried.—The Duke of Norfolk's Bill for a divorce thrown out, he having managed it very indiscreetly.—The quarrel

---

[1] Bishop Kidder.

between Admiral Russell and Lord Nottingham yet undetermined.

4th February. After five days' trial and extraordinary contest, the Lord Mohun was acquitted by the Lords of the murder of Montford, the player, notwithstanding the Judges, from the pregnant witnesses of the fact, had declared him guilty; but whether in commiseration of his youth, being not eighteen years old, though exceeding dissolute, or upon whatever other reason, the King himself present some part of the trial, and satisfied, as they report, that he was culpable, 69 acquitted him, only 14 condemned him.

Unheard-of stories of the universal increase of witches in New England; men, women, and children, devoting themselves to the devil, so as to threaten the subversion of the government.[1]—At the same time there was a conspiracy amongst the negroes in Barbadoes to murder all their masters, discovered by overhearing a discourse of two of the slaves, and so preventing the execution of the design.—Hitherto an exceeding mild winter.—France in the utmost misery and poverty for want of corn and subsistence, whilst the ambitious King is intent to pursue his conquests on the rest of his neighbours both by sea and land. Our Admiral, Russell, laid aside for not pursuing the advantage he had obtained over the French in the past summer; three others chosen in his place. Dr. Burnet, Bishop of Salisbury's book burnt by the hangman for an expression of the King's title by conquest, on a complaint of Joseph How, a Member of Parliament, little better than a madman.

19th. The Bishop of Lincoln preached in the afternoon at the Tabernacle near Golden Square, set up by him.—Proposals of a marriage between Mr. Draper and my daughter Susanna.—Hitherto an exceeding warm winter, such as has seldom been known, and portending an unprosperous spring as to the fruits of the earth; our climate requires more cold and winterly weather. The dreadful and

---

[1] Some account of these poor people is given in Bray and Manning's *History of Surrey*, ii. 714, from the papers of the Rev. Mr. Miller, Vicar of Effingham, in that county, who was Chaplain to the King's forces in the Colony from 1692 to 1695. Some of the accused were convicted and executed; but Sir William Phipps, the Governor, had the good sense to reprieve, and afterwards pardon, several; and the Queen approved his conduct.

astonishing earthquake swallowing up Catania and other
famous and ancient cities, with more than 100,000 persons
in Sicily, on 11th January last, came now to be reported
amongst us.

26th February. An extraordinary deep snow, after almost
no winter, and a sudden gentle thaw.—A deplorable earthquake at Malta, since that of Sicily, nearly as great.

19th March. A new Secretary of State, Sir John Trenchard;[1] the Attorney - General, Somers, made Lord - Keeper,
a young lawyer of extraordinary merit.—King William goes
towards Flanders; but returns, the wind being contrary.

31st. I met the King going to Gravesend to embark in his
yacht for Holland.

23rd April. An extraordinary wet spring.

27th. My daughter Susanna was married to William
Draper, Esq., in the chapel of Ely House, by Dr. Tenison,
Bishop of Lincoln (since Archbishop). I gave her in portion
4,000*l.*, her jointure is 500*l.* per annum. I pray Almighty
God to give His blessing to this marriage! She is a good
child, religious, discreet, ingenious, and qualified with all the
ornaments of her sex. She has a peculiar talent in design,
as painting in oil and miniature, and an extraordinary genius
for whatever hands can do with a needle. She has the French
tongue, has read most of the Greek and Roman authors and
poets, using her talents with great modesty; exquisitely
shaped, and of an agreeable countenance. This character is
due to her, though coming from her father. Much of this

[1] Of Bloxworth, in Dorsetshire. He had been engaged with the Duke
of Monmouth, but escaped out of England, and lived some time abroad,
where he acquired a large and correct knowledge of foreign affairs. He
was a calm and sedate man, and more moderate than could have been
expected from his previous party connection. He was the confidential
friend of King William, by whom he had been commissioned to concert
measures with his friends on tnis side of the water, and ensure his favourable reception. Previously to his appointment of Secretary-of-State,
the King had made him Serjeant-at-law, and Chief Justice of Chester.
He died in 1694, at the age of forty-six, and is buried at Bloxworth.
There is an engraved portrait of Sir John Trenchard in mezzotinto, by
James Watson, representing him in the dress of his office, and expressing a weakness which he had in his right hand and arm: also another
in armour, .from a miniature after the original, by Osias Humphrey,
R.A., engraved by Cantlo Bestland. See Hutchins's *History of Dorsetshire,* vol. iii.

week spent in ceremonies, receiving visits and entertaining relations, and a great part of the next in returning visits.

11*th May.* We accompanied my daughter to her husband's house,[1] where with many of his and our relations we were magnificently treated. There we left her in an apartment very richly adorned and furnished, and I hope in as happy a condition as could be wished, and with the great satisfaction of all our friends; for which God be praised!

14*th.* Nothing yet of action from abroad. Muttering of a design to bring forces under colour of an expected descent, to be a standing army for other purposes. Talk of a declaration of the French King, offering mighty advantages to the Confederates, exclusive of King William; and another of King James, with an universal pardon, and referring the composing of all differences to a Parliament. These were yet but discourses; but something is certainly under it. A Declaration or Manifesto from King James, so written, that many thought it reasonable, and much more to the purpose than any of his former.

June. Whit-Sunday. I went to my Lord Griffith's chapel; the common church-office was used for the King without naming the person, with some other, opposite to the necessity and circumstances of the time.

11*th.* I dined at Sir William Godolphin's; and, after evening prayer, visited the Duchess of Grafton.

21*st.* I saw a great auction of pictures in the Banqueting-house, Whitehall. They had been my Lord Melford's, now Ambassador from King James at Rome, and engaged to his creditors here. Lord Mulgrave and Sir Edward Seymour came to my house, and desired me to go with them to the sale. Divers more of the great lords, &c., were there, and bought pictures dear enough. There were some very excellent of Vandyke, Rubens, and Bassan. Lord Godolphin bought the picture of the Boys, by Murillo the Spaniard, for 80 guineas, dear enough; my nephew Glanville, the old Earl of Arundel's head by Rubens, for £20. Growing late, I did not stay till all were sold.

24*th.* A very wet hay-harvest, and little summer as yet.

9*th July.* Mr. Tippin, successor of Dr. Parr at Camberwell, preached an excellent sermon.

[1] At Addiscombe, near Croydon.

13th July. I saw the Queen's rare cabinets and collection of china; which was wonderfully rich and plentiful, but especially a large cabinet, looking-glass frame and stands, all of amber, much of it white, with historical bass-reliefs and statues, with medals carved in them, esteemed worth £4000, sent by the Duke of Brandenburgh, whose country, Prussia, abounds with amber, cast up by the sea; divers other China and Indian cabinets, screens, and hangings. In her library were many books in English, French, and Dutch, of all sorts; a cupboard of gold plate; a cabinet of silver filagree, which I think was our Queen Mary's,[1] and which, in my opinion, should have been generously sent to her.

18th. I dined with Lord Mulgrave, with the Earl of Devonshire, Mr. Hampden (a scholar and fine gentleman), Dr. Davenant,[2] Sir Henry Vane, and others, and saw and admired the Venus of Correggio, which Lord Mulgrave had newly bought of Mr. Daun for £250; one of the best paintings I ever saw.

1st August. Lord Capel, Sir Cyril Wyche, and Mr. Duncomb, made Lord-Justices in Ireland; Lord Sydney re-called, and made Master of the Ordnance.

6th. Very lovely harvest-weather, and a wholesome season, but no garden-fruit.

31st October. A very wet and uncomfortable season.

12th November. Lord Nottingham resigned as Secretary of State;[3] the Commissioners of the Admiralty outed, and Russel[4] restored to his office.—The season continued very wet, as it had nearly all the summer, if one might call it summer, in which there was no fruit, but corn was very plentiful.

14th. In the lottery set up after the Venetian manner by Mr. Neale, Sir R. Haddock, one of the Commissioners of the Navy, had the greatest lot, £3000 ; my coachman £40.

17th. Was the funeral of Captain Young, who died of the stone and great age. I think he was the first who in

[1] Mary of Esté, King James's Queen, now with him in France.

[2] Charles, eldest son of Sir William Davenant, joint inspector of plays, Commissioner of Excise, and Inspector-general of Exports and Imports. His chief work was called "Essays on Trade," in five volumes. Born 1656, died 1714.

[3] He was succeeded by Charles Earl of Shrewsbury.

[4] Edward Russell, afterwards Earl of Orford.

the first war with Cromwell against Spain,[1] took the
Governor of Havannah, and another rich prize, and struck
the first stroke against the Dutch fleet in the first war with
Holland in the time of the Rebellion; a sober man and an
excellent seaman.

30th November. Much importuned to take the office of
President of the Royal Society, but I again declined it. Sir
Robert Southwell was continued. We all dined at Pontac's,
as usual.

3rd December. Mr. Bentley preached at the Tabernacle,
near Golden Square. I gave my voice for him to proceed
on his former subject the following year in Mr. Boyle's
lecture, in which he had been interrupted by the importunity of Sir J. Rotheram that the Bishop of Chichester[2]
might be chosen the year before, to the great dissatisfaction
of the Bishop of Lincoln and myself. We chose Mr. Bentley again.—The Duchess of Grafton's Appeal to the House
of Lords for the Prothonotary's place given to the late Duke
and to her son by King Charles II., now challenged by the
Lord Chief Justice. The Judges were severely reproved on
something they said.

10th. A very great storm of thunder and lightning.

1693-4. 1st January. Prince Lewis of Baden came to
London, and was much feasted. Danish ships arrested
carrying corn and naval stores to France.

11th. Supped at Mr. Edward Sheldon's, where was Mr.
Dryden, the poet, who now intended to write no more plays,
being intent on his translation of Virgil. He read to us his
prologue and epilogue to his valedictory play now shortly to
be acted.

21st. Lord Macclesfield, Lord Warrington, and Lord
Westmorland, all died within about one week. Several
persons shot, hanged, and made away with themselves.

11th February. Now was the great trial of the appeal of
Lord Bath and Lord Montagu before the Lords, for the
estate of the late Duke of Albemarle.[3]

[1] See vol. i. p. 336.
[2] A mistake for Bath and Wells. Bishop Kidder is referred to; see
ante, p. 334.
[3] See *post*, pp. 356, 379.

z 3

10th March. Mr. Stringfellow preached at Trinity parish; being restored to that place, after the contest between the Queen and the Bishop of London who had displaced him.

22nd. Came the dismal news of the disaster befallen our Turkey fleet by tempest, to the almost utter ruin of that trade, the convoy of three or four men-of-war, and divers merchant-ships, with all their men and lading, having perished.

25th. Dr. Goode, minister of St. Martin's, preached; he was likewise put in by the Queen, on the issue of her process with the Bishop of London.

30th. I went to the Duke of Norfolk, to desire him to make cousin Evelyn of Nutfield one of the Deputy-Lieutenants of Surrey, and entreat him to dismiss my brother, now unable to serve by reason of age and infirmity. The Duke granted the one, but would not suffer my brother to resign his commission, desiring he should keep the honour of it during his life, though he could not act. He professed great kindness to our family.

1st April. Dr. Sharp, Archbishop of York, preached in the afternoon at the Tabernacle, by Soho.

13th. Mr. Bentley, our Boyle Lecturer, Chaplain to the Bishop of Worcester, came to see me.

15th. One Mr. Stanhope [1] preached a most excellent sermon.

22nd. A fiery exhalation rising out of the sea, spread itself in Montgomeryshire a furlong broad, and many miles in length, burning all straw, hay, thatch, and grass, but doing no harm to trees, timber, or any solid things, only firing barns, or thatched houses. It left such a taint on the grass as to kill all the cattle that eat of it. I saw the attestations in the hands of the sufferers. It lasted many months.—"The Berkeley Castle" sunk by the French coming from the East Indies, worth £200,000. The French took our castle of Gamboo in Guinea, so that the Africa Actions fell to £30, and the India to £80.—Some regiments of Highland Dragoons were on their march through England; they were of large stature, well appointed

---

[1] Afterwards Dean of Canterbury, a respectable and worthy divine, who made no scruple to praise and adopt what he found truly pious in the works of a Roman Catholic Priest. See *post,* p. 350.

and disciplined. One of them having reproached a Dutchman for cowardice in our late fight, was attacked by two Dutchmen, when with his sword he struck off the head of one, and cleft the skull of the other down to his chin.

A very young gentleman named Wilson, the younger son of one who had not above £200 a-year estate, lived in the garb and equipage of the richest nobleman, for house, furniture, coaches, saddle-horses, and kept a table, and all things accordingly, redeemed his father's estate, and gave portions to his sisters, being challenged by one Laws, a Scotchman, was killed in a duel, not fairly. The quarrel arose from his taking away his own sister from lodging in a house where this Laws had a mistress, which the mistress of the house thinking a disparagement to it, and losing by it, instigated Laws to this duel. He was taken and condemned for murder. The mystery is how this so young a gentleman, very sober and of good fame, could live in such an expensive manner; it could not be discovered by all possible industry, or entreaty of his friends to make him reveal it. It did not appear that he was kept by women, play, coining, padding, or dealing in chymistry; but he would sometimes say that if he should live ever so long, he had wherewith to maintain himself in the same manner. He was very civil and well-natured, but of no great force of understanding. This was a subject of much discourse.

24th April. I went to visit Mr. Waller, an extraordinary young gentleman of great accomplishments, skilled in mathematics, anatomy, music, painting both in oil and miniature to great perfection, an excellent botanist, a rare engraver on brass, writer in Latin, and a poet; and with all this exceeding modest. His house is an academy of itself. I carried him to see Brompton Park [by Knightsbridge],[1] where he was in admiration at the store of rare plants, and the method he found in that noble nursery, and how well it was cultivated.—A public Bank of £140,000, set up by Act of Parliament among other Acts, and Lotteries for money to carry on the war.—The whole month of April without rain.—A great rising of people in Buckinghamshire, on the declaration of a famous preacher,[2] till now reputed a sobc.

---

[1] Belonging to Mr. Wise. See *post,* p. 379.
[2] John Mason, who was presented to the rectory of Walter Stratford,

and religious man, that our Lord Christ appearing to him
on the 16th of this month, told him he was now come down,
and would appear publicly at Pentecost, and gather all the
saints, Jews and Gentiles, and lead them to Jerusalem, and
begin the Millennium, and destroying and judging the
wicked, deliver the government of the world to the saints.
Great multitudes followed this preacher, divers of the most
zealous brought their goods and considerable sums of money,
and began to live in imitation of the primitive saints, minding no private concerns, continually dancing and singing
Hallelujah night and day. This brings to mind what I
lately happened to find in Alstedius, that the thousand years
should begin this very year 1694 : it is in his Encyclopædia
Biblica. My copy of the book printed near sixty years ago.

4th May. I went this day with my wife and four servants
from Sayes Court, removing much furniture of all sorts,
books, pictures, hangings, bedding, &c., to furnish the
apartment my brother assigned me, and now, after more
than forty years, to spend the rest of my days with him at
Wotton, where I was born; leaving my house at Deptford
full furnished, and three servants, to my son-in-law Draper,
to pass the summer in, and such longer time as he should
think fit to make use of it.

6th. This being the first Sunday in the month, the
blessed Sacrament of the Lord's Supper ought to have been
celebrated at Wotton Church, but in this parish it is exceedingly neglected, so that, unless at the four great Feasts,
there is no communion hereabouts; which is a great fault both
in ministers and people. I have spoken to my brother, who
is the patron, to discourse the Minister about it.—Scarcely
one shower has fallen since the beginning of April.

30th. This week we had news of my Lord Tiviot having
cut his own throat, through what discontent not yet said

in 1674. Granger calls him a man of unaffected piety, and says that he
was esteemed to be possessed of learning and abilities above the common
level, till he became bewildered in the mysteries of Calvinism. Great
numbers of his deluded followers left their homes, and filled all the
houses and barns in the neighbourhood of Walter Stratford; and, when
prevented from assembling in their chosen field, they congregated in the
town. Three pamphlets on the subject were published in 1694, the year
after Mr. Mason's death, one of which has been privately reprinted by
the late Rev. Edward Cooke, Rector of Haversham, in the same county.

He had been, not many years past, my colleague in the commission of the Privy Seal, in old acquaintance, very soberly and religiously inclined. Lord, what are we without Thy continual grace!

Lord Falkland, grandson to the learned Lord Falkland, Secretary of State to King Charles I., and slain in his service, died now of the small-pox. He was a pretty, brisk, understanding, industrious young gentleman ; had formerly been faulty, but now much reclaimed ; had also the good luck to marry a very great fortune, besides being entitled to a vast sum, his share of the Spanish wreck, taken up at the expense of divers adventurers. From a Scotch Viscount he was made an English Baron, designed Ambassador for Holland ; had been Treasurer of the Navy, and advancing extremely in the new Court. All now gone in a moment, and I think the title is extinct. I know not whether the estate devolves to my cousin Carew. It was at my Lord Falkland's, whose lady importuned us to let our daughter be with her some time, so that that dear child took the same infection, which cost her valuable life.[1]

3rd June. Mr. Edwards, minister of Denton, in Sussex, a living in my brother's gift, came to see him. He had suffered much by a fire.—Seasonable showers.

14th. The public Fast. Mr. Wotton,[2] that extraordinary learned young man, preached excellently.

1st July. Mr. Duncomb, minister of Albury, preached at Wotton, a very religious and exact discourse.

The first great Bank for a fund of money being now established by Act of Parliament, was filled and completed to the sum of £120,000, and put under the government of the most able and wealthy citizens of London, All who adventured any sum had four per cent., so long as it lay in the Bank, and had power either to take it out at pleasure, or transfer it.—Glorious steady weather ; corn and all fruits in extraordinary plenty generally.

13th. Lord Berkeley burnt Dieppe and Havre-de-Grace with bombs, in revenge for the defeat at Brest. This

[1] See *ante*, pp. 222-228.
[2] The Reverend William Wotton. author of "Reflections upon Ancient and Modern Learning," "The History of Rome, from the Death of Antoninus Pius, &c.," and other works. Born 1666, died 1726.

manner of destructive war was begun by the French, is exceedingly ruinous, especially falling on the poorer people,
and does not seem to tend to make a more speedy end of th
war ; but rather to exasperate and incite to revenge.—Many
executed at London for clipping money, now done to that
intolerable extent, that there was hardly any money that was
worth above half the nominal value.

4th August. I went to visit my cousin, Georg Evelyn
of Nutfield, where I found a family of ten children, five
sons and five daughters—all beautiful women grown, and
extremely well-fashioned. All painted in one piece, very
well, by Mr. Luttereil, in crayon on copper, and seeming to
be as finely painted as the best miniature. They are the
children of two extraordinary beautiful wives. The boys
were at school.

5th. Stormy and unseasonable wet weather this week.

5th October. I went to St. Paul's to see the choir, now
finished as to the stone work, and the scaffold struck both
without and within, in that part. Some exceptions might
perhaps be taken as to the placing columns on pilasters at
the East tribunal. As to the rest it is a piece of architecture without reproach. The pulling out the forms, like
drawers, from under the stalls, is ingenious. I went also to
see the building beginning near St. Giles's, where seven
streets make a star from a Doric pillar placed in the middle
of a circular area; said to be built by Mr. Neale,[1] introducer
of the late lotteries, in imitation of those at Venice, now set
up here, for himself twice, and now one for the State.

28th. Mr. Stringfellow preached at Trinity church.

22nd November. Visited the Bishop of Lincoln [Tenison]
newly come on the death of the Archbishop of Canterbury,
who a few days before had a paralytic stroke—the same day
and month that Archbishop Sancroft was put out.—A very
sickly time, especially the small-pox, of which divers considerable persons died. The State Lottery[1] drawing, Mr.

---

[1] This Mr. Neale took a large piece of ground on the north side of
Piccadilly; of Sir Walter Clarges, agreeing to lay out £15,000 in building thereon; but failing to complete his engagement, Sir Walter himself,
after great trouble, got the lease cut of his hands, and built what is now
called Clarges-street. *Malcolm's London,* p. 329.

[2] State Lotteries finally closed October 18, 1826.

Cock, a French refugee, and a President in the Parliament of Paris for the Reformed, drew a lot of £1,000 per annum.

29th November. I visited the Marquis of Normanby,and had much discourse concerning King Charles II. being poisoned. —Also concerning the *Quinquina* which the physicians would not give to the King, at a time when, in a dangerous ague, it was the only thing that could cure him (out of envy because it had been brought into vogue by Mr. Tudor, an apothecary), till Dr. Short, to whom the King sent to know his opinion of it privately, he being reputed a Papist (but who was in truth a very honest good Christian), sent word to the King that it was the only thing which could save his life, and then the King enjoined his physicians to give it to him, which they did, and he recovered. Being asked by this Lord why they would not prescribe it, Dr. Lower said it would spoil their practice, or some such expression, and at last confessed it was a remedy fit only for kings.—Exception was taken that the late Archbishop did not cause any of his Chaplains to use any office for the sick during his illness.

9th December. I had news that my dear and worthy friend, Dr. Tenison, Bishop of Lincoln, was made Archbishop of Canterbury, for which I thank God and rejoice, he being most worthy of it, for his learning, piety, and prudence.

13th. I went to London to congratulate him. He being my proxy, gave my vote for Dr. Williams, to succeed Mr. Bentley in Mr. Boyle's lectures.

29th. The small-pox increased exceedingly, and was very mortal. The Queen died of it on the 28th.

13th January, 1694-5. The Thames was frozen over. The deaths by small-pox increased to five hundred more than in the preceding week.—The King and Princess Anne reconciled, and she was invited to keep her Court at Whitehall, having hitherto lived privately at Berkeley-house; she was desired to take into her family divers servants of the late Queen; to maintain them the King has assigned her 5,000*l.* a-quarter.

20th. The frost and continual snow have now lasted five weeks.

February. Lord Spencer married the Duke of Newcastle's daughter, and our neighbour, Mr. Hussey, married a daughter of my cousin George Evelyn, of Nutfield.

3rd February. The long frost intermitted, but not gone.

17th. Called to London by Lord Godolphin, one of the Lords of the Treasury, offering me the treasurership of the hospital designed to be built at Greenwich for worn-out seamen.

24th. I saw the Queen lie in state.

27th. The Marquis of Normanby told me King Charles had a design to buy all King Street, and build it nobly, it being the street leading to Westminster. This might have been done for the expense of the Queen's funeral, which was 50,000*l.*, against her desire.

5th March. I went to see the ceremony. Never was so universal a mourning; all the Parliament-men had cloaks given them, and four hundred poor women; all the streets hung, and the middle of the street boarded and covered with black cloth. There were all the Nobility, Mayor, Aldermen, Judges, &c.

8th. I supped at the Bishop of Lichfield and Coventry's, who related to me the pious behaviour of the Queen in all her sickness, which was admirable. She never inquired of what opinion persons were, who were objects of charity; that, on opening a cabinet, a paper was found wherein she had desired that her body might not be opened, or any extraordinary expense at her funeral, whenever she should die. This paper was not found in time to be observed. There were other excellent things under her own hand, to the very least of her debts, which were very small, and every thing in that exact method, as seldom is found in any private person. In sum, she was such an admirable woman, abating for taking the Crown without a more due apology, as does, if possible, outdo the renowned Queen Elizabeth.

10th. I dined at the Earl of Sunderland's with Lord Spencer. My Lord showed me his library, now again improved by many books bought at the sale of Sir Charles Scarborough, an eminent physician,[1] which was the very best collection, especially of mathematical books, that was I believe in Europe, once designed for the King's Library at St. James's; but the Queen's dying, who was the great

[1] See vol. i. p. 296.

patroness of that design, it was let fall, and the books were miserably dissipated.

The new edition of Camden's Britannia was now published (by Bishop Gibson), with great additions; those to Surrey were mine, so that I had one presented to me. Dr. Gale showed me a MS. of some parts of the New Testament in vulgar Latin, that had belonged to a monastery in the North of Scotland, which he esteemed to be about eight hundred years old; there were some considerable various readings observable, as in John i., and genealogy of St. Luke.

24th March. Easter-day. Mr. Duncomb, parson of this parish, preached, which he hardly comes to above once a year though but seven or eight miles off;' a florid discourse, read out of his notes. The Holy Sacrament followed, which he administered with very little reverence, leaving out many prayers and exhortations; nor was there any oblation. This ought to be reformed, but my good brother did not well consider when he gave away this living and the next [Abinger].

March. The latter end of the month sharp and severe cold, with much snow and hard frost; no appearance of spring.

31st. Mr. Lucas preached in the afternoon at Wotton.

7th April. Lord Halifax died suddenly at London, the day his daughter was married to the Earl of Nottingham's son at Burleigh. Lord H. was a very rich man, very witty, and in his younger days somewhat positive.

14th. After a most severe, cold, and snowy winter, without almost any shower for many months, the wind continuing N. and E. and not a leaf appearing; the weather and wind now changed, some showers fell, and there was a remission of cold.

21st. The spring begins to appear, yet the trees hardly leafed.—Sir T. Cooke discovers what prodigious bribes have been given by some of the East India Company out of the stock, which makes a great clamour.—Never were so many private bills passed for unsettling estates, showing the wonderful prodigality and decay of families.

¹ This was William Duncomb, Rector of Ashted, in Surrey, not Mr. Duncomb, of Albury, mentioned in pp. 343 and 349.

5th May. I came to Deptford from Wotton, in order to the first meeting of the Commissioners for endowing an Hospital for Seamen at Greenwich; it was at the Guildhall, London. Present, the Archbishop of Canterbury, Lord-Keeper, Lord Privy Seal, Lord Godolphin, Duke of Shrewsbury, Duke of Leeds, Earls of Dorset and Monmouth, Commissioners of the Admiralty and Navy, Sir Robert Clayton, Sir Christopher Wren, and several more. The Commission was read by Mr. Lowndes, Secretary to the Lords of the Treasury, Surveyor-General.

17th. Second meeting of the Commissioners, and a Committee appointed to go to Greenwich to survey the place, I being one of them.

21st. We went to survey Greenwich, Sir Robert Clayton, Sir Christopher Wren, Mr. Travers, the King's Surveyor, Captain Sanders, and myself.

24th. We made report of the state of Greenwich House, and how the standing part might be made serviceable at present for £6,000, and what ground would be requisite for the whole design. My Lord-Keeper ordered me to prepare a book for subscriptions, and a preamble to it.

31st. Met again. Mr. Vanbrugh[1] was made Secretary to the Commission, by my nomination of him to the Lords, which was all done that day.

7th June. The Commissioners met at Guildhall, when there were scruples and contests of the Lord Mayor,[2] who would not meet, not being named as one of the quorum, so that a new Commission was required, though the Lord-Keeper and the rest thought it too nice a punctilio.

14th. Met at Guildhall, but could do nothing for want of a quorum.

5th July. At Guildhall; account of subscriptions, about 7 or £8,000.

6th. I dined at Lambeth, making my first visit to the Archbishop, where there was much company, and great cheer. After prayers in the evening, my Lord made me

---

[1] Sir John Vanbrugh, the famous dramatist, architect of Blenheim and Castle Howard; also Clarencieux King at Arms, Comptroller of the Board of Works, and Surveyor of Greenwich Hospital. Born 1672, died 1726.

[2] Sir William Ashurst, Knt.

stay to shew me his house, furniture, and garden, which
were all very fine, and far beyond the usual Archbishops,
not as affected by this, but being bought ready furnished by
his predecessor. We discoursed of several public matters,
particularly of the Princess of Denmark, who made so little
figure.

11*th July*. Met at Guildhall: not a full Committee, so
nothing done.

14*th*. No sermon at Church; but, after prayers, the
names of all the parishioners were read, in order to gathering
the tax of 4*s*. for marriages, burials, &c. A very imprudent
tax, especially this reading the names, so that most went
out of the church.

19*th*. I dined at Sir Purbeck Temple's, near Croydon;
his lady is aunt to my son-in-law, Draper; the house exactly furnished. Went thence with my son and daughter
to Wotton.—At Wotton, Mr. Duncomb, parson of Albury,
preached excellently.

28*th*. A very wet season.

11*th August*. The weather now so cold, that greater frosts
were not always seen in the midst of winter; this succeeded
much wet, and set harvest extremely back.

25*th September*. Mr. Offley preached at Abinger; too
much of controversy on a point of no consequence, for the
country people here. This was the first time I had heard
him preach.'—Bombarding of Cadiz; a cruel and brutish
way of making war, first begun by the French.—The season
wet, great storms, unseasonable harvest weather.—My good
and worthy friend, Captain Gifford, who that he might get
some competence to live decently, adventured all he had in
a voyage of two years to the East Indies, was, with another
great ship, taken by some French men-of-war, almost within
sight of England, to the loss of near £70,000, to my great
sorrow, and pity of his wife, he being also a valiant and industrious man. The losses of this sort to the nation have

---

¹ This gentleman gave good farms in Sussex for the better endowment of Oakwood Chapel, a Chapel of ease for the lower parts of
Abinger and Wotton, both of which livings are in the gift of the owner
of Wotton; many of the inhabitants thereabouts being distant five
miles from their parish churches, and the roads also in winter being
extremely bad.

been immense, and all through negligence, and little care to
secure the same near our own coasts; of infinitely more
concern to the public than spending their time in bombarding and ruining two or three paltry towns, without any
benefit, or weakening our enemies, who, though they began,
ought not to be imitated in an action totally averse to
humanity, or Christianity.

29th September. Very cold weather.—Sir Purbeck Temple,
uncle to my son Draper, died suddenly. A great funeral at
Addiscombe. His lady being own aunt to my son Draper,
he hopes for a good fortune, there being no heir. There
had been a new meeting of the Commissioners about Greenwich Hospital, on the new Commission, where the Lord
Mayor, &c. appeared, but I was prevented by indisposition
from attending. The weather very sharp, winter approaching apace.—The King went a progress into the north, to
show himself to the people against the elections, and was
everywhere complimented, except at Oxford, where it was
not as he expected, so that he hardly stopped an hour there,
and, having seen the Theatre, did not receive the banquet
proposed.—I dined with Dr. Gale at St. Paul's school, who
showed me many curious passages out of some ancient
Platonists' MSS. concerning the Trinity, which this great
and learned person would publish, with many other rare
things, if he was encouraged, and eased of the burden of
teaching.

25th October. The Archbishop and myself went to Hammersmith, to visit Sir Samuel Morland,[1] who was entirely
blind; a very mortifying sight. He showed us his invention of writing, which was very ingenious; also his wooden
kalendar, which instructed him all by feeling; and other
pretty and useful inventions of mills, pumps, &c., and the
pump he had erected that serves water to his garden, and to
passengers, with an inscription, and brings from a filthy
part of the Thames near it a most perfect and pure water.
He had newly buried £200 worth of music-books six feet
under ground, being, as he said, love-songs and vanity. He
plays himself psalms and religious hymns on the theorbo.
Very mild weather the whole of October.

10th November. Mr. Stanhope,[2] Vicar of Lewisham,

preached at Whitehall. He is one of the most ac.ompplished preachers I ever heard, for matter, eloquence, action, voice, and I am told, of excellent conversation.

13*th November*. Famous fireworks and very chargeable, the King being returned from his progress. He stayed seven or eight days at Lord Sunderland's at Althorpe, where he was mightily entertained. These fireworks were showed before Lord Romney, master of the ordnance, in St. James's great square, where the King stood.

17*th*. I spoke to the Archbishop of Canterbury to interest himself for restoring a room belonging to St. James's library, where the books want place.

21*st*. I went to see Mr. Churchill's collection of rarities.

23*rd*. To Lambeth, to get Mr. Williams continued in Boyle's lectures another year. Amongst others who dined there was Dr. Covel,[1] the great Oriental traveller.

1*st December*. I dined at Lord Sunderland's, now the great favourite and underhand politician, but not adventuring on any character, being obnoxious to the people for having twice changed his religion.

23*rd*. The Parliament wondrous intent on ways to reform the coin; setting out a Proclamation prohibiting the currency of half-crowns, &c. ; which made much confusion among the people.

25*th*. Hitherto mild, dark, misty weather. Now snow and frost.

1695-6. 12*th January*. Great confusion and distraction by reason of the clipped money, and the difficulty found in reforming it.

2*nd February*. An extraordinary wet season, though temperate as to cold.—The Royal Sovereign[2] man-of-war burnt at Chatham. It was built in 1637, and having given occasion to the levy of Ship-money was perhaps the cause of all the after-troubles to this day.—An earthquake in Dorsetshire by Portland, or rather a sinking of the ground suddenly for a large space, near the quarries of stone, hindering the conveyance of that material for the finishing St. Paul's.

[1] Dr. John Covel, Master of Christ's College, Cambridge, and Chancellor of York. He wrote an account of the Greek Church, which he published just before his death in 1722 in his 85th year.

[2] See vol. i. p. 18.

23rd February. They now began to coin new money.

26th. There was now a conspiracy of about thirty knights, gentlemen, captains, many of them Irish and English Papists, and Nonjurors or Jacobites (so called), to murder King William on the first opportunity of his going either from Kensington, or to hunting, or to the chapel; and, upon signal of fire to be given from Dover Cliff to Calais, an invasion was designed. In order to it there was a great army in readiness, men-of-war and transports, to join a general insurrection here, the Duke of Berwick having secretly come to London to head them, King James attending at Calais with the French army. It was discovered by some of their own party. £1000 reward was offered to whoever could apprehend any of the thirty named. Most of those who were engaged in it, were taken and secured. The Parliament, City, and all the nation, congratulate the discovery; and votes and resolutions were passed that, if King William should ever be assassinated, it should be revenged on the Papists and party through the nation; an Act of Association drawing up to empower the Parliament to sit on any such accident, till the Crown should be disposed of according to the late settlement at the Revolution. All Papists, in the mean time, to be banished ten miles from London. This put the nation into an incredible disturbance and general animosity against the French King and King James. The militia of the nation was raised, several regiments were sent for out of Flanders, and all things put in a posture to encounter a descent. This was so timed by the enemy, that whilst we were already much discontented by the greatness of the taxes, and corruption of the money, &c., we had like to have had very few men-of-war near our coasts; but so it pleased God that Admiral Rooke wanting a wind to pursue his voyage to the Straits, that squadron, with others at Portsmouth and other places, were still in the Channel, and were soon brought up to join with the rest of the ships which could be got together, so that there is hope this plot may be broken. I look on it as a very great deliverance and prevention by the providence of God. Though many did formerly pity King James's condition, this design of assassination and bringing over a French army, alienated many of his friends, and was likely to produce a more perfect establishment of King William

1st March. The wind continuing N. and E. all this week, brought so many of our men-of-war together that, though most of the French finding their design detected and prevented, made a shift to get into Calais and Dunkirk roads, we wanting fire-ships and bombs to disturb them; yet they were so engaged among the sands and flats, that 'tis said they cut their masts and flung their great guns overboard to lighten their vessels. We are yet upon them. This deliverance is due solely to God. French were to have invaded at once England, Scotland, and Ireland.

8th. Divers of the conspirators tried and condemned.

Vesuvius breaking out, terrified Naples.—Three of the unhappy wretches, whereof one was a priest, were executed [1] for intending to assassinate the King; they acknowledged their intention, but acquitted King James of inciting them to it, and died very penitent. Divers more in danger, and some very considerable persons.

Great frost and cold.

6th April. I visited Mr. Graham in the Fleet.

10th. The quarters of Sir William Perkins and Sir John Friend, lately executed on the plot, with Perkins's head, were set up at Temple Bar, a dismal sight, which many pitied. I think there never was such at Temple Bar till now, except once in the time of King Charles II., namely, of Sir Thomas Armstrong.[2]

12th. A very fine spring season.

19th. Great offence taken at the three ministers[3] who absolved Sir William Perkins and Friend at Tyburn. One of them (Snatt) was a son of my old schoolmaster. This produced much altercation as to the canonicalness of the action.[4]

21st. We had a meeting at Guildhall of the Grand

---

[1] Robert Charnock, Edward King, and Thomas Keys.

[2] He was concerned in the Rye-House Plot, fled into Holland, was given up, and executed in his own country, 1684. See p. 208.

[3] Mr. Collier, Mr. Snatt, and Mr. Cook, all nonjuring clergymen.

[4] Pamphlets upon the subject were written pro and con, now altogether forgotten.

Committee about settling the draught of Greenwich Hospital.

23rd April. I went to Eton, and dined with Dr. Godolphin, the provost. The schoolmaster assured me there had not been for twenty years a more pregnant youth in that place than my grandson.—I went to see the King's House at Kensington. It is very noble, though not great. The gallery furnished with the best pictures [from] all the houses, of Titian, Raphael, Correggio, Holbein, Julio Romano, Bassan, Vandyke, Tintoretto, and others; a great collection of porcelain; and a pretty private library. The gardens about it very delicious.

26th. Dr. Sharp preached at the Temple. His prayer before the sermon was one of the most excellent compositions I ever heard.

28th. The Venetian Ambassador made a stately entry with fifty footmen, many on horseback, four rich coaches, and a numerous train of gallants.—More executions this week of the assassins.—Oates dedicated a most villainous reviling book against King James, which he presumed to present to King William, who could not but abhor it, speaking so infamously and untruly of his late beloved Queen's own father.

2nd May. I dined at Lambeth, being summoned to meet my co-trustees, the Archbishop, Sir Henry Ashurst, and Mr. Serjeant Rotheram, to consult about settling Mr. Boyle's lecture for a perpetuity; which we concluded upon, by buying a rent-charge of £50 per annum, with the stock in our hands.

6th. I went to Lambeth, to meet at dinner the Countess of Sunderland and divers ladies. We dined in the Archbishop's wife's apartment with his Grace, and stayed late; yet I returned to Deptford at night.

13th. I went to London to meet my son, newly come from Ireland, indisposed.—Money still continuing exceeding scarce, so that none was paid or received, but all was on trust, the Mint not supplying for common necessities. The Association with an oath required of all lawyers and officers, on pain of *praemunire,* whereby men were obliged to renounce King James as no rightful king, and to revenge King William's death, if happening by assassination. This

to be taken by all the Counsel by a day limited, so that the
Courts of Chancery and King's Bench hardly heard any
cause in Easter Term, so many crowded to take the oath
This was censured as a very entangling contrivance of the
Parliament in expectation, that many in high office would
lay down, and others surrender. Many gentlemen taken
up on suspicion of the late plot, were now discharged out
of prison.

29th May. We settled divers officers, and other matters
relating to workmen, for the beginning of Greenwich
Hospital.

June 1st. I went to Deptford to dispose of our goods, in
order to letting the house for three years to Vice Admiral
Benbow, with condition to keep up the garden. This was
done soon after.

4th. A Committee met at Whitehall about Greenwich
Hospital, at Sir Christopher Wren's, his Majesty's Surveyor-General. We made the first agreement with divers
workmen and for materials ; and gave the first order for
proceeding on the foundation, and for weekly payments to
the workmen, and a general account to be monthly.

11th. Dined at Lord Pembroke's, Lord Privy Seal, a very
worthy gentleman. He showed me divers rare pictures
of very many of the old and best masters, especially one
of M. Angelo of a man gathering fruit to give to a woman,
and a large book of the best drawings of the old masters.—
Sir John Fenwick, one of the conspirators, was taken.[1]
Great subscriptions in Scotland to their East India Company.—Want of current money to carry on the smallest
concerns, even for daily provisions in the markets. Guineas
lowered to twenty two shillings, and great sums daily
transported to Holland, where it yields more, with other
treasure sent to pay the armies, and nothing considerable
coined of the new and now only current stamp, cause such
a scarcity that tumults are every day feared, nobody paying
or receiving money ; so imprudent was the late Parliament
to condemn the old though clipped and corrupted, till they
had provided supplies. To this add the fraud of the bankers

[1] He was taken at a house by the side of the road from Great Book-
ham to Stoke Dabernon, in Surrey, near Slyfield-mill, as the first editor
of this work, Mr. Bray, was told by the great grandson of Mr. Evelyn.

▲ ▲ 2

and goldsmiths, who having gotten immense riches by extortion, keep up their treasure in expectation of enhancing its value. Duncombe, not long since a mean goldsmith, having made a purchase of the late Duke of Buckingham's estate[1] at near £90,000, and reputed to have near as much in cash. Banks and Lotteries every day set up.

18*th June.* The famous trial between my Lord Bath and Lord Montague for an estate of £11,000 a year, left by the Duke of Albemarle, wherein on several trials had been spent £20,000 between them. The Earl of Bath was cast on evident forgery.[2]

20*th.* I made my Lord Cheney a visit at Chelsea, and saw those ingenious water-works invented by Mr. Winstanley,[3] wherein were some things very surprising and extraordinary.

21*st.* An exceeding rainy, cold, unseasonable summer, yet the city was very healthy.

25*th.* A trial in the Common Pleas between the Lady Purbeck Temple and Mr. Temple, a nephew of Sir Purbeck, concerning a deed set up to take place of several wills. This deed was proved to be forged. The cause went on my lady's side. This concerning my son-in-law, Draper, I staid almost all day at Court. A great supper was given to the jury, being persons of the best condition in Buckinghamshire.

30*th.* I went with a select Committee of the Commissioners for Greenwich Hospital,[4] and with Sir Christopher Wren, where with him I laid the first stone of the intended foundation, precisely at five o'clock in the evening, after we had dined together. Mr. Flamstead, the King's Astronomical Professor, observing the punctual time by instruments.

4*th July.* Note that my Lord Godolphin was the first

[1] At Helmsley, in Yorkshire.
    "And Helmsley, once proud Buckingham's delight,
        Slides to a Scrivener or a City-Knight."—POPE.
[2] *Post*, p. 379.
[3] The ingenious architect who built the Eddystone Lighthouse, and perished in it when blown down by the great storm in 1703.
[4] Sir William Ashurst, Sir Christopher Wren, Sir Thomas Lane, Sir Stephen Evance, John Evelyn, William Draper, Dr. Cade, Mr. Johnson, Mr. Thomas, Captain Gatteridge, Mr. Firmin, Mr. Lake, and Captain Heath, constituted this Committee.

of the subscribers who paid any money to this noble fabric.[1]

• SUBSCRIPTIONS TO GREENWICH HOSPITAL; FROM MR. EVELYN'S PAPERS.

	£	s.	d.
The King	2,000	0	0
Archbishop of Canterbury	500	0	0
Lord Keeper Somers	500	0	0
Duke of Leeds, President of the Council . .	500	0	0
Earl of Pembroke, Lord Privy Seal . .	500	0	0
Duke of Devonshire	500	0	0
Duke of Shrewsbury, Secretary of State .	500	0	0
Earl of Romney	200	0	0
Earl of Dorset	500	0	0
Lord Montague	300	0	0
Lord Godolphin, First Commissioner of the Treasury	200	0	0
Mr. Montague, Chancellor of the Exchequer .	100	0	0
Mr. Smith, Commissioner of the Treasury .	100	0	0
Lord Chief-Justice Holt	100	0	0
Sir Ste. Fox, Commissioner of the Treasury .	200	0	0
Earl of Ranelagh	100	0	0
Sir John Lowther	100	0	0
Mr. Priestman	100	0	0
Sir Geo. Rooke	100	0	0
Sir John Houblon	100	0	0
Lord Chief-Justice Treby	100	0	0
Sir Wm. Trumball, Principal Secretary of State	100	0	0
Sir Robt. Rich	100	0	0
Sir Hen. Goodrick	50	0	0
Col. Austen	100	0	0
Sir Tho. Lane	100	0	0
Sir Patience Ward	100	0	0
Sir William Ashurst	100	0	0
Sir John Trevor, Master of the Rolls . .	100	0	0
Mr. Justice Rokeby	50	0	0
Mr. Justice Powell	50	0	0
Mr. Justice Eyre	50	0	0
Lord Chief Baron Ward	66	13	4
Mr. Justice Gregory	50	0	0
Mr. Baron Powell	50	0	0
Earl of Portland	500	0	0
Mr. Baron Powis	40	0	0
Sir Richard Onslow	100	0	0
Mr. Baron Lechmore	40	0	0,
	£9,046	13	4

The subjoined memorandum accompanies the foregoing list: "By the

7th July. A northern wind altering the weather with a continual and impetuous rain of three days and nights, changed it into perfect winter.

12th Very unseasonable and uncertain weather.

26th. So little money in the nation that Exchequer Tallies, of which I had for £2000 on the best fund in England, the Post-Office, nobody would take at 30 per cent. discount.

3rd August. The Bank lending the £200,000 to pay the army in Flanders, that had done nothing against the enemy, had so exhausted the treasure of the nation, that one could not have borrowed money under 14 or 15 per cent. on bills, or on Exchequer Tallies under 30 per cent.—Reasonable good harvest-weather.—I went to Lambeth and dined with the Archbishop, who had been at Court on the complaint against Dr. Thomas Watson, Bishop of St. David's, who was suspended for simony.[1] The Archbishop told me how unsatisfied he was with the Canon-law, and how exceedingly unreasonable all their pleadings appeared to him.

September. Fine seasonable weather, and a great harvest after a cold wet summer. Scarcity in Scotland.

6th. I went to congratulate the marriage of a daughter of Mr. Boscawen to the son of Sir Philip Meadows; she is niece to my Lord Godolphin, married at Lambeth by the Archbishop 30th August.—After above six months' stay in London about Greenwich Hospital, I returned to Wotton.

24th October. Unseasonable stormy weather, and an ill seed-time.

November. Lord Godolphin retired from the Treasury, who was the first Commissioner and most skilful manager of all.

Committee for the fabric of Greenwich Hospital, Nov. 4, 1696.—Expense of the work already done, £5,000 and upwards, towards which the Treasurer had not received above £800, so that they must be obliged to stop the work, unless there can be a supply of money both from the tallies that have been assigned for payment of his Majesty's £2,000, and the money subscribed by several noblemen and gentlemen; the Secretary was ordered to attend Mr. Lowndes, Secretary to the Lords of the Treasury, to move for an order that the tallies may be fixed on such fund as may be ready money, or that the Treasurer of the Hospital may be directed to dispose of them on the best terms he can; and that the Solicitor, with the Treasurer's clerk, do attend the noblemen and gentlemen that have subscribed, to acquaint them herewith."

[1] Afterwards deprived: see p. 366.

8th November. The first frost began fiercely, but lasted not long.—More plots talked of. Search for Jacobites so called. *15th—23rd.* Very stormy weather, rain, and inundations. *13th December.* Continuance of extreme frost and snow. 1696-7. *17th January.* The severe frost and weather relented, but again froze with snow.—Conspiracies continue against King William. Sir John Fenwick was beheaded.

7th February. Severe frost continued with snow. Soldiers in the armies and garrison-towns frozen to death on their posts.

(Here a leaf of the MS. is lost.)[1]

[1] In a letter to Dr. Bohun, dated Wotton, 18th January, 1696-7, Evelyn gives a minute and agreeable account of his domestic life and circumstances at this time :

"Having been told that you have lately inquired what is become of your now old friends of Sayes Court, the date hereof will acquaint you where they are, and the sequel much of what they do and think. I believe I need not tell you that, after the marriage of my daughter, and the so kind offer of my good brother here, my then circumstances and times considered, I had reason to embrace it, not merely out of inclination to the place where I was born and have now an interest.

"Amongst other things, I had paid £300 for the renewing of my lease [at Deptford] with some augmentation of what I hold from the Crown, which the Duke of Leeds was supplanting me of————but I am not here on free cost.

"My Lord Godolphin (my ever noble patron and steady friend, now retired from a fatiguing station) got me to be named Treasurer to the Marine College erecting at Greenwich, with the salary of £200 per annum, of which I have never yet received one penny of the tallies assigned for it, now two years at our Lady-day ; my son-in-law, Draper, is my substitute. I have only had this opportunity to place my old (indeed faithful) servant J. Strd. in an employment at Greenwich, which with my other business, not small, among so many beggarly tenants as you know I have at Deptford [is some provision for him]. I have let my house to Captain Benbow, and have the mortification of seeing every day much of my former labours and expense there impairing, for want of a more polite tenant.

"My grandson is so delighted in books, that he professes a library is to him the greatest recreation, so I give him free scope here, where I have near upon 22,000 [qu. 2000 ?] (with my brother's), and whither I would bring the rest had I any room, which I have not, to my great regret ; having here so little conversation with the learned, unless it be when Mr. Wotton [Dr. Bentley's friend] comes now and then to visit me, he being tutor to Mr Finch's son at Albury, but which he is now

17th August, I came to Wotton after three months' absence.

September. Very bright weather, out witn snarp east wind. My son came from London in his melancholy indisposition.

12th September. Mr. Duncombe, the rector, came and preached after an absence of two years, though only living seven or eight miles off [at Ashted].—Welcome tidings of the Peace.

3rd October. So great were the storms all this week, that near a thousand people were lost going into the Texel.

16th November. The King's entry very pompous; but is nothing approaching that of King Charles II.

2nd December. Thanksgiving-day for the Peace. The King and a great Court at Whitehall. The Bishop of Salisbury,[1]

leaving to go to his living, that without books, and the best wife and brother in the world, I were to be pitied ; but, with these subsidiaries, and the revising some of my old impertinences, to which I am adding a Discourse I made on Medals (lying by me long before Obadiah Walker's Treatise appeared), I pass some of my Attic nights, if I may be so vain as to name them, with the author of those Criticisms. For the rest, I am planting an evergreen grove here to an old house ready to drop, the economy and hospitality of which my good old brother will not depart from, but *more veterum* kept a Christmas, in which we had not fewer than three hundred bumpkins every holy-day.

"We have here a very convenient apartment of five rooms together besides a pretty closet, which we have furnished with the spoils of Sayes Court, and is the raree-show of the whole neighbourhood, and in truth we live easy as to all domestic cares. Wednesday and Saturday nights we call Lecture-nights, when my wife and myself take our turns to read the packets of all the news sent constantly from London, which serves us for discourse till fresh news comes ; and so you have the history of a very old man and his no young companion, whose society I have enjoyed more to my satisfaction these three years here, than in almost fifty before, but am now every day trussing up to be gone, I hope to a better place.

"My daughter, Draper, being brought to bed in the Christmas-holidays of a fine boy, has given an heir to a most deserving husband, a prudent, well-natured gentlemen, a man of bussiness, like to be very rich, and deserving to be so, among the happiest pairs I think in England, and to my daughter's and our hearts' desire. She has also a fine girl, and a mother-in-law exceedingly fond of my daughter, and a most excellent woman, charitable and of a very sweet disposition. They all live together, keep each their coach, and with as suitable an equipage as any in town."

[1] Burnet.

preached, or rather made a florid panegyric, on 2 Chron. ix. 7, 8.—The evening concluded with fireworks and illuminations of great expense.

5th December. Was the first Sunday that St. Paul's had had service performed in it since it was burnt in 1666.

6th. I went to Kensington with the Sheriff, Knights, and chief gentlemen of Surrey, to present their address to the King. The Duke of Norfolk promised to introduce it, but came so late, that it was presented before he came. This insignificant ceremony was brought in in Cromwell's time, and has ever since continued with offers of life and fortune to whoever happened to have the power. I dined at Sir Richard Onslow's, who treated almost all the gentlemen of Surrey. When we had half dined, the Duke of Norfolk came in to make his excuse.

12th. At the Temple Church; it was very long before the service began, staying for the Comptroller of the Inner Temple, where was to be kept a riotous and revelling Christmas, according to custom.

18th. At Lambeth, to Dr. Bentley, about the Library at St. James's.

23rd. I returned to Wotton.

1697-8. A great Christmas kept at Wotton, open house, much company. I presented my book of Medals, &c. to divers Noblemen, before I exposed it to sale.

2nd January. Dr. Fulham, who lately married my niece, preached against Atheism, a very eloquent discourse, somewhat improper for most of the audience at [Wotton], but fitted for some other place, and very apposite to the profane temper of the age.

5th. Whitehall burnt, nothing but walls and ruins left.

30th. The imprisonment of the great banker, Duncombe: censured by Parliament; acquitted by the Lords; sent again to the Tower by the Commons.[1]

[1] 25th Jan. 1697-8. Charles Duncombe, Esq., M. P., was charged with making false endorsements on Exchequer-bills, and was committed close prisoner to the Tower. 29th. Being ill, his apothecary and his brother Anthony Duncombe were permitted to see him. He confessed his guilt, and was expelled the House. A Bill was brought in for seizure of his estate, which was passed 28th Feb after great opposition, 138 against 108. It was entitled "An Act for punishing C. Duncombe, Esq., for contriving and advising the making false endorsements of several Bills

The Czar of Muscovy being come to England, and having a mind to see the building of ships, hired my house at Sayes Court, and made it his court and palace, new furnished for him by the King.[1]

21st April. The Czar went from my house to return home. An exceeding sharp and cold season.

8th May. An extraordinary great snow and frost, nipping the corn and other fruits. Corn at nine shillings a bushel [£18 a load].

30th. I dined at Mr. Pepys, where I heard the rare voice of Mr. Pule, who was lately come from Italy, reputed the most excellent singer we had ever had. He sung several compositions of the late Dr. Purcell.

5th June. Dr. White, late Bishop of Norwich, who had been ejected for not complying with Government, was buried in St. Gregory's churchyard, or vault, at St. Paul's. His hearse was accompanied by two non-juror Bishops, Dr. Turner of Ely, and Dr. Lloyd, with forty other non-juror clergymen, who would not stay the Office of the burial, because the Dean of St. Paul's had appointed a conforming minister to read the Office; at which all much wondered, there being nothing in that Office which mentioned the present King.

8th. I went to congratulate the marriage of Mr. Godolphin with the Earl of Marlborough's daughter.

9th. To Deptford, to see how miserably the Czar had left my house, after three months making it his Court. I got Sir Christopher Wren, the King's Surveyor, and Mr. London his gardener, to go and estimate the repairs, for which they allowed £150 in their report to the Lords of the Treasury.

made forth at Receipt of the Exchequer commonly called Exchequer-Bills." This being sent to the Lords, they desired a conference with the Commons, and not being satisfied, though he had acknowledged the fact, they discharged him from the Tower. 31st March, the Commons re-committed him. We do not find, however, in the Journals of the House of Commons, that anything further was done.

[1] While the Czar was in his house, Evelyn's servant writes to him: "There is a house full of people, and right nasty. The Czar lies next your library, and dines in the parlour next your study. He dines at ten o'clock and six at night, is very seldom at home a whole day, very often in the King's Yard, or by water, dressed in several dresses. The King is expected here this day; the best parlour is pretty clean for him to be entertained in. The King pays for all he has."

I then went to see the foundation of the Hall and Chapel at Greenwich Hospital.

6th August. I dined with Mr. Pepys, where was Captain Dampier,[1] who had been a famous buccaneer, had brought hither the painted Prince Job,[2] and printed a relation of his very strange adventure, and his observations. He was now going abroad again by the King's encouragement, who furnished a ship of 290 tons.[3] He seemed a more modest man than one would imagine by the relation of the crew he had assorted with. He brought a map of his observations of the course of the winds in the South Sea, and assured us that the maps hitherto extant were all false as to the Pacific Sea, which he makes on the south of the line, that on the north end running by the coast of Peru being extremely tempestuous.

25th September. Dr. Foy came to me to use my interest with Lord Sunderland for his being made Professor of Physic at Oxford, in the King's gift. I went also to the Archbishop in his behalf.

7th December. Being one of the Council of the Royal Society, I was named to be of the Committee to wait on our new President, the Lord Chancellor,[4] our Secretary, Dr. Sloane, and Sir R. Southwell, last Vice-president, carrying our book of statutes; the Office of the President being read, his Lordship subscribed his name, and took the oaths according to our statutes as a Corporation for the improvement of natural knowledge. Then his Lordship made a short compliment concerning the honour the Society had done him, and how ready he would be to promote so noble a design, and come himself among us, as often as the attendance on the public would permit; and so we took our leave.

18th. Very warm, but exceeding stormy.

[1] The celebrated navigator, born in 1652, the time of whose death is uncertain. His *Voyage round the World* has gone through many editions, and the substance of it has been transferred to many collections of voyages.

[2] Giolo, of whom there is a very curious portrait, engraved by Savage, to which is subjoined a singular narrative of his wonderful adventures; there is also a smaller one, copied from the above, prefixed to a fictitious account of his life, printed in a 4to pamphlet. Evelyn mentions him in his *Numismata*.

[3] Noticed in Parliament.   [4] Lord Somers.

1698-9. *January*. My cousin Pierrepoint died. She was daughter to Sir John Evelyn, of Wilts, my father's nephew; she was widow to William Pierrepoint, brother to the Marquis of Dorchester, and mother to Evelyn Pierrepoint, Earl of Kingston; a most excellent and prudent lady.

The House of Commons persist in refusing more than 7000 men to be a standing army, and no strangers to be in the number. This displeased the Court party. Our county member, Sir R. Onslow, opposed it also; which might reconcile him to the people, who began to suspect him.

17th February. My grandson went to Oxford with Dr. Mander, the Master of Baliol College,[1] where he was entered a fellow-commoner.

19th. A most furious wind, such as has not happened for many years, doing great damage to houses and trees, by the fall of which several persons were killed.

5th March. The old East India Company lost their business against the new Company, by ten votes in Parliament, so many of their friends being absent, going to see a tiger baited by dogs.

The persecuted Vaudois, who were banished out of Savoy, were received by the German Protestant Princes.

24th. My only remaining son died after a tedious languishing sickness, contracted in Ireland, and increased here, to my exceeding grief and affliction; leaving me one grandson, now at Oxford, whom I pray God to prosper and be the support of the Wotton family. He was aged forty-four years and about three months. He had been six years one of the Commissioners of the Revenue in Ireland, with great ability and reputation.

26th March. After an extraordinary storm, there came up the Thames a whale which was fifty-six feet long. Such, and a larger of the spout kind, was killed there forty years ago (June 1658). That year died Cromwell.

30th. My deceased son was buried in the vault at Wotton, according to his desire.

The Duke of Devon lost £1,900 at a horse-race at Newmarket.

The King preferring his young favourite Earl of Albe-

---

[1] Dr. Roger Mander was elected Master of his College, in the place of Dr. John Venn, deceased, 23 Oct. 1687. Wood's *Fasti Oxonienses*.

marle[1] to be first Commander of his Guard, the Duke of
Ormond laid down his commission. This of the Dutch
Lord passing over his head, was exceedingly resented by
every body.

April. Lord Spencer purchased an incomparable library[2]
of . . . . wherein, among other rare books, were
several that were printed at the first invention of that wonderful art, as particularly "Tully's Offices, &c." There was a
Homer and a Suidas in a very good Greek character and good
paper, almost as ancient. This gentleman is a very fine
scholar, whom from a child I have known. His tutor was
one Florival of Geneva.

29th. I dined with the Archbishop; but my business was
to get him to persuade the King to purchase the late Bishop
of Worcester's library, and build a place for his own library
at St. James's, in the Park, the present one being too small.

3rd May. At a meeting of the Royal Society I was nominated to be of the Committee to wait on the Lord Chancellor to move the King to purchase the Bishop of Worcester's
library (Dr. Edward Stillingfleet).

4th. The Court party have little influence in this Session.

7th. The Duke of Ormond restored to his commission.—
All Lotteries, till now cheating the people, to be no longer
permitted than to Christmas, except that for the benefit
of Greenwich Hospital. Mr. Bridgman, chairman of the
committee for that charitable work, died; a great loss to it.
He was Clerk of the Council, a very industrious useful man.
I saw the library of Dr. John Moore,[3] Bishop of Norwich,
one of the best and most ample collection of all sorts of good
books in England, and he, one of the most learned men.

11th June. After a long drought, we had a refreshing

---

[1] Arnold Joost Van Keppel, created Earl of Albemarle, Viscount
Bury, &c. in Feb. 1695-6; K. G. 1700; died in 1718, at the Hague
æt. 48.

[2] The foundation of the noble library now at Blenheim.

[3] Afterwards Bishop of Ely. He died 31 July, 1714. King George
the First purchased this library after the Bishop's death, for £6000, and
presented it to the University of Cambridge, where it now is. The gift
occasioned two epigrams on the Universities of Oxford and Cambridge:
a troop of horse being at this time sent to the former, holding high
Tory opinions; the books to the latter, holding those of the Whigs.
The reader will find them printed in Noble's *Continuation of Grainger.*

shower. The day before, there was a dreadful fire at Rother-
hithe, near the Thames side, which burnt divers ships, and
consumed near three hundred houses.—Now died the
famous Duchess of Mazarine; she had been the richest lady
in Europe. She was niece of Cardinal Mazarine, and was
married to the richest subject in Europe, as is said. She
was born at Rome, educated in France, and was an extraordinary beauty and wit, but dissolute and impatient of
matrimonial restraint, so as to be abandoned by her husband, and banished, when she came into England for shelter,
lived on a pension given her here, and is reported to have
hastened her death by intemperate drinking strong spirits.
She has written her own story and adventures, and so has
her other extravagant sister, wife to the noble family of
Colonna.

15th June. This week died Conyers Seymour, son of Sir
Edward Seymour, killed in a duel caused by a slight affront
in St. James's Park, given him by one who was envious of
his gallantries; for he was a vain foppish young man, who
made a great éclât about town by his splendid equipage and
boundless expense. He was about twenty-three years old;
his brother, now at Oxford, inherited an estate of £7000 a
year, which had fallen to him not two years before.

19th. My cousin, George Evelyn of Nutfield, died
suddenly.

25th. The heat has been so great, almost all this month,
that I do not remember to have felt much greater in Italy,
and this after a winter the wettest, though not the coldest,
that I remember for fifty years last past.

28th. Finding my occasions called me so often to
London, I took the remainder of the lease my son had in a
house in Dover Street, to which I now removed, not taking
my goods from Wotton.

23rd July. Seasonable showers, after a continuance of
excessive drought and heat.

August. I drank the Shooters' Hill waters. At Deptford, they had been building a pretty new church.—The
Bishop of St. David's [Watson] deprived for simony.[1]—The
city of Moscow burnt by the throwing of squibs.

3rd September. There was in this week an eclipse of the

_____
[1] Ante, p. 358.

sun, at which many were frightened by the predictions of
the astrologers. I remember fifty years ago that many were
so terrified by Lilly, that they durst not go out of their
houses.—A strange earthquake at New Batavia, in the East
Indies.

4th October. My worthy brother died at Wotton, in the
83rd year of his age, of perfect memory and understanding.
He was religious, sober, and temperate, and of so hospitable
a nature, that no family in the county maintained that
ancient custom of keeping, as it were, open house the whole
year in the same manner, or gave more noble or free entertainment to the county on all occasions, so that his house
was never free. There were sometimes twenty persons
more than his family, and some that stayed there all the
summer, to his no small expense ; by this he gained the universal love of the county. He was born at Wotton, went
from the free-school at Guildford to Trinity College, Oxford,
thence to the Middle Temple, as gentlemen of the best
quality did, but without intention to study the law as a
profession. He married the daughter of Colwall,[1] of a
worthy and ancient family in Leicestershire, by whom he
had one son ; she dying in 1643, left George her son an infant, who being educated liberally, after travelling abroad,[2]
returned and married one Mrs. Gore, by whom he had
several children, but only three daughters survived. He
was a young man of good understanding, but, over-indulg-
ing his ease and pleasure, grew so very corpulent, contrary
to the constitution of the rest of his father's relations, that
he died. My brother afterwards married a noble and
honourable lady, relict of Sir John Cotton, she being an
Offley, a worthy and ancient Staffordshire family, by whom

[1] Mary, daughter and co-heiress of Daniel Caldwell, of Horndon, in
Essex. See pedigree.

[2] In a letter to his nephew, George Evelyn, then on his travels in
Italy, dated 30th March, 1664, Evelyn tells him that his father complained of his expenses, as much exceeding those of his own, which
were known to the young gentleman's father, as all the money passed
through his hands. He says that when he travelled he kept a servant,
sometimes two, entertained several masters, and made no inconsiderable
collection of curiosities, all within £300 *per ann.*—In the same letter, he
desires seeds of the ilex, phyllera, myrtle, jessamine, which he says are
rare in England.

he had several children of both sexes. This lady died, leaving only two daughters and a son. The younger daughter
died before marriage; the other afterwards married Sir Cyril
Wych, a noble and learned gentleman (son of Sir ——
Wych), who had been Ambassador at Constantinople, and
was afterwards made one of the Lords Justices of Ireland.
Before this marriage, her only brother married the daughter of —— Eversfield, of Sussex, of an honourable family,
but left a widow without any child living; he died about
1691, and his wife not many years after, and my brother re-
settled the whole estate on me. His sister, Wych, had a
portion of £6000, to which was added about £300 more;
the three other daughters, with what I added, had about
£5000 each. My brother died on the 5th October, in a
good old age and great reputation, making his beloved
daughter, Lady Wych, sole executrix, leaving me only his
library and some pictures of my father, mother, &c. She
buried him with extraordinary solemnity, rather as a nobleman than as a private gentleman. There were, as I com-
puted, above 2000 persons at the funeral, all the gentlemen
of the county doing him the last honours. I returned to
London, till my lady should dispose of herself and family.

21st October. After an unusual warm and pleasant season, we were surprised with a very sharp frost. I presented my *Acetaria,*[1] dedicated to my Lord Chancellor, who
returned me thanks in an extraordinary civil letter.

15th November. There happened this week so thick a
mist and fog, that people lost their way in the streets, it
being so intense that no light of candles, or torches, yielded
any (or but very little) direction. I was in it, and in
danger. Robberies were committed between the very lights
which were fixed between London and Kensington on both
sides, and whilst coaches and travellers were passing.
It begun about four in the afternoon, and was quite gone
by eight, without any wind to disperse it. At the Thames,
they beat drums to direct the watermen to make the shore.

19th. At our chapel in the evening there was a
sermon preached by young Mr. Horneck,[2] chaplain to Lord
Guilford, whose lady's funeral had been celebrated magnifi-

[1] See Evelyn's "Miscellaneous Writings," pp. 721—812.
[2] Of the character of this gentleman's father, see p. 183.

cently the Thursday before. A panegyric was now pronounced, describing the extraordinary piety and excellently
employed life of this amiable young lady. She died in child-
bed a few days before, to the excessive sorrow of her husband, who ordered the preacher to declare that it was on
her exemplary life, exhortations and persuasion, that he
totally changed the course of his life, which was before in
great danger of being perverted; following the mode of this
dissolute age. Her devotion, early piety, charity, fastings,
economy, disposition of her time in reading, praying, recollections in her own hand-writing of what she heard and read,
and her conversation were most exemplary.

24th November. I signed Dr. Blackwall's election to be
the next year's Boyles Lecturer.

Such horrible robberies and murders were committed, as
had not been known in this nation; atheism, profaneness,
blasphemy, amongst all sorts, portended some judgment if
not amended; on which a society was set on foot, who
obliged themselves to endeavour the reforming of it, in
London and other places, and began to punish offenders and
put the laws in more strict execution: which God Almighty
prosper![1]—A gentle, calm, dry, temperate weather all this
season of the year, but now came sharp, hard frost, and mist,
but calm.

3rd December. Calm, bright, and warm as in the middle
of April. So continued on 21st Jan.—A great earthquake
in Portugal.

The Parliament reverses the prodigious donations of the
Irish forfeitures, which were intended to be set apart for
discharging the vast national debt. They called some great
persons in the highest offices in question for setting the
Great Seal to the pardon of an arch-pirate,[2] who had turned
pirate again, and brought prizes into the West Indies,
suspected to be connived at on sharing the prey; but the
prevailing part in the House called Courtiers, out-voted the
complaints, not by being more in number, but by the country-
party being negligent in attendance.

---

[1] *Post*, p. 371.
[2] Captain Kidd; he was hanged about two years afterwards with
some of his accomplices. This was one of the charges brought by the
Commons against Lord Somers.

1699-1700. 14*th January.* Dr. Lancaster, Vicar of St. Martin's, dismissed Mr. Stringfellow, who had been made the first preacher at our chapel by the Bishop of Lincoln [Dr. Tenison, now Archbishop], whilst he held St. Martin's by dispensation, and put in one Mr Sandys, much against the inclination of those who frequented the chapel.—The Scotch book about Darien was burnt by the hangman by vote of Parliament.[1]

21*st.* Died the Duke of Beaufort,[2] a person of great honour, prudence, and estate.

25*th.* I went to Wotton, the first time after my brother's funeral, to furnish the house with necessaries, Lady Wych and my nephew Glanville, the executors having sold and disposed of what goods were there of my brother's.—The weather was now altering into sharp and hard frost.

One Stephens,[3] who preached before the House of Commons on King Charles's Martyrdom, told them that the observation of that day was not intended out of any detestation of his murder, but to be a lesson to other Kings and Rulers, how they ought to behave themselves towards their subjects, lest they should come to the same end. This was so resented that, though it was usual to desire these anniversary-sermons to be printed, they refused thanks to him, and ordered that in future no one should preach before them, who was not either a Dean or a Doctor of Divinity.

4*th February.* The Parliament voted against the Scots settling in Darien as being prejudicial to our trade with Spain. They also voted that the exorbitant number of attorneys be lessened (now indeed swarming, and evidently

---

[1] The volume alluded to was *An Enquiry into the causes of the Miscarriage of the Scots Colony at Darien: Or an Answer to a Libel, entituled, A Defence of the Scots abdicating Darien.* See Votes of the House of Commons, 15th January, 1699-1700.

[2] Henry Somerset, the first Duke, who exerted himself against the Monmouth Rebellion in 1685, and in 1688 endeavoured to secure Bristol against the adherents of the Prince of Orange; upon whose elevation to the throne, the Duke, refusing to take the oaths, lived in retirement till his death.

[3] William Stephens, Rector of Sutton, in Surrey. After the censure of his sermon by the House of Commons, he published it as in defiance. See more of this and of him in Manning and Bray's *History of Surrey,* ii. 487.

causing lawsuits and disturbance, eating out the estates of people, provoking them to go to law).

18th February. Mild and calm season, with gentle frost, and little mizzling rain. The Vicar of St. Martin's frequently preached at Trinity chapel in the afternoon.

8th March. The season was like April for warmth and mildness.—*11th.* On Wednesday, was a sermon at our chapel, to be continued during Lent.

13th. I was at the funeral of my Lady Temple, who was buried at Islington, brought from Addiscombe, near Croydon. She left my son-in-law Draper (her nephew) the mansion house of Addiscombe, very nobly and com pletely furnished, with the estate about it, with plate and jewels, to the value in all of about £20,000. She was a very prudent lady, gave many great legacies, with £500 to the poor of Islington, where her husband, Sir Purbeck Temple, was buried, both dying without issue.

24th. The season warm, gentle, and exceeding pleasant. —Divers persons of quality entered into the Society for Reformation[1] of Manners; and some lectures were set up, particularly in the City of London. The most eminent of the Clergy preached at Bow Church, after reading a de- claration set forth by the King to suppress the growing wickedness; this began already to take some effect as to common swearing, and oaths in the mouths of people of all ranks.

25th. Dr. Burnet preached to-day before the Lord Mayor and a very great congregation, on Proverbs xxvii. 5, 6. "Open rebuke is better than secret love; the wounds of a friend are better than the kisses of an enemy." He made a very pathetic discourse concerning the necessity and advan- tage of friendly correction.

April. The Duke of Norfolk now succeeded in obtaining a divorce from his wife by the Parliament for adultery with Sir John Germaine, a Dutch gamester, of mean extraction, who had got much by gaming; the Duke had leave to marry again, so that if he should have children, the Dukedom will go from the late Lord Thomas's children, Papists indeed, but very hopeful and virtuous gentlemen, as was their father. The now Duke their uncle is a Protestant.

[1] *Ante,* p. 369.

The **Parliament** nominated fourteen persons to go into Ireland as Commissioners to dispose of the forfeited estates there, towards payment of the debts incurred by the late war, but which the King had in great measure given to some of his favourites of both sexes, Dutch and others of little merit, and very unseasonably. That this might be done without suspicion of interest in the Parliament, it was ordered that no member of either House should be in the Commission.—The great contest between the Lords and Commons concerning the Lords' power of amendments and rejecting bills tacked to the money-bill, carried for the Commons. However, this tacking of bills is a novel practice, suffered by King Charles II., who, being continually in want of money, let anything pass rather than not have wherewith to feed his extravagance. This was carried but by one voice in the Lords, all the Bishops following the Court, save one; so that near sixty bills passed, to the great triumph of the Commons and Country-party, but high regret of the Court, and those to whom the King had given large estates in Ireland. Pity it is, that things should be brought to this extremity, the government of this nation being so equally poised between King and subject; but we are satisfied with nothing : and, whilst there is no perfection on this side Heaven, methinks both might be contented without straining things too far. Amongst the rest, there passed a law as to Papists' estates, that if one turned not Protestant before eighteen years of age, it should pass to his next Protestant heir. This indeed seemed a hard law, but not only the usage of the French King to his Protestant subjects, but the indiscreet insolence of the Papists here, going in triumphant and public processions with their Bishops, with banners and trumpets in divers places (as is said) in the northern counties, has brought it on their party.

24th April. This week there was a great change of State-officers. — The Duke of Shrewsbury resigned his Lord Chamberlainship to the Earl of Jersey, the Duke's indisposition requiring his retreat. Mr. Vernon, Secretary of State, was put out.—The Seal was taken from the Lord Chancellor Somers, though he had been acquitted by a great majority of votes for what was charged against him in the

House of Commons.[1] This being in term-time, put some stop to business, many eminent lawyers refusing to accept the office, considering the uncertainty of things in this fluctuating conjuncture. It is certain that this Chancellor was a most excellent lawyer, very learned in all polite literature, a superior pen, master of a handsome style, and of easy conversation; but he is said to make too much haste to be rich, as his predecessor, and most in place in this age did, to a more prodigious excess than was ever known. But the Commons had now so mortified the Court-party, and property and liberty were so much invaded in all the neighbouring kingdoms, that their jealousy made them cautious, and every day strengthened the law which protected the people from tyranny.

A most glorious spring, with hope of abundance of fruit of all kinds, and a propitious year.

10th May. The great trial between Sir Walter Clarges and Mr. Sherwin concerning the legitimacy of the late Duke of Albemarle, on which depended an estate of £1500 a year; the verdict was given for Sir Walter.—19th. Serjeant Wright[2] at last accepted the Great Seal.

24th. I went from Dover Street to Wotton, for the rest of the summer, and removed thither the rest of my goods from Sayes Court.

2nd June. A sweet season, with a mixture of refreshing showers.

9th — 16th. In the afternoon, our clergyman had a Catechism, which was continued for some time.

July. I was visited with illness, but it pleased God that I recovered, for which praise be ascribed to Him by me, and that He has again so graciously advertised me of my duty to prepare for my latter end, which at my great age cannot be far off.

The Duke of Gloucester, son of the Princess Anne of Denmark, died of the small-pox.

[1] Post, p. 375.
[2] Sir Nathan Wright, appointed Lord-Keeper, who purchased the manor of and resided at Gothurst, near Newport Pagnell, Bucks. He lies buried in that church, in which are whole-length figures in white marble of the Lord-Keeper in his robes, and his son, George Wright, Esquire, Clerk of the Crown, in his official dress.

13th July. I went to Marden, which was originally a barren warren bought by Sir Robert Clayton,[1] who built there a pretty house, and made such alteration by planting not only an infinite store of the best fruit; but so changed the natural situation of the hill, valleys, and solitary mountains about it, that it rather represented some foreign country, which would produce spontaneously pines, firs, cypress, yew, holly, and juniper; they were come to their perfect growth, with walks, mazes, &c., amongst them, and were preserved with the utmost care, so that I who had seen it some years before in its naked and barren condition, was in admiration of it. The land was bought of Sir John Evelyn, of Godstone, and was thus improved for pleasure and retirement by the vast charge and industry of this opulent citizen. He and his lady received us with great civility.—The tombs in the church at Croydon of Archbishops Grindal, Whitgift, and other Archbishops, are fine and venerable; but none comparable to that of the late Archbishop Sheldon, which, being all of white marble, and of a stately ordinance and carvings, far surpassed the rest, and I judge could not cost less than 700*l.* or 800*l.*[2]

20th September. I went to Beddington, the ancient seat of the Carews, in my remembrance a noble old structure, capacious, and in form of the buildings of the age of Henry VIII. and Queen Elizabeth, and proper for the old English hospitality, but now decaying with the house itself, heretofore adorned with ample gardens, and the first orange-trees[3] that had been seen in England, planted in the open ground, and secured in winter only by a tabernacle of boards and stoves removable in summer, that, standing 120 years, large and goodly trees, and laden with fruit, were now in decay, as well as the grotto, fountains, cabinets, and other curiosities in the house and abroad, it being now fallen to a child under age, and only kept by a servant or two from utter dilapidation. The estate and park about it also in decay.

---

[1] *Ante*, p. 122.

[2] There is a print of this very beautiful monument in Lysons' *Environs of London*, article Croydon, vol. i. p. 193. In the same volume, p. 52, &c., will be found also an ample account of the family of Carew, named in the succeeding entry, of the house as it now is, with a portrait of Sir Richard Carew, views of the church, monuments, &c.

[3] Oranges were eaten in this kingdom much earlier than the time of King James I.

23rd September. I went to visit Mr. Pepys at Clapham, where he has a very noble and wonderfully well-furnished house, especially with Indian and Chinese curiosities. The offices and gardens well accommodated for pleasure and retirement.

31st October. My birthday, now completed the 80th year of my age. I with my soul render thanks to God, who, of His infinite mercy, not only brought me out of many troubles, but this year restored me to health, after an ague and other infirmities of so great an age, my sight, hearing, and other senses and faculties tolerable, which I implore Him to continue, with the pardon of my sins past, and grace to acknowledge by my improvement of His goodness the ensuing year, if it be His pleasure to protract my life, that I may be the better prepared for my last day, through the infinite merits of my blessed Saviour, the Lord Jesus, Amen!

5th November. Came the news of my dear grandson (the only male of my family now remaining) being fallen ill of the small-pox at Oxford, which after the dire effects of it in my family exceedingly afflicted me; but so it pleased my most merciful God that being let blood at his first complaint, and by the extraordinary care of Dr. Mander, (Head of the college and now Vice-Chancellor) who caused him to be brought and lodged in his own bed and bed-chamber, with the advice of his physician and care of his tutor, there were all fair hopes of his recovery, to our infinite comfort. We had a letter every day either from the Vice-Chancellor himself, or his tutor.

17th. Assurance of his recovery by a letter from himself.

There was a change of great officers at Court. Lord Godolphin returned to his former station of first Commissioner of the Treasury; Sir Charles Hedges Secretary of State.

30th November. At the Royal Society, Lord Somers, the late Chancellor, was continued President.

8th December. Great alterations of officers at Court, and elsewhere—Lord Chief Justice Treby died; he was a learned man in his profession, of which we have now few, never fewer; the Chancery requiring so little skill in deep law-learning, if the practiser can talk eloquently in that Court;

so that probably few care to study the law to any purpose.
—Lord Marlborough Master of the Ordnance, in place of
Lord Romney made Groom of the Stole. The Earl of
Rochester goes Lord Lieutenant to Ireland.

1700-1. *January*. I finished the sale of North Stoake in
Sussex to Robert Michell, Esq., appointed by my brother to
be sold for payment of portions to my nieces, and other in-
cumbrances on the estate.

4th. An exceeding deep snow, and melted away as suddenly.

19th. Severe frost, and such a tempest as threw down
many chimneys, and did great spoil at sea, and blew down
above twenty trees of mine at Wotton.

9th February. The old Speaker laid aside,[1] and Mr. Harley,[2] an able gentleman, chosen. Our countryman, Sir
Richard Onslow, had a party for him.

27th. By an order of the House of Commons, I laid before the Speaker the state of what had been received and
paid towards the building of Greenwich Hospital.[3]

Mr. Wye, Rector of Wotton, died, a very worthy good
man. I gave it to Dr. Bohun, a learned person and excellent preacher, who had been my son's tutor, and lived long
in my family.

18th March. I let Sayes Court to Lord Carmarthen, son
to the Duke of Leeds.—*28th*. I went to the funeral of my

---

[1] Sir Thomas Lyttelton, Bart.

[2] Robert Harley, Speaker in three Parliaments in the reign of Queen
Anne, Secretary of State, Lord High Treasurer; attempted to be
stabbed by Guiscard, a Frenchman, under examination before the Lords
of the Privy Council. Afterwards created Earl of Oxford and Morti-
mer; impeached upon the succession of the House of Hanover; died
1724.

[3] JOHN EVELYN, Esq. Dr. to GREENWICH HOSPITAL.

Received in the year		£	s.	d.
1696	. . . .	3,416	0	0
1697	. . . .	6,836	16	3
1698	. . . .	14,967	8	4
1699	. . . .	14,024	13	4
1700	. . . .	19,241	1	3
1701, June 16	. . . .	10,834	2	3
		69,320	1	5

Per Contra,

sister Draper,[1] who was buried at Edmonton in great state. Dr. Davenant displeased the clergy now met in Convocation by a passage in his book, p. 40.[2]

April. A Dutch boy of about eight or nine years old was carried about by his parents to show, who had about the iris of one eye, the letters of *Deus meus,* and of the other *Elohim,* in the Hebrew character. How this was done by artifice none could imagine; his parents affirming that he was so born. It did not prejudice his sight, and he seemed to be a lively playing boy. Everybody went to see him; physicians and philosophers examined it with great accuracy, some considered it as artificial, others as almost supernatural.

Per Contra, Creditor.	£	s.	d.
By the Accompt in			
1696	5,915	18	7
1697	8,971	10	4
1698	11,585	15	1
1699	19,614	9	8
1700	18,013	8	5
1701	8,000	0	0
Remain in Cash	219	1	4
	69,320	3	5
	69,320	3	5

Remain in Lottery Tickets } £11,434
to be paid in ten years . }
More in Malt Tickets . 1,000
69,320 ————
12,434

In all 81,754
Besides His Majesty 6,000, and Subscriptions.

[1] Mother of Evelyn's son-in-law.

[2] Charles Davenant, LL.D (son of Sir William). The book was, *Essays upon the Balance of Power,* and the objectionable passage was that in which he says that many of those lately in power have used their utmost endeavours to discountenance all revealed religion. "Are not many of us able to point to several persons, whom nothing has recommended to places of the highest trust, and often to rich benefices and dignities, but the open enmity which they have, almost from their cradles, professed to the Divinity of Christ?" The Convocation on reading the book, ordered papers to be fixed on several doors in Westminster Abbey, inviting the author, whoever he be, or any one of the man [?], to point out such persons, that they may be proceeded against.

4th April. The Duke of Norfold died of an apoplexy, and Mr. Thomas Howard of complicated disease since his being cut for the stone ; he was one of the Tellers of the Exchequer. Mr. How made a Baron.

May. Some Kentish men delivering a petition to the House of Commons, were imprisoned.[1]

A great dearth, no considerable rain having fallen for some months.

17th. Very plentiful showers, the wind coming west and south.—The Bishops and Convocation at difference concerning the right of calling the assembly and dissolving. Atterbury[2] and Dr Wake[3] writing one against the other.

20th June. The Commons demanded a conference with the Lords on the trial of Lord Somers, which the Lords refused, and proceeding on the trial, the Commons would not attend, and he was acquitted.[4]

22nd. I went to congratulate the arrival of that worthy and excellent person my Lord Galway, newly come out of Ireland, where he had behaved himself so honestly, and to the exceeding satisfaction of the people ; but he was removed thence for being a Frenchman,[5] though they had not a more worthy, valiant, discreet, and trusty person in the two kingdoms, on whom they could have relied for his conduct and fitness. He was one who had deeply suffered, as well as the Marquis his father, for being Protestants.[6]

July. My Lord Treasurer made my grandson one of the Commissioners of the prizes, salary £500 per annum.

8th. My grandson went to Sir Simon Harcourt, the Soli-

---

[1] Justinian Champneys, Thomas Culpepper, William Culpepper, William Hamilton, and David Polhill, gentlemen of considerable property and family in the county. There is a very good print of them in five ovals on one plate, engraved by R. White, in 1701. They desired the Parliament to mind the public more, and their private heats less. They were confined till the prorogation, and were much visited. Burnet gives an account of them.

[2] Afterwards Bishop of Rochester.

[3] Afterwards Archbishop of Canterbury.   [4] *Ante*, p. 372.

[5] Henry Rouvigné, Earl of Galway, in Ireland, son of the Marquis, who was Ambassador from France to Charles II. He was created a Peer by King William for his gallantry at the battle of the Boyne, where his brother also fought and was killed. He commanded afterwards both in Italy and Spain, where the fatal battle of Almanza put an end to his military glory. There is a mezzotinto portrait of him by Simon.

[6] *Ante*, p. 276.

eitor-General, to Windsor, to wait on my Lord Treasurer. There had been for some time a proposal of marrying my grandson to a daughter of Mrs. Boscawen, sister of my Lord Treasurer, which was now far advanced.

14th July. I subscribed towards re-building Oakwood Chapel,[1] now, after 200 years, almost fallen down.

August. The weather changed from heat not much less than in Italy or Spain for some few days, to wet, dripping, and cold, with intermissions of fair.

2nd September. I went to Kensington, and saw the house, plantations, and gardens, the work of Mr. Wise,[2] who was there to receive me.

The death of King James happening on the 15th of this month, N. S., after two or three days' indisposition, put an end to that unhappy Prince's troubles, after a short and unprosperous reign, indiscreetly attempting to bring in Popery, and make himself absolute, in imitation of the French, hurried on by the impatience of the Jesuits ; which the nation would not endure.

Died the Earl of Bath, whose contest with Lord Montague about the Duke of Albemarle's estate, claiming under a will supposed to have been forged, is said to have been worth £10,000 to the lawyers. His eldest son shot himself a few days after his father's death; for what cause is not clear. He was a most hopeful young man, and had behaved so bravely against the Turks at the siege of Vienna, that the Emperor made him a Count of the Empire.—It was falsely reported that Sir Edward Seymour was dead, a great man ; he had often been Speaker, Treasurer of the Navy, and in many other lucrative offices. He was of a hasty spirit, not at all sincere, but head of the party at any time prevailing in Parliament.

29th. I kept my first courts in Surrey, which took up the whole week. My steward was Mr. Hervey,[3] a Counsellor, Justice of Peace, and Member of Parliament, and my neighbour. I gave him six guineas, which was a guinea a-day, and to Mr. Martin, his clerk, three guineas.

---

[1] In the lower part of the parish of Wotton.
[2] Mr. Wise was the great gardener of Brompton Park, *ante*, p. 341. See Evelyn's " Miscellaneous Writings," pp. 714, 715.
[3] Of Betchworth.

31*st October.* I was this day 81 complete, in tolerable health, considering my great age.

December. Great contentions about elections. I gave my vote and interest to Sir R. Onslow and Mr. Weston.[1]

27*th.* My grandson quitted Oxford.

1701-2. 21*st January.* At the Royal Society there was read and approved the delineation and description of my Tables of Veins and Arteries,[2] by Mr. Cooper, the chirurgeon, in order to their being engraved.

8*th March.* The King had a fall from his horse, and broke his collar-bone, and having been much indisposed before, and agueish, with a long cough and other weakness, died this Sunday morning, about four o'clock.

I carried my accounts of Greenwich Hospital to the Committee.

12*th April.* My brother-in-law, Glanville, departed this life this morning after a long languishing illness, leaving a son by my sister, and two grand-daughters.[3] Our relation and friendship had been long and great. He was a man of excellent parts. He died in the 84th year of his age, and willed his body to be wrapped in lead and carried down to Greenwich, put on board a ship, and buried in the sea, between Dover and Calais, about the Goodwin sands; which was done on the Tuesday, or Wednesday after. This occasioned much discourse, he having no relation at all to the sea. He was a gentleman of an ancient family in Devonshire, and married my sister Jane. By his prudent parsimony he much improved his fortune. He had a place in the Alienation-Office, and might have been an extraordinary man, had he cultivated his parts.

[1] Of Ockham; but Mr. Wessell of Bansted (a merchant) carried it against Mr. Weston.

[2] *Ante,* vol. i. p. 224, 258, 296 ; ii. p. 34.

[3] One of these daughters became heiress of the family, and married William Evelyn of St. Cleer, in Kent, son of George Evelyn, of Nutfield. He assumed the name of Glanville; but there being only daughters by this marriage, he had two sons by a second wife, and they resumed the name of Evelyn. The first of those sons left a son who died unmarried before he came of age, and a daughter who married Colonel Hume, who has taken the name of Evelyn, but has no child ; the second son of Mr. Glanville Evelyn married Lady Jane Leslie, who became Countess of Rothes, in her own right, and left a son, George William, who became Earl of Rothes in right of his mother, and died in 1817, leaving no issue male.

My steward at Wotton gave a very honest account of what he had laid out on repairs, amounting to 1900*l.*

3rd May. The Report of the Committee sent to examine the state of Greenwich Hospital was delivered to the House of Commons, much to their satisfaction.—Lord Godolphin made Lord High Treasurer.

Being elected a member of the Society lately incorporated for the Propagation of the Gospel in Foreign Parts, I subscribed 10*l.* per annum towards the carrying it on. We agreed that every missioner, besides the 20*l.* to set him forth, should have 50*l.* per annum out of the stock of the Corporation, till his settlement was worth to him 100*l.* per annum. We sent a young divine to New York.

22nd June. I dined at the Archbishop's with the new-made Bishop of Carlisle, Dr. Nicolson, my worthy and learned correspondent.

27th. I went to Wotton with my family for the rest of the summer, and my son-in-law, Draper, with his family, came to stay with us, his house at Addiscombe being new-building, so that my family was above thirty.—Most of the new Parliament were chosen of Church of England principles, against the peevish party. The Queen was magnificently entertained at Oxford and all the towns she passed through on her way to Bath.

31st October. Arrived now to the 82nd year of my age, having read over all that passed since this day twelvemonth in these notes, I render solemn thanks to the Lord, imploring the pardon of my past sins, and the assistance of His grace; making new resolutions, and imploring that He will continue His assistance, and prepare me for my blessed Saviour's coming, that I may obtain a comfortable departure, after so long a term as has been hitherto indulged me. I find by many infirmities this year (especially nephritic pains) that I much decline; and yet of His infinite mercy retain my intellects and senses in great measure above most of my age. I have this year repaired much of the mansion-house and several tenants' houses, and paid some of my debts and engagements. My wife, children, and family in health: for all which I most sincerely beseech Almighty God to accept of these my acknowledgments, and that if it be His holy will to continue me yet longer, it may be to the praise of His infinite grace, and salvation of my soul. Amen!

8th November. My kinsman, John Evelyn, of Nutfield, a young and very hopeful gentleman, and Member of Parliament,[1] after having come to Wotton to see me, about fifteen days past, went to London and there died of the small-pox. He left a brother, a commander in the army in Holland, to inherit a fair estate.

Our affairs in so prosperous a condition both by sea and land, that there has not been so great an union in Parliament, Court, and people, in memory of man, which God in mercy make us thankful for, and continue! The Bishop of Exeter preached before the Queen and both Houses of Parliament at St. Paul's; they were wonderfully huzzaed in their passage, and splendidly entertained in the city.

December. The expectation now is, what treasure will be found on breaking bulk of the galleon brought from Vigo by Sir George Rooke, which being made up in an extraordinary manner in the hold, was not begun to be opened till the 5th of this month, before two of the Privy Council, two of the chief magistrates of the city, and the Lord Treasurer.

After the excess of honour conferred by the Queen on the Earl of Marlborough, by making him a Knight of the Garter and a Duke, for the success of but one campaign, that he should desire £5000 a-year to be settled on him by Parliament out of the Post-office, was thought a bold and unadvised request, as he had, besides his own considerable estate, above £30,000 a-year in places and employments, with £50,000 at interest. He had married one daughter to the son of my Lord Treasurer Godolphin, another to the Earl of Sunderland, and a third to the Earl of Bridgewater. He is a very handsome person, well-spoken and affable, and supports his want of acquired knowledge by keeping good company.

1702-3. News of Vice-Admiral Benbow's conflict with the French fleet in the West Indies, in which he gallantly behaved himself, and was wounded, and would have had extraordinary success, had not four of his men-of-war stood spectators without coming to his assistance; for this, two of their commanders were tried by a Council of War, and

---

[1] For Blechingley, in Surrey.

executed;¹ a third was condemned to perpetual imprisonment, loss of pay, and incapacity to serve in future. The fourth died.

Sir Richard Onslow and Mr. Oglethorpe (son of the late Sir Theo. O.) fought on occasion of some words which passed at a Committee of the House. Mr. Oglethorpe was disarmed.—The Bill against occasional Conformity was lost by one vote.—Corn and provisions so cheap that the farmers are unable to pay their rents.

February. A famous cause at the King's Bench between Mr. Fenwick and his wife,² which went for him with a great estate. The Duke of Marlborough lost his only son at Cambridge by the small-pox.—A great earthquake at Rome, &c. —A famous young woman, an Italian, was hired by our comedians to sing on the stage, during so many plays, for which they gave her £500; which part by her voice alone at the end of three scenes she performed with such modesty and grace, and above all with such skill, that there was never any who did anything comparable with their voices She was to go home to the Court of the King of Prussia, and I believe carried with her out of this vain nation above £1000, everybody coveting to hear her at their private houses.

. *26th May.* This day died Mr. Samuel Pepys, a very worthy, industrious and curious person, none in England exceeding him in knowledge of the navy, in which he had passed through all the most considerable offices, Clerk of the Acts and Secretary of the Admiralty, all which he performed with great integrity. When King James II. went out of England, he laid down his office, and would serve no more; but withdrawing himself from all public affairs, he lived at Clapham with his partner, Mr. Hewer, formerly

The Captains Kirby and Wade, having been tried and condemned to die by a Court-Martial held on them in the West Indies, were sent home in the "Bristol;" and, on its arrival at Portsmouth, were both shot on board, not being suffered to land on English ground.

² She was daughter and heir of Sir Adam Brown, of Betchworth Castle, in Dorking, and married Mr. Fenwick. This suit probably related to a settlement which she had consented to make, by which the estate was limited to them and their issue, and the heir of the survivor. They had one son, who died without issue, and she survived her husband, thereby becoming entitled to dispose of it.

his clerk, in a very noble house and sweet place, where he enjoyed the fruit of his labours in great prosperity. He was universally beloved, hospitable, generous, learned in many things, skilled in music, a very great cherisher of learned men of whom he had the conversation. His library[1] and collection of other curiosities were of the most considerable, the models of ships especially. Besides what he published of an account of the navy, as he found and left it, he had for divers years under his hand the History of the Navy, or *Navalia*, as he called it; but how far advanced, and what will follow of his, is left, I suppose, to his sister's son, Mr. Jackson, a young gentleman, whom Mr. Pepys had educated in all sorts of useful learning, sending him to travel abroad, from whence he returned with extraordinary accomplishments, and worthy to be heir. Mr. Pepys had been for near forty years so much my particular friend, that Mr. Jackson sent me complete mourning, desiring me to be one to hold up the pall at his magnificent obsequies; but my indisposition hindered me from doing him this last office.

13th *June*. Rains have been great and continual, and now, near midsummer, cold and wet.

11th *July*. I went to Addiscombe, sixteen miles from Wotton, to see my son-in-law's new house, the outside, to the coving, being such excellent brickwork, based with Portland stone, with the pilasters, windows, and within, that I pronounced it in all the points of good and solid architecture to be one of the very best gentlemen's houses in Surrey, when finished. I returned to Wotton in the evening, though weary.

25th. The last week in this month an uncommon long-continued rain, and the Sunday following, thunder and lightning.

12th *August*. The new Commission for Greenwich Hospital was sealed and opened, at which my son-in-law, Draper, was present, to whom I resigned my office of Treasurer. From August 1696, there had been expended in building £89,364 14s. 8d.

---

[1] His valuable library he gave to Magdalen College, Cambridge, together with his fine collection of prints, where they now remain in a handsome room, and are to this day among the more interesting of the treasures of that University.

31st October. This day, being eighty-three years of age, upon examining what concerned me, more particularly the past year, with the great mercies of God preserving me, and in the same measure making my infirmities tolerable, I gave God most hearty and humble thanks, beseeching Him to confirm to me the pardon of my sins past, and to prepare me for a better life by the virtue of His grace and mercy, for the sake of my blessed Saviour.

21st November. The wet and uncomfortable weather staying us from church this morning, our Doctor officiated in my family; at which were present above twenty domestics. He made an excellent discourse on 1 Cor. xv., v. 55, 56, of the vanity of this world and uncertainty of life, and the inexpressible happiness and satisfaction of a holy life, with pertinent inferences to prepare us for death and a future state. I gave him thanks, and told him I took it kindly as my funeral sermon.

26-7th. The effects of the hurricane and tempest of wind, rain, and lightning, through all the nation, especially London, were very dismal. Many houses demolished, and people killed. As to my own losses, the subversion of woods and timber, both ornamental and valuable, through my whole estate, and about my house the woods crowning the garden-mount, and growing along the park-meadow, the damage to my own dwelling, farms, and outhouses, is almost tragical, not to be paralleled with any thing happening in our age. I am not able to describe it; but submit to the pleasure of Almighty God.

7th December. I removed to Dover Street, where I found all well; but houses, trees, garden, &c. at Sayes Court, suffered very much.

31st. I made up my accounts, paid wages, gave rewards and new-year's gifts, according to custom.

1703-4. January. The King of Spain[1] landing at Portsmouth, came to Windsor, where he was magnificently entertained by the Queen, and behaved himself so nobly, that everybody was taken with his graceful deportment. After two days, having presented the great ladies, and others, with

---

[1] Charles the Third, afterwards Emperor of Germany, by the title of Charles the Sixth.

very valuable jewels, he went back to Portsmouth, and immediately embarked for Spain.

16th January. The Lord Treasurer gave my grandson the office of Treasurer of the Stamp Duties, with a salary of £300 a-year.

30th. The fast on the martyrdom of King Charles I. was observed with more than usual solemnity.

May. Dr. Bathurst, President of Trinity College, Oxford, now died,[1] I think the oldest acquaintance now left me in the world. He was eighty-six years of age, stark blind, deaf, and memory lost, after having been a person of admirable parts and learning. This is a serious alarm to me. God grant that I may profit by it! He built a very handsome chapel to the college, and his own tomb. He gave a legacy of money, and the third part of his library, to his nephew, Dr. Bohun, who went hence to his funeral.

7th September. This day was celebrated the thanksgiving for the late great victory,[2] with the utmost pomp and splendour by the Queen, Court, great Officers, Lord Mayor, Sheriffs, Companies, &c. The streets were scaffolded from Temple Bar, where the Lord Mayor presented her Majesty with the sword, which she returned. Every Company was ranged under its banners, the City Militia without the rails, which were all hung with cloth suitable to the colour of the banner. The Lord Mayor, Sheriffs, and Aldermen, were in their scarlet robes, with caparisoned horses; the Knight Marshal on horseback; the Foot-Guards; the Queen in a rich coach with eight horses, none with her but the Duchess of Marlborough in a very plain garment, the Queen full of jewels. Music and trumpets at every City Company. The great officers of the Crown, Nobility, and Bishops, all in coaches with six horses, besides innumerable servants, went to St. Paul's, where the Dean preached. After this, the Queen went back in the same order to St. James's. The City Companies feasted all the Nobility and Bishops, and illuminated at night. Music for the church and anthems composed by the best masters.

---

[1] There is a very good Life of him, with his portrait prefixed, by Thomas Warton, Fellow of Trinity College, and Poetry Professor at Oxford.

[2] Over the French and Bavarians, at Blenheim, 13th August, 1704.

The day before was wet and stormy, but this was one of the most serene and calm days that had been all the year.

October. The year has been very plentiful.

31st. Being my birthday and the 84th year of my life, after particular reflections on my concerns and passages of the year, I set some considerable time of this day apart, to recollect and examine my state and condition, giving God thanks, and acknowledging His infinite mercies to me and mine, begging His blessing, and imploring His protection for the year following.

December. Lord Clarendon presented me with the three volumes of his father's History of the Rebellion.

My Lord of Canterbury wrote to me for suffrage for Mr. Clarke's continuance this year in the Boyle Lecture, which I willingly gave for his excellent performance of this year.

9th February. I went to wait on my Lord Treasurer, where was the victorious Duke of Marlborough, who came to me and took me by the hand with extraordinary familiarity and civility, as formerly he was used to do, without any alteration of his good-nature. He had a most rich George in a sardonyx set with diamonds of very great value; for the rest, very plain. I had not seen him for some years, and believed he might have forgotten me.

21st. Remarkable fine weather. Agues and small-pox much in every place.

11th March. An exceeding dry season.—Great loss by fire, burning the outhouses and famous stable of the Earl of Nottingham, at Burleigh [Rutlandshire], full of rich goods and furniture, by the carelessness of a servant. A little before, the same happened at Lord Pembroke's, at Wilton. The old Countess of Northumberland, Dowager of Algernon Percy, Admiral of the Fleet to King Charles I., died in the 83rd year of her age. She was sister to the Earl of Suffolk, and left a great estate, her jointure to descend to the Duke of Somerset.[1]

May. The Bailiff of Westminster hanged himself. He had an ill report.

On the death of the Emperor, there was no mourning

[1] This Duke had married Elizabeth Percy, widow of Lord Cole, only daughter and heir to Joceline Percy, the eleventh and last Earl of Northumberland.

worn at Court, because there was none at the Imperial Court on the death of King William.

18*th May.* I went to see Sir John Chardine,[1] at Turnham-Green, the gardens being very fine, and exceeding well planted with fruit.

20*th.* Most extravagant expense to debauch and corrupt votes for Parliament members. I sent my grandson with his party of my freeholders to vote for Mr. Harvey, of Combe.[2]

1704-5. 4*th January.* I dined at Lambeth with the Archbishop of Dublin, Dr. King, a sharp ready man in politics, as well as very learned.

June. The season very dry and hot.—I went to see Dr. Dickinson[3] the famous chemist. We had long conversation about the philosopher's elixir, which he believed attainable, and had seen projection himself by one who went under the name of Mundanus, who sometimes came among the adepts, but was unknown as to his country, or abode; of this the Doctor has written a treatise in Latin, full of very astonishing relations. He is a very learned person, formerly a Fellow of St. John's College, Oxford,[4] in which city he practised physic, but has now altogether given it over, and lives retired, being very old and infirm, yet continuing chymistry.

I went to Greenwich Hospital, where they now began to take in wounded and worn-out seamen, who are exceeding well provided for. The buildings now going on are very magnificent.

October. Mr. Cowper[5] made Lord Keeper. Observing how uncertain great officers are of continuing long in their

[1] See p. 201.　　　[2] Sir Richard Onslow and Sir William Scawen were the other candidates, and succeeded. Harvey was a violent Tory.

[3] Edmund Dickinson, of Merton College, Oxford, took the degree of Bachelor of Arts, 22nd June, 1647. He was living in Westminster, in 1692, in good repute for his practice in the faculty of physic. He published several things. Wood's *Fasti Oxon.*, p. 741.

[4] He was afterwards a Fellow of Merton. He died in 1707, aged 84. Campbell, in his edition of the *Biog. Brit.*, speaks very highly of him; but Kippis, in the new edition of that Work, differs much from the Doctor's opinions, though he allows him to have been a very learned man. Evelyn must have mistaken Dr. Dickinson as to his not knowing who Mundanus was, for in 1686 the Doctor printed a letter to him with his answer from Paris; and in the latter, Mundanus says he made two projections in his presence *Biog. Brit.* art. Dickinson.

[5] William Cowper, created a Baron in 1706, and Lord Chancellor afterwards Viscount Fordwich and Earl Cowper, by George the First.

places, he would not accept it, unless £2000 a-year were given him in reversion when he was put out, in considera-tion of his loss of practice. His predecessors, how little time soever they had the seal, usually got £100,000 and made themselves Barons.—A new Secretary of State.[1]— Lord Abington, Lieutenant of the Tower, displaced, and General Churchill, brother to the Duke of Marlborough, put in. An indication of great unsteadiness somewhere, but thus the crafty Whig party (as called) begin to change the face of the Court, in opposition to the High Church-men, which was another distinction of a party from the Low Churchmen. The Parliament chose one Mr. Smith, Speaker.[2] There had never been so great an assembly of members on the first day of sitting, being more than 450. The votes both of the old, as well as the new, fell to those called Low Churchmen, contrary to all expectation.

31st *October*. I am this day arrived to the 85th year of my age. Lord teach me so to number my days to come, that I may apply them to wisdom !

1705-6. 1st *January*. Making up my accounts for the past year, paid bills, wages, and new-year's-gifts, according to custom. Though much indisposed and in so advanced a stage, I went to our chapel [in London] to give God public thanks, beseeching Almighty God to assist me and my family the ensuing year, if He should yet continue my pilgrimage here, and bring me at last to a better life with Him in his heavenly kingdom. Divers of our friends and relations dined with us this day.

27th. My indisposition increasing, I was exceeding ill this whole week.

3rd *February*. Notes of the sermons at the chapel in the morning and afternoon, written with his own hand, conclude this Diary.

₊ Mr. Evelyn died on the 27th of this month.

[1] Charles, Earl of Sunderland.
[2] John Smith, Esq., Member for Andover.

END OF THE DIARY.

APPENDIX.

ILLUSTRATIONS.

I.

(See p. 244.)

FEB. 1687-8, there was printed what was called "A true and perfect narrativ; of the strange and unexpected finding the Crucifix and Gold-chain of that pious Prince, St. Edward the King and Confessor, which was found after six hundred and thirty years' interment, and presented to his most Sacred Majesty, King James the Second. By Charles Tay-lour, Gent. London, printed by J. B., and are to be sold by Randal Taylor, near Stationers' Hall, 1688."

He says, that "on St. Barnaby's Day (11 June), 1685, between 11 and 12 at noon, he went with two friends to see the coffin of Edward the Confessor, having heard that it was broke; fetched a ladder, looked on the coffin and found a hole as reported, put his hand into the hole, and turning the bones which he felt there, drew from under the shoulder-bones a crucifix richly adorned and enamelled, and a golden chain of twenty-four inches long to which it was fixed; showed them to his two friends; was afraid to take them away, till he had acquainted the Dean; put them into the coffin again. But the Dean not being to be spoke with then, and fearing this treasure might be taken by some other, he went two or three hours afterward to one of the choir, acquainted him with what he had found, who accompanied him to the monument, from whence he again drew the crucifix and chain; his friend advised him to keep them, until he could show them to the Dean (the Bishop of Ro-chester): kept them three weeks before he could speak to the Bishop; went to the Archbishop of York, and showed them; next morning, the Archbishop of York carried him to the Archbishop of Canterbury at Lambeth, and showed them. After this, he procured an exact drawing to be made of them; showed them to Sir William Dugdale.—6th July, the Archbishop of Canterbury told the Bishop of Rochester, who, about four that afternoon, sent for him, and took him to Whitehall, that he might present them to the King; which he did accordingly. The King ordered a new strong wooden coffin to be made to inclose the broken one. The links of the chain oblong, and curiously wrought; the upper part joined by a locket, composed of a large round knob of gold, massy, in circumference as big as a milled shilling, half an inch thick ; round this went a wire and half a dozen little beads, hanging loose, running to and again on the same, all of pure gold, finely wrought; on each side of the locket were set two large square stones (supposed to be rubies). From each side of this locket, fixed to two rings of gold, the chain descends, and, meeting below, passes through a square piece of gold, of a convenient bigness, made hollow for the same purpose. This gold, wrought into several angles, was painted with divers colours, resembling gems or precious stones, to which the crucifix was joined, yet to be taken off by help of a screw. The form of the cross nearest that of an humettée flory (among the heralds), or rather the botany [botonée]; yet the pieces not of equal length, the perpendicular beam being near one-fourth part longer than the traverse, as being four inches to the extremity, whilst the other scarce exceeds three; yet all neatly turned at the ends, and the botons enamelled with figures thereon. The cross of the same gold as the chain, but exceeds it by its rich enamel, having on one side the picture of our Saviour Christ in his passion wrought thereon, and an eye from above casting a kind of beam on him ; on the reverse, picture of a Benedictine monk in his habit, and on each side of him these capital Roman letters :—

On the right,
(A)
Z A X
A

And on the left,
P
A C
H

This cross is hollow, to be opened by two little screws towards the top, wherein it is presumed some relic might have been conserved. William I. commanded the coffin to be enshrined, and the shrine covered with plates of gold and silver, adorned with pearls and precious stones. About one hundred and thirty-six years after, the Abbot resolved to inspect the body, said to be incorruptible, and, on opening, found it to be so, being perfect, the limbs flexible : the face covered; Gundolph, Bishop of Rochester, withdrew the cover, but, with great reverence, covered it again, changing the former vestments, and putting on others of equal price. In 1163, Thomas à Becket procured a canonisation of the King, and in the ceremony the Abbot opened the coffin, found the body lying in rich vestments of cloth of gold, having on his feet buskins of purple, and shoes of great price; the body uncorrupted; removed the whole body from the stone repository to another of wood, some assisting at the head, others at the arms and legs ; they lifted it gently, and laid the corpse first on tapestry spread on the floor, and then wrapping the same in silken cloths of great value, they put it into the wooden chest, *with all those things that were found in the former*, except the gold ring which was on the King's finger, which the Abbot, *out of devotion, retained*, and ordered it to be kept in the Treasury of the Abbey.

" In 1226, King Henry III. again removed the coffin to a chapel built for the purpose."

II.

EVELYN'S PUBLICATIONS.

THE SUBJOINED LIST IS FROM A LETTER OF EVELYN'S TO DR. PLOT, DATED 16 MARCH, 1682-3.

Translations.

1. Of Liberty and Servitude, Lond. 1644, 12mo.
2. The French Gardener and English Vineyard, 1658, 12mo. 3rd edit.
3. An Essay on the first Book of Lucretius, 1656, 8vo.
4. Gaspar Naudæus, Instructions concerning Libraries, 1661, 8vo.
5. A Parallel of the Ancient Architecture with the Modern, with a treatise on Statues, &c. 1664, folio.
6. An Idea of the perfection of Painting, 1668, 8vo.
7. The Mystery of Jesuitism, 2 parts, 8vo.
8. St. Chrysostom's Golden Book for the Education of Children, out of the Greek, 1659, 12mo.

Original Works.

1. An Apology for the Royal Party, 1659, 4to.   Three Editions.
2. Panegyric at his Majesty's Coronation, 1661, folio.
3. Fumifugium, or a prophetic Invective against the Fire and Smoke of London, with its Remedies, 1661, 4to.
4. Sculptura, or the History of the Art of Chalcography, 1662, 8vo.
5. Public Employment, and an active life preferred to Solitude, 1667, 8vo.
6. History of the Three late Impostors, 1669, 8vo.
7. Kalendarium Hortense, 1664, 1679, 8vo.   Six Editions.
8. Sylva, 1679, folio.   Three Editions.
9. Terra, 1679.   Two Editions.
10. Tyrannus, or the Mode, 8vo.
11. The Dignity of Man, &c., not printed, nearly ready.
12. Elysium Britannicum, not printed, nearly ready

Prepared for the Press.

A Discourse of Medals.—Of Manuscripts.—Of Stones.—Of Reason in Brute Animals.[1]

In a letter to Dr. BEALE, 11 July, 1679, Evelyn says, "I have sometimes thought of publishing a Treatise of *Acetaria,* which (though but one of the chapters of *Elysium Britannicum*) would make a competent

---

[1] Of the four Treatises here enumerated, the Discourse on Medals only has been printed.   There is at Wotton a copy of that on Manuscripts in thirteen leaves, 4to., which seems to contain all he intended ou this subject.   There is also a chapter of an essay, entitled, "De Baculis," which from the proem seems to have been intended as jocular, but it begins with great gravity.

volume, accompanied with other necessaries, according to my manner; but whilst I as often think of performing my so long-since promised (more universal) Hortulan work, I know not how to take that chapter out, and single it for the press, without some blemish to the rest. When again I consider into what an ocean I am plunged, how much I have written and collected for above these twenty years upon this fruitful and inexhaustible subject (I mean Horticulture) not yet fully digested to my mind, and what insuperable pains it will require to insert the (daily increasing) particulars into what I have already in some measure prepared, and which must of necessity be done by my own hand, I am almost out of hope, that I shall ever have strength and leisure to bring it to maturity, having for the last ten years of my life been in perpetual motion, and hardly two months in a year at my own habitation, or con versant with my family.

"You know what my charge and care has been during the late un happy war with the Hollanders; and what it has cost me as to avoca- tions, and for the procuring money, and attending the Lord Treasurer, &c., to discharge the quarters of many thousands.

"Since that, I have upon me no fewer than three executorships, besides other domestic concerns, either of them enough to distract a more steady and composed genius than is mine.

"Superadd to these the public confusions in church and kingdom (never to be sufficiently deplored), and which cannot but most sensibly touch every sober and honest man.

"In the midst of these disturbances, who but Dr. Beale (that stands upon the tower, looks down unconcernedly on all those tempests) can think of gardens and fish-ponds, and the *delices* and ornaments of peace and tranquility? With no little conflict and force on my other business, I have yet at last, and as I was able, published a third edition of my 'Sylva,' and with such additions as occurred; and this in truth only to pacify the importunity of very many (besides the printer), who quite tired me with calling on me for it, and above all, threatening to reprint it with all its former defects, if I did not speedily prevent it. I am only vexed that it proving so popular as in so few years to pass so many impressions, and (as I hear) gratify the avaricious printer with some hundreds of pounds, there had not been some course taken in it for the benefit of our Society. It is apparent, that near £500 has been already gotten by it; but we are not yet economists.

"You know what pillars we have lost: Palmer,' Moray,[1] Chester,[2] Oldenburg,[3] &c.; and through what other discouragements we still labour; and therefore you will excuse the zeal and fervour of what I have added in my Epistle to the Reader, if at length it be possible to

[1] Dudley Palmer, Esq., born in 1602, and died in 1666, and Sir Ro- bert Moray, Knt., who died July 4, 1673, two of the first Council of the Royal Society.
[2] John Wilkins, D.D., Bishop of Chester He died Nov. 19, 1672.
[3] Secretary to the Royal Society who died in September, 1677.

raise up some generous soul to free us, or emerge out of our difficulties. In all events you will see where my inclinations are fixed, and that love is stronger than death; and secular affairs, which is the burial of all philosophical speculations and improvements: though they can never in the least diminish the great esteem I have of your friendship, and the infinite obligations I daily receive from your favours."

Of Books which he had designed to publish, we find various Memoranda in his letters, &c.

In a letter to Mr. BOYLE, 8 August, 1659, he says he had intended to write a *History of Trades*; but had given it up, from the great difficulty he found in the attempt.

In another, 23rd Nov., 1664, he says, "One Rhea [qu. Ray?] has published a very useful book concerning the Culture of Flowers; but it does nothing reach my long-since attempted design on that entire subject, with all its ornaments and circumstances, but God only knows when my opportunities will permit me to bring it to maturity."

In the Preface to the "Acetaria," published in 1669, he mentions a Work in which he had spent upwards of forty years, and his collections for which had in that time filled several thousand pages. The author of the "Biographia Britannica" believes that this was the work, part of which he had showed to his friends under the title of "Elysium Britannicum," but which in that Preface he calls "The Plan of a Royal Garden," &c.; and that his "Acetaria" and "Gardener's Kalendar" were parts of it. This is confirmed by the preceding letter to Dr. Beale.

Amongst the MSS. at Wotton there are parts of two volumes with the running title of "Elysium Britannicum," consisting of miscellaneous observations on a great variety of subjects, but nothing digested, except a printed sheet of the contents of the intended Work, as follows:

ELYSIUM BRITANNICUM

IN THREE BOOKS.

Præmissis præmittendis, &c.

BOOK I.

Chap. I. A Garden derived and defined, with its distinctions and sorts.—2. Of a Gardener, and how he is to be qualified.—3. Of the Principles and Elements in general.—4. Of the Fire.—5. Of the Air and Winds.—6. Of the Water.—7. Of the Earth.—8. Of the Celestial Influences, particularly the Sun, and Moon, and of the Climates.— 9. Of the Four Seasons.—10. Of the Mould and Soil of a Garden.— 11. Of Composts and Stercoration.—12. Of the Generation of Plants.

BOOK II.

Chap. 1. Of the Instruments belonging to a Gardener, and their several uses.—2. Of the situation of a Garden, with its extent.—3. Of fencing, enclosing, plotting, and disposing the Ground.—4. Of a Seminary, and of propagating Trees, Plants, and Flowers.—5. Of Knots, Parterres, Compartments, Borders, and Embossments.—6. Of Walks, Terraces, Carpets, and Alleys, Bowling-greens, Malls, their materials and proportions.—7. Of Groves, Labyrinths, Dædales, Cabinets, Cradles, Pavilions, Galleries, Close-walks, and other Relievos.—8. Of Transplanting.—9. Of Fountains, Cascades, Rivulets, Piscinas, and Waterworks.—10. Of Rocks, Grots, Cryptas, Mounts, Precipices, Porticos, Ventiducts.—11. Of Statues, Columns, Dials, Perspectives, Pots, Vases, and other ornaments.—12. Of Artificial Echos, Music, and Hydraulic motions.—13. Of Aviaries, Apiaries, Vivaries, Insects.—14. Of Orangeries, and Conservatories of rare Plants.—15. Of Verdures, Perennial-Greens, and perpetual Springs.—16. Of Coronary Gardens, Flowers, and rare Plants, how they are to be propagated, governed, and improved; together with a Catalogue of the choicest Trees, Shrubs, Plants and Flowers, and how the Gardener is to keep his Register.—17. Of the Philosophico-Medical Garden.—18. Of a Vineyard.—19. Of Watering, Pruning, Clipping, Rolling, Weeding, &c.—20. Of the Enemies and Infirmities to which a Garden is obnoxious, together with the remedies. —21. Of the Gardener's Almanack, or Kalendarium Hortense, directing what he is to do Monthly, and what Flowers are in prime.

Book III.

Chap. 1. Of Conserving, Properating, Retarding, Multiplying, Transmuting, and altering the Species, Forms and substantial qualities of Flowers, &c.—2. Of Chaplets, Festoons, Flower-pots, Nosegays, and Posies.—3. Of the Gardener's Elaboratory, and of distilling and extracting of Essences, Resuscitation of Plants, with other rare Experiments.—4. Of composing the Hortus Hyemalis, and making books of Natural Arid Plants and Flowers, with other curious ways of preserving them in their Natural.—5. Of planting of Flowers, Flowers enamelled in Silk, Wax, and other artificial representations of them.—6. Of Hortulane Entertainments, to show the riches, beauty, wonder, plenty, delight, and use of a Garden-Festival, &c.—7. Of the most famous Gardens in the World, Ancient and Modern.—8. The Description of a Villa.—The Corollary and Conclusion.

Amongst the MSS. at Wotton also, on a separate paper, are the following Memoranda in Evelyn's handwriting:

"Things I would write out fair and reform, if I had leisure:—

Londinum Redivivum, which I presented to the King three or four days after the Conflagration of that City, 1666.

Pedigree of the Evelyns.

The three remaining Meditations on Friday, Saturday, and Sunday, being the remaining course of Offices; to which belongs a Book of Recollection bound in leather.

A Rational Account of the True Religion, or an History of it. With a packet of Notes belonging to it.

Oeconomist to a Married Friend.

The Legend of the Pearl.

Some Letters of mine to Electra and to others in that packet.
The Life of Mrs. Godolphin.
A book of some Observations, Politica's, and Discourses of that kind.
Thyrsander, a Tragi-Comedy.
Dignity of Mankind.
My own Ephemeris or Diary.
Animadversions upon Spinosa.
Papers concerning Education.
Mathematical papers." [1]

Of the works by Mr. Evelyn actually published, the list now finally subjoined, comprising many which are included in the collection of Evelyn's *Miscellaneous Writings* edited by Mr. Upcott, will, it is believed, be found tolerably accurate.

1. Of Liberty and Servitude, 1649, 12mo.

2. A Character of England, as it was lately presented in a Letter to a Nobleman of France; with Reflections upon Gallus Castratus, 1651, 3rd edit. 1659.

3. The State of France. London, 1652, 8vo.

4. An Essay on the first Book of Lucretius de Rerum Naturâ, interpreted and made into English Verse, 1656, 8vo. The frontispiece designed by his lady, Mary Evelyn.

5. Dedicatory Epistles, &c., to "The French Gardener." London, 1658, 12mo.—The third edition, in 1672, was illustrated by plates.—In most of the editions is added "The English Vineyard Vindicated, by John Rose, Gardener to King Charles II."

6. The Golden Book of St. Chrysostom, concerning the Education of Children. London, 1659, 12mo.

7. An Apology for the Royal Party, written in a Letter to a person of the late Council of State: with a Touch at the pretended Plea of the Army. London, 1659, in two sheets, 4to. Three editions.

8. The late News from Brussels unmasked. London, 1660, 4to.

9. The manner of the Encounter between the French and Spanish Ambassadors at the landing of the Swedish Ambassador.

10. A Panegyrick at his Majesty King Charles's Coronation. London, 1661, folio.

11. Instructions concerning the erection of a Library. Written by Gabriel Naudé, published in English with some improvements by John Evelyn, Esq. London, 1661, 8vo.

12. Fumifugium; or the Inconveniences of the Air and Smoke of

---

[1] Of the "things" mentioned in this list as reserved for attention and revision in Evelyn's leisure, the Diary and Letters and Life of Mrs. Godolphin (see also p. 124 of this volume) have since been given to the world; and the work entitled "A Rational Account of the True Religion, or an History of it," edited from the MSS. at Wotton, has more recently been published. It embodies the researches and reflections of Evelyn's life on the all-important subject to which it relates.

London dissipated. Together with some remedies humbly proposed by John Evelyn, Esq. London, 1661, 4to., in 5 sheets, addressed to the King and Parliament, and published by his Majesty's express Command.[1]

13. Tyrannus; or the Mode; in a Discourse of Sumptuary Laws, 1661, 8vo.

14. Sculptura; or the History and Art of Chalcography and Engraving in Copper and Mezzo-tinto. Lond. 1662, 8vo.

15. Sylva; or a Discourse of Forest-Trees. Lond. 1664, fol.; 2nd edition 1669; 3rd in 1697; 4th in 1733, also in folio.—Pomona is an Appendix; 3rd edition, 1679; 4th, 1706; 5th, 1729.—This learned work has since been several times republished by Dr. A. Hunter, an eminent physician in York, who has rendered it still more valuable by adding to it the observations of later writers.

16. Dedicatory Epistles, &c., to "Parallel of Ancient and Modern Architecture." London, 1664, folio. 4th edit. 1733, fol.; with the Elements of Architecture by Sir Hen. Wotton.

17. Ditto to "Μυστήριον τῆς 'Ανομίας;" another part of the Mystery of Jesuitism. Lond. 1664, 8vo. Two parts.

18. Kalendarium Hortense, Lond. 1664, 8vo.—The 2d and 3d edit. was in folio, bound with the Sylva and Pomona; also reprinted in octavo in 1699.

19. Public Employment and active life preferred to Solitude, in reply to Sir Geo. Mackenzie. Lond. 1667, 8vo.

20. History of the Three late famous Impostors. Lond. 1669, 8vo.

21. An Idea of the Perfection of Painting, translated from the French of Roland Freart. Lond. 1668, 8vo.

22. Navigation and Commerce, their Original and Progress. Lond. 1674, 8vo.

23. Terra; a Philosophical Discourse of Earth. Lond, 1675, fol.; and 8vo. 1676.

24. Mundus Muliebris. Lond. 1690, 4to.

25. Monsieur de la Quintinye's Treatise of Orange-Trees, and Complete Gardener, translated from the French. Lond. 1693, fol.

26. Advertisement to the Translation of the Compleat Gardener, by M. de la Quintinye, 1693.

27. Ditto to M. de la Quintinye's Directions concerning Melons.

28. Ditto to M. de la Quintinye's Directions concerning Orange-Trees.

29. Numismata: a Discourse on Medals. Lond. 1697, fol.

30. Acetaria: a Discourse on Salads. Lond. 1699, 8vo.

31. An Account of Architects and Architecture—a tract.

32. Letter to Viscount Brouncker, concerning a new Engine for Ploughing, &c. 1669-70.

33. Dedication to Renatus Rapinus of Gardens, 1673.

34. Letter to Mr. Aubrey, concerning Surrey Antiquities, 1670.

---

[1] Reprinted in 1772, in quarto, with an additional Preface.

35. Abstract of a Letter to the Royal Society concerning the damage done to his Gardens in the preceding Winter, 1684.
36. The Diary and Letters. 1818, 1825.
37. Miscellaneous Writings, collected and edited by Mr. Upcott.
38. Life of Mrs. Godolphin. 1849.

Evelyn had likewise etched, when he came to Paris from Italy, five several Prospects of Places which he had drawn on the spot between Rome and Naples, to which he prefixed also a frontispiece, intituled,

"Locorum aliquot insignium et celeberrimorum inter Romam et Neapolin jacentium, ὑποδειξεις et exemplaria.

"Domino Dom. Thomæ Hensheaw Anglo, omnium eximiarum et præclarissimarum artium cultori ac propugnatori maximo, et συνοψάμενῳ αὐτῷ (non propter operis pretium, sed ut singulare Amoris sui Testimonium exhibeat) primas has ἀδοκιμασίας aquâ forti excusas et insculptas, Jo. Evelynus Delineator D. D. C. Q."   *R. Hoare excud.*

I. Tres Tabernæ sive Appii Forum, celebre illud, in sacris Litteris. Act. 28.

II. Terracinæ, olim Anxuris, Promontorium.

III. Prospectus versùs Neapolin, à Monte Vesuvio.

IV., V. Montis Vesuvii Fauces: et Vorago, sive Barathrum internum.

He etched also a View of his own Seat at Wotton, then in the possession of his brother, George Evelyn; and Putney ad Ripam Tamesis —corrected on one impression, by himself, to Battersea.

END OF VOL. II.

LONDON: PRINTED BY WILLIAM CLOWES AND SONS, LIMITED, STAMFORD STREET AND CHARING CROSS.

, in
f Gla
of hi
scawi
ma:

.

———

r.   .

CATALOGUE OF
BOHN'S LIBRARIES.

729 *Volumes,* £159 2s. 6d.

The Publishers are now issuing the Libraries in a NEW AND MORE ATTRACTIVE STYLE OF BINDING. The original bindings endeared to many book-lovers by association will still be kept in stock, but henceforth all orders will be executed in the New binding, unless the contrary is expressly stated.

New Volumes of Standard Works in the various branches of Literature are constantly being added to this Series, which is already unsurpassed in respect to the number, variety, and cheapness of the Works contained in it. The Publishers beg to announce the following Volumes as recently issued or now in preparation:—

Cooper's Biographical Dictionary, containing Concise Notices of Eminent Persons of all ages and countries. In 2 volumes. Demy 8vo. 5s. each.
[Ready. See p. 19.]

Goethe's Reineke Fox, West-Eastern Divan and Achilleid. [Ready. See p. 5.]

North's Lives of the Norths. Edited by Rev. Dr. Jessopp. [In the press.]

Johnson's Lives of the Poets. Edited by Robina Napier. [In the press.]

Hooper's Waterloo. [Ready. See p. 5.]

The Works of Flavius Josephus. Whiston's Translation. Revised by Rev. A. R. Shilleto, M.A. With Topographical and Geographical Notes by Colonel Sir C. W. Wilson, K.C.B. 5 volumes. [See p. 6.]

Elze's Biography of Shakespeare. [Ready. See p. 8.]

Pascal's Thoughts. Translated by C. Kegan Paul. [Ready. See p. 7.]

Björnson's Arne and the Fisher Lassie. Translated by W. H. Low. [Ready. See p. 20.]

Racine's Plays. Translated by R. B. Boswell. [Vol. I. ready, see p. 7.]

Hoffmann's Works. Translated by Lieut.-Colonel Ewing. Vol. II. [In the press.]

Bohn's Handbooks of Games. New enlarged edition. In 2 vols. [See p. 21.]
Vol. I.—Table Games, by Major-General Drayson, R.A., R. F. Green, and 'Berkeley.'
II.—Card Games, by Dr, W. Pole, F.R.S., and 'Berkeley.'

Bohn's Handbooks of Athletic Sports. In 4 vols. [See p. 21.]
By Hon. and Rev. E. Lyttelton, H. W. Wilberforce, Julian Marshall, W. T. Linskill W. B. Woodgate, E. F. Knight, Martin Cobbett, Douglas Adams, Harry Vassall, C. W. Alcock, E. T. Sachs, H. H. Griffin, R. G. Allanson-Winn, Walter Armstrong, H. A. Colmore Dunn.

For recent Volumes in the SELECT LIBRARY, see p. 24.

BOHN'S LIBRARIES.

STANDARD LIBRARY.

331 *Vols. at 3s. 6d. each, excepting those marked otherwise.* (58l. 14s. 6d.)

ADDISON'S Works. Notes of Bishop Hurd. Short Memoir, Portrait, and 8 Plates of Medals. 6 vols.
This is the most complete edition of Addison's Works issued.

ALFIERI'S Tragedies. In English Verse. With Notes, Arguments, and Introduction, by E. A. Bowring, C.B. 2 vols.

AMERICAN POETRY. — *See Poetry of America.*

BACON'S Moral and Historical Works, including Essays, Apophthegms, Wisdom of the Ancients, New Atlantis, Henry VII., Henry VIII., Elizabeth, Henry Prince of Wales, History of Great Britain, Julius Cæsar, and Augustus Cæsar. With Critical and Biographical Introduction and Notes by J. Devey, M.A. Portrait.

— *See also Philosophical Library.*

BALLADS AND SONGS of the Peasantry of England, from Oral Recitation, private MSS., Broadsides, &c. Edit. by R. Bell.

BEAUMONT AND FLETCHER. Selections. With Notes and Introduction by Leigh Hunt.

BECKMANN (J.) History of Inventions, Discoveries, and Origins. With Portraits of Beckmann and James Watt. 2 vols.

BELL (Robert).—*See Ballads, Chaucer, Green.*

BOSWELL'S Life of Johnson, with the TOUR in the HEBRIDES and JOHNSONIANA. New Edition, with Notes and Appendices, by the Rev. A. Napier, M.A., Trinity College, Cambridge, Vicar of Holkham, Editor of the Cambridge Edition of the 'Theological Works of Barrow.' With Frontispiece to each vol. 6 vols.

BREMER'S (Frederika) Works. Trans. by M. Howitt. Portrait. 4 vols.

BRINK (B. T.) Early English Literature (to Wiclif). By Bernhard Ten Brink. Trans. by Prof. H. M. Kennedy.

BRITISH POETS, from Milton to Kirke White. Cabinet Edition. With Frontispiece. 4 vols.

BROWNE'S (Sir Thomas) Works. Edit. by S. Wilkin, with Dr. Johnson's Life of Browne. Portrait. 3 vols.

BURKE'S Works. 6 vols.

— **Speeches on the Impeachment** of Warren Hastings; and Letters. 2 vols.

— **Life.** By J. Prior. Portrait.

BURNS (Robert). Life of. By J. G. Lockhart, D.C.L. A new and enlarged edition. With Notes and Appendices by W. S. Douglas. Portrait.

BUTLER'S (Bp.) Analogy of Religion; Natural and Revealed, to the Constitution and Course of Nature; with Two Dissertations on Identity and Virtue, and Fifteen Sermons. With Introductions, Notes, and Memoir. Portrait.

CAMÖEN'S Lusiad, or the Discovery of India. An Epic Poem. Trans. from the Portuguese, with Dissertation, Historical Sketch, and Life, by W. J. Mickle. 5th edition.

CARAFAS (The) of Maddaloni. Naples under Spanish Dominion. Trans. by Alfred de Reumont. Portrait of Massaniello.

CARREL. The Counter-Revolution in England for the Re-establishment of Popery under Charles II. and James II., by Armand Carrel; with Fox's History of James II. and Lord Lonsdale's Memoir of James II. Portrait of Carrel.

CARRUTHERS. — *See Pope, in Illustrated Library.*

CARY'S Dante. The Vision of Hell, Purgatory, and Paradise. Trans. by Rev. H. F. Cary, M.A. With Life, Chronological View of his Age, Notes, and Index of Proper Names. Portrait.
This is the authentic edition, containing Mr. Cary's last corrections, with additional notes.

CELLINI (Benvenuto). Memoirs of, by himself. With Notes of G. P. Carpani. Trans. by T. Roscoe. Portrait.

CERVANTES' Galatea. A Pastoral Romance. Trans. by G. W. J. Gyll.

—— **Exemplary Novels.** Trans. by W. K. Kelly.

—— **Don Quixote de la Mancha.** Motteux's Translation revised. With Lockhart's Life and Notes. 2 vols.

CHAUCER'S Poetical Works. With Poems formerly attributed to him. With a Memoir, Introduction, Notes, and a Glossary, by R. Bell. Improved edition, with Preliminary Essay by Rev. W. W. Skeat, M.A. Portrait. 4 vols.

CLASSIC TALES, containing Rasselas, Vicar of Wakefield, Gulliver's Travels, and The Sentimental Journey.

COLERIDGE'S (S. T.) Friend. A Series of Essays on Morals, Politics, and Religion. Portrait.

—— **Aids to Reflection. Confessions** of an Inquiring Spirit; and Essays on Faith and the Common Prayer-book. New Edition, revised.

—— **Table-Talk and Omniana.** By T. Ashe, B.A.

—— **Lectures on Shakspere and** other Poets. Edit. by T. Ashe, B.A.
Containing the lectures taken down in 1811-12 by J. P. Collier, and those delivered at Bristol in 1813.

—— **Biographia Literaria; or, Bio**graphical Sketches of my Literary Life and Opinions; with Two Lay Sermons.

—— **Miscellanies, Æsthetic and** Literary; to which is added, THE THEORY OF LIFE. Collected and arranged by T. Ashe, B.A.

COMMINES.—*See Philip.*

CONDÉ'S History of the Dominion of the Arabs in Spain. Trans. by Mrs. Foster. Portrait of Abderahmen ben Moavia. 3 vols.

COWPER'S Complete Works, Poems, Correspondence, and Translations. Edit. with Memoir by R. Southey. 45 Engravings. 8 vols.

COXE'S Memoirs of the Duke of Marlborough. With his original Correspondence, from family records at Blenheim. Revised edition. Portraits. 3 vols.
*** An Atlas of the plans of Marlborough's campaigns, 4to. 10s. 6d.

—— **History of the House of Austria.** From the Foundation of the Monarchy by Rhodolph of Hapsburgh to the Death of Leopold II., 1218-1792. By Archdn. Coxe. With Continuation from the Accession of Francis I. to the Revolution of 1848. 4 Portraits. 4 vols.

CUNNINGHAM'S Lives of the most Eminent British Painters. With Notes and 16 fresh Lives by Mrs. Heaton. 3 vols

DEFOE'S Novels and Miscellaneous Works. With Prefaces and Notes, including those attributed to Sir W. Scott. Portrait. 7 vols.

DE LOLME'S Constitution of England, in which it is compared both with the Republican form of Government and the other Monarchies of Europe. Edit., with Life and Notes, by J. Macgregor, M.P.

DUNLOP'S History of Fiction. With Introduction and Supplement adapting the work to present requirements. By Henry Wilson. 2 vols., 5s. each.

ELZE'S Shakespeare.—*See Shakespeare*

EMERSON'S Works. 3 vols. Most complete edition published.
Vol. I.—Essays, Lectures, and Poems.
Vol. II.—English Traits, Nature, and Conduct of Life.
Vol. III.—Society and Solitude—Letters and Social Aims—Miscellaneous Papers (hitherto uncollected)—May-Day, &c.

FOSTER'S (John) Life and Correspondence. Edit. by J. E. Ryland. Portrait. 2 vols.

—— **Lectures at Broadmead Chapel.** Edit. by J. E. Ryland. 2 vols.

—— **Critical Essays contributed to** the 'Eclectic Review.' Edit. by J. E. Ryland. 2 vols.

—— **Essays: On Decision of Charac**ter; on a Man's writing Memoirs of Himself; on the epithet Romantic; on the aversion of Men of Taste to Evangelical Religion.

—— **Essays on the Evils of Popular** Ignorance, and a Discourse on the Propagation of Christianity in India.

—— **Essay on the Improvement of** Time, with Notes of Sermons and other Pieces. N. S.

—— **Fosteriana:** selected from periodical papers, edit. by H. G. Bohn.

FOX (Rt. Hon. C. J.)—*See Carrel.*

GIBBON'S Decline and Fall of the Roman Empire. Complete and unabridged, with variorum Notes; including those of Guizot, Wenck, Niebuhr, Hugo, Neander, and others. 7 vols. 2 Maps and Portrait.

GOETHE'S Works. Trans. into English by E. A. Bowring, C.B., Anna Swanwick. Sir Walter Scott, &c. &c. 13 vols.

Vols. I. and II.—Autobiography and Annals. Portrait.
Vol. III.—Faust. Complete.
Vol. IV.—Novels and Tales : containing Elective Affinities, Sorrows of Werther, The German Emigrants, The Good Women, and a Nouvelette.
Vol. V.—Wilhelm Meister's Apprenticeship.
Vol. VI.—Conversations with Eckerman and Soret.
Vol. VII.—Poems and Ballads in the original Metres, including Hermann and Dorothea.
Vol. VIII.—Götz von Berlichingen, Torquato Tasso, Egmont, Iphigenia, Clavigo, Wayward Lover, and Fellow Culprits.
Vol. IX. — Wilhelm Meister's Travels. Complete Edition.
Vol. X. — Tour in Italy. Two Parts. And Second Residence in Rome.
Vol. XI.—Miscellaneous Travels, Letters from Switzerland, Campaign in France, Siege of Mainz, and Rhine Tour.
Vol. XII.—Early and Miscellaneous Letters, including Letters to his Mother, with Biography and Notes.
Vol. XIII.—Correspondence with Zelter.
Vol. XIV.— Reineke Fox, West-Eastern Divan and Achilleid. Translated in original metres by A. Rogers.

—— **Correspondence with Schiller.** 2 vols.—*See Schiller.*

GOLDSMITH'S Works. 5 vols.
Vol. I.—Life, Vicar of Wakefield, Essays, and Letters.
Vol. II.—Poems, Plays, Bee, Cock Lane Ghost.
Vol. III.—The Citizen of the World, Polite Learning in Europe.
Vol. IV.—Biographies, Criticisms, Later Essays.
Vol. V. — Prefaces, Natural History, Letters, Goody Two-Shoes, Index.

GREENE, MARLOW, and BEN JONSON (Poems of). With Notes and Memoirs by R. Bell.

GREGORY'S (Dr.) The Evidences, Doctrines, and Duties of the Christian Religion.

GRIMM'S Household Tales. With the Original Notes. Trans. by Mrs. A. Hunt. Introduction by Andrew Lang, M.A. 2 vols.

GUIZOT'S History of Representative Government in Europe. Trans. by A. R. Scoble.

—— **English Revolution of 1640.** From the Accession of Charles I. to his Death. Trans. by W. Hazlitt. Portrait.

—— **History of Civilisation.** From the Roman Empire to the French Revolution. Trans. by W. Hazlitt. Portraits. 3 vols.

HALL'S (Rev. Robert) Works and Remains. Memoir by Dr. Gregory and Essay by J. Foster. Portrait.

HAUFF'S Tales. The Caravan—The Sheikh of Alexandria—The Inn in the Spessart. Translated by Prof. S. Mendel.

HAWTHORNE'S Tales. 3 vols.
Vol. I.—Twice-told Tales, and the Snow Image.
Vol. II.—Scarlet Letter, and the House with Seven Gables.
Vol. III. — Transformation, and Blithedale Romance.

HAZLITT'S (W.) Works. 7 vols.

—— **Table-Talk.**

—— **The Literature of the Age of** Elizabeth and Characters of Shakespeare's Plays.

—— **English Poets and English Comic** Writers.

—— **The Plain Speaker.** Opinions on Books, Men, and Things.

—— **Round Table.** Conversations of James Northcote, R.A. ; Characteristics.

—— **Sketches and Essays,** and Winterslow.

—— **Spirit of the Age;** or, Contemporary Portraits. New Edition, by W. Carew Hazlitt.

HEINE'S Poems. Translated in the original Metres, with Life by E. A. Bowring, C.B.

—— **Travel-Pictures.** The Tour in the Harz, Norderney, and Book of Ideas, together with the Romantic School. Trans. by F. Storr. With Maps and Appendices.

HOFFMANN'S Works. The Serapion Brethren. Vol. I. Trans. by Lt.-Col. Ewing. [*Vol. II. in the press.*

HOOPER'S (G.) Waterloo : The Downfall of the First Napoleon : a History of the Campaign of 1815. By George Hooper. With Maps and Plans. New Edition, revised.

HUGO'S (Victor) Dramatic Works: Hernani—RuyBlas—The King's Diversion. Translated by Mrs. Newton Crosland and F. L. Slous.

—— **Poems,** chiefly Lyrical. Collected by H. L. Williams.

HUNGARY: its History and Revolution, with Memoir of Kossuth. Portrait.

HUTCHINSON (Colonel). Memoirs of. By his Widow, with her Autobiography, and the Siege of Lathom House. Portrait.

IRVING'S (Washington) Complete Works. 15 vols.

—— **Life and Letters.** By his Nephew, Pierre E. Irving. With Index and a Portrait. 2 vols.

JAMES'S (G. P. R.) Life of Richard Cœur de Lion. Portraits of Richard and Philip Augustus. 2 vols.

—— **Louis XIV.** Portraits. 2 vols.

JAMESON (Mrs.) Shakespeare's Heroines. Characteristics of Women. By Mrs. Jameson.

JEAN PAUL.—*See Richter.*

JOHNSON'S Lives of the Poets. Edited by R. Napier.   [*In the press.*

JONSON (Ben). Poems of.—*See Greene.*

JOSEPHUS (Flavius), The Works of. Whiston's Translation. Revised by Rev. A. R. Shilleto, M.A. With Topographical and Geographical Notes by Colonel Sir C. W. Wilson, K.C.B. Vols. 1 to 3 containing Life of Josephus' and the Antiquities of the Jews.   [*Just published.* Vols. IV. and V. containing the Jewish War, &c.   [*Immediately.*

JUNIUS'S Letters. With Woodfall's Notes. An Essay on the Authorship. Facsimiles of Handwriting. 2 vols.

LA FONTAINE'S Fables. In English Verse, with Essay on the Fabulists. By Elizur Wright.

LAMARTINE'S The Girondists, or Personal Memoirs of the Patriots of the French Revolution. Trans. by H. T. Ryde. Portraits of Robespierre, Madame Roland, and Charlotte Corday. 3 vols.

—— **The Restoration of Monarchy** in France (a Sequel to The Girondists). 5 Portraits. 4 vols.

—— **The French Revolution of 1848.** Portraits.

LAMB'S (Charles) Elia and Eliana. Complete Edition. Portrait.

LAMB'S (Charles) Specimens of English Dramatic Poets of the time of Elizabeth. Notes, with the Extracts from the Garrick Plays.

—— **Talfourd's Letters of Charles** Lamb. New Edition, by W. Carew Hazlitt. 2 vols.

LANZI'S History of Painting in Italy, from the Period of the Revival of the Fine Arts to the End of the 18th Century. With Memoir of the Author. Portraits of Raffaelle, Titian, and Correggio, after the Artists themselves. Trans. by T. Roscoe. 3 vols.

LAPPENBERG'S England under the Anglo-Saxon Kings. Trans. by B. Thorpe, F.S.A. 2 vols.

LESSING'S Dramatic Works. Complete. By E. Bell, M.A. With Memoir by H. Zimmern. Portrait. 2 vols.

—— **Laokoon, Dramatic Notes, and** Representation of Death by the Ancients. Frontispiece.

LOCKE'S Philosophical Works, containing Human Understanding, with Bishop of Worcester, Malebranche's Opinions, Natural Philosophy, Reading and Study. With Preliminary Discourse, Analysis, and Notes, by J. A. St. John. Portrait. 2 vols.

—— **Life and Letters,** with Extracts from his Common-place Books. By Lord King.

LOCKHART (J. G.)—*See Burns.*

LONSDALE (Lord).—*See Carrel.*

LUTHER'S Table-Talk. Trans. by W. Hazlitt. With Life by A. Chalmers, and LUTHER'S CATECHISM. Portrait after Cranach.

—— **Autobiography.**—*See Michelet.*

MACHIAVELLI'S History of Flo- rence, THE PRINCE, Savonarola, Historical Tracts, and Memoir. Portrait.

MARLOWE. Poems of.—*See Greene.*

MARTINEAU'S (Harriet) History of England (including History of the Peace) from 1800-1846. 5 vols.

MENZEL'S History of Germany, from he Earliest Period to the Crimean War.   Portraits. 3 vols.

MICHELET'S Autobiography of Luther Trans. by W. Hazlitt. With Notes.

—— **The French Revolution** to the Flight of the King in 1791. *N. S.*

MIGNET'S The French Revolution, from 1789 to 1814. Portrait of Napoleon.

MILTON'S Prose Works. With Preface, Preliminary Remarks by J. A. St. John, and Index. 5 vols.

—— **Poetical Works.** With 120 Wood Engravings. 2 vols.

Vol. I.—Paradise Lost, complete, with Memoir, Notes, and Index.

Vol. II.—Paradise Regained, and other Poems, with Verbal Index to all the Poems.

MITFORD'S (Miss) Our Village. Sketches of Rural Character and Scenery. 2 Engravings. 2 vols.

MOLIÈRE'S Dramatic Works. In English Prose, by C. H. Wall. With a Life and a Portrait. 3 vols.
'It is not too much to say that we have here probably as good a translation of Molière as can be given.'—*Academy.*

MONTAGU. Letters and Works of Lady Mary Wortley Montagu. Lord Wharncliffe's Third Edition. Edited by W. Moy Thomas. With steel plates. 2 vols. 5*s.* each.

MONTESQUIEU'S Spirit of Laws. Revised Edition, with D'Alembert's Analysis, Notes, and Memoir. 2 vols.

NEANDER (Dr. A.) History of the Christian Religion and Church. Trans. by J. Torrey. With Short Memoir. 10 vols.

—— **Life of Jesus Christ, in its Historical Connexion and Development.**

—— **The Planting and Training of** the Christian Church by the Apostles. With the Antignosticus, or Spirit of Tertullian. Trans. by J. E. Ryland. 2 vols.

—— **Lectures on the History of** Christian Dogmas. Trans. by J. E. Ryland. 2 vols.

—— **Memorials of Christian Life in** the Early and Middle Ages; including Light in Dark Places. Trans. by J. E. Ryland.

OCKLEY (S.) History of the Sara- cens and their Conquests in Syria, Persia, and Egypt. Comprising the Lives of Mohammed and his Successors to the Death of Abdalmelik, the Eleventh Caliph. By Simon Ockley, B.D., Prof. of Arabic in Univ. of Cambridge. Portrait of Mohammed.

PASCAL'S Thoughts. Translated from the Text of M. Auguste Molinier by C. Kegan Paul. 3rd edition.

PERCY'S Reliques of Ancient Eng- lish Poetry, consisting of Ballads, Songs, and other Pieces of our earlier Poets, with some few of later date. With Essay on Ancient Minstrels, and Glossary. 2 vols.

PHILIP DE COMMINES. Memoirs of. Containing the Histories of Louis XI. and Charles VIII., and Charles the Bold, Duke of Burgundy. With the History of Louis XI., by J. de Troyes. With a Life and Notes by A. R. Scoble. Portraits. 2 vols.

PLUTARCH'S LIVES. Newly Translated, with Notes and Life, by A Stewart, M.A., late Fellow of Trinity College, Cambridge, and G. Long, M.A. 4 vols.

POETRY OF AMERICA. Selections from One Hundred Poets, from 1776 to 1876. With Introductory Review, and Specimens of Negro Melody, by W. J. Linton. Portrait of W. Whitman.

RACINE'S (Jean) Dramatic Works. A metrical English version, with Biographical notice. By R. Bruce Boswell, M.A., Oxon. Vol. I.
Contents:—The Thebaïd —Alexander the Great--Andromache—The Litigants— Britannicus—Berenice.

RANKE (L.) History of the Popes, their Church and State, and their Conflicts with Protestantism in the 16th and 17th Centuries. Trans. by E. Foster. Portraits of Julius II. (after Raphael), Innocent X. (after Velasquez), and Clement VII. (after Titian). 3 vols.

—— **History of Servia.** Trans. by Mrs. Kerr. To which is added, The Slave Provinces of Turkey, by Cyprien Robert.

—— **History of the Latin and Teu-** tonic Nations. 1494-1514. Trans. by P. A. Ashworth, translator of Dr. Gneist's 'History of the English Constitution.'

REUMONT (Alfred de).—*See Carafas.*

REYNOLDS'(Sir J.) Literary Works. With Memoir and Remarks by H. W. Beechy. 2 vols.

RICHTER (Jean Paul). Levana, a Treatise on Education; together with the Autobiography, and a short Memoir.

—— **Flower, Fruit, and Thorn Pieces,** or the Wedded Life, Death, and Marriage of Siebenkaes. Translated by Alex. Ewing. The only complete English translation.

ROSCOE'S (W.) Life of Leo X., with Notes, Historical Documents, and Dissertation on Lucretia Borgia. 3 Portraits. 2 vols.

—— **Lorenzo de' Medici, called 'The** Magnificent,' with Copyright Notes, Poems, Letters, &c. With Memoir of Roscoe and Portrait of Lorenzo.

RUSSIA, History of, from the earliest Period to the Crimean War. By W. K. Kelly. 3 Portraits. 2 vols.

SCHILLER'S Works. 7 vols.
Vol. I.—History of the Thirty Years' War.
Rev. A. J. W. Morrison, M.A. Portrait.
Vol. II.—History of the Revolt in the
Netherlands, the Trials of Counts Egmont
and Horn, the Siege of Antwerp, and the
Disturbance of France preceding the Reign
of Henry IV. Translated by Rev. A. J. W.
Morrison and L. Dora Schmitz.
Vol. III.—Don Carlos. R. D. Boylan
—Mary Stuart. Mellish—Maid of Or-
leans. Anna Swanwick—Bride of Mes-
sina. A. Lodge, M.A. Together with the
Use of the Chorus in Tragedy (a short
Essay). Engravings.
These Dramas are all translated in metre.
Vol. IV.—Robbers—Fiesco—Love and
Intrigue—Demetrius—Ghost Seer—Sport
of Divinity.
The Dramas in this volume are in prose.
Vol. V.—Poems. E. A. Bowring, C.B.
Vol. VI.—Essays, Æsthetical and Philo-
sophical, including the Dissertation on the
Connexion between the Animal and Spiri-
tual in Man.
Vol. VII. — Wallenstein's Camp. J.
Churchill. — Piccolomini and Death of
Wallenstein. S. T. Coleridge.—William
Tell. Sir Theodore Martin, K.C.B., LL.D.

SCHILLER and GOETHE. Correspondence between, from A.D. 1794-1805.
With Short Notes by L. Dora Schmitz.
2 vols.

SCHLEGEL'S (F.) Lectures on the
Philosophy of Life and the Philosophy of
Language. By A. J. W. Morrison.
—— **The History of Literature,** Ancient
and Modern.
—— **The Philosophy of History.** With
Memoir and Portrait.
—— **Modern History,** with the Lectures
entitled Cæsar and Alexander, and The
Beginning of our History. By L. Purcel
and R. H. Whitelock.
—— **Æsthetic and Miscellaneous**
Works, containing Letters on Christian
Art, Essay on Gothic Architecture, Re-
marks on the Romance Poetry of the Mid-
dle Ages, on Shakspeare, the Limits of the
Beautiful, and on the Language and Wis-
dom of the Indians. By E. J. Millington.

SCHLEGEL (A. W.) Dramatic Art
and Literature. By J. Black. With Memoir by A. J. W. Morrison. Portrait.

SCHUMANN (Robert), His Life and
Works. By A. Reissmann. Trans. by
A. L. Alger.
—— **Early Letters.** Translated by May
Herbert.

SHAKESPEARE'S Dramatic Art.
The History and Character of Shakspeare's
Plays. By Dr. H. Ulrici. Trans. by L.
Dora Schmitz. 2 vols.

SHAKESPEARE (William). A
Literary Biography by Karl Elze, Ph.D.,
LL.D. Translated by L. Dora Schmitz. 5s.

SHERIDAN'S Dramatic Works. With
Memoir. Portrait (after Reynolds).

SKEAT (Rev. W. W.)—*See Chaucer.*

SISMONDI'S History of the Litera-
ture of the South of Europe. With Notes
and Memoir by T. Roscoe. Portraits of
Sismondi and Dante. 2 vols.
The specimens of early French, Italian,
Spanish, and Portugese Poetry, in English
Verse, by Cary and others.

SMITH'S (Adam) The Wealth of
Nations. An Inquiry into the Nature and
Causes of. Reprinted from the Sixth
Edition. With an Introduction by Ernest
Belfort Bax. 2 vols.

SMITH'S (Adam) Theory of Moral
Sentiments ; with Essay on the First For-
mation of Languages, and Critical Memoir
by Dugald Stewart.

SMYTH'S (Professor) Lectures on
Modern History ; from the Irruption of the
Northern Nations to the close of the Ameri-
can Revolution. 2 vols.
—— **Lectures on the French Revolu-**
tion. With Index. 2 vols.

SOUTHEY.—*See Cowper, Wesley, and
(Illustrated Library) Nelson.*

STURM'S Morning Communings
with God, or Devotional Meditations for
Every Day. Trans. by W. Johnstone, M.A.

SULLY. Memoirs of the Duke of,
Prime Minister to Henry the Great. With
Notes and Historical Introduction. 4 Por-
traits. 4 vols.

TAYLOR'S (Bishop Jeremy) Holy
Living and Dying, with Prayers, containing the Whole Duty of a Christian and the
parts of Devotion fitted to all Occasions.
Portrait.

THIERRY'S Conquest of England by
the Normans ; its Causes, and its Consequences in England and the Continent.
By W. Hazlitt. With short Memoir. 2 Portraits. 2 vols.

TROYE'S (Jean de). — *See Philip de
Commines.*

ULRICI (Dr.)—*See Shakespeare.*

VASARI. Lives of the most Eminent
Painters, Sculptors, and Architects. By
Mrs. J. Foster, with selected Notes. Por-
trait. 6 vols., Vol. VI. being an additional
Volume of Notes by J. P. Richter.

WERNER'S Templars in Cyprus.
Trans. by E. A. M. Lewis.

WESLEY, the Life of, and the Rise
and Progress of Methodism. By Robert
Southey. Portrait. 5s.

WHEATLEY. A Rational Illustra-
tion of the Book of Common Prayer, being
the Substance of everything Liturgical in
all former Ritualist Commentators upon the
subject. Frontispiece.

YOUNG (Arthur) Travels in France.
Edited by Miss Betham Edwards. With
a Portrait.

HISTORICAL LIBRARY.

22 Volumes at 5s. each. (*5l. 10s. per set.*)

EVELYN'S Diary and Correspondence, with the Private Correspondence of Charles I. and Sir Edward Nicholas, and between Sir Edward Hyde (Earl of Clarendon) and Sir Richard Browne. Edited from the Original MSS. by W. Bray, F.A.S. 4 vols. *N. S.* 45 Engravings (after Vandyke, Lely, Kneller, and Jamieson, &c.).

N.B.—This edition contains 130 letters from Evelyn and his wife, contained in no other edition.

PEPYS' Diary and Correspondence. With Life and Notes, by Lord Braybrooke. 4 vols. *N. S.* With Appendix containing additional Letters, an Index, and 31 Engravings (after Vandyke, Sir P. Lely, Holbein Kneller, &c.).

JESSE'S Memoirs of the Court of England under the Stuarts, including the Protectorate. 3 vols. With Index and 42 Portraits (after Vandyke, Lely, &c.).

—— **Memoirs of the Pretenders and** their Adherents. 7 Portraits.

NUGENT'S (Lord) Memorials of Hampden, his Party and Times. With Memoir. 12 Portraits (after Vandyke and others).

STRICKLAND'S (Agnes) Lives of the Queens of England from the Norman Conquest. From authentic Documents, public and private. 6 Portraits. 6 vols. *N. S.*

—— **Life of Mary Queen of Scots.** 2 Portraits. 2 vols.

—— **Lives of the Tudor and Stuart** Princesses. With 2 Portraits.

PHILOSOPHICAL LIBRARY.

17 Vols. at 5s. each, excepting those marked otherwise. (*3l. 19s. per set.*)

BACON'S Novum Organum and Advancement of Learning. With Notes by J. Devey, M.A.

BAX. A Handbook of the History of Philosophy, for the use of Students. By E. Belfort Bax, Editor of Kant's 'Prolegomena.' 5s.

COMTE'S Philosophy of the Sciences. An Exposition of the Principles of the *Cours de Philosophie Positive.* By G. H. Lewes, Author of 'The Life of Goethe.'

DRAPER (Dr. J. W.) A History of the Intellectual Development of Europe. 2 vols.

HEGEL'S Philosophy of History. By J. Sibree, M.A.

KANT'S Critique of Pure Reason. By J. M. D. Meiklejohn.

—— **Prolegomena and Metaphysical** Foundations of Natural Science, with Biography and Memoir by E. Belfort Bax. Portrait.

LOGIC, or the Science of Inference. A Popular Manual. By J. Devey.

MILLER (Professor). History Philosophically Illustrated, from the Fall of the Roman Empire to the French Revolution. With Memoir. 4 vols. 3s. 6d. each.

SCHOPENHAUER on the Fourfold Root of the Principle of Sufficient Reason, and on the Will in Nature. Trans. from the German.

SPINOZA'S Chief Works. Trans. with Introduction by R. H. M. Elwes. 2 vols.

Vol. I.—Tractatus Theologico-Politicus —Political Treatise.

Vol. II.—Improvement of the Understanding—Ethics—Letters.

TENNEMANN'S Manual of the History of Philosophy. Trans. by Rev. A. Johnson, M.A.

THEOLOGICAL LIBRARY.

15 Vols. at 5s. each, excepting those marked otherwise.   (3l. 13s. 6d. per set.)

BLEEK. Introduction to the Old Testament. By Friedrich Bleek. Trans. under the supervision of Rev. E. Venables, Residentiary Canon of Lincoln. 2 vols.

CHILLINGWORTH'S Religion of Protestants. 3s. 6d.

EUSEBIUS. Ecclesiastical History of Eusebius Pamphilius, Bishop of Cæsarea. Trans. by Rev. C. F. Cruse, M.A. With Notes, Life, and Chronological Tables.

EVAGRIUS. History of the Church. —*See Theodoret.*

HARDWICK. History of the Articles of Religion ; to which is added a Series of Documents from A.D. 1536 to A.D. 1615. Ed. by Rev. F. Proctor.

HENRY'S (Matthew) Exposition of the Book of Psalms. Numerous Woodcuts.

PEARSON (John, D.D.) Exposition of the Creed. Edit. by E. Walford, M.A. With Notes, Analysis, and Indexes. .

PHILO-JUDÆUS, Works of. The Contemporary of Josephus. Trans. by C. D. Yonge. 4 vols.

PHILOSTORGIUS. Ecclesiastical History of.—*See Sozomen.*

SOCRATES' Ecclesiastical History, Comprising a History of the Church from Constantine, A.D. 305, to the 38th year of Theodosius II. With Short Account of the Author, and selected Notes.

SOZOMEN'S Ecclesiastical History. A.D. 324-440. With Notes, Prefatory Remarks by Valesius, and Short Memoir. Together with the ECCLESIASTICAL HISTORY OF PHILOSTORGIUS, as epitomised by Photius. Trans. by Rev. E. Walford, M.A. With Notes and brief Life.

THEODORET and EVAGRIUS. Histories of the Church from A.D. 332 to the Death of Theodore of Mopsuestia, A.D. 427 ; and from A.D. 431 to A.D. 544. With Memoirs.

WIESELER'S (Karl) Chronological Synopsis of the Four Gospels. Trans. by . Rev. Canon Venables.

ANTIQUARIAN LIBRARY.

35 Vols. at 5s. each.   (8l. 15s. per set.)

ANGLO-SAXON CHRONICLE. — *See Bede.*
ASSER'S Life of Alfred.—*See Six O. E. Chronicles.*
BEDE'S (Venerable) Ecclesiastical History of England. Together with the ANGLO-SAXON CHRONICLE. With Notes, Short Life, Analysis, and Map. Edit. by J. A. Giles, D.C.L.

BOETHIUS'S Consolation of Philo- sophy. King Alfred's Anglo-Saxon Version of. With an English Translation on opposite pages, Notes, Introduction, and Glossary, by Rev. S. Fox, M.A. To which is added the Anglo-Saxon Version of the METRES OF BOETHIUS, with a free Translation by Martin F. Tupper, D.C.L.

BRAND'S Popular Antiquities of England, Scotland, and Ireland. Illustrating the Origin of our Vulgar and Provincial Customs, Ceremonies, and Superstitions. By Sir Henry Ellis, K.H., F.R.S. Frontispiece. 3 vols.

CHRONICLES of the CRUSADES. Contemporary Narratives of Richard Cœur de Lion, by Richard of Devizes and Geoffrey de Vinsauf ; and of the Crusade at Saint Louis, by Lord John de Joinville. With Short Notes. Illuminated Frontispiece from an old MS.

DYER'S (T. F. T.) British Popular Customs, Present and Past. An Account of the various Games and Customs associated with different Days of the Year in the British Isles, arranged according to the Calendar. By the Rev. T. F. Thiselton Dyer, M.A.

EARLY TRAVELS IN PALESTINE. Comprising the Narratives of Arculf, Willibald, Bernard, Sæwulf, Sigurd, Benjamin of Tudela, Sir John Maundeville, De la Brocquière, and Maundrell ; all unabridged. With Introduction and Notes by Thomas Wright. Map of Jerusalem.

**ELLIS (G.) Specimens of Early En-
glish Metrical Romances, relating to
Arthur, Merlin, Guy of Warwick, Richard
Cœur de Lion, Charlemagne, Roland, &c.
&c. With Historical Introduction by J. O.
Halliwell, F.R.S. Illuminated Frontispiece from an old MS.

**ETHELWERD. Chronicle of.—*See
Six O. E. Chronicles.***

**FLORENCE OF WORCESTER'S
Chronicle, with the Two Continuations:
comprising Annals of English History
from the Departure of the Romans to the
Reign of Edward I. Trans., with Notes,
by Thomas Forester, M.A.

**GEOFFREY OF MONMOUTH.
Chronicle of.—*See Six O. E. Chronicles.***

**GESTA ROMANORUM, or Enter-
taining Moral Stories invented by the
Monks. Trans. with Notes by the Rev.
Charles Swan. Edit. by W. Hooper, M.A.

**GILDAS. Chronicle of.—*See Six O. E.
Chronicles.***

**GIRALDUS CAMBRENSIS' Histori-
cal Works. Containing Topography of
Ireland, and History of the Conquest of
Ireland, by Th. Forester, M.A. Itinerary
through Wales, and Description of Wales,
by Sir R. Colt Hoare.

**HENRY OF HUNTINGDON'S His-
tory of the English, from the Roman Invasion to the Accession of Henry II.;
with the Acts of King Stephen, and the
Letter to Walter. By T. Forester, M.A.
Frontispiece from au old MS.

INGULPH'S Chronicles of the Abbey
of Croyland, with the CONTINUATION by
Peter of Blois and others. Trans. with
Notes by H. T. Riley, B.A.

**KEIGHTLEY'S (Thomas) Fairy My-
thology, illustrative of the Romance and
Superstition of Various Countries. Frontispiece by Cruikshank.

LEPSIUS'S Letters from Egypt,
Ethiopia, and the Peninsula of Sinai; to
which are added, Extracts from his
Chronology of the Egyptians, with refer-
ence to the Exodus of the Israelites. By
L. and J. B. Horner. Maps and Coloured
View of Mount Barkal.

MALLET'S Northern Antiquities, or
an Historical Account of the Manners,
Customs, Religions, and Literature of the
Ancient Scandinavians. Trans. by Bishop
Percy. With Translation of the PROSE
EDDA, and Notes by J. A. Blackwell.
Also an Abstract of the 'Eyrbyggia Saga'
by Sir Walter Scott. With Glossary
and Coloured Frontispiece.

**MARCO POLO'S Travels; with Notes
and Introduction. Edit. by T. Wright.

**MATTHEW PARIS'S English His-
tory, from 1235 to 1273. By Rev. J. A.
Giles, D.C.L. With Frontispiece. 3 vols.—
*See also Roger of Wendover.***

**MATTHEW OF WESTMINSTER'S
Flowers of History, especially such as relate to the affairs of Britain, from the beginning of the World to A.D. 1307. By
C. D. Yonge. 2 vols.

**NENNIUS. Chronicle of.—*See Six
O. E. Chronicles.***

**ORDERICUS VITALIS' Ecclesiastical
History of England and Normandy. With
Notes, Introduction of Guizot, and the
Critical Notice of M. Delille, by T.
Forester, M.A. To which is added the
CHRONICLE OF St. EVROULT. With Gene-
ral and Chronological Indexes. 4 vols.

**PAULI'S (Dr. R.) Life of Alfred the
Great. To which is appended Alfred's
ANGLO-SAXON VERSION OF OROSIUS. With
literal Translation interpaged, Notes, and
an ANGLO-SAXON GRAMMAR and Glossary,
by B. Thorpe, Esq. Frontispiece.

**RICHARD OF CIRENCESTER.
Chronicle of.—*See Six O. E. Chronicles.***

**ROGER DE HOVEDEN'S Annals of
English History, comprising the History
of England and of other Countries of Europe from A.D. 732 to A.D. 1201. With
Notes by H. T. Riley, B.A. 2 vols.

**ROGER OF WENDOVER'S Flowers
of History, comprising the History of
England from the Descent of the Saxons to
A.D. 1235, formerly ascribed to Matthew
Paris. With Notes and Index by J. A.
Giles, D.C.L. 2 vols.

**SIX OLD ENGLISH CHRONICLES:
viz., Asser's Life of Alfred and the Chroni
cles of Ethelwerd, Gildas, Nennius, Geoffrey of Monmouth, and Richard of Cirencester. Edit., with Notes, by J. A. Giles,
D.C.L. Portrait of Alfred.

**WILLIAM OF MALMESBURY'S
Chronicle of the Kings of England, from
the Earliest Period to King Stephen. By
Rev. J. Sharpe. With Notes by J. A.
Giles, D.C.L. Frontispiece.

YULE-TIDE STORIES. A Collection
of Scandinavian and North-German Popular Tales and Traditions, from the Swedish,
Danish, and German. Edit. by B. Thorpe.

ILLUSTRATED LIBRARY.

84 Vols. at 5s. each, excepting those marked otherwise. (20*l.* 18*s.* 6*d.* *per set.*)

ALLEN'S (Joseph, R.N.) Battles of the British Navy. Revised edition, with Indexes of Names and Events, and 57 Portraits and Plans. 2 vols.

ANDERSEN'S Danish Fairy Tales. By Caroline Peachey. With Short Life and 120 Wood Engravings.

ARIOSTO'S Orlando Furioso. In English Verse by W. S. Rose. With Notes and Short Memoir. Portrait after Titian, and 24 Steel Engravings. 2 vols.

BECHSTEIN'S Cage and Chamber Birds : their Natural History, Habits, &c. Together with SWEET'S BRITISH WAR-BLERS. 43 Coloured Plates and Woodcuts.

BONOMI'S Nineveh and its Palaces. The Discoveries of Botta and Layard applied to the Elucidation of Holy Writ. 7 Plates and 294 Woodcuts.

BUTLER'S Hudibras, with Variorum Notes and Biography. Portrait and 28 Illustrations.

CATTERMOLE'S Evenings at Haddon Hall. Romantic Tales of the Olden Times. With 24 Steel Engravings after Cattermole.

CHINA, Pictorial, Descriptive, and Historical, with some account of Ava and the Burmese, Siam, and Anam. Map, and nearly 100 Illustrations.

CRAIK'S (G. L.) Pursuit of Know- ledge under Difficulties. Illustrated by Anecdotes and Memoirs. Numerous Woodcut Portraits.

CRUIKSHANK'S Three Courses and a Dessert ; comprising three Sets of Tales, West Country, Irish, and Legal ; and a Mélange. With 50 Illustrations by Cruikshank.

—— **Punch and Judy.** The Dialogue of the Puppet Show ; an Account of its Origin, &c. 24 Illustrations and Coloured Plates by Cruikshank.

DIDRON'S Christian Iconography ; a History of Christian Art in the Middle Ages. By the late A. N. Didron. Trans. by E. J. Millington, and completed, with Additions and Appendices, by Margaret Stokes. 2 vols. With numerous Illustrations.

Vol. I. The History of the Nimbus, the Aureole, and the Glory ; Representations of the Persons of the Trinity.

Vol. II. The Trinity ; Angels ; Devils ; The Soul ; The Christian Scheme. Appendices.

DANTE, in English Verse, by I. C. Wright, M.A. With Introduction and Memoir. Portrait and 34 Steel Engravings after Flaxman.

DYER (Dr. T. H.) Pompeii: its Buildings and Antiquities. An Account of the City, with full Description of the Remains and Recent Excavations, and an Itinerary for Visitors. By T. H. Dyer, LL.D. Nearly 300 Wood Engravings, Map, and Plan. 7*s.* 6*d.*

—— **Rome :** History of the City, with Introduction on recent Excavations. 8 Engravings, Frontispiece, and 2 Maps.

GIL BLAS. The Adventures of. From the French of Lesage by Smollett. 24 Engravings after Smirke, and 10 Etchings by Cruikshank. 612 pages. 6*s.*

GRIMM'S Gammer Grethel ; or, German Fairy Tales and Popular Stories, containing 42 Fairy Tales. By Edgar Taylor. Numerous Woodcuts after Cruikshank and Ludwig Grimm. 3*s.* 6*d.*

HOLBEIN'S Dance of Death and Bible Cuts. Upwards of 150 Subjects, engraved in facsimile, with Introduction and Descriptions by the late Francis Douce and Dr. Dibdin.

HOWITT'S (Mary) Pictorial Calen- dar of the Seasons ; embodying AIKIN'S CALENDAR OF NATURE. Upwards of 100 Woodcuts.

INDIA, Pictorial, Descriptive, and Historical, from the Earliest Times. 100 Engravings on Wood and Map.

JESSE'S Anecdotes of Dogs. With 40 Woodcuts after Harvey, Bewick, and others ; and 34 Steel Engravings after Cooper and Landseer.

KING'S (C. W.) Natural History of Gems or Decorative Stones. Illustrations. 6*s.*

—— **Natural History of Precious** Stones and Metals. Illustrations. 6*s.*

KITTO'S Scripture Lands. Described in a series of Historical, Geographical, and Topographical Sketches. 42 coloured Maps.

KRUMMACHER'S Parables. 40 Illustrations.

LINDSAY'S (Lord) Letters on Egypt, Edom, and the Holy Land. 36 Wood Engravings and 2 Maps.

LODGE'S Portraits of Illustrious Personages of Great Britain, with Biographical and Historical Memoirs. 240 Portraits engraved on Steel, with the respective Biographies unabridged. Complete in 8 vols.

LONGFELLOW'S Poetical Works, including his Translations and Notes. 24 full-page Woodcuts by Birket Foster and others, and a Portrait.

—— Without the Illustrations, 3s. 6d.

—— **Prose Works.** With 16 full-page Woodcuts by Birket Foster and others.

LOUDON'S (Mrs.) Entertaining Naturalist. Popular Descriptions, Tales, and Anecdotes, of more than 500 Animals. Numerous Woodcuts.

MARRYAT'S (Capt., R.N.) Masterman Ready; or, the Wreck of the *Pacific.* (Written for Young People.) With 93 Woodcuts. 3s. 6d.

—— **Mission; or, Scenes in Africa.** (Written for Young People.) Illustrated by Gilbert and Dalziel. 3s. 6d.

—— **Pirate and Three Cutters.** (Written for Young People.) With a Memoir. 8 Steel Engravings after Clarkson Stanfield, R.A. 3s. 6d.

—— **Privateersman.** Adventures by Sea and Land One Hundred Years Ago. (Written for Young People.) 8 Steel Engravings. 3s. 6d.

—— **Settlers in Canada.** (Written for Young People.) 10 Engravings by Gilbert and Dalziel. 3s. 6d.

—— **Poor 'Jack.** (Written for Young People.) With 16 Illustrations after Clarkson Stanfield, R.A. 3s. 6d.

—— **Midshipman Easy.** With 8 full-page Illustrations. Small post 8vo. 3s. 6d.

—— **Peter Simple.** With 8 full-page Illustrations. Small post 8vo. 3s. 6d.

MAXWELL'S Victories of Wellington and the British Armies. Frontispiece and 4 Portraits.

MICHAEL ANGELO and RAPHAEL, Their Lives and Works. By Duppa and Quatremère de Quincy. Portraits and Engravings, including the Last Judgment, and Cartoons.

MILLER'S History of the Anglo-Saxons, from the Earliest Period to the Norman Conquest. Portrait of Alfred, Map of Saxon Britain, and 12 Steel Engravings.

MUDIE'S History of British Birds. Revised by W. C. L. Martin. 52 Figures of Birds and 7 coloured Plates of Eggs. 2 vols.

NAVAL and MILITARY HEROES of Great Britain; a Record of British Valour on every Day in the year, from William the Conqueror to the Battle of Inkermann. By Major Johns, R.M., and Lieut. P. H. Nicolas, R.M. Indexes. 24 Portraits after Holbein, Reynolds, &c. 6s.

NICOLINI'S History of the Jesuits: their Origin, Progress, Doctrines, and Designs. 8 Portraits.

PETRARCH'S Sonnets, Triumphs, and other Poems, in English Verse. With Life by Thomas Campbell. Portrait and 15 Steel Engravings.

PICKERING'S History of the Races of Man, and their Geographical Distribution; with AN ANALYTICAL SYNOPSIS OF THE NATURAL HISTORY OF MAN. By Dr. Hall. Map of the World and 12 coloured Plates

PICTORIAL HANDBOOK OF Modern Geography on a Popular Plan. Compiled from the best Authorities, English and Foreign, by H. G. Bohn. 150 Woodcuts and 51 coloured Maps.

—— Without the Maps, 3s. 6d.

POPE'S Poetical Works, including Translations. Edit., with Notes, by R. Carruthers. 2 vols.

—— **Homer's Iliad,** with Introduction and Notes by Rev. J. S. Watson, M.A. With Flaxman's Designs.

—— **Homer's Odyssey,** with the BATTLE OF FROGS AND MICE, Hymns, &c., by other translators including Chapman. Introduction and Notes by J. S. Watson, M.A. With Flaxman's Designs.

—— **Life,** including many of his Letters. By R. Carruthers. Numerous Illustrations.

POTTERY AND PORCELAIN, and other objects of Vertu. Comprising an Illustrated Catalogue of the Bernal Collection, with the prices and names of the Possessors. Also an Introductory Lecture on Pottery and Porcelain, and an Engraved List of all Marks and Monograms. By H. G. Bohn. Numerous Woodcuts.

—— With coloured Illustrations, 10s. 6d.

PROUT'S (Father) Reliques. Edited by Rev. F. Mahony. Copyright edition, with the Author's last corrections and additions. 21 Etchings by D. Maclise, R.A. Nearly 600 pages.

RECREATIONS IN SHOOTING. With some Account of the Game found in the British Isles, and Directions for the Management of Dog and Gun. By 'Craven.' 62 Woodcuts and 9 Steel Engravings after A. Cooper, R.A.

RENNIE. Insect Architecture. Revised by Rev. J. G. Wood, M.A. 186 Woodcuts.

ROBINSON CRUSOE. With Memoir of Defoe, 12 Steel Engravings and 74 Woodcuts after Stothard and Harvey.

—— Without the Engravings, 3s. 6d.

ROME IN THE NINETEENTH CENtury. An Account in 1817 of the Ruins of the Ancient City, and Monuments of Modern Times. By C. A. Eaton. 34 Steel Engravings. 2 vols.

SHARPE (S.) The History of Egypt, from the Earliest Times till the Conquest by the Arabs, A.D. 640. 2 Maps and upwards of 400 Woodcuts. 2 vols.

SOUTHEY'S Life of Nelson. With Additional Notes, Facsimiles of Nelson's Writing, Portraits, Plans, and 50 Engravings, after Birket Foster, &c.

STARLING'S (Miss) Noble Deeds of Women; or, Examples of Female Courage, Fortitude, and Virtue. With 14 Steel Portraits.

STUART and REVETT'S Antiquities of Athens, and other Monuments of Greece; with Glossary of Terms used in Grecian Architecture. 71 Steel Plates and numerous Woodcuts.

SWEET'S British Warblers. 5s.—See Bechstein.

TALES OF THE GENII; or, the Delightful Lessons of Horam, the Son of Asmar. Trans. by Sir C. Morrell. Numerous Woodcuts.

TASSO'S Jerusalem Delivered. In English Spenserian Verse, with Life, by J. H. Wiffen. With 8 Engravings and 24 Woodcuts.

WALKER'S Manly Exercises; containing Skating, Riding, Driving, Hunting, Shooting, Sailing, Rowing, Swimming, &c. 44 Engravings and numerous Woodcuts.

WALTON'S Complete Angler, or the Contemplative Man's Recreation, by Izaak Walton and Charles Cotton. With Memoirs and Notes by E. Jesse. Also an Account of Fishing Stations, Tackle, &c., by H. G. Bohn. Portrait and 203 Woodcuts, and 26 Engravings on Steel.

—— **Lives of Donne, Wotton, Hooker,** &c., with Notes. A New Edition, revised by A. H. Bullen, with a Memoir of Izaak Walton by William Dowling. 6 Portraits, 6 Autograph Signatures, &c.

WELLINGTON, Life of. From the Materials of Maxwell. 18 Steel Engravings.

—— **Victories of.**—See Maxwell.

WESTROPP (H. M.) A Handbook of Archæology, Egyptian, Greek, Etruscan, Roman. By H. M. Westropp. Numerous Illustrations.

WHITE'S Natural History of Selborne, with Observations on various Parts of Nature, and the Naturalists' Calendar. Sir W. Jardine. Edit., with Notes and Memoir, by E. Jesse. 40 Portraits and coloured Plates.

CLASSICAL LIBRARY.

TRANSLATIONS FROM THE GREEK AND LATIN.

103 *Vols. at 5s. each, excepting those marked otherwise.* (25l. 4s. 6d. per set.)

ÆSCHYLUS, The Dramas of. In English Verse by Anna Swanwick. 4th edition.

—— **The Tragedies of.** In Prose, with Notes and Introduction, by T. A. Buckley, B.A. Portrait. 3s. 6d.

AMMIANUS MARCELLINUS. His- tory of Rome during the Reigns of Constantius, Julian, Jovianus, Valentinian, and Valens, by C. D. Yonge, B.A. Double volume. 7s. 6d.

ANTONINUS (M. Aurelius). The Thoughts of. Translated literally, with Notes, Biographical Sketch, and Essay on the Philosophy, by George Long, M.A. 3s. 6d.

APOLLONIUS RHODIUS. 'The Ar- gonautica.' Translated by E. P. Coleridge.

APULEIUS, The Works of. Comprising the Golden Ass, God of Socrates, Florida, and Discourse of Magic. With a Metrical Version of Cupid and Psyche, and Mrs. Tighe's Psyche. Frontispiece.

ARISTOPHANES' Comedies. Trans., with Notes and Extracts from Frere's and other Metrical Versions, by W. J. Hickie. Portrait. 2 vols.

ARISTOTLE'S Nicomachean Ethics. Trans., with Notes, Analytical Introduction, and Questions for Students, by Ven. Archdn. Browne.

—— Politics and Economics. Trans., with Notes, Analyses, and Index, by E. Walford, M.A., and an Essay and Life by Dr. Gillies.

—— Metaphysics. Trans., with Notes, Analysis, and Examination Questions, by Rev. John H. M'Mahon, M.A.

—— History of Animals. In Ten Books. Trans., with Notes and Index, by R. Cresswell, M.A.

—— Organon; or, Logical Treatises, and the Introduction of Porphyry. With Notes, Analysis, and Introduction, by Rev. O. F. Owen, M.A. 2 vols. 3s. 6d. each.

—— Rhetoric and Poetics. Trans., with Hobbes' Analysis, Exam. Questions, and Notes, by T. Buckley, B.A. Portrait.

ATHENÆUS. The Deipnosophists; or, the Banquet of the Learned. By C. D. Yonge, B.A. With an Appendix of Poetical Fragments. 3 vols.

ATLAS of Classical Geography. 22 large Coloured Maps. With a complete Index. Imp. 8vo. 7s. 6d.

BION.—See Theocritus.

CÆSAR. Commentaries on the Gallic and Civil Wars, with the Supplementary Books attributed to Hirtius, including the complete Alexandrian, African, and Spanish Wars. Trans. with Notes. Portrait.

CATULLUS, Tibullus, and the Vigil of Venus. Trans. with Notes and Biographical Introduction. To which are added, Metrical Versions by Lamb, Grainger, and others. Frontispiece.

CICERO'S Orations. Trans. by C. D. Yonge, B.A. 4 vols.

—— On Oratory and Orators. With Letters to Quintus and Brutus. Trans., with Notes, by Rev. J. S. Watson, M.A.

—— On the Nature of the Gods, Divination, Fate, Laws, a Republic, Consulship. Trans., with Notes, by C. D. Yonge, B.A.

—— Academics, De Finibus, and Tusculan Questions. By C. D. Yonge, B.A. With Sketch of the Greek Philosophers mentioned by Cicero.

CICERO'S Orations.—Continued. —— Offices; or, Moral Duties. Cato Major, an Essay on Old Age; Lælius, an Essay on Friendship; Scipio's Dream; Paradoxes; Letter to Quintus on Magistrates. Trans., with Notes, by C. R. Edmonds. Portrait. 3s. 6d. -

DEMOSTHENES' Orations. Trans., with Notes, Arguments, a Chronological Abstract, and Appendices, by C. Rann Kennedy. 5 vols.

DICTIONARY of LATIN and GREEK Quotations; including Proverbs, Maxims, Mottoes, Law Terms and Phrases. With the Quantities marked, and English Translations. With Index Verborum (622 pages).

—— Index Verborum to the above, with the Quantities and Accents marked (56 pages), limp cloth. 1s.

DIOGENES LAERTIUS. Lives and Opinions of the Ancient Philosophers. Trans., with Notes, by C. D. Yonge, B.A.

EPICTETUS. The Discourses of. With the Encheiridion and Fragments. With Notes, Life, and View of his Philosophy, by George Long, M.A.

EURIPIDES. Trans., with Notes and Introduction, by T. A. Buckley, B.A. Portrait. 2 vols.

GREEK ANTHOLOGY. In English Prose by G. Burges, M.A. With Metrical Versions by Bland, Merivale, Lord Denman, &c.

GREEK ROMANCES of Heliodorus, Longus, and Achilles Tatius; viz., The Adventures of Theagenes and Chariclea; Amours of Daphnis and Chloe; and Loves of Clitopho and Leucippe. Trans., with Notes, by Rev. R. Smith, M.A.

HERODOTUS. Literally trans. by Rev. Henry Cary, M.A. Portrait.

HESIOD, CALLIMACHUS, and Theognis. In Prose, with Notes and Biographical Notices by Rev. J. Banks, M.A. Together with the Metrical Versions of Hesiod, by Elton; Callimachus, by Tytler; and Theognis, by Frere.

HOMER'S Iliad. In English Prose, with Notes by T. A. Buckley, B.A. Portrait.

—— Odyssey, Hymns, Epigrams, and Battle of the Frogs and Mice. In English Prose, with Notes and Memoir by T. A. Buckley, B.A.

HORACE. In Prose by Smart, with Notes selected by T. A. Buckley, B.A. Portrait. 3s. 6d.

JULIAN THE EMPEROR. By the Rev. C. W. King, M.A.

JUSTIN, CORNELIUS NEPOS, and Eutropius. Trans., with Notes, by Rev. J. S. Watson, M.A.

JUVENAL, PERSIUS, SULPICIA, and Lucilius. In Prose, with Notes, Chronological Tables, Arguments, by L. Evans, M.A. To which is added the Metrical Version of Juvenal and Persius by Gifford. Frontispiece.

LIVY. The History of Rome. Trans. by Dr. Spillan and others. 4 vols. Portrait.

LUCAN'S Pharsalia. In Prose, with Notes by H. T. Riley.

LUCIAN'S Dialogues of the Gods, of the Sea Gods, and of the Dead. Trans. by Howard Williams, M.A.

LUCRETIUS. In Prose, with Notes and Biographical Introduction by Rev. J. S. Watson, M.A. To which is added the Metrical Version by J. M. Good.

MARTIAL'S Epigrams, complete. In Prose, with Verse Translations selected from English Poets, and other sources. Dble. vol. (670 pages). 7s. 6d.

MOSCHUS.—*See Theocritus.*

OVID'S Works, complete. In Prose, with Notes and Introduction. 3 vols.

PAUSANIAS' Description of Greece. Translated into English, with Notes and Index. By Arthur Richard Shilleto, M.A., sometime Scholar of Trinity College, Cambridge. 2 vols.

PHALARIS. Bentley's Dissertations upon the Epistles of Phalaris, Themistocles, Socrates, Euripides, and the Fables of Æsop. With Introduction and Notes by Prof. W. Wagner, Ph.D.

PINDAR. In Prose, with Introduction and Notes by Dawson W. Turner. Together with the Metrical Version by Abraham Moore. Portrait.

PLATO'S Works. Trans., with Introduction and Notes. 6 vols.

—— **Dialogues.** A Summary and Analysis of. With Analytical Index to the Greek text of modern editions and to the above translations, by A. Day, LL.D.

PLAUTUS'S Comedies. In Prose, with Notes and Index by H. T. Riley, B.A. 2 vols.

PLINY'S Natural History. Trans., with Notes, by J. Bostock, M.D., F.R.S., and H. T. Riley, B.A. 6 vols.

PLINY. The Letters of Pliny the Younger. Melmoth's Translation, revised, with Notes and short Life, by Rev. F. C. T. Bosanquet, M.A.

PLUTARCH'S Morals. Theosophical Essays. Trans. by C. W. King, M.A.

—— **Ethical Essays.** Trans. by A. R. Shilleto, M.A.

—— **Lives.** *See page 7.*

PROPERTIUS, The Elegies of. With Notes, Literally translated by the Rev. P. J. F. Gantillon, M.A., with metrical versions of Select Elegies by Nott and Elton. 3s. 6d.

QUINTILIAN'S Institutes of Oratory. Trans., with Notes and Biographical Notice, by Rev. J. S. Watson, M.A. 2 vols.

SALLUST, FLORUS, and VELLEIUS Paterculus. Trans., with Notes and Biographical Notices, by J. S. Watson, M.A.

SENECA DE BENEFICIIS. Newly translated by Aubrey Stewart, M.A. 3s. 6d.

SENECA'S Minor Essays. Translated by A. Stewart, M.A.

SOPHOCLES. The Tragedies of. In Prose, with Notes, Arguments, and Introduction. Portrait.

STRABO'S Geography. Trans., with Notes, by W. Falconer, M.A., and H. C. Hamilton. Copious Index, giving Ancient and Modern Names. 3 vols.

SUETONIUS' Lives of the Twelve Cæsars and Lives of the Grammarians. The Translation of Thomson, revised, with Notes, by T. Forester.

TACITUS. The Works of. Trans., with Notes. 2 vols.

TERENCE and PHÆDRUS. In English Prose, with Notes and Arguments, by H. T. Riley, B.A. To which is added Smart's Metrical Version of Phædrus. With Frontispiece.

THEOCRITUS, BION, MOSCHUS, and Tyrtæus. In Prose, with Notes and Arguments, by Rev. J. Banks, M.A. To which are appended the METRICAL VERSIONS of Chapman. Portrait of Theocritus.

THUCYDIDES. The Peloponnesian War. Trans., with Notes, by Rev. H. Dale. Portrait. 2 vols. 3s. 6d. each.

TYRTÆUS.—*See Theocritus.*

VIRGIL. The Works of. In Prose, with Notes by Davidson. Revised, with additional Notes and Biographical Notice, by T. A. Buckley, B.A. Portrait. 3s. 6d.

XENOPHON'S Works. Trans., with Notes, by J. S. Watson, M.A., and others. Portrait. In 3 vols.

COLLEGIATE SERIES.

10 *Vols. at* 5s. *each.*   (2l. 10s. *per set.*)

DANTE. The Inferno. Prose Trans., with the Text of the Original on the same page, and Explanatory Notes, by John A. Carlyle, M.D. Portrait.

—— **The Purgatorio.** Prose Trans., with the Original on the same page, and Explanatory Notes, by W. S. Dugdale.

NEW TESTAMENT (The) in Greek. Griesbach's Text, with the Readings of Mill and Scholz at the foot of the page, and Parallel References in the margin. Also a Critical Introduction and Chronological Tables. Two Fac-similes of Greek Manuscripts. 650 pages. 3s. 6d.

—— or bound up with a Greek and English Lexicon to the New Testament (250 pages additional, making in all 900). 5s.
The Lexicon may be had separately, price 2s.

DOBREE'S Adversaria. (Notes on the Greek and Latin Classics.) Edited by the late Prof. Wagner. 2 vols.

DONALDSON (Dr.) The Theatre of the Greeks. With Supplementary Treatise on the Language, Metres, and Prosody of the Greek Dramatists. Numerous Illustrations and 3 Plans. By J. W. Donaldson, D.D.

KEIGHTLEY'S (Thomas) Mythology of Ancient Greece and Italy. Revised by Leonhard Schmitz, Ph.D., LL.D. 12 Plates.

HERODOTUS, Notes on. Original and Selected from the best Commentators. By D. W. Turner, M.A. Coloured Map.

—— **Analysis and Summary of,** with a Synchronistical Table of Events—Tables of Weights, Measures, Money, and Distances — an Outline of the History and Geography—and the Dates completed from Gaisford, Baehr, &c. By J. T. Wheeler.

THUCYDIDES. An Analysis and Summary of. With Chronological Table of Events, &c., by J. T. Wheeler.

SCIENTIFIC LIBRARY.

51 *Vols. at* 5s. *each, excepting those marked otherwise.* (13l. 9s. 6d. *per set.*)

AGASSIZ and GOULD. Outline of Comparative Physiology touching the Structure and Development of the Races of Animals living and extinct. For Schools and Colleges. Enlarged by Dr. Wright. With Index and 300 Illustrative Woodcuts.

BOLLEY'S Manual of Technical Analysis; a Guide for the Testing and Valuation of the various Natural and Artificial Substances employed in the Arts and Domestic Economy, founded on the work of Dr. Bolley. Edit. by Dr. Paul. 100 Woodcuts.

BRIDGEWATER TREATISES.

—— **Bell (Sir Charles) on the Hand;** its Mechanism and Vital Endowments, as evincing Design. Preceded by an Account of the Author's Discoveries in the Nervous System by A. Shaw. Numerous Woodcuts.

—— **Kirby on the History, Habits,** and Instincts of Animals. With Notes by T. Rymer Jones. 100 Woodcuts. 2 vols.

—— **Whewell's Astronomy and** General Physics, considered with reference to Natural Theology. Portrait of the Earl of Bridgewater. 3s. 6d.

BRIDGEWATER TREATISES,— *Continued.*

—— **Chalmers on the Adaptation of** External Nature to the Moral and Intellectual Constitution of Man. With Memoir by Rev. Dr. Cumming. Portrait.

—— **Prout's Treatise on Chemistry,** Meteorology, and the Function of Digestion, with reference to Natural Theology. Edit. by Dr. J. W. Griffith. 2 Maps.

—— **Buckland's Geology and Miner-** alogy. With Additions by Prof. Owen, Prof. Phillips, and R. Brown. Memoir of Buckland. Portrait. 2 vols. 15s. Vol. I. Text. Vol. II. 90 large plates with letter-press.

—— **Roget's Animal and Vegetable** Physiology. 463 Woodcuts. 2 vols. 6s. each.

—— **Kidd on the Adaptation of Ex-** ternal Nature to the Physical Condition of Man. 3s. 6d.

CARPENTER'S (Dr. W. B.) Zoology. A Systematic View of the Structure, Habits, Instincts, and Uses of the principal Families of the Animal Kingdom, and of the chief Forms of Fossil Remains. Revised by W. S. Dallas, F.L.S. Numerous Woodcuts. 2 vols. 6s. each.

CARPENTER'S Works.—*Continued.*
—— **Mechanical Philosophy, Astronomy, and Horology.** A Popular Exposition. 181 Woodcuts.

—— **Vegetable Physiology and Systematic Botany.** A complete Introduction to the Knowledge of Plants. Revised by E. Lankester, M.D., &c. Numerous Woodcuts. 6s.

—— **Animal Physiology.** Revised Edition. 300 Woodcuts. 6s.

CHEVREUL on Colour. Containing the Principles of Harmony and Contrast of Colours, and their Application to the Arts ; including Painting, Decoration, Tapestries, Carpets, Mosaics, Glazing, Staining, Calico Printing, Letterpress Printing, Map Colouring, Dress, Landscape and Flower Gardening, &c. Trans. by C. Martel. Several Plates.

—— With an additional series of 16 Plates in Colours, 7s. 6d.

ENNEMOSER'S History of Magic. Trans. by W. Howitt. With an Appendix of the most remarkable and best authenticated Stories of Apparitions, Dreams, Second Sight, Table-Turning, and Spirit-Rapping, &c. 2 vols.

HIND'S Introduction to Astronomy. With Vocabulary of the Terms in present use. Numerous Woodcuts. 3s. 6d.

HOGG'S (Jabez) Elements of Experimental and Natural Philosophy. Being an Easy Introduction to the Study of Mechanics, Pneumatics, Hydrostatics, Hydraulics, Acoustics, Optics, Caloric, Electricity, Voltaism, and Magnetism. 400 Woodcuts.

HUMBOLDT'S Cosmos ; or, Sketch of a Physical Description of the Universe. Trans. by E. C. Otté, B. H. Paul, and W. S. Dallas, F.L.S. Portrait. 5 vols. 3s. 6d. each, excepting vol. v., 5s.

—— **Personal Narrative of his Travels** in America during the years 1799–1804. Trans., with Notes, by T. Ross. 3 vols.

—— **Views of Nature ; or, Contemplations of the Sublime Phenomena of** Creation, with Scientific Illustrations. Trans. by E. C. Otté.

HUNT'S (Robert) Poetry of Science ; or, Studies of the Physical Phenomena of Nature. By Robert Hunt, Professor at the School of Mines.

JOYCE'S Scientific Dialogues. A Familiar Introduction to the Arts and Sciences. For Schools and Young People. Numerous Woodcuts.

JOYCE'S Introduction to the Arts and Sciences, for Schools and Young People. Divided into Lessons with Examination Questions. Woodcuts. 3s. 6d.

JUKES-BROWNE'S Student's Handbook of Physical Geology. By A. J. Jukes-Browne, of the Geological Survey of England. With numerous Diagrams and Illustrations, 6s.

—— **The Student's Handbook of** Historical Geology. By A. J. Jukes-Brown, B.A., F.G.S., of the Geological Survey of England and Wales. With numerous Diagrams and Illustrations. 6s.

—— **The Building of the British** Islands. A Study in Geographical Evolution. By A J. Jukes-Browne, F.G.S. 7s. 6d.

KNIGHT'S (Charles) Knowledge is Power. A Popular Manual of Political Economy.

LILLY. Introduction to Astrology. With a Grammar of Astrology and Tables for calculating Nativities, by Zadkiel.

MANTELL'S (Dr.) Geological Excursions through the Isle of Wight and along the Dorset Coast. Numerous Woodcuts and Geological Map.

—— **Petrifactions and their Teachings.** Handbook to the Organic Remains in the British Museum. Numerous Woodcuts. 6s.

—— **Wonders of Geology ; or, a** Familiar Exposition of Geological Phenomena. A coloured Geological Map of England, Plates, and 200 Woodcuts. 2 vols. 7s. 6d. each.

SCHOUW'S Earth, Plants, and Man. Popular Pictures of Nature. And Kobell's Sketches from the Mineral Kingdom. Trans. by A. Henfrey, F.R.S. Coloured Map of the Geography of Plants.

SMITH'S (Pye) Geology and Scripture ; or, the Relation between the Scriptures and Geological Science. With Memoir.

STANLEY'S Classified Synopsis of the Principal Painters of the Dutch and Flemish Schools, including an Account of some of the early German Masters. By George Stanley.

STAUNTON'S Chess Works. — *See* *page* 21.

STOCKHARDT'S Experimental Chemistry. A Handbook for the Study of the Science by simple Experiments. Edit. by C. W. Heaton, F.C.S. Numerous Woodcuts.

URE'S (Dr. A.) Cotton Manufacture of Great Britain, systematically investigated ; with an Introductory View of its Comparative State in Foreign Countries. Revised by P. L. Simmonds. 150 Illustrations. 2 vols.

—— **Philosophy of Manufactures,** or an Exposition of the Scientific, Moral, and Commercial Economy of the Factory System of Great Britain. Revised by P. L. Simmonds. Numerous Figures. 800 pages. 7s. 6d.

ECONOMICS AND FINANCE.

GILBART'S History, Principles, and Practice of Banking. Revised to 1881 by A. S. Michie, of the Royal Bank of Scotland. Portrait of Gilbart. 2 vols. 10s. *N. S.*

REFERENCE LIBRARY.

30 *Volumes at Various Prices.* (9l. 5s. *per set.*)

BLAIR'S Chronological Tables. Comprehending the Chronology and History of the World, from the Earliest Times to the Russian Treaty of Peace, April 1856. By J. W. Rosse. 800 pages. 10s.

—— **Index of Dates.** Comprehending the principal Facts in the Chronology and History of the World, from the Earliest to the Present, alphabetically arranged ; being a complete Index to the foregoing. By J. W. Rosse. 2 vols. 5s. each.

BOHN'S Dictionary of Quotations from the English Poets. 4th and cheaper Edition. 6s.

BOND'S Handy-book of Rules and Tables for Verifying Dates with the Christian Era. 4th Edition.

BUCHANAN'S Dictionary of Science and Technical Terms used in Philosophy, Literature, Professions, Commerce, Arts, and Trades. By W. H. Buchanan, with Supplement. Edited by Jas. A. Smith. 6s.

CHRONICLES OF THE TOMBS. A Select Collection of Epitaphs, with Essay on Epitaphs and Observations on Sepulchral Antiquities. By T. J. Pettigrew, F.R.S., F.S.A. 5s.

CLARK'S (Hugh) Introduction to Heraldry. Revised by J. R. Planché. 5s. 950 Illustrations.

—— *With the Illustrations coloured*, 15s.

COINS, Manual of.—*See Humphreys.*

COOPER'S Biographical Dictionary. Containing concise notices of upwards of 15,000 eminent persons of all ages and countries. 2 vols. 5s. each.

DATES, Index of.—*See Blair.*

DICTIONARY of Obsolete and Provincial English. Containing Words from English Writers previous to the 19th Century. By Thomas Wright, M.A., F.S.A., &c. 2 vols. 5s. each.

EPIGRAMMATISTS (The). A Selection from the Epigrammatic Literature of Ancient, Mediæval, and Modern Times. With Introduction, Notes, Observations, Illustrations, an Appendix on Works connected with Epigrammatic Literature, by Rev. H. Dodd, M.A. 6s.

GAMES, Handbook of. Comprising Treatises on above 40 Games of Chance, Skill, and Manual Dexterity, including Whist, Billiards, &c. Edit. by Henry G. Bohn. Numerous Diagrams. 5s.

HENFREY'S Guide to English Coins. Revised Edition, by C. F. Keary, M.A., F.S.A. With an Historical Introduction. 6s.

HUMPHREYS' Coin Collectors' Manual. An Historical Account of the Progress of Coinage from the Earliest Time, by H. N. Humphreys. 140 Illustrations. 2 vols. 5s. each.

LOWNDES' Bibliographer's Manual of English Literature. Containing an Account of Rare and Curious Books published in or relating to Great Britain and Ireland, from the Invention of Printing, with Biographical Notices and Prices, by W. T. Lowndes. Parts I.-X. (A to Z), 3s. 6d. each. Part XI. (Appendix Vol.), 5s. Or the 11 parts in 4 vols., half morocco, 2l. 2s.

MEDICINE, Handbook of Domestic, Popularly Arranged. By Dr. H. Davies. 700 pages. 5s.

NOTED NAMES OF FICTION. Dictionary of. Including also Familiar Pseudonyms, Surnames bestowed on Eminent Men, &c. By W. A. Wheeler, M.A. 5s.

POLITICAL CYCLOPÆDIA. A Dictionary of Political, Constitutional, Statistical, and Forensic Knowledge ; forming a Work of Reference on subjects of Civil Administration, Political Economy, Finance, Commerce, Laws, and Social Relations. 4 vols. 3s. 6d. each.

PROVERBS, Handbook of. Containing an entire Republication of Ray's Collection, with Additions from Foreign Languages and Sayings, Sentences, Maxims, and Phrases. 5s.

—— **A Polyglot of Foreign.** Comprising French, Italian, German, Dutch, Spanish, Portuguese, and Danish. With English Translations. 5s.

SYNONYMS and ANTONYMS; or, Kindred Words and their Opposites, Collected and Contrasted by Ven. C. J. Smith, M.A. 5s.

WRIGHT (Th.)—*See Dictionary.*

NOVELISTS' LIBRARY.

13 *Volumes at* 3s. 6d. *each, excepting those marked otherwise.* (2l. 8s. 6d. *per set.*)

BJÖRNSON'S Arne and the Fisher Lassie. Translated from the Norse with an Introduction by W. H. Low, M.A.

BURNEY'S Evelina; or, a Young Lady's Entrance into the World. By F. Burney (Mme. D'Arblay). With Introduction and Notes by A. R. Ellis, Author of 'Sylvestra,' &c.

—— **Cecilia.** With Introduction and Notes by A. R. Ellis. 2 vols.

DE STAËL. Corinne or Italy. By Madame de Staël. Translated by Emily Baldwin and Paulina Driver.

EBERS' Egyptian Princess. Trans. by Emma Buchheim.

FIELDING'S Joseph Andrews and his Friend Mr. Abraham Adams. With Roscoe's Biography. *Cruikshank's Illustrations.*

—— **Amelia.** Roscoe's Edition, revised. *Cruikshank's Illustrations.* 5s.

—— **History of Tom Jones, a Foundling.** Roscoe's Edition. *Cruikshank's Illustrations.* 2 vols.

GROSSI'S Marco Visconti. Trans. by A. F. D.

MANZONI. The Betrothed : being a Translation of 'I Promessi Sposi.' Numerous Woodcuts. 1 vol. 5s.

STOWE (Mrs. H. B.) Uncle Tom's Cabin ; or, Life among the Lowly. 8 full-page Illustrations.

ARTISTS' LIBRARY.

9 *Volumes at Various Prices.* (2l. 8s. 6d. *per set.*)

BELL (Sir Charles). The Anatomy and Philosophy of Expression, as Connected with the Fine Arts. 5s.

DEMMIN. History of Arms and Armour from the Earliest Period. By Auguste Demmin. Trans. by C. C. Black, M.A., Assistant Keeper, S. K. Museum. 1900 Illustrations. 7s. 6d.

FAIRHOLT'S Costume in England. Third Edition. Enlarged and Revised by the Hon. H. A. Dillon, F.S.A. With more than 700 Engravings. 2 vols. 5s. each.
Vol. I. History. Vol. II. Glossary.

FLAXMAN. Lectures on Sculpture. With Three Addresses to the R.A. by Sir R. Westmacott, R.A., and Memoir o Flaxman. Portrait and 53 Plates. 6s. *N.S.*

HEATON'S Concise History of Painting. New Edition, revised by W. Cosmo Monkhouse. 5s.

LECTURES ON PAINTING by the Royal Academicians, Barry, Opie, Fuseli. With Introductory Essay and Notes by R. Wornum. Portrait of Fuseli.

LEONARDO DA VINCI'S Treatise on Painting. Trans. by J. F. Rigaud, R.A. With a Life and an Account of his Works by J. W. Brown. Numerous Plates. 5s.

PLANCHÉ'S History of British Costume, from the Earliest Time to the 10th Century. By J. R. Planché. 400 Illustrations. 5s.

LIBRARY OF SPORTS AND GAMES.

7 Volumes at 5s. each. (1l. 15s. per set.)

BOHN'S Handbooks of Athletic Sports. In 4 vols. [*In the press.*

Vol. I.—Cricket, by Hon. and Rev. E. Lyttelton; Lawn Tennis, by H. W. Wilberforce; Tennis and Rackets, by Julian Marshall; Golf, by W. T. Linskill; Cycling, by H. H. Griffin.

Vol. II.—Rowing and Sculling, by W. B. Woodgate; Sailing, by E. F. Knight; Swimming, by Martin Cobbett.

Vol. III.—Athletics, by H. H. Griffin; Rugby Football, by Harry Vassall; Association Football, by C. W. Alcock; Skating, by Douglas Adams; Lacrosse, by E. T. Sachs; Hockey, by F. S. Cresswell.

Vol. IV.—Boxing, by R. G. Allanson-Winn; Single Stick and Sword Exercise, by R. G. Allanson-Winn and C. Phillipps Wolley; Gymnastics, by A. F. Jenkin; Wrestling, by Walter Armstrong; Fencing, by H. A. Colmore Dunn.

BOHN'S Handbooks of Games. New Edition. 2 volumes.

Vol. I. TABLE GAMES. 5s.

Contents:—Billiards, with Pool, Pyramids, and Snooker, by Major-Gen. A. W. Drayson, F.R.A.S., with a preface by W. J. Peall—Bagatelle, by 'Berkeley'—Chess, by R. F. Green—Draughts, Backgammon, Dominoes, Solitaire, Reversi, Go Bang, Rouge et noir, Roulette, E.O., Hazard, Faro, by 'Berkeley.'

Vol. II. CARD GAMES. [*In the press.*

Contents:—Whist, by Dr. William Pole, F.R.S., Author of 'The Philosophy of Whist, etc.'—Solo Whist, Piquet, Ecarté, Euchre, Poker, Loo, Vingt-et-un, Napoleon, Newmarket, Rouge et Noir, Pope Joan, Speculation, etc. etc., by 'Berkeley.'

CHESS CONGRESS of 1862. A collection of the games played. Edited by J. Löwenthal. New edition, 5s.

MORPHY'S Games of Chess, being the Matches and best Games played by the American Champion, with explanatory and analytical Notes by J. Löwenthal. With short Memoir and Portrait of Morphy.

STAUNTON'S Chess-Player's Handbook. A Popular and Scientific Introduction to the Game, with numerous Diagrams and Coloured Frontispiece.

—— **Chess Praxis.** A Supplement to the Chess-player's Handbook. Containing the most important modern Improvements in the Openings; Code of Chess Laws; and a Selection of Morphy's Games. Annotated. 636 pages. Diagrams.

—— **Chess-Player's Companion.** Comprising a Treatise on Odds, Collection of Match Games, including the French Match with M. St. Amant, and a Selection of Original Problems. Diagrams and Coloured Frontispiece.

—— **Chess Tournament of 1851.** A Collection of Games played at this celebrated assemblage. With Introduction and Notes. Numerous Diagrams.

BOHN'S CHEAP SERIES.

Price 1s. each.

A Series of Complete Stories or Essays, mostly reprinted from Vols. in Bohn's Libraries, and neatly bound in stiff paper cover, with cut edges, suitable for Railway Reading.

The only authorised Edition; no others published in England contain the Derivations and Etymological Notes of Dr. Mahn, who devoted several years to this portion of the Work.

WEBSTER'S DICTIONARY
OF THE ENGLISH LANGUAGE.

Thoroughly revised and improved by CHAUNCEY A. GOODRICH, D.D., LL.D., and NOAH PORTER, D.D., of Yale College.

THE GUINEA DICTIONARY.

New Edition [1880], with a Supplement of upwards of 4600 New Words and Meanings.

1628 Pages. 3000 Illustrations.

The features of this volume, which render it perhaps the most useful Dictionary for general reference extant, as it is undoubtedly one of the cheapest books ever published, are as follows :—

1. COMPLETENESS.—It contains 114,000 words.
2. ACCURACY OF DEFINITION.
3. SCIENTIFIC AND TECHNICAL TERMS.
4. ETYMOLOGY.
5. THE ORTHOGRAPHY is based, as far as possible, on Fixed Principles.
6. PRONUNCIATION.
7. THE ILLUSTRATIVE CITATIONS.
8. THE SYNONYMS.
9. THE ILLUSTRATIONS, which exceed 3000.

Cloth, 21*s.* ; half-bound in calf, 30*s.* ; calf or half russia, 31*s.* 6*d.*; russia, 2*l.*

With New Biographical Appendix, containing over 9700 Names.

THE COMPLETE DICTIONARY

Contains, in addition to the above matter, several valuable Literary Appendices, and 70 extra pages of Illustrations, grouped and classified.

1 vol. 1919 pages, cloth, 31*s.* 6*d.*

' Certainly the best practical English Dictionary extant.'—*Quarterly Review*, 1873.

Prospectuses, with Specimen Pages, sent post free on application.

⁕ To be obtained through all Booksellers.

www.ingramcontent.com/pod-product-compliance
Lightning Source LLC
Chambersburg PA
CBHW031100110726
47900CB00003B/1007